Praise for G. Cabrera Infante

"Cabrera Infante is the first Latin American master of puns and word games, an essential part of the English language literary tradition; by creating his own *Spunish* language, he assaults the Spanish language with a slew of oddities allowing the language to renew, recognize, and contaminate itself; but, by doing so, his writing destroys the deadly nature inherent in the insular tradition of our prose."

—Carlos Fuentes

"*Three Trapped Tigers*—a work that I never tire of re-reading—is, like *Paradiso*, *Terra Nostra*, or *Conversations in the Cathedral*, an essential point of reference of the Latin American novel of the second half of the twentieth century."

—Juan Goytisolo

"A ferociously verbal book, an apolitical satire masquerading as erotic memoir, a kind of medley, of Marx (Groucho, not Karl), Frank Harris and James Joyce, with some Laurence Sterne and Jonathan Swift, a little Lewis Carroll and a pinch of Petronius and Marcel Proust, all set in the triste tropics."

—*New York Times*

"A lavishly erotic book. . . . *Infante's Inferno* is a mammoth political statement on behalf of individual freedom. It should help Cabrera Infante to be recognized as one of the three or four finest novelists from Latin America."

—*Observer* (London)

"*Infante's Inferno* is a funny, lubricous, autobiographical novel of a would-be rake's progress."

—*New York Review of Books*

Other Books by G. Cabrera Infante in English Translation

Guilty of Dancing the ChaChaChá
Holy Smoke
Mea Cuba
Three Trapped Tigers
A Twentieth Century Job
View of Dawn in the Tropics
Writes of Passage

Infante's Inferno

G. Cabrera Infante
Translation by Suzanne Jill Levine
and the Author

Dalkey Archive Press
Normal · London

Originally published in Spain under the title *La Habana para un Infante difunto* by Editorial Seix Barral, 1979
Copyright © 1979 by Guillermo Cabrera Infante
Translation copyright © 1984 by Guillermo Cabrera Infante and Suzanne Jill Levine

First Dalkey Archive edition, 2005

Library of Congress Cataloging-in-Publication Data:

Cabrera Infante, G. (Guillermo), 1929–2005.
  [Habana para un infante difunto. English]
  Infante's inferno / by G. Cabrera Infante ; translation by Suzanne Jill Levine with the author.— 1st Dalkey Archive ed.
    p. cm.
  ISBN 1-56478-384-7 (alk. paper)
  I. Levine, Suzanne Jill. II. Title.

PQ7389.C233H313 2005
869'.64—dc22

2004063485

Partially funded by grants from the National Endowment for the Arts, a federal agency, and the Illinois Arts Council, a state agency.

Dalkey Archive Press is a nonprofit organization located at Milner Library (Illinois State University) and distributed in the UK by Turnaround Publisher Services Ltd. (London).

www.dalkeyarchive.com

Printed on permanent/durable acid-free paper and bound in the United States of America.

CARL DENHAM *(after taking a good look at the natives)*
Blondes seem to be pretty scarce around here.
—KING KONG

Trivia laughs among the nymphs eternal.
—Dante's *Paradiso*

Movies is a very good place—you can hold hands.
—Preston Sturges

THE HOUSE OF CHANGES

It was the first time I climbed a staircase. Few houses in our town had more than one floor, and those that did were inaccessible. This is my inaugural memory of Havana: climbing marble steps. Before the staircase there's the memory of the bus station and the Plaza del Vapor market across the street, both arcades, but there were colonnades in our town too. Thus, my first real memory of Havana is of this sumptuous staircase, which is dark until you reach the second floor (so that I don't recall the first floor, only the staircase winding once again after the landing), opening beyond a baroque whorl onto the third floor, into a different, filtered, almost mauve light, and an unexpected sight. Facing me (my family had already disappeared in my amazement) was a long corridor, a narrow tunnel, a hallway like none I had seen before, lined with doors. The doors were always open but you couldn't see the rooms, hidden by curtains leaving open a space above and below. A breeze moved the colored curtains that hid the various households: even though it was midsummer, it was cool in the early morning and drafts came from within the rooms. Time stopped at that vision: going into the house marked Zulueta 408 was a vertical move: I had stepped from childhood into adolescence on a staircase. Many people talk, dream, or even write about their adolescence, but few can pinpoint the day it began, childhood expanding into a shrinking adolescence or vice versa. I can say precisely that on July 25th, 1941, my adolescence began. Of course I would continue being a child for a long time yet, but essentially that day, that morning, that moment when I faced the long hall of curtains, contemplating the interior view which would frighten even a veteran of the lower depths, the primitive painter Chema Bue—a visitor who years later refused to remain in it for even a minute, horrified by the corrupt beehive architecture of the building, on whose entrance a sign enticed the unwary: "ROOMS FOR RENT—SOME WITH FREE DAYS"—that day marked the end of my childhood. It was not only my entry into that institution of Havana lowly life, the *solar,* the tenement (a word I heard there for the first time, and

1

learned as I had to learn so many others: the city spoke another language, poverty had another vulgate, and it was like entering another country), but what for me was to be an education had begun.

We advanced apprehensively, all together now, down the corridor to the only closed door, which faced another longer corridor. (The inside of the building was designed like a tall T with a flourish at the end and to the left, a kind of serif where we would later find the bathrooms and collective toilets, a nasty novelty.) That door was ours, for a while. My mother had persuaded a family from our town, who went back every summer, to lend us the room for a month. My father (though it should have been my mother) opened the door and we were struck by a hidden, hideous smell we would always associate with that room, that family, who had never smelled when we visited their big house back home. Later my mother discovered that it was produced by some powerful powder they used, although we never knew for what. That smell, like the perfume worn by the first prostitute I slept with, was typical of Havana, and though the whore's whiff was the fragrance of the forbidden, tempting and pleasing, this other memorable odor coming out of the room could be called offensive, an evil stench—the stink of rejection. But both smells are the smell of initiation, the incense of adolescence, a stage in my life I wouldn't wish to live again—and nevertheless, it leaves a lot to remember.

We settled in this rumpled room ruled by the exotic essence, with all our baggage (merely cardboard boxes tied with rope), and my mother, obsessed with cleanliness, began to put the chaos in order. I remember the month we lived there as an endless succession of trolleys during the day. I was fascinated by trolleys, vehicles for which I knew no equal, with their rigid path along rails shining from the constant traffic: the trolley looked like a railroad car abandoned to its momentum as some sort of fate, its long double antennas contacting the cables above, parallel to the tracks, producing scintillations like brief sparks of life. Of the nights I remember the flashing red and blue light from the neon sign hanging outside, right next to our balcony, which said off and on "SARRÁ DRUGSTORE —THE BIGGEST." That incessant two-toned sign colored my sleep, dreams inhabited by flashing red and blue trolleys, by motley moons, by the infrared life of midnight.

The great adventure began earlier in the evening in Havana by night, with the novelty of its outdoor cafés and its unusual all-women orchestras (I don't know why the orchestras that entertained the cafés along the Paseo del Prado, just around the corner from us, were always female but funny: a woman blowing a saxophone produced in me a disturbing hilarity) and its lush lighting: city lights: streetlights, spotlights, lamps, lanterns, neon signs: lights making day by night. We came from a poor town, and though my grandparents' house was on Calle Real there were only a few candles in a bulb on each corner of that measly main street, barely lighting the area around the lamppost, making it seem even darker from corner to corner. The streetlamps were so poor back home that they couldn't even afford moths.

But there were lights all over Havana, not only for utility but for luxury, adorning the Paseo del Prado in particular, and also the Malecón, that prolonged promenade along the coast, where cars sped by, their headlights shining on the asphalt while streetlamps along the sidewalk bathed the wall across the street, a glowing tide in contrast with the invisible waves on the other side. Lights shone everywhere and anywhere, on the streets and sidewalks, over the roofs, even on trees, lending a radiant beam, a lustrous glow to the most trivial things, making them relevant, giving them a theatrical importance, highlighting a palace that by day would become an ugly, flat, and common building. During the day the wide avenues offered an unlimited perspective, since the sun was less blinding than back home, where its light reverberated relentlessly off the white clay of the streets. Here the black pavement absorbed the same sun, its radiance relieved, besides, by the shade of tall buildings and the sea air from the nearby Gulf Stream, refreshing the tropical summer and providing an illusion of winter that would be impossible back home. That free Havana landscape alone compensated for our cramped life in a room, since in our town, even during the poorest times, we always lived in a house. The constantly closed door (my mother had not yet learned the art of using the curtain as a partition) forced me, us, to the balcony, the only free opening although also a place of terror: my mother had continued her custom, older than I can remember, of reaching the climax of any domestic quarrel (for example, if my brother had accidentally stained his pants) with a suicide threat, now almost followed by an action: "I'll throw myself off the balcony and end it all, for good!" But I don't want to write about the negative life (though its metaphysics will intrude upon my happiness more than once) but about the bit of positive life contained in those adolescent years, begun when ascending a solid marble staircase of convoluted design and baroque banisters.

The first person I met in Havana was unique: a man my father took us to meet—even the manner of meeting him was unusual. According to my father he was an extraordinary human being. "A real character," he explained but did not sufficiently prepare us. The meeting took place a few days after our arrival, and the place was typically Havanan, thus unusual. We all walked down to the corner that I would later learn was the corner of Aguila, Reina, and Estrella (that is, Eagle, Queen, and Star Streets) where Fixed Prices, a big store, stood. There we stopped to wait not for a person but for a bus or, in my father's now Havananized words, a *guagua* and *guagua* was what we would call the bus in the future. This word, to which some backyard philologist would attribute an indigenous origin—imagine the syphilitic Ciboneys or taciturn Tainos traveling in their pre-Columbian cars, they who weren't even acquainted with the wheel!—probably comes from the American occupation at the turn of the century, when the first collective carriages came into use, drawn by mules and called in the American way *wagons*. In Havana parlance *wagons* became *guagons*, and from there they were easily assimilated to the indigenous *guagua*, its feminine gender determined not only by the ending but because all English vehicles are female, even abroad. The fact that in Chile, Peru, and Ecuador they call all babies *guaguas* would produce, for Cubans, moments of raving-mad surrealism like this sentence, read in a Chilean book, "He took the *guagua* out of the river and carried it in his arms." Another Hercules, nay, another Atlas would be needed to find someone capable of not only taking a bus out of a river single-handed but of carrying it in his arms!

We waited for the *guagua* but not any old *guagua:* it would be a Route 23 bus with a particular number on it that my father knew by heart. The appointed chariot finally arrived and my father made the stop signal, a cross between a greeting and a Nazi salute: I'd always remember that outstretched Havana hand, usually used to verify if it was raining or had stopped raining. Upon my father's mandatory sign (he was worried, this first time, that he had missed the bus, but it was *the guagua*), the compact, colorful vehicle stopped and we got on. It turned out that the person my father was taking us to meet was not the bus driver but the ticket seller, who in Havana was called a *guagüero,* a position that was not only modest but which went with a particular psychology, an attitude toward life, a behavior, a way of talking. In one word, a conductor: not a very high profession in Havana's stratified social spheres. But of course I didn't know these distinctions then and I looked at the family friend as one looks upon a hero: from below, almost with reverence, and he looked like a Scandinavian god: tall, blond, blue-eyed, in marked contrast with my father, who introduced us to Eloy Santos, a very appropriate name. Eloy Santos gave us all a grand reception, but my mother in particular, whom he had met before. Needless to say, we didn't pay for the ride. This generosity with the company's money would cost Eloy Santos his job years later: he often forgot to register the passengers' fare and pocketed the five cents whenever he could, justifying this pocket money with a saying he adopted as his own: "Rob the rich and give to the poor," and as the rich was the bus company and the poor, Santos, he saw himself as a rolling Robin Hood. He looked in fact like William Demarest.

Eloy Santos had been, like my parents, a founder of the clandestine Communist party back in the early thirties. Unlike his country cousins, he had been a pioneer in Havana, years back when he had been a sergeant in the navy and had offered to organize, for the party, a mutiny on the ship in which he (theoretically) sailed, one of our few seaworthy warships. This naval plot of his was never on the ocean but always at sea. Eloy Santos had planned to take command of the ship, sail it out of the Casablanca docks, navigate the narrow port entrance, steer his course for some blocks (with such a ship one couldn't even speak in terms of nautical knots or miles), ply to windward in front of the Malecón, lie to, and

4

fire the single starboard cannon upon the Presidential Palace, bombarding the tyrant until he surrendered or fled. As you see, his plan was a heady mixture of Russian revolutionary myths, like the mutiny on the battleship *Potemkin* and the rebellion of the cruiser *Aurora,* the dictator Machado being sixty percent Tsar Nicholas II and forty percent President Kerensky.

But the mutinous theory never became target practice. The party (which planned in those days to reach a political agreement with Machado) expressly prohibited any "seditious movement" (party words—or Eloy's) and Seaman Santos, who offered imposing arguments in favor of the mutiny, fell into a sort of stubborn disgrace once Machado had fled, and left the navy (for reasons he never explained), to enter a kind of political limbo in which he lived forever after. He was still a Communist. He would be one his whole life: what's more, he was a staunch Russophile, who insisted, years later, that I read the most orthodox works of Russian realism: through his persistence and so as not to disappoint him, I had to read the abominable Soviet novel *Nights and Days.* But I decidedly refused to praise Stalinist architecture, of which he showed me photos, exalting it while abusing colonial Cuban mansions, describing them as decadent. When the 1944 cyclone knocked down a beautiful palace in Old Havana, more cadent than decadent, he explained: "That wouldn't happen in the Soviet Union." This phrase was so cryptic (he said no more) that I never knew if he was referring to the architecture or to hurricanes.

This Eloy Santos was my father's best Havana friend. A true Havanan, he had an accent that immediately struck me as the funniest way of speaking Spanish I had ever heard, and his stories were the stuff legends are made of. In his Havana time machine, the bus, we traveled the whole course of Route 23, from Aguila and Reina and Estrella to El Vedado. I don't know what my father and mother talked about with Eloy Santos since I was busy the whole time watching the petrified urban landscape go by on both sides, like a fast forest. I remember, though, that we didn't do the whole route to the El Vedado stop but that we got off at Maceo Park, leaving Eloy Santos to complete his urban *via crucis*, stuck in the struggle of determining to what extent he could neglect the ticket meter as if it were a stopped clock and at the same time avoid the exact accounting of the examiners he would be seeing at the most unexpected places, inspectors, specters.

That evening becomes confused with another voyage with Eloy Santos, this time on foot, his stature reduced but not his legend, telling tales of the unexpected in the expected while we strolled along the Malecón in the area of Maceo Park. That day Eloy Santos told my mother (but me in particular, since I was the one collecting it in my memory) how he returned from the dead. He had a *chiquita* (it was the first time I heard this Havana diminutive for girlfriend) who was really a prostitute, and I thought he meant destitute: he was a Communist, wasn't he? It was one of the first times I heard him refer to risqué subjects with the most careful language, using euphemisms each time he had to say something crude, though he was the first person I heard utter the word *pederast*. Eloy employed it to personally humiliate the aristocracy: "All aristocrats are degenerates. Lord Byron, to name one, was a pederast." I had to look in a dictionary to see what *pederast* meant, but it took me more time to identify Lord Byron, since Eloy Santos had said: "Lor Birion was a pederast."

"That girl burnt me with the pox," added Eloy Santos. Years later I came to understand that burnt meant in Havana slang to catch a venereal disease.

But this narration was memorable not because of the language but because of the incredible story Eloy Santos told. He realized too late that he was syphilitic and when he went to the doctor he was already terminally sick. "Your number's up" was the diagnosis: they couldn't even save him with Salvarsan. "I died," he said simply, though they were alarming words for me because it was obvious he wasn't telling tales. Given up for dead, he was taken to the stiffs' ward (i.e., hospital morgue) and it was pure luck that an intern passed by. This doctor's disciple noticed with a sharp eye a slight movement of the big toe, the only visible part on the now dead Eloy Santos, the only living portion of his body, protruding from under sheet and shroud. The young doctor had him taken out of the mortuary and into the operating room and discovered that Eloy Santos was more dead than alive but still somewhat alive.

More as an experiment than with experience the intern tried to revive him, using a desperate method. They were doing repairs in the hospital, or perhaps building another ward, but for one reason or another there was a blowtorch nearby and the dilettante doctor, a probable pyromaniac, had them bring it into the operating theater. They started the blowtorch and he applied it directly to Eloy's heart, producing third-degree burns, of course. Eloy Santos told us that they'd told him that the smell of burnt flesh was unbearable. After one or two applications (not many because he could have burnt the heart itself) the orderly, medic, or doctor in bloom applied his stethoscope (I imagine that the crackling of crispy flesh probably produced interference) and heard Eloy Santos's heart beating—and beating it continued from then on. "So," was the corollary of his story, "I came back from the other side." But syphilis had done more damage than the old flame, which had left a charred scar the length of his chest. He showed it to us to prove that his was a true story. Eloy Santos had lost his vision in one eye, the other eye being partially damaged—this explained Eloy Santos's light-blue Scandinavian eyes, but did not diminish his hero's stature.

From the Malecón one could see the neon signs shining on the west side of Maceo Park, and though they couldn't be compared with the glittering lights in Central Park (especially the scanty Jantzen bathing-suit ad with the bathing beauty diving from the intermittent springboard

6

into the shimmering, shining waters), the other signs that lit up the opposite sidewalk cast a unique unforgettable magic spell over the Havana night. I still remember that first bath of lights, that baptism of pale fire, the yellow radiance enveloping us with the luminous halo of night life, the fatal phosphorescence that was so promising: street life and free days all. The phosphorescence of Havana was not a foreign light from the sun or reflected like the moon's: it was a light that came from the city itself, created by Havana to bathe in and purify itself of the dark that remained on the other side of the wall. From that Maceo bend of the Malecón one could see all the way to the Havana waterfront landscape, day and night. I would take this path later in life again and again, without thinking of it as a unique atmosphere, without reflecting on its possible end, imagining it infinite, believing it deceptively eternal—though perhaps it is eternal after all in memory.

We walked the evening from Maceo Park to the crossroad of the Malecón and Prado, by La Punta Castle, where the night became more luminous in life though not in memory, and we went up Prado, strolling more than walking under the trees that form a leafy arcade over the central walled promenade. It was the first time I saw day changing this way: becoming a long electric twilight. In our town there had been only day and night, the blinding day, the blind night.

A few days after our arrival in Havana, the first visitor from home appeared. Or rather, almost from home because he was a *guajiro,* a hick from Potrerillo, the sugar-cane farm near town. Like all farmers he was melancholy but had transparent yellow eyes that saw—or at least looked at—everything. He was one of those farmers whom my mother, in her proselytizing zeal, had converted to Communism. But I feared that he was in Havana not for party reasons but for partying reasons—that is, he was after my mother, who was then a Communist beauty. This hick found a new sport in the big city: like us, he had never known tall buildings, and now he amused himself on the balcony by spitting at the wayfarers passing below. Fortunately his spittle was off target but in spite of his bad aim he insisted on practicing each time he saw someone approaching on the sidewalk. My mother never managed to convince him that this wasn't done (he was a real *montuno* type and even the word portrays primitive nature in all its splendor), that he could make trouble for us if someone was hit. To which the spitting image of a bombardier responded that he'd dare 'em, meaning he, *muy macho,* would challenge the other to a machete duel, so frequent in the Cuban countryside. He had forgotten that he had left the machete in his hut in Oriente, but just the same he would challenge whomever to a punching match—he was made of what gauchos, cowboys, and Mexican rancheros are made of: stud stuff.

This hick's presence was providential, nonetheless, a gift of the gods, from Juno but also from Eros. My father was working then on the newly-created newspaper *Hoy,* the organ of the Communist party. But, contaminated, they paid as if they were capitalist scoundrels: three pesos a week. Though the equivalent of three dollars then, it was still almost nothing. The newspaper *Hoy* meant another step down for my father. He had been an editor of the town paper, press secretary of the local party, speech writer for the secretary general, and an impeccable editor of copy: all this had made him assistant to an incompetent journalist, always assigned to subordinate tasks. Not even the discovery of what would be my day and nighttime habitat, a newspaper office (and its marvelous machine—after the plain press back home—the rotary printing press, an automatic hen, newspapers coming out from under it like illustrated flat eggs) would make me forget the offensive shame that my father was submitted to on a daily basis. He who had been a political prisoner because of the Communist cause, a true believer in Marx and Engels, in Lenin and even Stalin, disciplined to the point of blind obedience, devoted to the point of appearing humble, militant to the point of becoming inconspicuous in the rank and file of the party. It was because he so zealously toed the party line that he went unnoticed: he was such a good Communist that he managed to go from being red to being invisible. But we were very visible, and not even with his family in Havana did my father manage to get a raise. So the final day arrived when we had to leave the room, return it to its lawful owners back from the country, and find a room of our own. But my father didn't have a cent. It was my mother who thought of borrowing money (or rather receiving a gift: how and when could she return it?) from the hick who visited us every day to try his luck at spitting on target. And so one night (why at night? it never occurred to me to ask why we couldn't leave the room during the day: why the drama of a last-minute escape?) we left that strange house —to which we would fatally return one day: we were destined to it, like a sentence one must carry out.

We went out to look for a place to spend the night, my father supplied with money from the hick (who disappeared in the night and from our lives forever: *hic jacet:* I never saw him again and I don't think my father paid him back: for many years we would be the kind who always borrow —money, salt, sugar—and never pay back), trying to find a hotel in the vicinity. We didn't go in the direction of the luminous Prado but in the opposite direction, toward murky Montserrate, full of cheap hotels, leaving behind a café called Castillo de Farnés (of A. Dumas & Son), going down Obrapía past the corner of Bernaza. (One day, many days, I would stand there on erotic guard under a balcony, waiting for only a glimpse of Gloria Graña, the strange blue-eyed brown-haired girl who was so aloof on her balcony that she would become my first distant love in Havana—my ideal love, until the vengeful day she appeared vulgar to me, Dulcinea walking down Bernaza carrying Aldonza Lorenzo on her back.) A little further down Obrapía we found the hotel whose price was right, fit for our fixed finances. We went up the staircase decked in tiles that were so lovely I felt like running my hand along their glossy surface, until my mother smacked my hand away, gently advising me not to do it.

We got to our room, the four of us procrustinated in one bed. At least in the tenement room (I'm getting ahead of myself linguistically: in my vocabulary the word *tenement* did not yet exist. I have already gotten ahead of myself before, but that was the introduction while now we're *in medias res*) we had slept in two beds. But since I was no longer a child there was no way I could complain. So I decided to go to sleep. As soon as I tried I was awakened (I didn't get to fall asleep really: it wasn't insomnia—that malady is a habit acquired in adulthood—but rather that we had gone to bed too early) by strange noises, difficult to define. They were human but seemed animal, as if from large cats with hands. The meows dissolved into improbable sobs, then resurged elsewhere: we were surrounded by cries—or rather howls, although I must say that at one moment I managed to identify them specifically as female howls. The hooting owls were women, but sometimes the female meows were accompanied by male bellows. I already knew about animals but these were weird unknown beasts. I also heard words here and there, phrases I couldn't identify, uttered perhaps in another language. The bellows and meows went on most of the night as I lay awake. I remembered the hideous Mexican horror film *The Howler,* in which a wandering soul in hell comes to earth to disturb the actors and terrorize the spectators. I thought of the zoo across from Maceo Park with its exotic animals. But neither memory nor thought could explain to me the series of sounds heard that night. Was it the wind?

The next day we left the hotel very early. My father seemed annoyed but my mother was amused. What's more, she was laughing. These reactions of my parents were not directed at each other but at the building: my mother laughed at the hotel, my father was bothered by its façade. Years later I found out that we had spent the night in a *posada,* as it is called in Havana: a *hotel de passe,* a blue house, an infamous inn. My father was pissed, annoyed by his choice: it was evident that night and necessity had confused him and made him choose a *hotelito* as a hotel, an explicable confusion not only because the terms, and the architecture, are so similar but because my father had never known such a place. He was not a heathen in a house of pleasure but was there for Marxist motives, that is, economic reasons. My mother was amused by the adventure in the inn because she was much more liberal than my father. She used a bad word when she had to, and in her youth consumed novels that were considered erotic then, like the *Dalliances of Mr. Delly.* It was she who explained to me the incident of the *hotelito* taken for a hotel. What's more, to annoy my father, she told all our friends in Havana, when we acquired them, and the friends from town when they came to visit, after immigrating to the city, before one could say Havana!

From the inn that sounded like an Aeolian cave we somehow ended up, I don't know how, on the other side of Havana, in Lawton Lawns, a misnomer if ever there was one, a neighborhood on the outskirts, one of the poorest haunts in the whole city, to live with—whom else?—with Eloy Santos. His was not the dwelling place of a hero: it was just another room, this time a back room on the ground floor of a small boardinghouse, near the Route 23 bus stop. There we touched bottom. Though I never knew or even suspected it, we couldn't have been poorer.

The family's economic decline had begun that year but now it had reached its lowest point ever: there was nowhere to go but up—theoretically, that is. I remember that stay in the Lawton Lawns lair, since I had a new adventure there: I joined up with a local youth gang. I had seen youth gangs in the movies (in *Dead End,* for example, or in the mysterious *The Devil Is a Sissy,* which was intriguing because there had been a power failure in town halfway through the movie and I never learned what finally happened to those romantic dare-devil boys) but there were no gangs in our town. That was another Havana invention, like the red-light district or continuous showings at the movies. Thus I entered enraptured into the ranks of the Lawton Lawns gang. I can't remember what my brother was up to during that period. He who had been so ubiquitous, so involved in my affairs, my inseparable appendix, spoiling hide-and-seek games, I look for him in my memory and don't find him. At least he wasn't there when the gang put me to the test on a daring raid.

Together we all went to steal guavas from a nearby orchard, which one reached after climbing a steep slope—my version of Bunker Hill—next to some gas tanks, obviously about to explode and engulf me in flames. From there one went down a kind of precipice, which I naturally did not do. I fixed it so that they left me to guard those dangerous, dizzying heights, since descending into the abyss of the guava orchard had to be even more vertiginous. From my lookout I saw the other boys busy harvesting the forbidden guavas. What I didn't see was the watchman, who was doggedly pursuing the thieves among the trees, they zigzagging around the orchard, then heading for the open field toward my watch-tower, climbing agilely up the hill, hasty climbers all, arriving safe and sound but without a single guava, blaming *me,* more a spectator than a guard, for the failure of the raid. Right then and there ended my brush with gangland, by mutual disagreement. I spent the rest of the time at Eloy Santos's place, quietly in the room or sitting silently on the sidewalk, watching an occasional old car go by, since there weren't even electric trolleys to admire in the domain of bus Route 23. Only late at night could I hear, as on a distant radio, the whistle of a train, probably never on time.

Those days were not memorable because I had to sleep on the floor. I, my father, and Eloy Santos were bedfellows without a bed since on his only cot slept my brother, my mother, and Eloy Santos's wife: they were newly wed or newly coupled as he himself said, since he didn't believe in legal liens and, much less, religious marriages—I forgot to say that Eloy Santos's *nom de guerre* was not a Cuban copy of Stalin's steel man: Eloy Santos baptized himself Iconoclast and that he was: a heretic who denied all images, sacred or profane. But they were days to remember because the same Eloy Santos, image hater, took my brother and me to the movies and this was an inauguration: the first time I went to the movies during the day. I underwent the marvelous act of passing from the vertical blinding afternoon sun, into the theater that was blinded throughout except for the screen, the luminous horizon, my eyes flying like moths to the fascinating fountain of light. We saw a double feature, that other novelty: in our town they always showed only one movie. At one point the movie repeated itself, obsessively, and Eloy Santos murmured: "This is where we came in," and he got up as if it were the end of the show. Neither my brother nor I understood. "It's a continuous show," explained Eloy Santos. "We've got to go." "Why?" I asked, almost fresh, I'm afraid. "Because the movie repeats itself." "And what's so bad about that?" I wanted to know. "It's the rules of the game," said Eloy Santos. "We've got to go. Let's go!," and as it sounded like an order, we got up and left.

That Sunday of expectations and revelations (it had to be Sunday, and if it wasn't, memory declares it a holiday) we, I saw *Souls at Sea,* the story of a shipwreck, and, more important, *The Whole Town's Talking,* of which I later learned the English title, forgetting the inadequate Spanish (sub)title, all of which signified the double encounter with an actor who would become one of my favorites, Edward G. Robinson. More than the unforgettable Paul Muni of *Scarface,* Robinson would come to personify the gangster, the crafty villain, as well as the opposite, the naïf, the innocent good guy. Here were two in one, knowledge and ignorance, the bad guy and his double negative. We went, I went to the San Francisco Theater, which was the first moviehouse I visited in Havana but to which I would never return.

I will always remember it, however, with its petite-pleasure-palace architecture, an unpretentious neighborhood theater, friendly and noisy, dedicated to offering its movie mass magnificat, but caught between two eras: too late to be an Art Deco temple, like the theaters built in the late thirties, which I would later discover in downtown Havana, and not pretentiously simple like the theaters from the end of the fifties, the last commercial cinemas built in Cuba. The San Francisco was an ideal place for the initiation. The Los Angeles, not too far away, could have been better, or the Hollywood, to which I never went. But the San Francisco, its name reminding me of one of my favorite movies that I had seen back home, was a gift of Eloy Santos, who, despite his poverty and overwhelmed by the sudden visit that fell upon him from the astronomical, not theological, heavens, had the consideration to invite us, initiate me at the movies in Havana that auspicious August Sunday of '41. Years later Eloy Santos would introduce me to another initiation, perhaps more important but not more unforgettable.

My parents disappeared during the day—my father to work and my mother relentlessly roaming the roads of Havana, desperately seeking a place for us. Soon, however, she found what was for her an ideal spot: a room in an annex facing the Unique Market at Monte 822. An *annex,* another new word, was in Havana a variation on *tenement.* The annex was usually located in an alley. The alley was of course a passageway that went from one street to another but with houses on both sides, while *annex* meant that instead of houses there were rooms on either side of the alley. This room of ours (I don't know where my father got the money to pay the month's rent in advance and the month's deposit they demanded) was located at the entrance of the annex on the first floor of one of the rooming houses. But to get to it you had to go up a spiral staircase of rusty iron: another discovery in the field of elevation. (At first I had a hard time learning how to go up and down the narrow spiral, but I was soon an expert in running up it, grabbing its whorls at a whirling speed.)

The room was in the back but had a window that faced an air shaft —surprise!—connecting to the Esmeralda Moviehouse. It took some time before my father could pay for my movies, but on many days I was content with the noises coming up the ventilator, an organ of arias from the new opera: precious scraps of sound tracks, the exotic murmur of American actors, movie music.

Neither do I know where my father got a bed—he was becoming a loan magician: somewhere in Havana was a cornucopia top hat from which he pulled out funds without limits and no obligations. I do know where the dining table came from: Eloy Santos knew a black carpenter, also a Communist, who brought some planks evidently from shipping boxes, and other thick pieces of wood and, before our spectators' eyes, my brother's and mine, the marvelous erector built a table on which we ate for a long time.

Monte 822 had other advantages besides being across the street from a market (I was never bothered by the smell of rotten fruit mixed with stale fish and spicy fragrances—animal or vegetable smells have never bothered me but human stench is what offends me) and on saturnine Saturdays, many years later, when I worked for *Carteles* and earned a salary that as a boy would have not only seemed fabulous to me but highly improbable, I would go to the Unique Market with several artist friends to eat the delicious soup at the humble Chinese restaurant or, rather, eatery, on the first floor there where you could shop cheap.

Our place was also a few blocks from the newspaper. Around the corner, on the same block, was the primary school I thought was called Rosa Inn but in reality was Rosaín, the most famous public school in Havana because of its high level of education. Even before September my father enrolled my brother and me in that school, which was fortunately, for the sake of temptation and titillation, coed. But what made the location of our house perfect for me (I would never get out of the habit of calling the rooms we lived in houses) was its door-to-door proximity to the Esmeralda, where I made that great discovery of the dream as adventure: the serials of the forties. I was an old (in a manner of speaking) hand at the serials of the thirties, and the most memorable of them has been mentioned elsewhere. I would soon be a fan of *The Green Hornet* (I fell in love, for the first time, with a car, the two-seater driven by the Hornet), *The Green Archer* (continuing my blind addiction to the color green—in black-and-white film) and, last but not least, *Captain Marvel*—Sham Shazam! All that would come later, though. At the beginning of life at the rooming house all that reached me from the Esmeralda screen were the sounds, I a buff of the blindman's movie.

My father finally received a raise at the newspaper, Communist consideration: he now earned five pesos a week, a measly salary but one that allowed us to change rooms, as soon as there was a vacancy at the annex. Our next room was much larger, and instead of the dungeon window it had a door to the interior of the house and another that went out onto a small walled terrace. On the other side of the wall was the vast roof of the north annex and facing us across the alley, and matching our rooming house, was a Chinese community. They were not Chinese Cubans, which would have made them a family, but rather Chinese from China, isolated and silent. They barely talked among themselves, and they'd come out on the roof, in tunics and sandals. In their windows one could see them smoking short, fat bamboo pipes, from which they drew a barely visible smoke. They weren't burning sandalwood. My mother shocked my father by saying that they were probably smoking opium: "The smoke that makes you dream, rather than merely sleep." My mother must have gotten this sententious knowledge out of her readings of the mysterious M. Delly. Soon two uncles joined us, my mother's brothers, which made the new room as small as the previous one but also livelier. One of my uncles, Toñito, a carpenter, had strange sleepwalking dreams, in which he would pursue imaginary thieves around the room, house, and roof, at midnight. There was nothing to steal in the house, but the less one has the more one's possessions are treasures and a temptation for those the newspapers comically called *cacos,* friends of their neighbors' private property.

When we lived in the first room, my mother received a box of fruits and vegetables from my grandmother back home. As the bananas were green, my mother hung a bunch out our window to ripen, but from the next floor up, from a window the next room over, someone cleanly swiped our bunch of bananas, to my mother's perpetual anger and my sustained surprise, intrigued by such skillful thievery. I used to explain to my brother the most complex theories on how they had carried out the robbery, ahead of my own readings of Poe: the purloined hand.

I don't know how or when (at least my memory didn't jot it down: they must have arrived at night) townspeople appeared not only in Havana (the city wasn't mine alone) but also at the very rooming house at Monte 822, hidden as it was, inside the annex alley, stashed away under the street portico, whose sign said Máximo Gómez, not Monte, lined with torn rather than Tuscan columns. They arrived magically. Many of these visitors from the outside world came not to visit but to stay, among them a family of certain standing back home. They had lived down the hill near the principal plaza and were different from those of us who lived on the hill—the heights there meant a descent—where our grandparents had a house. (Our last refuge had been the high hill: down below was the high society, the posh in our town.) This family occupied a luxury room in the annex, with a balcony facing the street—not exactly the street but the portico, with its wide corridor and columns—their luxury a form of destiny.

María Montoya, a widow, was the head of this household (and her alliterating name had been a source of tags among the town wags in town), consisting of her son Marianín, constantly called Marianín Montoya though his real name was Otero (his father's name should have come first) and her daughter, Mercy. María and Marianín were good friends of my parents, and Mercy, only a little older than I, was the first girl I had seen wearing glasses (glasses then were only for men and old people), which barely disguised her crossed eyes. Another new boarder, in one of the poorer rooms, was Rubén Fornaris, a mulatto carpenter in the tradition of the decent Negro, some sort of Cousin Tom because he was so good and innocent. His innocence was perhaps reduced (it could never be totally eliminated) by my mother. Rubén's room was for sleeping only, since he didn't know how to cook. Somehow he had made an agreement with María Montoya (the Montoyas were rather racist) that he would eat with them for a fee that must have been reasonable (or perhaps scanty) for María Montoya but excessive for Rubén's wages. María Montoya managed it so that Rubén wouldn't eat with her family (an arrangement perhaps suggested by Rubén himself) and Rubén would always eat later. The agreement worked to everyone's satisfaction. But it happened that one day another neighbor, a native Havanan light-skinned *mulata* named Victoria, very thin because she suffered as she herself said from "weak lungs," without ever admitting the tuberculosis evident in her cough and consumptive air, told my mother that she wanted to show her something and took her to the kitchen—but not to give her a cooking lesson. There she showed my mother some plates with leftovers and told her: "That's what María serves your friend Rubén and all because he's a poor mulatto." My mother was really more a friend of María Montoya's than of Rubén and thought that the accusation was inverted racial prejudice on the part of Victoria. "How do you know?" "Because I've been watching them for days," answered Victoria. "You'll see. Stay with me and pretend we're cooking together." My mother didn't have time to waste but she was less patient with injustice and decided to investigate Victoria's terrible accusation.

After the two had been in the kitchen awhile María Montoya came in, said something trivial, and began bustling around with her dishes. My mother looked while pretending not to and saw that, effectively, she had emptied the plates with the leftovers into a pot and was heating up this potluck. After completing her concoction she left the kitchen with a plate of food apparently freshly served. Convinced, my mother had no choice but to agree with Victoria and call Rubén to tell him he couldn't continue eating at the Montoyas'. "But why?" Rubén asked, puzzled. "They've agreed to have me eat with them." My mother didn't know what to say and was silent, thinking, and thought so much about what to say tactfully that finally she exclaimed: "They're giving you leftovers!" From my mother's tone, Rubén realized she was telling him the truth. He knew her honesty and perhaps that was how he had learned other lessons in life: he lost enough innocence to be able to tell María Montoya that he wouldn't eat in her house anymore, but of course he didn't burst out in anger or complain or even tell her the real reason for ending their arrangement. The shame of being deceived, however, forced him to move from Monte 822, and for a while we thought we wouldn't see him again. But we were wrong, and when we later moved back to Zulueta 408 again he would become an important, perhaps essential, person for me. At least for a while.

In Monte 822 there was another incident with María Montoya, but it wouldn't be a secret misdemeanor. On the contrary, the event would spread and become such a legend in the Havana colony from our town (because soon, attracted by job opportunities in the big city and repelled by economic difficulties at home, or compelled by their curiosity to know Havana, many displaced persons made their place in the capital, having left what they affectionately called the White Village, now almost a ghost town) that many former town folk believed this story to be an ingenious invention.

It happened that María Montoya sent her daughter, Mercy, on an errand, perhaps to the market. But Doña María (as she was addressed) forgot to order something extra or had a sudden inspiration and, as Mercy was not yet far away, her mother went out on the balcony and began to shout to her: "Mercy, Mercy." Mercy didn't hear her but the wayfarers below did and perhaps the people in the moviehouse too— ticket seller, doorman, patrons. Soon a general alarm was provoked by those cries for help emitted by a matron in distress: people gathered beneath Doña María's balcony, which wasn't high up, she still shouting: "Mercy! Mercy!" this time louder because Mercy was already up the street—but the relentless rabble didn't know that.

Soon a policeman appeared (they're always near when they're not needed), who addressed Doña María with authority and respect: "What's the matter, madam?" Doña María, now in her role as María Montoya, annoyed because she hadn't reached Mercy despite her shouting, disturbed by this interruption, answered: "With me? What do you mean what's the matter? Nothing!" The officer didn't like this reply. In fact he found it a little short-tempered: "Then why are you asking for help?" "I have not asked for help, my good man," said María Montoya, even more

15

annoyed, accustomed to calling her daughter Mercy without connecting her name to a desperate emergency. "Yes, madam," said the policeman, piqued because he had been lowered from his rank to mere man, "you were crying for mercy, I heard you." "No, sir," insisted María Montoya, "I was calling my daughter, whose name is Mercy." The police officer did not want to accept an absurd excuse or dangerous joke—gags being totally unacceptable to the police. "You know, madam, that one doesn't fool around with the law," said the policeman. María Montoya, perhaps prepossessed by her own preeminence in our town, which meant total anonymity in Havana, haughtily replied: "Look, leave me alone and don't stick your nose in other people's business." The policeman tried to find the entrance to the house of that insolent woman, who, besides, talked in singsong like a provincial from Oriente. But fortunately at that moment Mercy returned and María Montoya called her by her name and she replied: "Yes, mama?" The policeman, who hadn't found the entrance, now found a way out, was convinced that it had all been a misunderstanding. The people, more pressing than impressed, continued on their way, María Montoya became Mother of Mercy and the policeman went back to his *posta,* which in Havana meant the beat of an officer of the law and which, back in the sticks, meant the place where donkeys, mules, and sometimes asses were tied up.

Yet another incident occurred with those magnificent Montoyas, which was a revelation. This time the protagonist was not María but her son Marianín. Rare rumors about Marianín had circulated in town, in vague adult conversations which I had overheard. María Montoya, a widow after all, now adored her only son Marianín, who reciprocated this love with interest. He was decidedly a good son and was thus praiseworthy, back in town. But the rumors continued. The sore point was the sure evidence that Marianín, already a grownup, was not interested in women or rather was interested in a strange way. He was capable, for example, of describing a woman's dress with unusual precision for a man—unless he's a novelist. He would also use words uncommon in a man, even a novelist. For example, his favorite phrase was "There's some detail here," and, upon describing any occasion, he'd always add: "But there's one little detail," and his appraisal or objection would follow. Once, it seems, he managed to fuse his preciousness with his fashion mania to an extreme degree and described a skirt thus: "Lovely. But there's one little detail in the width of the hem." I took note of these details of Marianín's in my mother's conversations with her women friends. Marianín was, on the other hand, tall, strong, with abundant black hair (though he already had a receding hairline, which mortified him terribly) and eyes with unusually long lashes. He described them as velvety and always added: "You know, like Tyrone Power's"—and he also had a thin, well-groomed mustache, copied from Don Ameche, who became his idol after he saw him in *In Old Chicago.* "I'm sorry to have to betray Tyrone," he said smiling.

16

One day, one evening rather, after work (Marianín was a wood varnisher—he described himself as a cabinetmaker—but you'd never imagine that he did that kind of work since he washed his hands so scrupulously that they were always white, without a trace of varnish, and he was proud of them, especially the long nails of his pinkies. This cleanliness carried to the last, as he would say, detail was admired by my mother, who contrasted him favorably with my uncle Toñito, who always returned from the same carpenter's shop as immaculate Marianín, covered with sawdust to his lashes, prematurely graying from cedar dust) Marianín told my mother he had a surprise for her that he would give her later. My mother had no idea what it could be and was wondering what the surprise was when there was a knock on the door. She opened it and before our eyes (mine were there to register everything) was a girl in black high heels, emphasizing her amply-curved legs, and a purple dress. She also had on deep red lipstick, a little too much mascara on her thick lashes, and a high black hat. The girl was Marianín, dressed—attired, as he would specify—in his mother's clothes, so well transformed that he could fool my mother. But one detail betrayed him: his thin but visible mustache beneath the makeup. Marianín burst into laughter, which was echoed by María Montoya appearing behind him. My mother, her surprise over, also laughed heartily. I don't remember if my father was present, perhaps to show his definite disapproval, or if my uncles did or didn't join in the laughter of my mother, Marianín, and María Montoya. I do remember my innocent amazement: I had just seen my first drag show and didn't know it. The occasion would not be repeated until a quarter of a century later.

I was also going to meet up with my first real book of pornography in Monte 822. Pure pornography is a strange literary mechanism that enters the eyes (or ears: more later), acts upon the mind, and impels the pubes, producing erections, titillating tits, and stimulating clits. I don't know who lent the book in question to my uncle the Kid, who hardly knew anybody in Havana and didn't have money to buy anything. It couldn't have been the innocent Rubén Fornaris. I don't think my uncle the Kid would have admitted such a loan from marked Marianín. Perhaps it had been Nila, a woman (really a girl: she was not yet twenty but I continued using my childhood measures and females were divided into little girls, girls, and women), who had moved to our old back room but who seemed to have money and was quite daring. At least she had a radio, and not even María Montoya possessed such a precious talking machine. Nila had a husband named Reynaldo. I overheard my mother say once that he looked like a prime pimp, which in the newspapers was always a procurer. But this didn't make Nila a whore, because rather than living with her, Reynaldo visited her. He was a tall man, who impressed me because he always dressed so well, in dazzling white suits and an eternal light straw hat: "A panamá," my mother explained, "the most expensive hat there is," and it was said that the panamá hat was virtually indestructible: I immediately associated the quality of the hat with its owner.

Nila had become friends with us, particularly with the Kid, my uncle. When she was alone, Nila would amuse herself by having long chats with the Kid. Sometimes those conversations got very intimate and worried my mother, who feared that Reynaldo would catch them together one day. "That man is dangerous," my mother used to warn, and I attributed his attire to the danger: each time I saw someone in an expensive white suit and a panamá hat, I'd invariably think: "That man is dangerous," and later I learned the phrase in English, "He's dressed to kill."

Sometimes Nila's entertainment was merely going to the movies, accompanied by me of course—I've always managed to go to the movies for free. I remember having gone with her to the scandalous Scarlet Salon (its name had connotations that were apparently so obscene that, at the request of the decent families in the neighborhood, it was soon changed to the Starlet Salon), which had the arbitrary architecture of facing the seats toward the entrance, the screen placed where the projection room usually is, and vice versa. I could never find an explanation for that whimsical inversion.

There we saw more than one unforgettable movie, I entranced with the film when I should have laid my eyes upon the starlet or scarlet beauty beside me. This woman, girl, Nila must have lent the book to my uncle the Kid, of course she did, now I have no doubt it was her licentious loan. (Her hidden hands handed to my uncle the book in red he read with such secrecy.) I don't know how I managed to steal—not steal: borrow without asking, which is what I did, returning it as stealthily as when I picked it up: thus I learned to mask my joy—*Memoirs of a Russian Princess,* from its very title an object of scandal to my father. Already on the first page, without preambles which would be an obstacle, the sexual descriptions were generated, degenerated, regenerated by the princess named Vávara, who enjoyed the most obscene adventures, fucking more and more profusely, intricately, involving more and more people in each successive *tableau.* The book excited me sexually, free of complications, and if I had known how to masturbate (I was always a retard in sex though advanced in love) I would have done it, in spite of not having a refuge like the distant outhouse back home. I would have had to hide in the shared bathroom (a phrase I learned from my mother in Havana, which I'm using ironically now: please note: a shared bathroom, according to the home-appliance publicity of that era, was an apartment bathroom placed between two rooms: in this rooming house there were one shower and one toilet for all the tenants, the bathroom as collective as the kitchen, but I don't want to discuss this sweeping discomfort but rather the lack of a good place to masturbate—if I had known how), however, I limited myself to a merely passive reading.

Though Monte 822 was an intermezzo, an intermission, I continued my apprenticeship in love, begun back home with a cousin famous in the family for her green eyes—but that's another story and belongs elsewhere. Love complications arose on the Monte, in this temporary tenement, which was really a return to the childhood I had lost at Zulueta 408. Complications took the form of a quartet, a triplet rather, involving three girls, one of them a real little girl. They lived next door, in the room facing the kitchen, and were the daughters of the driver of a taxi (called a hired car then) named Pablo Efesio. A bald mustachioed mulatto, he was dark and dangerous, and not a fake danger like Nila's husband, a postcard villain, but an ex-jailbird as he himself admitted. He didn't inspire much respect in me because I knew his weakpoint: his daughters, who were by no means self-Ephesians. You already know their mother: Victoria, Rubén Fornaris's stealthy avenger, who was dying leisurely of a languid tuberculosis. The three sisters couldn't have been more different from one another: Esther, the youngest who was actually ten years old, was lame in one leg, had a slightly long nose, and wore her hair, straighter than her sisters', in curls. Then came Rachel, who had enormous eyes and a big Negroid mouth, with plenty of black curls in her more wavy hair: she was precociously naughty for her twelve years. Finally there was Magdalena, tall, thin, with perhaps a touch of the tuberculosis that would kill her mother a few years later: she was very serious and her fourteen years seemed twenty to me.

Esther was the one I fell in love with, initiating my passion for impossible loves, looking for perfection in the imperfect woman. My anonymous love had such a need to express itself that I took nature as my witness: on a family trip to the neighboring town of Cuatro Caminos, to the house of relatives of my father, I somehow managed, probably following some boring romantic movie I saw with Nila, to carve Esther's and my initials on a tree in the patio, which I surely crippled with the big entwining heart. I don't know how I tattooed that totem since knives had been forbidden by my father: I must have used a penknife. When I returned to the rooming house I was going to tell Esther about this lover's feat but her father was at her door as the ubiquitous ursine usher. And then Rachel got in the way.

It was after school, as I was playing parcheesi with Esther, Rachel, and Magdalena, that the first of a series of perturbing incidents occurred, blurred in my memory by subsequent sequels. The parcheesi board was on a small table (where they probably ate since there was no place in the room for a bigger table) and the game was at its most intricate, with all the squares occupied, when I felt someone touching me between the legs and it wasn't a casual touch because that member was looking for my member. I looked at Esther, beside me, then at Magdalena on the other side: both were too involved in parcheesi to be thinking about my weenie. Then I looked at Rachel: she had to be the one with the tactile foot since it couldn't be their mother sitting at the window, sewing and coughing faintly. But Rachel was looking down, at the parcheesi. Suddenly she raised her eyes and didn't wink at me but rather laughed without moving her lips, her eyes shining daringly: she was the one. She didn't touch me

19

again but afterward confessed that she had been the one: she had taken off a shoe and with her bare foot had touched me right on my sex. From that moment on my erotic direction changed—but not my love, faithful till death or at least till we changed residence. My love was for Esther, who didn't understand erotic games: she didn't even let me touch her breasts, perhaps because they didn't exist, but there was her flat chest which she didn't let me fondle. She let herself be kissed softly, however, with her long-lashed eyes closed, looking like the true image of chastity.

With Rachel there were other more and more intimate games. I don't know how I found a place for us—and I'm speaking not only of space but of time in the reduced rooming house, watched as she was, not only by her mother but by Magdalena. But we found the time and the place. The game got more serious on one of these occasions, when I went with Rachel to get some alcohol far from home—the war had begun and they were rationing alcohol. Rachel and I went up distant side streets around Monte, near Cristina Street and the Starlet Salon, dark and hostile roads where I was afraid of meeting up with some gang. Can time turn dreams into nightmares? In six months the gangs, one of which I had briefly belonged to, had changed from friendly to threatening associations. They all seemed to have their habitats, their territories, in the outskirts, and the most dangerous were, who knows why, those from the Luyanó neighborhood, forbidden terrain for me until one day, more to show my bravery than out of necessity, I crossed the whole length of it with all the fear in the world, and with a schoolmate, only to reach an anticlimax: we survived the adventure not only without a scratch but without even a menacing gesture. On those eager searches for alcohol (not a drinking potion for my abstemious father but fuel for cooking on a Havana invention called the headlighter, which didn't reflect light but rather produced heat: it was a miniature stove, extremely dangerous with its diet of alcohol and a turbulent tendency to explode, more Molotov cocktail than oven: my mother cooked on one of those alcohol contraptions until my father bought a portable kerosene stove) Rachel always came with me and had the habit of putting one of her hands (in reality, little hands) in one of my pockets, not taking refuge from the cold but rather taking advantage of my intimacy and, sheltered by the dark (I don't know why this far-flung foray for fuel was always at night or late in the afternoon when it was nearly dark, propitious for our departure to the promised land of love and alcohol), she'd feel me fully, trying to caress my little penis, which was already erect—the mere placing of her hand in my pocket produced an erection. Just to leave the house with her was already an erotic trip. As these searching parties were frequent (those stoves were like alcoholics: not only precarious but avid for booze), I was clever enough to open a hole at the bottom of the pocket so that Rachel could stick her little hand in and find my little penis. I don't remember any ejaculations but I do remember wandering the streets parallel to Monte, from Rastro—a source of alcohol—to Cuatro Caminos (a city crossroads, not the town of the same name many kilometers away), not only a dangerous but a busy corner and, what's worse (I never before thought I would hate the lights of the Havana night), very illuminated, in a bewitched wanderlust, in complete surrender to sex, still incipient but already powerful, entrancing, enthralling, an invisible halo but no less radiant than the phosphorescence of the city.

The climax of my relationship with Rachel (which we disguised so well with adult dexterity) occurred one day when I was bathing in the tiny bathroom, which had a side window that was always closed, with an opening on top, the wall of the door ending about two yards above it. I was in the shower when I heard a voice calling my name. All I could think of was to look for its source in the walled-up window. The voice then said, "Up here," and I looked up and there was Rachel, looking and laughing at me, precariously holding on to the top of the wall. I didn't know what to say, I who was so used to bathing alone, so determined not to be seen naked by anyone. Perhaps I even tried to cover myself, with ridicule. Rachel, very content with her daring deed, laughed like a madwoman. On top of that she suggested that I do the same (look, not laugh) when she was bathing. "I'm not going to cover myself," she said encouraging me, but I never dared to imitate her, perhaps fearful of her fierce father, or of the forbidden naked body.

It must be remembered that (without posing as irresistible) I was the only boy in the rooming house. So what happened afterward probably won't seem so strange. Rachel and Esther must have been at school but Magdalena, who took care of her mother, was cooking something in the kitchen. I don't know why I wasn't at school too, but somehow I managed to be passing by the kitchen (I had no business in that part of the house: our room was far from the kitchen; perhaps I was seeking, as I often did, the sound of the radio from Nila's room) and suddenly I found myself inside the kitchen, talking to Magdalena. The conversation was trivial: we had nothing to say to each other, and I even kept a certain distance since she was a big girl, almost a woman. Suddenly she said: "Why do you like Esther and Rachel?" and the question didn't end there, but rather she paused and asked, "and not me?" I was shocked. I didn't know what to say, how to answer her, to deal with such a direct question. "Is it because they're darker?" She surprised me, but not for long since the explanation was in plain view: Magdalena, unlike her sisters and more like her mother than her father, was almost white. Hers was an inverse racism that I would find often in the future: she resented not being as dark as her sisters. *Mulata* mania did exist in Cuba, especially for sex, but this was a male obsession. Black-haired women with dark skin and eyes (and a variation: dark women with green eyes, praised in popular mythology, mentioned in many songs, folk forms of poetry) were much admired but usually they were white women with dark skin. Meeting with this male admiration expressed by a woman, however, made it all more complicated. Magdalena was a complicated girl, not with Esther's complica-

21

tions as a cripple, but rather of a complexity nourished by the neurosis of her mother's consumptive complications, tuberculosis being a neurotic's malady.

It was too complex for my twelve years even though I was used to adult conversations. I had been educated by my mother (to the posthumous horror of Uncle Matías I ended up educated by my mother's heart, not my father's brain), by my father's political associations, by my Uncle Pepe's arguments, and by the overheard conversations of my mother and her girlfriends, gathered around her while she embroidered upon her eternal Singer sewing machine. But it was really too complex. I didn't know how to tell Magdalena that I liked her a lot (I really didn't: there was a nunlike quality about her, so devoted to her mother, so serious) and I couldn't do a thing. Magdalena must have guessed because she said: *"Pera,"* the Havana way of saying wait a minute, and she quickly left the kitchen and, before I could realize that she had abandoned me, she was back. Later I thought she had gone to see her mother but at the moment I didn't have time to think.

Magdalena had zoomed back into the kitchen just as she had left, her long, thin body slipping through the doorless doorway, and come silently toward me. Without a word she grabbed me by the arm and led me to an empty part of the wall next to the stove (which was really a cement platform to prop a headlighter or kerosene stove, center of the collective kitchen: it's curious: town poverty was more individual or all in the family, while urban poverty had first introduced me, in Zulueta 408, to communal showers and toilets and now, in Monte 822, to the collective kitchen. I can say that the rest of my adolescence was dominated, among other desires, by the longing to return to small-town individuality—not to the town though, a mere passing fancy or rather wish—in order to regain privacy, doors that would close and exclude a neighbor's possible intrusion, a toilet, bathroom, kitchen of one's own, the feeling of being singular again. But another of my longings was now about to be fulfilled by Magdalena, to get to the point) and in that corner she leaned over me, cornering me against the wall, pressing her lips against mine in the first adult kiss I was given in my life. I didn't open my mouth (I didn't know how) and neither did she open hers, but it wasn't an adolescent kiss: more than a girl, Magdalena was a woman. But, instead of delight, I felt confusion. I didn't know why she was doing what she was doing: it all happened silently, without preliminaries, without a motive. It's true that we saw each other often and played (with her sisters: domestic games, not yet drawing-room games but not the childhood games played back in town either), talked, shared life at the rooming house, but she had always seemed distant and cold. She wasn't like childish Esther, for whom "boy and girl" was yet another game, nor like Rachel with those naughty eyes and big white teeth behind her liver-lipped smile, the smiler with a secret under her skirt. Magdalena was very reserved. Even her thin lips showed this reserve, inherited from her mother, who kept even her ill-

22

ness silent, without ever letting herself be exposed by a loud cough. Esther and Rachel had their father's large mouth and had inherited his temperament, attenuated in Esther by her childishness but about to explode in Rachel, who was almost what was popularly known as a hot *mulata,* a creature of Havana's erotic mythology. Thin, pale Magdalena was as reserved as her mother, but was now kissing me as none of her sisters had ever done. Only Esther had really kissed me, a little girl's kisses, while Rachel was only interested in my penis: making it erect, touching, seeing it. Magdalena embraced me but her hands never went below my chest, revealing a passion I would qualify years later as romantic. I'm not going to be so vain as to believe that her passion, so sudden, was for me: it was an ancient, almost atavistic passion, expressed in my direction because I was the only boy who lived in the rooming house; the other young person was my uncle the Kid, and she must have realized there was something between the Kid and that Nila vamp, or perhaps she considered him too old.

I barely paid attention to what she was telling me amid the kisses or the long-sustained kiss, she speaking that esperanto of love, the language which expects more than it expresses, I being deaf because I was more interested in the kiss itself than in its literature. (Years later I would have been able to say that I paid more attention to her tongue than to her mother tongue.) In reality I was trying to touch her breasts, to bring my hand down between her legs, to caress her buttocks—all of which she prevented, controlling my arms with her embrace, kissing me, murmuring between the kisses words I didn't understand. When I noticed that the seconds passed as do certain seconds which seem more like minutes, and she didn't separate from me, I began to worry that someone might come into the kitchen, perhaps her quiet mother entering silently. Or even worse, her ferocious father, a hasty and reckless taxi driver, could return home ahead of time, that is, in evil hour. As I thought more and more of those possible enemy ambuscades, I must have transmitted my fear to Magdalena—a fear greater than love—because she left off kissing with an action as sudden as the one with which she began, and departed from our embrace and the kitchen like a single solid shadow. I remained there breathless, motionless, absolutely surprised, amazed at Magdalena's attack. (Yes, it had been an attack, a rape of kisses.) But I was also waiting: wanting her to return, waiting for her to return, longing for her to return —but she didn't. After a while (minutes with the waiting weight of hours) I left the kitchen and tried to find Magdalena somewhere in the house, unsuccessfully. Of course I didn't look for her where I would have found her, in her room—the contradictions of a captive of both love and fear.

That was the first and last time I had intimate relations with Magdalena. She even seemed to appear distant afterward (she had never been very close, but she had always been accessible when addressed). Later, much later, when we moved back to Zulueta 408 and the sisters came to visit, only Rachel and Esther appeared. Childish Esther was the same and seemed angry because of her slightly jutting jaw—perhaps she resented her maimed leg—but Rachel had changed: by becoming more of a woman she had become conscious of a particular fault and seemed to have a racial inferiority complex. I remember that when we met on the roof with some boys from the building she gave me the impression that she was afraid I had told about our escapades on apparent errands that were really errant practice sessions of secret sports. But before, those sexual adventures not only didn't bother her but she even wanted them to be known. Once she even asked me—I'll never forget—all smiling big teeth and fat lips: "And you didn't tell your uncle?" but really saying: "Why didn't you tell your uncle?" On that sole visit (they never came by anymore and later I learned that their mother had died) Magdalena didn't come and I never saw her again.

We left Monte 822 (significantly in the month of April though the significance is totally personal) to return to first base, the first stop, the starting point: in some way we were destined for Zulueta 408. From the moment we left that phalanstery my father had been trying to return, among other reasons because it faced the Havana Institute, where I was to begin my baccalaureate, a reason that always seemed an excuse to me. My mother too liked to live in downtown Havana, even if it had to be in that bizarre building with its depraved architecture. (My friend Silvio Rigor, an acquaintance when I was already a student at the Institute, was one of my first friends to visit the room, the domicile which I hid the best I could, hiding from my schoolmates the fact that I lived in a tenement. Silvio called it the House of Changes and never referred to the place where I lived by any other name: with time I have come to understand that no name could be more apt.) But before moving from Monte 822 I came up in a conversation between Pablo the taxi driver and my mother, on the rooming-house terrace where the neighbors would always meet to chat. I had overheard conversations before but now I could hear it clearly: Pablo was warning my mother with his husky voice, in futile whispers, that what I needed more than an education was for them to make a man out of me. He was sincerely worried because he had seen me playing with his little girls a lot, perhaps too much for a boy, definitely not good for a future man. "A boy shouldn't play with girls," he pronounced. I remember that even then I managed to wonder what would happen if this dangerous man, a didactic daddy, knew what games I really played with his dear daughters.

I had come several times to this part of Havana with my mother, to visit an old friend from our town and her grown-up daughter (the two had been obliged to leave town because the mother had had relations with a stranger and become an unwed mother; her daughter, an old-fashioned beauty named Carola, died mysteriously in Havana, of tuberculosis we were told), also to visit my godfather, a dentist who had an office on Compostela Street, and to fly like a moth to the light of the Actualidades Theater, its lights and shadows sometimes accompanied by the new American music, swing. I had traversed the Paseo del Prado several times and attended, at the end of the promenade, many live radio shows on station CMQ, but even though I had sailed around that future island I had never returned. Let's say then that I came back from beyond to Zulueta 408, this tenement, this phalanstery, which would be pivotal in my life, of which I still dream dreams that have the shape of nightmares, and which I had entered—or rather, penetrated—as a child and would leave as a man, which created at the same time it consumed my adolescence.

I think I should give a rough sketch of the building now that we were installed there more or less definitely (at first I thought indefinitely, then I believed eternally), and I had all the time in the world to explore it. It had (or still has: its perverse structure seemed to be made to last forever) three floors, without a ground floor. (Here there was only a utility room near the enormous entrance to keep the cleaning equipment.) The first floor was gloomy because it was submerged in constant darkness, and all the rooms were closed except the double room of the superintendent, the *encargada*, the concierge, who was also a stand-in for maid, janitor, and Cerberus: her door a great iron grille of a gate, which allowed her to observe with ubiquitous eye all the movements of the inner corridor onto which it faced, and the landing after the first flight of stairs. The second floor was where we lived, which I now saw (I had never left it, really) bathed in an ashen light coming from the open rooms, the light filtered through curtains that were also doors, and up above was the third floor, reached by an old open wooden staircase, which was also the access to the vast roof, where the neighbors would hang their clothes out to dry. There were only five roof rooms, and they seemed precarious, with their wooden frames. But on the second floor there were fifteen rooms, where as many families lived. The room my father had rented (the cell to which we had been sentenced) didn't have a window and opened onto the long inner corridor. Another door led to a kind of rundown terrace (where the open staircase was), with an inner patio, a little square facing the bathrooms, the toilets and, more important, the so-called font. This was another new word for me (the only font I knew then was the marble baptismal font in the town church) and this dismal font now was really a rusty old faucet with a cement basin below, almost a square meter in shape, surrounding the tap up to a meter high on three sides. The fourth side was a fifth column supporting the faucet, which seemed to have a chronic cold: drip drip dripping: thus its font name was not a bad metaphor after all. Behind that basin was a large square transom, several meters long and wide, which let some faint light through to the house downstairs, an alien domain. This giant transom, made of wire netting and wood, protected the lower depths from dust and debris, foul manna from above. The basin, the toilet, and the bathroom roofs (as well as the huge transom, of course) all faced the open air, flanked by the adjoining building's wall. Topping that wall was a semicircular opening, an in-

25

verted *arc-en-ciel* through which one could see the nearest high wall of the Payret Theater, yellow with green mold like an old backdrop, and, if you strained, the cloudless tropical sky.

Along the south face of that cliff climbed a runaway chimpanzee one day: the wretched creature, mistreated by his tamer training him in the patio of the theater, near the men's outhouse, scaled the whole wall and got onto the roof to then come down the wooden staircase and stroll about, tottering yet majestic, a sad human version of an ape. Yet he was sufficiently simian to wreak havoc everywhere and to create panic among the women, especially the young and beautiful. Even though many of these *solar* beauties were incapable of feeling fear for their supposedly endangered maidenheads—ape's rape—the hairy beast made that theater wall a memory to treasure: our Mutia Escarpment. Or even better, the poor ape's Empire State.

An all-seeing eye to the lower floors, the treacherous transom was dangerous and therefore fascinating. After negotiating its iron railing, any daring boy (and lightweight too: I was skinny then and could have run the risk, as many of my mates did, but I never dared) could dash across the old pinewood frame to hang for a breath-taking moment above the man-made chasm, transforming the wooden crossbeam into a flying trapeze, the wire mesh a false safety net. But the strange skylight (a square bull's eye through which light and sounds could pass *partout*) imparted a double vision more dangerous to the spirit than to the flesh that dared to crawl across its threshold: it was a keyhole that had no door, you see.

The first person I met at Zulueta 408 was, inevitably, the nearest neighbor, in this case the next-door neighbor. Her name was Isabel Scribé, who without the accent fulfilled in her surname my future sentence. Isabel Scribé most probably descended from Catalans (many Cubans have Catalan names) but she had enough drops of black blood in her veins for her skin to have that iodine color I associate with certain young beauties who go often to the beach or who have the same black mixture —half and half half-castes, *mulatas à la mode.* But Isabel Scribé was for me almost an old lady (she must have been forty-five or environs) seen from my twelve years. She was old-fashioned enough to let it be known more often than not and with the legitimate pride of a wife, that she had been the mistress (that is, the official paramour) of Don Domingo Rosillo —with full certainty that all of us knew who Domingo Rosillo was. I, of course, had not the faintest.

It must have been my father then who informed me that Domingo Rosillo, already an "older man" at the time, was a pioneering aviator, a hero of Cuban aviation: he had crossed, solo, the Florida Strait in 1913— more than a quarter of a century before! This exploit only made Isabel older than I thought. Around the time I knew Isabel Scribé, Rosillo was of course a former lover, she perhaps one more loop in his flying memory. Isabel Scribé, whom I began calling Doña Isabel, following the town custom (to her dismay: she finally forbade me to continue calling her Doña), is important to me not only because I felt attracted to the remains of her beauty, as if visiting ruins, but because she was a *real* mistress: I finally knew one. I had heard my mother talk of many mistresses abroad (different from the women in town who had lovers and were merely kept women, plebeian), indiscreetly catching the information in full flight while pretending to be playing around her Singer sewing machine. Mistress meant mystery. I didn't know then that it was only the feminine form of master.

Next to Isabel Scribé, and next to the bathroom, lived a family composed of Gerardito (the neighborhood barber, whose barbershop was on the ground floor beside the big entrance door), his wife, Dominica, his sister, Leonor (who one or two years later was going to die suddenly, run over by a trolley a few weeks before her wedding: elements of melodrama forming a true family tragedy: she was, besides, an Andalusian beauty and didn't deserve to die), and the couple's daughter, Elsita, a fat dwarf who had to have God knows how many baby teeth removed. When Isabel Scribé moved (Doña Isabel was the first person who could abandon the phalanstery for a decent apartment, giving me the hope that it was possible to leave Zulueta 408), Gerardito's family transferred into her room. The room they left was rented by Rosendo Rey, a very serious Spaniard, who always wore a white hat, which my mother informed me was not made of real jipijapa (making him a dangerous fraud) and who would produce one day a scandalous revelation—if anything, by that time, could scandalize me (or anybody) at Zulueta 408.

Dominica, unlike her sister, was an ugly woman: she had a tough face, with a large thick jaw, thin lips, sparse lashes, and thick eyebrows. She looked Galician enough, but she had tremendous tits, which never failed to impress me then. Afterward, with time and knowledge, I would become an expert on tits and would come to appreciate small tits, almost absent breasts—like Elsita's. Though the idea never went through my head nor the desire through my body for that little girl full of loose baby teeth, always insisting that I pull them out. "You should study to be a dentist," Dominica said to me after each painless extraction as if that were an uplifting prospect. Dominica used to talk to me a lot, perhaps compelled by her solitude, with Elsita at school, Gerardito cutting hair down below, her sister dead. I think she was the first person in the tenement in whom I noticed loneliness, so inappropriate in such a jampacked place, where life was so promiscuous. She didn't listen to me read like a river, or chat like Isabel Scribé, sorry widow.

Dominica didn't have iodine-colored skin and used to talk not about airplanes and daring pilots but about everyday subjects which bored me to yawns and tears, but with Isabel Scribé, aviatrix (when I first heard this word I thought it meant the wife of an aviator), I had begun to cultivate an interest in older women: a decidedly sexual interest. Of course I had my eyes on girls my own age, as in that vision converted into

27

distant passion and never, alas, requited by Gloria Graña, alliterative and arrogant, beneath whose balcony I was a daytime and remote Romeo and never called by my name in the name of love. Dominica, with her big head and big teeth, could not be a passion but could become an interest. I began to suspect that she was somewhat more than amused by our conversation when one day she interrupted her chatter, lively until then, because Elsita came back. Another day (my visit must have taken place in the morning) she became very agitated at the unforeseen return of Gerardito, father figaro.

It wasn't till years later that I adopted the custom of imagining the possible, impossible sexual act of couples, single people, and bachelors, of friends, acquaintances, and even total strangers, and now I think that Gerardito's coitus must have been spectacular: so big, so fat, always breathing through his mouth—because of a nasal malady that would bring death upon him. He died suddenly, and when they did his post-mortem they discovered an enormous hairy ball which obstructed his stomach: he had absorbed the hairs from his customers, breathing through his mouth while cutting. Red from high blood pressure, this lubricious Leviathan must have spouted like a sperm whale, up and down, up and down, almost crushing Dominica, some sort of siren, a Sirenian.

Time passed and my visits became more scarce: I didn't dedicate all my attention to Dominica: constance is not among my virtues, at least in regards to love. But I visited Dominica an afternoon here or there and it was my custom (learned at the university of Zulueta 408) to enter her room at any hour—if of course Elsita wasn't there with some loose baby tooth or the corpulent Gerardito occupying now the whole space of the room, stretching toward the little terrace, expanding throughout the tenement, which was like saying the universe then. One time I raised the curtain, entered, and caught Dominica in her slip. She didn't make any move to complete her attire with even a blouse or by covering herself with a towel: she simply sat there next to the window, covered by a curtain. As soon as I saw her my perturbation turned into conversation: a trait of my timidity since, though laconic by nature, shyness made me garrulous. I don't remember what I said: I only remember that Dominica answered me but there was no place for conversation for either of us: it was a mere scrap, a piece of crap like the curtain, to mask the situation. I had remained in the same place I had occupied when entering: seeing Dominica in her slip I ventured to the middle of the room, which wasn't very large but whose halves were in relation to its proportions: despite my first giant step I still had another half to cross to Dominica sitting beside the window, evidently just bathed, still half dressed, apparently waiting. I didn't even think she was waiting for me but rather for Elsita or Gerardito, though I knew that at three in the afternoon it was dubious that either of the two could return and even if they could—why wait for a daughter or husband in a slack slip, more naked than dressed? But, question without an answer, why wait for me, now an occasional visitor —a mature woman waiting for a barely adolescent boy, for a risky rendezvous, a trying tryst?

We spoke (or rather, I spoke) and while I talked I saw the down on her upper lip perspiring despite her recent bath, she still in profile, answering my questions and occasionally asking questions I was supposed to answer in turn—questions and answers that had nothing to do with what was happening. I imagined an arm longer than mine (monstrously longer, in fact) like a daring hand reaching the edge of her slip salaciously and gently caressing her breasts. Her ugliness did not detain me (though even in profile it was possible to notice the narrow forehead, protruding eyebrows, ball-point nose and great distance between this and the upper lip, which together with the lower formed a muzzle more than a mouth: all this was blurred by the promise of her breasts and, more important, her sex) but rather respect for my elders. What if I touched her and she was shocked, the boy electric? Or if she wasn't frightened but simply told my mother, who would then be the author of the scandal? Or if she threw me out of the room and out of her life? But if those social considerations stopped my short hand my penis did not peter, prolonging all this digressive time and now aggressively raising my pants. So much so that Gerardito's sudden entrance, his rapid glance (in my guilty imagination that look could only be toward one place on my clothed anatomy but denouncing, announcing nudity) would reveal what was happening, or worse: what was going to happen, even if he didn't notice that his wife was in her slip (I dreamt awake that she wasn't wearing panties underneath, that she was naked except for this piece which made her partial nudity more exciting, that she was dressed like this on purpose, and I even fantasized that it was I she wanted to tantalize), that between us was a tension, a sure sexual current.

Dominica and I stopped speaking at the same moment. There was a pregnant silence in which the licentious noise of my penis could be heard, compelling, impelling me to act. I think I moved a foot. I'm not certain. I was moving between the imagined mediate future and the immediate present: time that abolished space. At that moment Dominica, no longer in profile, mistress of her place, turned toward me. She looked at me and must have noticed my turgescence: I presumed it was as visible for everybody (everybody was then Dominica) as it was for me: I felt its thrust through the tropical fabric of underpants and pants, my pushing penis: an enormous appendage to me, my monument, as evident in that moment as an obelisque in a square. Dominica was looking at me in silence but I can't say whether she was looking at me or my penis, though the two of us were one. Now she said, in an amazingly sweet but unrefined tone: "I think you better go."

I heard her but didn't want to believe what I had just heard: this woman who had been in a closed room (the curtains kept both stage and actors out of view: everything in the tenement happened backstage), half naked, suggestive, exciting me with her nudity (or with the partially dressed promise of becoming totally nude), but also with her conversation (the fact that she had talked about nothing, remaining as impassive with her lip as in her slip was a form of verbal excitement), she who had made my penis grow out of near nonexistence—isn't there a saying that says what you don't see doesn't exist?—until becoming a presence that could connect us both, was now playing the role of decent housewife (her room her theater), sending me away, dismissing me. I couldn't understand it. I simply couldn't understand it. I even thought that she must have felt flattered that with her ugliness and years (she was probably only thirty) she had managed not only to interest but to excite me to the point of indiscretion. But today I tend to think that decent Dominica did the right thing in exiling my obscene presence with a sweet but sweeping voice. After all, I could have been completely mistaken and have taken a mere social gesture to be sexual interest. I certainly left the room, confused but no longer fearing Gerardito's imposing intrusion, running, snorting, straining to save his wife's honor, or her telling my mother or Elsita arriving untimely, in time to see my pitched tent and ask: "What's that?," to discover sex just when her first baby teeth were coming out, her toothdrawer also her tutor in maturing prematurely, she reaching public puberty through my private part.

Many years later I discovered a painting by Quentin Matsys, unknown to the ignoramus me in Cuba despite my interest in painting since boyhood, called "The Ugly Duchess," a portrait of Margaretha Maultasch, supposedly the ugliest woman of her time. When my wife declared, "I've never known anybody so ugly," I thought immediately of Dominica, dubious duchess but ubiquitously ugly, turning a dizzying double somersault of centuries and continents, from a rich Belgian museum to the Old Havana phalanstery, and I said, "Well, I did."

But I didn't say that I had desired her ardently once. I left to never again enter that room—three walls and a curtain—which had awakened my desire (remembered or imagined, directly or vicariously) for two older women, one who could have been my grandmother, the other who could have easily been my mother. But if I had felt a vicarious form of desire for Isabel Scribé, thinking back on how desirable she must have been when young (even with her slightly crossed eyes, which I just thought to mention only now), the other, despite her ducal ugliness, managed to awaken in me true desire. I didn't return to her room, though she welcomed me more than once and I had to take out another of forever repellent Elsita's baby teeth. She seemed to produce loose teeth at a faster pace than my capacity to pull them out, Dominica, the mother nurse, intervening to grab the still bloody tooth and keep it, putting it away like a treasure and at the same time exclaiming, paying me off with her favorite phrase: "You really should study to be a dentist."

My attention turned, like my footsteps, in the direction of the third room facing the little patio, to the left of ours. I don't remember who lived there before Zenaida and her fertile family moved in. Besides her parents there were several brothers and sisters but Zenaida was the eldest, the best. She turned, in a matter of days, from a plain girl into a woman of rare beauty: fair, with reddish-brown hair and violet eyes, an eye color foreign to Havana. In her features she preceded the popular image of a European movie star, Alida Valli, captured and christened by Hollywood's marvelous lie machine with her Italian half-name. This falling star—declining as an actress, not as a woman—was never more beautiful than when I saw her years later, a mature woman, in Mexico. There, in a fashionable nightclub where an Indian singer sang hoarse boleros, a Mexican producer introduced me to her, and I, who never knew how to dance a step, impelled by alcohol and enthusiasm, went out on the floor with Valli and was able to hold her desirable flesh though not as desirable as when she was a face on a screen, as Gregory Peck desired her. I tried, a dancing fool, to pick her up, unaware that seated at our same table in the low light was her secret husband, a silent spectator, an anonymous American photographer: they had married secretly to preserve her star status. When I learned that they were an incognito couple, my shame doubled, because of both the fiasco of trying to seduce the actress and the presence of her hidden husband. I felt like Joseph Cotten felt. But a triple love absolves me of the double guilt: my love for the movie star, the real woman, and the memory of Zenaida.

Older than I, she never looked upon me except as a young neighbor, and then she married Bautista López, my father's cousin, who met her while visiting us and who was noteworthy because even though he was quite young he had gray hair. My mother said that Bautista was very handsome, that the gray hair made him interesting: "He looks bleached blond." Zenaida must have thought the same because they started going together immediately.

Nevertheless, I once held this simple Valli, as with her double, in my arms, though not thanks to alcohol or the dark but because of an idiotic, dangerous and (must I add?) adolescent joke. She too was an adolescent. How green was my Valli then! Zenaida was always saying that she was mortally afraid of mice and nobody believed the extent of her fear, which was all a comic convention. One day Chino (one of the tenement boys), another boy (I don't remember who: perhaps Cuco), and I prepared a culinary surprise for Zenaida. We invited her to Chino's, facing the street (the same room with the exotic smell where we stayed upon our arrival in Havana, inherited by Chino's family, relatives of the former tenants), made her go out on the balcony before the meal, and Chino appeared with a dish covered by another and saying, "Look, Zenaida—alive and kicking!," he raised the upper dish to uncover a dead mouse. Zenaida screamed upon seeing it and the joke almost ended badly, since in her panic she tried to jump off the balcony to the street three floors below. I was the one who had the double luck to grab her, both preventing her death and having her in my arms alive, only a moment but enough to feel

31

her body trembling, not from my embrace but for the dead animal, not for love but out of her harassing horror of mice, her fear no less impulsive than my desire. Zenaida forgave my participation in the practical joke but I didn't forget my part. It consoled me later in my envy of Bautista, knowing that I too had held Zenaida's flesh, similar to the Italian actress's but younger, more tender, though no less reluctant toward my embrace, both women a single myth.

Before traversing in memory the long central corridor, longer now in my recollections, and entering again the rooms I frequented during eight adolescent years (my adolescence would actually extend beyond adulthood, lasting lingeringly), I want to tell of my encounter with evil and pleasure made into the same flesh: evil for others, pleasure also for others, but for me a memorable meeting. It occurred upon my return from that summer in my hometown: it was still summer because I wasn't going to school and that September was when I began to audit classes at the Institute. In my absence my mother had become friends with a girl whom nobody else on the floor had dealings with because she was a whore. There was another whore in the tenement but she was what I would learn later was a luxury prostitute, who had a rented room but didn't live in it, or only visited it. But Etelvina (the girl's name) was what was known as a *fletera,* a streetwalker, a word learned in Havana. Only my mother, with her terrible tolerance, broke the social fence in which they had all enclosed Etelvina. When I said that Etelvina was a girl I wasn't euphemizing and should have told her age: Etelvina Marqués wasn't any older than fourteen and had confessed to my mother that she had been a whore for two years. She had escaped her mother's manor in Camagüey at that age, and had come to settle in Havana. She was the niece of Senator Marqués, notorious years back for his mysterious murder, probably a political assassination. I remember the headlines: "MARQUES MURDERED." Etelvina had told my mother who she was, her real age, and how she had escaped home.

Unlike many whores, Etelvina didn't have a pimp and was extremely independent. She was a tall blonde (peroxide blonde, not platinum or honey-colored but rather an intermediate though definite blond tone characteristic of bleached dark hair, like burnt blond), pretty and quite happy, so much so that she justified the epithet "daughter of joy." Moreover, she was amazingly adult, so much so that no one would guess she was fourteen—which doubtless had permitted her to escape the law against the corruption of minors. My mother, perhaps to show that she wasn't afraid of Etelvina's social leprosy, had appropriated the cuckoo's job of waking her up in the morning: since she got up early (or rather, never slept, an insomniac all her life) she made sure that Etelvina didn't sleep past eleven.

When I came back from home my mother entrusted me with this tedious task: now I had to wake up Etelvina every day, knocking hard on her door until she declared shouting that she was awake. But by no means should I enter her room. My mother warned me that, although Etelvina was a good girl, she could have bad diseases, which was the general expression for all the gonorrheas, blennorrheas and plural syphilis of the scarlet woman. What's more, the phrase "bad woman's disease" was the one used by my mother, despite her liberalism. She also led me to believe, through veiled words, that all the evil of Havana was concentrated in Etelvina's room. (Though our town was big, there was only one whore, curiously: also scandalously blonde, Gloria Cupertino was so contagious that the mere mention of her splendid name was enough to infect you.) I woke Etelvina dutifully many times, knocking on her door not like a cuckoo but like a woodpecker—no pun intended.

But one day I went to wake her and knocked on the door not once but several times and still no one answered. I knocked once again and saw that the door, as in mystery movies, was ajar. I thought something had happened to her during the night, and thus the door had been left open. Even though we'd sometimes sleep in the summertime with the door open, protected only by the constant curtain, Etelvina didn't have a front curtain. I pushed the door and it opened more, all the way, and from the door frame I could see the whole room, but I didn't even look at it: I only had eyes for Etelvina. She was lying face down on the bed—totally naked. I don't know what precisely led me to enter, either uncertain curiosity or definite desire. I went to the bed and touched her body (her shoulder) because, my morbid mind!, I thought she was dead, perhaps felled by the foul woman's disease. As I touched her I felt her warmth (almost heat: she was alive: ever since the death of my baby sister years before, I had learned that dead bodies, saints or sinners, are always cold) and now I shook her shoulder.

Etelvina woke up, turned around slowly, and, upon seeing me, she smiled. "I came to wake you," I said. She yawned: unlike mine and my family's teeth, hers were a complete and healthy set: the disease had not attacked her through the mouth. "It's just that last night," she explained to me between yawns, which I had learned were in very poor form and she, after all, was the niece of a senator, though now deceased: perhaps street life had infected her not only with a bad disease but with mean manner: "I went to bed very late." Then I noticed that all this time she had remained nude, without making the slightest gesture to cover herself, a hirsute vagina before me: the first I had seen in my life. She was showing her tits, which seemed enormous to me: the only ones I had seen naked till now, my mother's, eyed surreptitiously, were not even a third as large as Etelvina's, who was not a woman but a mere girl. "Sit down," she said, leaving a side free for me on the bed, and I obeyed her more rapidly than if I had intended to sit down, impelled as always by my timidity. I must add here that I was careful, upon seeing Etelvina naked on the bed, to close the door behind me: perhaps I did it so that she couldn't be seen naked from the corridor, perhaps it was another act of shyness, but I never had the intention of creating an intimacy: Etelvina

33

was evil for me and besides she was dead, remember?

I forget what she talked about and maybe she didn't talk about anything else but what she was talking about, which was, what else? sex: she was a sexual creature: natural selection. I remember the naughty eyes she flickered at me as she spoke (her eyes were made up with what was beginning to be called Maybelline, real American mascara, but she had no lipstick on: perhaps sleep—or someone—had erased it), her suggestive voice saying, suddenly: "So, you jerk off yet?" I pretended not to know what she was talking about: I couldn't tell her that I did know what masturbation was, an art I had learned recently, but unlike other arts I had learned it well. Of course I would have preferred to study it with Etelvina rather than with my anonymous informant: having as my instructor all that naked flesh spread on the bed would have been much more pleasant than Nano, a nil initiator.

But I said nothing. I didn't say if I knew or didn't know: I kept mum. "You don't know how it's done?" Etelvina asked and sat up in bed. Her breasts, which before fell to the sides of her body, now sat erect with her, like glowing golden domes over her Bosphorus. "It's very easy," she continued. "You take it out," pointing to my fly, which was as flat as my penis was flaccid: fearful, retreating, reduced by the terror of so much nearby nude flesh, "and you jerk your dickie and you come." For a moment I feared—but also desired—that she would do a demonstration for me, right there. *Quod eros demonstrandum.* But she didn't carry it out: she remained sitting on the bed, her legs bent between her arms, her sex almost open or perhaps open but not clearly seen by my alerted eyes. "But you have to do it yourself, though," she advised, "if not, it's not jerking off."

Now I was assaulted by the fear that my mother would come in: I had been too long at the task of waking up Etelvina when three knocks were enough (for two knockers), but I didn't feel at all like leaving the room, not on my own steam. Etelvina was the first woman I had really seen naked (when I saw my cousin naked she was a child and, to boot, I think she had only raised her skirt, and the three little amorous *mulatas* never got undressed for me: one of them did it in the bathroom but I didn't have the courage to jump over the barrier of modesty which was the protective wall and watch her take a shower), and though I had found Etelvina naked (it's not the same to see a woman denuding as to see her already in the nude) it was still exciting, despite my timidity, my fear, my apprehension of the impending arrival of my mother, who was then (regarding Etelvina) the sex police. I was thrilled to the point of hearing my telltale heart beat at the sight of that girl with the big (for me grandiose) tits, with already womanly hips, with that smile as naughty as her eyes, talking immodestly of pricks, jerking off, and coming as if talking about flowers while sitting naked in a garden.

I don't know how I left the room, how I could go away from the bower of that unveiling, how I could abandon such bliss and leave gorgeous golden Etelvina nude, looking at me with her salacious eyes, smiling with her public lips (even her private lips must have been smiling then though I didn't know how to locate them), leaving behind this sweet and happy whore. She wasn't the only happy whore I met in my life.

Years later, working for *Carteles,* next to one of Havana's brothel districts, on its very border, an easy access—acsex, Silvio Rigor would say then—to the cathouses, I got to know true daughters of joy. I don't know why my literary sources didn't recognize this epithet. Perhaps the erroneous notion of the unhappy whore was learned in *Nana*—whatever Zola wants, Zola gets. But it was not my good fortune to awaken Etelvina anymore. Maybe my mother noticed my delay that day or saw in my face that I had said hello to evil. I don't know, but the truth is that I never again saw all that splendid young flesh, naked and easy. (See sassy.) A short time later she moved to a better street and when I saw her it was always from a distance. One day, she crossed the gardens of the Institute, her hair gilded in the sun like Belisa, an anagram, the mute muse of the baroque bard, and with the naked fragments she offered to the voyeur—arms, legs, neck protruding from her dress—I composed her bare body. Another day she was at the fruit stand on the corner of Teniente Rey, buying canistels that copied her golden color. I don't think she saw me this time either. She was as pretty as ever though it surprised me that she was up so early: it was barely eleven then.

But Etelvina left her true trace as a truce upon Raúl de Cárdenas, an eternal student who had been in love with her (perhaps he had been a customer, perhaps she simply gave him her goods: Etelvina was a generous whore) and who came to visit one day, as he often would. My mother found him pale and poorly, and Raúl confessed that Etelvina had infected him with an incurable disease: the feared word was whispered secretly, sibilant: *syphilis,* and I noticed my mother's alarm, and compassion for poor Raúl the victim, though she never put the blame on guilty Etelvina. When poor Raúl left, my mother immediately washed with alcohol the seat where he'd been sitting. My mother didn't know much about venereal diseases, viruses, or bacteria, but I knew less than my mother then and if I caught anything from poor Raúl, or beauteous Etelvina, it was the terrible terror—like Zenaida and her mice—of whores, which would turn out to be more harmful to me than having been infected with syphilis upon sitting on the edge of Etelvina's bed to chat.

Directly facing our room lived a man, his wife, and two Chinese daughters. But the daughters were already women—or at least seemed so to me. It was a queer family. The wife must have had Chinese ancestors because not only was she Chinese but the force of her race had strained through to her two daughters, slanting their eyes and their looks. They were all native *habaneras* but one of the daughters, named Gloria, was a typhoon, a dragon in the shape of a woman, our version of Dragon Lady. I never saw her smile, much less laugh. But I did see her burst into anger with everything and against everyone, especially her white target: her father, whose name was, curiously, Amparo, which not only spelt Shelter but also meant the first man I ever met who had a woman's name. Of course I had heard the names José María and Jesús María and their variants, in which the feminine name of María was like a complement and a compliment to the Virgin. But a man called Amparo was weird. Poor Amparo was demure, as determined by his name, outnumbered by the Chinese dames in his den. His far east room (it faced the sun) was the empire of Celeste, his commanding wife, and her demanding daughters. The eldest, Gloria, was what one could call *solariega,* an adjective coming from the Havana word *solar,* meaning tenement. From the original, aboriginal *solar* (meaning also wasteland or empty plot), the adjective *solariego* was easily derived, referring to everything having to do with the tenement but having nothing to do with the former manorial houses or *solariegas.* This adjective was a derogatory way of describing someone's character or ways: it meant an extreme form of the vulgar, the scandalous, the lowly. Gloria did not inherit the withdrawn, reserved character of the Chinese: she was boisterous, common, scrutable. Gloria was definitely *solariega.* She was the first person in whom I found this urban quality.

Gloria was a verbal-abusive *solariega.* She not only insulted her father but also insulted the next-door neighbors and once gratuitously insulted my mother: she was obviously capable of insulting the heavenly gates. After she insulted my mother we all stopped speaking to her. Or, rather, we had never really spoken to her because communication with these ever-evident neighbors (you only had to lift the curtain and there they were) took place through Delia, Gloria's sister. Delia was a real beauty: she was perhaps less curvaceous (another word I learned in Havana, where I had to learn so many that Spanish became exotic to me) but more statuesque (new word) than Gloria, and had a pallor probably inherited from her Chinese grandfather, since Amparo was white but dark and their mother was a tanned brunette, as was Gloria. Another contrast: Delia was sweet and spoke with a very pleasant voice, almost caressing: a difficult voice to find in the tenement. She was not at all strident and was truly sensual but modest. Gloria used to exhibit herself, going to the bathroom in her loud petticoats. I'd hide then behind my safety curtain, not daring to look for fear of offending the dragon in underwear and turning to stone. Delia, on the other hand, was very chaste. The two went out together a lot, however, especially to night balls. They loved to dance and sometimes came home very late and we'd hear them—in summer with the curtain as our only night door—chatting. Gloria clanging with her gong voice, Delia murmuring like a fan: they seemed to belong to different dynasties. During the day Delia almost disappeared and it was a feast for my eyes when I'd see her emerge from the curtain, which I considered a chinoiserie though it was probably as *habanera* as our own stage curtain.

One day she called me and I was charmed by the way she pronounced my hateful name, emphasizing the inevitable diminutive as an intimacy. Perhaps it was to send me on an errand, one of the curses of Zulueta 408: I had to go on errands not only for my mother but for all the neighbors and the city too. But it never bothered me to run an errand for Delia. I was especially charmed when she deposited the money in my hand: that brief contact of her Chinese lacquered nails on my open palm lasted delightfully. But more than these fleeting moments I remember an occasion that is unforgettable, almost eternal. I was leaving our room and there blew a sudden propitious wind, which did not abolish Chinese chance: the air lifted the bamboo curtain and I could see Delia in her slip: her arms bare to her pale shoulders, the beginning of her breasts, her naked legs way above the knee, turning there into well-rounded sighs (I still didn't know that was what they were called in Havana but that's how I heard them), all her Asiatic beauty, with enough Cuban blood to make her sensual. This descendant of concubines (that's what I think today, when the names of Shanghai and Canton and Szechuan come to mind: what I remember yesterday is an unnamable Delight) was seen only one memorable moment, I wishing I had left previously, before the revealing wind of the East blew like a blessing, since she was evidently preparing to go out and I might have been able to see her in panties and bra or, who knows, to coincide with the precise, precious moment when she was all nude, in the raw, unmentionably stark-naked: a heavenly body. Here was a Chinese beauty bare, the first I must have seen in my life. There had been Chinamen in our town, but I never saw a Chinese girl: there simply wasn't a single Chinese girl visible in our town! Which made me reach the early but firm conclusion that Chinese women did not exist. Delia, in all her Asiatic splendor, undid my childhood theories, initiating with her half-nakedness (total nudity in my memory) my delirious desire for Chinese beauty. The glorious Delia (she should have been called Gloria and not her sinister sister), the one I surrounded with a longing wall of looks, ended up as a concubine, a Chinese destiny. She left but did not return to China. The whole family moved from the tenement, with great fanfare, to a Chinese block. Later we found out that it was all thanks to the delicious Delia, who became the main mistress, by proximity, of a senator who would become a minister to end up as president! But Delia did not accompany him along the entire road to his political triumph: her fate remained hidden in an impenetrable mystery. The vision of Delia (a long single vision interrupted by the curtain or many minimal misses) became not a fixity but a fixation. Where could one find a penetrable China doll?

In the next room lived Georgina, the only pure black (with the exception of minuscule Elsita, a fiddlestick on the roof) who inhabited the tenement. She was the tallest woman on the premises: her perfect, fine-featured black face, obviously Nubian in origin. She had several daughters, and the eldest, Marta, had gotten her fine features from her mother but was even blacker and more perfect, a retrogression to beauty. I have always regretted not seeing Marta as a grown girl and I've often imagined that she must have been a splendid nubile type. Her mother was married to a big mug-faced black sailor, an older man branded with the exotic name of Tartabull: he must have descended from the slaves of a Catalonian colonist. Tartabull was seldom at home at first because of nautical duties. (Which was a strange cargo since the Cuban navy was still as tiny as in the quasi-heroic times of Eloy Santos and his impotent *Potemkin.* The warships consisted only of two cruisers, the *Cuba* and the *Patria,* always anchored at port, one of them apparently in dry dock, the other with a problem of dry rot. But later it was known that Tartabull, poor, old, and ugly, also had naughty duties and permitted himself the lechery of having two girls in one port. Georgina was not his wife but had been demoted to mistress, more luxury liner than warship.

Georgina liked me and used to greet me on the days when I would sit in the patio outside our room, feeling blue, denied essence and ape, resigned to looking into the mauve void, and she would say, "Hey, you got up a lunatic today?," without knowing that she was alluding to my future self. I felt affection for Georgina too, but I was always segregated from her black beauty by a sure and serious barrier of innate decency: she was a kept woman, even a secondhand woman, but she acted like a first lady. Besides, despite her beautiful face and long lambent legs, which could weave (as Silvio Rigor said another time at another place of another woman) like lascivious black mambas, I preferred the promising sorcery of her daughter in effigy. Once or twice I had the twelve-year-old Martita sitting on my lap. But these moments were as innocent, I can swear, as the blonde apparitions of the vestigial virgin on the lap of the English reverend—or perhaps as guilty?

I was even more interested in the room next to Georgina's where Serafina lived. Serafina was the daughter of another of the tenement Marías, María the Asturian, who lived in one of the rooms with a balcony on the street. Serafina was enveloped in perfumed mystery, living alone and visiting more than occupying her room. She was already a mature woman (though today I think she probably wasn't even thirty-five but for me then thirty-five was my mother's age: respectable), was very white and had very black hair (evidently dyed), used lots of makeup and had nocturnal flesh like a deep-sea fish, so much so that Georgina had baptized her the Bass.

Serafina's mystery, which with the wake of her whiff she didn't make much of an effort to hide, was that she was a *horizontal:* thus my mother qualified her: a posh prostitute, not a streetwalker like that happy-go-fucky hooker Etelvina Marqués—and I'll bet her contact wasn't contagious either. De luxe or luxuriant, Serafina was a whore and yet she had a good relationship with her mother, a stern, hard-working old woman, who had another daughter, Severa, very severe (sexually speaking), and some equally decent sons. Serafina exercised her profession with a certain decorum, and though she knew how to laugh and be friendly, she kept her distance, even with her immediate neighbors. There was never any intimacy with her, not to say any *relajo,* such a good Cuban word to describe what the Spanish dictionary calls dissolute behavior, and now I think the more dissolute it is, the better: give me libertinism or give me death.

But I didn't think that way then: I was obviously born a puritan, or made one (by my father, my uncle Pepe, my uncle Martías: brainy friends, sexual enemies) and only the sexual education I received at the school for scandals that was Zulueta 408 saved me from a fate worse than death, that of a denizen becoming a decent citizen. And I used to watch Serafina from afar, bass fiddling. Though at times I dared to approach her perfumed flesh: her mouth always painted a loud, lewd red, her necklines showing the beginning of her big white tits, promising revelations I was never able to witness, and her wide buttockless hips—she was not Cuban, thus a bass relief. Later the urban university would teach me to appreciate big fat buttocks, asses, the esthetics of steatopygia, but it was obviously an acquired taste: what's more, I lost it at the movies soon after. It's Hollywood's fault that I lost my love of lasses with asses, the movies being a gallery of bottomless figures, a museum in two dimensions, to which I managed to gain access not only through Isabel Scribé's beloved doorman, who ushered me in free, but through other interventions of chance, that tutelary goddess.

Allow me to make a parenthesis in my topographic guide to sex in a tenement in order to reveal this propitious occasion. Rubén Fornaris knew our address (all the people in our town who had made their way to Havana seemed to know it) and often visited us. One day he showed up in a state. He who was so calm and peaceful was now frantic, his triple timidity accentuating his vacillating delivery, his pauses, the usual stammering of his phrases now total incoherence. He finally exploded and explained himself, smiling shyly: he had come downtown to go to the movies, but before, as he often did, he had had lunch in the restaurant, a mere joint, next to the Payret Theater.

On the same street was a *quincalla,* a small store in a closet on a corner, where you could buy everything from cigarettes to condoms, from hairpins to cigars, lottery tickets, colored pencils, and dreadful pens, and next to this cheap Havana store was the urban well of seltzer water, a soda fountain, an exotic source which was actually a fountainhead of miracles, my local Lourdes. There I witnessed the birth of the ice-cream soda, whose ingredients emerged, thanks to pistons and siphons, from metal and marble urns, distilling green and red and orange oily liquids, the upside-down sodawater then bursting into the large glass: a true source for the sweet-toothed believer. As part of the reconstruction of the happy Havana of the forties, reconstruction here meaning destruction, the old building of the Payret Theater was torn down, the crashing crane also razing the sweet and soda fountain of joy. There were daily, deadly

39

demolitions in that era but this was the first I registered and the one that mattered most to me.

Apparently Rubén had committed a gastronomic excess upon ordering a new dish (Veal à la Chanfaina: I never knew exactly what this delicacy was, and I'll never know since I haven't managed to find it in the numerous cookbooks, Cuban, Spanish, and European, which I've consulted). "Very delicious," Rubén added, but when the check came he discovered he couldn't pay it. (Now I know he was only a few cents short.) Somehow he persuaded the owner or manager to let him go out and get money, and he came to see us, my mother, to see if we could lend him the necessary change to pay for his untimely extravagance, Rubén always caught between leftover meals and luxury lunches. As usual, there wasn't a cent at home: the little money we had my father had on him: that was his custom, his only independence a dependence. Sorry, we couldn't help Rubén. But my mother thought of a solution that was both a way out and a trap: springing Rubén while ensnaring me. Why didn't I substitute for Rubén in the restaurant while he went home to get money? Rubén's house, unfortunately for me, was now on Santos Suárez, beyond La Víbora and near the Calzada of Jesús de Monte, as far as it sounds— farther even.

God knows how long I spent sitting in that joint—supposedly a restaurant—sharing a table with several flies, mere acquaintances that by now had become friends with me, a prisoner more than a stand-in, with the sole occupation of shifting my eyes from the moving flies to the sedentary flies on the stains on the tablecloth, watching the air become thinner as the lunch aromas, thick as thieves, dissipated before my very eyes. Some lazy waiters were looking at me maliciously or mischievously, then wagging their heads and smiling since I was the center of attention of the manager or owner (evidently they couldn't afford a maître d'), and finally the door opened miraculously and I saw Rubén Fornaris, the real culprit, enter with his everlasting shy smile. The decently dire mulatto had been saved from embarrassment but condemned to eternal poverty even in the fat fifties, despite his talent as a carpenter (or cabinetmaker, as Marianín would say, adding perhaps that Rubén lacked that little detail), but in those lean forties Rubén Fornaris was rich compared to us.

Thus, as a retribution for my doing time for him, he offered me an escape: he began to invite me to the movies every Sunday. I don't know why Rubén had chosen the Fausto Theater (with which I was unacquainted) as his favorite (the Favorito was another theater in Havana: if he had chosen this one it would have become my *Faust de mieux* theater). It was on the Paseo del Prado, far from the bus routes going by his house, which was in a neighborhood with many movie houses, more accessible to him. But Rubén's difficulties were my facilities, my felicity. The Fausto Theater, fatal in the future, then showed only one kind of movie, which Rubén seemed to prefer, and which would later be called, in another culture, *film noir.* I enjoyed these movies without knowing that they would nourish what would become my nostalgia, I fell in love with the sweet, sad shadow of Gail Russell, with her unforgettable green eyes (I learned in black-and-white movies to distinguish green eyes from blue, red hair from brown, honey-colored skin from dark), adult eyes that were almost identical to those of my little cousin who introduced me to love—and jealousy. Rubén came to our house every Sunday at two, conveniently after lunch and without the inconveniences of debts: he was now an expert gastronomic navigator, who could avoid the strait of temptation and sail the seas of troubles like a Drake. Together we'd go off to the continuous showings at the Fausto, to meet up with Alan Ladd and his love—as well as mine—who had long blond locks and a passionate wave over one of her insolent little eyes, that husky voice emanating from the lisping lips of her miniature mouth. Her body was so tiny that I myself could have handled her like Alan Ladd—yes, another little love, Veronica Lake.

Rubén and I went often to the Fausto Theater and I discovered other Faustian phantoms, other shadowy loves, not other actresses but other women: Priscilla Lane, Anne Sheridan, Joan Leslie, Brenda Marshall, Ida Lupino, and the false and *fatale* Mary Astor: a girl in every part. Rubén always invited me, even after the rescue from the restaurant had passed into oblivion. After years of these Sunday sorties to movie dreamland, Rubén suddenly became strange. He would often suffer from what was still known as a bad cold. But he wasn't really suffering from a cold: he was an imaginary invalid, as I later discovered, and much more hypochondriacal than I, who have a long history of hypochondria since early childhood.

At first, when his absences were not caused by a common cold or almost fatal flu, we thought he had a girlfriend. But Rubén didn't seem to have a girlfriend in Havana (he would later find his mate back in town and have a stable marriage), and when he'd reappear he'd tell us the most implausible stories about strange maladies. But we always found our way back to the Fausto and its *films noirs.* He disappeared again, this time for a longer stretch, and when he resurfaced he made an extraordinary revelation. He told my mother, to whom he always enumerated his ills: "Zoila, I'm becoming homosexual." My mother was startled, although she assured Rubén that his conversion wasn't possible: nobody becomes homosexual: homosexuals are born, not made. But she obviously believed Rubén's revelation because when he left (this time we didn't flee to Fausto) my mother told me to invent any excuse so as not to return to the movies with Rubén. Queer that my mother would react with such intolerance when a few years later she would be gracious hostess to most of my homosexual friends.

Our room even became the convenient dressing room for an itinerant theater company that performed briefly a brief block away, in Central Park. These Thespians were more homosexual than lesbian, and my mother received them with as genuine an affection as the feeling she professed for Marianín. What's more, Rubén Fornaris's last visit to Zulueta 408 (he'd still return from time to time though we didn't go to the movies) ended with my mother's intervention when he behaved in a really rude macho manner. Rubén was at the house during the visit of a new friend of mine, a strong Spanish emigrant who didn't seem at all homosexual (though in time he would be one, and with such sexual success that I declared him a *homo satient*) and was very sensitive and shy. Rubén stared at my friend as he spoke with his Spanish accent, and didn't say a single word, but suddenly, out of nowhere, exploded with a plosive: "You seem to me to be a pansy." Fortunately my friend still didn't know what *pansy* meant (if Lorca hadn't been shot in Spain at the time, he would have known), but he must have sensed the meaning from my mother's discomfort as she practically ordered, not invited, Rubén to leave the house, that is, the room, immediately. Thus my free visits to the movies ended regrettably, and would not return until Germán Puig and Ricardo Vigón founded the Cuban Cinemateque—except for the times I was invited by Fina (the daughter of the janitor, who would later marry my uncle the Kid) to the updated Payret Theater because she knew the manager, and to the America Theater where she obtained courtesy passes. The first time I visited this high temple of my religion (with heavenly bodies on the ceiling) the tall priestess and voluptuous vestal was Ingrid Bergman. This was beginner's luck, for she had been my perverse and pervasive love ever since I saw her morbidly marked bare shoulder in *Dr. Jekyll and Mr. Hyde,* doggedly adored by Mr. Hyde, against whom I conceived a jealousy displaced only by the envy I felt for Humphrey Bogart, her reluctant seducer in *Casablanca.*

The two sisters of Zulueta 408 were not like the Pablovian three sisters of Monte 822. They lived alone with their mother and maintained a certain distance, either because they weren't nearby neighbors or because they were reserved, though in the end they seemed quite open, each in her own way. The first time I realized the existence of one of them (the younger of the two, nicknamed Beba: curiously, I never knew her real name) was when she was arguing with her mother in public, which the two had a habit of doing, and she said: "What I should do is go live with Pipo." Those were the early spring days, when the tenement light was still fresh, giving everything a twilight, mauve aura. I remember my excessive reaction to her misfeasance, with my male morality. I was scandalized because this very young girl was threatening to run away with her boyfriend—at least he must have been her boyfriend by the way she said Pipo so sweetly. Some time passed before I realized my mauve mistake and discovered that Pipo was the name she gave her father, a common form of saying papa in Havana, which I had never heard before. But this made me notice Beba, illuminated by the false twilight and even falser notion: she was a brown brunette beauty, with slightly slanty large eyes and a meaty mouth, which often revealed big white even teeth that she'd come to brush in the sink three times a day. It was impossible to ignore her visits to the bathroom because she was always singing, as she strolled by, what seemed to be the same sad song. She was really singing boleros, old habaneras, even current guarachas, all of which in her low off-pitch voice acquired a funeral air—even if the original melodies were joyous—like *triste* trite tangos. Perhaps they reflected the essence of Beba, who during some time was magnificently indifferent to me.

But her sister Trini was different. Her name was obviously Trinity, alluding to the three people living in the room, but she did not form an identical duo with her sister. Trini was whiter and shorter than Beba and her hair wasn't wavy but straight. If Beba's nose was gracefully long, Trini's was prominently hooked, almost hanging like a canopy over her thin lips adorned by a slight fuzz: that puss became, with the years, I imagine, a mustachioed muzzle. Instead of having Beba's passive nature, Trini had an active bad humor, which burned brightly in quarrels with her mother, Manuela Mauri. Manuela worked outside (I guess as a maid or cook since she wasn't very bright: in fact, she was dull and dotty) and was divorced from her husband—the Pipo of Beba's once distressing threat. More than short, Trini was dumpy, with wide hips and small breasts, which didn't need the support of bras, though then, theory of the thirties or a practice of poverty, none of the women in the tenement whom I remember watching wore bras. The fashion would change (or perhaps it was the fruit of her father's extra work: he was a painter whose paintings I had once hoped to see, though I later learned he was really a Lautrec of lettering, painting the poster titles outside the Majestic and the Verdun, neighborhood movie theaters) because I do remember Beba wearing that invisible enemy of visible breasts, that nipple-erasing machine which hid one of the attributes of the female sex. (Silvio Rigor used to say that if men had vaginas and tits instead, he'd become a bugger.)

Trini and I were joined by our love for the comic strip, those comics that could be comical but also serious, with melodrama, drama, and, for me, erotic escapades. This Arcadia of comic strips was procured by Trini every Saturday and so we decided on an arrangement: I bought the newspaper for her and she let me read the cartoons, or rather, balloons. (You see, at that time it was not proper for a young lady to go on errands, and even less to buy newspapers. Trini, though she lived in a promiscuous tenement, was a young lady.) I often bought the newspaper for Trini— I don't remember how often but I do remember a particular Saturday.

An April shower had begun, a typically tropical raucous rainfall, as abrupt in beginning as in ending: a beginning and end without relation to the intensity of the rain, a true torrent. Though the newsstand was just downstairs, protected by the portico, if anything can be a shelter against a rainstorm in the tropics, I waited for it to stop before going out to buy *El Pais* for Trini. I entered the room after the ritual "May I?" that my mother had taught me as one of the social rules of the tenement and, on the other side of the curtain, I found her alone: perhaps Beba was visiting

43

in another room or had gone for good to her painter parent's pad. But it didn't matter where Beba was: what mattered was that Trini was alone and, maybe because of our shared passion for the comics (which took precedence over hers, a mere fan) or because Beba was remote, I felt attracted to the demoted Trini though there was no warning of what would happen that day—except perhaps the rain. She was wearing a skirt and blouse, a kind of shirt with a little pocket on one side, and when I asked her for the newspaper money she said: "It's here in my pocket." I didn't understand why she hadn't taken it out and given it to me, but she didn't give me time to repeat my request. She said: "Take it." It became obvious that the little pocket (like all pockets in feminine clothing a mere ornament, meant to contain nothing) was very tight even for my adolescent and hesitant hand, and so I paused, paw poised. She said again: "Go ahead, take it." I still hadn't caught on, even though I knew it was impossible to take the money out without brushing her breast. But I did what she asked and put my hand in her little pocket. I felt immediately the transparent material upon my almost naked contact with her cup, then the nipple and then cupping her whole breast: one of the sensations I've always treasured: that soft, round, promising cornucopia was something I'd never been offered before. Of course I took my time and didn't fish for the money right away but rather latched leisurely onto the breast she offered by proxy. I tried then with the other hand, compelled by timidity but also by sex, that totalitarian titillation impelling one not to settle for the parts but to reach for the whole, to grab her other breast, unbutton her blouse, to see more than to touch what would be tits out in the open, and warm in the wet afternoon.

But Trini moved, her breasts slithering out of reach, and removed my hand from her pocket. Then I made a mistake. I tried to kiss her, to feel her thin lips against mine, to experience again that sudden sensation Magdalena had produced in me so unexpectedly with her strange strong kiss. But Trini had no intention of letting me kiss her though she didn't completely reject me either. I was conscious of my protuberance and prescient that the curtain would presently rise and Beba, or worse, old Manuela, would come in, a curtain call catching me in the act. But the agony didn't last long, nor the ecstasy (yes, Trini's brief offering was an ecstatic moment, the touch of the one component of her sex, which for me at that time was the only element of sex with which I had had contact, even if only visual, barring my brief valuable venereal vision of naked Etelvina, of her hairy harbinger contrasting black with her blond hair), since she took out of the propitious pocket the money, a mere five-cent coin, a nickel, the price of the newspaper, and gave it to me: "You'd better get the paper," she said.

Thus ended my brief, brusque intimations with Trini. I tried to find her favorable again but she was never in the mood for the magic trick of the hidden coin that turned into a ticket to mystery. On the contrary, she established a relationship, if not intimate at least conspiratorial, with Pepito, one of the tenement boys who was younger than I. I wondered then what Trini found in a little boy who, besides, didn't even like the funnies. However, I kept buying *El Pais* for her on Saturdays: after all, if I didn't have a sexual venture at least I had the consolation of those surrogate adventures.

I suffered jealousy with Trini, because of her preference for Pepito, but her sister Beba made me even more jealous. Beba and I grew up together but separate: while she became more of a woman, I became more of an adolescent. I was now used to her daily walk to wash her tantalizing teeth, her funereal march as she sang with that voice which each day became huskier, her slow majestic (or tired) step, to the beat of her languid song in eternal adagio, her skirts both covering and revealing her curved thighs in front, unveiling her full, straight legs, her body in profile showing her small but beautiful breasts, barricaded behind brassières now, slips gone with the wind of fashion.

It was the mid-forties when I became interested in observing that siren whose song had not haunted me but whose body had. I can't say how Beba and I became friends (despite Trini's sisterly sarcasm: she had developed an open animosity toward me) when we didn't even share the designed delights of the comics, now tragics for Trini and me: Trini's scorn showed in the way she tightened her lips and flared her nostrils, and in the way she left the room when I visited, whistling and whipping by like a sudden serpent. Now I spent the afternoons after school (I had more time when classes ended in the morning and when I didn't have physical education, executing the stupid contortions of Swedish gymnastics), those bewitching hours until it was time for English school, in Beba's room—it effectively became her room since Trini would abandon it completely on my arrival. We talked about those few things that interested her (like Trini, Beba had gone only as far as primary school, so that there wasn't much to talk about with them, but since childhood I had been used to the chitchat of women, having always been close to my mother, and to this day I prefer the conversation of an idiotic girl to that of an intelligent man: babes backchat better and, besides, beneath the conversation there's always the underlining undercurrent of sex) and, searching, Beba and I found a common interest: songs.

I've always been fascinated by popular music and can still sing the songs, the vivid Viennese waltzes, the vague boleros in vogue when I was four or five years old. From that age I can remember with identical intensity only certain movies, the weekly comic strip, and the lullaby of life. As a child I was charmed by the late-night Latin serenades in town, to the sound of the *tres,* the six-stringed native guitar, and virile voices of venery or brass bands in the main square on Sunday evenings. But I didn't discover the American musical until I was an adolescent in Zulueta 408 (there had been a preview, *Sun Valley Serenade,* at the Actualidades Theater, which I walked very far from Monte 822 to see and, especially, to hear), not only in movies but on nickelodeons such as

45

the radiant, rainbow chrome Wurlitzer—like a metaphor of the city—in the center of the Martí Theater lobby, among numerous pinball machines with their electrical accomplice's wink and lighted funny figures, a combination of sport and game of chance, which must have served to attract me. But as I entered that captivating cave, I was caught by another time machine, that juke box which I'd stick to, virtually glue myself to, as with the movies. This robot phonograph bewitched me with its selection system and rotating records, these mechanical musical movements which preluded more than preceded the slaving, sensual sound. Though I first had to wait for someone with money (I never had any) to come and drop a nickel in the machine, and choose, if I was lucky, as in a lagniappe lottery, my favorite of all favorites first, "At Last." I became a fan of the Glenn Miller band (the initial fault, or original sin, had been with the *Sun Valley Serenade*), by the new sound, swing. But I couldn't talk about this to Beba.

Beba and I came to enjoy an idyllic intimacy, despite Trini's toy, coy interruptions. She had already left behind child's play with Pepito and had become the girlfriend of a man—who will remain incognito because he was insignificant—who worked at the Presidential Palace, a fact which she and her mother granted great importance although he was only some sort of glorified waiter, a palace butler. "But he sees the President," was the exciting raison d'être of that fiancé, and of Trini and her mother en passant, but not Beba's: she was different—despite her act of duplicity toward me she was still different from her family. We played first up in Beba's room, sometimes in ours, any game: post office, spin-the-bottle, Chinese checkers: all pretexts for proximity. One day, one afternoon (I know precisely by the shadow cast by the sun, now fading over the edge of the high wall) she was finally alone on the roof with me.

On this particular occasion we gradually stopped talking and I looked at her nose, the only imperfection in her face: it was one of those noses that seem split by nature, but it's because they have a broken bridge, and this single Michelangelic defect gave her perfect face all its charm, with its long oval shape, little ears, and high forehead. I remember that she lowered her eyes, showing her eyelids ending in luscious lashes (she barely used makeup then), and above, her unplucked, naturally curved eyebrows. At that moment active contemplation became passive action, and my timidity, my motor, made me lean my face near hers and brush with my mouth her long, large lips—and she didn't move. She didn't return my kiss but allowed herself to be kissed and this for me was a victory, the compensation for years of wondering how to kiss her fleshy mouth, ever since she was a little girl until now when she was a woman, her lasting lips never changing, and if they were large in her little girl's face before, now they completed and adorned her adult beauty. I didn't know how to kiss, I admit, but I think it was the perfect kiss, the one I was supposed to give her, the one she was perhaps awaiting (I never knew exactly) and I don't think that she suffered it passively, merely

46

tolerating it, but that she returned it in her fashion. I had never seen Beba with a boyfriend or noticed any interest in a particular man, and the fact that she paid attention to me, a mere boy, was a major event more than a minor exception. I never kissed her again because a few days later foreign facts came to interrupt my idyll.

Many kinds of Communists came to our house, of course, but one day a new specimen appeared: a professional: a proselytizer who worked exclusively for the party and was paid for his services. His name was Carlos Franqui and it's curious that this occasional visitor came to have so much importance in my life, especially when one considers that our mutual acquaintance, our first meeting, took place under the worst auspices. Franqui was an activist of the Sole Section (a mysterious designation, it seems to me, almost an accessory), one of the city cells of the Cuban Communist party. Zulueta 408 was in that sector. (It was called Heel not Sole.) Franqui, naturally, visited the tenement and chose our room as a base not only because my parents were Communists from way back but because my father worked at *Hoy,* the newspaper upon which Franqui, a secret writer, had his sites set.

I didn't like Franqui at all the first time I saw him, which was natural in me since I always mistrusted the kindness of strangers. Or perhaps I already foresaw that he would be an intruder. On his second visit Franqui met Beba and was interested in knowing this remote rose from up close. Franqui (never a typical Tenorio but rather the contrary of a Casanova: he had never even had a girlfriend before, I believe) fell in love with Beba, declared his love to her, and she accepted! I don't know if they ever kissed (I suppose so, of course, and at that time I became enraged at the mere idea that another man would touch those lips larger than life, especially this visitor from Hegel's History) and they became formal fiancés. I, who have never been prone to tears, not even at the death of my little sister or great-grandmother, whom I loved so much, locked myself up in one of the bathrooms to cry in anger and jealousy, forgetting the fermenting fumes in my pain of unquenched love, stronger than the stench.

Then I got a fever which lasted a few days, and I have no doubt that its origin was viral not venereal. But laid out in bed, feverish, almost delirious (I've always been easy prey to deliriums, which Dr. De Quincey would attribute to opium, the smoke that induces dreams), hallucinating that my hands turned into bare bones and my blood curdled into sand thinner than water, suffering narcotic nightmares at noon, I nevertheless sensed that someone was coming slowly and stealthily toward me and, expecting my mother, I saw upside down the still-beloved face of Beba, full of full lips. She came closer, lowering her head to whisper in my ear. "I know why you're sick. You're sick because of me. But I want you to know that I don't love anybody else but you," she said simply, and left. Fury cured me of the fever! I got up and looked all over the room for her like a maniac, but she had disappeared! She had gone but not my anger!

She was a double-crossing traitor: she had betrayed me with Franqui and now she was betraying Franqui with me. I would have been able to forgive Beba for leaving me for another (after all, that other was a full-grown man who had a job: I was nobody and had nothing), but now she was unforgivable, sinful, an evil woman. Fortunately her courtship with Franqui didn't last long.

Later Franqui confessed to me that she was distant and cold and, he suspected, frigid. It all ended the day Franqui invited old Mauri—the remote Pipo of yesteryear—and Beba to a concert at the Philharmonic. The program's *pièce de résistance* was *The Fire Bird* and, to Franqui's embarrassed amazement, the *artiste* Mauri, when the concert was over, people leaving the hall, musicians abandoning the orchestra, remained seated. Franqui asked what he was waiting for and the musical Mauri answered: "They haven't played *The Fire Bird* yet." Mauri looking for the firebird abroad and having it on his program! I never laughed so much. I doubled over with double laughter for a double crosser. I don't know if Franqui considered this a hereditary trait or contagious idiocy, or if he was already disenchanted with Beba, a disappointment augmented by her family—Trini proud of her palatial boyfriend, her *raison d'état,* Manuela so ignorant and vain, Mauri a pretentious painter of poor posters—but I do know that the engagement was broken off around that time. I never asked Franqui what Beba's silly slow songster's reaction was to a symphonic suite, but I can imagine: classical music, funeral music, all out of key.

Needless to say, I never again was intimate with Beba. We continued being distant neighbors until her sister Trini married the presidential garçon and they moved to an apartment on Industria Street, not far from the Verdun and Majestic theaters, their father's turf. As far as I know, Beba never married. Franqui and I became close friends, later. But that's another story. That's another story about knowledge, though not the carnal kind. But I never told Franqui that I had been in love with Beba before him, that I had kissed that perfect, passive, perverse mouth before he had. Neither did I tell him about her covert visit to my sickbed—a secret between Beba and me until now. After all, that apparition could very well have been a dream.

I should mention, I believe, a previous occurrence on the roof. It must have been before my romance (or anti-romance) with Beba, but it happened on the same roof: the prairie of a roof, that vast space which united Beba and me for a moment in a kiss. I was never very robust, and though I was addicted to sports, as a game, I was not a healthy boy and was often sick. On one occasion I had a particularly bad cold, some form of flu—when it was no longer known as the grippe but was not yet known as influenza—which left me very weak. This insidious feeling of illness persisted like a Chinese curse, and I remember spending days sitting in a corner without moving, without wanting to do anything. I had no appetite, which really had my mother worried, envisioning in my shrunken figure the ill-fated image of death. She was afflicted by my illness, not knowing how steadfastly the sick live on and that she herself, who had never been sick a day in her life, would precede me by decades to the grave. Her affliction lasted until the intervention of Eloy Santos, who always seemed such a great authority, perhaps because he spoke and acted slowly (I never saw anyone take as much time as he to drink Cuban coffee, a demitasse, and he was perhaps the only Havanan to let his coffee calmly turn tepid in the cup, despite the tropical heat, and to end up drinking it cold, hours after it was served, to my mother's eternal chagrin) and pronounced his words clearly despite his syncopated Havana accent and by virtue of his parsimonious delivery and artful articulation.

Eloy Santos concluded his endless paragraph saying that I needed sunbaths—obviously, a tempting tautology in the tropics. But the sun never enlightened the tenebrous tenement of Zulueta 408, where there was only an ashen, mauve light, and our room, without windows to the world or a street balcony, was dungeon dark. My mother decided immediately to follow Eloy Santos's slow but sure advice and chose the place for my sunbaths: the roof, of course. To there I climbed with indecisive, indirect, incredulous step, carrying a dark old blanket, which I spread out over the tiles eternally covered with soot, and I lay down. The wide roof bordered a great bright void on one end—that is, the alley which connected Zulueta to the Paseo del Prado. On the other side of this passage was the hotel inevitably called the Pasaje. Between our roof and the presumptuous penthouse of the hotel, a structure of rusty iron rose like the ruins of a bridge, supporting a glass roof—a crystal palace now completely in ruins, with vitreous blades still sticking to the metallic frame. These dangerous man-made stalactites, veritable guillotines, sometimes came off and crashed against the floor of the alley. Only Havana luck prevented them from beheading some wayfarer, ignorant of the dangers threatening those who crossed the perilous passage.

At first I didn't see this decidedly evil construction because my eyes were shut against the blinding sun. After lying face up for what seemed hours, but was probably no more than minutes (while I would have given my immortal or immoral soul to prolong Beba's kiss, which had lasted a legato eternity in a single second) I turned around and then crept adeptly along the edge of the roof in search of visual distraction amid the monotonous shimmering of the sun. It now burned on my back as I looked toward the Pasaje Hotel and its rooms with windows opening onto balconies that hung over the arcade. When my eyesight got used to the magnified magnesium glare from above I saw that the rooms across the way were all empty. The neighborhood rumor was that the decadence of the Hotel Pasaje followed or preceded the deterioration of the glass roof over the alley, whichever came first. But I continued scanning the hotel façade: a file of open uninhabited rooms. Suddenly, in the corner room of the building, distant and yet visible, the bed in the middle was, unlike the other rooms, occupied: a woman lay upon the sheets—naked. She lay face down, one arm under her blond head, the other extended along her legs opened almost in a Y. Her body was small, suntanned, superb: I didn't know if she looked dark because of the contrast of the sheets or of her light-colored hair. Only her hair was out of tune—artificial blond, for sure—the peroxide bleach in shocking opposition to her iodine skin, an impossible chemical compound made possible only by modern fashions.

This woman (I want to believe she was a girl, almost a little girl or miniature nude, though perhaps this was an optical illusion created by distance: bodies, even feminine ones, tend to diminish as the observer moves further away until they reach the vanishing point) had thighs that were not fat but full, and a smooth small back with a thin waist ending in slim hips that made her buttocks bigger—a callypigian Calypso. Her spinal column, slightly paler, nearly met the dark slit of her ass: like Etelvina's vagina, a dark, mysterious canal zone. Her whole body shone as if anointed with Vaseline or, better, butter, and her flesh was tight and tan. She was the second woman I had seen naked—the third, including my mother—and if the first two had been distanced by the taboos of incest and infection, this one was not only distant but remained enveloped in a third threatening taboo: what if she turned around and saw me looking at her? This could unleash her fury and alarum, alarming the hotel and even alerting the penthouse watchdogs. I didn't move from my position, which repeated hers as if she were underneath me, face down, a fucking figure I wouldn't form for another twenty-five years. I became motionless so as to become invisible, following nature's rule in which the hunted doesn't move, a camouflage to avoid being seen by the hunter: only movement is visible. But I would have liked to see her face—which I never saw.

The single vision of that nude, which still seems ideal to me (in color, flesh, and form), cured me of my cold and cataplexy. The cure consisted in a more public than pubic masturbation (higher buildings had a view of the tenement roof, as well as the hotel penthouse, and there was the risk of a neighbor coming up to hang out her wash), which I began as soon as I returned to the maternal blanket, now face up, defying face to face the possible witnesses, the ceaseless sun, and high sky. After the ejaculation (the spasmodic climax of my anonymous homage to a goddess supine), I didn't return to the edge of my lookout, of course, but rather went downstairs to clean the mess: which is why I hate jerking off recumbent.

I went up to my Zolarium the next day and the next and the next, supposedly to continue my sun cure but really to look for that apparition, which I never saw again, alas. She flew away and into my memory. I vainly strained to search the whole room: it was still open, but there was only the empty bed, no bed of roses. That unique vision is nevertheless a treasure: I kept it with me all these years and it's only now, with sudden generosity, that I share it. But the episode has a happy, almost humorous, ending, provided by my poor, unwitting mother. Eloy Santos returned to the house days later to ask how my cure had gone, and my mother's answer was an involuntary double entendre: "A handy remedy."

In the corner to the left of the T there lived a violinist, from the Philharmonic. He was tall, thin, and strawberry blond. Very refined, with a slight lisp, he complained often to my mother about the sour surroundings, meaning the tenement. He was what was then called a pansy, later called queer and finally, in the late fifties, he was made a queen. In a word, he was a fruit. He shared his room with a younger man, also tall and thin, but dark, who looked like a professional Andalusian—perhaps because he was learning to dance flamenco and spent the hours tap-dancing *jondo* and playing the castanets. Despite the fact that Havana was a notoriously noisy city, the tenement at Zulueta 408 was relatively quiet, especially early in the afternoon, and the only sound that broke the silence of the few people remaining in the building, with the men out to work, was the constant heel tapping and castanet clicking, shattering an occasional siesta. The castanet—with its two chattering wooden shells— was an instrument which I had always considered a feminine prop, associated with the corny curls and intense eyes of Imperio Argentina, a false Andalusian film female of the thirties. The future flamenco dancer was, of course, a flaming fag. Both *artistes* lived, practiced their respective instruments—at different hours—and presumably made love behind doors, discreet and distinguished. They were the only fags on our floor but they weren't alone in the phalanstery.

Our floor was hemmed in between two floors that were teeming with fairies, to each a story. In the rooms on the roof lived (aside from Elsita, a tiny and ugly black girl) Eliseo, a mature, serious, rather funereal fag who, when talking to my mother, used to say: "Zoila, those of us who have this defect," alluding to his homosexuality like Hamlet to his "particular fault." Eliseo used to hang around the high window looking over our bathrooms, trying to spy through the screens that aired the showers, ogling the bathers, male only. More than once I saw him looking furtively at the shower I was in, his sad face first avid and then livid because he couldn't penetrate with his gimlet eyes the wire screens, now walls of rust and dirt and dust. In contrast with saturnine Eliseo there lived up-stairs for a while a small bony black man, who wore tiny glasses with a metal hoop frame and was a tailor. He looked like a venereal version of the venerable Gandhi and his name was Tatica, but he had himself called Tatica the seamstress. Tatica was a hard-core delinquent who had been in jail several times and would tell my mother (she was very good at listening to the true confessions of mature females and ripe fruits) what good times he had at the Castillo del Príncipe. "Zoila," he would say, "I've spent the best years of my life at the Castle," and he'd smile as if talking about the Palace and not a hideous prison for men. "They treat me like a real princess at the Príncipe." Tatica spent little time in his roof room. One day two cops came to fetch him (we never knew what crime he had committed this time), and as he went down the stairs as if they were the marble staircase of the Palace, he said good-bye to Eliseo, Elsita, and my mother, shouting: "So long, sisters. I'm off to the Príncipe for a summer vacation. Boy, am I going to have a grand time!" and he in fact seemed happy to return to jail. The other roof tenant was Diego, Tiny Tina's paid lover but also a stud, who went to bed with men for money. At the time I shared the popular sexual superstition in Havana that a bugger, since he was the active member of the couple, was not a pederast. Now I know that he was as homosexual as the guilt-ridden Eliseo and the innocent Tatica and that his profession was just a cover-up, a sexual alibi. Anyway, sleazy Diego went from beggary to buggery and struck it rich, sort of.

The floor downstairs, the first floor, that dark and remote place like Uranus where not even the ashen light reached, was completely inhabited by homosexuals. There is no rational explanation for that congregation of queers. There were a few female tenants among them: Venancia the janitor and her daughters Fina and Chelo, Nersa and her mother, and Emiliana (a middle-aged blonde with long tresses and too much makeup, a solitary spinster who nonetheless gathered around her girls from the neighborhood and the building, assembling them in a circle of which she was the center, reading—or perhaps inventing—romantic stories for them: rumors rumbled that she was a dike and had a conclave of young lesbians, an unseemly Sappho of Zulueta 408: it was never proven that this was true but then I, a pure Puritan, was shocked, though now I think the rumor was right: Zulueta 408 was a sexual colony), and old Consuelo Monfort, who had been a popular singer half a century ago and whom I respected for her musical knowledge, which went beyond the Spanish zarzuela (one day I hummed a melody for her that I had heard on the radio and that haunted me as only melodies can, and she said immediately: "Schubert's Serenade"), but aside from these active women, the remaining rooms were occupied by passive pederasts. They maintained, like the married musicians, an acceptable appearance for Cuban standards of machismo, though many of them were the kind of Havana homo who proclaims with voice, walk, ways, and exaggerated feminine airs, their condition as reigning queen, aggressive socially in their sexual passivity. One of the fags downstairs was a mulatto already advanced in years, bald, very discreet—but who broke his vow of silence one Christmas Eve when he got drunk and started shouting along the corridors: "Fire! Set me on fire!," instructing us not to send for the fire brigade but, on the contrary, to light his fire. Ever since then he was called Atlanta. *Gone With the Wind* was still playing then.

The incident that ended the dire discretion of the queens of Zulueta 408 made the building notorious not only in Havana but in the whole country. The protagonist was an organist at the Salud Church, a very serious, very Catholic, very moderate man. This organist, who would be posthumously known as the organ grinder, had picked up a young man in Lovers' Lane. (Should it be given its real name, Martyrs' Mall, or perhaps should one call it Monument to the Martyrs of Love?) To judge by the photographs, the pickup was quite ugly, and had an almost jailbird face according to mugshots. In the newspaper his victim looked saintly or disgusting. It all depended if it was printed in a morning edition or an evening paper.

We heard on the radio one morning that someone had found, under the Asturian Center colonnade, half a block from home, two human thighs carelessly wrapped in newspaper. We thought it was another political crime, so common then, the terrorist organizations of the thirties having degenerated into gangs, bumping each other off on the streets of Havana. It wasn't difficult to imagine that the corpse to whom those spoils belonged was an assassinated leader, though the usual weapons were guns, not knives. Later the radio announced that two arms had been found under another portico not far away. Around noon the news came that some boys had found a human torso (and, an unlikely detail in a man of action, a slipper) in the Institute garden. When I went with my father to the newspaper (I had gotten a temporary job butchering English for the magazine section of *Hoy*), we saw a group of people in the garden and we also drew near to catch a glimpse of a curious thing, a quartered human torso. The police hadn't yet picked up the corpse (or the missing member), waiting for the coroner, who, like a deceived husband, is the last to arrive at the scene of the crime. Poorly wrapped in newspaper, surrounded by flies and people, what I saw could easily have been the chest of a cow: nothing human was left in those remains. I wasn't particularly upset because I didn't associate that chunk of meat with a person.

At night we found out that the head of the quartered man, absent till now, had turned up in the toilet of the Payret bar, around the corner. We commented on the news with the same excitement we had had in our town, in the early forties, when everyone was talking about the hacking of Margarita Mena by her policeman lover, Officer Hidalgo. It had happened here in Havana, on Monte Street, a few blocks past Monte 822 toward El Cerro. I still remember my father pointing out to me the site of the crime: an enormous, ugly gray building, perhaps a phalanstery like ours. We talked about the case of the dismembered (our speech contaminated by journalistic prose), identified definitively as an older man. We discussed it with the morbidity that atrocious crimes always awaken, but without suspecting how close those hacked limbs were to us.

Sunday afternoon (it was summer and my brother was back home with my grandmother) I went to the movies, as usual. I now had the money to give myself a treat and see the opening of *State Fair,* with one of my movie loves, the lovely, groomed redhead, Jeanne Crain. But Dick Haymes sang all the way. More than the movie, more than the music, more than the color image of Jeanne Crain's kisser being kissed forever, I remember leaving the theater, heading toward Central Park, and then the utter surprise of meeting my parents, apparently out walking, though their faces revealed worry and something else: fear. "We came to get you," my mother said, confirming what I already sensed. "Something terrible has happened." At that time nobody else was living with us, which is why I thought something had happened to my brother in our town. My mother didn't give me time to ask. "The butcher lives in our house," as she, and I, called our room and the whole building. "The man who was butchered, too. That poor fellow I once had a fight with over the water." Water was getting scarce in that part of Havana, and the pressure could barely get it to the third floor, never mind the roof of our building. The neighbors had to go to the second-floor basin with buckets, and at times the line didn't stay in stable order because the water seekers, like nomads of the desert divining the mirage of an oasis, worried that there wouldn't be enough water left to fill their pails, would go into screaming scrimmages. On one of these unruly lines, the organist tried to get in front of my mother. I wasn't there because it happened very early in the morning, but according to her, the man had been disagreeable, almost nasty. Now I was escorted home by my parents, one on either side of me like bodyguards to protect me from the murderer's knife. The main entrance, always open until ten, was guarded by a uniformed policeman, and the small side door, which had a lock, now seemed barred. There were more policemen and photographers and other men, probably the secret service and reporters, spread out along the corridor of the second floor, the real scene of the crime. We went up to our floor, where there were shock and fear: I remember that my parents didn't let me go out alone at night for weeks after. But the most alarmed of all were the inhabitants of the room across from us.

After the Chinese left, to become conspicuous concubines, a black family had moved in. It consisted of the venerable Valentín (who wasn't so venerable: we owe the adjective to alliteration); his wife Angelita, who belied her name—she was a big, fat black woman, always smiling, laughing heartily, shaking and shouting; her sister Fermina; and the couple's three children: Eloy, always ready to sing a guaracha or a rumba, Nela, a *mulata* by spontaneous combustion, tall and not at all homely, with one of the most voluminous pieces of ass I've ever seen, a steatopygia that made her very popular in the neighborhood, and her kid sister, who was so tiny and lively that they called her Little Cummin. Cum laude. This happy family was poorer than the poor, but rich in lore and love. Venerable Valentín became famous in the tenement for his sound advice on hurricanes. "Against high winds," he used to say, "there are only three remedies: nails, water, and candles. In that order." A motto he repeated ad nauseam during one of the many cyclic cyclones that threatened Havana but crossed other parts of the island instead, to his disappointment. Fermina, her fascinating face full of tiny warts, had the habit of Cubanizing all the names of her favorite American actors. Thus, Robert Taylor became Roberto Tilo. Gregory Peck was Gregorio Peca and Clark Gable, of more difficult domestication, became Clarco Gabla. One day they all had a dilated discussion (the whole family, except for Little

54

Cummin, who couldn't speak, were given to arguing) on semantics and jet engines, in which venerable Valentín insisted that the expression was jet impulsion, Angelita said it was jet expulsion, Fermina was in favor of jet repulsion, and Eloy for jet emulsion. Nela didn't participate, never interested in words unless they were of love. (This made me happy because I had had my eye on her for some time and she was not indifferent to my glances—at one remove from glans.) There was great consternation and contrariness in the family when venerable Valentín called me in to mediate, as an expert on words, and I declared that nobody was right, that the technical term was jet propulsion—a word nobody had remotely considered. They all laughed. They were a happy bunch, now become unhappy individuals. They were, like all of us, more than most of us, full of fear.

Everything was in the newspapers—except, of course, the truth. It took the police only forty-eight hours to solve the case, which is not surprising, considering the stupidity of the murderer, who had managed to scatter the pieces within a radius of less than a hundred meters—exactly one block from his lair. But one must credit the investigative know-how of the police (aided by the priest at the Salud Church, who reported the organist's unaccountable absence from work) in finding the victim's abode so soon. They obtained an extra key from Venancia to enter his room (following a deduction that was more an intuition). They didn't notice anything abnormal until someone from the crime squad— a "criminologist" the newspapers called him—found traces of blood on the wall. When he applied his chemical detectors he found that practically the whole room had been stained with blood, and the stains had been carefully washed off afterward—a feat in itself, considering the scarcity of water in the building. They left the room as they had found it and closed the door, and two officers sat in the janitor's outer room, whose gate permitted a view of the whole corridor. There were other detectives posted on the street, all awaiting the presumed murderer. He finally appeared, walking calmly, a common, ordinary man, without a weight on his conscience or a particularly heavy-handed appearance. When he went down the corridor, Venancia (who saw everything) said that he was the organist's roommate. They grabbed him before he entered the room. He did not offer the least resistance. He confessed immediately, at the headquarters of the chief of the secret police (the only investigative police force then, peaceful times when the uniformed police only had to maintain order and direct traffic). He had met the organ player (regrettably reduced to organ grinder in the popular prose of the press: part of the following story is reconstructed from the newspapers of that era) in Lovers' Lane and the organist had offered him his room, and board. And he had also promised him (thence, the origin of the crime) that he would give him some extra money. They had a more or less stable relationship for several months (the murderer was very careful to establish his identity as the bugger, active achiever, the organist defined as a fag, passive partner, very important distinctions for the popular machistic mentality and, more decisive, for his status during his undoubtedly long stay in prison), but lately the organist seemed uninterested in his future assassin. Not only did he not give him the promised money but he even began to refuse to cover his expenses.

The day of the crime (or rather, the afternoon), the murderer-to-be had had a verbal but violent argument with the organ player, who became particularly unsavory. The imminent murderer asked him for money one more time and the murdered-to-be said, no, definitely not, no money: "Go look for work in the park." Furious with this comment, the emergent murderer picked up a handy kitchen knife (his victim was sitting comfortably in his rocking chair, wearing his usual pajamas, still smiling sarcastically) and without vacillation violently thrust it into his chest. (The knife blow was so fierce that it went straight through the victim, who died instantly, and the knife stuck to the back of the chair: but the killer didn't realize the depth of the wound or its aftermath until hours later.) He left the room, took a bus on the corner, and went to Marianao beach, visiting all the joy joints there, and he didn't return to the tenement until late at night. When he entered the room he was surprised not only by the obvious death of his protector but by the fact that he was there in his pajamas, sitting in the same rocking chair, motionless, his eyes opened, a smile on his lips, and the knife still stuck in his chest. He decided to do something about it, and what he thought of, to cover up the crime and get rid of the corpse, was to hack it into pieces. (The crime journalist described the butchery as "the macabre task.") He used the same knife with which he had killed him, which took some effort to pull out. To carry out the dismemberment, which was time-consuming, he first took off all his clothes. When he finished cutting up the corpse he discovered that there was a great deal of blood spread around the room, the floor, and all the walls. He took on the job of washing it, dressing to go out and throwing the dirty water down the drain. He didn't find anybody in the corridor during the many trips to the end of the floor. Finally he wrapped the loose limbs in old newspapers and began to distribute them. He didn't go very far since the members tended to slip out of their precarious wrapping. (He never realized that one of the feet still had on a slipper.) Thus he had to leave the thick thighs under the portico of the Asturian Center and the torso in the southernmost garden of the Institute—only twenty-five meters from the entrance of the building.

What gave him the most trouble was the head, curiously, which he tried to hide in the toilet of the Payret bar. First he threw it up into the high cistern, but it always bounced back. ("A kind of macabre basketball," added the crime columnist.) Tired of fumbling with the head and afraid that someone might enter the men's room, he tried to force it down the toilet—obviously impossible. But his crazy mission was not aborted by any idea of impossibility but by the fact that the now wet newspaper came off and the visible naked head still had its eyes open: that stare scared him and he fled. Nobody saw him get rid of his parcels (what the yellow journalist called "macabre cargo") but on his various trips to the street, carrying the members, he always found standing at the side door a little black boy, who cheerfully greeted him each time, in and out. He began thinking that this innocent witness might suspect something and wondered if he wouldn't have to kill him as well. This little black boy was Eloy, enjoying the cool breeze of the evening, as he often did during the long, hot Havana summer. Thus the origin of the fear after the fact, nurtured by the newspapers, that Eloy and his family shared with all the tenants, horrified by the crime.

One of the best-known journalists of Havana, of Cuba, wrote a front-page editorial, which justly condemned the murder but unjustly called the tenement "that den of Zulueta 408" (venerable Valentín's family had discussions, of course, about the exact meaning of the word "den," forgetting fear in their thirst for definitions), accusing the building—and implicating its occupants—of being a breeding place for criminals capable of housing other murderers (and not other victims?), a past and future habitat of what he called "dregs in drag." Though many tenants didn't understand this last phrase, they all shared the fury against the verbal injustice of being called delinquents, of being branded criminals, of being condemned without having been judged—especially since their only misdemeanor was to have been the unwitting neighbors of a hideous killer. It took them longer to forget the moral condemnation than the crime. But life goes on, more persistent than words.

One must admit, however, that there was something haunting about the yellow building, in its very air and ashen light—perhaps because of the provoking promiscuity, or the Cuban character or what the song called the Havana heat haze—that set the stage for sordid sex and all its possible passionate variations (including murder) and which made the phalanstery a nasty nest of nexus. For instance, the room where the velvety violinist and the flamenco fag had lived (they had left shortly after the case of the hacked organist, perhaps for musical motives: they had moved suddenly and silently after so much fiddling in the afternoon and castanet clacking), that corner of sexual sounds, passed into the hands of a quiet older man, very serious and respectable-looking, who sported a little mustache and tortoise-shell eyeglasses. His name was Neyra but he called himself Dr. Neyra, the Dr. before his name conferring even greater respectability, and his room was called his office. (He also lived there but insisted that he had his own townhouse in another part of the city, indicating in passing that it was in a good neighborhood.) He was the first tenant to enjoy what we in Zulueta 408 considered a technological luxury, the telephone.

Neighbor Neyra thought of himself as a very important man, as did many neighbors who came to consult him on complicated transactions —whose nature was a misty mystery to me. After the proper transactional time had passed, Dr. Neyra invited us grownup boys on the floor to his office, apparently on a day off. Now he called the room his bureau and I saw the desk, lamp, and telephone but also noticed the narrow night bed against the wall. Almost immediately Dr. Neyra began to make August confessions about his life and miracles. He was the first person I knew who could make sexual use of the telephone, Graham Bell reduced (or raised) to the position of pimp. According to Dr. Neyra (and we didn't doubt him then) he'd call any number (sometimes from the directory but mostly he dialed numbers at random), and if a woman answered, he would greet her politely and begin to banter, making small talk but eventually arriving at bigger issues, such as intimate subjects (here Dr. Augustine Neyra's voice became softer, lower, more mellow, his confession as intimate as the conversation), and he ended up having an affair with her, all by telephone, without ever meeting in person. It never failed. He had a girl right now (I don't know how he knew her age, since his amatory art consisted mainly in not knowing his other 'alf) who got so hot on the telephone when he spoke to her that she would jerk off. (It was the first time I heard someone say that women could jerk off like men, and I remember that for a while I didn't believe a word of what Dr. Neyra was saying, simply because I couldn't conceive of a masturbating female, the memberless sex.) "And I remain cool and collected," added Dr. Neyra. "My mission, gentlemen"—that was the phrase he used—"is to make them come like maniacs!" I never learned exactly how phony Dr. Neyra resolved his sexual needs. Maybe he didn't have any: having a phone was enough for him. Love on an engaged line.

Of the other people living in the T of the corridor who had an extraordinary sex life (aside from the ordinary sex life of Pepito's mother, Joaquina, a single parent who apparently had an understanding with the baker boy who went up every morning to sell bread in the building), none was more amazing than Tiny Tina. She was almost an old lady without a tooth in her mouth, who was old Don Domingo's maid. (That wasn't his name but we called him Don Domingo because every Sabbath he went out dominically dressed in his Sunday best to take a stroll down the Prado.) He looked like a senator (according to our naïve notion of a senator then: a father of the country, a patrician, a legislator of and for the people), walking tall and erect, with abundant white hair and pale skin, and was a little thick around the waist where the rest of us were slum slim. He passed our room every day on his way to the bathroom, dressed in a bathrobe whose threadbare plush did not diminish its former elegance, a true toga, his towel around his neck like a white scarf. He'd return from his bath with identical apparel and the same proud and elegant pace. On both trips Tiny Tina preceded him with the bucket of water and empty washbasin.

One had to use, abuse, one's imagination to believe that someone living in Zulueta 408 could have a servant and, even less imaginable, that a man alone would maintain a maid. But in our circle the unimaginable was the everyday and Tiny Tina was in effect his housemaid. What's more, on one occasion Don Domingo referred to her as "my housekeeper." Doubtless a case of delirious delusions since nobody was wild enough to imagine that between them there was a relationship other than man and maid, that any hideous hanky-panky was going on between Don Domingo—such a proper and proud gentleman—and Tiny Tina, the epitome of what the editorialist titled all the tenement tenants: dregs in drag. No one knew how much Don Domingo paid Tiny Tina, just as no one knew the exact job or profession of Don Domingo, who slept late and went out early every night, returning well past midnight. He couldn't possibly have been a procurer (and never a mere pimp: the word wasn't grand enough for his white airs), and he came back too early to be a night watchman. Besides, such work was beneath him. At times I thought he could be a smug smuggler, who went on audacious and rapacious raids every evening. But those fantasies were dominical dreams induced by the Sunday opium of "Terry and the Pirates," and the problem to solve was Tiny Tina's title role—was she just a crone or an old Caribbean reincarnation of the daring Dragon Lady who pursued souls at sea off the coast of China? We knew Tiny Tina earned money because she kept Diego, who lived on the roof, where she'd often openly visit. One day, bursting into one of those loud attacks of crude confessions contagious among the tenants (still inexplicable to me though I had already witnessed many public paroxysms affecting, for example, Gloria the churlish Chinese chick, who on one occasion shouted at the top of her vicious voice in the patio: "Oh, there's nothing like a fuck!"), Tiny Tina came down from the roof—from Diego's room as we all knew—booming with all stops pulled out: "Oh boy oh, have I been well sucked!" Don't think that Diego was the least embarrassed: a little while later he came calmly down the wooden stairs, vigorously clicking against the creaking steps, accentuating the masculine ending for all the world to know. So that not only did Don Domingo have a housekeeper but she, a far-from-menopausic old crone, had a gigolo—and this wasn't the Riviera but Zulueta 408.

I had a brief but unforgettable encounter with the incredible sexuality of Tiny Tina. Though I didn't have good balance, I persisted in rushing down the stairs at great speeds, and shortly after moving into the building, I fell in the stretch between the first floor and the street, breaking my finger in an attempt to grab the banister. And then I fell again, less seriously but more momentously: I banged myself on the back, my spine crashing against a stone step, and, probably because of some effect on my spinal nerves, I remained motionless upon the stairway, in the reclining position in which I had fallen. I was paralyzed but I could talk to myself and even shout out, though the secretiveness of the first floor, full of fags who preferred to remain anonymous, made any call for help useless. So I lay still but not stunned, my arms crossed and my legs stretched out, a living Y. Thanks to chance, or the good god Eros, Tiny

59

Tina came in from the street shortly after, and seeing me recumbent she rushed up to me. She asked what I was doing in such a queer position. I told her all about the fall. "Got to get help," she said right away but didn't move from her spot. At first she didn't do anything, but what she did next was surprising: as if about to auscultate me, a dubious doctor without a stethoscope, she began to explore my belly manually and then moved her hands down to my fly, rubbing my parts with both hands. Not even if I had been in a normal state would I have responded to Tiny Tina's sexual scrubbing, so old, so toothless, and so repellent a chronic manhandler was she. The terror that she would open my pants, take out my penis, and begin to perform (I didn't doubt that she would suck it, a bland blow job with her toothless mouth), was greater than the fear of being paralyzed, perhaps forever, reduced to a wheelchair or to crutches. But a greater horror struck me: Tiny Tina had declared that she was a well-sucked servant: maybe she was also a good sucker, and I already knew that, despite my paralysis, the penis had a life of its own—what if it responded to the totally tactile temptation of Tiny Tina and erected in its own erector? At that moment she raised her head and said, looking over my head: "He fell." She wasn't talking to me but to Venancia (who heard everything: she hadn't heard my racket upon falling but heard Tiny Tina's efforts to arouse or raise me), who had now come out of her rooms, her headquarters. Venancia seemed alarmed and together they lifted me up (I was skinny when young) and carried me to her room, laid me on the bed, and Tiny Tina announced that she would go get my mother—to my mental and physical relief. When my mother came in, frightened, I was able to get up before her doubly incredulous eyes (first, because I'd been hurt, and second, because I was now all better) and walk and even say: "It was nothing." I never had any other effect from the fall except my erotic encounter with Tiny Tina—and the repugnant recollection.

At the other end of the T lived another María, María the Asturian legend, mother of the luxurious prostitute but also of Severa, who was Severe in her fashion. Severa had an uncommon beauty for her family. She didn't have her sister's or mother's big blue eyes: hers were beady black, instead, like her jet-black straight hair, parted down the middle, falling around her long triangular face with its prominent dimpled chin. This was her greatest grace, since her lips were thin and her nose long and straight, curiously giving her a more Mediterranean profile than Cantabrian—or perhaps even Aegean. There was something ancient about Severa's head. She had big tits and a long neck like her sister Serafina, but she was on the tall side. Her most defined trait was her temper, which I learned to respect early on, and which was peculiar to many Cuban women. This characteristic consists of an almost masculine aggressiveness, a way of talking, moving, confronting any person who presents a challenge, especially men, above all men. But it is not of

Severa that I wish to speak but of her niece Rosa, forever Rosita, my last love at Zulueta 408.

Rosita was the daughter of a brother of Severa, and for some unknown and uncomfortable reason lived in the room of her grandmother, María the Asturian. We met when she was very little and practically grew up together, but I never paid her the attention I gave, for example, to Beba, until the day I saw that she had become a girl. She was not beautiful but pretty, or rather cute and coy. She wasn't very tall, which suited me fine: I'm short, though I didn't know it then, and I didn't feel the attraction for tall women that I would suffer from later in life. Rosita continued being chubby as a girl as she had been as a little girl, but more gracefully now. She was very busty, which made her seem even shorter, and she had a round head and naturally blond curls, blue eyes, and a smile, ending in dimples, that was as pleasant as it was frequent. She was a life-sized version of Shirley Temple. I don't remember how I began talking to her one day but I found that we tended to talk alone, despite the almost perpetual presence of Severa, whose vigilance seemed more suspicious than solicitous. Rosita studied business (which actually meant typing and shorthand and a little arid arithmetic) in an academy on San Lázaro at the end of the Prado, a half block from the Malecón. One day she gave me permission to go with her to that exotic Havana Business Academy. I accompanied her, then escorted her, and later asked her if I could wait for her after school. She assented and so I found myself killing time sitting on the last bench along the promenade, there where the false laurel trees truly die because of the sun and the brine.

I learned by heart every detail of the monument with statute of the poet Juan Clemente Zenea in bronze and marble, more memorable for his unjust execution (but is justice ever just?) during the Spanish Colonial period than for his published poems—as opposed to his unforgettable unpublished poetry? The monument consisted of more than the poet's eponymous effigy. On the base was a naked muse (supposedly Euterpe but more reminiscent of Erato) of immaculate white marble, whose mount of Venus was blackened by unseen and obscene hands, making it a shallow shadow of the feminine sex, a venereal verism which city workers continuously erased, perhaps being men especially trained for the job. But the anonymous charcoal artists always returned to draw a blackface mons pubis upon the white statue. There I was, faced with the poet martyr and his muse, proper one day, impudent the next, my constant vigil allowing me to view indecency and decency in those labors of love, through the explicit or implicit image of sex. Later, fearful that I would be accused of obscenity (I always had that unfounded fear, which would finally founder me one day), since I wasn't one of the cleansing agents of that filthy statue but yet felt that I was a private correspondent in that public war, I changed benches.

Finally, tired of watching the hours dance down the promenade (before, at least, I had the feminine forms of the muse and the uncertain battle over whether or not her pubes would remain in private or public domain), I told Rosita I would come to get her after school: she didn't object to my intention, nor did she correct me for saying "get her" instead of "wait for her," passing from a passive to an active verb, in sexual semantics.

But Rosita wasn't my type. Though I didn't have a definite kind of woman in mind yet, I did prefer the thin ones (wide-hipped Beba, tending toward the robust figure she rounded out in her twenties, I imagine, was a historical or rather, social selection) or the svelte, to be more tactful. Now, however, I was content to hold Rosita by one of her burnished arms, when crossing the street or stepping down the promenade—I didn't dare manifest, of course, any other improper propriety—squeezing her soft, smooth, white flesh. We barely talked.

My interest not only in sculpture but in culture (being so young an extremist was a condemnation devoutly to be wished) had already begun. I couldn't stand trivial conversations, a chat for chat's sake, shitchat. In a word (which always means more than a sentence) I began to find that I had little to say to the girls I knew, and though I've always preferred conversation with women (not only are they more beautiful than men, usually, but they're more true though less truthful), I couldn't find a woman after my own mind, except for one or two high school classmates —who were unfortunately so ugly that I had to make a big effort to look at them when we talked, my nose forced to forget the halitosis so that I could literally become all ears.

The short, silly, blonde, busty and hopelessly proper Rosita was nevertheless delicious: in flesh and features she was the spitting image of a character I had abducted from a novel years ago, which I had read first as pure pornography and then as a primal source, my best bedside book. In this story the hero (the novels I read then had heroes) progressed from the disgrace of extreme poverty (like mine) to grace and glory, thanks to women and journalism (to which condition I aspired). This winner was my ideal hero for some time and, even though I was far from being tall, blond, and handsome, and French!, I identified with this fortunate opportunist's tastes in love: he always had in store a small, trivial, talkative, and tart mistress, with more sex than sense: thus I imagined Rosita: my incarnation of a literary lady, a vulgar virgin version of Madame de Marelle. *Ma boule de Swift.* My Stella Rosae.

Rosita became my love, perhaps a little one-sidedly, though I came to think that she secretly shared my sentiments. My surprise was therefore great when Rosita one day, out of the blue of her eyes, declared: "You'd better not accompany me to school anymore." A pitcher of cold water in my hot face, that's what it was! Besides, I didn't accompany her to school but rather took her home from school. Useless to point out to her, of course, the syntactical distinction: she wouldn't have noticed the difference. She did realize, though, that she had been somewhat abrupt. "You see," she said, "they're starting to say things in the building." Like me, she avoided calling Zulueta 408 by its real name, tenement, and thus the staircase, the corridor, the balconies, rooms, showers, toilets, sinks, were, platonically, a single soul, *the* building. I was going to tell her that it didn't matter what people said, that only the truth mattered—and the awful truth was that all I did was to wait, platonically again, for her at that remote academy, whose distance I blessed: it gave me more time to accompany home that bundle of perfumed flesh.

Rosita always smelled good, as if she had just taken a bath, but particularly when she went to school she smelled of verbena soap, of Florida water, of scented talcum powder. I've always had a fixation about human smells, perhaps because of my mother's obsession with personal hygiene —she would sometimes bathe twice a day—and her use of fragrant soaps and perfume, always called scent in my home town. Even in the days of greatest poverty, my house was frequently fragrant and there's nothing I hate more than a person who stinks, especially a foul-smelling woman, though in the heat of the chase I've managed to overlook this obsession —odor or ardor—with two or three women, who didn't smell precisely like otto of roses. But not my Rosita. Dimpled Rosita, with her blond curls and blue eyes, was in her soft way a very decisive person and her request became almost an order: I could no longer escort her. The most I could do was to calculate the precise time when she would cross Central Park and meet up with her. Or visit her grandmother's room to talk to Severa, hearing her spin her salacious tales, while awaiting Rosita's return.

One day when twilight had suddenly become night (it must have been winter and, though the difference of temperature is barely noticeable in Cuba, I'm very sensitive to the changes of light and winter sunsets can be surreptitious), Severa and I were talking on her balcony, which faced not the passageway but the massive gray building of the Havana Institute, the edifice I was about to abandon, leaving behind scholarly studies for an apprenticeship in literature and life. I don't remember what nonsense we were saying, Severa cracking jokes or perhaps subtly satirizing my amorous situation. I only remember that she suddenly left me alone and went back in the room without any pretext, where there was nobody, her mother maybe visiting her sons—or at a Communist meeting. I was busy looking at the street, following the parallel courses of the trolleys toward the infinite where they meet, thinking, perhaps desiring the imminent entrance of my Madame Marelle, when I was suddenly embraced from behind and felt two hard tits nailing me in the back. I remained paralyzed, like the considerate caterpillar victim of an ichneumon wasp, and at the same time was delighted with what I thought was a surprise attack by Rosita, returning to repeal her decision, demonstrating her overwhelming love.

My surprise was even greater when I heard Severa's voice whispering waspishly in my ear: "What would the newspapers say if the balcony fell right now and the two of us landed dead in the street in each other's arms?" I couldn't answer. Or, rather, the question was actually rhetorical and it was her action that made my surprise so severe. Severa was, in my mind, a sexually unassailable woman because of the fortress of her character, her very jokes and double-entendres, her playful yet serious spirit: Severa stereotyped as the virago and as Rosita's eternal aunt. She let go of me immediately, the paralyzing sting having done its job, and flew back into the room. At the same moment, as in a mediocre melodrama, Rosita really returned. Her entrance had an extraordinary effect. Never before I had welcomed her perfumed presence with indifference, but now it was inconvenient, intrusive, obnoxious: in one second I had come to desire Severa more than I had ever desired Rosita. Had I ever really desired her? Or had it all been a vicarious vision? A labor of literary love?

The incident, the furtive embrace on the balcony, was never repeated and remained like some secret between Severa and me. More than a secret an enigma: I was never able to decipher Severa's attitude, but with a single gesture and phrase she had erased the many exchanges, which I believed significant, between her niece and me. Suddenly this girl had ceased to exist, becoming the specter of Rosita. Was it because of that strange embrace? At the time I couldn't explain it. I have reached the conclusion today that Severa's seduction was only some form of parody.

The history of my erotic life in Zulueta 408, that stretch of my sexual *via crucis,* that station on my road to passion seems like a long and languid initiation to failure: there are too many encounters with scornful, falsely difficult, and difficult but easy women. But one must remember that I'm speaking of the forties, an era when tropical sexuality had not been fully assumed, at least by Havana women, as in the American fifties. There were still many throwbacks from that Spanish town morality, which, in my childhood, decreed that a woman who dyed her hair, painted her lips, and wore rouge was scarlet. This was also true in Havana, and despite the propitious promiscuity of Zulueta 408, profoundly hypocritical habits prevailed beneath the apparent sensual ease. All my girlfriends regarded virginity as a precious gift, a kind of dowry. But there was also what would later be known by the exotic and exact name of cockteaser (translation), a concept not at all Cuban but Spanish and very apt to describe these girls and women I knew close up but, alas, not with the intimacy I desired. One of these women was, not by chance, a girl from our town.

Another of these phony virgins was, curiously, a woman, not a girl, who might have been in her late twenties, possibly early thirties. She lived alone apparently, with a young daughter, opposite Beba and Trini. Her room had an open door with a curtain and she sewed for a living. Like my mother who embroidered, she was "riding the machine" (a phrase copied from my mother) most of the time. But she didn't look at all like my mother. Today I would say that she was beautiful, but then she seemed merely exotic to me. *Exotic* in Cuba is supposed to mean Swedish or German, but my vocabulary was taken from the movies, and thus Hedy Lamarr, with her dark, heavy makeup, was exotic in her immortal coy casting as Tondelayo, the native girl of Malay. But Elvira (that was her name: I never knew her last name: in Zulueta 408, as in the Communist party then and in Hollywood, everyone was called by his or her first name) was exotic in her way but didn't look like Hedy Lamarr, my loud love in two dimensions. My contact with Elvira took place way back, before the days of Beba and Rosita, when I was still very young. I don't know what my excuse was for entering her room. Though one didn't need an excuse to visit a neighbor in the tenement, I still kept my country customs. Elvira was tall and thin and wore her slightly wavy hair down to her shoulders, in the style of the era: Elvira was aping María Felix or perhaps prefiguring her because María Felix was not known in Cuba yet: María Felix incarnated the epitome of beauty those days in Latin America. She was celebrated as Pretty María and even Ave María, while Elvira was not considered desirable by the men in the building and I don't think she was beautiful according to Cuban criteria either. Like my mother, she would talk as she sewed, and one day she suddenly asked me if I had a little girlfriend. I said no, which was the truth. "You should have one: you're old enough. Besides, you're not bad-looking." (That statement was repeated, to my double amazement—like a double mis-understanding—by Beba, who once said to my mother: "Zoila, how is it you have such handsome sons?," including my brother in the question, which was a form of double praise, but alluding directly to me. It was that observation which encouraged me enough to approach Beba with second thoughts, because I considered myself utterly ugly, so much so that when La Niña, one of the girls from our town who lived in the tenement, declared in front of our room, belying someone who derided the man who would later be her fiancé: "I like my men ugly," I said to myself that even I could have a pretty girlfriend.) And here Elvira, living alone, without a male acquaintance aside from her daughter's remote father, going further than La Niña, almost as far as the future Beba, announced to me that I wasn't bad-looking.

She and I were talking one day, I remember, and she made me move from where I was sitting to a place not closer to her machine in perpetual motion but more propitious to progressing from mere acquaintanceship to personal intimacy, with the pretext (now I think it was a pretext, but then it was a motive) that I was in her light. Upon getting up and sitting down again I saw her open dress (or blouse: women didn't wear shirts then), allowing one to see her flat chest and the beginning of her breasts. She wasn't wearing anything on them, perhaps out of poverty, perhaps because the garment was so strange, so hot, that even its Cuban name is strange: *ajustadores.* Adjust what, bills or boobs? I always preferred the word imported from the United States—like so many other things—*bras-sières,* though the word "bra" is brief and you can play with it: *bras dessous, bras dessus.* (But that I discovered years later. More cumber-some, I think, is the French word, *soutien gorge.*) Her bodice, like all those previous words, was forebodingly absent. I looked well and saw, while she sewed, more than just the tops of her breasts: I saw one of her little tits: she bent forward, attending to her sewing or accommodating my vision, and I saw her whole tit, to the pointy nipple. The view of a tit has always moved me (also that of two tits: double commotion), and that day I began to feel that my mind had become matter and was located between my legs, my matterhorn. It hadn't happened before with Elvira, with whom I had a certain friendship, but for whom I felt nothing. She bent over even more, to sew, and I looked eagerly, forgetting her daughter playing on the balcony and remembering that we were protected from the neighbors by the curtain that was always a closed door. Looking, now wordless, conversation cut off by the vision, I could see that, without stopping her work, Elvira was watching me, attentive to my reaction, and I can swear that she was smiling to herself. Elvira, who according to my mother had the reputation for being a slob, apparently suffered that poetic form (at least its Cuban name is pleasing to me) of leucorrhea, white flower. Despite her infamous malady, this cool customer became, to me, a female in such heat that I would have taken her from the moving machine and thrown her on the bed—and ended there and then my virginity—always bearing in mind that she was at least ten years older than I: a generation gap that then seemed a lifetime, an eternity. Elvira's archaic smile on her contemporary face made it obvious that I was the clear object of her desire. Impelled by sex, I became immodest and stood up to impale her, facing the machine, which meant facing her with my bulge, showing her the evident erection she had provoked with her stories of mandatory girlfriends, her esthetic opinions on boyish beauty, and her displacing of my body to facilitate in fact a better view of her breasts. Now Elvira stopped sewing for the first time since I had visited her room, which was an event: would changes take place? She looked at my face, then down at my mole or mountain and at my eyes again. "Now sit down," she said finally, as if saying: Well, I see what you're capable of, and now what?, but she added, "You're distracting me from my sewing." Her tone was so indifferent that I felt insulted. Elvira's scorn had cooled my corn, had frozen over my hot horn. The erection deflated instantly, the bulge collapsed, no more mountain, but I didn't sit down. I turned around and walked out of the room—never again did I cross Elvira's threshold. So touchy was I then.

But the worst—or maybe best—was Lucinda, cock-*teaseuse extraordinaire.* She was the sister of Balbina, Carlitos's sister-in-law, Payeye's aunt and La Niña's younger sister, all folks from our hometown. Balbina, Lucinda, and La Niña, the savior of us freaks, who had married a monster of a man, all lived in the room that revealed to me Etelvina, the precocious prostitute, the syphilitic streetwalker, my naked *maja.* The father of the three sisters was a Spaniard, probably Asturian, but their mother was a backward *mulata,* who had left a dark mark on her daughters and especially on her sons, which only La Niña managed to hide with her bleached hair, an early fake blonde. They were all madly in love with their father, a respected figure in town, the owner of a downtown café in which all the sons worked. In a way, Havana had been a step down for the family, condemned as they were to live forever in the tenement (they were still there when we moved) and because of Carlitos's poor salary as a traveling knife sharpener. Balbina was mature and attractive, though she had the flattest buttocks this side of Ingres, surely an Asturian trait. From our youthful, almost childish, days, when Carlitos was the object of jokes cracked behind his back ("Carlitos, the knife swallower"), Balbina was the paradigm of the no-ass woman, and buttocks à la Balbina became a category in the museum of female measurements. Lucinda was not as tall as Balbina: she was quite short, with slim hips, and her ass wasn't flat like Balbina's but rather prominent. Her figure was graceful though it lacked something: she didn't have bad breasts, but simply had none, not even a drop: her tits were as ironed as Balbina's buttocks and never, before or since, have I seen anybody with less breasts, except, of course, a man. I saw her in all sorts of clothes, dresses, blouses, even in a slip one day, and all I saw were the pleat marks on the satin. Her face looked Polynesian—au Gauguin—which is common among *mulatas,* with large fleshy lips and slanty eyes. She had naturally wavy hair and a short but cute nose. The only blemish on her pleasing face was the few pimples that appeared periodically. She had done everything to eliminate them, even practicing for a while a disgusting antidote: each night she put saliva on them and washed it off carefully in the morning. I had never heard of such a remedy, and I must say this ugly ointment didn't do her much good. Despite pimples, saliva salve and all, Lucinda was very attractive, but for some reason (her imperfect skin?) she never had a boyfriend, and when she finally did, the results were disastrous. The infamous fiancé was a cabdriver from the Puerta Tierra hackstand, which was also the bus terminal contrarily called Golden Arrow: the buses couldn't be slower or filthier. Her suitor's name was Alberto Prendes and he was young, quite good-looking, and so serious and quiet that he seemed taciturn. They nicknamed him the Turk, perhaps, I thought, because he looked like Turhan Bey, María Montez's Levantine lover. But Prendes led a double life, and when the astounding assault on the Paseo del Prado bank occurred, sensational because this was the first bank ever held up in Havana and because the robbers carried off the record loot of a million pesos (the exact equivalent then of the same amount in dollars), it was discovered that the driver of the getaway car was known as Turk Prendes, taxi driver. Miraculously, Lucinda wasn't connected to the robbery, which would have dragged Zulueta 408 into the crime columns again, perhaps inciting another insidious editorial on this center of infamy, where even the women are dangerous.

Long before the bank robbery (which obliged the ashamed Lucinda to go back to our town for a while: an unwitting gun moll cooling it off in her hideout), long before she met the fascinating and fatal Prendes in

Aleppo, urbane and malignant Turk, and became in my eyes María Montez for a day, I used to have a close relationship with her, but not as close as I wanted. I liked Lucinda, with her acute cutis, bare breasts, and all. Despite Balbina, Carlitos, and Payeye—almost an audience—the two of us would often be alone together in her room. One day she said that she'd like to peruse a novel and I thought of Maupassant, even Chekhov, but I couldn't yet think of Corín Tellado (my innocent penny-dreadful pornographer to be). "You know," she specified charmingly, "the ones where they do things." Even before she told me exactly what she meant ("where they do things to each other"), I knew that her favorite reading was what was then known as naughty novelettes, defined by their anonymous authors as "gallant gaucheries." I found an esoteric specimen—titled *The Lust of a Moron*—curiously under the mattress of my parents' bed. An unexpected find, considering how puritan my pater was, and I suspect that its pornographic presence was produced by my mother's curiosity, but I'm sure that she, an eager reader, didn't buy it because of the insurmountable difficulties a woman would have had in the purchasing process in those days. I could never unveil the major mystery of that found manuscript, which emerged amazingly from the backlands of bedbugs beneath the mattress. That little book, which I read again and again, opened an erotic door through which I entered. (The *Memoirs of a Russian Princess* and even more remote *Satyricon* were far from this genre, which could be considered a new rather than renewed experience.) Other nymph novelettes followed this initiation, now bought by me though their sale was prohibited by the law (always severe about sex) and one had to discover the precise secondhand bookstore (a particularly well-stocked one on Neptuno Street faced the Rialto Theater, two temptations face to face: the turgid printed word and animated shadows) in which they sold books firsthand, more than under the counter, in the back room: a licentious library without a license. I read each little volume over and over, all of them handmade for masturbation. The plots varied, but the fornicatory formula was invariable: the narrator (or even better, the narratrix, as in *Bunny's Buns*) always ended up in bed with everybody, innocent or guilty, even the butler, who did quite well for himself. There was an early sample which for some particular reason was a gushing source of erotic fantasies for me. In it two wanton women (or adventuresses, as they called themselves) were going skating in Maine Park, on the Malecón, wearing incongruous overcoats because it was winter (overcoats, winter, in Cuba!) and skating, not on the impossible to imagine Cuban ice, but on rollers. One of the gracious girls showed, through an opening in the coat, that she had absolutely nothing on underneath. This precious discovery was made by a man (a gourmet, obviously, not in search of clove and cinnamon buns but strawberry blondes) who shrewdly happened to pass by and right there, in the public park, he floored and fucked the two of them! You see, it was very early in the morning and nobody else was around, so that the trio (two tribades and a stud) committed all sorts of indecent acts and even a few against nature, out in the open.

This was one of the novelettes I read to Lucinda, maybe the first. Needless to say, I was excited by this oral sex—but not like Lucinda. My excitement wasn't as great because I had to do the reading and at the same time watch the door, attentively observing the curtain in case some family member came in unexpectedly. Not Carlitos, who always came home at five o'clock sharp, but maybe Balbina, and on one occasion Payeye popped in early from school, and because of his entrance I had to quickly hide the reading material (a maneuver that was almost a magic trick in itself), disguise my mounting excitement and, to top it off, begin a conversation that would seem like a continuation and not a beginning or an end. Lucinda became enormously excited with this libidinous literature. But I think my excitement excited her most: despite the role of reader or because of it, I interpreted the part of the steady stud who fornicates everything that moves. Such a stimulus was initiated by the erotic adventures in the novel and increased by Lucinda's presence, by the half smile on the full moon of her face as she listened, always sitting in her chair, without any sign of her state other than her Mona License smile. Her nonexistent tits could not become erect, her absent nipples would not swell, her legs were eternally in the same position, closed, squeezed against each other, and her eyes kept shining with malice without ever revealing anything—thus it was her large mouth, those big spread lips, that indicated her degree of pleasure. At times my excitement became unbearable because I imagined I was Lucinda's lecher *de main,* the pornographer and protagonist of these amorous adventures in which she accompanied me in each tableau—in all the positions and often in profile. But what returned me to the written page was that Lucinda never let me get near her in this perpetual heat induced by the reading, which I had to start again each time I attempted to get nearer than a meter and a half away, a distance apparently imagined but very real for her: she not only controlled herself but was very guarded. The furthest I got was to sneak up to this iMaginot Line and take out my big Bertha and show her, from my point of view, my formidable member, almost for her inspection: swollen, purple, adolescent-looking: my cannon as imaginary as her borderline. She looked at it with almost medical curiosity, with no erotic interest at all, and didn't let me shake it, much less touch it herself: the penis can be perilous. As soon as I began rubbing, forgetting the vigilant Balbina, the pubescent Payeye, and even Carlos the Blade and his now menacing knives: bang! swish! off with a single stroke, she said: "No, no, you're not going to make a mess here." She wasn't referring to our reading relationship but to the floor, the room, her domestic universe, because you see, Lucinda—her sister, her whole family, like my mother—had the tidy town malady: cleanliness, even in her libido.

That was the only time I penetrated her intimacy with my penis, but we continued our sexual contact through the worm of words, my libidinous lipservice. Now I saw myself forced, the tyranny of sex more than of women, to abandon my male friends, my playmates, my schoolmates, with the wildest excuses (the truth once more stranger than my fictions) in order to read to Lucinda—literary labors, as they say. I had to sneak into her room—be doubly sneaky, if you include the reading, triply, if you include the trip to the clandestine bookstore—without being seen. Plus I had to take the little savings I had for the movies and spend them on new novelettes—but it was worth it. I thank Lucinda for these labors of love and lust, even though she enjoyed my situation of impotent potency, listening attentively, looking curiously but always remaining carefully outside the situation. Even though she never gave me the satisfaction of a sign of her excitement, with her immobility and Mona Licentious smile, I covered all the expenses, even the vain erections, thinking, imagining the things she'd do when she was left alone. The randy readings lasted awhile, until Alberto, alias the Turk, Prendes entered her life.

I had begun to leave living and loving for reading and writing but there was a moment in which love and literature joined, though one didn't win over the other—or rather blood was stronger. Not metaphoric blood but the real thing: family blood. Though I'm not going to talk about my long battle with tooth pain, I do want to record my puzzlement at how literature has neglected something as present and pressing as dental neuralgia. I remember only three novels *(Anna Karenina, À Rebours* and *Buddenbrooks)* where a toothache is a sinister ill. Perhaps it's because a toothache seems like such a vulgar thing, but, curiously, those three novels are tidy, elegant, refined books. On the other hand, tuberculosis has been meticulously described in literature and, being familiar with it, I don't think that consumption is a particularly glamorous or chic disease: the patients live, choke, and die amid sputum and blood. Can one really exalt any disease?

I have suffered greatly from molar maladies, worse than moral maladies. On one occasion I had had another wisdom tooth extracted at four o'clock, blood in the afternoon, and though I've always tended to bleed, I know the difference between slight bleeding and a real hemorrhage. As always, I began to obsess over the fact that hours after the extraction the wound was still bleeding (my mother, the expert, called it a caesura, not to be confused with a Caesarean section), and to find out if I was bleeding or not, I touched the wound with my tongue. It always bled when I did that, and besides, I had to suck innocent blood. My parents went to the movies (which my father hated then, like people now who hate television: reactionaries of the image) and my brother must have been on vacation again in our town.

But I wasn't alone. My cousin then lived with us, the girl with the obsessively green eyes whom my mother adopted, the one I loved like a sister (my mother and I were always in search of the family female, twice found, and twice lost in early death), the legendary little girl with whom

I discovered both love and jealousy at the age of six, with whom I had my infantile initiation, incomplete incest interrupted not only by the severe and sudden appearance of my, of our grandmother, but also by the natural incapacity for sex that one suffers at six and at sixty. That night I went to bed but couldn't sleep, not only because of the bleeding but because I was suddenly aware that I was alone with my first cousin in the same room, enveloped in protective but now guilty darkness. From my bed I stretched my arm toward my cousin's bed, touched her leg, and she didn't move. My hand continued advancing to her knee, up her thigh, and discovered that what was visible to the eyes in daylight was only really revealed to me at night: my cousin had grown up: that little girl of rare beauty, our version of Shirley Temple with the big green eyes and the beautiful mouth, the pride of the family, was no longer my little cousin. She was obviously awake, and she let me touch her without responding, when as a little girl she had always taken the initiative.

Suddenly I felt the flow of blood and had to get up to spit it out. I saw that it wasn't too much blood. On my way back I didn't return to bed or to my incestuous impulse but rather felt that I had to sit down to write. I had already written one or two stories and now that I knew I was going to die, before bleeding to death, like Petronius, I had to leave a last message, a communication of extreme importance, a testimony. I turned on the light, picked up pencil and paper, and began to write a story that mixed in my still potent passion for ball games and recent readings. Thus an old ballplayer, the only one who could save his team from defeat, batted a homer, hitting the ball further than ever before and than anybody else, and while he ran he suffered a heart attack and almost fell. But he continued running the bases, stumbling, dying, but with great effort he managed to reach home, and as he stepped on the rubber plate, winning the game, he died. Writing this double testament I was convinced that there was no doubt that I was a writer, perhaps a great writer who was composing his masterpiece before dying.

I was taken from this awkward assignment by my cousin, sitting up in bed and saying: "What are you doing now?" I don't know if she referred to the occasion or the hour. "Come here"—and I never knew if she meant my bed or hers, while I looked at those luscious lips, which several generations of my family, Infantes, Castros, Espinozas and Reynaldos, had managed to compose, producing the masterpiece of her now open mouth. I felt that I had to go to her and at the same time knew that I should finish my story. I was shaken from this vacillation by a flow of blood greater than the previous, and I had to get up to spit what was an evident hemorrhage but to me seemed a Chopin-like hemoptysis: I still didn't know what Keats or Chekhov had died of: my only references to glorious deaths in which heroes vomited blood were movie images. The story remained unfinished and, to my momentary sorrow and future relief, my cousin's virginity remained intact for her eventual marriage: my parents returned.

I didn't know what movie theater they were coming from, they who hardly ever went out and never returned unexpectedly. I only knew the time because my mother exclaimed: "What are you doing awake at this hour?" To which I could answer, without lying, without resorting to false excuses and inventing moral alibis to save the honor of the family, whose monument I had been about to profane: "I have a hemorrhage." My mother, an expert in molars and migraines, a malady I've inherited from her, invented a homemade remedy to stop the blood, but I continued bleeding and still toward dawn bled, now in rapids. "You'll have to take him to the dentist," my mother announced, as always giving orders, and my father began to dress to take me to the dentist's office. We went along dark, empty, silent streets: the dentist lived on San Nicolás but I don't know why we took so many side streets—or I do know: my father was an urban Daedalus and knew the art of making Havana a maze of zigzagging streets.

It took some effort to awaken the dentist, who came out on his balcony, alarmed: who's that knocking on my door so late? When he opened the door he denied the evidence of a hemorrhage, saying that it was all in my mind, and despite his halitosis I felt flattered that someone would confer supernatural powers upon my imagination. He had given me the faculty of producing the effect of imaginary blood flooding out of the hole where my wisdom tooth had once been, filling my mouth and making me spit true torrents. But when he lit up his office he saw that I really had a hemorrhage and without alarm said: "We're going to end it immediately, my boy," and singing softly (unlike birds and tenors, dentists can make music at any hour) he began to prepare a bitter solution, which he placed in the hole: "Tannin powder," he explained and plugged it all up with cotton. "Finished," he finally announced.

I don't know how I left the dentist's den, but I do remember, the sun now coming up, that my father took me to a dairy store on San Lázaro Street, where he ordered a quart of milk and made me drink it all down. It was one of the few times I was close to my father since we had come to Havana, where I began to grow distant, for obscure reasons: maybe I was growing up. Then he explained: "It washes the blood." For a moment I thought he meant the blood in my veins, then I thought it was the family blood, which made me and my cousin one, and finally the blood of the writer who had proven himself that night—but he only meant the blood from the wisdom hole that I had swallowed, a vampire of myself.

I had already been in all the carnal chambers (even my own) at least twice. Now everything would happen in the little patio facing our room. One of the surprising sexual revelations of my adolescence took place there, though it had nothing to do with me, a mere spectator. The protagonist of the midday mystery was Rosendo Rey, who had been for years the peaceful tenant in the last room on the floor, next to the bathrooms, which he had rented after Dominica and her family vacated it. He was the most serious man in the tenement and passed by every day

72

after work (I never figured out what his work was), walking erect, always in a white or beige suit, his white hat of false jipijapa pulled down properly in a straight angle. He was not as imposing as Don Domingo but neither was he such a poseur, a false serious man. His advantage over Dr. Neyra was that he was taller and not a chatterbox—he was, indeed, a man of few words, laconic, almost hermetic. When he tripped one day and fell in front of our room, his virile verticality becoming a hectic horizontality (it was a noisy fall, which had grave results as he later realized), falling as dead men fall as he slipped upon the wet cement (my mother having carried her mania for cleanliness too far this time), he got up without a complaint and limped away. All the material witnesses of his crashing fall felt sorry for him, even more so when we found out he had broken his coccyx bone. My mother, perhaps a little guilty, always showed interest in him and often asked how he felt, Rosendo Rey responding with his strong Spanish accent: *"Mejor*—improving," showing in passing his Spanish stoicism since he was getting worse: the fracture had complications and it took him months to get better. When I was younger, my playmates and I would suspend our game around the fascinating transom when we saw him coming, and almost always ended the game then, since we knew that Rosendo Rey had to go to bed early, to get up at dawn and go to work. His reputation as a serious man grew with time, and we never saw women going to his room, who would have had to be whores since Rosendo Rey was no longer young and despite his poise was far from good-looking: only his resonant name was handsome.

Since he was such a perfect gentleman, as my mother decreed, our surprise (the witnesses included this time my mother, of course, Dominica, and possibly Zenaida) was so much the greater. That afternoon he returned home earlier, almost at midday, and in bad company —that is, followed by Diego. Both passed by without a word: Rosendo Rey didn't greet us as he always did; slippery Diego, who never greeted anybody, had a slight smile on his face, which, for a moment, we didn't understand. Rosendo Rey opened his door and went in. Behind him went Diego and the door closed completely: Rosendo Rey had no use for a curtain. The door was closed for quite a while. All of us in the patio waited, almost knowing what was going on. After a long while, the door opened and Diego came out alone (or accompanied by his sly smile) and passed us, showing off bills in his hand, two, perhaps three, with the satisfaction of one who has pulled off a good trick. We immediately knew what smirking Diego was up to in the house of Rosendo Rey, with whom he had never had a relationship or the slightest contact. Diego, besides being Tiny Tina's gigolo, was a professional pederast.

The respectable Rosendo Rey, with his serious mien and air of a Spanish gentleman, had suddenly revealed that he was a fag. I don't know if he had always been one, but till now he had conducted his private life quietly as his own affair, or discreetly enough so that no one would guess his sexual secret. (I even thought that he became queer after his fall and the fracture of what was commonly known in Cuba as the small bone of gaiety. In any case he was a king without a crown now, checkmated by a poisoned pawn. But Silvio Rigor had the last word when he learned of this event years later, uttering as a verdict his favorite phrase about the double fall: "It was obviously a profanation of the sacrum.") From then on Diego was a common visitor to that last or first room, in which the two locked themselves up for a while but not for long: the love that dared speak its name now was always rapid. Nothing changed in Rosendo Rey's appearance, which intrigued me. I naïvely expected that he would start to tweeze his eyebrows, wear rouge and lipstick, and dye the gray hairs of his sideburns, which showed from under his perennial pseudo-panama hat: he wasn't von Aschenbach but, come to think of it, neither was slimy Diego a Tadzio. Except for that day when he revealed himself (or rather, I think, exposed us), he continued greeting everybody as always and soon all the witnesses of his erophany got used to the idea that he practiced in his cloisters his *ars amatoria.*

That little patio was the place of an event that concerned me directly. But first I must mention, briefly, the literary magazine founded and edited by several friends and me, some of them classmates at the time. I won't be a moment. The idea of the magazine was Carlos Franqui's and it almost succeeded. The publication didn't last more than four issues and sank into total oblivion, which is greater than literary oblivion but not worse. Soon Franqui invented a smashing successor, a kind of artistic and literary society that was called (with the same intentions as the magazine, with identical pretensions and almost the same name: the magazine was called *New Generation*) *Our Time,* which brought together budding intellectuals, writers, artists, musicians, and a few spectators.

I made my greatest friendship among the amateur musicians, my love for music winning over an old passion for painting. Among the musician-composers, I met a young lawyer who had been a diving champion in Cuba years back but who committed his first musical peccadillo by hatching a little egg titled "Sad Song," more Lecuona than Schubert, which I never let him forget now that his musical pretensions were less ambiguous and more ambitious. Juan Blanco, short but blond with pale blue eyes, was a big success among the musical women, although with his half harelip he was rather ugly. Around that time I had finally overcome my hangups about living in a tenement. Now all my friends, old and new, would come to visit me in my house, our room, to enjoy my mother's hospitality, to drink her coffee, and gather in the patio, which was now an agora.

Juan Blanco was among those who came most often. I was therefore not surprised that one of his muses suddenly came to visit us one day. What intrigued me was how she had gotten the address. Her name was Gloria Antolitía and she seemed as Italian as her name, though perhaps she was merely Italianate. In any case Juan Blanco finally married her

74

—perhaps exhausted by the hot pursuit (it was summer again), she a driving Delilah after this small Samson of sex. That particular day (which was going to change so many things in my life) Gloria Antolitía came in the company of her half sister, who was on her Easter vacation before returning to convent school. The sister was a tall, very thin brunette with deep-seated but radiant eyes and, without smiling, she sometimes showed sweetly a protruding tooth. Her lips were irregular—the upper too thin, the lower too fleshy—and, when facing front, her nose had a bridge that was too broad. But her long neck, her gracefully pointed chin, and the outline of her nose made a delicate profile. The contradictory combination (front vs. profile) was attractive to me, and though I didn't seem like much to her that first time, this girl (she was very young then, probably seventeen) came to be my first flirt, my first fiancée, my first wife. None of this seemed possible that day, so much so that I haven't marked it among my memorable meetings. But it was perhaps the most significant day of my life in the *solar,* the tenement, the phalanstery: that strange ashen mauve light had become familiar by now, the nightmarish atmosphere was an everyday dream, the alien or dangerous inhabitants were now friends, sex had become love and then sex again. But leaving was still a salvation.

A few months later we moved away from Old Havana, leaving behind her shores without saying so long but rather farewell, to live in El Vedado, at the poorer end but amid flowers and trees, on a garden avenue where we could go out and see the sky. Although we weren't more affluent (for some time we had less money than ever, my father having lost his job, my brother's tuberculosis getting dangerously worse, almost fatal), it was a sea change. Our phase at Zulueta 408, more than a season in hell, had been a whole lifetime and was to remain behind like night. But it was really an umbilical cord which, cut off forever, remains in the navel's memory.

LOVE THYSELF

I'm not going to talk about self-esteem but about that well-known love which, like charity, begins at home, in the home of one's own body: that sexual battlefield in which I had early victories and in which I never suffered a single defeat. I'm talking about masturbation, which at the beginning is called jerking off (for a long time it was only jerking off, later it became a swank wank), a game of solitaire in which, through which, thanks to which I conquered my solitude. With my hand I never felt alone, and I still remember the most lasting moment of love I ever felt in my whole life the day when, after apprentice years of jerking off, in one of the bathrooms at Zulueta 408, I produced, alone with my hand, a moment that lasted longer than a moment, temporal immortality, the lapse of time it took to come, delayed many times, interruptus like coitus, my penis coming out of my hand, my hand releasing my penis at the last moment, until the climax became overwhelming and the damp cement floor was sinking, space disappearing (no more floors, walls, door, the ceiling rising thousands of meters above the melting shower as the sky was my limit), the moment made completely of time, a song on a distant radio sounding as celestial songs must sound, the music of the spheres, perfect chords for a perfectly pitched ear, sinking, sunken, falling weak-kneed, yielding beneath my torso (because my belly had disappeared into thin air) but my right hand still existed, welded to my solid parts at that moment—monument of my religion—and my whole body ceased to exist, universal plexus, pulsating like an enormous lonely heart throbbing its last beats, trembling like flesh in a final tremor, last gasps of the I, the self gone with the semen splashing spasmodically against the now materialized door a meter and a half away, not knowing then that never again would I feel so intensely what was not yet called orgasm, that which was the cum of cums.

LOVE THY NEIGHBOR

There was an old saw back home that said, "Your neighbor's grass is where it's green." It must be a rusty saw by now but I've never forgotten its golden meaning: no matter whom a man loves he'll always want someone else whose flesh is fresh. Perhaps it also means that the man who hasn't been happy loving just one woman suffers the pangs of loving them all—as Don Juan does. But for a long time, even though I fell in love every other week, the saying could be applied to me because of my quest for the right girl—green is where I found her. My only pursuit was to walk the streets and watch the girls (then they were all girls) go by and follow one for a while, but a while sometimes turned into the longest day and even night.

At first I didn't dare speak to them: I'd just follow, a shadow in love. Then, in time, I dared to come up to them and say hello, trying to be a polite alien, for I was a stranger in their paradise, you see. Sometimes I succeeded in getting an answer, other times a pregnant silence: Narcissus without his Echo. Or a killer look or haughty Havana hash, worse than sticks or stones: "Get lost!" "Who do you think you're talking to!" "The nerve!"

All that was in the future. Then (I don't know when then was now because what struck me as extraordinary in Havana was the custom of making passes that didn't exist back home, where the boys made contact with the girls in the park while walking around in circles—we'd circle the square without realizing it—each boy finding his girl and love, locked silently in looks. Nobody would say a thing, especially not those foul words of Havana men, whose passes were intended as flattery of the flesh but were public insults to private parts) I'd look at the girls, follow and speak to them or not speak to them, but they were all my lady loves—I mean I was in love with all of them. Whenever there was a fight at home (or rather when my mother was at war with everybody) or any family trouble or the *solar* looked like a bleak house, I'd head for the street to walk my worries away, and as soon as I saw a woman or rather a girl, the gloomy mood would pass, my balloon filled again with hot air. At first I wasn't very discriminating, and I'd go after a girl whom years later I would have never looked at. But around that time I was a colt in search of green grass.

My fleeting love for any woman linked up with my eternal passion, the movies, and I became a taster of foreign flesh, a tickler, a touch artist in the moviehouses. But it wasn't my original idea to search for forbidden fruit at the movies. A ripe Eve put the idea in my head, on an occasion that was really an initiation rite. I was with my brother at the old Lira Theater. It would later change its Apollonian name pretentiously into a Tiberian caprice, Capri, though it continued to be a small aisle of Rite. I was watching an unusual cartoon (a full-length film based on *Gulliver's Travels,* which was reduced to Gulliver's magnified stay in Lilliput) and the theater was full of kids. When I was able to see my surroundings (it was a nonstop show, in the afternoon, and the theater was a veritable *camera oscura*), I saw that I had sat down next to a woman with child attached. The woman was big and fat, grown-up in more than one sense. I returned to the adventures of Gulliver, now accepted by the Lilliputians as a friendly giant, but I lost the thread of what was going on on the lively screen because the live woman had put her hand on my thigh. A truly novel sensation. But it didn't last long because she withdrew her hand, as if she had touched me by mistake. I stayed seated without doing a thing, without even watching the cartoon, which interested me so much because it was the counterpart of a favorite fable—tiny Jack, the giant killer—and at this point the giant was being astute enough to conquer the pugnacious little dwarfs when the woman leaned toward the arm of my seat (it was her left arm, my right, that is, the one that belonged to me by rights: I learned movie protocol very early on since in my town there used to be quarrels and even fist fights over which armrest belonged to whose arm, and my neighbor was no Venus de Milo) and stuck all her flesh against my restless arm. She was up against me like a wall of fat for a while, and then she moved away, as if bored. But she made contact again with all her flesh and fat (the zone right under the armpit, the back part but not quite her back) and I realized what she wanted. My brother was immersed in the movie and I couldn't get a glimpse of the woman's little boy, probably following the animated mannikins so that he couldn't be looking in our direction because of the double obstacle: the translucid screen and his opaque, massive mother—and I let my arm accidentally fall on her fat thigh. No reaction. She didn't even look at me, her eyes staring straight ahead, and so I began to move my hand uphill, toward her crotch: her thighs had now become arduous slopes. I brushed my hand against her crotch, where her mountain of Venus was supposed to be located, but I didn't feel anything because it was a homogeneous surface, without reliefs, not even bas-reliefs. Years later, I figured that she must have been wearing a girdle, but that orthopedic artifact was unknown to me then: the women in my family (my mother and my cousin) were always thin. I brushed my hand against the tense toile but couldn't grab onto anything. Then the woman opened her legs and I felt an inviting draft: I couldn't see this propitious movement because all this time, while my hand caressed her skirt in vain, I didn't look in her direction but rather had my eyes glued to the blank screen. She was cuing me on my next move, however. I lowered my hand to the edge of her dress —and touched flesh. (I felt skin this time but other times, with other women, I would feel only the veiny varicose viscosity of nylon, which I've always detested, insidious silk.) I began to dig now beneath the cloth and over her thighs, which she tried to open in welcome, but the skirt was narrow (or she was fatter under her clothing) and my hand came to a halt in a cul-de-sac. I fought against the firm fabric and at the same time felt her trying to open her legs. But I was unable to penetrate the fleshy frontier and her open legs had become an impossible invitation. My hand was sweating (my palms have always sweated during all the decisive moments of my life) and her thigh was also damp, which made my labor even more difficult. I was in the midst of that fight for flesh when I felt someone pulling on my other arm. For a moment I thought it was some-one from the theater or worse, the police: I had already heard tales of police terror against flesh feelers and touch smugglers, whether all hands or mere voyeurs, and I always knew there was a secret police of sex. But a voice that immediately became familiar shouted in my ear: "This is where we came in." My brother, of course, all eyes and ears, was announcing to me that we had entered the theater at this point in the movie. I had to leave my labor of lust, neither won nor lost but begun, and abandon my corner on the flesh market. But before leaving the theater I could see, in the spare, intermittent Lilliputian light, the southern face of my unconquered Everest, that is, her profile, which is all that she had shown me, and I thought she was smiling—but it's difficult to make out the outline of a smile.

I don't know if it was this alpine experience or a natural interest in girls (though there's nothing natural about sex) that made my neighborly love move away from the sunny or desolate streets to the dark rooms of the movies. (I almost always went to the movies in the afternoon: in the pitch-black theaters, platonic caves before the screen, the pursuit of sex interfered with my passion for films, the contact of flesh awakening me from my movie dreams.) I continued chasing skirts out in the open, of course—the city a hunting ground for fuckers—walking block after block behind a girl for the simple pleasure of following in her perfumed wake, eternal timidity preventing me from coming up to her. There was also the maneuver of leaving a bus caught a few blocks earlier, leaping off at a run (abandoning the moving vehicle and landing safe and sound on asphalt was a Havana trick I had to learn and learn quickly, like all the other trade techniques of love) for a girl glimpsed in passing. Or the art of bus riding, in which one had to find a vacant seat beside a girl, first sit down carefully on the edge of the seat, to then start edging toward the passenger pigeon, capturing more and more vital space until reaching the promised leg, often to find a fiasco. (In the future, though, far in the future, I myself would cause promising encounters to abort in failure.)

But the movie theaters, more than the movies, are primordial places, the mortification of the solid sexual search interrupting the enjoyment of the screen shadows. There was a technique to getting one's eyes used to the dark of the theater after the blinding light outside: sitting in the last row, where I had never sat before. Since childhood, like all true movie fans, I had sat in the first row or as close as possible to the screen. Later in life I'd come seeking solitary female spectators. This was hard to find at first because it was not the custom in Havana for women (much less girls) to go alone to the movies, but around the mid-forties, especially during the day, lonely girls started going alone. One had to proceed with caution. The search became even more difficult if my brother was with me, insisting that either we sit down front from the beginning—he too was a fan—or that we stay where we were for the whole show—more *engagé* to his seat than *enragé*. Many of my early failures were the fault of this obligatory company, having to be my brother's keeper. After the possibly approachable girl had been sighted, then came getting up, finding the right row, getting into it, and sitting next to her as if it were the most natural thing in the world, and not a carefully planned landing. Now came the perilous approach, which meant putting some part of myself in contact with a foreign body, usually my half-naked arm (I always wore short-sleeved shirts, until it became pressingly fashionable to wear the guayabera, an unfortunate garment that makes fat men look obese and thin ones emaciated) against the often stark-naked arm of my neighbor. By that time I could guess her features from the close profile. Sometimes I was shockingly disappointed, which is why there's nothing more disturbing to me than a profile that doesn't agree with the frontal features. But the body was still a mystery, perhaps partially revealed by the visible bust above the shadow line from the row in front. Perhaps my arm could become glued to her elbow, horny not thorny flesh. Or my foot might touch her calf if I crossed my leg skillfully. (I know I'm dismembering my girl, but she's not my victim and mine is a labor of love, not hate.) The rarest of contacts was my thigh against her hip, almost always prohibited by the long arm of the seat. Often, after the first—never innocent—contact (Havana women, tropical all, were always conscious of their bodies, their skin a sly detector of intruders), the lady would move to the end of her seat or, even worse, abandon her place for the next seat or move a few rows away. Or leave. One was always running the risk of a scandal, an uproar, the angry protest that would draw the presence of the usher, the manager, the owner, the police, God knows who. This never happened to me, though a fabulous revelation did take place in the Rialto: a mishandled woman raised Cainite mutiny and the lights went on—to reveal several presumed spectators who were each missing a shoe. The crime mystery of the shoeless singles is unveiled as soon as I explain that one of the toucher's techniques in the movies was to insert a bare foot into the crack of the seat, the opening between back and seat, to seek the buttocks stuffed into the hard wood. But I wasn't seeking simply contact in the dark but love, love, that body counter.

In the same Rialto, this time after dark—it was opening night of *The Razor's Edge*—I casually sat down (nothing happened by chance with women in the movies: it was all knowhow) beside a girl who was a beauty in the dark. More than once, when the lights went on, or out in the street, I discovered that my presumed prey was a young version of the witch in *Snow White*. While trying to follow Tyrone Power's indecision, between Gene Tierney's possessive beauty and his search for truth (there's no doubt about what I would have chosen between the physical and the metaphysical), I tried at the same time to gain access to my beautiful neighbor, a virgin version of Gene Tierney. The show ended, the lights went on, and I could see that she was beautiful even under harsh light scrutiny. But between us came a male impersonator who thought he looked like Tyrone Power and had seen the movie already, obviously, because he was carrying on his arm a useless or at least unusual raincoat. When it rains in Cuba, it rains: no one, except the hicks in the country with their oil slickers, tries to protect himself from the rain. In Havana, at least this part of Havana where the Rialto is (which is neither Old nor New Havana, both naked cities, ignoring the tropics), prudent and knowledgeable architects built arcades, colonnades, passageways, making it possible to walk for blocks under the thickest rain without getting wet. This newcomer, this tropical Tyrone Power (whom through the years and friends in common I got to know personally: he wasn't a bad guy, just conceited) chose to sit in the empty seat on the other side of this tender Tierney. She no longer had eyes for the screen (especially not the empty screen of the intermission) because the stranger was tall, dark, and handsome. She opted for his attention (which was scarce: whatever seeped through the cracks in his wall of narcissism) instead of doing the right thing and choosing me. Because of her decision, she gained only this rough sketch. But I'd betray the memory if I didn't admit that she was instantly beautiful—though not as beautiful as the eternal Tierney up there, my favorite face then.

There were many attempts to grope for love in the dark of the movie theater, perhaps repeating the events on the screen—and some were sour gropes. But to tell all, even just to list them, would be uselessly tedious, because even memories can be betrayed by memory. Sometimes there's only a fragment not of memory but of a woman, like that night in the Alkazar Theater, where I never saw the face of a girl sitting in front of me—only her back and shoulders. She was wearing one of those dresses (or rather, blouses) which began to be fashionable around then, when the strapless cut, under the arms and just over the bust, left part of the back and shoulders uncovered, tauntingly tantalizing. Hers was a perfect back (perhaps too languid a line for my present taste, her shoulders drooping slightly) and it was right there in front of me, within hand's reach. I was unable to watch the movie or don't remember watching it, but I remember this soft, solid back that even in the gray penumbra of the theater was cinnamon-colored, seeming so smooth to the sight that I could almost see its fragrance in the dark. My finger brushed the back of her seat, a few centimeters—less, millimeters—beneath the girl's bare back. (She had to be a girl: she couldn't be a woman with such surging young flesh.) I again passed my finger from left to right along the surf of her skin, going a little higher but not enough for her to feel the shadow of my hand. I don't remember her hair nor can I say why I didn't stay until she got up, alone or accompanied, and left her seat, in order to glimpse her full frontal. Maybe that shoulder was enough. I tend to remember the many legs I've looked at or seen in my life, and of course I can't count them all, but this back that night in the Alkazar pleasure palace presents itself as a unique vision. Surely life has mistreated her, time soiling, spoiling her splendor, the years disfiguring her face, but they can't age the memory: that back will always be on my mind: I did well in not touching it, not reaching for it with my finger because its destiny was to be the epitome of all the backs I've ever seen, desired, recorded, and there's only one other that I remember with such fervor upon seeing it naked for the first time—but that memory belongs to another time, another place, and will be revived elsewhere, in another book where I won't be me.

Then there's the relevant occasion when I had money (I don't remember how I got hold of that bundle) to leave what was called in Havana the *tertulia* and in our town had been officially called Paradise or the chicken coop by its occupants—the cheapest seats high up, close to the ceiling—to sit in the orchestra of the Radiocine Cinema. They were playing *The Seventh Veil,* a complex story about an almost incestuous love affair between a sour Oedipus and his niece in custody. I've seen the movie since but I remember the first time I saw it because my carnal will made me sit next to a girl with a little boy she was taking care of— fortunately on the other side of the barrier of beauty. I was not sitting next to her precisely because between her and me was an empty seat like an abyss. I couldn't make leg contact with her. I could only look at her, and only from time to time at that, to keep her from noticing my offensive and therefore from defensively changing seats. Or so that she wouldn't call the usher—or worse, usheress—or that feared, fearful manager who was almost a law enforcer of the libido. I think she returned the look once or twice, as if it had been on loan. Or perhaps I imagined the whole thing. But I kept looking at her when the movie was over. It was at night, not in the afternoon, at a continuous showing, rightly called so in Havana: I had to watch nonstop more than once to enjoy later the privilege of seeing in the clear light of day the object of my desire in the dark. We left together. She had seemed beautiful to me in the theater, but on the street I found her radiant under the bright lights of the night: her black hair framed her face in a new wave, her pouting wet lips shone and her black eyes looked deeply into the dark, becoming darker as they looked, not absorbing the light but reflecting it, enigmatically, as in a looking glass darker. She walked up Galiano Street (the indirect route for me: the longest distance between two points) and I dared to greet her and she, echo or source, answered me. We managed to start a coded conversation during which I received the message that she was the daughter of a proctor at the Institute. Now I can consider a proctor a uniformed janitor but then, in my high school days, he was an authority, like a rector: among other horrors (like a movie manager) he could take one to the principal, which usually meant expulsion ipso facto. For a four-eyed student like me, inoffensive because I didn't belong to any of the armed gangs, gunsels in distress, who had made the Institute their hideout, it was, as always, a risk to be innocent. When she told me she was a proctor's daughter I began to think our conversation could be dangerous (I've always tended to think of conversations as dangerous when told) and I was glad I hadn't attempted any active approach in the theater. But I liked her more now in the street light and she seemed to be alone (that is, without a steady, having gone to the movies with a little boy who could be her younger brother) and anxious for company. At long last the perfect love I was looking for everywhere, but especially at the movies, in the darkroom of my development. Walking and talking we landed on the street where she lived. Before saying good-bye I managed to get her to tell me where we could meet again. She chose the Institute, hostile hinterland, where she would show up—those were her words—one of these days.

In response to her vagueness I waited for her visit with precise anxiety. I didn't know which of the several proctors was her father, but she told me that he worked in the principal's office, meaning that he wasn't one of those who stood guard at the main door and that he might be posted at the side entrance. At every recess I went to the principal's door to see if I would ever again see my newfound flesh, who hereinafter should be called the girl or the girl with the black eyes like dark mirrors or the Radiocine Cinema girl—because, you must remember, she had not told me her name. Asking a girl her name was devilishly complicated those days. It was improper, like trying to borrow some private property, and except for the girls at school (whose names I knew from the roll call) or the tenement girls (collective property) or the girls in my home town (whose names were familiar patrimony) I didn't know the names, never knew the names, of most of the girls I fell in love with. I remember, for example, routine excursions after school to the girls' school at the Galician Center, to see a particular girl who came out every day at five to walk from Dragon and Zulueta streets to Teniente Rey and Bernaza streets, where she lived, followed by the luminous trail left behind by her body in motion. She strolled in beauty and I remember following her stellar course for months, never even knowing the girl's name. She was always the Dark Girl of the Horse (descending from the Dark Lady of the Sonnets) because one day she wore on the blouse of her uniform a brooch with a stamping stallion, an adornment that became a label. This Andalusian beauty has remained fixed in my memory like a juvenile jewel and as such has a name in my imaginary harem that has nothing to do with her real name.

I was now looking for the other girl, from Radiocine, every day, between the principal's office and the short stone staircase leading to it. I never entered the principal's: that would mean entering not an enclosure but a maze: I remember having been in those offices only two or three times. Once, memorably, to register when I entered the Institute. Another time, also unforgettable, I got only as far as the vestibule, dressed in an improbably nylon raincoat when it wasn't raining, wearing its transparent skin as a sheath. I had a kitchen knife in my belt. I was accompanying my friend Armando Arnaz in order to rescue his friend Alberto Acevedo, who had taken refuge in the principal's because the gangsters of the SA were outside waiting for him and had threatened to kill him. You see, Alberto had stated flatly that the Cuban flag was merely a colored rag. The SA, native Nazis, were members of the Students' Association.

But I don't want to speak of politics now but rather of love in the place of expulsions. I also prowled around the miniature gardens of that wing of the building: there was no enclosure there, surrounded by confusing hedges, where she could hide: the only labyrinth was time. I had to make sneak visits to that amorous zone between one class and the next, bolting downstairs like a man possessed as soon as the lesson was over—except in the afternoons when I had free time. Some afternoons, though, three times a week, I had to go as far as Martí Park to become paralyzed doing gymnastics for the physical-education course. I don't know how much time I spent in that search. I even thought of returning to Radiocine, which was a more stupid exercise than Swedish gymnastics. One day, however, my search finally paid off and suddenly I found—on the staircase, next to the staircase, around the staircase?—the girl of the seventh veil in all her dark beauty, her black eyes shining bright in the morning, as luminous as the tropics, her lips more pouting and wet than in the night, features which exalted the glossy frame of her hair. I don't remember her body because I didn't pay any attention to the body then: only heads and faces counted as points of attraction: beauties being all busts. She was talking to a woman, not a girl or student but an older woman. Later I found out that a couple took care of the Institute and lived in the building. I figured that her father the proctor and the woman were the nightwatch couple, but the woman didn't seem to be her mother and, besides, I knew that she, my girl, did not live at the Institute. I waited almost hidden (in memory the scene seems to belong to the Golden Age theater, in which the actors hide from one another amid the sparse scenery, an impossible hiding place in real life, but what does memory have to do with reality?) in the garden or at the side of the staircase—

divided into two sets of Spanish steps, fearful symmetry—farthest from the principal's door.

After an endless interlude (recess was now over, of course, and probably even the next recess was already over) the Radiocine girl left the woman (fortunately she wasn't with the little boy, intruder in the night) and walked toward me, by then not at all hidden but rather quite visible in the tropical morning, which makes everything crystal clear. I stepped forward: "How are you?" I said to her, a greeting of course. She stopped a moment and stared as if she were seeing me for the first time. Maybe night had favored me. I realized she had forgotten and I said: "Don't you remember me, from Radiocine, from *The Seventh Veil?*" She continued to look at me but her look changed slightly and she opened her delicious lips as if to say something—but said nothing. A tic perhaps. I thought she didn't understand the movie reference. *"The Seventh Veil,"* I declared didactically, "the movie in which the perverse uncle falls madly in love with his nice niece who becomes Salome, hence the title"—I stopped in time: if not, I would have told her the whole traumatic story showing my Freudian slip. She continued looking at me, but now closed her magnificent lips. (I know that age is particularly cruel with lips, wrinkling, reducing, consuming them, but I want to think that this dark lass, the true protagonist of *The Seventh Veil* and not the faded lipless blonde in the movie, has maintained her bold lips as I saw them the first time, in profile, and as they were seen now, facing front, though closed). Then she opened them again, this time to speak—a tic douloureux—which she should never have done. "I never saw you before in my life" was all she said. But she didn't have to say more. I was completely stunned, deflated, incapable of uttering a word and thus, with my mouth still open in amazement—a tic amoureux—I saw her turn around and disappear into the morning, perhaps to the corner of the Institute building, perhaps in the direction of the Galician Center, perhaps crossing Zulueta toward the arcades—though she could just as well have been on her way to oblivion.

This did not keep me from going to the movies to look for my love, for the possible girl I knew was waiting for me in the dark to share other delights that were something more and something less than those to be seen on the screen.

I remember all the girls seen alone or accompanied conveniently by appropriate chaperons (little boys, for example, or other, younger girls) at the movies during that loveless age, as I remember almost all the movies I saw then. At times I remember a movie without remembering a particular girl, and it's because the movie was romantic, that is, it dealt with love, the romance I had recently discovered and was capable of appreciating whereas before I only liked adventure, suspense, or music. There's a movie that is doubly remembered because it's doubly lost. Today I know it's called *Humoresque,* but then it was called *Melodía pasional* and I remember its first run, as I remember the theater in which it opened and which ceased to exist long ago. With it disappeared one of my milestones, the old Encanto, sited right in the middle of my field of vision and nevertheless, for a long time, inaccessible like a mirage because it was an elegant theater and more expensive to enter than other theaters, with the exception of the America. In the Encanto Joan Crawford died of a long melody, which I later learned was the epitome of romantic music, "The Death of Love" from *Tristan and Isolde.* I was already becoming interested in European music, which I would later know to be classical music, and *Humoresque* made a lasting though false impression on me: remembering the movie is better than seeing it. \

Another movie I went to for the music (not because it was a musical comedy, to which I am still addicted, but because classical music was its theme) was *Carnegie Hall.* But at this première, by chance or by design (I had developed such a technique that I no longer knew if I was sitting next to a girl because I had meant to or out of sheer luck, like a Yukon prospector in search of a streak to make a strike), I sat next to a girl and despite my intense interest in the music I managed to talk to her, carnal knowledge being more urgent than Carnegie Hall, asking such urgent and decisive questions as "Do you like classical music?" The most amazing thing is that she interrupted her pleasure to produce mine by saying yes, she liked classical music. A lot. Between the tenuous plot and endless music I got a conversation going, but for some mysterious reason or perhaps because of the girl's very appearance or the tone of her voice I did not try to touch her arm with mine or make foot contact with her leg or look at her intensely. Thus, by the time the coda sounded and the movie was over we were like friends and left together—to suffer a shock. The glamour glow of the semi-dark hall (it was the America Theater with its planetarium ceiling, where twilight always gleamed, adding to the lights and shadows from the screen) faded as soon as we were out on the street, exposed to crude electric light. I had seen her profile in the theater (for me the rows of moviehouses were files of profiles) and she had seemed no beaut but cute (that's an adjective I use now, but in those days I wouldn't have been caught dead with it) and her short hair seemed what was called then a page boy. I saw nothing of her body but I've already said that bodies didn't exist in the movies, spiritist sex sessions. On the street the snub nose and Prince Valiant haircut became the features of a ninny. I had already noticed something twangy about her voice in the theater but now it was definitely an idiot's voice. She was moronic and more. Perhaps she wasn't a total imbecile because they wouldn't have let her go to the movies alone, but she was on the border of Mongolia. While walking (I went on walking with her: I wasn't going to leave her abruptly alone; besides, I wasn't heartless with women then: I can't even be that way now) underneath the arcades she told me her brother's name was Miguel Miguez and that he was in high school. It so happened I had a friend (not a close friend because he was a year ahead of me) named Miguel Miguez and there couldn't be two alliterating Miguel Miguezes studying at Havana High at the same time: it would be carrying onomastic coincidence too far. I was glad I hadn't made the slightest effort to get either physically or sentimentally close to that poor girl, for whom one could only feel pity. I even thought she limped—or was it my poor eyesight? It was a pitiful situation and cured me of my enthusiasm for romantic adventures at the movies forever—for a while.

Approaching girls in the movies when I went with my brother, which was often, was literally a pain in the ass: it was hard to change seats or rows or cross half the theater, as I would do when I saw a girl sitting by herself. But the maneuver became a real nuisance when I'd go with a friend (which I avoided as much as possible: I always liked to go alone, not only for the possible girls but to enjoy the solitary pleasure of the movies) and these complications became a total mess, an impossible confusion and a perilous excursion, when I went with my mother. She liked the movies so much that back home, when I was a boy, she already had a saying, which was a proposition to forget dinner in favor of the visual nourishment of a movie, and she'd say, for us to choose: "Movie or gravy?" In Havana I went to the movies with my mother a lot, which produced problems that were more than mere mother fixation. So just imagine the obstacles I had to go through when I went to the Universal, up to its family circle, with a friend, my mother, and even my father, who never went to the movies. I don't remember why he decided to go with us this time. It wasn't because they were playing *Man's Hope,* a Spanish Communist film, because I remember clearly the night of its only showing (an opening and closing-down case) in the same Universal Theater in the Plaza de las Ursulinas, an occasion in which they searched the women's handbags and frisked the men as if a second Spanish civil war were about to occur in the theater, confusing spectacle and spectator. The truth is I don't remember what we went to see en masse at the Universal that time: the movie is forgotten but not the move.

We sat (my parents and my friend Franqui) in the second section of the family circle, right next to the projection room, underneath the arcs. I had still not discovered my near sight. (Schoolmates had already been complaining that I hadn't responded to their greetings at night on the Paseo del Prado or late in the late afternoon—the worst hour for my myopia, the dusty dusk adding fog to poor sight.) That night in the Universal I realized I couldn't see from so far, and in the middle of the movie, to my mother's surprise, I got up and said: "I can't see!" She was alarmed, thinking that a sudden attack of blindness had come over me, a tropical Oedipus. "I mean," I said, "that I can't see well from here." My father, as always, didn't express any opinion and Franqui was up to his eyes in images. "What are you going to do?" asked my mother, Zoilícitous. "I'm going to sit further down." Down the aisle I went with these words, seeking to see better but also attentive to my hunt of vixen. I found a seat, right next to a girl who seemed to be alone, and although there was someone seated to the right of her (I don't remember if man or woman, but it must have been a woman, if not zealous always jealous) I knew, with my sixth sense of sex, that she was alone. I had arrived in the middle of the movie and it seemed like a calculated movement (it had really been my least-calculated movement with respect to a girl in the movies) to sit next to her. She looked at me. I was already looking at her. She wore her hair long in a way that was so fashionable in the forties (not falling in a fringe over the forehead and molding her face, like the girl of the seven veils), perhaps with a permanent, perhaps natural, and she seemed pretty. She looked very classy and, though I sat down to continue seeing the movie, after a while my neighborly love was more than I could handle and slowly I began to move up close to the girl, to her arm (which was not on the armrest but rather hanging next to it) until I felt the body warmth that warned me that a foreign arm was nearby, a third arm that completed me. I had learned to measure thermically the nearness of another body in the movies with quasi-scientific precision. It was a help that no girl wore long sleeves and the flesh was nude, radiating erotic heat to my arm like vibratile antennas. I stuck my arm toward her arm and she didn't withdraw hers, not even eluding with a sideways movement, the easiest form of disdain. I brought my arm closer and now we were in contact, skin against skin, her warmth now mine, both arms one. As always my face must have been red, the palms of my hands sweating, my heart beating (so loudly that I thought it could be heard in the whole theater over the soundtrack), my stomach agitated, my penis swollen: my whole body waiting for an enemy action and at the same time seeking a friendly response—or at least a passive attitude equivalent to a positive declaration of peace. In one word, an armistice.

My next move in this chess game of love would be to put a hand on her thigh: king's paw to queen. But I didn't do it because even though she was within reach she still looked like class. What I did was to speak to her. All this time, from the moment I had crossed the board and sat beside her in a gambit at a game of chance, I was conscious of what surrounded me: the nearby neighbors, the audience all over the place, who were for me the enemy or at least the opposition: they were surrounding this girl to comment on her actions—and consequently on mine. So it took me as much trouble to talk to her as to touch her arm with mine, verbal contact a form of oral sex. The same thing always happened: I was very sensitive to the possible comment of a neighbor but at the same time, as a compulsion, I couldn't avoid looking for girls at the movies, sitting near them, making Cuban overtures (a musical term that has another meaning in a sexual contact: approaching a female with an ulterior motive, which in my case, during those years of my life, was the leitmotiv) and anxiously awaiting the response. I spoke to the girl in the Universal Theater (there was none other around) and, lo and behold! she answered me. She had a pleasant voice but, though I was as fanatic about the radio as I was about talking pictures, it didn't leave a lasting impression on me: what impressed me was her face when she turned to me to answer my question, which was, how original of me, if she liked the movie (of which I had seen little, what with my budding myopia that sitting toward the rear of the rear had turned into a critical case and now with my attention totally turned toward my nice neighbor), and she replied yes. A lot. Did she come to this theater often? Yes, she did. Did she come alone? (A way of knowing if she was on her own, of which I wasn't yet sure: remember the ogress beside her, so attentive to our conversation.) Almost always. But she added: "Though my father doesn't approve." This last statement seemed like an omen to me, not only because of her father's disapproval of her going alone to the movies, but because I immediately imagined an ogling ogre dedicated to watching over his daughter with a hundred eyes—if this creature of my erotic mythology exists: the ogre with an Argus eyesight. However we—far from her father's century eyes—continued talking. I had already developed a speaking style at the movies so as not to bother the other spectators. In Havana then there was as little urge to be silent at the movies as the Pekinese have to chat and eat during a Chinese opera. What's more, the Havana spectators not only spoke among themselves but often embarked on monologues which seemed like dialogues with the apparition on the screen. One of my treasured memories of the movies did not occur on the screen but rather among the spectators. It happened at the Radiocine, during a showing of *The Devil and the Body*, a literal translation of the Spanish title of the French film *Le Diable au corps*. It was in the scene in which the leading character, who really has no character, finds himself in the enviable position of dictating the letters that his Parisian mistress writes to her husband at the battlefront. Then when she asks: "What shall I put?," a boy in the back suggested, in a gravelly voice: "Dear Hornelius."

Now I had stopped talking to the girl beside me, whom I had been trying to force—skillfully—into a violent verbal relationship, in order to look at her. She showed me her intermittent profile, eclipsed by the screen shadows and at times bathed in the light shining from the scarce blank spots in the picture, which was obviously a melodrama with more oscuri than chiari. But if I couldn't see her face well, I could guess it because sometimes she looked at me out of the corner of her only eye. An egress. Finally the film was over: without looking at the screen, without following the action, I knew the end was near by the intensity of the music: movie musicians, unlike Victorian children, should be heard and not seen.

"Where can I see you?" I asked.

"Please," she said, suddenly turning to me, "don't come with me."

She, an expectant spectator, also knew the movie was over.

"My father will see me," she added.

I insisted: "But I want to see you again. What should we do?"

She thought in profile and still in profile said: "I live on San Isidro Street, near the Terminal. Number 422. I go out on the balcony sometimes. You can see me there."

I wanted to tell her that I didn't want to see her from below, my eyes clinging to a balcony like two myopic Romeos. I wanted to have her near again, as near as in the movies now, at the movies again, my favorite place for romance, not only for love adventures on the screen but for love adventures far from the aisle. But she didn't give me time: as soon as the loud chords sounded indicating the second coming of the cast, she was already getting up, going, gone. I also stood up. Other people got up. I thought of my parents up there as I was going out after this moving target, the light on already, I trying to get past the spectators bursting toward the only exit, thinking, fearing that my family and friend could see me, but nevertheless determined to go after this girl who under the vertical lights dropped from the ceiling (until now I had only seen her hit by the horizontal lights of the screen) looked almost beautiful or at least pretty though I hadn't been able to see her whole face, before a sole profile, now only the back of her head. But by now there were more people around her, a veritable crowd coming between her and me: patrons leaving their seats, the opposition, the mob swamping her suddenly. Outside, on the sidewalk, I lost sight of my star because of the extras. I didn't hesitate for a moment. I crossed Sol Street and continued up, or down, Montserrate: I don't know when this damn road is going up or down, this street with too many names: Montserrate first and later Egido to end at the Malecón, almost calling itself Avenue of the Missions and whose official name, on the street signs, is Avenue of Belgium: a labyrinth of titles. Without the benefit of all these reflections, then hindrances, a drag, more tortoise than hare, I was already crossing Luz Street and I didn't see her anywhere, neither on Sun nor Light. I continued walking along Montserrate, leaving behind the theater, family, and friend, going toward San Isidro after my prey, in a drag hunt, walking faster and faster, looking anxiously ahead without seeing her, without even glimpsing her dress (which I didn't notice before, which I can't describe now but I'm sure I could have distinguished it on the dimly-lit street: it's curious how Montserrate, like Zulueta, got darker as it got closer to the Terminal although this building was a well-lit palace), crossing other side streets, until I sighted the square with the Wall, a piece of it, a ruin, a relic, already reaching San Isidro.

The city had swallowed her. It was not hard to find number 422, just as it wasn't hard to remember: they were the digits of the day and month of my birth. The building, false phalanstery, was almost on the corner of Montserrate and San Isidro. But I didn't see her or any lighted window that would indicate her presence: nobody in sight, all balconies empty, the house in darkness. Might it be that she hadn't yet arrived, that I had passed her en route without seeing her, that she had taken another street? I decided to wait. I don't know how long I waited: I didn't use a watch then: I didn't have the money to buy one: thus there was no need to use one. I waited a little more. Suddenly I remembered my parents, my friend—and I turned around and returned to the theater. When I got there all the lights were out but at the entrance I could see my parents and friend, waiting, still looking toward the Universal door as if waiting for me to emerge, Jonas of the movies, from the insides of the dead Leviathan: there's nothing more lifeless than a closed movie theater. They saw me: first my father, who, as always, seemed indifferent or at least resigned, and then my mother, who came to life like a fury: "Where the hell have you been?"

I didn't know how to explain what I had done. Fortunately, she didn't let me speak: "First you leave us and then you disappear without a trace!"

Franqui, my friend, smiled, not at my mother's fury but at my disappearance: he guessed where I'd been. He knew I had gone off with a girl but didn't know the failure that had been my fugue: not an exercise for ten fingers but for two feet. My mother possessed a bad temper—like a poorly-bottled genie—and now not only fright but fury had taken over. Or rather fury had substituted for fright, as always happens with groundless fear. I had disappeared in a sequence that had struck her with anxiety. First I had left the seat next to her to go down to the front of the family circle without rhyme or reason. Second, I had bolted from the theater without her seeing me. Third, I had vanished into thin air while they waited like idiots outside the theater for me to come out, and when the last spectator had gone (or perhaps the ushers, the doorman, the ticket lady, even the projectionist), they were still waiting for me to reappear, now coming from the direction they had least expected: from the Terminal, a traveler's not a spectator's route. My mother didn't shout (she never shouted when she was furious), she only hissed her Spanish phrase "Where were you?" My father didn't say a word but rather, between the silences of my mother's repeated question, cleared his throat of the imaginary phlegm of embarrassment, and Franqui smiled like a sage his wise-guy smile: he knew where I had been. But I couldn't tell my mother where I had been, at least not in detail. I knew her temperament, what she was capable of doing in her fury, her temper on the loose: I had seen, not long ago, in a domestic discussion with my uncle, who was a grown man, how she slapped him resoundingly, accenting her arguments with a final blow. Nevertheless, seeing that we were alone in the deserted Plaza de las Ursulinas, that there was no one there to embarrass me, no girl to witness my humiliation as an aspiring adult reduced to a scolded child, I said: "I accompanied a girl home," which, if not the whole truth and nothing but the truth, was the truth in part and in art.

"So you accompanied a girl home?" my mother said, turning my declaration into a doubt.

"Yes," I said, affirmatively.

"And us here like fools looking for you all over the place, while you accompanied a girl home." She sounded even more furious now, if that were possible, though less hissing.

"Yes," I got ready to lie, "a schoolmate I met by chance in the theater."

"A schoolmate?"

"Yes."

"Whom you met in the movies just like that?"

"By chance."

"By chance?"

"Yes."

I thought my mother's next action would not be verbal but that she would slap me in the face right on the street—or squarely on the square. I could not call upon my rights because with my mother I had none. I couldn't even legally claim my rights because I wasn't eighteen yet and at that time in Cuba a person's rights began at twenty-one. I opted for silence, imitating the night and my father. My mother continued with her interrogation, which, police style, consisted of asking the same question several times. But suddenly she started walking, crossing the Plaza de las Ursulinas, homeward bound, followed obediently by my father, and in the rear guard Franqui accompanied me, still smiling, half wise, half wiseguy. The incident had ended, apparently.

But only my mother's rage was spent, not my love, which had unleashed her fury as it chained me. I decided to go along San Isidro Street to try to see the girl in motion (all I had to remember her by was her fleeting profile in the shadows), who lived at 422. I went at all hours. In the morning, escaping the Institute, furtive love. In the afternoon, a fugitive from the gym gang and from what was more appealing, almost an obsession, the ball game, I still trying to form if not part of the intermural team then at least part of the Havana High team, which some years played against others. I even missed, for the first night, my radio program *The Spirit,* which was my favorite not only because it was an adaptation of one of the best comics ever but because its musical theme, a lethal Lethe leitmotif, delighted me (I would later learn that it was a motif from the *New World Symphony*), and I was leaving behind all those dear habits to go see if I would again get a glimpse of that girl, a going concern. There were times when I even went at night (telling my folks that I was going to the movies) and I spent hours in front of the building, waiting to see her peer out a window, come out on the balcony, perhaps enter the house. In another season that vigilance which became a vigil would have been dangerous, but these were balmy days—though not for that time of year. September became October and it began to rain, persistent if not Proustian rains, which put a damper on my search for the lost. Not that rain mattered to me—all that could happen to me would be to get wet, soaked, risk a cold, perhaps catch double pneumonia and die. What is all that compared to love, which lasts beyond the grave? But there was an insoluble problem: how to justify standing on the corner all that time? I couldn't even pretend I was waiting for the streetcar because it didn't go by that street but rather along Montserrate, a few feet beyond my post. Finally, unable to sustain my untenable position, a sentimental sentry, seeing the imminent checkmate, I gave up, declared the game lost, and never returned to my constant corner. I never again saw the gentle, accessible, and cute spectator of the Universal Theater, the—why not say it?—pretty good liar.

Nil desperandum, as Horace says. Or was it Mr. Micawber? There were other theaters, other haunts. If Zulueta 408 had one advantage, apart from its promising promiscuity, it was being in the then downtown Havana, where we were surrounded by movie houses, as well as other spectacles like the theater of life, the human comedy, and so there was little bread but lots of circuses. Right next to our phalanstery of funambulists, with its grand and grotesque guignol, stood the Payret Theater. It was so close that one could jump from our wide roof onto the brief back terrace of the theater, and I often went over there—first to study, then to read, and sometimes to look toward Central Park, some fifty meters away from the door. The Payret Theater then showed Spanish movies, but some years later they remodeled it, destroying in passing its interior with box seats and the pit of the orchestra and the pendulum of wings, built during colonial times, to turn it into a modern moviehouse of dubious distinction. Next to the Payret, separated only by the passageway and the Hotel Pasaje, was the small Nice Theater, which I never entered because very early on I was warned (I don't know if by my father or my mother but it must have been my mother, in charge of my social and sexual education) that it wasn't so nice a theater. Not only because of the movies they played (which later proved to be as innocent as their titles: *How Ladies Bathe, Blemished Butterflies,* and *Children Should Know*—which according to my mother was what her children shouldn't know) but because of the audience, apparently made up completely of degenerates —though she never explained to me their particular degeneration. (According to those who knew—there was always some friend who went to the Nice—the movies were quite disappointing, especially the children's feature, full of syphilitic ulcers and sick penises as illustrations of venereal maladies.) Exactly a block away, on the same sidewalk, was the MonteCarlo Theater, which had as bad a reputation as the Nice: depravities on the screen, the depraved in the audience. The theater further south, the Belgium, was another I never visited because of its infamous fame, with the worst audience of all the nasty moviehouses in Havana. It should have been called the Ostende, to form a deformed trio of moviehouses as casinos. Across the street was the Universal, left behind by my story, not by chronology. Returning to the Prado, a little to the right of the Payret, was the National Theater, within the Galician Center and since colonial times a theater with better reputation than acoustics, now entirely devoted to showing Mexican and Argentine movies. Further down the Prado was the Lara, alliterating ally of the Lira, which is on my erotic itinerary, but for dark, twisted reasons. On the opposite sidewalk was the Plaza Theater, pleasant to attend, pleasantly attended until destroyed by television, almost a future metaphor, and converted into a studio-theater for Channel 4. Across the way was the Negrete, a long tube of poor visibility, like an inverted telescope, to which I went mainly for the

93

quality of the movies it showed in the early fifties. The northernmost and last theater on the Prado was the Fausto, to which I went a lot in the early forties, where I saw more than one unforgettable movie thanks to the patronage of Rubén Fornaris, a fatal Faust one day. Toward the east the furthest theater was the Havana, in the Plaza Vieja, where I went a few times. Closer to home was the Cervantes, on Lamparilla Street, to which I also seldom went. The Ideal was on Compostela Street but I went only once, leaving it to oblivion. Back in the neighborhood, there was the Actualidades, to which I had traveled since the time I lived at Monte 822, a trip that was a treat. Afterward I continued going, of course, because it was only three blocks from home. Closer was the Campoamor, but one had to be physically careful: the degenerate here was the architecture, with such a sloping peanut gallery that it was dangerous: a lost step on a peanut in the dark could be your last. The Campoamor had the pretensions of being a real theater. But the only live performance I ever saw there was an American erotic parade, Minsky's Burlesque, my first strip-tease show, with the unforgettable Bubbles Darlene, probably a decrepit grandma in Amarillo, Texas, by now but then bursting out all over, like the Yellow Rose. She was also beautiful and brave: she paraded down Old Havana in the nude (or as naked as a stripper could go then, in the so-called G-string, a plastic figleaf which in Havana became a Band-aid), wearing only a transparent green raincoat on top, walking along the downtown streets until she was arrested by the police for attempts against Catholic Cuban customs, when all she did, poor girl, was to end civil boredom. I've already spoken of the Lira—opposite the Campoamor —as the place of my first explorations in amorous alpinism. Parallel to it, on San Rafael Street, was the Cinecito, which showed newsreels and cartoons. Also on San Rafael, as the crow flies, was the double movie-house called Rex Cinema and Duplex. The Rex ran only news and documentaries, but the Duplex showed movies. (Both had a large lobby in common that would one day be my erogenous vestibule.) Almost parallel, at the beginning of Neptuno Street, one could see the Rialto and further up the Encanto, and diagonally opposite, on Consulado Street, there were three theaters. Two of them, the Majestic and the Verdun, seemed to be in the same building, the Verdun having the tropical novelty of a sliding roof to let the nocturnal spectators watch a movie "under the stars," as its slogan said. Closer to the Neptuno was the Alkazar and I can't say which of these I frequented more. Further up Galiano Street (really the Avenue of Italy but never called by this name: in Havana, particularly Old and downtown Havana, and in many neighborhoods, all the old neighborhoods, they never accepted the new names of streets but continued calling them by their names from way back, even as far as colonial days, oral tradition conserving these former names and contradicting the street signs) was the Radiocine, and next to it the best moviehouse in Havana in the early forties, the America. (It was the most luxurious, most expensive, and offered the best first runs: only with a free pass was

I able to go there, many years after moving to Havana.) The most westerly theater was the Neptuno, on Neptuno Street, of course, but it was much further up and I rarely went. On the southwest border was the Reina Theater, on Reina Street naturally. There were other theaters where I rarely went, like the Favorito and the Belascoain on Belascoain Street, of course, and the Astral and the Infanta on, oddly enough, Infanta Street. And then there were the theaters in the outlands, outposts like the Los Angeles in Santos Suárez, where I went more than once, or the Apollo on *calzada* Jesús del Monte. But these were excursions and I want to talk about intimate incursions, make a map of the moviehouses I lived in, describe the topography of my found paradise and sometimes my stalls. I went to all these theaters in search of entertainment, the marvel of the movies, the white-and-black magic—but also led by the yearning for love.

It was in the lair of the Lara that the hunter was hunted. The Lara was at the beginning of the Paseo del Prado but was situated, on the moral map, in a twilight zone to which the Lira also belonged (or had belonged: the Lira was gradually regenerated, more and mores, until, rehabilitated by architects, it began a new life, with another name, as a capricious film club on Sundays. But the Lara never suffered that salvation of the army of art). My brother and I went often to the Lara because it was cheap and we could see good movies badly there, many of them recent first runs at the Fausto or Rialto. One night (or perhaps it was afternoon outside) the two of us were enjoying a drama or melodrama or voyage, all ventures, adventures, misadventures, forgetting the heat and the closed-in space of the theater, the poor visibility precluded by our concentration on what was happening on the screen (events on the screen always happened, were never told, narration replaced by images and music and sometimes the human voice crept in), alien to all that surrounded us, all eyes—when suddenly I felt a hand alight on my thigh. I almost jumped in surprise but first looked to see who the owner of the hand was (thinking that perhaps I had been touched by feminine grace as in the initiatory Lira). I immediately saw that the hand was enormous (maybe it was a huge woman, the size of the actresses on the screen, made flesh), but the hand continued up into a thick hairy arm, belonging to some old ogre: a man, an old man in fact, an aging giant who had put his hand on my thigh. There was no doubt about this manhandler's attentions. I wasn't surprised that it was a man at all because few women went to the Lara: the shock was that a man had touched me. I decided that it was better not to offend him by making a fuss (it might have been dangerous to cry Wolf on this island of immoral men) but rather to prepare a retreat. So I told my brother: "We better change seats." "Why?" My brother always wanted to know the reason for any new situation or change of plans. I couldn't explain because I was afraid that the old man next to me would hear me referring to his action. He was so big that I was frightened by his mere bulk, his presence more scary than what he had done or tried to do. "I don't see very well from here," I answered. "But I

95

see well," he said. "But I don't," I replied. "Then we'd better change," he agreed, so reasonable at times, and we got up and went to sit elsewhere, closer to the screen of course, amid inoffensive flat giants. I didn't even dare to look the touchy old man in the face but I never forgot his formidable appearance or the fact that he was truly old, accustomed as I was to seeing homosexuals as young and delicate or as passive pansied middle-aged men.

Other brief encounters with aggressive pederasts occurred in the Lara, but I don't think they were the degenerate kind my mother had alluded to. After the incident with my enormous neighbor and his hairy hand I started to realize that the Lara was a theater of queer gestures: weird movements, permutations, tropical tropisms: people who frequently changed seats and went down to sit in the first rows. They weren't movie fans but rather spectator lovers: their spectacle did not occur within the double dimension of the screen but rather in the 3-D world of seats and armrests and arms. One of these restless customers was Japanese. I don't know how I knew he was Japanese and not Chinese, considering that the proportion of Chinese and Japanese in Havana overwhelmingly favored the former. Perhaps World War II had something to do with my guess and with the fact that for me this Jap was evil, as the movies of the era showed: since they were always hiding in the shadows waiting to ambush the Americans and shove steel bayonets into their bellies, a good Jap was a dead Jap. This movie Jap was waiting in the shadows to put his hand below your belly: he was a compulsive cocksucker, ready to practice a faggot's favorite fun, fellatio. When I was sitting in the second row one day (perhaps because the first row was taken: by now I was an inveterate veteran of the first row: the larger the shadows the better, unlike real life), suddenly, in a dream which wasn't occurring on the screen, one of the spectators in the first row turned his head—it was the ubiquitous Jap! He looked me up and down, swung his arm over, and dropped his kamikaze hand on my crotch now crouched. I was as shocked as when the old giant put his hand on my thigh, though by then I had learned to recognize Japanese judo. I was alone in the movies, without my brother or a friend or my mother, so that I had to confront the perfidious enemy all by myself, like Robert Taylor in *Bataan*. But I didn't know what to do with that hand already touching me except remain inert as under the ogre's hand. And what if my treacherous penis fraternized with the enemy? I couldn't change seats because I was in the middle of the row, or make a row as I was trapped between my neighbors, all Axis allies, evidently Italians and Germans. (I obviously could have stood up, and the fact that I didn't think of this or that I felt inhibited, almost paralyzed, requires further explanation.) But, in the nick of time, I managed to seize the Jap's hand by the wrist. It wasn't very thick or hairy like the hand of the Cyclops—whom I imagined looking at the screen with a single central eye—or slimy, like all movie Japs: it was a human hand. I picked it up from between my legs to deposit it

calmly on the back of his seat, without haste or hate. The belligerent bandit was now disarmed—the arm from which his hand hung now rested on the back of the seat—and could have cried Banzai if he wished, using his hand in a masturbatory harakiri. The obliging Jap turned toward the screen but didn't get a chance to look at the movie because he immediately got up and left—not the theater, I assume, but rather to look for another Western spectator who wouldn't resist his Oriental advances.

The third strange occurrence in this theater (not so strange, really: what was strange was that nobody had forewarned me that going to the Lara—like the Belgium, the MonteCarlo or the Nice—could be, as my friend Rigor said, a "dangerous emission") was more major than the attack of the judicious Jap or the advances of the old Cyclops caveman. One day, or night, but most probably one August afternoon, I was in the proper derangement of my senses in the Lara when I suffered the overwhelming desire to urinate, from peep to pee, and I had to go to the john that didn't even have a sign saying "MEN'S ROOM." I knew how repulsive the restrooms in neighborhood theaters could be, ever since I began the education of my sphincters in the Esmeralda, a rank gem. Furthermore, I was already used to the always wet water closets of Zulueta 408, which smelled of all the perfumes of Araby and none was attar of roses. I went to the bathroom—or fecal pit—which was ill-lit by a single naked lightbulb: the light was unreal, or perhaps what was happening there was unreal and the source of light was your average lightbulb. In that men's sana there were three urinals and, toward the back, an open toilet in full view without door or curtain to excuse one's private parts. There was nobody in the room except for a busily occupied couple near the first urinal. At first I didn't see them clearly and assumed that one was urinating while the other waited his turn. But upon proceeding to the second urinal (or perhaps the third: I've always found it difficult to urinate with witnesses, shyness of the penis) I sensed that something unusual was going on in the first stall and I turned to look. I saw an older man (not as old as the perversely elderly giant nor as young as the Japanese pervert, so he was probably thirty years old) bending over the other man and I noticed that his arm was going up and down almost as religiously bent as in Millet's *Reaper*. The second figure was much smaller than the first man and for a moment I thought he was a gnarled gnome. But I observed attentively and realized that he wasn't a shorter man but rather a boy. I must have been seventeen then and I was at the stage when anyone who wasn't my age was either a kid or an old gent, but I was able to realize that this boy couldn't be over twelve years old. Now, the man was masturbating him and the boy let him do it with great joy, two getting a mutual pleasure out of the masturbation of one. The man didn't masturbate himself nor did the boy in turn masturbate the man. It was only the man who did all the masturbating and I could see the ecstatic expression on the boy's face. I couldn't see the man's face, bent as he was over his work, applying himself with arduous art to the minor's pleasure: an anony-

97

mous artisan of sex, a blind harvester, a real Jack the Reaper. Now the
man turned to me to whisper: "One downward twist, a turn of the wrist
and the wound is incurable." Shit!

Suddenly the Lara's true identity was revealed to me: it was a house
for homos. Those who were considered at my age the most dangerous
kind of perverts were buggers, the sort that chased after small boys. In
this case, though, the chaser was a queen and the boy, straight, passively
active, and satisfied, had agreed to the queer relationship. Anyway, the
Lara was for pederasts, as I discovered in this third experience, I the only
spectator in this theater of crudeness. But it didn't keep me from going
to the Lara, of course: they played so many movies so cheaply that the
depraved couldn't deprive me of the only movie theater where it wasn't
possible to find, along with the movie venture, the adventure of an accessible girl in the house—except for Gloria Grahame, a carnal shadow.

Some time later I returned to the movies with my mother (her temper
tempered by my wit), this movie lover who took me to the town theater
when I was twenty-nine days old, creating for me a second umbilical
cord, a tether to the theater (movies mostly), I almost born with a silver
screen in my mouth, she alienated by the bedsheet with film shadows—
a faithful wife capable of being unfaithful to my father with the pro-
jected specters of Franchot Tone, Charles Boyer, or Paul Henreid. Now
the two of us were going, as in the first days, as in the era of flick or treat,
on our way to the Orphic cave. We were going through lean years. Many
were the hard times we passed through then and there were still more
to come, but who could complain about daily life when we had the opium
of the movies, dreams in black and white and sometimes, as in dreams,
even in color. Only oblivion and memories were possible for us addicts.
Hard times were no hindrance, but rather a force of gravity that impelled
us to free-fall into the movies. This time my mother and I went alone to
the gods' heights of the Actualidades Theater, which had once been so
auspicious. That night Fate was a lady, or rather sat me beside an actual
Eve who even in the light of the white nights of the movies looked like
a Petersburgian blonde beauty. I did nothing at first except look at her
out of the corner of my eye, a practice I was expert at, my movie glance.
But after a while I put my elbow on our common armrest: what's more,
it belonged to me exclusively since she was sitting on my right. Her arm
wasn't resting there but was nesting nearby. My elbow advanced a little
and then some, groping, creeping, until I made contact with her naked,
warm, promising flesh—the promised limb. She left her arm where it
was. Confident, I advanced my elbow some more so that the contact
would be complete. (There was still the question of what to do with her
once conquered, accompanied as I was by my mother, but before the
conquest came the exploration. Colonizing that unknown territory was
not a problem I had thought of yet—it wasn't even among my immediate
plans.) Now my elbow was the hard tentacle of the octopus that swam
between the white and dark waters of the alternate light and shadow of

the show. I felt her flesh, or rather her skin in contact with mine, my daring young elbow trying to reach one of her budding breasts, since I'd already taken the arm for vanquished. I'm telling this as fast as you read it, but it took many minutes of masked advance so as not to frighten my prey away to the other end of her seat. I had already perfected these techniques before, sitting next to other girls, and now that I had put them into practice and the strategy had become tactics (a word related to *tactile, contact,* and, of course, to *tact*) I was not going to throw it all away on a gauche move. Besides, my mother was right next to me, though as always she looked totally immersed in what was happening in the movie, while I was submerged in the moviehouse—as much among the shadows of the screen as amid the figures in the seats. Next to the girl were her parents, doubtless, accompanying, escorting her, sitting on the other side of her precious presence: a girl who allowed anyone to make a pass at her.

Suddenly I felt an electric contact on my encroaching elbow: a cold sting that shocked flesh and bones, a piercing pain that immediately spread along my arm and forearm, reaching my hand and fingers. My reflex reaction was to withdraw my elbow and whole arm, pulling it away jerkily, quickly, violently. But I controlled myself. I stood the stab (the sting had now defined itself as a stabbing pain), and I left my arm just where it was. I looked, however, at the girl and saw that she had her hand very close to my elbow but without touching it. I turned toward her and saw that she held her hand in the same position and that she repeated her near contact with my elbow. It was when I saw her smile that I realized what had happened and I felt the pain even stronger, more piercing. She had stabbed my elbow. In cold blood she had stuck a *pin* in my arm. (Like many murderous women of the screen—beautiful Barbara Stanwyck in *Double Indemnity,* luminous Lana Turner in *The Postman Always Rings Twice*—she had executed her action coldly, deliberately, perfidiously.) Now it was hurting like hell. I knew that it would continue to hurt me because she was not taking her hand away from my elbow, burying the pin almost caressingly up to its head. Very slowly, as if it were nothing, a slight wound, almost as if I hadn't realized, as if bitten by a mosquito, I, a movie stoic, gradually removed my elbow that had been so close to her tits, its destiny. It now brushed her arm in passing and finally came to rest on my armrest, where it should have stayed in the first place. I saw her quickly pull the pin out of my flesh and now, avenged, she had become so calm (or rather, remained as she had been, because she hadn't changed in the slightest: she hadn't moved to stick the pin, perhaps a safety pin, in me), a cool customer, seemingly amused by what was happening on the screen (the sufferings of Ella Raines—that brunette beauty with translucid eyes capable of piercing crusty Charles Laughton had to be she), still smiling as if answering a question put to her by her solicitous father, "Do you like it?," she saying yes, a lot, apparently referring to the movie but he could have very well

been asking her about the pleasure of sticking knives into her neighbor's flesh.

All I remember about that night, the rest of it, was that I was worried about getting tetanus from the pin, probably rusty, that had pierced me deeply, not suffering so much from the pain, an injection in lean flesh, as from the doubt over whether or not I would survive tetanus, possibly gangrene, surely symptoms of septicemia, which I would suffer as soon as I got home. I must add now that I am extremely apprehensive, an incurable hypochondriac, terrified by all possible and some impossible diseases. In a metaphor, I am not made for those adventures at the movies that begin when entering a long dark passage, at the end of which a door opens onto an arena lit by blinding light, with unseen spectators who sit waiting—among whom I finally glimpse a figure I'm attracted to because of its posture, its sinuous, insinuating movements. I try futilely to trap it, close in on it, a maneuver I repeat often, always ending up a brave bull but killed by *descabello:* not with the sword but by a stiletto.

So, just as there are evil Eves and ingenuous ingénues in the movies, there were bad beauties and good girls in the movie theaters. When I least expected, I met one who couldn't be defined as an ingénue but neither was she a femme fatale. I was coming, that day, from the house of my mentor, the one who had accepted my first story (a heavy-handed and pretentious parody) and promised to publish it. Not only did he keep his promise but he was sincerely concerned about my literary education which would have been more thorough, probably, if I hadn't preferred living life over studying storytelling. Besides, he offered me my first solid job. Up until then I had been an erratic reader of proofs, a galley slave, picking up the jobs dropped along the wayside by Franqui, either because he was going off, like the first time, on an aborted armed expedition against Trujillo the tyrant in the Dominican Republic, or, safer and closer, to get a better job—also proofreading. I became my mentor's little night clerk, his nocturnal amanuensis, his secret secretary. If this job made it difficult for me to get to the night movies (some of them of the essence, like the Cine Club screenings, or elusive, like the art and cinema series at the University), it had the advantage of leaving me the whole day to study. But I am speaking of the day, the afternoon, I left his house nestled on the corner where amiable Amistad Street meets turning Trocadero, on the border of Colón, the *bayú* zone. (By the way, *bayú* is that mysterious Havana word for brothel. Nobody knows its origin, its etymology, but its sound suggests the attraction of sin and its spelling is like a graph of evil. The *bayús* were almost next to his house, not only to his disgrace but to the posthumous disgrace of our Discoverer, after whom Colón, the red-light district, was named. The name was there before the infamous professionals raised their tents, horizontal improprieties, and the name lasted longer than the sin, when a government minister expelled the "officiators of vice," as he called them in his purple prose, dispersing them, spreading them throughout Havana: thus the

neighborhood lost its immoral mystery and only charm.)

I, so fascinated with Colón, now crossed it fast and fearfully on my way to the Rex Duplex. In those days I used to imitate a one-arm bookish bandit and carry under my arm all the books my mentor had lent me that day. It was he who persuaded me to study journalism and forget medicine, a career I was about to commence. Finally, when *Bohemia* bought out its rival *Carteles* and my mentor was named editor-in-chief, he took me on as movie critic, which for years was my professed vocation—but that's in the future. In the present are the books loaned to me that afternoon when I left his house—it must have been a Saturday, I'm sure it was Saturday. After hearing his long literary litany (that is, our conversation), I left his house and crossed Colón, a name and place fallen from grace into sin, along Amistad toward virtuous Virtudes to reach my anxious goal, the Rex Cinema.

I walked rapidly, squeezing the books, because my mentor's exterior monologue had delayed me and I was afraid of arriving late to the show that united in a single motion picture my old love for Disney and new love for so-called classical music, which should have been called romantic. I rushed across the theater entrance to the box office, asking, buying, paying by putting my money in the small slot that made the booth into a blind little lobby, and upon executing all these motions, which were a single bullying action, I didn't notice I was trampling upon another customer, a bouncer in reverse. When it was almost too late I realized there was a woman there. I looked and saw a girl paying for her ticket before me. She looked at me and I, stammering, excused myself, recoiled, retrieved my money, removed myself, and waited until they gave her her ticket. I don't remember if she smiled at me then. I finally bought mine, entered the vast vestibule, and dashed toward the left lobby where the Duplex door was—and I found her on the way, not having entered yet.

The Rex Duplex (unlike the Rex Cinema, which was a long hall with only stall seats) had an orchestra and a first floor called the balcony, which even though they cost the same had independent entrances. The girl almost crushed by my rush handed in her ticket and began to climb the stairs to the balcony. I've already said many times how much I like to sit in the first row and I think I said how I hated going up to the peanut gallery when I didn't have enough peanuts to go downstairs. Now, nonetheless, I began to climb the stairs to the balcony like a robot and I entered the movies with her. I was far, that day, from an amorous ardor, from erotic escapades, by love not possessed: my libido was in the library or at least in the books I carried. Otherwise I was more interested in enjoying the film I had waited for so long: *Fantasia* had its debut in Havana in the early forties but, like *Gone With the Wind*, it disappeared astutely from the expensive first-run theaters, adding expectation to the spectacle, to now reappear at the Duplex in sections, like the invisible man: that day they were showing the "Nutcracker Suite," a fascinating film fragment and a blaring beacon to boot. So I can't explain what made me go upstairs after the girl. Or perhaps now I can: the old hard habit, the provoking woman alone at the movies, my ancient search for the unholy girl.

I saw her disappear in the dark but my movie eyes, a pair of used ushers, followed her to where she sat down. I didn't hesitate to sit down beside her. For a moment I paid attention to the screen, where some motley mushrooms were dancing a wacky waltz. Here is where my Russian revolt against Tchaikovsky began to turn my sympathies toward not his Fourth or Fifth Symphony but his Sixth, the Pathétique. Maybe that's what made me approach that Mexican-looking girl, who was rather short, if not squat, not at all thin, with gentle eyes and a sinuous half smile, which is what I had seen fleetingly in front of the ticket booth and a moment later when she gave her ticket to the doorman.

It was hard to speak when all the spectators were interested in what they could hear from behind the screen, some kind of mystical music (for those viewers who were all ears), at times soft, almost pianissimo, but I said to her what was *de rigueur:* "Do you like classical music?" I could have asked her if she liked Tchaikovsky or Walt Disney or even have made a synthesis of the musical thesis and the drawn antithesis, inquiring if she liked *Fantasia.* But that was all I could think of asking: if there's anything more predictable than a Don Juan it's an apprentice Don Juan. "Yes," she murmured, and, after a pause that seemed falsely pregnant to me, she added: "A lot." "I do too," I said immediately, enthused by her response. (Please note that when my amorous approach was verbal there were no attempts to move near the girl or to extend an exploratory elbow or daring digit.) But now she said "Ssh" gently, beatifically indicating that one didn't speak when Tchaikovsky was playing— or at least that's what I understood. I felt very good beside her, watching *Fantasia* (around that time I began to reject Disney, my pet cartoonist for many years, ever since his silly symphonies), perhaps enjoying its virtues, which twenty years later in another city, another country, on another continent would become a discovery—but gratefully gratified to share that corner of the theater with that girl, at whom I glanced from time to time.

Our interlude on the Duplex balcony was a brief one: suddenly the "Nutcracker" was over and the lights went on. She said to me, as a kind of good-bye: "I'm going." "So soon?" I said swiftly. "Yes," she explained, knowingly: "the rest is newscasts." No "Nutcracker" no more. Now newsreels would come or perhaps documentaries, and then they would repeat the fragment of *Fantasia* as if composing a whole. I got up to let her pass. We had occupied an area of the balcony that was quite empty, directly above the staircase, and when she chose that locale I thought it promised transformations, as Silvio Rigor would say. But nothing happened: I couldn't even smell her perfume. When she passed me, I decided to follow her downstairs. Impulsively I took her arm for a moment. "Are you coming next week?" I asked her politely, my advance more physical than

102

verbal. "Yes," she said, "I'm seeing all of *Fantasia.*" "Me too," I announced before extracting a response that could be a promise: "The same day?" "Yes," she answered, "the same day." I wanted to know her name because somehow I intuited that once she had crossed the magic threshold and was out on the real road, she was not going to converse but rather the reverse. I didn't know how to say: "What's your name?" since this question implied a familiarity that would make me too forward and I preferred to be the gentleman. I know I'd been daring on other occasions, that I had even become fresh, but not with this girl—whose arm I still held, however. My verbal vacillations led me to a minimal expression and I said: "Name?" She must have thought that she was hearing only a fragment of a question or perhaps she didn't even think because she said instantly: "Esther Manzano."

I can still hear her and it happened over thirty years ago. I remember her somewhat chubby figure or maybe I owe this impression to the dress she wore, a kind of tailored look. I remember her voice, which was low, and her slightly buck teeth that smelled of apples when she pronounced her name. I remember her eyes, which were perhaps her only beautiful feature. But what I remember most is her given name (I don't even have the touch of her arm in my memory because of her dress), written by me with *th* because many Havanan women write it that way, more cinematic than Semitic. But perhaps I remember her name because it was the only thing she conceded, all that she gave me. To nobody's surprise (not mine then, nor yours, good reader, now) I never saw her again: when I let go of her arm she left me forever. I continued going to the Duplex, completing *Fantasia* in weekly sections, but she never appeared again. I don't know why she didn't keep the promise she had made to herself more than to me. I hope that she hasn't died, run over by a car as I had almost run her down when I met her, love destroyed by speed. Esther Manzano disappeared from my life as she had appeared: suddenly at the Duplex Theater, one Saturday, on the verge of seeing *Fantasia,* having seen *Fantasia,* or rather, a fragment of *Fantasia.*

What has remained of this encounter is the sweetness of a girl's voice, the dubious color of her eyes, and the certainty of her name. Only that, and maybe even the name was false. Perhaps a screen existence was more solid and Gail Russell was more real than Esther Manzano. But man can bear a great deal of unreality. That occasion didn't keep me from dreaming of other possible encounters, perhaps imagining the impossible: in a neighborhood moviehouse, not far from home, an accommodating woman, or rather a girl, was waiting for me, she compelled to go to the movies out of the same desire. I didn't go to the movies now to enjoy the picture as I had done as a boy, or to view motion pictures as I would later on (when the names changed for me and my art, and a movie became a film), but rather to seek the love which I knew existed, that I was sure of finding, that awaited me in some friendly neighborhood theater.

103

And so, after many maneuvers and scarce skirmishes, I found myself going to the Majestic and, as at other times, I've forgotten the movie but not the occasion. Oblivion is justified this time because what happened on this side of the screen was more transcendent. This didn't happen often: almost always what took place on the screen was for me real life, and the theater, the audience, and the seats became a spectral zone that had no consistency: as in séances, the specters were mere shadows. It all began as at other times at the entrance, but without any promise of anything, the extraordinary veiled by the ordinary. I reached the door at the same time a girl was entering alone. I don't know how I saw her with my night sight: the dark theater became a thick black wall after the violent light outside. But I saw her sit in the middle of the orchestra. The spectators who let her pass by to get a seat were still standing up when I hurried through to sit next to her. The Majestic and its twin, the Verdun, cheap, unlike the Alkazar or the Duplex, had a lousy projector and the reflections from the screen were not intense but rather like dying light, as in *Gaslight.* Thus I saw her enveloped in shadows. She wore her hair long, down to her shoulders, as they did in the forties, influenced perhaps by Rita Hayworth. I didn't think of that possible model then but rather tried to see her face or at least define her profile, which I couldn't see clearly, as with the girl in the Universal, but she seemed to have a short, somewhat turned-up nose. I couldn't distinguish the shape of her lips, not pouting perhaps but more like those of the true protagonist of *The Seventh Veil,* the veiled blonde. I could barely make out her eyes (deepset? popping out? what color?) fixed upon the line of the dramatic horizon, but she probably didn't have the long Disney-like lashes of Esther Manzano.

Up until this point she hadn't paid the slightest attention to me. She didn't even seem to notice that I had sat next to her, that I was there, alive, looking at her. I couldn't even see her pupil travel to the corner of her eye in an animated glance. I really can't say what pressed me to approach her, I a pirate after prey and a prayer. Probably it was because she was alone or the two of us were alone in the same darkness or both things or, perhaps, a technical consideration. Other moviegoers were in front of us and suddenly, without thinking, I said to her: "Can't see anything from here." She turned toward me and said: "What did you say?" There was an aggressive tone in her question, so much so that it inhibited my technique for a moment. Finally I got up the courage to answer her: "I said that it's hard to see anything from here"—true enough, with all those heads in front making one dream of a horizontal guillotine. "You're right," she said, turning back to the screen. Then I did something that shyness, which at times makes us daring, compelled me to do: I grabbed her by the arm. "Eh!" she said. "What's this?" A veritably verbal *habanera.* Now all the neighbors knew some pussy-footing was afoot between us but nobody said or did anything, perhaps used to discord between couples (after all we had come in together), or perhaps too busy watching the movie. "We're going to change seats," I announced to her—I swear I

104

had never been so firm! My audacity and energy still amaze me, considering my age at the time, the way I had been brought up, and my timid nature. She then did something that turned the tide in my favor, saving me from drowning in embarrassment: she stood up and let me lead her by the arm. We left the row, trampling upon spectators, stepping on feet, even kicking knees. Now in the aisle I began looking for a place where we could be alone. I found a sufficiently solitary and distant place and led her there. We sat down and it was then that I realized my mistake. We had sat next to the entrance of the ladies' restroom, the light of the gender sign falling directly on us, bathing our bodies—and my lean body received an extra quota of light since I was closer to the forbidden zone. But nothing could be done. Another change of seats could inconvenience my near conquest. I call her that because I still didn't know if she was a conquest or not. But I suspected she was because it had been so easy to lead her away (or astray) from her seat. Moving would bring upon me God knows what problems, so I decided to stay the way we were.

We began to talk but I must have uttered the tritest trifles, truisms, and trivialities because I don't remember a thing that I said. I only remember that between my monotonous monologue and the actors' distant dialogue I had passed my arm around the shoulders of my girl (I was sure she was a girl, not a woman), who talked to me in a voice I remember as young but not very pleasant. There was something of the crow, magpie, or parrot in her strong Havana accent. I could still detect it despite having lived so many years in Havana. It was the same harsh accent that had seemed so strange when I met its shrill sound for the first time in Eloy Santos, a surly idiom full of coarse consonants and, curiously, a singsong, even though Havanites always claimed that we country folks sang a song. Years later, on a visit to my home town after nine years' absence, I was able to verify this: the provincials did sing, and I reached the conclusion that languages are not spoken but sung, arias rather than recitatives. Now neither of us was looking at the movie, too busy looking at each other. She was the apple of my eye, but what could this girl be seeing in the double screen of my pupils? Suddenly (memory shares these leaps with dreams and movies, and in those days all of them—memory, dreams, movies—were colorless, in black and white) we were kissing. I who had just recently kissed a girl for the first time, just a baby kiss, or rather Beba's kiss, was kissed back intensely: it was she who was kissing me now, trying to open my mouth to insert her flesh, a tongue kiss which I had never been given. (I knew of it through references, among them literary ones, the gallant novelettes, but not through my favorite literary source: the movies, where nobody kissed with an open mouth, despite passion, firmly in check by censorship.) This kind of kissing didn't seem hygienic, a high preoccupation with me because of my double maternal and paternal heritage. Hygiene was the only protection against poverty, which is like saying against life since I lived in poverty. That is, poverty was life.

The rules began with the mandatory hand washing before dinner. My father used to insist, when we first moved to the city—capital of vice and viruses—that I do it every time I came in from the street. But he had to make compromises in his war against germs: one of the conditions of poverty at Zulueta 408 was that the running water ran spasmodically and we had to wait for it to burst out like Bernadette's source, a repeated miracle once or twice a day, after which it would cease to flow. So we'd have to go downstairs for it or gather at dawn at the public fountain three blocks away in the Plaza de Alvear—a just justice. Alvear was the builder of the aqueduct and not only was his eponymous monument in this little square but also his anonymous public shame: this was the same famous artificial fountain that appears at the beginning of a noteworthy novel and a notorious movie. A born have-not, I was always worried, obsessed, about fetching the day's water early in the morning (in two full buckets, which murdered my hands) before the haves, the students, began to gather at the Institute door. There were always some, more haves than half-haves, who were already waiting for the door to open at seven-thirty sharp. There were invariably one or two acquaintances among these and, what's worse, a female friend, a she-have or two. Among the unspoken rules (because my father was as fanatic about hygiene as he was about Communism and my mother was also crazy about cleanliness, which for both doubtless meant that oral sex was taboo) was the injunction against the kind of conjunctive kisses this girl was now giving me, her tongue seeking mine, avidly and violently, pushing me back in my seat (she was almost on top of me), and I was worried not so much about hygiene as about the light falling directly on this now erogenous zone of seats. Then she irresistibly unbuttoned, undid one by one, the buttons of my fly (the days of the zipper were not yet upon us) and felt around, with both hands, in my underpants until she found my whatchamacallit, that independent instrument of desire which has so many names in Havana, all of them fallaciously feminine (but since the female sex has male names one must declare the world of words to be the strangest paradise), some as esoteric as *levana,* a sexual sound of fury signifying nothing. A doubtless con- cocted cocktail of a word because even the most exotic sword words are in the dictionary—like *pinga,* defined as a pole used mostly in the Philip- pines! The dictionary doesn't know that it's used more in Havana than in Manila but not precisely as a pole or perch. But where does *levana,* perhaps better written as *lebana,* to the envy of *lesbianas,* levitate from? Lesvos? Lavana? The Levites rising up in revolt? Meanwhile, she was seeking my blind, Cyclopean, Polyphenomenal appendix, finding and pulling on it since she couldn't extract it gently in her urgency and my turgescence, and what with the narrow passage of my underpants first and then of my fly, fingering, tugging, trying to take it out (no dice, no dick) without ceasing to kiss me. As soon as the suite of *balanus,* prepuce, and glans was finally outside, she began fiddling, playing with me, mas- turbating me. But it was really more like jerking me off: I masturbated, she jerked me off. *Voilà la différence.* And though there was more art in my way, hers was a more effective manner because she was immediately obtaining that inaudible murmur a second before coming, that agitation which precedes ejaculation, that moment when the penis seeks penetration only existing in the imagination of its glans, seeking a cunt it now knows it won't find, a fixed idea that the prepuce finally discards and alone, a circumsized *balanus* without vagina, as if it had a life of its own (individuality, in fact) it produces those same movements, always abrupt, upward, convulsive, which pass onto the body in symphonic sympathy, panning back to the baton-penis, which in a final masterstroke, unlike the forced faucet in the Plaza de Alvear, becomes a spout, a sprinkler, a natural bursting fountain, flowing, spraying its surroundings, rinsing the row in front, becoming a shaft shooting a stream toward the clean screen, erasing the actors, bathing the actresses, blurring the stars, my killer sperm sticking to the backs of the seats in front, falling, spilling over my legs.

What's left in her hand is an inverse erection, the aspergillum of my penis barely casting aspersions now, when I first hear the Latinate words this girl has been saying, murmuring at first, then speaking out loud, then shouting: "Youllsee." In her Havana dialect this came off as a dial-a-lecture, she at the lectern, holding my mike and belting out: "You'll see," making it more emphatic: "You'll see what a woman can be!" This last phrase rhyming only, perhaps, to my literary ear but uttered ferociously to intimidate my intimacy while she masturbated me as she bit my lip and pierced my ear. I realized then that this was no girl beside me (I can't say in my arms, since I was in her arms) but rather, quoting her, a woman, perhaps the first woman I had encountered—excepting the sierra madre of the Lira Theater, whom I had climbed without reaching her treasure, and the Greek chorus of Roman women at Zulueta 408. (But these were figments of fantasy and never existed sexually.) My captor (I was doubtless her prey) became a woman all over me, Dr. Jekyll transformed into Mrs. Hyde upon drinking my bitch's brew—from the rain of cream some drop must have fallen upon her avid mouth, a drunk trunk —Lana Turner turning into Ingrid Bergman in the last reel to finally fuck Spencer Tracy. This intertwining pythoness, this anaconductress, this serpent in a sea of gruel continued masturbating me as if masturbating herself. Actually, I hadn't seen a woman masturbate herself yet—a tit and clit massage. I already suspected there wasn't much difference between male and female masturbation without knowing that the latter was horizontal manipulation and the former a vertical rubbing, without realizing the nonexistence of a member or noticing the existence of a sketch of a horn of plenty, that anatomical clitoris, the alpine penis according to Gray's, called *pepita* in Havana, as if it were a pea nugget from a treasure trove.

But that digital data didn't occur to me then, enjoying, coming, almost satisfied as I was: now shaking, rattling, and rocking my powerful, pitiful penis, its porous body already flushed of the flood of yesteryear, becoming in her hard hand a sherbet-soaked cone melting downward—but it is a neighbor's voice that ends our wet encounter. Someone is saying: "How horribly hideous!" "The things one sees!" More voices blare and declare how disgusting, what scum, you can't even go to the movies anymore— and we're suddenly aware (she awakening fresh from her beauty sleep) that we are surrounded by ladies, mothers, families (excuse me, madam) with children at the matinée, and that we had offered a sideshow, an early happening, an old tableau vivant, aided and abetted by the light of the sign saying (if signs could talk) almost ironically "LADIES" (first and foremost). Afraid of the law as always, even before I went to jail for committing "English profanities" to paper, I was wary that the usher of the house might fall upon me like another bird of prey. But was there an usher in the Majestic? I don't remember, but I don't think they could afford the luxury of a vigilant Virgil for every damn Dante. Or a dog-matic doorman. Or a malevolent manager, accompanied by lewd officers, impregnable policemen who personify poetic justice in such a way that any private infraction, if caught in action, becomes a public insult, assault. Meanwhile, my peeved penis hid away in its lair, obeying my silent order and, taking advantage of its submission, I buttoned up my fly for fear of insubordination from my seditious, desirous, vicious member. I sat correctly, remembering with foreplayfulness the lessons I will one day receive from a professor of cinematography, a pretentious reviewer who was more like an expert in good manners. He lectured on how one should sit at the movies: back straight and against the seat back, legs together and touching at the knees, feet pointing forward, head erect facing the screen, eyes staring at the spectacle. End of show. I forced my companion, through my restorative reaction, to abandon her amorous embrace and sit properly in her seat. The alarm died down, the exclamations lost their point, the drones became willowed whispers, and finally, not Universal, but Majestic silence reigned again. Lady mothers could now take their lady daughters to the restroom or powder room, though that dirty place was never neither. The patient public, an amiable audience, could again assume its passivity. We, this woman whose name I didn't know and whose only words had been threats of love, and I, who finally found what I had sought so many years at so many movies, joined the majority and from lascivious lovers became serene spectators.

I don't remember if she saw the movie in that stopgap performance. I don't think I did. I do know that we went out when it was still light, and at the entrance, still blinded—this time by the vertical sun, another projector of images—I could see in big closeup my momentary lover, who wasn't a woman. She was a girl on her way to womanhood but still very young. I regret to say that the princess turned into a Cinderella. She was no Rita Hayworth: she was anything but beautiful. Her hair style was Split Ends, a cruel coiffeur. She didn't have a cute turned-up nose like Judy Garland, as I had thought in the theater, but was snub-nosed, pug-nosed, bulldog-like. Her eyes were not like Gail Russell's. They weren't ugly but what framed them wasn't beautiful: her look was a frown. Her mouth seemed thinner than thin, a sin, now smudged by smeared lipstick —which she didn't think of fixing before leaving the theater. She was rather tall and thin but poorly dressed. Her hands (which she hadn't washed after the flood) were long perhaps but the only thing about them that attracted, or rather distracted, me was that they had dark sunspots that went from the back of her hand to her arm—and they weren't exactly freckles. She saw me looking at her hands, the blotches, and said to me as an explanation: "Lard." This cryptic word explained the spotted hands, the yellow stains, everything: she was a char and had given me a cook's tour. "I always come on Sundays," she said next and it was, in fact, Sunday. "You comin' next week?" she asked, promising a seminal date. I said yes but before answering I'd decided I wouldn't see her again. I can't say what brought on that decision. Certainly not the fact that she was a cook. A short time later my favorite hobby would be the slavey trade, chasing after maids. Perhaps it was her offer to teach me then what a womanly woman was? I had been looking for that possible, impossible schoolmistress for years—how could I reject her now? Perhaps it was the certainty that our next encounter would end inevitably in bed. Was I ready for horizontal sex? I'm sure that my refusal has an explanation and that the causes can be found somewhere above. But to this day I have not succeeded in finding out why I never returned to the Majestic on Sundays. Perhaps I feared such knockout knowledge, as expressed by that rusty old saw sayer, the rigorist Silvio. Earlier, when I told him the story of the beautiful smiler with the killer pin under her cloak, he said: "One night you're going to find your Nemesis at the movies."

LA PLUS QUE LENTE

Claude Debussy has had a striking influence on Cuban popular music: I'm referring to a certain kind of Cuban popular music, not to classy classical or false folklore, but to that piano style best represented by Lecuona or Bola de Nieve, snowballing over the black and white keys. It's not that these musicians, or others like Frank Domínguez and Meme Solis, consciously imitate the composer of *Images* (curiously, there's a popular Domínguez bolero with the same title, and it was the favorite of an exquisite English writer who visited Havana in its heyday) but simply that Debussy's resonant style has influenced popular piano music, perhaps by way of the Spaniard Albéniz and his unconsciously persistent pedal. Debussy's broken chords, languishing harmonies, and fluid arpeggios have vanished, of course, but the sounds he elicits from the piano, especially in the higher notes and in his *forti* more than in his *pianissimi,* remain. I am reminded immediately of the hesitant melodies of "La plus que lente" waltz, which Debussy confessed to composing *"dans le genre brasserie."* Lecuona didn't possess the parodic power that sways Debussy in his slow little waltz, but if you listen carefully to his "Comparsa," for example, there are moments when Lecuona sounds like the Debussy of the café-concert genre that works so well in "La plus que lente," that slower than slow waltz.

What's curious is the role Debussy has played in my love life, his music more than himself. The first time I made love—the gallicism is a double-entendre—it was, to my amazement, with the most beautiful girl my Cuban eyes had ever seen, and to keep things going I had to caress her eardrums with Debussy's music, penetrating them gently with that soothing perforator, luring her into a swooning ecstasy that, believe me, wouldn't have occurred without a foreplay of waves at exactly eleven-fifteen in the morning—but that memory belongs to the future and now I'm talking about the present, that is, the past.

There was another amorous occasion in which Debussy, his music, intervened, but it ended in failure. A propitious part was played by Olga

Andreu, music matchmaker from noon to night, reclining hostess of our dialogue of hot wind and hand waves. But more than Olga, the culprit was her record collection, composed mainly of classical or rather impressionist music, a musical movement in which she involved Ravel, whom Satie nicknamed Ravol, adding insult to injury by claiming that Ravel believed firmly that, in music, theft is mere rubato. For Olga, Ravel was more than an impressionist, much more than an imitator: he was a parodist, a poet of pastiche and panache. "He also composed the *Bolero,*" said Olga and I asked: "Did you know he was a female impersonator?," remembering Ida Rubinstein, that fair virago. But Olga didn't say a thing. She didn't even mention the ultimate waltz, *La Valse,* so far from Debussy and yet so near. It wasn't the grand *valse,* though, but rather the smallest waltz, "La plus que lente," that comes to the foreground of love, forever unforgettable. I remember that the version was for violin and piano, or perhaps a violin solo, played by Jascha Heifetz. Whenever I hear "La plus que lente," even in its original form for piano, I remember the then idealized girl, my fair lass. Her name was (still is, I assume) Catia Ben Como. She was a friend of Olga's and lived in the same building, the Palace, which is on what would later be, on three different occasions, my cornerstone: on Avenida de los Presidentes, in El Vedado. Through Olga, I, we all, met Catia. "We all" were the group of friends who went to Olga Andreu's house to listen to music and chat with her on music and other less logical arts: Mademoiselle Olga Récamier fawning in the afternoon on her favorite fauteuil, a find, almost a historical miracle: a girl whom one could talk to, who wasn't corny or pretentious, a curiosity in Havana, the Vain, then.

Catia wasn't really beautiful, or even pretty, but she had the grace of her fifteen *habanero* years, which, two or three years later (she must have been eighteen, I not yet twenty), she still conserved in conversation. Besides she had a nice body, cute, they'd say (a word used to describe dolls in their houses), which means, more than in the dictionary, both pleasing and amusing. She was on the short side, and smiled very charmingly: her smile was not a rictus or a ritual but a state of mind. Like Olga she was intelligent and could hold her own in conversation with my friends and me, who were all the same, making constant jokes and puns, suffering insufferably from paronomasia as not only an incurable but contagious disease. I remember that one of the first times I saw Catia she was wearing that kind of dress with suspenders called a jumper, made of a material that imitated leopard skin, and for a few days she became Leopardina Como, the beastly beauty. We also performed combos on her surname, calling her Catia Lo Comotive, and wondering what a comotion there'd be if Catia Como married Perry Como, all appropriate to that adolescent, high-school humor which, like love, I would never give up. Catia withstood it all patiently, almost joyfully, and even reached the point of collaborating on jokes on her name or clothes, a truly catialyzing agent.

Those were the days when Roberto, born Napoleon, Branly, who joined the group as a specialist in vitreous humor, was said to have a friend named Leo Tiparillo, and another called Chinchilla, and we couldn't tell the surnames from the nicknames, doubting that Chinchilla's hide was genuine and wondering how many matches it would take to light Tiparillo. I remember the day Branly became notably noticed by Olga Andreu. He came to see her bowl of brand-new goldfish, and asked with almost scientific curiosity: "Are they adults?" But Olga (christened Volgar by Branly) made Branly's game into a set from her settee, a repartee à la Satie:

"Adulterers," said Olga. "They're fiendish fish."

"What are their names?" asked double Branly: "Daphne and Chloë?"

"No," said Olga, "Debussy and Ravel."

"Oh, I get it," said Branly, approaching the golden bowl but not bowled over. "Debussy must be that one with the flaxen scales."

"Algae."

"Olgae?"

"Vaguely vegetal floating filaments."

"Are they from the impressionist school of fish?" asked Branly.

"Yes, Debussy even composed *La Mer,* an impression."

"Quite impressive," Branly said. "Though I doubt he did. Nobody at sea composes *La Mer* and a goldfish wouldn't compose *The Fishbowl* either, I hasten to add."

Olga wanted to scare Branly: "The other one, Ravel, a composer of waltzes and boleros, wrote the *Pavane for a Dead Punster.*"

Branly pretended not to feel the hook and had the last word-fish: "I suppose that one afternoon Debussy will write *L'Après-midi d'un poisson d'or.*"

Catia, almost overcome, turned to ask me: "Is he crazy?"

"Merely enthusiastic."

The most curious thing is that we were all terribly timid, but we felt comfortable with Olga and Catia. Since they were always together, Branly christened them the Andreu Sisters, who were, for anyone who listened to swing in the fortunate forties, a *sonata à trio,* the allusion now an illusion, the triplet reduced to a golden duo. Inevitably some of us fell in love with Olga and others with Catia. I fell into the Mensheviks (the minority) who were in love with Catia. At first, love was only the desire to talk to her alone, without Branly and Olga, without witnesses, not even a fish. (It was all Debussy's fault—not the silent, circular one in the golden bowl but the resonant and no less obsessive one on the record with his "Plus que lente," which I'd listen to endlessly, no longer a hesitant waltz but an infinite melody, perpetual motion on Olga's record player. Her mother, Selmira—sometimes called Rossini's Selmiramis—would move in and out of the living room, both watchful and indifferent, while from the back room Finita, Olga's grandmother, an alert ninety-year-old woman who still smoked, would sometimes come in to join our conversation, lively and interested in our mad echolalia). I began to feel like being alone with Catia all the time and finally I fell stupidly in love, which is the only way to fall.

I remember exactly how it happened. Catia was visiting Olga as always and we were listening to (what else but?) "La plus que lente," with its hesitant notes, its pregnant silences and its disguised waltz air. Night was falling and as I was leaving, Catia accompanied me to the elevator. Since I came from the tenement at Zulueta 408 with its scatological staircase, I thought it very chic to live in an elevator building, and the ultimate in glamour to have a girl accompany me to what Catia called "the lift." "Not a lift, now, but a letdown," I corrected her. It was then that I decided, in turn, to accompany Catia to her apartment on the next floor, directly below Olga Andreu's B flat, thus delaying the separation and the sorrow. It occurred to me to ask if I could look out the hallway window facing south. (Neither the window nor the view nor the south belonged to her, of course, but I asked her permission as if she owned everything.) The twilight was still reflected down there, and from the balcony one could see the city traffic going downhill where the Avenida de los Presidentes meets its monument and begins to descend the cliffs of the Castillo del Príncipe (my jail and my cell for a day) and the new building of the Filosofía and Letras College, which I never attended, on the other side. At this point we could hardly see anything except the red lights of the cars going downhill and the white lights of those coming up.

We continued the conversation while we watched Havana by night. I don't remember what we talked about, but I know that we did talk a lot. Catia liked to listen and I, having conquered my shyness, loved talking to her, but the conversation was soon a domestic disturbance. It was dinnertime and Catia's family had begun to call her. First they went of course to Olga's house or called her on the telephone, and Olga must have said that Catia had gone down to her house hours ago. But Catia wasn't in her own apartment, which was obvious. She must be in the lobby then (that building, with its strange architecture, later identified as Edwardian, even had a lobby: for me further proof of Catia's class). Perhaps she was on the sidewalk in front of the building, where the boys and girls of the neighborhood often got together. She was of course with me loitering on the balcony, the two of us submerged in the friendly darkness at the end of the hallway, she watching the traffic (perhaps she caught my car fever, my scarlet passion for motion) or, most probably, staring into the night, while I tried to see her black eyes crossing a little when they looked at me closely. I tried to move nearer to those near-sighted eyes, to move their mistress, Catia, closer toward love. Not that we spoke of love: I was too shy to do so and she wouldn't have allowed it—at least I firmly believed she would never allow it. I don't remember when we spoke of love nor do I know if we really did. Yes, we must have, because she said "no" to my love, which was like saying, for me, "no" to love. But we didn't speak of love then but rather later, when my feelings for her changed to

113

love and from love to a passion no less overwhelming for being youthful. But, unfortunately, she was not to be my first girlfriend.

We continued talking and only stopped when she realized how late it was. I don't know how: she didn't wear a watch (it wasn't right for girls to wear watches then—time was for men only) and I was too poor to have a watch. I do know that she said it was late and that she had to go to dinner. Her family always ate together. It was a solemn occasion. At Zulueta 408, on the other hand, supper was a moveable feast. I took her to the door of her apartment, only twenty steps away from our cozy niche. She knocked on the door (a well-bred single girl didn't have the key to her house, though this rule, like others, was derided and broken daily by Olga: Andreu the Anarch, as Branly called her), or rather, she twisted the mechanical bell—not electrical but a Spanish caprice of the Cuban architect—which I can still hear squeaking, neither gaily nor sadly but simply squeaking. Her grandmother opened the door. Now I know it was her grandmother, but at that moment she was just an old woman opening a door while the good little rich girl said: "My grandmother," as if introducing a venerable old lady, who promptly expanded the introduction into a cue of complaints: "Where were you, child? The whole family's been looking for you all over the place. Where were you? What have you done? What time do you think it is?"

The confrontation made Catia look like a rich heiress in danger of being kidnaped. Catia managed to say, "There," pointing to the dark end (now black as a big bad wolf's mouth, black as the murky night, black as my true love's hair) of the hallway and the black balcony. The grandmother in turn used her skinny arms to express her disapproval (Catia might be a good little rich girl but grandma was no grand dame), and in one of her wavings, a tired conductor in her note row, I grabbed her hand, a movement coinciding with Catia's voice, again saying: "My grandmother," a ritornello. My reaction was an action that perhaps some hidden manual of manners often compels me to do: at the slightest provocation I will grab the extended hand of any stranger and shake it effusively. Thus I have found myself, almost in amazement, shaking the hands of doormen, emcees, ushers, of all sorts of people in that town of gesturing jesters that is Havana. I can safely say I've shaken the hands of half the city, half the populace, half the universe, believing that a mere gesture was a hand extended in friendship. Suddenly I saw myself with the old lady's little hand (I should say "old hag" but I am still preserving the respect I had for Catia's unknown family) in my damp but still warm hand, shaking it as if I could pump a cup of kindness yet from the dry old dame with this rather hydraulic procedure. But, worse still, Catia's grandmother saw her hand imprisoned in mine and almost screamed in horror, seeing herself caught by the dark stranger, possibly a kidnapper asking for ransom, who appeared so abruptly with her missing granddaughter.

The scene, the introduction, whatever it was, ended with a brief farewell from Catia: there ended, as well, my opportunity to be something more to Catia than a mere amusing acquaintance. I know that her grandmummy's tirade against her disappearance before the holy supper, our untimely appearance, and the confusion that both events produced, waxed into hostile intensity through my act of grabbing as mine the crowing crone's fluttering hand. I didn't need to hear what was said to know that it wasn't in my favor. God knows what Catia had to explain to make her disappearance seem decent. (Don't forget that the whole time she was missing from the family reunion we were hidden in the dissolute dark.) All I know is that everything changed after that luminous afternoon which suddenly turned to black night. Up until then everything had been uplifting. From then on it was all downhill. I went down the elevator to the lonely street, alone.

I didn't see Catia again until the next day. Already my love from the night before had become infatuation (as I said, I wasn't yet twenty and still an amorous adolescent). I waited for her after work at the electricity company, but following my lilt logic we didn't meet at Monte and Monserrate but across the street from the Palace Building. I must have given my visit a casual air, though I had crossed the whole city to create such a circumstance, because she gladly accepted to meet me under the flashy cement canopy of her Palace. It would have seemed more natural, of course, to meet her three blocks from home at the electricity company on Monte and Monserrate, but love is made of contradictions as well as contractions and expansions. But nothing was left of the Catia of the night before, although I didn't know it then. (I think I did know it because I wrote or began to write—but I never finished it—a story about Catia. It wasn't a story but rather a prose poem, an exercise in language into which night, the dark, the headlights, her shiny eyes, the bold balcony, and our intimacy entered, all accented by the sinuous sounds of "La plus que lente." Those notes were among my papers for a long time and finally meant more than my love for Catia: literature lasts longer.) We chatted a bit on the strange steps and she immediately went upstairs to her house, perhaps as a preventive measure against what happened the day before (a love story always repeats itself: first as a tragedy, then as a tragicomedy, finally as a comedy), perhaps as self-defense against my love, against the pseudo-kidnapper become real. I don't know, all I know is that she stole herself into the building.

My uncle the Kid's marriage to Fina took place around that time. The ceremony was in the Monserrate church, across from the America Theater, and afterward there was a party in Venancia's quasi-suite on the first floor, but the party extended, spilling out inevitably on the little square across from our room. I don't know how or when Olga and Catia, among others, appeared, but that day only Catia mattered to me. I'm sure Catia's presence was Olga's doing. Olga was getting interested in my brother, a promising young painter, and was also fascinated by our way of life, which she saw as preciously artistic in a terribly hostile house: baroque pearls cultured in an ornery oyster. There was drinking at the party, and for the first time in my life I got drunk. Two drinks and Catia's presence (another kind of alcohol) made me literally dance for joy, I who can't dance for beans. My joyous jig was a kind of left-footed hoofing, flawed flamenco, demented tap dancing which had the vertiginous virtue of frightening our Ready, the faithful image of the good dog, intelligent and tame, Argus alive, who because of my leaps, hops, and bounds, turned into a sudden savage beast and in his frenzy bit a little girl visitor. The wedding party ended right there, my mother furiously fighting with me for getting drunk, and, what was worse according to her, for making a fool of myself. I didn't know how or when Catia left (not sensing the essence of her absence) but I do know I mustn't have looked too good, drunk, and dancing like a Pan demon doing the pan pandemonium. Moreover I had shown Catia yet another faulty facet of my character, which, to boot, was false—I was anything but a drinker and the dual drinks it took to make me foolishly kick up my heels show how little alcohol agreed with me. But this was, fatally, not the impression Catia took with her—and who could convince the bitten girl that Ready was a good boy of a dog? Nevertheless, our meeting was the worst, not for Catia but for me.

It happened before a ballet performance at the Auditorium Theater. I had gone with my mother and Carlos Franqui (who previously had given me the necessary money to see my first ballet: I say this in passing since I had not planned to talk about dance but I must inevitably make a note of it), and there, to my delight, I met Catia accompanied by Olga. The night, however, turned out to be as moving as the evening spent together on the baroque balcony or the funny afternoon of the merry wedding—and I'm not referring to the movements on stage. As in (the Greek) tragedies a sudden messenger came to tell Franqui that his grandmother had died in their home town and that he had to go to the wake. Franqui didn't have money (and neither did we, of course) for the train ticket and we had to quickly pass the hat among all our friends in the theater. The collection determined my tarantella turmoil all over the theater (we were in the first balcony), going from friend to friend in a frenzy. For better (for my eyes) or for worse (for her eyes) I had to see Catia up close more than once. I should explain this double vision. I felt very good seeing Catia, but in some way my face must have shown the ravages of unrequited love (and not sorrow for a friend's misfortunes) because Catia's eyes, which were very expressive, showed me that she saw me suffering without being able to do anything about it apparently —and I don't think she contributed to the collection. The ballet, which interrupted my unhappiness with the mirth of the music and movement of the bounding bodies, was *La Sylphide,* featuring Alicia Alonso, all the female members of the ballet corps, plus some girl students from her school and perhaps the cleaning lady of the building—and a solitary male dancer. Branly barely let me see the ballet with his irreverent remarks. "It'll be a miracle," he said pointing to the solo male, "if that boy doesn't turn out a sissy." When *La Sylphide* ended, with the same slight slowness with which it had begun, the whole troupe moving a few steps at a time, Branly bantered: "Chopin has not died," he paused to then add: "He's only sleeping," another pause: "bored stiff." Even at the end when we all got together outside to comment on Franqui's worries, a friend in need, Branly was able to interpolate: "What I can't stand about *La Sylphide* is its machismo," declaring definitively: "Though you can't deny that Alicia Alonso knows how to mobilize her Afrika Korps de ballet." Everybody guffawed but I laughed less than anybody because, alas, Catia was not among us to laugh or even smile sweetly. She had left some time before, escorted by her brother (like a good little rich girl) and other friends whom I didn't know, Olga Andreu assured me. I wished with all my heart that Jacobsen, the mysterious, was not among them.

I don't know why I thought of Jacobsen then. I had heard Catia speak of Jacobsen several times. Her commentaries were almost made in passing, of no importance, always addressed to Olga, like "Today Jacobsen called me" or "I saw Jacobsen yesterday" or "Jacobsen will be there." But on one occasion Catia spoke about how attractive (and in my presence!) this Jacobsen was, a man without a first name, whom I had not seen, whom I never wanted to see, whom I never got to see but who was always in the way, like an alien line in my well-designed plans for happiness. He was almost a version of the inimical hand of Catia's grandmother, variations of an enigma. Perhaps that fateful night of the ballet, which began on the wrong foot, she mentioned Jacobsen once again or had seen him in the theater—although Jacobsen didn't seem to me the kind of person who liked ballet, who even listened to music, or who could much less appreciate the relationship between Catia and "La plus que lente." He was surely not even remotely capable of discovering Debussy's influence on Cuban music. I didn't doubt that the sinister son of a bitch had unexpectedly appeared, lurid, lurking in the shadows. Jackass Jacobsen! I felt like putting on a mask of black silk (during Carnival) and approaching the fortunate fellow to invite him to taste my vintage sherry and then take him to the treasure trove in my vaults, where already I had the trowel and mortal mortar ready—but how to recognize him? To this day I don't know what he looked like. Nor did I ever find out if he was nice or nasty, modern or medieval, or a moron, which were the categories that mattered then. Was he tall and thin or short and fat? Did he have a red beard or curly strawlike hair? Was Jacobsen a legendary, lonely Dane or just a Jew?

The third time I went out with Catia (the only time really, since the two previous times I had not gone out with her, and the day of my uncle the Kid's wedding she came to the party but left without me, I remaining with benevolent Bacchus and my mother's fury) it was to see Catia's profile (or rather, *The Asphalt Jungle*) at the Riviera. Between gasp and gap I remember the comments of Olga Andreu, who went with us (Catia, a good little rich girl, did not go out alone with a boy without a chaperon), though I don't remember who her companion was. During the movie Olga said: "That's the fall guy." She always liked to affect slum talk, despite her money. "He's cute!" Good God, calling Brad Dexter cute! It was a punch line enough to knock me down and make me die laughing, but that night I was already down, dying of love and jealousy over Catia. The double duress was so great that I couldn't stand it, and on the way out, under the spreading excuse of going to the "can" (as Olga called the powder room), I slipped away down under the covered staircase of the restaurant next door and returned home stealthily. Mum was the word to them. Then, when I saw Catia again the next day, I asked her if she hadn't been surprised by my disappearing act (during the whole bus trip I enjoyed the possible amazement of Catia and Olga, especially of Catia, who would think of my exercise in escapology, I thought, as "neat"), and she told me yes, it had seemed strange to her, but she had asked for me and finally decided that I had been bored by the movie. (But never by her, how conceited!) I still remember her exact words: "We looked for you. I asked: Have you seen a short boy? But nobody in the movies or in the restaurant had seen you." What hurt me most was not that nobody had noticed my absence, but that Catia, *cara* Catia, out of all descriptions of my person had chosen the adjective "short." I'm not tall but neither was Catia a Valkyrie, and that night we could have gone out with Bulnes, an admirer of Olga's from below, who was a little over five feet tall, if that. Angel Bulnes, almost a dwarf, had made of his short size a rare trait and used to say that he was angel-sized. Bulnes, more gnome than clone, told us the story of how, during an argument with his boss, he got so furious that he lost control: "I climbed onto a chair and slapped him twice." That inbulnerable Bulnes—merry midget—could have been Olga's toy companion, but all Catia had to say to identify me was: a short boy. These words were what finally convinced me that Catia would never love me, even if the social differences did not exist, if the family barrier were overcome, if the invisible but ubiquitous Jacobsen disappeared for good —and I stopped seeing her but not dreaming of her.

That is, it wasn't the last time I saw her—it's never the last time one sees anybody. I saw her several times afterward, and then we moved, a truly Hegelian leap (as Silvio Rigor played it) to Twenty-seventh Street and Avenida de los Presidentes, almost facing (tilting to the side) the Palace Building: from our balcony one could see the windows of Olga Andreu's apartment. Catia's windows would have also been visible if she hadn't moved a short time after—the whole family avoiding me perhaps? Inverted paranoia aside, I think they moved even before we pitched our tent in the neighborhood. As I said, I saw her other times and she even typed a story for me in which she dared to criticize *my* character, a little girl, who uses certain verb tenses which, according to her, the great grammarian, weren't appropriate in an infant. But by then my love, a curable disease, was gone. Perhaps it wouldn't have passed, recurrent fever, if she had condescended to look at me with only a little love in turn, with a fleeting sign of the loving look I saw that night on the bald balcony. But she never did. On the other hand I never forgot her: "La plus que lente" was there, recurring, to make me remember, and I'd often ask Olga Andreu to play the record one more turn. Then time took its toll and not even "La plus que lente" could make me sigh for Catia.

The years passed: I think ten or at least five years went by. I was already married, living in a posher part of El Vedado, and I had a daughter. She (I mean Catia) was also married (though luckily not to Jacobsen, as far as I know—I was never sure about that damn ghost). I almost didn't remember her when one morning, on my way to work in my convertible, I had to stop on the corner of Twenty-first Street and Avenida de los Presidentes to let the traffic pass down the avenue. Waiting for a bus on that corner was a rather short, fat or at least buxom woman with a long thick bulbous nose, wearing an off-white frock that was big on her, and arched eyeglasses: the epitome of the vulgar Vedado housewife. It was Catia Ben Como. At first I had a hard time detecting the slowest waltz under that *habanera* but when she saw me looking persistently at her, she looked at me, then recognized me, and waved. I waved to her too— but I didn't invite her into my car to take her wherever she was going and there she stayed, at the bus stop, waiting. I went on my way almost dancing with joy: I had felt happy to see coy Catia converted from a model miss, my youth's yearning, a unique object of love, into a common Cuban cow and ugly at that: it was an almost savage or at least unhealthy joy, which lasted the rest of the day.

LOVE CONQUERED BY ALL

Amor vincit omnia: love conquers all. So said Virgil. He knew heaven and hell (above all hell) but he didn't know a thing about love. If Virgil's phrase were true I wouldn't be able to look back in pain at the time when my love was conquered by everything. It happened more than once, not only with the disappointing Catia Ben Como. (Was she really Jewish or just teasing?) I must tell you now that I got rejected a lot. My lot. When it came to love and me, a dame was the spur—and the spurn.

For instance, there's the failure, the fiasco, the final defeat with Carmen Silva, the one with the name like a waltz, waltzing Carmela. She cut quite a figure at the Lyceum, I must say. She seemed to emerge from its evening music hall like Venus among the Marthenot Waves. I had seen her before, of course. I've always seen them all before somewhere, types more than prototypes. I discovered her when she was leaving the old Auditorium Theater. Lyceum, Auditorium, by Jove! So many Latinate names almost justify the twisted quote from Virgil and my Venusian metaphor—Greek by way of Latin rather. It's better to suffer from Greek love than to be called a Latin from Havana!

The Lyceum was where I fell in love with her, during the intermission of a chamber music recital. The program probably included Ravel's *Introduzione e allegro* but I don't remember the rest of that concert of concertanti rippling with ripieni and a continuous basso continuo. I do remember that I went with my mother, memorable music lover, almost a melomaniac. It had rained that afternoon: one of those downpours I love, intense, sudden, fleeting like passion: such a summer shower had once turned Lorca into a spectator of Havana. The evening now had a tranquil transparency, like a pond after rain. I suppose that all tropical nights are like that, but for me they are *the* Havana night. I listened to the first part of the concert and then, leaving my mother in her seat, I went to join some friends (acquaintances, rather). Among them was a long, thin, dark mulatto from Jamaica who played the bass fiddle at the Philharmonic, his bow a continuation of his skeletal arm: Longfellow

120

and his long bow are playing tonight. He introduced me to Carmen, then called "Carmen Silva." "A name to dance to," I said, gracefully I thought, but she urged me to call her Carmina there and then, "Like all my friends," and that's been her name ever since.

Atone (pardon my typewriter) at one moment of the conversation she, who was then so impulsive and charming (as I told her later, all charm comes from Carmen, but she could have annihilated me by flashing her killer smile and muttering, "By Bizet?"—women were learning to be wits very fast then in Havana, at least the women I knew), asked to borrow my handkerchief. I tried to retaliate with some punning about hankering chiefs and turbaned Othello, but she let my pass pass. You see, she had no need for disdain and didn't have to make a fool of me—I was a ready-made one. All she did was to raise my handkerchief—white flag of my surrender—to her mouth and press it between her lips, leaving the clear imprint of a kiss. For me it was a social surprise (Longfellow, also shocked, almost said, "Fiddlesticks!"), and when she returned the hand-kerchief to me, I couldn't say a thing (I didn't know whether to thank her or not) but kept the embossed, bussed handkerchief in my hand, without knowing what to do with it though really knowing I should treasure it always—and that's what I did, even though I didn't have many handker-chiefs then. (If you haven't lived in the tropics, you can't know how necessary handkerchiefs are there.) I put it away with the trace of her carmine-red lips (surely the color of Carmina's kiss). But before the kiss of love on linen faded, love faded.

On another occasion, in the Lyceum of course, probably in the library after a rehearsal, I dared to offer to accompany her home. Only a shy oxymoron like me could have been so daring. We got on the trolley, which was almost empty, and for hours (though they seemed like minutes to me) we were traveling on rails and beneath cables as if along a stave, thanks to Carmina's musical conversation. She lived in Santos Suárez, which meant that, from the Lyceum in El Vedado, she had to travel to the antipodes. The antic podium. Carmina advised me to remain at the trolley stop and not accompany her to her house because her parents were "old-fashionable" as she said, taking fashionable for fashioned. But I decided to forget what I had heard and concentrate on what I saw: a beauty with black hair, parted down the middle, and blue eyes. Though she looked like an imitation of Hedy Lamarr, my favorite feminine *fétiche* (for many Havana beauties then, Tondelayo was no joke), her image was very much her own and not on loan. Furthermore, there were her indelible lips that laughed a lot, revealing her white, perfect, healthy teeth, which were her greatest asset. How could I accuse her of making her old-fashioned parents fashionable, with all her charms, and body besides, those big breasts that she barely bared (another paternal pat-tern, probably) though one could sense their feather weight? But later I would discover Carmina not only committed verbal sins (maternal mo-rality excluded language) but that she constructed maudlin metaphors.

121

One day, pointing to a plane in the sky, she exclaimed: "Look at that steel bird!" I let it pass for contrary reasons: by then I wasn't in love with Carmina anymore. But even today, when I see a plane in flight, I can't help saying to myself: "Look at that steel bird!" and laugh at the slight (slight then, but now, like that passing bird, lofty) corniness of Carmina, contrary to Catia.

Yet another memorable occasion with Carmina took place at the Conservatory. How musical I was then! Always in pursuit of a recital or rehearsal, since I was too poor to have records and, much less, a record player! A small group of us had gotten together in the office of Affan Díez who, though a musician (he also played the bass: all my friends were in the string section those days: Eloy Elosegui, viola player at the Philharmonic, was also at the gathering), was in charge of the Conservatory publications, writing program notes and designing billboards and posters. That day Silvano Suárez, a buddy and budding writer, was with me, but the only woman in the group was Carmina. Whenever I think of her I see her alone, though on the night of the kiss by proxy at the Lyceum there must have been other women, aside from my mother. She was sitting with her legs crossed and skirt raised over her knees, which was very daring then, moving her shapely white legs and at the same time throwing her head back and laughing at everything, even when it wasn't a joke, to show off her tit-like teeth. Then and there I felt real love for Carmina, vitality incarnated: a fascinating life force, the florid fountain of youth.

The night I saw *The Third Man* I walked from the Infanta Theater to Zulueta 408, which was really far. I mulled over Joseph Cotten's impossible love for Alida Valli, so evident in the last scene, when she's coming from the distance to the foreground, taking her time in the void to walk the endless stretch and passing in front of him, faithfully waiting for her on the side of the road—and she doesn't even look at him. Walking back home, I felt just like calamitous Cotten, a writer deceived by his only friend and despised by the woman he loved, still drunk on zither music (which I knew by memory long before I saw the movie, after having gone with Germán Puig to one of the perilous port pubs just to hear the "Theme of Harry Lime"), carrying with me its unhappy ending all the way. When I got home, a telegram was waiting for me (a message that had greatly alarmed my mother, for whom telegrams were sinister signs) which said "HAPPY BIRTHDAY" and was signed "CARMINA." I don't know who told her it was my birthday (it wasn't) and even less my address, which I never gave her. But the cordial cable touched me deeply despite the puzzlement it provoked. I couldn't communicate my feelings to Carmina (I didn't have her telephone and even her address was vague) but the next day I went to her street, looking for her house without knowing the number, knowing only that it was on Venusberg (her own Wagnerian name for the hill where she lived). I walked up and down, the sun beating mercilessly upon my head, and when I was about to return home I saw a girl coming out of a house on the hill and I thought from afar (I was on the lower part of the street) that she was Carmen, it had to be she and I hurried uphill. But as I approached the girl she looked less and less like Carmina. She was no girl but a woman and of course not Carmen.

I tried to see her at the Conservatory that afternoon. I went there without hope, as a last resort, but as soon as I entered I bumped into her in a corridor, talking to a boy who was obviously a music student. In fact there was something of the metronome in the way he swayed his head as he spoke: he was not agreeing, he was keeping time. I don't know what face I put on to express my joy over the telegram, but Carmen got me out of the bind—at the same time smashing the magic of the moment to smithereens—by saying: "It's a truffle." (Did she want to say it was a trifle, perhaps? Or was she alluding to an exquisite mushroom and not to triviality? One had to interpret Carmen's cant carefully.) But her white, even teeth, twinkling when she laughed, made me forget the malapropism of her tongue. We didn't go on a date that day, I merely took her to the trolley, since she didn't even want me to go with her anywhere near her house, her father being a scout out for my scalp.

Around that time a good friend indeed was Harold Gramadié, a composer of serious music (to separate himself from popular music: I suppose that mambo and bolero composers would usually laugh themselves to tears at the keyboard) and a counterpoised professor of counterpoint and harmony at the Conservatory. As he was leaving our house one day, after a visit, I decided to accompany him to the bus stop on Prado and Neptuno. Along the way (under the afternoon sun heating my head as much as the midday sun near Carmen's house, evidently the same Havana sun) I decided to ask his opinion of Carmina. I wanted to know about her character, her personality, and I was ready to confess to Harold that I had fallen in love with her when he answered:

"Carmina? She has lots of talent and if she worked harder she'd be a good pianist. She's very musical, you know that? Very expressive. She has good hands and memorizes pieces easily. If she were more serious she could be a concert pianist."

See what I mean? The question I asked couldn't be taken in a musical sense and yet Harold's answer was typical: he never thought of the woman, only of the musician. I of course didn't say a thing. If I wanted to know anything about Carmina I would have to ask someone who hadn't composed a *Serenade for Giuletta* (as Harold had), in which you couldn't find one single theme of a girl on a balcony in the moonlight. I then thought of asking Affan Díez, who wasn't a friend of mine but who was at least a mutual acquaintance who might know something about Carmina's life. But I decided against this. What could Affan know about Carmina when she wasn't even his student?

Then came the inspired days when the orchestra of station CMQ was going to give an all-Bach concert, I mean Johann Sebastian Bach—to avoid baroque confusions with his rococo sons. At that time the ostinato

123

war was still on between the Pro-Arte Musical group and the Philharmonic on one side and a little group of Cuban composers who were barricaded behind the white façade of the Conservatory. Now, like a grave guerrilla group, the CMQ Orchestra joined in, never having been involved in such a commendable quarrel for producing music other than Beethoven, Brahms, or Bruckner, who were the composers drafted by Pro-Arte and the Philharmonic. As a sign of belligerence against the Three Bs the CMQ became a battle station and its orchestra retaliated with the Big B, Old Man Bach himself. (By now you can sense the bombastic nature of this musical warfare, in which Bach was considered a subversive!) I went with Harold to all the rehearsals, war games rather. Till then, Harold had laughed at the musical pretensions of the CMQ conductor, who had Italianized his name from Martínez Mantisi to mere Manticci. But that week it was Harold in Italy all right. It wasn't the first time I had heard Bach (his *Toccata and Fugue* had even been in that zoo of *Fantasia*) but I had never heard his Brandenburg Concertos, masterpieces all: "Best that bit!" Nor his sweet suites. Now the CMQ was going to debut—baroque Bach in the tropics—the Brandenburg Concerto No. 4 and Suite No. 3. For me these rehearsals were a memorable moment. One reason was the conductor's performance on his podium (or rather, political platform), from where he could shout to the orchestra during the rehearsals of the Suite in D, demanding only of his musicians: "Forte!" "Piano!," making me laugh sotto voce, thinking that at some confused moment he would shout: "Pianoforte!" and hang himself on a solo string. The real reason (apart from the real revelation—since then the Brandenburg Concerto No. 4 has been one of my favorite fugues, escapist music) was that, during one of the rehearsals (they almost always took place in the afternoon, when the studio was empty), which lasted till night, Carmen appeared (literally, like an apparition), dressed in a low-cut white dress that revealed almost half her breasts, by reflection allowing one to imagine the other half spheres. I left Harold during a break in the rehearsal and approached her. I don't remember if she was alone or accompanied as usual but I only see her, a radiant remembrance, and she smiled her white, wide, beautiful smile, lips in sordino, a silent laugh. I sat next to her, and when the rehearsal was over I didn't even say goodbye to Harold but left, we left, going down La Rampa which wasn't yet La Rampa, walking that stretch of Havana where El Vedado ends and Infanta begins, then down San Lázaro, a dark street that she lit up, and a few blocks further she said to me: "I have to call home," which was good news: calling home meant she would stay with me—and that's what happened. On the telephone she lied with a sudden knowhow: "I'm with a girlfriend," she said. "We've just come out of a rehearsal intermission" —"Rehearsing the intermission?" I thought but didn't broadcast—"and they're going to finish the rehearsal, so I'll be home a little later. Is that all right?"

It was all right and she hung up. I would have liked having money to invite her to dinner but all that I could buy as food was bread (she was calling from La Candeal bakery, which became a monument in my memory: to a bread unknown) or perhaps two rolls and offer her one—or was it half of one, the miracle of breaking bread? She seemed happy eating with her carmine mouth and biting the universal dough as if it were the fruit of the tree of knowledge. We walked from San Lázaro to Maceo Park and then down the whole Malecón to the Prado and along Prado up to Neptuno, where she caught her tram late. A good long walk, during which Carmina didn't make a single commentary that could be considered corny or say one malapropism or call the poet with his marble muse Juan Clemente Zanaco. Or perhaps Zany? Only in one momentous musical moment did she comment: "I think Bach is about to become famous." What could one say to that? But it wasn't a grave note. I mean it didn't spoil the perfect night, and when she got on her trolley I should have gotten on with her, accessible as she was. But the corner was a block away from home, and besides I had so little money that I was afraid to repeat what happened one Sunday morning on my way to the Philharmonic, to hear Brahms or Bruckner, with just enough money for the cheapest seat and my return trip, when a girlfriend, or rather an acquaintance, got on the bus, and I was forced to pay her way. Coda: I had to return home on foot from the Auditorium, hobbling along the cobble. Poverty, as we well know, does not allow for gallantry. That night I was more in love with Carmina than ever.

We saw each other again that week, but then two weeks passed in which Carmina didn't appear anywhere. She didn't go to the Conservatory during the week, or to the Philharmonic on Sunday, and there was virtually nobody I could ask about her whereabouts. Finally she reappeared one day, with her widest, whitest smile, her eyes bigger and more beautiful than ever, and she said to me: "Guess what."

What could it be?

"Haven't the foggiest," I said.

"Come on, guess." She was a sphinx with a secret.

"I can't."

"I'll give you a clue. The University, the movies, summer school."

No clue would do, I told her, wishing she would devour me with her mouth of Carmine lips.

"But it's all there," she assured me.

"I give up," I said.

"Okay," she said, "since you're being so octuse."

She probably meant to say obtuse but she almost called me an octopus: I who would be for her all eyes but never hands or limbs.

"I'll spell it out for you: I got a scholarship to study film at the University summer school."

That was a surprise! The sphinx produced a revelation. I knew how one applied for scholarships: you had to write a review of some first-run film and send it to the university and among the applicants they awarded ten scholarships—I knew because I had won a scholarship the year before. But that Carmina would win a scholarship with a film review seemed to me not only improbable but impossible. What's more, I doubted that she could even write a note, not musical but critical. The sphinx with a secretary. She should have read all this in my face, scrutable Oriental that I am, but only saw surprise.

"I surprised you, right?"

I had to admit that I was surprised, though I was really dumbfounded.

"Tomorrow I have to register," she said and I took this as an invitation to accompany her. "At ten A.M.," she added. "It's going to be great to be in that course," she said with enthusiasm. "I can't wait for it to begin!"

"Yes," I said, to say something, "you'll like it. They show a lot of movies during the course."

"That's right," she said, "you're an inveterate."

Possibly she wanted to say a *veteran* or an *initiate* and combined the two words and it came out *inveterate,* one word for two. It's possible but what is certain is that she said *inveterate.* That was almost her last word.

The next morning I was sitting in Cadenas Square, in the middle of the University, facing the registration offices, long before ten. The peaceful atmosphere of the little square was very pleasant, the sparrows around the bench, vivacious and shy and at the same time fearless—urban birds. While waiting for Carmina I thought of a story, which I later wrote, about love's long wait. But she delayed less in life than in fiction and I saw her going up the steps to the offices. I ran to her, and before she entered the building, breathless but not handless, I grabbed her arm.

She seemed surprised and said: "Oh, it's you!" as if she had been expecting another person. She added: "I'm going to immatriculate."

Was I hearing right? Im! So early in the morning, besides.

"I know," I said. "I came to help you."

"Oh, no, silly," she said. "Don't bother, I know how to do it. It's just like in the Conservatory."

True, it was easy to register in the summer school, though there was always a little confusion with the scholarship winners.

"I'm going in now," she said.

"Well," I said, "I'll wait for you to finish,"

She seemed a little upset. "It might take a while. You can go if you like."

"No," I said, more adhesive than aggressive, "I'll wait for you. Look," pointing, "I'll be sitting in the square."

"Okay," she said, but in her tone doubt was mixed with resignation.

I walked slowly around the square and sat among the sparrows, old Havanans (imported), and beneath the sun that was already intense, the morning sun like the midday summer sun. But I liked the sun, even the Havana sun, which at ten in the morning is as hot as fire and at twelve is a formidable flamethrower. After a while, which seemed a long time to me, Carmina reappeared, walking down the building steps, smiling to herself, or rather, laughing to herself, reaching me almost in a state of hysterics.

"It's all irresolved now," she said. How come she didn't realize it? Prefixes to verbs deny more than reaffirm. I don't know why but the truth is it was, how shall I say? irritating. She sat next to me and looked at the ground.

"You know," she said, "I have something to tell you," and then said nothing. Typical. Have a Havanan. Have not.

"What is it?" I asked.

"Well it's just that, you know, I'm waiting for someone."

It surely had to be a girlfriend. A celesta or harp player from the Conservatory, all of them celestinas and harpies.

"Who?" I asked.

"Well," she said, "it's a person you know."

What friend or foe of hers could I know? I couldn't think of any because I had met her among men and had always seen her with men around.

"I have," she hesitated, "I have to tell you that it's a special person." A miracle she didn't say specialized.

"But who is it?"

"Well," she said and then stopped. Who was it? A musical mystery: "You'll see and then you'll know."

Why all that intrigue, her reticent announcement of a masked person? I didn't understand at all. But then, from the end of the square, crossing the academic arcade of doric or ionic columns (I can never tell the difference between these Greek orders), the University's classical façade, emerged a figure that vibrated in the strong morning sun as if with a light of its own for a moment, becoming clearer, then familiar and finally incongruous: it was Affan Díez, sometimes called Celloaffan because he played the bull fiddle like a cello. I wondered what he was doing so far from the Conservatory, his greenhouse. When he got closer he greeted me both pleasantly and abruptly, as if it were he who hadn't expected me. I responded to his how are you with a fine thank you and how do you do. I felt I always had to be formal with Affan Díez. We had met a while back. I had even visited him in what he called his refuge (I was glad he hadn't said *lair*), which was a kind of studio in scarlet (the walls) in the Plaza del Vapor, above the fetid fish market, which he shared with a friend, Arturo Kammer, a graphic designer memorable only because his brother was a composer, of Kammermusik. I simply couldn't be informal with Affan as much as I tried. It was a compulsion with me. Now he addressed Carmina: "All set?"

"Oh, yes," said Carmina, "a while ago. We were just taking in the fresh air."

Sunbathing is what she should have said! No fresh air there, despite the altitude of Cadenas Square on what was called, a Cuban cliché, University Hill or, changing classics, the Seventh Hill as if Havana were

Roma when Havana was all amor. Affan came closer and sat down on the bench, next to Carmina. The situation, inexplicably, became tense. He didn't say or talk about anything—and that was weird. Though perhaps not so weird. In fact, one of Affan Díez's traits was that he spoke sparingly. An idiosyncrasy for which I envied him, since by barely speaking, when he did open his mouth, even to yawn, everybody was ready to listen to him: the opposite of what happens with me. I talk too much and nobody listens. All of a sudden (I swear it happened suddenly) I had a revelation: the sphinx unveiled: Affan was her amanuensis: he had written the review with which Carmina won the scholarship: they had an old understanding: Carmina and Affan were lovers! I remembered the occasion when Carmina was visiting Affan's offices at the Conservatory, the only woman among us, when I fell definitively in love with her. Now it was clear that I was the outsider in this gathering in the hostile square: I had invited myself. Affan was not an intruder in the duo or the third party: one didn't have to play the theme of Harry Lime for him: he was there on his own right: Carmina belonged to him. I was the odd man out. Never in my life have I suffered a more fulminating revelation: it was a direct impact on the plexus. Nexus. It has often happened to me that my mind puts two and two together and that I reach the truth in a sudden way, knowing that the odds and ends that appear unconnected are intimately linked. The hidden truth was now made evident: Affan and Carmina were linked intimately. Odd ending.

I don't know how I got out of that menace à trois, how I abandoned Cadenas Square in chains, how I left the University, how I passed through portal and portico in a *portamento,* how I went down the murderous steps which, upon going up, had been like musical scales, and how I returned to Zulueta 408, my den. Somehow I did it, feeling ridicule like another layer of skin all over my body, recognizing the falseness of my position, knowing that my love had been invested mistakenly in Carmina. Having taken her for the virgin of La Víbora, I found out—no, intuited—that she and Affan had already gone to bed together, that it wasn't a purely platonic pastime, that she didn't give her kisses on handkerchiefs but on his mouth. But Affan Díez was married! I said to myself, like an idiot, and inside me a second voice corrected me: So what? But for one part of my being, then, married men were faithful till death do them part and girls like Carmina remained virgins till marriage, untouchables till then. Now it turned out that none of this was true, that my second voice, my cynical censor, was right.

It was this interior voice turned inner ear that allowed me to hear Carmina's confession one concert night in the Conservatory, when she came to see me and took me out of the concert hall (concerts at the Conservatory seemed never to begin: all composed of un-begun symphonies) to an adjoining classroom. She told me how much she loved Affan, how they had been in love for a long time and the only thing that came between them was his marriage, his wife, a teacher at the Conservatory, who made Carmina's life impossible because she knew that she and Affan loved each other for never and never. "Like Tristan and Desirée," said Carmina wisely confusing Isolde. That night she asked me not to leave her because she couldn't bear the idea that Affan's wife was at the same concert. Fear of dissonant chords perhaps? I was tempted to ask her but it would have been cruel, considering Carmina's nervous state, tense like a string on a viola—or a bass fiddle. I also observed that she had put on too much makeup, losing the fragrant freshness of her skin, which was her trademark: she no longer looked as beautiful as when I met her.

Some time later Carmina suffered a religious crisis. Perhaps the loss of her virginity and living in sin had to do with her missionary mania. I got a glimpse of it from something she mentioned but it was so early in the morning that it was impossible for me to catch what she said. She got into the habit of calling me (by then we had moved from downtown Havana to El Vedado and we had a telephone, technology as a luxury) terribly early on Sunday mornings to tell me to stop living in sin (the first day I thought, obviously an echo, that she said, "Stop living in Sing-Sing") and to go to mass, communion, and confession: all of this said in an agitated voice. She sounded as if she had very little time—not on the telephone but to live. But she had a lot of life left. I found this out one morning, after leaving the Philharmonic with Juan Blanco, stopping for some reason at a café on Tenth Street almost on the corner of Línea (perhaps because Harold Gramadié lived there), far from the Auditorium and near the cemetery: we saw Carmina crossing the street, almost unrecognizable because of the many masks of makeup she was wearing, her blue eyes painted black, the face of a forty-year-old woman when Carmen probably wasn't even twenty. I was going to greet her but Juan Blanco, who was well-acquainted with Carmina, Affan Díez, and his wife, Carmen (an ironic touch: there was no way Affan could betray himself: he could use one name for his two women, one a pianist, the other a composer: quite an arrangement), said to me: "No, let her be. She's completely crazy." I asked him to explain why Carmina had gone crazy in such a short time. Juan, who's quite ironic, replied with a clash of cymbals: "The reason she lost her reason is musical, her Affan-fare."

But this wasn't the last time I saw Carmina. I saw her many more times, some crazy and some sane, and the story ended well for her though not for me. Carmen agreed to divorce Affan so that he could marry Carmina, which is what they did and they lived, as Carmen would say, happily never-after. (Do I hear laughter? As Shakespeare said: "At lovers' perjuries, they say, Jove laughs." Let's be like Jove then, and laugh!)

There was another occasion in which all, or rather she, conquered my love. It happened shortly before Carmina and her name was Virginia Mateus. She was blonde, and surprisingly the only natural blonde I ever met—though it's possible she was no natural blonde either. Virginia (her real name was Carmen Virginia but we've had a plethora of Carmens already) had gone to Havana High, meaning, of course, that she was no longer there. Now her family representative at school was her sister, prettier (Virginia wasn't beautiful: she was pale and attractive, as people would later say) but remote. All the boy students liked her but she maintained her distance from us with her aloof air. Virginia, however, was a very warm person and the first woman with whom I had a real relationship of any kind. The rumor ran around the school that our classmate's sister (that is, Virginia) had been married and divorced in less time than it takes to say "I do." I didn't believe it: when I met her I only thought that she was an independent girl, who cared very little about what people said, very sure of herself—which made her a woman.

I didn't meet Virginia at the Institute. I don't even think she went back there to visit, though perhaps she might have visited the girls' waiting room: a woman's privilege. We boys didn't have a waiting room, except for the Students' Association clubhouse, which was more like a hideaway. I met her at the Asturian Center library, nearby but far away. I had already been enlightened, that is, I had ceased to study in order to educate myself: I had deserted the classrooms for the libraries. As the Institute library was not well stocked, I went often to the Asturian Center, to read books in several tongues. Maybe it was mere chance that our readings led us to the same table or perhaps I played the game of chance. The truth is that we were sitting almost face to face, I trying to get deeper into a jungle of exotic words but distracted by her foreign head, seeing only the top of her blond iceberg, when she suddenly raised her eyes from the book and with them her golden helmet, asking me, as if we'd known each other all our lives: "What are you reading?"

Her question surprised me as much as if she had shouted "Furr!" in Old Norse or, still more adequate, "Stop!" to me, a thief of furtive glances.

"Who, me?" was what I said.

"Yes," said Virginia, who was not yet Virginia, only a girl of medium height (I saw that when she stood up but sitting down she looked rather small), blonde, not pretty, and yet . . .

"Ah," I finally said, recovering my poise if not my purpose, "Burroughs."

"Who?" said she, puzzled, or rather lost like the world in the jungle.

"Edgar Rice Burroughs. *Tarzan of the Apes.*"

"Oh," she said, "Tarzan. I thought that was only movies and comic strips. I didn't know there were books too."

"They were books before anything," said I, explaining more than excusing my choice of readings. (This happened before I had discovered literature; my passion for Tarzan led me to the Asturian Center library where they had the obsessive oeuvre of Edgar Rice Burroughs, bound in monkey skin as a homage to the ape man.) I suspected that it was my turn to become interested in what Virginia was reading even though she still wasn't Virginia.

"And what are you reading, may I ask?" I asked with this seemingly pedantic, Dantesque attitude, which has always prevented me from speaking informally to a new acquaintance—even a beaming Beatrice.

"Why so formal?" said Virginia. "My name is Carmen Virginia Rodríguez Mateus, but everybody calls me Virginia."

I told her my name.

"I like it," she said.

"I hate it," I said, "but it's a family heirloom."

"How's that?"

"I inherited it from my father."

She didn't register. She never did. "Well, I like it. It has character. I'm reading *Les Fleurs du mal.* Baudelaire."

"I know," I said smiling. *"Flowers of Evil."*

"Of course you do," she said, "but I like to make myself crystal clear." What did she mean?

"Unlike all that mystery with *Tarzan and the Apes,"* she said, smiling. Oh, I got it. She continued, "The good thing about this library is not that you can read but that you can talk."

"Maybe the librarian is deaf. The one at the Institute is one-eyed."

"Yes," she said, "old Polyphemus. Poor thing. He's the nicest person."

"Then you also study at the Institute?"

"Studied. The one who studies there now is my sister."

She told me her sister's name, which was different, simpler than hers, and that's how I found out she was the sister of the reserved, reluctant, radiant beauty, Rosaura Rodríguez.

"Oh, yes," I said, "we're in the same class."

"We don't look alike at all, right?"

"Wrong," I lied, "there's a certain family resemblance."

"No, there's not, you," she insisted, speaking in that familiar Havana way, Olga Andreu–style. "My sister is beautiful and good and even modest. I'm none of those things. All that we share in common is our blond hair and even in that we're different."

It was true. Her sister's hair was a mane that fell down her shoulders, soft and silky to the eye. Virginia wore her hair short, like a curly casque, curled with a permanent—or with curlers.

"Do you have brothers?" she asked.

"Yes," I said, "one."

"Older or younger than you?"

"Younger."

"Ah, just like my sister. Then you know what Cain suffered on account of Abel. A real godsend."

I didn't say a thing. I wasn't going to talk so soon about my family and about biblical relations.

"Did you think that Cain and Abel were exclusively male? Well, I want you to know that there's also Caina and Abela. Like my sister and me. She, poor thing, is so sweet, so shy, so well-mannered. I'm the black sheep of the family, so much so that I've been tempted to dye my hair

131

black more than once. If it weren't for all the trouble it takes."

She was quiet for a moment.

"*Je vais m'occuper de mon jardin,*" she said and was kind enough to translate it for me: "Time to go back to my flowerbed." Shit! *Je vais cracher sur la tombe de Couperin,* I should have said, but she had opened her book and was reading with a kind of fury now, verse versus verse. I imitated her, scaling the Mutia Escarpment with the agility of a seasoned reader of adventures on parole. Suddenly she stood up: a violent Virginia.

"I'm going," she announced. "Are you staying?"

Was it an invitation to accompany her? I wasn't completely sure but I decided against the book and in favor of Virginia—of life.

"Yes," I said, "I'm going too."

We went to the reception table together, handed the books in, meandered through the baroque recesses of the Asturian Center, and descended the musty stairs to the street. There were no people around the Institute: it was too late for day classes and too early for night school (the mere mention of this nightwatch depressed me).

"What do you have to do now?" she asked.

"Me? Nothing. Why?"

"Let's take a walk around Old Havana, then."

"Okay," I said, thinking that she lived in Old Havana. "What street shall we take?" I asked her. Standing on the corner of the Asturian Center we had many possibilities open to us in the triple O of Obrapía, Obispo, and O'Reilly streets.

"Let's go down Obispo," she said, "less gas fumes from *guaguas.*"

The Havana word for bus suddenly sounded silly, coming from this reader of Baudelaire in French. We walked along Obispo, flanked by bookstores. In a book I discovered Virginia and now we walked among books—and of books we spoke that afternoon.

"What do you think of Baudelaire?" she asked me. Today I could tell her: "I'm more interested in Nadar, his contemporary, also a con man," and thus clear the air after such a momentous question. But I told her the truth, Ernest as I was: "I haven't read him."

"You haven't read him!" She stopped in her tracks to say this, incredulous and shocked. "How is that possible?"

I had the nerve to say: "That's life." I was going to add that I was lost with Tarzan in the African jungle but I didn't.

"You mean his life, of course," she enlightened me. "A terrible life, I must admit. Women weren't good to him." A pause and then she added: "I could have helped Baudelaire."

I would not have believed this statement if I hadn't heard with my own eager ears! But, despite her petulance, Virginia was intriguing. She was capable of dressing in black and white, and explaining: "I'm in half mourning for life," but she also seemed capable of a passionate intensity. She herself was intense. There was, besides her spiritual side, her body: she had an erect bust and her legs looked strong and shapely as she walked in her sandals. She wore a high-necked dress, which was tight-fitting around her waist, widening below, but one could still divine her divine tits and firm buttocks beneath the summer fabric. Years later, when I had read Baudelaire, it occurred to me that I would have liked seeing her *corps mis á nu.*

Before we had finished walking down Obispo Street I was already in love with Virginia—it was amazing how easily I fell in love those days. I would fall in love with any girl on the street, and at school I had fallen for several, though mine was an anonymous affliction. Perhaps the most prominent (in my affection) was Corona Docampo, a Galician gal with black hair and black eyes, who always wore an immaculate gym uniform. By the evil design of the gym teachers, the boys and girls not only did exercises in separate gyms but also on different days, and, if they had had their own way, we would have done calisthenics on distant planets! Corona, under her white, aseptic skirt, had long, athletic legs. I fell in love with her as soon as I could but of course I never told her so. Only after her drama, which was worse than a tragedy, could I approach her, and it was to ask her, as everyone did, how she was. Here is her event: during a carnival parade Corona had crowned a float which caught on fire and she was seriously burned—not on her face, but on her neck, arms (so stainless, before), and legs—her legs! Perhaps she had burns elsewhere but if her body hadn't changed much, her behavior certainly did. Now she was no longer the triumphant Corona of yesteryear, but rather there was sadness in her young eyes that had seen death so closely: several girls on the float had died in the flames. But I have not come to talk about Corona Docampo but rather of Virginia Mateus, who behaved somewhat like Corona after the accident. There was something sad about her, maybe a tragedy in her future: an inversion that made me fall in love with her. In those days poetry had a strong effect on me and if it wasn't Baudelaire, it was the boleros: with bolero lyrics, the wait in the park for Carmina, and Virginia's legs and golden hair, I wrote a story, its title from a sign in a movie-theater entrance.

But now—that is, then—still walking down Obispo, I felt good (though the bookstores had been left behind) listening to Virginia talk about life: "Haven't you ever thought about life?"

I didn't answer because it was clearly not a question: it was rude rhetoric.

"I mean," she said, "from the edge of death?"

I could tell Virginia many things about life and death: about how at age twelve I had already contemplated suicide when I thought I'd failed the entrance exam for high school: sitting near a window on the third floor of the Institute I thought of the possibility of climbing over the desks and hurling myself into the street. But I wasn't walking with Virginia to make revelations to her, or even to tell her how women always saved me from death in the last reel of the perils of Plotinus, how I'd leave the house depressed about life, obsessed with suicide and, upon crossing in

133

front of a skirt, a pair of legs, and two tits (it didn't seem to matter if it was a whole or hole) my mood would change and the half-Hamlet would turn into a never whole Don Juan.

"Baudelaire is the only man I know," Virginia was saying as if she knew Baudelaire personally (Charlie to her), "who understands women."

I didn't say anything then (how could I, not knowing Baudelaire, almost without knowing Virginia?) but today I could have said, *esprit de l'escalier du temps,* that if hate is a form of knowledge, then Baudelaire understood women. I would have added his phrase *célèbre* stating that woman is natural and therefore abominable. He sums her up as the opposite of his ideal, the dandy.

"It matters not to me if you're good! Be sad but beautiful!" Virginia was citing, reciting down Obispo Street. "He's saying that to me, don't you see?"

I didn't see or know how Baudelaire could communicate with her without a medium, but I tended to agree with the psyphilitic poet in recommending that she be beautiful and sad and keep quiet. *Tais toi. Tête, toit.* Now I know that Virginia could never be beautiful but then, during that long afternoon's walk into twilight, I found her beautiful and it seemed very appropriate that she be sad. "Yes," I said, trying to show that I understood. The next thing she said was astounding, but only in the context: *"Voilà* my bus!" and without even saying good-bye she ran toward the vehicle, which was already moving, at the end of Obispo: we were now almost at the Malecón, having passed the Hotel Ambos Mundos, Town Hall, and the Plaza de Armas: I hadn't realized, so submerged was I in Virginia's aura, bathed totally in her temperament, going, gone, fallen deep in love so suddenly—what she would call, if she spoke my French, *un coup de foutre.*

When would I see her again? Had I lost her? Perhaps eloping with Charlot Baudelaire in Nadar's balloon? She would probably return the next day to the library of Bebel: woman was born free and we find her imprisoned everywhere. I walked all along the Malecón to the Paseo del Prado and up Prado, leaving behind the scandalous monument to the scanning poet Juan Clemente Zeugma and his marble mass. I returned home, not without first looking at the ill-lit windows of the Asturian Center library with a certain sadness. Ah, *le spleen de La Havane!*

The next day I didn't go to class but set up shop nice and early at the Asturian library. This time I didn't move, man imitating ape, from vine to vine, but rather buried myself in *Leaves of Grass,* so that if she insisted upon communing with Baudelaire, I could converse with Old Walt. Around then I was passing through a stage, doubtless influenced by Silvio Rigor, in which my heroes were all old: old Ludwig van, old Johann Sebastian, old Wolfgang Amadeus, old Claude Achille, and of course old Richard All Maniac, to fuse more than confuse. But she didn't appear that afternoon. I went by the Institute to see if I'd see her, since she admitted that she sometimes visited the building, "Nostalgia," she explained. "Neuralgia," I thought. "A pain in the neck." But though I walked slowly down the hall, looked toward the waiting room, and saw some girls, none was the vivacious Virginia. In the library (at that hour I wasn't going to enter any of the classrooms, in the middle of a class) I bumped into Silvino Rizo, a pretty good friend of mine, who would continue being so for many years until he committed a slight (or serious, depending on how you look at it) betrayal. But what are friends for if not to betray? Silvino was studying, I think, I'm sure. He was a bit of a jerk; that's why he was such a good student. I interrupted him in his mute combat with some textbook. (I detest texts and tests.) I talked to Silvino as much as one could in the Institute library, where the one-eyed librarian was all ears. Cycle of the Cyclops. I asked him if he knew by chance Carmen Virginia Rodríguez Mateus—and I immediately realized all those names made too much noise. He said yes, though his answer really was: "Peachy." Silvino Rizo was used to talking in low Havanese, so he added: "A blonde bombshell." (His idiom sounds dated now, I know, but it was all the rage then. Thus dies slang: killed by time.) Of course he knew her and he whispered (not out of discretion but of fear of our Polynfamous's ubiquitous eye) everything he knew about her.

The first thing he said, naturally, was that she was her sister's sister which made me impatient: there's nothing older than old news. But he gave me new, important, and almost virginal information. One bit in particular: Virginia was not a virgin, she was divorced. Dedée was a divorcée. On top of that, Silvino considered her easy. This was almost an insult to me, but I tolerated it not as gossip but as information. Virginia, said Silvino, had stopped going to school (she was a year or two ahead of us: "She," he added unnecessarily, "is getting on in years, you know") to get married, but she had tired of married life even sooner than school. "Seeking," sibylline Silvino hissed, without clarifying for what: perhaps she was looking for her lost paradise. Silvino knew no more but added, nosing around in what was none of his business, "You're not falling in love with her, are you?" Of course I told him: "Of course not." He added: "You're on the right track. Just follow her scent." I decided to talk about something else, but when he insisted on talking about his homework, I told him I had to go, adding: "I'll be seeing you." To which he answered, pure Havana-cigar style: "See ya."

I went home, which merely meant crossing the street between trolleys: parallel lines, parallel lives. As it was already close to five, the hour when the students would leave the Institute—that is, many of my classmates—I entered my building stealthily. I had developed a technique to carry out this maneuver, which consisted in walking under the arcade, flat against the wall, and pretending to be continuing up or down the street, and then suddenly entering the main door with a sideways jump. That's how I did it this time (besides there was the possibility that Virginia might be around) and I went up the two flights of stairs but didn't go into our room: I continued to the end of the hall and climbed up the wooden stairs that led to the roof. Up there I went over to the wall, near the iron base of the neon sign, and looked toward the street: I could see (from there) the side façade and part of the southern wing of the Asturian Center. I could also go onto the adjoining roof and see Central Park and the whole monumental hulk of the Asturian Center. This time I stayed on our side, watching the students come out and looking at the windows of the Asturian Center (precisely the library windows) to see if I could see Virginia. The last students poured out of the entrance gate of Havana High, and then Zulueta Street was deserted, revived occasionally by trolley tortoises and automobile hares in their crazy race, which the loser always wins. I stood at the parapet for a while, waiting for God knows what, actually suffering that joy—or enjoying that pain—namely the love that rejoices in saying its name. Night fell everywhere, though our neon light was blind to the fact, and I went downstairs to home before they closed the roof door.

I saw Virginia again, of course. Back at the Asturian library, she was still reading the continuing poems of Baudelaire. She looked beautiful that day with her short, straight blond hair. (Yes, I know I'm contradicting myself: I said before that she had a permanent, but I remember her with short, straight hair the second time I saw her. Perhaps she never had a permanent or straight hair, but I have to be faithful to my memory even though it may betray me.) She greeted me with a happy, almost joyful smile. I sat facing her to see her better though sitting next to her would have been better for talking: the round table came between us now. Suddenly I remembered I had forgotten to request my book and I went to the librarian's desk to take out the same old Whitman from the day before. I was chatting with her (I don't remember about what, trite trivia terribly important to me) when the librarian came over and said: "Here you are, *Leaves of Grass*," and he handed me the book, rustically. The grass looked greener.

At that moment Virginia said: "Oh, you're reading Walt Whitman," pronouncing the poet's name perfectly.

"Yes," I said as an old joke, "I'm behind in my readings."

"That's very good," she insisted. "Very good."

"What's good? Whitman, *Leaves of Grass,* or what?"

"Catching up," she said.

There was a silence—provoked by me, of course—and after a while she said: "That's why you interest me." I said nothing. "Not for reading Whitman, but because you have an interesting mind."

How the hell did she know, she who hadn't even spoken twenty words —including her quotations from Baudelaire—with me? But when she looked at me with her caramel-colored eyes, I was overcome, overwhelmed. There could be no anger or discomfort: I was in love with Virginia. Almost imperceptibly, her foot brushed my leg and I had an instant erection, totally unexpected, since my love for Virginia was spiritual, pure and sweet. I'm incurably platonic. But she crossed her legs

136

again, and again her shoe rubbed against my pants and my leg for a moment. "Excuse me," she said, making note that she had touched me. "Excuse what?" I said and she smiled smartly. Smart tart. Now I know she knew more than Carmina with her kerchief kisses and mouthed malapropisms. I remembered Silvino's confidential data that Virginia was divorced and easy, and I looked at her with newfound eyes.

When the afternoon was ending and she had finished studying *Les Fleurs du mal* petal by petal (it seemed to me she was tarrying too long on each line, on each sonnet, on each page), learning Baudelaire by heart, when she finished her Beaudelaire, I suggested taking a walk. "Ah, yes," she said, "that's a good idea." The best route was to go down Prado, thus going away from my house and getting closer to Martyrs' Mall, also called, let's not forget, Lovers' Lane. We returned our books and left the Asturian Center, crossed Central Park and went along the Paseo del Prado. The birds had already begun to perch on their trees: they came by the hundreds and thousands, darkening the sunset and sky over Prado and Neptuno. They were mocking magpies, who chose these trees at the beginning of the Prado just to perturb the evening with their loud, multiple chirping, and then, when they'd finally settled down early in the night, they'd shit on both Paseo and passersby: cursed birds of evil omen that expelled doubly damned droppings. But now, as we walked under the trees and along the prominent promenade, there were no ornery owls and I considered this a good omen. Virginia almost didn't talk the whole way. Could she have forgotten Baudelaire dead as Nadar had in life? At that moment she was one of the women who tormented Baudelaire with her emptiness and I incarnated the *poète maudit.* These are, of course, present reflections. Then I thought only of reaching the longed-for Lovers' Lane and suggesting that we take a seat on a bench, preferably far from the Prado and its machine-made noise and, especially, far from the streetlights. For a moment I thought of holding her hand but I was foiled by my timidity. I was thinking all the time how to hold her hand, thinking so intensely that I even started thinking indistinctly of the verb *to hold* and the noun *hand.* I thought so much of hands and holds that I put my hand on her hand, but before she could reprimand me from bad to verse, before she could look at me, before she could even turn her head in my direction I let go of her hand as if it were made of asbestos. It was then that she spoke:

"You want to hold my hand?"

"Oh no," I replied, like a jerk, "it was only an uncontrollable impulse."

I was going to add that I had already managed to dominate the bolting beast of desire, that patient who hides in every doctor—a galloping metaphor, it seemed even then. What I did say was: "I don't like people who hold hands on the street," but I didn't complete the sentence with its complement: "as if they were wearing handcuffs." I was lying and in those days, I bashfully believed, a gorgeous Goebbels, that the shorter the lie, the more believable. She believed me. At least I believed she did.

"Isn't that funny," she said, "I don't either."

She meant that she didn't like to see people holding hands as if hand-cuffed either, but I had to insist.

"What?"

"What about what?" she said, smiling.

"What don't you either?"

"Oh. I don't like to hold hands on the street with anybody. Either. Especially with a man."

I was alarmed. Was she a lesbian? A Sapphic lover of the poet? Baude-laire's beau on Lesbos? But no, she was too young, too feminine, even fay. I noticed that she had said *man* instead of *boy*, as any girl her age would have said: marrying had not made her a wife but divorcing had made her a woman. We came to the end of the Prado. We crossed in the direction of the Castillo de la Punta and couldn't avoid going through the Mall of the Martyred Lovers. We had to cross the street first, of course, eluding traffic, Havana then being a city of many cars and few lights. Now in the park I suggested, an impromptu which was really an étude:

"Why don't we sit for a little while?"

The use of *little* bothered me, but what I meant was that we wouldn't be sitting there enough time to allow darkness to descend on us, imposing thus its procuring presence. (Now I mock my pathetic fallacy but then I thought in those terms.) She looked at me and smiled: "Okay," she said. We sat on the first bench we found: they were all empty: it was not yet time for lousy lovers, still time for the timid. Seated now, she crossed her leg (her white body beneath a yellow dress: I think it was yellow or maybe white with yellow polka dots, but there was no doubt about her body: it was white: a milky way) and I could see her fleshy calf from firm ankle to round knee. I looked up at her face, which seemed almost beautiful in the twilight. "I must tell her," I said to myself. "After all, she reads Baudelaire." But I decided some time ago not to pay any attention to you now, my friend, and then I didn't pretend to have read Baudelaire. In-stead I popped her the question I often ask women, a more profound form of "a penny for your thoughts."

"What are you thinking about?"

She looked at the autumn sun now fallen violently behind the horizon and the mirror of the sea and, without turning around, she said to me: "Oh, nothing special."

I was going to say, "But you were thinking about something" when she said, without waiting for my next question: "Well, I was really thinking that I had never sat in this park."

She spoke with a slight tone of scorn, even rejection, perhaps disgust —and she was right about feeling uncomfortable. Though the park was clean it was a polluted place, perhaps from old ejaculations, and it wouldn't have been surprising to see a used condom on the grass, like an evil-smelling if not evil flower. Before the flowers of evil faded, evil faded. Even I faded. Fazed I asked her: "You want to go?"

138

"That's just what I was going to suggest. Please, escort me to the bus."

The combination of the urbane verbs *suggest, escort,* so un-Havanan, with the noun *guagua,* an urban bus, was typical of her conversation: Baudelaire's reader lived in Havana. We skirted the east edge of the park until passing the Ministry of Foreign Affairs, a rococo palace in rocaille, and then the amphitheater, a classic pastiche, both exotic buildings in a city that ignored it was in the tropics: architects must read in Braille. We continued along other parks of tame palm trees, now walking in the dark when it would have been so good to hold her hand. I fantasized letting go of her hand to pass my avid arm behind her consenting *corps mis en plis,* thus holding her close to me, from time to time to kiss her face, that immaculate complexion. Virgin complex. All we did, awful awakening, was to march to the corner bus stop, where the *guaguas* almost always come to a dangerous halt. There I waited for her to catch that violent vehicle, going God knows where—isn't it curious that I never asked Virginia where she lived? She looked as if she lived in El Vedado or maybe La Víbora, but not like someone who lived beyond the river and across La Sierra, in Miramar or the suburb of Kohly, there where all is order, peace, and opulence. Where the silent minority dwells. Perhaps she lived alone, now that she was divorced. Most probably, good bourgeois that she was, she lived with her family, her mother and her sister. In any case she didn't suggest solitude (I caught this from her conversation) and I think I felt I had been too daring already, taking hold of a fleeting hand, seating her precarious ass in Lovers' Lane, to ask her in addition where she lived. Perhaps that's why I didn't travel with her uninvited—or maybe because I didn't have any money. In any case I watched her climb onto her Route 15 bus and saw her white, robust legs disappear. Her white dress (she always wore white or almost white, making the whiteness of her skin whiter), her blond ponytail moving from side to side as she walked, without having the *nature-morte* stillness of her sister's hair, her restless mane and her whole exotic self disappeared into the interior of the Havana bus. I walked home via O'Reilly Street without wondering what that unusual and unexpected Irish intruder was doing in the middle of my Havana.

The next day I went, as always, to the Asturian Center library, and found Virginia in the reading room—but not alone. It wasn't the eternal Baudelaire who accompanied her but another man. Beside her was Krokovsky and the two of them talked in a whisper, belying the librarian's dull deafness. They were having a conversation, and since I wanted to interrupt, I just sat facing her.

"Hello," she said happily. "Do you know each other?"

"Yes, of course," said Krokovsky before I could answer, though he would have spoken first in any case: I had decided not to talk to anybody that afternoon, not even to her. What could they have been talking about when I arrived? Baudelaire? French poetry? I doubted it from Krokovsky's face, and also from his accent, in which a slight drawl made his appearance even more foreign. I was annoyed to see her talking to Krokovsky, because it showed such poor taste on her part. At least if it had been somebody less ugly! Krokovsky, with his big head, enormous nose, and sour sweat, was almost obscene. Please understand: I have nothing against Jews. What's more: many of my friends, schoolmates from Havana High and from before, when I took night courses in English on Havana Street (Havana within Havana) between Muralla (the poor man's Wall Street) and Sol—the very heart of the Jewish neighborhood —were Jewish and I was very close to them there and in high school, to roll call:

Moisés Chucholicki
Rodolfo Stein
Salomón Lutzky
Max Szerman (which he later spelled Sherman)
León Silverstein (who would become Larry Silvers in the U.S.A.)
Isaac Cherches
Samuel Cherson
Emmanuel Krichter
Saúl Entenberg
Morris Karnovsky
Aarón Rosenberg
Manuel Maya
David Pérez
Salomón Mitrani

and the unforgettable Cheyna Beizel, with her huge tits, always crescent and always full moons. Croissants.

There are many more Jewish colleagues whose names I forget, but I can't forget Krokovsky's (as I can't manage to forget the name of Boris Borovsky, the only Jewish schmuck I knew, to my misfortune), never shithead Krokovsky; Krokovsky the cunt, cause of the ruin of my monument (or moment) of love for Virginia. Crowkovsky. The unforgettable Krokovsky got up and announced: "I have to go."

"So soon?" said Virginia as if Krokovsky were another, as if his accent were French, as if he were another Baudelaire.

"Yes," he insisted, "I have things to do."

He didn't say he had to study because he knew that was the only *verboten* verb at the Institute: if you pronounced it you were condemned without a trial: you were immediately accused of being an egghead, a condition worse than the word: one wasn't supposed to study at high school or at least you had to pretend you weren't studying. That's why Silvino Rizo would hide in the library during classes, as in a gentile ghetto. This was why Krokovsky said he had things to do, like a dutiful housewife, when he really had to study.

"My pressure," he said, and the pun, for once, was not intended. I didn't say a word: I wasn't going to talk that afternoon.

"We'll see each other tomorrow perhaps," and, you guessed it, he was addressing Virginia.

"Yes," she said smiling, "of course. We must."

Krokovsky finally left, smiling with his swelled head, and I remained there, deflated, facing Virginia, slumped in my chair, without saying a word—looking at her without seeing her.

"How are you doing?" she said. I wasn't going to talk that afternoon but mellow Virginia spoke to me so sweetly that I had no choice but to answer automatically:

"Fair," which was neither here nor there: it didn't indicate any mood in particular. Certainly not my mood, bluer than blue.

"I didn't know you knew Krokovsky," she said.

"Yes," I said, which was the least I could say about Krokovsky.

"He has an interesting mind"; it was Virginia speaking, of course. Everybody had an interesting mind according to her and there was even more reason to suspect that Krokovsky's big continental *Kopf* contained a proportional quantity of interesting mind: all matter, as gray as the personality of its owner. Why didn't I speak to her about great empty eggheads? I should have said that Anatole France's brain was as small as that of an adult penguin. Perhaps the mention of France, of literature, of French literature, would have interested, retained, and detained her from doing what she was doing now, which was gathering up her books (Baudelaire, I presume), or rather her only book (Baudelaire, I presume), the one she was reading or learning by heart: *par coeur mis à nu.*

"You're going already?" I asked, more jealous than sluggish.

"Yes," she said, "I have to get home early."

She got up, handed in her book, and left—or rather, both of us left. You see, all this time I had accompanied her without saying a thing and, as I hadn't asked for a book, they hadn't given me any, and so I had no book to return. Here I was, a man free of books but prey to his passion. We descended the stairs and right there, on the Asturian Center corner, was the stop of all the buses in Havana and the world: with one movement Virginia abandoned the sidewalk and alighted on a moving bus so rapidly that I couldn't even tell what rotten route it was. She only had time to announce: "Good-bye." It was appropriate that she said "good-bye" and not "so long" because I never saw Virginia again. Close up, that is. I saw her from afar, from the roof, now a nest of hate, the next day at five in the afternoon. I didn't want to see her but I saw her leave Havana High, which was unusual. She wasn't alone: she was with Krokovsky, which was grotesque. Grotesky. Krokovsky, who had, like me, an interesting mind, followed her more than accompanied her. Virginia always walked briskly, even on the walks with me. If I didn't mention it earlier it's to conserve the pleasant memory of a stroll, now not a pleasure *via crucis* upon seeing them enter the Asturian Center together. I followed them with my eagle eyes, peering from my promontory, my mute escarpment. Actually, my glasses helped as much as going up on the Payret Theater roof, to observe the library window. There I saw them finally sitting next to each other, chatting, whispering unnecessarily, mouth into ear, intimate—hypocritical readers, not my equals, never my brothers.

It wasn't Beba Far who cured me of that evil reader called Virginia: before the flowers of Eve faded, Eve faded, and she became a faint ardor, a jaded odor of virgin's bower, the sounds of her virginal, fade-out music. But Beba Far inspired my next lost labor of love, a defeat more everlasting than a victory. Perhaps the chronology is not exact, but my memory is the device that measures my time. In memory the first time I saw Beba, barely glimpsed, was in the lobby (or rather the screening room) of Royal News, where Germán Puig and Ricardo Vigón ran all the showings of their Primer Cine Club de la Habana. This heroic enterprise had an enormous name for its tiny quantity of dream reality: the small projection room of the Royal News Reel—also a bit pretentious with its royal British name and its pun on the real. At their headquarters, one horrid, torrid night (the Royal News couldn't stoop to the common luxury of air conditioning though more than imperious it was necessary), in that chamber of film fervor, I saw Beba from afar though we were virtually on top of each other. This fleeting vision has lasted longer in my memory than the venture, adventures, and misadventures of Buster Keaton on screen, even though it was the very first time I had seen this unique comedian in a portrait of the American clown as an artist. The occasion was a homage to his art but we were the ones honored by his precious presence on the screen. Meanwhile . . .

I saw her in the lobby before the show began. This cubicle had a wall of mirrors, perhaps to deceptively magnify its size. By doubling the expectant bodies, all pregnant with social noises, it added to the promiscuity, justified only once: when screening the melancholy anatomy of Beba Far in all her static splendor. Though she must have been around my age (seventeen or eighteen), she was a woman, much more of a woman physically than Virginia Mateus and completely opposite in appearance: despite her marble-white skin she had jet-black hair and was what one called a "royal beauty" (nominal contagion from the Royal News, perhaps?), with fleshy but very shapely arms, and legs even shapelier than her arms, with wide hips, a narrow waist, and a prominent, voluminous bust—in short, a regal beauty. But that first double vision was of no consequence. How was I to imagine that Beba Far would be so important, so decisive, so total to me that I would fall in love with her, would love her madly, that she would bring me near the brink of death by love?

I had met her sister, quiet Queta, first. She was a calm, bovine blonde, perhaps too passive. She often went to the National Library, then located in the Castillo de la Fuerza, the oldest military fort in America—the pen unintentionally mightier than the sword. I used to go to this library sometimes to study in hiding. But that was long long before I discovered books. In the day and age when I met Queta, I went there no longer to

most ruined the show—but the anonymous caresser didn't own up.

If I am detained at this theatrical interlude it's because it has something directly to do with my fatal encounter with Beba Far: if one hadn't existed, the other wouldn't have taken place. The performances—successful, of course, since they were free and given in that center of idleness, Central Park: obligatory crossroads of pedestrians, vehicles, and transients—ended in an incident which only the times (the foul forties) explain. It happened with the performance of *Don Cristóbal's Tableau,* which Lorca meant for puppets and which Morín saw as slapstick comedy. Thus, on this occasion, the playlet was performed by players, the director prevailing over the poet. But this time the farce had as its stage the whole of Havana. Now we enjoyed the technical advantage of loudspeakers which broadcast the actors' voices all over the park, the neighboring houses, the Paseo del Prado, magnifying the droll delivery. This emission was pure magpie madness (theater as radio) but then all of us were culture-crazy. So imagine the surprise for the unwary pedestrians when they heard coming out of nothingness—or everything, such was the uproar of the voices: ". . . and in my little ass/Have I a little stash/A nice roll of hard cash." Or, even worse: ". . . I want a girl that's fit/A redhead big and sassy/With her two plump little tits/And her marvelous assy." Or the worst ever: "And you're the haggard old crone/Wipes her ass with a paving stone." Just imagine (especially in Cuba where the worst curse word is *ass*) the shock! What with Don Cristóbal's lascivious lechery, and Rosita in heat, with her hot-to-trot tits and asses popping up everywhere like molasses. It was almost the scatological secret of the Shanghai Theater divulged by loudspeakers—in Central Park. Right there and then the free theater season ended: the Ministry of Education (that is, the Board of Culture) decided to give better use (silent not deadly tools) to the booth, which was for a few weeks (we didn't last more than a month) our deflated version of the Globe.

But my theater days didn't end, and though I want to talk only about Havana, about urban ventures, misadventures, and adventures, there was an occasion—inverse invasion—when the city went to the country. It was almost Holy Week, which was celebrated with special splendor in Trinidad. This was a magnificent city in colonial times, now a kind of museum—against the will of the Trinidarians, of course, since no one wants to live in a museum. Mysteriously (enveloped in the same mist of mystery, cloud, or cloak, with which he obtained the Central Park place), Franqui got a special invitation from the Town Hall of Trinidad for the Prometheus Company—and its constant companions, among them myself. The group was to go put on a religious play, some version of the Passion, whose author has remained in oblivion: perhaps Judas himself. Anyway, it was no Gospel. Town Hall would pay our train fare to Trinidad the Remote. There was no highway to the reclusive colonial city and going there was like traveling in time. I had already been there on a high-school excursion, an Institute expedition with the so-called "revolutionary students" (actually armed assailants), who controlled the Student Association and cornered the funds: there they spent their days putting together and taking apart pistols as if they were Meccano sets. (I remember at least one of these spurious students, the alliterate Arsenio Ariosa, illiterate, who killed himself with a bullet in his temple as he played Russian roulette and lost.) They even managed to kill a poor pedestrian who unfortunately passed the offices during homicide hours. Nobody intervened, not even the police, especially not the police. They were violent times, as Havana times always were. My fellow travelers were violently disappointed to find stone pavements and tile-roofed houses and whitewashed walls, ruins to them. In revenge they composed and howled a farewell song, an instant hit: "Trinidad, I shit on your mother's heart/I'm not coming back, Trinidad!," shouting, threatening to shoot up the whole town. (How I found myself in such company would be another story, though I can sum it up in one phrase: love of the past, which was passed over by love: in Trinidad I would spend my first honeymoon, a loveless trip, but this second time around I would be by love ambushed at a crossroads.) Back to our outing: besides the train tickets we would have free meals and lodging. The Group grew with the promise and there were now almost more spectators than actors in it. To my good (or perhaps ill) fortune, among the freeloaders were Queta and Beba Far.

The day, or rather the night, of the departure arrived, and we were already in the Terminal when Franqui confided to me that his man Becker (the unknown Becker, of whom I knew years later that his name wasn't Bécquer of the *rimas,* as I believed, but that it was a corruption of an American named Baker, the Spanish poet turned dime-a-dozen Baker: I knew Becker well) had sent him a telegram informing him that the town had canceled the invitation. We never found out why: lack of funds was considered, but our stay in Trinidad would prove this wasn't true or at least accurate. What to do? Franqui decided to act the conquistador, Cortés ignoring Velázquez: ignore the telegram and continue on to the train, taking Trinidad by storm. *Affaire accomplie.* But: not a word to anybody, especially the actors, all fickle faggots. Only Franqui, Morín, Silvano, and I would know the awful truth: the quartet of the secrét. Thus, already seated on the train, waiting for its departure which seemed never to arrive, we heard on the loudspeaker an obscene call: "Calling Carlos Franqui." Franqui, sitting next to me, looked at me and we both knew at once what the message meant. Franqui, Cortesian, pretended not to hear it. But the announcement was repeated and sweet Dulce Velazco, an actress who seemed eternally (despite her blond permanent) forty years old and had, besides, a funny face, looked at Franqui. She was so affected that she became the perfect image of the meddlesome middle-class lady (now I wonder, what could Dulce Velazco do in the Passion, be it according to Saint Mark or Saint Matthew or an anonymous author?), and accordingly she left her seat to come mincing over to Carlos to tell him, almost confidentially: "Excuse me, Franqui, but I think they're call-ing you." I was about to say, "It's another Franqui," when the frank Franqui got up suddenly and went down the aisle toward the exit of the car. I went with him, and Morín and Silvano followed me. On the plat-form there was a small summit meeting. We agreed that if Franqui answered the call—which had to be from the mysterious Becker—we'd have to cancel the trip. The best was to proceed as with the telegram and pretend not to notice any messages; thus the arrival in Trinidad would be a consummated fact. *Fête accomplie.* The other alternative was to accept defeat and forget all those days of rehearsal, the wardrobe (ac-quired by Morín from God knows where, the devil knows how) and, most important, the enthusiasm, more necessary than all the rest: it is essen-tial to go with God to Christ. The Cortés character of Franqui's tactics did not escape Silvano as he proposed: "We can also burn the ships, that is, the train." Cartesian all, we returned to our seats. Once again before leaving we could hear the loudspeakers transmitting, as embarrassing as in Central Park: "Urgent call for Carlos Franqui." I saw Dulce Velazco on the verge of rising, coming toward us, and saying with the face of a late Christian: "I hear voices." Vae Becker, those about to depart salute thee! *Fait a accomplices.*

We reached Trinidad in the morning and the first thing we did in group formation—Prometheus bringing the light of Havana to the dark ages of Trinidad—was to walk to Town Hall, which in Trinidad was in the midst of some winding streets that always seemed to me like circular ruins. It was Franqui first and frank-heartedly who entered the hallowed hall. He was inside a while and then returned saying: "We have to see Becker," cryptic and predictable, and we followed him. We came out of the labyrinth of stone-paved streets onto a square near a stone house. Franqui went up the stairs and I scaled a step or two behind him, hearing him say again and again to a woven more than wrought-iron grate: "Bé-quel?" in his lambdacic pronunciation, free of r's, typical of the legion, region. But Becker or Bécquer or Béquel, phantom of Morse, never materialized. From there Franqui, followed by all, went to a house that seemed a private palace and came out in a few minutes, smiling his sly smile. Everything was set. We were going to stay at a kind of old folks' home that had been left free—a flight of fossils, a geriatric journey?—just a few days earlier and we would eat at a municipal eatery. It was obvious that they were treating us like an order of mendicants, as if we had made vagabond vows. Apparently, Franqui had gone to see the mayor in his house, since he was never at Town Hall in Holy Week, of course: Trinidad was a Catholic city, not pagan like Havana.

All this time I had barely noticed Beba. What's more, if someone had asked me if she had come with us, I wouldn't have been able to give a clear yes or no. I was going to pay for this ignorance: she was going to make her mark on me, as a rotund revelation. Lunchtime arrived fortu-nately (we hadn't had breakfast) and we went to a kind of country restaurant without trees, the tables with smelly oilcloth: our collective dining room. Quiet waiters served us rice, beans, and sweet potatoes, no dessert. I was reminded of the doubly (in Trinidad, on Holy Week) blasphemous story about Christ, when he multiplied the bread and the fish and, after this marvelous miracle, one of the diners dared to ask Jesus: "But, Lord, is there no dessert?" Dulce Velazco suffered a similar fate: upon seeing the food she exclaimed in disgust: "Starch, starch, starch," her thick voice getting louder on each starch until she was shouting her protest. It was all she said and she didn't eat. The rest of us ate that common Cuban food turned ambrosia by hunger and not a mere miracle. We spent the afternoon touring the city with Franqui as our guide: having been a Communist delegate to Trinidad, he knew it well. Considering myself a connoisseur, I decided to see it on my own, accompanied by Rine Leal, now cultural attaché like me but who would later be a Roman centurion in the Passion. He explained his theatrical technique thus: "Playing centurion is like playing the part of the century." Of course, as soon as I left Franqui behind, I got lost in that city which for me was an island—Crete, not Trinidad, the Aegean and not the Caribbean. After many concentric turns, in the marrow of the labyrinth, I found a burro. Rine found another. Both donkeys were for rent, and as they cost very little we rented them. The burros knew their town like a manger and took us out to see the walls, or one long wall in ruins. All was going well, I a boy on my burro, righteous rider, when in a cul de sac a little boy appeared, then another, and finally it was a band: a gang of dead-end kiddies. They decided to fall upon us for sport, jabbing the burros in the belly with rustic sticks, and from vulnerable bellies they passed on to private parts. The burros began to stomp and kick but couldn't eliminate such asinine annoyance, so I decided to intervene and threaten the roughnecks with worse reprisals. This inspired a bellicose brat to stick his prick in the ass of the ass—who then stood on his two front legs and threw me off. From the ground I could hear not only the ruffians' laughter but Rine's too: it was useless to put the enemy in his place when even one's friends were on their side. After getting up and trying to dismount Rine with a forceful look, without success, I kicked in the direction of the nearest scoundrel and hit air. But his friends replied by throwing stick and stones and I was barely able to take refuge behind the donkey, the burro's back getting the barrage. The incident ended when one of the stones hit Rine in the chest and he charged his donkey against band and bandits, disbanding in flight, obviously less dangerous than the Havana High gangs. We returned (I walking, with donkey in tow, guided by Rine's donkey, which he was still riding: *tres* burros) to the place where we rented them. Thus ended the afternoon.

That night we knew what discomfort was, added to the injury of the hostel, really an asylum, an old old house: nothing was ever new in Trinidad. It's not that there were bedbugs (like the Blefusco bugs which assaulted me in another provincial city in my pollster days) but that there was a sudden cold wave, unusual for Holy Week, when there's always a southerly wind, called precisely the Lent Wind. This time the northerly was whipping the whole province of Las Villas, particularly the region of Trinidad, particularly our lodging. When they led us there, we were so happy to have a roof that we didn't notice the beds were stripped naked except for bare mattresses—no sheets or pillows, much less blankets. We would sleep—theoretically—according to a code of conduct: the men downstairs, women upstairs. Havana would teach Trinidad group morality: we would be Prometheus but not promiscuous. I said theoretically because nobody could sleep that night, even with our clothes on, those garments of the Havana summer we had left behind. The next day, as a remedy for the cold—homeopathic histrionics—someone proposed an excursion to the top of cool Collantes, a nearby mountain where there was a sanatorium for consumptives (a tropical version of the Magic Mountain) begun ages ago and never finished. Everything in Trinidad was in ruins, the past and the future. We had to get there by car: old cars, or rather the only jalopies to be found in the city, which awkwardly climbed the vertical road. In our car Beba and I coincided for the first time, in close company (we did everything squeezed together on that Trinidad trip), along with Margarita Fiallo, Ernesto Miret, Franqui, Morín and the local chauffeur crushed against the steering wheel. Miret was in such a good mood, making jokes the whole trip, that he put me in a bad mood. Frowning more and more, black-browed, I was so intolerant, intolerable that at one point Morín told me I was so deadly serious because I had let Miret steal the show. Not true. I knew the truth later, to my surprise: I was jealous, anticipating jealousy because Beba was laughing with her beautiful buck teeth at anything Miret said. The mountain trip, with its antediluvian ferns, wild orchids, and exotic plants, became a kind of torture, not the sweet pain of jealousy but rather the confused feeling that anticipates jealousy when there still isn't love.

As performance day drew near (Holy Thursday) we continued to devote ourselves to being tourists. We went to Casilda, Trinidad's seaport. Trinidad itself is located inland and during colonial times it was through Casilda alone that merchandise entered (and left) the city. At one end of the port, open to the Caribbean Sea, is the beautiful peninsula of Ancón (trivial travelogue). There we went (in a slow sloop) to establish a beachhead on this "Varadero of the South" (in Cuba all beaches are versions of Varadero, hyped prototype), which became unforgettable in more than one sense. The sun kept us from feeling the cold, not as intense that day as the first night, and we decided to go swimming. The men wore underpants since nobody had thought, symbolic logic, of bringing swimsuits. The women, in turn, improvised their bathing apparel with scarves tied around their underwear. Only Queta bathed in her slip. You have to have known that hypocritical era in order to know how daring she was to swim in only that intimate, so seductive, garment. At first, as she sunbathed, it looked discreet because it was a satin slip, but when she entered the water—or rather, came out—her nude body was revealed through transparency: appointed nipples. Nevertheless, I only had eyes for Beba, who made an exclusive bikini with two scarves but didn't go in the water, her incredibly white skin, in the double sun of the sky and the radiant sand's reflection, in sharp contrast with her black hair. Tired of seeing this dry mermaid, two of us (male) bathers went over to her, determined to baptize her: *jeux d'eaux, jet á deux.* I think it was Silvano who grabbed her under the arms (retrospectively, two days later, what wouldn't I have given to have been in his place); I grabbed her by both feet—why not the legs? perhaps too much intimacy intimidated me—and then someone else came to carry her in the middle. She, laughing, barely protested. We went down to the shore with our precious cargo, into the sea, and dropped her, the ducking making a big splash. But when Beba recovered from her dive and emerged smiling from the waters, the rush became a ruse, all the noisy frolickers suddenly silent, paralyzed, frozen by her presence—seeing her was seeing Venus rise (and now it wasn't a mere metaphor) from amid the waves. It seemed to me that I had never seen such a beautiful woman before in my life.

That night two unconnected though related events occurred, having nothing to do with my path to perfecting the art of love. Mere diversions: *per aspera ad amor.* A group of us, including Beba and Queta, went off on our own to have dinner. The restaurant didn't seem even remotely like any in Havana (even the poor Havana dives that I could frequent on my not very sound summer salary), but we ate well, including Beba, who seemed to have a hard time choosing anything. Queta was impossible: she ate only rice. When we left, walking down the dimly lit streets, Queta confided to me that she couldn't eat meat because every time she cut into a steak she saw the cow on the verge of being slaughtered. I agreed with her that it was inhuman (Queta corrected me: "Unanimal") to eat meat, though my guts were full of cow meat: vetoing vague vegetarian visions. Beba was walking in front with Silvano, and in the bare light from the houses I could see her body moving harmoniously as she stepped between stones. I don't know if I was completing her image in my memory but I liked more and more to see Beba around me, even though she was much less of a girl than Virginia and Virginia was already all woman. I, not yet nineteen, looked like an artless young man without a portrait.

When we got to the hostel (or whatever it was) we noticed strange goings-on. A melodramatic incident had occurred, which ended well, even hilariously. Several actors had gone to a calm café in the center of town. Soon a hostile atmosphere formed around them: municipal machismo manifested itself crudely against the newcomers, all too fine-mannered for those rough folk. The oldest of the group, none of them character actors, immediately realized the error of entering and tried to right it by an immediate exit: a bad move, as always happens with actors who have poor parts. But he whispered to his friends: "Gentlemen"—later he told me he had almost said, as always, "Girls," but this time he told it this way—"big black cloud formations are gathering around us. Storm warnings, you know. Pay as nonchalantly as you can and let's get out of here, one by one." They did this but the café crowd followed them into the street and halfway across town. The city-slick actors walked rapidly, but their campfollowers, who knew every rounded corner, became pursuers. Soon they were running for dear life, the amateur actors turning into record-breaking runners. The fugitives reached the hostile hostel, turned refuge, taking shelter in their asylum—where Franqui was sleeping and Ernesto Miret, a heterosexual actor, was sitting on his bed: "Smoking in bed," he explained, city-wise. When they heard the racket Franqui got up and Miret accompanied him to the front door, where the breathless thespians were trying to reconstruct, dramatically, their ordeal. But they didn't have to tell about the hunt: the hounds had just arrived, ready to finish off their prey. Franqui didn't have to think twice: he armed himself with the crowbar that locked the door—instead of closing it he threw it open and rushed out on the sidewalk. Miret followed him, easily picking up the first cobble. When the ruffians saw themselves faced with armed men, they turned around and started running, pursuers now pursued. Franqui almost reached them, forgetting that he was still in his underpants and even that he was on the main street, near the principal park. It was Miret who caught up with him to convince him of the convenience of returning to the hostel. He had to reveal to Franqui his present state. A half-naked stranger with a stake in his hand was certainly not the correct appearance for a cultural envoy from Havana who had come with a theater group to stage the life, passion, and death of Jesus Christ. Upon hearing the story, completed by Miret in his scatological style, Silvano laughed his head off. Though in the near future he would have a painful experience with Cuban scum in action, when the Prometheus Group—Morín unbound again—went to act in a movie theater not far from Havana and actors and director found that the performance had to take place at the end of the movie and their audience was to be the town ruffians, who from the Gods expelled them from the stage and at the theater exit bombarded them with stones. One of the projectiles got Silvano in the shin, and he was now not only incapable of walking without a limp but of laughing painlessly. I heard the celebrated two-part story and also laughed. Later one of the accosted actors, whose name shouldn't be mentioned because he's rich and famous now, looking faggishly at Franqui, now dressed, said to me, entranced at the entrance: "What a man!" This pithy passion didn't prevent him from marrying, two years later, the Passion's heroine, a myopic Mary Magdalen.

At long last, the night of the mess *en scène* (as Miret would later call the performance of the Passion) arrived. It took place on the portico of the Brunet Palace, its pillars playing the stage and its interior serving as wings and dressing rooms. Miret would be Christ. This mocking actor had taken his role so seriously, to everyone's surprise, that he appeared ludicrous, as always happens with the Passion. In this play the protagonist invariably comes to believe he is not a version of Jesus but the Nazarene himself, incarnate. Unfortunately, Miret had to tiptoe barefoot from backstage in the dark and he bumped into one of the floor stones that stuck out and he couldn't avoid exclaiming, as he came out on stage: "Jesus Christ!" The audience almost heard it and I never forgot this private spectacle of seeing Christ cursing while at the same time announcing his entrance. Curious to know what happened to Christ, I stayed till the end. The performance was moving, at least for the Catholic taste of the Trinidarians, who filled the street and the spacious square, applauding with an *ecco in lontano.* After the show there was the anticlimactic feeling of having come so far for only one performance. "The same thing happened to the Lord, ladies and gentlemen," said Miret, consoling the actors, "and still he said: 'Forgive them, God, for they know not what they do.' He, the best drama critic of all times, could well have been referring to all of us." Fortunately we weren't going to have to put up with an actor bearing Christ's cross. Miret was wittier that night than on the trip to the mountain: he obviously enjoyed his double passion, his love for theater and humor. Despite his good looks, his natural distinction, and his charm he didn't make it as an actor, as all of us thought he would: he ended up as a Havana bus driver. But I'm sure he turned his omnibus into a dramatic vehicle: *la commedia é infinita.*

The next day we left Trinidad by train, in the twilight. We left behind the colonial mansions, the Cuban baroque museum, and the strange nostalgia that remote city produces with time. We left behind the starch, the inhospitable hostel, and the discomfort of that enforced excursion (Becker was never Baedeker), but I also left the close contact with Beba, since I found out, gradually, that it wouldn't be the same in Havana. We occupied the caboose doubling as observation car—it was now night—and I went out on the platform despite the cold, which became more intense after the heights of Cumbres, which for me were wuthering. Weathering out there I didn't hear the door opening behind me but I did hear the voice saying softly: "Looking at the scenery?" There was no scenery to see, you see, much less to look at: all was darkness without, but I felt joy within upon recognizing the voice: it was Beba. I think I said "uhuh" or perhaps something more explicit: I used to be then, when I could, quite garrulous with women, especially with women. I know I had turned around and seen her full figure filling the frame of the door and my round pupils. I immediately suggested that we sit on the ladder of the platform, a stairway to the void now—"Have a step"—and she accepted. The rungs were very narrow and by necessity we were in contact, her thighs touching mine, her dress raised to her knee, revealing the legs of a beautiful *habanera* (today I would find them fat but then they seemed form-and-flesh perfect), molding her lilting more than heaving hips when she walked. Now all that was nearby—perhaps too close for comfort. "You like to look at nature," she said, as if seeing her body with my eyes. "Just like me," she added. She referred of course to the open country, the vast spaces, perhaps the steppes beyond, but there was no nature at all to look at or even to glimpse, except for the yellow shrubs growing alongside the tracks, revealed rapidly by the lights of the train. Nevertheless, the sound of her words fascinated me: she spoke gently, quietly, in a very personal way, and could be heard above the rhythmic racket of train and tracks, a scene with stereophonic sound before its time, creating an instant intimacy out there, the two of us alone.

It was the first time I had been alone with Beba and it was then that I fell in love with her: it had to be then: it was then, then. Regrettably our train for two was a brief vehicle without any stopover. Queta came out on the platform, followed by another girl from the excursion. I don't remember which but she wasn't an experienced actress like María Suárez, who would have realized instantly that, if three are a crowd, four are a promiscuity—and love is an enemy of promiscuity: two form a couple on its way to becoming one, platonic perfection. Inevitably our dialogue had to turn into a conversation, innocuously inane, but I remember that Queta, looking at the tracks, said: "Trains produce a horizontal vertigo," a new notion to me. It was then I noticed that Beba and I (especially I, now without Beba's support) were precariously seated on the steps with all those dangerous curves. Centripetal force could have thrown us clear off the train, and I felt good imagining the two of us flying out together in each other's arms, like a duo, into a ditch and there—from this imagined intimacy Beba's voice brought me back to the car, saying: "I'm going inside." I wanted to ask her to stay a while longer in our *dolce Far niente,* but the other girls were there and I didn't say anything. The three entered the car together and I remained on the deserted platform, sitting sour, solitary. Then I stood up and walked to the other side, down the steps along the side of the train, where the pull of the last car was worse, lurching, holding onto a railing, looking darkly ahead. We were crossing a bridge noisily and I felt a great desire to throw myself off the train. A sickly, silly desire, unlike the daydream with Beba, thinking now of what would happen to me upon falling, feeling my body crash with brutal violence against the iron arches of the bridge, lying in a gutter, ditch, or gulch—trying to figure out what they'd all say when I was gone. But especially imagining what Beba would say, think, feel—and I had to exercise a lot of control over myself, aided by that identical interior incubus that impelled me, in order not to leap out of the train, which now seemed to be going at a velocity of vertical vertigo.

Back in Havana my prime occupation was following Beba around, everywhere. The Cine Club had left the Royal News to take refuge in some precarious place on the Paseo del Prado, next to the Plaza Moviehouse, kind competition. I went to a screening, sure of finding Beba there, but what I found was the obituary notice broadcast gaily by Germán Puig that Beba was "apparently in love" with Juan Blanco—who wasn't a man then but a name. I was alarmed, though, that Beba Blanco sounded possible. I couldn't believe it, as I couldn't believe Germán's contrary statement that Beba was really in love with Beba. "She's a narcissist," Germán said, and I remembered with displeasure her solitary pleasure on the beach, lying in the sand while all of us went swimming. She was smiling, happy to be in the open air, or so it seemed. But I never thought of her happy with how she appeared not to others but to herself, imagining alone on the beach her body lying somewhere in space, between her mind and the deep blue sea, her mirror. The night's desolation was culminated and yet becalmed by Bernardo Iglesia, who knew the inside dope on the actors of the Prometheus bond. Bernardo was an oculist (still not my oculist but he would soon be, you'll see), and he had a senseless sense of humor sans lenses. That night he came to tell me confidentially: "There's a prometheus loose in the loo," and he added: "Come with me, please, I'm afraid to go alone." I went with him to the men's room and he entered one of the infamous cubicles, but as soon as he closed the door he shouted: "No, prometheus, don't do anything to me! Prometheus, the flesh is weak! Prometheus, I promise you the fire next time. Please, I beg of you! Prometheus!" He shouted so loud that some of the moviegoers rushed to the restroom, so unrestful now, and found me in the doorway, while from the closed cubicle came sounds of a mist match. Suddenly the little door opened and Bernardo came out, slickly sedate, saying to the double spectators: "It was a prometheus but he decided to go to the theater instead," Bernardo Iglesia taking refuge in his holy name— which didn't save him, as nothing saves anybody from nothingness.

Then came the times of *Our Time*. Gestation and birth of a notion and its further development, all conceived and carried out by Franqui. From the meetings in the Conservatory, Carmina's karma, it progressed to the old studios of Mil Díez, or One Thousand Ten, the Communist radio station closed down by the government three years back, and inherited by Our Time, thanks to Franqui, Carlos the Entrepreneur. The station had a studio-theater and a hall and offices, but we had to clean and air out the premises, major and minor, which had been closed for so long. (We all took on this task, the group of friends who had originated the magazine *New Generation*, long faded into oblivion), all faggots and folks from Prometheus, and other new (at least to me) artists and models, now supplied with brooms, mops, and buckets of water. We all had the time of Our Time. But, of course, I don't want to speak of them but of my love object: Beba Far wearing pants. Women in Havana didn't wear trousers then—except when there were hurricanes. These sartorial saunterers were called Cyclone Eves, and they created the storms they came to see amid the voyeurs watching them and not the typhoon. They were true meteoric Venuses, born from wind waves. I remember once when I went to watch the Cyclone Eves watching a cyclone, despite the alarming storm warnings that the cyclone would circle over Havana. The announcement came from the National Observatory, which is why we didn't take it seriously: meteorologists don't know anything about weather. A heavy sea began to surge while I was watching a thin girl in tight pants watching the arrival of the cyclone, and we were both hurricane happy. But the young Cyclone Eve reported me to a policeman, stationed on the Malecón to keep an eye on voyeurs who perturbed with their eyes the Cyclone Eves, preventing them from enjoying the spectacle of hostile nature by becoming, with our friendly act, indecent onlookers. I was put in prison right then and there and locked up in a dungeon nearby. Soon the sea level rose and the water flooded the cell and I was up to my neck, already about to drown when they opened the cell and the police let me go out of Christian compassion. Not for being innocent: all looks are guilty. But, an obsessed observer, I returned to the Malecón, to watch Cyclone Eves. I found none but I did find one hell of a storm: the hurricane in full force. Houses were flying to bits and pieces, roofs first, then walls, finally doors all around me: Havana was being razed to the ground. From the Malecón I miraculously made it to one of the squares and, seeking protection among the trees, I grabbed onto the naked trunk of a wild palm, smooth and hard and curvy like a mature woman. I embraced that curvaceous trunk as my only salvation, but the violent wind whipped through, tearing to pieces the leaves of the palm tree as if cropping off a girl's hair, then pulled the trunk up by its roots and, along with the airborne root hairs, I flew over parks and *prados,* above lots and plots, holding fast to that dismembered body in a vertiginous flight—gone with the hurricane.

But back to Beba, to her body naked though fully trousered, her flesh seeming even more perfect: "She's a lot of woman for you," Silvano, almost Silvino, had whispered in my ear, a revelation that could have ended our friendship. But sometimes, on the beach in Trinidad, or now in tight trousers as she cleaned the walls of the future Our Time, with her tender tail-end turned toward me, I also got to thinking: "That's a lot of woman. What a lot!" I'd say, cursing my lot.

Our Time brought us together in its inception but spared her and separated us once the society began to function: I saw Beba less, Beba far from me. She also had some strange sickness that made her even more aloof. Years later, it was known that she had schizophrenia, a malady those days described in psychiatry books, and visualized in movies but not in real life: *The Snake Pit* was a memoir and a motion picture, and all mentally ill women looked like Olivia de Havilland, a sick shadow. In her real-life crisis Beba saw herself divided in two. Not two Bebas but two half Bebas looking for each other in vain. Such was the familiar story but whether it was true or false I never knew. I even became friends with Juan Blanco, who admitted to me one day that he had never been really interested in Beba. When she returned to our culture circle she had changed: the same shape contained a different woman. I remember that I came over to her and that she sent me away without a gesture, segregating herself inwardly. Even though we were alone together again, in Our Time, it was never like that distant night on the Trinidad train, on the rear platform, sitting on the scarce steps, she stuck to me, I almost holding her hand: two together, far from everyone else, motionless while the earth moved around us in an inverted vertigo. Now she alone was remote, Beba Faraway.

There was one more occasion on which we were together but I wished then that it hadn't occurred. Ironically, Juan Blanco gave a little open-house party to celebrate his new apartment in El Vedado, almost outside the neighborhood on Paseo and Zapata Street, a corner that would be fatally familiar to me in the future. (More later.) Juan Blanco's other pretext for the occasion was a recorded performance of the Ninth Symphony (in its entirety) and so he brought together a group of friends—more girls than boys, obviously. That's where Queta did her notorious double somersault, with an immortal remark, as she fell back on the rocking chair—the only piece of furniture (except for the expensive record player) in the living room. Her famous final phrase was, moments before reclining emphatically on the precarious rocking chair: "That Beethoven is a chained monster!" She completed her ensnaring metaphor with an end link in the air, falling backward, her head knocking against the floor, the heavy rocking chair overturning upon her to everyone's dismay—which turned into laughter when they realized that Queta was safe and sound and still entangled in the Beethoven chain, chair. But there was another intimate and no less uproarious phrase which had the insidious virtue of damping my love for Beba, which she herself uttered with more noise and frenzy than the binding sentence threatening Beethoven's freedom and Queta's life. The two of us went out on the balcony, I perhaps looking for the platform of the lost last car, and Beba with a distant look said: "Look at Venus, the morning star!" I looked and didn't see Venus (which couldn't be either the morning or evening star because it was nine o'clock at night and it was winter) but rather a lightbulb shining bright and vulgar on a neighboring roof. That beat of Venusian beatitude seemed intolerable to me then and almost tore to shreds my love for Beba, the perfect woman: her shape, her shapes were there but the content had changed utterly. Nevertheless it wasn't herself, her antibody or her soul, that inoculated me against my malady but rather her body, which had made me identify her with Venus—not the morning star but the goddess of love.

To celebrate the opening of the society there was an art exhibit in the halls of Our Time, but, typical of our Havana, there was also an inaugural ball. I went to the exhibition but not to the ball because, though I liked to watch dancing, I didn't want to see Beba dancing—inevitably with someone else. On both occasions the president of Our Time was present. Predictably it was Harold Gramadié (the most presentable, most presidential of us), one of the society's creators and one of its destroyers when he placed himself at the service of the Communist party and Franqui and I and several others left what had almost been a pre-Fidelite brotherhood, now a Communist front. But it is not of politics or culture or even of cultural politics that I've come to speak but of love, of its shapes and of the shapes of my love—even of the empty shell of love. At the ball Harold danced with Beba: he was a serious composer but also a good dancer. He told me so afterward, and when I thought he was going to talk about diffuse semiquavers and demisemiquavers and perfect chords, he spoke to me dissonantly of Beba, perhaps because the rhythms were Cuban and the melodies had nothing to do with baroque counterpoint and harmony, his specialty. He went to dance some later *danzón* with her (it could have also been a middle-period mambo and even an early chachachá in that year, 1950), and on one cadence Beba, a dandy dancer, delayed too long, and as it wasn't the stop-and-go of the old *danzones* (in which the *fin-de-siècle* dancer was permitted to stop and let his partner *se donner un coup d'éventail à la Mlle. Mallarmé)*, Harold wanted to know what was holding her up, when he saw facing them a large mirror —Beba had simply stopped dancing to look at herself longingly in the mirror. Harold saw that she was pleased with what she saw and was right to be so: Beba was really beautiful that night. But at the same time he realized that he had in his arms the cold mirror image: Beba was not Echo but a female Narcissus. Harold Gramadié, triple traitor, who had been so exclusively and so excessively technical in his evaluation of Carmina, extended himself in considerations that concerned me but which I didn't want to hear because they pained me. He spoke about how Beba was incapable of loving anyone who wasn't herself and, a sudden sexologist, he said that the only sex possible for the narcissist was masturbation—but here his penetrating comments stopped. I wasn't seduced by Beba's sex: I only wanted her love, though it meant being an Echo to her inverted Narcissus. Now I returned to Virgil and saw he was truly wise. Let us surrender to love, he says, since it conquers all: *"Et nos cedamus amori: omnia vincit amor."*

YOU ALWAYS CAN TELL

In Havana, boys had to go through two initiation rites in order to pass from adolescence to adulthood, or rather "manhood"—and one of those ceremonies was more a circus than a circumcision, a balmy bar mitzvah. This first rite of passage was pure pornography, but pornography Havana style included joking as a form of fucking and obscene humor as a way of life. The first temple of initiation—gaining entrance allowed you to don the viral toga—was a theater. The Shanghai, as spectacle, descended directly from the colonial comedy of bad manners, but by now had adopted bad words as the highest, and perhaps only, form of oral expression, and the most private plays as public display. It was really a degradation of the old Alhambra Theater, famous in the twenties and thirties, but, like all degenerates, its decadence was a change, a transformation, a form of creation. The characters and situations became true originals in these pornographic productions. Thus one might easily find on stage an elegant, high-class lady as the sorrowful participant of a funny funeral, which plodded along in bereavement until Blackie and the Spaniard—traditional comic characters, from as far back as the gay nineties—uninvited mourners, inexplicably showed up at the wake, and soon turned it into a sexual soirée. At some point in the play the lady says, as she hands the duo a ceremonious calling card: "Please come visit us soon. My husband is so moody and, therefore, a sodomite." A sudden revelation of pure perversion that makes Blackie leap up and shout: "Fuck you!" and the Spaniard gets excited too and exclaims noisily at this unveiling of a habit—presumably common only in Cuba—"If I'll be fucked!" Then come more or less complicated adventures in the skin trade, which Blackie and the Spaniard resolve by simulating a (standing) coitus, either with the stuck up lady (an adjective Blackie might have received with an obscene: "Stick it up, boys!") or with some old woman who had switched suddenly from menopause to nymphomania. (And Tiny Tina in Zolaueta 408 was a fool's proof that the burlesque was not a farce but a naturalistic version of our own slice of life.) The show would

158

end with the whole company on stage (including a Chinaman, nick-named Chunk, a fag called Toothy Fruity, a virgin primed to lose her virginity at any point, named Mary or some other Christian name, and a dirty old man called Old Man, a label completed by the actor's *nom de guerre,* Daguerre) dancing bawdyville numbers, which included a rumba invariably titled "Let's All Come Together Now." During inter-mission there were "Artistic Interludes," which were only *tableaux* denuding the chorus girls in a strip without the tease, that is, letting it all hang out.

Eloy Santos took me to this mythical rite of the spring of life, with my father's grumbling disapproval. (My father never cursed, drank, or smoked, and still doesn't at seventy-five. But, despite Eloy Santos's proph-ecy that one day he'd be a dirty old man, we would not have to wait so long for this prediction to come true.) At the door of the Shanghai Thea-ter—on Zanja Street, inside the walls of Chinatown—already in the thea-ter (there was no vestibule or preamble: one entered this show directly) there was a literary section where they sold "gallant novelettes" illus-trated with explicit pictures and drawings that left nothing to be desired: one obscene image is worth a thousand erotic words. I remember an illustration that impressed me in spite of myself because it showed a sex act between two women—and at that time I considered lesbians to be man's worst enemy. This notion must have come from the scandal at Havana High when they discovered that a school of lesbians was holding its general quarters in the recreation room, where boys were not allowed, a veritable *zenana*. Some of the older sisters had tried to seduce one of the novices. But she revealed herself to be, unlike others, a reluctant bride and so decidedly heterosexual that she brought about the discovery of the secret society, which Silvio Rigor, with his usual verbal *rigueur,* denounced as a "tribe of tribades," a phrase as impressive as the porno-graphic illustration. Sometimes words are worth an image. In this photo one woman was on top of the other in a double cunnilingus, but the lower lesbian held her sex up high as she raised her torso and belly with vertical arms and legs, producing a pleasure plane upon which the upper woman, extending her own arms and legs, could land. Thus the two of them formed an octopod, the veritable image of an erotic Arachne, the double kiss of the spiderwoman. Never again have I seen that photo on my frequent forays in the unknown lands of Erotica, on my private pas-sages to Afrodisiac countries, on my observant visits to sexual inconti-nents, but I don't think it was made in Havana because of its contrasts (the women were milky white and had black hair), its visual and techni-cal sophistication far superior to the usual dirty photographs in the naughty novelettes. I described the photograph to a woman some time later, much later.

I went fearfully to the Shanghai Theater, with that adolescent appre-hension of forbidden doors—anxious that they may open at any moment —now about to be opened by a mentor with a memento or by a master

159

of the ceremonious mysteries of life. I crossed the entrance into the salacious salon, not without first confronting the sensational surprise of old Don Domingo, a senior citizen acting as doorman, a servile Cerberus who seemed not to recognize me. I'm sure he pretended not to know me in order to maintain his dignity back home, in the common commune known as Zulueta 408. Recuperating from my discovery that our serious senator was in another congress, letting people pass like laws, I crossed the mysterious threshold and found myself suddenly in the sanctuary of sex, inside the comic cupola of copulation, where that strange union of sex and humor was possible. A pagan miracle, since there is no act more ceremonious than coitus—as there is nothing graver than death. It really was fun, especially the parodies of popular songs, ingeniously twisted by the grafting of bad words onto good verses, forming a row of double-entendres that had a single sense. Thus the bolero "Forever Hand in Hand" was manhandled as "Forever Prick in Hand," and the lyrics "you were meant for me" became "you were bent for me." The former lady of the wake was there, now a melodious *mulata* intoning a long monotone on "purple parts," which appeared wherever she went, leaving behind another wake of deep-purple penises, and which I took as a pictorial (or picturesque) reference to syphilis, Venus's curse. There are other more outrageous examples, but to quote them would be list making—besides, there's the problem of the copyright laws.

That first test of Havana manhood I passed with flying colors and, even after marrying, I went often, alone or accompanied but never by a woman—they were not to be seen among those pornogravid audiences. During carnival, mysterious hooded figures often attended these shows: not Montrésors but treasures: curious women disguised in order to penetrate an exclusive clan's club: "For gentlemen only," as a sign on the door warned, and could have added: "She who enters should cast her sex aside." I always found fun at the Shanghai sex dynasty, and it was even illuminating on one occasion. Years later I went with an Italian filmmaker who was doing a documentary to be called *Havana for a Night,* and I was surprised at the exit, as Don Domingo had surprised me at the entrance, when the filmmaker compared the Havana spectacle to Naples's Pìccolo Teatro! But then again, the Italian didn't know Spanish.

The second test was more trying because I had to switch from spectator to actor—and even leading man. It was my first trip to a brothel. Carlos Franqui took me, thinking there wasn't much difference in initiating me in Faulkner or fucking. We were accompanied by Pepito, another debutant, more than a friend—a twin, a neighbor at the phalanstery. You already know that I was familiar with the Colón colony, but only superficially, crossing it as if it were some seductive Spanish steppes, full of perfumed but poisonous flowers. I had passed the neighborhood for the first time with some showoff schoolmates, true truants who would heckle the whores on their daytime rounds. One of the favorite jokes of the most daring of these companions, Guido Canto, who didn't last long at Havana

High, was to get an erection at will. (I don't know how and I still can't explain it, which is why I tend to believe the story by Frank Harris, fabricator, in which Maupassant made a similar demonstration.) Guiding the visible but veiled erection in the direction of a whore standing defiantly in a doorway or bashfully behind a whorish jalousie, Guido would point to the bulk beneath his pants and ejaculate: "It's yours, fucker. For free," earning our invariable reaction of laughter and the wayward woman's variable swear words. But I had never been in a brothel before. That night was not only the first time I would enter a cathouse, but the first time I would go to bed with a woman.

We went first, inescapably, to the pseudo-literary meeting that took place every evening on the reactionary sidewalk of the Diario de la Marina building, opposite the illuminated copy Capitol, but the night did not luminesce like my first Havana nights, its new streetlamps projecting now an intense, harsh light. Franqui, Pepito, and I were killing time with words before heading for Colón, our destiny, destination, the private testing theater. It must have been later than eight and earlier than ten, but I don't remember hearing the blank but noisy nine o'clock cannon blast from La Cabaña. Finally we left the corner of Teniente Rey, went down Prado to Virtudes Street and from there (from virtue to sin) to Crespo and the corner of Trocadero, the hidden but throbbing heart of Colón. The street, the corner, the houses were dark. We knocked (that is, Franqui knocked) on the door of a colonial mansion and the thick door opened immediately a crack, as if automatically activated—or so it appeared to me. A *mulata* peered out and, looking at us, Pepito and me, asked:

"Are they the right age?"

"Yes," lied Franqui.

"They don't look it," said the *mulata,* who must have been looking at me more than at Pepito.

"Well, they are," insisted Franqui, "the ripe age."

"Look here, we don't want no trouble with them police."

"There will be, if we continue standing here."

This circular argument seemed to convince the concierge, a constant Cerberus. (There are many references in this area to that hideous mythological creature: it's just that the Shanghai and *barrio* Colón were mythical Havana hotbeds of what the virtuous called vice, and sin can send you packing to Hell.) She opened the door to let us in and there was a contrast, like coming out of the movies, between the dark, quiet street and the light inside the cat *bayú,* and its boisterous noise: the exuberant joy of the gay (as in Paree) life. It was a three-story building, with an inner patio and a running balcony facing onto what was meant to be a garden: the usual manorial house of Old Havana turned house of pleasure. The place was topsy-turvy with women dressed scantily, and to say scanty for some of the "pupils" was to say a lot: one or two wore only panties and at a certain moment the door of one of the closed rooms opened and a woman—or rather, a girl—appeared naked like Eve, her pubic bush her figleaf. Everything seemed to happen at once, and while Franqui spoke to the matron—a word which had degenerated in Havana from the dictionary's "noble and generous mother" to madam of a brothel—I was watching the show, my eyes all pupils. Never had I seen so many women together in the altogether except on the distant stage of the Shanghai or in my wildest erotic fantasies, and all of them ready for what so many refused: the gay science of screwing. Nevertheless, from amid my fascination I could hear Franqui saying something sounding like it's the first time and the stabat matron answering you can count on me, but I can't swear that was the exact exchange because I only had ears for the sumptuous sound of women crossing the salon to the beat of a mambo from the variegated Victrola, a light-and-sound sideshow, but a beacon in this whoredom by the sea. Now the madam addressed me, I mean us—I had forgotten about Pepito with all that flesh around—and shouted for somebody called Mireya, a name which has remained in my ears as very whoresome. She came over to us before big mother could add: "And Xiomara," another whorish name from then on. "Take good care of the boys," she ordered, pointing to Pepito and me, though there was no need for that index finger: one could see that all the other clients in the den of dames were bona-fide men.

Pepito chose Mireya, or rather Mireya chose Pepito, and I remained with Xiomara. I could have chosen another of those evidently ladies-in-waiting, scattered throughout the room. But I liked Xiomara of Xanadu, with her shapely body everywhere, hips, tits, and thighs: pleasure domes. Perhaps the exoticism of her name now forces the romantic association —I was already a young man of letters. Besides, her face, though not pretty, could not be called ugly, framed by her bleached-blond hair, and something about her—features, expression, walk?—made her seem (later I realized she only seemed) very young. Xiomara wore a satin slip for a dress and smiled at me as I went with her: she didn't have good teeth. We crossed the salon and went, or rather she went—she was my guide and I limited myself to following her—to the back staircase, which led to the second floor. It was a common staircase in this kind of house in Old Havana, but I insist upon remembering it, who knows why, as a spiral staircase: perhaps it's not memory but vicious circles in my imagination. After going down the brief hallway, which seems longer to me in my mind, she opened a door to a dark room, and, when she turned on the light, became a room with an empty but not very well-made bed: someone had been lying in it not long ago and had not bothered to make it—my mother would have objected to such balled-up sheets. From this reflection on a blank sheet I was shaken by Xiomara, who, as she entered the room, as if activated by a spring (reminding me of the instant opening of the brothel door) took off her slip and was completely naked. Though apparently more modest than the naked whore who had crossed the salon, Xiomara did not wear panties, but her nudity was visible for only

162

a second: she turned off the light as quickly as she had gotten undressed. Nevertheless, in that flash I could see her flesh, her body that reminded me—though vertical and facing me—of the almost therapeutic vision I had had on the roof, of the naked girl lying on the bed of the Pasaje Hotel room. Xiomara the whore recovered for me, now, momentarily, that lost horizontal. But it was only a memorable moment: a moment later she, Xiomara, was in bed, professionally waiting for me to form the familiar (theoretically) mythical two-backed monster, the missionary position, which I had never completed, she hurrying me with her visible stare in the now not so dark room. Her attitude made it obvious that she was hurrying me to undress, which I did, as far as she was concerned, desperately slowly (I heard her decayed teeth grate), but at breakneck speed for me. You see, the bottoms of my pants always get stuck on the heels of my shoes and almost make me lose my balance, which I recover with a step or two to one side and then to the other, as if dancing a conga all by myself. I was getting closer to the moment when I would penetrate, cross the threshold of the only mystery of life we can ever know and which I had yet to unveil, leaving aside childhood's instincts, my imperfect discoveries, and later learnings that were mere scratches upon the hairy door of knowledge. I rushed into bed and climbed upon Xiomara with my habitual alpine ability (climbing, I smell her perfume, cheap pomade mixed with a vague fragrance: whore's whiff in Havana lexicon but for me the odor of desire), but upon raising myself over her, the fire I felt at first when seeing this fair hetaera naked deserted me upon covering her, and instead of bulging I was limp, powerless for the promised penetration—a promise for me, for her the wages of fucking. She struggled with me, now a dead weight, but didn't do what was necessary: not to be merely physical but pleasant, offering affection, giving love if only for sale. Thus we remained in that false coitus a few minutes, which seemed to me sojourns in eternity, she rubbing the inert me uselessly against her pubes, the two of us less lewd than the lesbian spiderwomen. She got tired of fighting the whore wars: "Well, get off," was what she finally said, an ominous order, and I obeyed. She jumped out of bed and slipped her sweating body back into her satin slip. Then she turned on the light crudely and opened the door while I was still dressing, my pants now tangled above the heels of my bare feet: she ready for the next customer, I unprepared to meet my friends.

I've spoken lightly now about what was for me a collision with failure. I had expected anything—a premature ejaculation instead of capable intercourse, or more minor mishaps—but my total incapacity to function. How, after multiple masturbations, countless erections from only speaking to Beba, oral orgasms with Lucinda, how could I be practically impotent, I, presumably powerful and potent? It was all as unreal as the atmosphere of the brothel, but both are totally tactile in my memory. Before leaving the room, while trying to pay her her unearned salary of sin which I looked for vainly in my pockets, another frustrating fragment of futility, my hands now tangled in all the empty interstices of my pants, deeply humiliated, finally finding it at the last moment, I managed to say without looking at her: "Please don't let my friends find out," and she replied, almost automatically: "Don't worry." Now in the hallway's naked light I could see that she wasn't so young, that there was a big gap between her and the sleeping beauty lying face down in the Pasaje (the siesta of a nymph), whose face I had never seen but which was joined, a yellow head in my imagination, to her iodine body in the memory, altogether unforgettable. The initiation had been a failure of the real but a triumph of memory.

Two weeks later I returned with my friend Franqui and pal Pepito, den mate, to the same *bayú,* to the same Xiomara (she and frustration were one and inextricable: the two had become an obsession: I had to return and conquer) and the same things happened: my timidity winning over my will, the limp battle for the bulge being fought and lost, the repeated failure a fiasco. I think I attributed it to a greater cause: the fear of whores instilled in me by my mother, by the whole wholesome family, by a few friends: harlots had turned into leper women. Presiding over those physical fears a great, almost metaphysical fear was induced by a terrible term: syphilis. But Xiomara, now a nurse, had another diagnosis. Charging again for work she hadn't done ("Your money will not be returned if the performance is canceled"), she said: "You should go see a doctor," and she scared the hell out of me because she meant something was wrong with my body (unless she was perceptive enough to imply that something was wrong with my head), but the fright lasted only a moment: the time it took to close the door behind me, to leave the flophouse on Crespo Street, in corrupted Colón—and get back to Virtud. I knew nothing was wrong with my sex that love couldn't cure.

Some time later—I don't remember exactly: the rememberer alone knows that time is elastic, Eleatic—the third repetition of my second initiation occurred but this time I was my own master of the ceremony. It was Christmas Day and we had been drinking at home, in our room of the polluted palace at Zulueta 408. Rine Leal had brought a bottle of exotic wine—or perhaps domestic rum: I don't remember, I only remember that the high content of alcohol was measured by my father's discontent, expressed in mumblings, throat clearings, and piercing glances—and we were drinking it in the company of Matías Montes, a writer in bloom, and with Rine, a critic but less of a critic than my father. Finally I decided that the adverse ambience with my father playing the boring boor was unbearable, and the three of us left the room, the tenement, the empty bottle: decent people didn't drink in the street, especially from an empty bottle. The tippling trio reeled more than walked in the late night and down the precarious edge of Old Havana—it was difficult to keep one's balance in that borderline zone that day—which was Zulueta Street, on Christmas Night (or perhaps Eve: nobody celebrated Christmas Day in Cuba but rather Nochebuena, Christ having been born the

night before), under an unusual shower instead of the snowstorm fore-
cast in all Christmas cards, even Cuban Christmas cards. We weathered
young men were certainly disappointed by the absence of snow, and our
disapproval could be heard in dual and sometimes triple hocus hiccups
in the rain. We weren't far from home, barely two blocks, walking now
under the Apple Arcade (and it's strange how often in my sleep I again
pass under this colonnade, which the dream turns into an endless building, but in that part of Havana the columns really form the urban horizon, an infinite landscape of arcades), protected from the rain but not
from temptation that Eve under the Apple Arcade. It was there that I
came face to face with the loveliest black woman I had seen in my life
—and I had seen quite a few black beauties before, believe me. In the
future there was yet to come my encounter with a veritable Afro Venus.
This one was not a woman but a tall, slender girl, who became even
younger when I got to know her—and upon seeing her I knew I had to
follow behind her footsteps and try to get as intimate as her insteps. So
I simply said to Rine and Matías: "I'll be seeing you," turning around and
walking off immediately, an alacrity which they didn't think alarming.
It wasn't the first time I had left my friends, their company, deserting
friendship for affection, to fall upon a woman from behind, often without
succeeding in offering her my erring love, an erratic arrow. But this time
I quickly joined up with the black girl, who smiled at me as I greeted her:
I was made, as the saying went in Havana when something turned out
well, as if one had to be completed and only success did the trick.

"Out walking alone so late," I said, making the sentence neither a
question nor a statement: simply a fresh approach in the night.

"So it seems," she said, in the same tone.

"Why's that?"

"That's life, for you," and she smiled again: her smile evidently enclosed or unveiled a mystery and it wasn't her teeth that she revealed and
hid, lighting up and darkening her beautiful black face. She knew something I didn't know but should guess.

"Where are you going?" I asked her, finally familiar.

"Oh, just around."

"Nowhere special?"

She stopped and faced me (now we were protected from the rain by
the procuring porticos of the Centro Asturiano). Although she wasn't
confronting me, still smiling or smiling again, using her only, devastat-
ing question upon so many harmless questions of mine, she answered:
"What do you want?"

My heart fell to my feet. So it wasn't a conquest but a bill of sale: she
was a prostitute, a streetwalker, *fletera*—that strange Havana word
whose origin no one has been able to explain. What did a *fletera* have to
do with a fleet, follow the fleet? Or streetwalker with flirt, if the deriva-
tion was English? Did *flete* come from fleeting moment? But I wasn't in

165

shape for etymology exercises, and the recent rum (or wine) made me ask, leaping over my timidity: "How much?"

(You will ask how I had known she was a prostitute just by her behavior and a pointed question. But you don't have her before you as I did. Her question was a lead, her manner a calling card, her face a letter of credentials.)

She smiled again and said in a low voice, so low that the rain almost prevented me from hearing: *"Un peso,"* which meant a dollar, of course, but was more than that then, at least for me (the theory of relativity applied to economics), though it was extraordinarily cheap even for the forties. "But," she added, "you must pay for the room."

It wasn't difficult to find a cheap hotel: I didn't have enough money for more. The one I chose on Obrapía Street, near that fancy Floridita Bar, was a seedy hotel, and the room's squalor made the bordello room in Colón look like a suite in the Ritz: instead of a bathroom, a pitcher stood on a basin stand in a corner. (We had passed another *hotel de passe*—the same in which the whole holy family had slept one August night in 1941. But I didn't go in, to avoid closing the cycle of my sexual sojourn: I thought it would end up costing me more than the one I finally chose.) We took off our clothing—I don't remember asking for a room or entering it or having closed the door, which is why we could very well be undressing in public—and this time I could see how a woman stripped (off stage), which I had never seen before. I had seen women naked but not taking their clothes off piece by piece: before this present denudement, what the anaphrodisiac Xiomara had done was vulgar and violent: this girl disrobed with deliberate leisure, and as it was winter she had a lot of clothes to take off. It was a veritable unveiling. When she was finally nude, I looked speechless at a body of rare perfection: long lean legs and the bulging buttocks black women have, high and protuberant, and then those little tits that made her almost the negative of a Venus by Cranach. Are there medieval Negresses? I think of this now: then I thought she was the promised gift of Marta, Georgina's daughter, a young Georgina incarnate in this black girl. Although I was still drunk I could enjoy her nudity the marvelous moment it lasted: she ran to the bed, in African flight from frost, and jumped under the sheet, leaving outside only her Hottentot head, which looked blacker in the dark. (I can't remember who turned off the light, or perhaps the hotel was so poor they couldn't afford a lightbulb? Or maybe I had turned the switch? But I'm sure there was no light.) Naked I went and got under the sheets or sheet—there was only one copy—and then on top of her, feeling her tender young bones yield under my body, which did not weigh much then. I think that for a moment I wondered if this was how I'd lose my virginity, precious despite myself, with a whore and not with the beloved woman I believed in, wanted, willed. Then there was a false penetration because of what happened, which had never happened to me in the long years of penis practice, of being a master masturbator, when I thought that the hand was

166

man's best friend; what I feared would happen with my first true wife, even with a professional prostitute, came to pass with this amateur *fletera* or hetaera: a premature coitus (*ejaculatio precox* is the technical term according to the manuals).

"Already?" asked the nubile Nubian almost timidly upon noticing my limp state. The sight of her young face was enough to make me ask her the question *de rigueur,* according to the precepts of prostitution. That is, what was a mere girl like her doing in an adult's job, to thus continue, now covering my own embarrassment, how long had she been doing the streets, how had she gotten into the business—and those many long questions were my answer to her brief: "Already?" She told me how she had been practicing prostitution for two years—"whoring" she said, better, more direct—that she had begun at the rape age of sixteen, initiated by a country cousin who took part in her earnings in the beginning, but now, for the last few months, she was on her own, without having to account to anyone, a freelancer. It wasn't such a bad life. "They call us bad apples, rotten to the core, but there's nothing so bad about us," she said and smiled, her mouth becoming an arcade of white teeth. She earned good money these nights and now she could buy clothes and shoes and perfume. (Her cheap perfume was more powerful than Xiomara's, but this black Venus—I never learned her name, not even her *nom de nuit*—smelled much better than the white whore's whiff.) "Besides," she said, "do I have fun!" (I've already said it: I even found happy whores.) From here she returned without transition to concerning herself with me: "How about another bout?" she asked, meaning another coition: she was generous: the first didn't even have the right to be called a bout or even a fuck. But for some reason I was content. It may have been the white wine (or Rine's rum) or the realization that I hadn't completely lost my virginity: I could still await that perfect love, aspire to it, deserve a wife. I don't know. I only know that I gave her all my money, leaving a little to be able to pay the smoking, silent, suave Chinaman who opiated a chink in the street door for us. We stepped out onto Obrapía Street, where it was still raining: it was raining on Obrapía and on Monserrate Street, on Zulueta Street and on the Prado, on Jésus del Monte and in El Vedado: it was raining all over Havana, our snow for Christmas.

"And I thought I wouldn't do any business tonight," she said, still on Obrapía.

"You see," I said to her, leaving the phrase in the damp air so that she could complete it with the saying:

"You never can tell."

167

THE MOST BEAUTIFUL GIRL
IN THE WORLD

Will you pardon the hyperbole? You must, for I was young then and the young always blow everything out of proportion. Even if she wasn't the most beautiful girl in the world, that's the way she looked to me. Silvio Rigor used to say she was so sexy that you felt like starting right from the left leg of her bed—though this pithy phrase dates to a later era when we dared exaggerate about sex, and to another girl who's now dead. But the time I'm speaking of, we were much more timid in our talk about girls, especially if they were important and we were impotent. If they didn't matter much, then what we said (or thought) about them didn't matter much. The girl I'm talking about, Julia Estévez (I always called her Juliet), mattered more than a lot because she really was the most beautiful girl in high school.

There might have been another girl with a prettier face, or one with a better body, but none had both, face and body, as she did. Though she was short, she had a perfect figure like a Tanagra figurine. (I learned these words later: at the time she was just a doll.) She'd been elected Girl Freshman of the Year, which showed that I wasn't the only one at the Institute who appreciated her beauty. I met her during sophomore year (I had first seen her freshman year, and had learned immediately to recognize her from afar) when we attended the same class. I particularly noticed her at the school party (held on the last day of class before Christmas vacation), when she went on stage to do her act. She recited a popular poem with a funny, phony Spanish accent, saying: "When you step on ripe grapes, my black beauty, how painfully they burst!" What made the poem more ludicrous than her accent was that she was blonde—maybe not pubic blonde but fair enough to seem like a natural blonde.

It was when I began to lose interest in my studies and spend all my class time in the library reading books that I became friends with her, since she also read in the library sometimes. I'd watch her as she read at the same time I was being watched by our Polyphemus's penetrating pince-nez: one glass was dark, thus becoming a monocle, hence the nick-name. One day I saw her playing hooky with Ricardo Vigón, who had just become a friend of mine. Maybe not yet a friend, but when he did become my friend I recalled their exit together and how jealous I got. That's how I knew she was more interested in boys than most girls her age and from her class (in an academic, not social, sense: however, as far as I'm concerned, the ambiguity has its duplicities). After that I saw her several times with the man (to me a man because he was two or three years ahead of us in high school) who later became her husband. Another time we both happened to be at the Lyceum library, which I had just discovered, I the Columbus of culture, traveling so far from home that day to become a member of this library. The crowded reading room had large windows that let in light and the breeze and rustling of the trees but also, intruding physically, the sound of tennis balls being bounced by rhythmic racquets—but to the readers, trees, racquets, and the racket were invisible. There was fair Juliet, more golden than bronzed: she looked adorable, and thus adored. Isadored—more in a moment. Unfortunately, there was another person with her, Martha Pompa, whom we peacefully called Martha Plumpa because she was big and fat, and later, because of her blond tresses and blue eyes and passion for music (and because of my, our, knowledge of Wagner's operas), she was nicknamed the Walking Walkyrie, a light motive.

From all the subjects in the world (it's curious how much one could talk in Havana libraries those days) we chose to talk that day about beauty. I pedantically quoted Plato quoting Socrates in order to contradict her idea that beauty cannot be found in small things, choosing the mosquito as my biting bait. The mosquito is small but as beautiful as the butterfly (I guess I chose the butterfly because the mosquito is not only smaller but its beauty is not openly, visibly, gratuitously displayed like the butterfly's) and besides, it can have a fatal effect. Juliet would have been a better example but I would have committed the double sin of personalizing my theory and revealing my feelings: pathetic fallacies both. It was pure provocation, of course, and Juliet reacted to my words as I would have liked her to react to me. We also talked about art—to her, Art with a capital—and I said that art was a lie to which the artist gave an appearance of truth. (I didn't know Wilde then and Oscar was to me a golden statuette, just like Juliet, except more famous.) She was almost furious (and more beautiful than the first time I saw her beauty shine) and, very excited, she said: "How can you say such a thing! Art is real!" The true lie was my argument and the truth was she had read with more passion than attention Isadora Duncan's *My Life* (then almost all the girls interested in Art had read *My Life* more than once, swearing by Isadora Duncan as I later swore by Isadore Ducasse), a book I had also read, mostly for its erotic passages. I knew, above all, all about Isadora's affair with the ugly, small, hunchbacked violinist, a Quasimodo d'une Autre Dame, with whom she does it in her car, driven by his intense

169

desire for her, despite her repulsion, revulsion even. I treasured this anecdote—especially having in mind the girls who had read Isadora (always called Isadora by them, as if adoring Isis), who were all pretty or at least attractive. Consider this, said I to myself, if the humpbacked violinist could conquer his darling dancer, I, who didn't even have a crook (or play the violin, I must admit), could certainly hump some of those priestesses of that goddess of free love.

The thought of writing my own version of *My Life (Eyes I Adore)* did of course cross my mind. I realized, however, that my life would be a closed book, which, when opened, would prove to be full of innocent acts described with guilty words. That was my plan, my pet project, but my fulfillment now lay with Juliet Estévez, who answered with passion, argued with graceful gestures, stressing her points charmingly, making me forget my arguments (mere adornments, cosmetic constructs, as Silvio Rigor would say) in order to concentrate fully on her beautiful face. All I remember, at this symposium in which Socrates ate his last supper, is that the awful Walking Walkyrie, joining Juliet, made the duo a duet of contralto and soprano against my arguments, against nature, while I beat a silent retreat, shutting my mouth and becoming all eyes to admire Juliet's beauty: truth more beautiful than fiction.

From then on I began to seek out her company, despite my timidity —and I sought and found her. I knew she lived on Inquisidor Street, not far from the Alameda de Paula, Paula's still unrestored promenade, with its decadent beauty (ruins will never move me: I'm more interested in live beauty), and though I didn't know the number of her house, I deduced—*expertus crede* Romeo—where I could find Juliet: on the corner of Inquisidor and Sol at the trolley—now trollop—stop. It was a good place to wait for her without making it obvious that I was looking for her—and it was there I found her one day, on a summer afternoon (it was always summer then in Havana), a glorious afternoon though she wasn't Gloria Graña. Juliet saw me and smiled, surprised: she had to know I had nothing to do in that part of Havana. At least that's what I thought she thought, seeing through me, man of glass that I am, a licentious show window, *licenciado vidriera.* We talked and though I didn't tell her what I was doing in that Havana, she revealed to me her secret: she was waiting for the tram. We continued talking, and when the streetcar named coincidence (for her, for me named intention) arrived, I got on after her. Juliet realized, of course, that I got on because of her, not because I had to go anywhere. I don't know where she or where we both went: I only remember that, wherever it was, I went with her. The afternoon becomes golden in my memory but it's because it really was golden, the houses in sunset colored like a Bellini painting, contrasting with the luminous sky. (I can continue forever with this picture writing, describing the picturesque landscape and making time a tempera, but I prefer to talk about the flesh made Word.) Juliet spoke of many things. Of poetry, for instance, which interested her so much. Though captivated by the sound of her voice, I was able to participate, making her monologue a dialogue, not to tell her that a lot of poetry was only rhyming prose, but to agree with her, seeking in her discourse not a discussion but an intimate course, an intercourse. When we bade farewell we promised to meet again, but I don't remember if the promise was expressed or merely implied.

I found her again many times, without knowing then that she was destined to play an important if not decisive role in my life. Not only would I give her my love (I'd give that in a pass to any passing stranger) but I would bestow upon her my virginity. (Much later I would learn that she had been a mutual muse for different friends, even friends who didn't yet exist, future friends.) Time passed and our meetings became frequent but they didn't seem to lead to anything—how shall I say?—palpable. But one day I received a telephone call. Not on my telephone since we didn't have or even think or dream of having one, but rather the phone of Fina, my uncle the Kid's fiancée (they hadn't married yet) and Fina came upstairs to tell me I had a call. I was absolutely amazed, but when I asked who it was and Fina said it was a woman, my amazement doubled, and when she added "someone named Julia" (for a moment I couldn't connect that name with the image of Juliet) my amazed heart did a triple somersault. Summer sault, for it was June. I never figured out how Juliet found Fina's number or how she knew she was my uncle's fiancée. Perhaps she asked the operator, giving my address, which she knew, despite my resistance, more than reticence, to give people my address in those days, not out of a sense of privacy but rather the opposite: I lived not in a private house but in a public building, publicized even in the editorial pages of a morning newspaper. Not to mention the crime columns. I don't know why I gave her my address, that slanderous stamp, Zulueta 408. Or I do know why: I wanted to be in direct communication with her body, to be within her reach, I wanted her to know all she could about me—a *coup de data* to abolish chaff. I went to the telephone wary of the perpetual presence of Venancia, my uncle the Kid's future mother-in-law, but her voice, Juliet's, sounded so sweet to my only ear that I forgot the proximity of my Uncle the Kid's mother-in-law. She, Juliet, wanted to see me. Could I come to her house? Of course I said yes as soon as possible I was already on my way—which I was. Down Teniente Rey to Compostela Street, passing Sol to reach the light of Luz, which led me onto Inquisidor, I was thinking that she must be alone and that's why she was calling me. Of course there would be conversations, dialogues, variations on the theme of love—who knows, we might even get to the blooming bed. I was dreaming all that until I rang the bell of her apartment. She lived in one of those Old Havana houses which, nevertheless, had been built in this century: a long apartment with living room and balcony facing the street, then a narrow exterior corridor, which led to the four bedrooms, ending in a dining room and a kitchen in the back. (This small topographical digression on the site of love is not for the sake of my architectural zeal of approval but rather to help you visualize a later scene on this same domestic stage.) She opened the door: waiting for me anxiously, prettier than ever, in a low-cut yellow dress, which revealed the top of her cleavage. She looked like a Golden Delicious apple. She smiled, showing her even perfect teeth, gums as rosy as her lips, her ruby-red tongue now a soft dart.

"How quickly you came!" she said as a greeting.

"Yes," I admitted, "I came quickly."

I didn't say I had practically come running, not only because I was eager to see her but because it was raining. She closed the door and walked toward the living room. She sat on the sofa, inviting me to sit next to her. A settee for two. I did so quickly, sitting almost before she did. There didn't seem to be anybody in the house. Was she really alone? Would we get anywhere? Would there be transfigurations, figurations, figures? Soon I suffered a double deception. Someone, clattering Cuban heels, came from the back into the living room, saw me, went to the door, opened it, and went out, down the stairs, into the street and Old Havana and the rain. I never knew who that passing shadow was, whether a close friend or poor relative. The second shock was when she expressed a *tolle lege:* from some part of her body she pulled out a book and said:

"Here, read."

So it sounded. She didn't even say please. It was a royal command: she handed me the book and I was to read it. The book, when I took it in my hands, became a poetry anthology—in English. The page was marked, with her index finger stuck in the book. Before I could see it, she said to me: "It's Eliot. You must read his poem to me."

In effect, her fingerprint on the page indicated that it was the section of the English poetry anthology dedicated to Eliot and the poem she had pointed out was *Ash Wednesday*—but how could I read it to her? Besides, was this the big emergency she had called me for? Not "come up and see me sometime" but come up and read to me now? I should mention that even today my pronunciation of English is more reminiscent of Conrad's than of Eliot's—I usually call him Elliott—who, talking of Conrad, remembered only the novelist's thick Polish accent, an oral halitosis for that effete American poet who spoke a fake British English. In that era my English was an unclear or rather too clear garble in my dreadful Havanan accent, and though I could read it very well to myself, I had never, except in class, dared to read it to anyone else. I tried to convince Juliet that one couldn't read Eliot just like that. But she didn't understand my Spanish or pay any attention to my arguments. "I want to hear how it sounds," she ordered me. I finally gave in to her command (it was never a request, nor even a plea, especially not a plea) and I began to read:

"Bee caused eyed doe not to hop to turn a game," my pronunciation producing a cruel parody of April in Eliot. I finally finished the poem in Gibberish, where I was born. She found the poem and my reading excellent, exciting: obviously, even though she was now an actress (she would

172

later act quite successfully, especially in Ionesco's *The Lesson*, playing the part of the little girl who, despite a toothache, gives and receives a lesson while the spectators learn that culture leads to the worst excesses if not abscesses), she had a tin ear. My reading was a disaster, leaving a taste of ashes in my mouth that Wednesday. A double disaster now that it was clear she had called me only to read her the poem and, knowing that she could be very firm, I didn't try to steer the visit to the Waist Land of Sex.

Several years passed between establishing a relationship with Juliet and achieving my goal, the only goal I had in mind, the great goal. High school came to an end and our friendship survived the separation: I went to journalism school and she studied acting. There were other unexpected invitations, no less literary than the reading of Eliot's poem. One was an excursion to the Colón cemetery (Colón meaning Columbus, after whom Havanans named cities of love and death). Juliet was as attracted to cemeteries as to sex, and she said she knew a corner of Colón that was ideal for both. I steadfastly refused to go to the Colón cemetery: white horses couldn't drag me there alive. Not even if I could have done over a flat tombstone what I intended to do in a bed would I have gone to the Colón cemetery with her. I hate cemeteries and detest people who say they like cemeteries. Juliet was an exception: her beauty made one forgive all the demands her Slavish soul made upon her body.

Around that time Juliet introduced me to her girlfriend (curiously, Juliet didn't really have any girlfriends) Silvia Saénz, who was a sculptor or beginning to sculpt. I went out with Silvia several times, and one of these times we went to the quarries (to be expected: as if Michelangelo would ever invite his friends to any place other than Carrara) of Casablanca, to see if, as in Galatea, marble could turn to flesh. Apart from one or two revelations about Juliet (which in passing unveiled Silvia, as with a statue: it soon became evident that she was more interested in women than in men) nothing happened, and after those versions and diversions our friendship languished noticeably because of her Sapphic choice. But through Silvia I found out that ever since Juliet was a little girl, she had showed her whims and vanity. The two had gone to the same private school and Silvia clearly remembered the summer day when Juliet entered the classroom with an enormous yellow ribbon in her blond hair and told, not asked, the teacher: "Isn't it true, miss, that I'm the prettiest girl in school." Juliet must have been ten or twelve then, but she already revealed her confidence in her beauty. There was also the day when they caught her "doing things" (as Silvia said) with a boy who was visiting the all-girls school: the boy (or rather, little boy: according to Silvia he was much younger than they and Juliet was the seductress, which I believe) was the headmistress's relative.

Silvia told me other stories and confessions but I already knew some from Juliet, like her relationship (which apparently went both ways: one of Silvia's few excursions into heterosexuality) with Noel Noel (that was, surprisingly, his real name), painter by profession, who affected a perennial tuberculosis that never became galloping consumption. He always dressed in mourning (all in black, in Havana! a double defiance: Havanan humor didn't let such extravagances go unpunished), and with his trim beard and romantic mane they sometimes called him Dada Noel. Other times, Victor Hugo Norrhea. Others, Van Goghnorrhea. One of the stories (which Juliet had already told me: she loved to recount her adventures) placed Noel in a boat with Silvia and Juliet on either end, rowing near Cojímár, defying not only the sunny sea but the seaworthy humor of some seamen reacting to the rower's attire. The story ended, according to Silvia, when she asked to get out, embarrassed more by the painter's immodesty than his inexperience, then losing sight of Juliet and Noel— not out to sea but down in the boat. In the bottom one bottom up. Juliet's story, however, contains an incident which changes Silvia's story. Noel, a poor painter who should have been a decadent poet, insisted that Juliet kiss Silvia (almost innocently according to Juliet), and her refusal bothered Silvia so much that the latter demanded to be landed immediately. I tend to believe Juliet's version not only because of her honesty but because she had a definitively heterosexual vocation and various stories she told me confirm this. One of these stories has as its protagonist a friend of mine, the hermetic poet Orlando Artajo, and his wife (who was not his wife then) María Escalante, an actress. According to Juliet, when Orlando and María were fiancés or partial partners they invited her to visit Orlando's bachelor flat on the corner of Malecón and Prado, in a house which for diverse reasons had been inhabited by many actual artists and not a few fags, and very often the same tenant would practice both activities—the artist as pederast. Leonard'or. Our erotic adventuress, after chatting awhile in the only room, which was studio, living room, and bedroom, was invited by Orlando to try the bed. She, Juliet, whose habit it was never to be surprised by any expression of sex (and she had no doubt that Orlando was not inviting her to sleep in the afternoon), was puzzled by Orlando's proposition, in front of María, since they were on the verge of marriage. As she showed her amazement it was María herself who asked Juliet to lay down on the bed (María was always choosy in her choice of verbs and men); Orlando had made the invitation for her: it was María who wanted to go to bed with Juliet! The exclamation is mine, not Juliet's: I was the one shocked by this story since I couldn't imagine María (I knew her well: she had been at high school with us) as a lesbian, but the years proved that Juliet's story was not only plausible but possible. María, who married Orlando, was driven by a "Lesbian license." (Orlando, furious, described it to me in these words, one night of confidential confessions.) Apparently, Orlando had made her debut possible, though he chose the wrong bedfellow. Juliet confessed to me that she got undressed and into bed with both more because she liked Orlando than out of any inclination for María and though she had the pretext of alcohol (they had been drinking wine, as exotic as it

174

is toxic in the tropics) the trio managed to go no further than tresses and caresses by María—which, according to Juliet, didn't have the slightest effect on her—and Juliet in turn touched Orlando's thing, more to her liking (licking) than María's massages and moans. But it didn't go beyond a critical point with Orlando, since if there was something Juliet took care in conserving (despite her liberated libido) it was her virginity. That was preserved for her husband, that is, for marriage—perhaps before betrothal but in any case she was reserving herself for her boyfriend.

The third Sapphic sacrifice she suffered (in her words) was when Dora Darío (her *nom de plume* as she said, that is, her pen name, taken from her two idols, Isadora and Rubén Darío), the lesbian poet who wrote "The Words of the Tribade," an ode to Sappho, invited her to the movies. Juliet went because she was interested in the film (the first run of *Beauty and the Beast*) but she almost couldn't admire its poetry because of the prosaic annoyance of Dora's constant caressing and crossing of legs. Finally, seeing she was getting nowhere in the stalls, Dora invited her to the ladies'. There Dora insisted that Juliet kiss her. She did, to see if she'd leave her alone, content with a kiss. Juliet didn't feel a thing and, bored, she clearly showed her desire to return to her seat and finish seeing the film, a French version of the virago and the virgin. "That's it," she said, "it's the last time I'm going out with a lesbian, even if I am considered backward." This was one of Juliet's pet preoccupations: though she wasn't a snob, she never wanted to seem as if she wasn't up-to-date. Those were Juliet's only Sapphic sallies, to date.

Juliet spoke to me of impossible passions, among which her heart had been ensnared in the memory machine of Felix Isasi. I knew of Felix only by hearsay. First because he was a friend of Ricardo Vigón and later, when I knew him personally, because he always insisted on saying Foul-kelner instead of Faulkner, whenever he spoke of his favorite author. These were traits that distinguished Felix from many other people I knew briefly at that time. But the passion he provoked more than produced in Juliet made me see him with other eyes. Felix was a tall, bony fellow with broad shoulders and long legs, but his thin lips and Dantesque nose made him utterly ugly. Juliet confessed to me that she fell madly in love with him when she noticed him one day in the reading room of the National Library. There, amid the musty, moisty odor of old books, in this ancient fortress overpowered by venerable volumes more than by a new weapon, was Felix reading (probably his frequent Foulkel-ner) and smiling, not at the book but at his reading. (How she could distinguish between book and reading is one of the major mysteries of Juliet's relationship with literature.) That radiant reader's sweet, silent smile was enough to produce in Juliet an overwhelming passion—never consummated. This time it wasn't because Juliet insisted upon preserving her *virgo intacta*. She would have surrendered it a thousand times to Felix so that he would rape her as he did French infibulated editions. Frail Felix suffered from an incurable illness he didn't wish to transmit to Juliet, the image of good health. I suppose this dread disease (Juliet didn't have the virture of being explicit in her stories or was explicit spasmodically) must have been syphilis, the malady *d'amour* that was no longer the venereal virulence which had threatened my early adolescence. Pox-facto Felix suffered this illicit and incurable ill (pale protozoa in the moonlight, just like orchids) more romantically than stoically, and he and his Juliet had to resign themselves to loving without ever consummating the act of love. According to Juliet, they got into bed many times. In poor Felix's poor room I suppose: he earned his living taking pictures on the street with an old box camera *(Daguerre c'est Daguerre),* prints that he tried to sell to the weary, wary wayfarers, *dei ex machina.* But the two always limited themselves to going to bed naked one beside the other, without further sexual contact than holding hands, Felix's flimsy fingers, stained with acid (or nicotine) intertwined with Juliet's golden digits, since Felix's culpa manifested itself in his dread or threat of transmitting his insidious illness in a kiss to ever-eager Juliet. *Non, non inmissio.* Long bedfellow.

Juliet's passion for Felix ended abruptly just when Felix was cured of his incurable disease, whatever it was, a cure occurring at the very moment Juliet didn't want to see him ever again. She developed a pox on him: I always felt sorry for Felix, photographer, and regretted that he had been cured of his pox-romantic disease. At least he was a friend (or a friend of a friend) and it was preferable that he go to bed with Juliet rather than an enemy, like Paret, who almost did. That's the movie critic Xavier Paret, whom I detested for his daily reviews and general attitude toward movies. (Talking about *Un Chien andalou,* this Catalan critic dared to say that it was "an early send-up of a later flight of genius!") With this old, bald, and bad-breathed admirer (he must have been around forty then), who was *in extremis* unpleasant, she also got involved. Although Juliet swore to me (not on the Bible, nor on her own bible, *My Life*) that it never went beyond a kiss between the wings of *The Flies (sic)* by Sartre, fascinated by his intelligence (Paret's, not Sartre's), and at the same time guarding her virginity, I now add, reserved for her steady boyfriend—and here, at long last, I must speak of Juliet's boyfriend, who was no Romeo, as he never was, I believe, her love for life.

His name was Vicente Vega, whom I knew as a gymnast from the Institute team and whom I learned to respect for being one of the few who defended viva voce (others did so sotto voce) the Jewish students when, as a false hazing, the hoodlums controlling the Students' Association made them swear by the Cuban flag. This oath to the flag was a pretext to rob the Jews, charging them a fee for not swearing, which was increased according to the relative affluence of the student's appearance. Some had money but others were completely broke. I don't remember knowing anyone poorer than Mitrani, a Sephardic Solomon, a companion in classes, games, and our love for medicine, and one of the few persons I met in my adolescence who was poorer than I. Hazing the Jews

176

was a way of demonstrating these gangsters' machismo and exhibiting their presumed superiority as Cubans over the Jews. A sign of the times (a Swiss swastika?): this happened when it had just been revealed that the Nazis were systematically annihilating the Jews of Europe. Vicente Vega protested against these pledges of allegiance to the flag and had a fist fight with one of the extortionists, who later became real murderers, though they considered themselves political militants and called themselves revolutionaries. He was a menacing mulatto mauler named Manasé (Manazas) Pérez, and he knocked Vicente unconscious on the sidewalk at the entrance. Vicente was lucky not to have been confronted by an armed dwarf but his defeat then was honorable.

Not so honorable was his defeat at the feet of Juliet, his former fiancée, who put horns on him even before marrying him. What's more, she covered him with mortal ridicule by trying to make him immortal. She took him off the gym team, where Vicente was a star and really shone with his own light (he was a champion in interschool gymnastics), to turn him into a mediocre painter, because Juliet couldn't marry anyone who didn't belong to the world of Art—or, as she said, "who wasn't an artist." Not only did she make him into a Sunday painter but she persuaded him to sign his paintings with the simple name of Vincent.

But, but Juliet was beautiful. Her beauty contradicted not only Socratic aesthetics but Aristotelian ethics. I forgave her then for all her moral faults because of her physical perfections, as long as she looked at me with her big *crème caramel* eyes, allowing me to admire her long blond hair, her tasty teeth whenever she smiled, her shapely mouth, which drove Vicente to despair when Vincent tried to portray her in repeated, distorted paintings, and her figure: a white Venus: venereal Venus since it wasn't Botticelli or Velázquez who tried to copy her parabolic curves, created by nature out of the froth of kisses, made of love for love, her graceful geometry repeated in the cupolas of her sheltering breasts. I know because one day I held one of those cups in my hand. That was the moment I swore I would go to bed with Juliet even if I had to make a pact against nature: more decisive than selling my soul to the devil was surrendering my virginity to Juliet. She knew or suspected my intention to go to bed with her or at least she knew the size of my triumph if I did. What she never guessed was that my virginity—voluntarily or by sheer chance—was hers for the taking. But I don't think she even knew I was being deflowered (if one can use that word for a man) when I went to bed with her for the first time. Before then, of course, to my despair, there were other interrupted encounters.

A particularly dangerous intermission occurred in the very living room of her house where I had betrayed (not translated) Eliot on another wet afternoon. This time I went to visit her and I remember that she sat down to chat with me in a rocking chair between the memorable, deplorable sofa and the chair where I was now sitting. We conversed (a conversation full of spasms: mine more than hers) and suddenly Juliet looked at me with her creole *crème caramel* eyes and said softly but firmly: "Give me a kiss." I didn't want to believe what I was hearing (which is what I wanted) and I was almost going to ask her to repeat the phrase (which was an order) when I decided to get up and believe my ears with my lips. She didn't move from the rocking chair, which is why I had to bend down to her mouth, to erase her smug smile from her painted loud lips. We kissed. She kissed hard, with apparent passion, biting my lower lip with her even eight teeth. I responded to her kisses with anxious ardor when I felt her feeling for my fly without ceasing to kiss me, opening that sartorial barrier, that chaste encasement, button by button. Codliverpiece. I had my Sweeney erect since we'd started kissing and now she pulled it out and took it without hesitation to her smiling mouth. Into it. Like lipstick. Not for her lips but for me it was an unexpected act, which is why I bolted up straight—but she continued her felicitous fellatio. *Is it safe?* I was worried about the distant noises, voices coming from the back of the house, now clearer because of some strange sound effect. Acousticks. And what if someone suddenly appeared, coming down the open corridor, catching us in flagrante. What could we do? Still more difficult, what could I say? None of this seemed to worry Juliet, who, though her back was to the apartment, didn't concede the slightest importance to what could occur there, occupied here. She continued sucking, from time to time aided and abetted by the rocking chair, moving back and forth like a procuring swingboat (pathetic fallacy) according to the movements of Juliet's head and mouth in orderly, almost monotonous rhythm. But being blown exalted me, lifting me up and away above my station in sex. The whole in the hole. Indeed it seemed impossible that all of me could leave through that orifice! That's exactly what I felt as her mouth went round and round, to and froth, her lips revolving, her tongue licking all sides of my penis, a delicious dart directed at the glans, she returning to take it all in her mouth while I, almost motionless at times, at other times moving my body to her bawdy beat. I held her by the head, her hair falling in disarray, a clear cascade, over her face and over what remained of my member—the little that wasn't inside her carnal cavern. Cyclops. Nevertheless I managed to keep observing the long, still lonely corridor to the back, and I was all ears (if I could be something that wasn't pure penis at that moment) to the background murmurs, longwave periphony, the house radio. But Juliet made me attentive to her again with a crisscross caress of her thick lips and thin, penetrating tongue. Finally, almost crying out but controlling myself (those neighboring noises!), I felt myself going but it was that I was coming obstreperously, not with sensuous sounds but in epileptic silences that were like a racket on a rock, like a run, like a river: in a flow. She received it all in her mouth, drinking my licorice lickety-split, licking the lollipop, right down to the last drop of liqueur. She swallowed swiftly. Avidly. When it was all over, my legs, thighs, trunk, arms, and hands trembled like a figleaf as I quickly put away the corpus deliriums, buttoning up rapidly.

I was more afraid that the sinful act would be discovered now that it was over than when committing the crime. *Crème et châtiment.* Punishing, vanishing cream. She looked at me intently, intensely from her rocker, never off it, and said:

"Let's talk about pounds."

Was she suddenly some Soho slut? I couldn't believe she wanted to talk about currency at a sterling moment like this. Perhaps she meant weight lifting.

"About what?"

"Tell me about Razpound."

This was even more incredible!

"Ezra Pound?"

"Yes, tell me about his imprisonment. I've heard that he was locked in a cage."

Poets and Pisans! After that glorious blow job, that *mamada madre*—making me into a blowfish—she wanted me to talk about Ezra Pound. Good goddess! She should have said Ez Rapallo. Were we going to end the afternoon talking about poetry and Pound? But I was interested, fascinated, obsessed by a question coming before hers. Mine: "And what if they had come?"

"What do you mean?"

"What if someone in your family had come into the room?"

She smiled. "They weren't going to come."

"How do you know?"

"I know."

"But what if they had come?"

"They weren't going to come."

"And if they had?"

"They would have witnessed a beautiful bond," she said and smiled again. "It was beautiful, wasn't it? You who were watching while doing it can't say no. Was it or wasn't it beautiful?"

"I suppose that for us it was. But what about the others?"

"They've done it too, and if they haven't we've shown them what they're missing. Now tell me all about Ezra."

She said it with such charm that I had no choice but to gratify her wish and I spoke about the poor poet on the losing side, victim of the winners' justice, of his six months in an iron prison that was a cage out in the open, where he lived, slept, defecated, and composed his Pisan cantos—but I didn't speak about what the losers, if they'd been winners, would have done with the poets (and everybody else) on the other side. Our side. While I gave my lecture I thought of how sure she'd been that nobody would intrude upon her oral copula and I felt jealous. So this wasn't the first time the wench had committed fellatio in her own house! —apart from other places, of course. It seemed to be a running act because of her knack in performing, in her clever use of the rocking-chair rhythms—apart from the precise knowledge that she could do it without

179

the risk of being found out. All this entered my mind, my thoughts interrupted not by my talk but by the funny feeling that went wet in my pants, a sign of the past event—and I then felt content. I had finally achieved more than contact, an act, though limited, a sexual action with her, with that Juliet who now seemed, listening to me, more beautiful than ever. Not only more beautiful than when I arrived but more beautiful than when she had looked most beautiful, even when I saw her for the first time. This was another first time: and it was reflected in her radiant, somewhat triumphant, face, my conquistadora, my most magnificent mistress! Of my will and my voice now saying: "But if he was a prisoner, poetry liberated him." All lies, of course. Madness, real or pretended, exonerated Ezra, but that Pounding peroration was what Juliet—sexual mistress but slave of the arts—wished to hear. I never knew how I moved from where she had placed me when that casual coitus began, or how I returned to my assigned seat or when I left her house. Now, trying to remember the tryst, from the moment of orgasm it's all a silent void, a vacuum. Only the single sound of our dialogue crisscrossed over the double damnation of my fear and her thirst, for sex and culture, extracting from me her Pound of flesh.

There was another coitus interruptus that was more like an impromptu. One evening we were in the Lyceum concert hall, listening to Miari de Torre making his strange sounds, staring at his outlandish appearance, his air of final triumph over all the adversities of his life—when sex came up, out, into the picture. Miari de Torre was an unknown maestro, a musician, introduced to Franqui by the painter José María Mijares. Franqui and I had met Mijares at the same time, on the corner of Prado and Virtudes, where the artists hung around the portals of the Crystal Salon Café, a club where there were more aspiring *artistes* than true artists and writers. There were also visitors from Havana's night life, joined usually by the occasional gangster imported from across the street, from the Paseo or from the benches of the Prado promenade, where those dangerous night birds of prey gathered. After having met skin-and-bones Mijares, it seemed an exaggeration to meet someone with more bones than Mijares, introduced by Mijares, almost with Mijares's same name—but this robed skeleton was the musician Miari de Torre, seemingly fresh from Auschwitz. Miari had given in his youth, way back in the twenties, a piano concert at Carnegie Hall (playing piano was Miari's major artistic activity) and now he still used this achievement as his endorsement, or epithet: *Miari de Torre, concert pianist of Carnegie Hall.* His poverty made us all (Mijares, Franqui, me) seem obese and opulent. He lived not in a Bohemian attic but in an ancient apartment in Old Havana, or long room rather (larger, to be sure, than the room I lived in with my whole family: speak to me of Promiscuity, I knew her well), dominated by a small upright piano, its white keys yellow from the passage of time, God's metronome, its black keys all gray now, like his hair. On this untouchable instrument, worn down by fingers, years, and termites, Miari played his music, but there were more notes, strings, hammers missing on this pedal-less piano than those present. To hear him play was like listening to an unfinished, unbegun melody, a harmony without resolution, pieces of pieces, bit by bit. The lame execution lent an extra mystery to the strange chords the pianist extracted from his instrument—which should remain nameless. On a visit to Miari and his martyr muse we met his wife instead: dumb, distracted, and so disoriented that she would still get lost, after twenty years of living there, if she went a few blocks from home by herself, the concentric ruins of Old Havana a local labyrinth to her. Miari had to go on periodic expeditions to find his lost wife, Smetana, who on many occasions had gone only for salt. Their daughter, Isolde, with her big blue eyes, her singularly serene beauty, and her even stranger naïveté was, at fifteen, passing through life like an immaculate concept of Miari's. This Isolde used to go out with my brother, a *triste* Tristan, who was then barely sixteen and still hadn't gotten over the tuberculosis he had contracted at fourteen. Isolde's destiny was circular, as Havana was to her mother. On one of these visitations with Mijares, when Franqui and I were trying to decipher Miari's compositions, increasingly cryptic not because of their harmonies but rather thanks to his comatose piano, we decided to organize a concert-homage to Miari de Torre of Carnegie Hall, now quoting from the succinct tickets all of us friends, baroquely broke, took charge of selling. While Miari got hold of the three musicians needed to perform his quartets (the program was four quartets, I don't know if for esthetic reasons or just plain superstition), Franqui reserved the Lyceum hall and Mijares announced the event standing on a soap box, a megaphone in hand and mouth, a disease on the corner of Virtudes. My brother and I managed to sell a few tickets to the few people (with means who weren't mean) we knew outside of our circle. We were all trying to inflate Miari's ego, if not his body, but in his state he was nearer to the Styx with each passing beat of his metronome. Miari, a precocious pianist, couldn't have been over forty but looked like a seventy-year-old man: he obviously didn't have much energy to spend, though this concert was to be, for a while, his reason for living if not his fountain of youth, before that final swansong, death. Sick transit, Gloria Swansong.

After all the hustle and bustle, the evening of the concert finally arrived, but the audience didn't. The only people at the Lyceum were Mijares, Franqui, Señora Smetana, Isolde, my brother, me, and Juliet. I had interested her in the event and she, mellow melomaniac, had been excited by the possibility of hearing unheard, unpublished, and never before performed music: the melody of memory played by an amnesiac. Satieric. Nobody else came, as far as I remember, except for the intimate musicians. When the curtain opened, Miari appeared on stage in an old frock coat, as gray as the black keys on his household piano, with three musicians, one more emaciated than the next, borrowed from a sanatorium more than from the conservatory, inmates more than intimate.

They began to play, following the program (God knows where Franqui, magician without a top hat, got the primitive printing press to print a program). The first piece was a sonata a quattro *"d'après Leopardi,"* after the program notes. The sounds starting to pour out of the grand piano (an ebony-black shiny Steinway: it must have been an eternity since Miari had even touched, let alone played, such an instrument) and out of the violin, viola, and violoncello were weird, to say the least. Hoarse noises rose from the lower keys of the piano, a discordant accompaniment to the right hand's arpeggios, sometimes in curious, cursive counterpoint with the strident string trio, on occasions achieving a unison reached more by chance than by art. Finally the sonorous novelty faded before friendship faded and one quartet *("d'après Petrarca")* followed another distressing (doubtless *d'après Dante*) dissonant litany, overshadowed by pity, an infinite malady, a lament for the poor talent of poor Miari. Deceased. Then all sound sank into tedium—but the disconcerting concert continued—forcibly forever.

To dissipate my aural boredom I began to look at the disturbingly shapely legs of Juliet. We were both sitting in the first row, far from the others, spread about the small concert room now augmented by the absence of an audience: almost Carnegie Hall. The listless listeners were trying to hear the unheard-of, while I wanted to get in touch with the palpable. Her skirt offered a generous view of her golden knees. It occurred to me to communicate with her with the only instrument I had at hand: my eyeglasses. I had taken them off for a moment to blur the music and I brushed her right arm with them, by mistake, an oversight. But I felt more than saw (I was already very near-sighted) the shiver going through her when the arm of my spectacles touched her. She turned slightly toward me (without ceasing to look at the musty musicians) and crossed her left hand over her right arm, letting it hang there half-closed: through this opening, intentionally now, I inserted my horny-rimmed glasses, touching the palm of her hand. She softly grabbed that arm, now something else, an amorous bond, and allowed me to impose a metronomic movement, back and forth, brushing her fingers and touching the palm of her hand. I repeated this friction with better rhythm (though the music, decidedly distant, as if coming from the past and not the stage, languished more and more and didn't accompany my positive piston), my melody now mimicking a coitus between her hand and my instrument, now presto, then molto presto, then prestissimo. My bow continued copulating with her viola d'amore, more and more intensely—until she turned toward me and said softly in my ear: "Please don't continue, I'm all wet": the only and last words before the finale of the concert, which now became the most unbearable of tortures: quartered by quartets. At the end we managed to escape. I muttered some words of consolation to Miari's wife, now widow, as if it had been a funeral and not a gala event. Almost without looking at Isolde and my brother, at circumspect Franqui and circumstantial Mijares, the two of us left the music hall rapidly, abandoning the Lyceum, rushing along the almost dark streets of that part of El Vedado.

"Where do we go now?" she asked me.

"Say the word," I proposed.

"Wherever you want."

I recited:

> "Let us go then, you and I
>   When the evening is spread out against the sky
>   Like a patient etherised upon a table."

"Yes," she said, "let's"—without recognizing the quotation. "But take me to the sea." By the sea, by the sea, by the beautiful Debussy.

We went down Calzada (or rather up) because we were leaving behind Eighth Street to reach Tenth in my hurry, turning in the direction of the sea, down to the shore. The Malecón still wasn't extended that far and it was possible to walk down to the water in that part of El Vedado, if you knew how to walk over reefs—or "dog teeth" as they were ferociously called in my town. Juliet seeking the sea, apparently; I beside her, my arm now passing from timidity to audacity to hold her by the waist, feeling her flesh beneath the subtle dress with my feverish, restless hand, not inert now. *Coup de main.* But the sea didn't appear in the black of night. Finally she went over to some broken column (what did it commemorate?) near the reefs, perhaps erected on them, not far from the maddening light of a streetlamp. There she turned around and kissed me in her vehement way: putting her tongue in my mouth, biting my lips, hanging on to my lower lip as if she wanted to tear it off. Meanwhile she was seeking me, groping for my fly, the strip that trips, finally pulling out the stuck swollen stick. Simultaneously, she lifted her skirt: she wasn't wearing, as I already sensed, panties, bloomers, or undies. However, I wasn't preoccupied by the name of what didn't exist but rather was occupied in seeking with my hand the unnamable essence, absence, her hole, which I finally found and it was, in fact, wet as the sea, but a strange, underground, and invisible sea, a sweet sea. While wild desire moved me to act, it didn't keep me from thinking she was a virgin, not Vicente's yet, perhaps, and thus I was close to being the happy immortal (or maybe unhappy mortal) to have the honor to be what poxmarked Felix could never be. But easier said than done standing. She was shorter than I and therefore I had to lower myself vertically as I grew horizontally to reach her opening that my harried penis sought for hurriedly, trying to put it in her and almost succeeding—but I was interrupted in my quasi-coitus by a shout I didn't understand. I couldn't figure out at first where it was coming from, but when it was repeated I realized it wasn't Juliet screaming from pleasure. It was not the actress but rather some unexpected spectators: we were the target of angry pedestrians, apparently forming an enraged mob. Sour grapes of wrath. I made it known to her, still at sea. *Ad astra per ardor.*

"What's up?" she asked me.

"The natives," I translated. "They want the golden girl," I said in my best imitation of Captain Engelshorn.

"Are they referring to me?" she asked, using her choice vocabulary.

"I would say they're slurring us," I said, catching her verbal disease. The shouts became voices and we heard things like "Apes!" "Go to a hotel!" "Bitch!"

"I think we'd better leave," I suggested. "They're sailors, troublemakers all."

She said: "Yes, you can't reason with the rabble," but immediately she faced the enemy and responded to the anonymous insults, hidden in the dark and wet, invisible to us. Disembodied voices are always like that.

"Vulgarians!" she shouted. "Don't you know what love is?"

That's how she was, and I, being myself, beat an immediate retreat, without further exchange with the nagging neighbors. She agreed to follow this time and we recoiled laterally, coastal crabs, leaving the truncated column, which we had almost made our monument. Fearing that someone, fishing or foul, would cast the first stone, we slipped out of the limey light to reach the street far from what she would have called —invoking the ghost of Gertrudis Gómez de Avellaneda, spinner of spicy island stories—"the diligent mob." And that's the closest I got to fucking with her in that era, folks.

But there are two consequences of that encounter. One is that between her ardor and the mob's anger, I had had an opportune orgasm, an ejaculation amid jaculatories, without realizing it. When I noticed the wet stain it was too late: I was already marching down Línea Street. I cleaned my pants, the crotch, my left leg, as well as I could without drawing the attention of the curious, meaning any citizen of Havana. The handkerchief became a damp, sticky mass, which I put in my pocket, not preserving my semen like Carmina's kiss but rather segregating my seed. The other consequence was indirect but more onerous. The next day I was to have an exam in logic, which was both easy and difficult: enjoying the jism in syllogisms I let the premises become major and the result was that I would have to study that whole night through, if I wanted to pass. The alternative of course was to fail. But Juliet's was too too solid flesh to renounce empirical knowledge of her for theory's sake. Fortunately for the theory of knowledge (and unfortunately for me) she suggested going by way of her house. When we got on the trolley, now seated, I could notice a budding principle of contradiction in her. Was she merely being contrary? I asked her when we would see each other again, meaning our next meeting. Her negative answer produced my surprise, not because of the negation itself but because of what she now said.

"I don't know," she said. "You know, I'm getting married next Monday."

I didn't know, nor did I suspect, though I feared it from time to time.

184

But I wasn't going to show my amazement, much less one final contradiction: "Yes, of course I know."

"I don't know when I'll see you again," she said, finally.

Those were not our last words exchanged before she married, before she got off the tram rather, but it's not worth reproducing the wordless sentence that left our now no longer longing lips. I got off the streetcar before her: I lived in the periphery of Old Havana, while Juliet lived in its center—which she called the heaving heart of its labyrinth.

I spent the night blanked out, not studying as I should but remembering our seaside sex interrupted by shouting sailors, how it almost ended in *inmissio penis*. Relieved, I continued to relive the moment and kept the handkerchief in my pocket—not as a souvenir, but to wash my stigmata in enigmata when everyone was asleep. I did so in secret silence, and after leaving it spotless I stuck the wet rag on the mirror of the dressing table so that it would iron out into a clean handkerchief again as it dried. The next morning, before I went off early to my exam, my mother asked me what had happened to the ironed handkerchief (she noticed everything) and I had to invent a complicated cover-up about it getting so dirty that it was too disgusting to wash: a phallacy: I was trying to spare her that disgust. Which wasn't far from axiomatic truth: all handkerchiefs get dirty eventually, but some get filled with semen. Thus, no handkerchief is ever starched. The exam was, of course, a major disaster, but I don't want to talk about logic or my academic life, but rather about my illogical love life. So, back to Juliet, the married virgin.

I didn't go to the wedding (I don't think she even invited me), but I did know about her honeymoon. She wrote me a letter from the Isle of Pines, in which she said she was collecting twilights (not sunsets, which are common in Cuba) and among other curiosities she informed me that she had sent me a piece of her favorite beach. I had no idea what she was referring to, but I searched the whole letter for something that could look like a beach: there was nothing. Then I examined the envelope with my naked eye (the myopic eye, optic irony, becomes a magnifying glass close up) and found strange grains of sand: thus I deduced that she was sending me sand from her beach, extravagant but logical. I found out what it really was days later, when she was back from her honeymoon and we saw each other again: she had sent me a seashell. (Symbolic to a Botticellist but not to me.) What I found in the letter was seashell powder, reduced to sand by the postmaster's stamp—or hedgehammer. But even stranger than the piece of white beach was the piece of purple prose that Juliet sent me in her short letter. She said, a propos of nothing, "I imagine you in a mauve interior, magenta and yellow, like an Oriental by Van Gogh." I treasured that phrase for years, savoring its unintentional humor (and strange sense of color), as I kept the letter which contained other examples of Juliet's spirited style. For example: "You say that art is a lie. Is the sea a lie?" Then I lost it in a move and regret not having it with me for many reasons, among private ones the public possibility

185

of reproducing it now instead of scribbling these measly quotable quotes.

Some time later Juliet told me about an occurrence on the Isle of Pines (she insisted on calling it, after Robert Louis Stevenson, Treasure Island) that Stevenson himself would never have dared dream or invent as a nightmare. But for her it was all a dream. "Like a dream in a dream," as she recalled for me. She knew (we all did, as a matter of fact) that René Hidalgo, *el descuartizador* (the man who hacked his *mulata* mistress to pieces and then delivered his chosen morsels in neat parcels wrapped in old newspapers all over Havana), was still doing time in the island's infamous *presidio*. He was a double lifer with a *cadena perpetua,* which in Spanish means in chains forever. Hidalgo had already done fifteen years but still had twice as much time to do—and then some. He was our first *descuartizador* ever, so he had to pay the price all pioneers must pay.

She visited the prison, naturally, and asked the *alcaide* about Hidalgo. He told her that it was possible for her to visit with Hidalgo or for him to bring the prisoner to her in the warden's office. As she wished. She petitioned to be allowed inside the immense penitentiary for vicious male criminals. To observe Hidalgo in his habitat—my addendum. Then she informed Vicente that she intended to go see Hidalgo alone. He was a gentleman, no doubt. Didn't his name mean son of something? A some-body at least. What did she want to go in there alone for? asked Vicente. *I* know but Vicente never knew. "For the sake of the experience," she answered. Was she lying? I should say not. Anyway he agreed to her demand. Vicente Vega was nothing if not an agreeable young man. So she went into the penitentiary. Not like Little Red Riding Hood into the woods nor as pure as the lamb. She was escorted by the warden and an armed guard.

She traversed the vast edifice with the same leisurely pace she used to walk along Inquisidor Street sashaying on her way downtown, fol-lowed by the ogling eyes and the dirty ditties of all those perennially sex-starved men in the streets of Havana. When she arrived at Hidalgo's cell she requested to go in all by herself, as if on a visit. Request granted. In she went full of anticipation that for Juliet was always sex expecta-tions: at long last, love and death in one man. "It was," she said, telling me what doing solitary is, "some sort of private room and he was all by himself. After all, the man had been a policeman, hadn't he?" But she confessed to instant disappointment. She had expected a virile, vigorous male, capable not only of killing his wife with a single blow (actually she slipped in the bathroom, fell against the washbasin, knocked herself out, he thought her dead and panicked—the rest was a mess) but also of dismembering her with just a kitchen knife. (Knife, wife: you don't have to tell me, reader. I noticed too.) Then he proceeded to quarter the half-caste into legs, arms, and a torso that included the beautifully bare breasts which the photos showed in gruesome detail in every newspaper. All that and her handsome head too. "So Gauguin-like," she remarked, "even in black and white." She was a *mulata,* wasn't she, I said. But Juliet

186

didn't catch the joke, probably because it was on her. Or was my *humor* too *negro*? All she said was: "I believe she was, yes. But does it matter really?" Besides, he had had the courage to distribute her head and limbs (and her torso, added I) all over the city. "Always dressed as a policeman," she recollected, mysteriously. Instead of all the dash and dare of the romantic *tueur de femmes* (Landru in love) she met an incurably mediocre man—and what Juliet hated most was mediocrity. He was gray-haired, old at forty, pallid and submissive, almost subservient, speaking in subdued tones: a criminal who couldn't own up to his crime. He was still handsome, yes, but with blandly beautiful features: much like Vicente's. (That was me thinking, not her speaking.)

What really astonished Juliet on *la isla* (as if Cuba weren't island enough) was that she had to walk across the central, circular cement yard facing all cells (all the rooms had a view to the concrete in Presidio Modelo, a model prison), ahead of both warden and warder, twice—and twice she felt the eyes of the twelve thousand odd prisoners (a hungry hundredfold Argus indeed!) gawking at her: watching that insult of a girl go by, our Io, lusting after her, as they desired her, as I desired her too. She didn't have to tell me: she was wet all the way.

But I didn't see Juliet again until I came back from a tour of Cuba. It wasn't that I suddenly became a now Cuban voyager: what really interested me was to explore Havana. It's just that I took on a job as an investigator (according to Rigor I was a pollster guy), which consisted of asking strangers questions (alarming for my timidity but it paid well and they covered the expenses) all over the island. The questionnaire was simple: I only had to ask who they were going to vote for in the next elections, if they knew the Minister of Education (the presumed President, who was also the one paying for the survey—and not out of his own pocket) and to note down the social status of each person interviewed and his possible race. (If any.) This peripathetic poll, with its ramifications, is a complicated, almost Canterbury tale, but I'll tell only about the part of the trip that has to do with Juliet though in that era my whole life seemed to revolve around Juliet.

I shared a hotel room in Camagüey with Roman Mesonero, another pollsman, who was my age but big and fat, and he looked older as long as he didn't open his mouth. Talking late one night we got onto the inevitable subject of love—that is, sex. Mesonero asked me if I had gone to bed with a woman yet. I lied and said yes and when he inquired how many times I said two and when he wanted to know if she had been a decent girl or a whore I answered, adopting the bravado air I had acquired in high school, that whores never count. "That's true," said Roman, proceeding to ask me what she was like, if I didn't mind answering. I told this curious pollster that I didn't mind and I gave such a vivid description of Juliet that I smelled her fragrance, heard her voice, saw her eyes, and felt her vague but distinct vagina, hairs and all. I almost had an erection. Upon portraying Juliet I swore to myself that as soon as

187

I returned to Havana I would go to bed with her, whatever the cost—and I came back, saw, and was conquered.

But it wasn't as easy as I tell it. First I had to catch up with Juliet. I called her house, saying it was the Institute calling (the survey had served me in the art of impersonating a surrogate: "We are a survey firm from Havana and we would like . . .") and that we wanted to know if this was still the address of Juliet Estévez. (Of course it was no longer, but in the war of love, lying is permitted.) "It's our pleasure to send her an invitation to the school party, madam." Juliet never finished high school, so it wasn't unusual for the Institute to be asking about her. The voice on the other end of the line (it seemed to be one of her sisters, the only one who was still single) told me that Juliet didn't live there anymore and that she had moved to Lamparilla Street. "Could you give me the number, please?" "She doesn't have a telephone." "No, I mean the number of her house." She gave me not one but two numbers: the apartment and the building. As I knew that Vicente, now her husband, worked in a bank in Havana and painted on Sundays, when he was Vincent, I calculated that at ten in the morning he wouldn't be home but that Juliet would.

I can get lost in a little town like Trinidad, but I always find my way around Havana. I found her address: she lived in an inner apartment of a huge building whose boxlike architecture was enhanced by the fact that it was a fake phalanstery. I knocked on her door nervously, since at the eleventh hour I thought that Vicente might not have gone to the bank that morning, to paint yet another sunflower. But there was no turning back: I had knocked once, twice now, impulsive compulsive that I am. At first there was no answer, which made me more nervous and also disappointed: perhaps no one was there. But somebody was there! Juliet herself opened the door, more beautiful than ever, tanned, her hair and body bronzed gold, her smile more open and luminous than before, and she was wearing an apron—tied under her breasts, which bulged beneath her blouse. She had smiled, laughed almost from the moment she saw me, perhaps with some amazement, but she didn't ask how I had found her address. Maybe it seemed natural to her: many things that seemed extraordinary to me seemed ordinary to her. She said, simply: "Come in, come in," and closed the door behind me. The apartment was rather small, at least what I saw, which was the tiny living room. I had already sat down when she said: "Sit, sit down." Juliet talked that way sometimes, repeating words for emphasis: very *habanera* of her, though she didn't consider herself any old *habanera*—and she really wasn't. I've talked about Juliet with Germán Puig, who was also involved with her (or vice versa), and we reached the reasoned conclusion that she was truly exceptional. Aside from the importance she had in our lives, we spoke of her intrinsic virtues (we didn't use those words, of course), both of us remembering our common past marked by Juliet's presence, like a musical motif. Germán's relationship with Juliet, however, ended tragicomically in an argument on the Malecón, years back, or later, Juliet taking a deep breath before every utterance, as she always did when she was furious. Her pronouncement, more like a premeditated curse, upon Germán was: "Your life is a fraud: you don't read anymore," a final phrase which Germán and I used to repeat for years, in unison, as the ultimate punch line, a mournful motto. But I must return to that morning marked by an enormous white stone: Juliet amid the sheets like a memorable monument, my *memento vivi.*

I sat down and Juliet (broom in hand but looking more like a fairy than a witch) stopped doing her chores, both amused and attentive, to ask if I wanted some coffee. Of course I wanted coffee, I always want coffee. But now I was laughing, smiling, staring at Juliet, who looked like she was playing house. She obviously had not been born to be a housewife, innate *innamorata:* Laura of all the sonnets, Beatrice of all the comedies, Juliet in her play went to make the coffee. When she returned, cup in hand, she was without her household apron and looked better now: her body to be contained only in the dress that molded so well her thighs and hips. I drank the light and bitter cold coffee, apparently savoring it but really trying to figure out my next step. There was a silence between us ("An angelus passed by," said Carmina on a similar occasion), Juliet seated in another chair which made a set with mine—it was hard to tell which was uglier: Vicente must have chosen the furniture. There I was, sipping the bitter brew, as if concentrating on the coffee, but thinking of something else: the only thing I could think of in Juliet's company. It was the same thing I had thought the day I found her catching that traumatic tram or when she trounced upon the poetic grapes on the stage of Room 2 or upon seeing her in another class at the Institute, or perhaps thought even before meeting her: when we were students together but she had seemed like a woman already: the most beautiful girl at school. I don't know what Juliet was thinking but she looked at me and didn't say a thing. I didn't either. Perhaps we both knew what had to be said and therefore we refused to speak. Though beneath my desire was the fear that what happened—or hadn't happened—to me with the three whores, or one repeated whore and the other whore, would happen again. But somehow I knew it couldn't happen again and suddenly I found myself thinking that I was going to lose my virginity (though I didn't think of it in those terms but in a grosser, funnier way) with the most beautiful girl in the world—at least in my world, which was the only possible world to me. Suddenly Juliet spoke and, as other times, shocked me with what she said, but she didn't make me declaim Eliot or explain Pound. She said: "Do you want to make love?" Those were her precious, precise words and that's the way she was. I never heard her refer to sex with vulgar words, as she never said anything vulgar. Her strongest insult, as you have seen, was to call something or someone vulgar, vulgarian.

Now I wasn't sure I had heard right: perhaps it was a hallucination or an aural form of desire—or the effects of the coffee. But she said: "Do you?," repeating the offer: that's the way she was: she would take the initiative throughout our relationship. From the very beginning she took the initiative to initiate me. I heard myself saying, "Okay," as if she had offered me another cup of coffee and not the greatest offering anybody could have made me in my life, that only she could, would ever make. Juliet got up and opened a door to a room and put her broom back in it: it was a closet. Then she opened a second door: it was the bedroom. She entered and I followed her into the small dollhouse room, fit for Juliet. She didn't make a tedious ceremony of taking off her clothes and in a strip second she was naked in front of me, her body beautiful more perfect than what I had imagined or touched or seen over her clothes. She was not a natural blonde. (And I liked that even better: if there was something I would have changed in Juliet's apparent appearance it was her blond hair.) She sailed around the bed, a covered island, uncovering it, taking off the bedspread carefully and folding it on a chair. She now spread out, or rather reposed in a pose: one leg slightly bent, the other straight, one arm under her head, slightly crooked, and the other along her body: she became even more desirable, in a position that was both staged and pictorial. (What she had done I only realized seconds later: she was imitating Goya's Maja, a golden maja: that was Juliet, conscious of Art even when she should be least so, at her most momentous. Though this initiation was only for me, really: she had been married for a while. Anyway, who's to say that she hadn't already done it with others besides Vicente? I thought with world-wide jealousy.) But jealousy didn't keep me from taking off my clothes—which I did with alacrity. I mean, as quickly as my legs, and feet, would allow me. I felt embarrassed, however, naked in front of Juliet, not only out of modesty (converted into nightmares in dreams where I found myself naked in the middle of the street), but also because I was really skinny then—somewhere between Mijares and Miari—and didn't like to show my body. I couldn't forget that Juliet was married to an athlete. I would have preferred it to be night, but what could I do: it was day and Juliet was the sun, the promised flesh, the beauty that could become mine just by reaching out—and I leapt, not stepped, into bed. Ouch! The sheets were cold. It was winter and, even if winter in Havana is hyperbolic, there are days when it's as cold as Trinidad, since the houses are insulated only against heat. But Juliet didn't seem to feel cold in her almost etherised pose in bed, and I wasn't going to stop desiring her even though I was shivering. Actually, I don't think it was so cold, but rather just another sign of the power of dark nerves over my body. But there was another body, Juliet's, to make me forget my own.

I got on top of her and, without even kissing her, almost without letting her forsake her Goyesque abandon, I penetrated her and she responded immediately, moving with a movement that I could only appreciate years later. At this moment I realize I have penetrated her, sex has triumphed, she has just initiated me in the other life, there where the alter ego lives. I feel a great joy in the pleasure Juliet knows how to give me with her rotary movements, regular at times, different at others, sinking into me to let me float in her, making the bed downy, either down, she weightless or defying gravity bodily, levitating as she comes back up to the neon-lit diving board from the luminous water like Jansen's gravid bathing beauty—and suddenly she's moaning, as if wounded by a soft dagger, groaning now, crying now, howling now, and amid the screams she says to me softly in my ear, panting, murmuring, whining: "Now! Hurry!" and I don't know what she wants, what she's asking for. I'll be damned if I know where I must hurry off to! But I say sí (the shortest way to assent) and I say sí again and again sí and it's then that she cries out: "Hurry Finn is!" And I finally understand: she wants me to ejaculate. I, an amateur in her lexicon, have kept it back but I can ejaculate in a moment, precocious as I am. (Actually I could have come before, but I instinctively repressed myself to delay the end of the pleasure Juliet was giving me: lessons of my hand when masturbatory.) I'm ejaculating, I ejaculate, jaculate, and despite myself moans like Juliet's come out of my mouth, except hoarser, more moos than moans. We're trapped in the same net, the two of us one, revolving over ourselves without going in circles, but rotating universally, both sun and moon. Juliet looks at me and asks: "Can you continue?" "Yes, of course," I say, and she opens her eyes and mouth to ask me again: "Without taking it out?" "Yes, of course," I repeat, and she doesn't say anything but I should say to her that I prefer to stop a moment, which I don't say, but it's just that I want to stop to record this eternal hour or at least lasting lull, the exact moment when I lost my virginity: to see if she circumcised me, to check if I lost my frenum in her frenzy, if I'd been cured of my famous phimosis.

But I'm still on top of Juliet and she's already beginning to move again. As will always happen, the second time is better, now not so conscious of Juliet's cries, only of the vibrations of her vulva. Never vulga. A third time follows the second, without taking it out, and Juliet, avid vagina, low voice, live kisses, *vae* vampire, sucks me all over: member, tongue, lips, foreskin, skin. When I finish, both of us coming at the same time, I get off and lie down beside her, hitting the ceiling but exhausted. *Fornicare stanca.* Juliet turns toward me, looks at me, and says: "Can you always do it three times?" I'm not going to tell her it's the first time I've gone to bed with a woman properly (speaking), that I've been a (reluctant) virgin till now, that I've just had my baptism of uterine fire. So I say to her, trying to sound not gauche but adroit: "So it seems." "You know something," she confides, "Vicente can do it only once." Her confidential info reminds me of the existence of Vicente and his unique coitus reminds me of the unicorn and the horny hour and I am alarmed because as I don't have a watch I don't know what time it is: nor do I know when Vicente comes home for lunch—but I suspect that he must do it at lunchtime.

"What time does Vicente return?"

"Oh, around twelve," says Juliet, who ignores time. Time is consuming and therefore vulgar.

"And what time is it?"

"Around eleven," says Juliet with the same vagueness and same indifference for Vicente that she has for time. Vicente is vulgar.

"Then I'd better be going."

"If you wish," she says, and I get up and begin to dress, impregnated with Juliet's penetrating odor. Attar of rosebuds. After putting my clothes on I look at her and see that she's still in bed: reclining, naked, *corpus deliciae.*

"When shall we meet again?" I ask her, meaning to say something else, of course.

"Oh," she says, "whenever you want. But, do you know something? I'd like to hear the sea while we make love."

"All right," I say, "we'll have to look for a waterfront hotel."

Juliet seems peeved. "It's not that."

"A beach resort then," I say, remembering that she collects twilights and seashells.

"My! You really are silly! I mean Debussy's *Sea, La Mer.*"

"Oh," I say, affecting an attitude of not being amazed at whatever this amazing woman who never gets amazed says. Or does.

"Don't you know someone who could lend you a Victrola? We don't have one."

It's as if she had asked me if I knew someone who could lend me a desk. A Victrola was a piece of furniture and the gramophone the Pino Zittos (also called the Pini Zitti) had was, in fact, a roll-top desk, with drawers for the speakers, shelves for the records, and a sliding panel for the turntable. But then I think of Olga Andreu and remember her portable record player, a square suitcase.

"Maybe," I say. "We also need the record."

"Of course," she says, as if it were as easy as pie. Olga Andreu has just recently bought *La Mer,* it so happens, during her impressionist phase, impressed by Debussy but especially by Ravel. I don't mention Ravel to Juliet so as not to provoke her desire to ball to the beat of *Bolero,* coitus as a sequence, the rhythm repeated in different pitches by my instrument in crescendo until reaching orgasm a tutti.

"You think you could bring it tomorrow?" She's referring to *La Mer,* but her question implies record, record player, and a few trips abroad.

"I'll try," I say to her.

"Yes," she says, "try," and we say good-bye with a kiss, she still lying in bed, bare, pornography on her way to being graphic, after recapturing the lost pose. Jealousy makes me hate the fact that she's going to receive Vicente just like that.

Despite the idea that making love (as Juliet said) to the sound of the sea, or rather *La Mer,* seemed as *recherché* to me as visiting the cemetery to see graves, I tried *pour l'esprit de son corps,* using all my persuasive gifts and then some, to get Olga Andreu to lend me her compact record player and new long-playing record of *La Mer*. Like Vicente she worked in a bank, appropriate symmetry, and couldn't play her records during the day. Her sour mother was indifferent to music and her (deaf then, now deceased) grandmother Finita only attended her granddaughter's gatherings for the pleasure of the company, not because she could hear the conversations or background music. I told Olga that there was this poor invalid boy in Old Havana who was wild about the sea, which he couldn't see from his dark garret, really a cell for a forced spiritual retreat. Since he couldn't see the sea he wanted, at least, to hear it. All lies, of course, except for the fact that someone in Old Havana wanted to hear *La Mer*. Olga could have easily told me to get a conch shell for this islander who longed for the sea. This would have been ironic since it was I who by listening to *La Mer* got myself a conch. But finally she agreed to the loan on the condition that I would return the record player that very afternoon, which was fine by me. I wasn't going to leave the record player in Juliet's house, enough evidence for Vicente to evince Juliet. Late request and early agreement occurred the night of that day, and the next morning I had to go from my house on the Havanan frontier of El Vedado, where Olga Andreu lived, take, under Selmira's watchful eye, record and record player, and return to Old Havana, where Juliet lived. I was so poor then that making all those trips around my world in half a day spelt ruin, though each trip cost only five cents. Thus I arrived in ruinous state at Juliet's house, but it didn't show because of the triple triumph: I had obtained the record player and the musical *mer* and could have Juliet if only for an hour (the trips had consumed almost all my money and time), despite the fact that we wouldn't be alone, now accompanied by Debussy, who never imagined that his music could be an aphrodisiac. (But it was more than a love philter. In Juliet's letter to me on her honeymoon she said: "You say that art is a lie. Is the sea a lie?" Though she hadn't capitalized or underlined the sea, I was now sure that she was referring to Debussy's *Sea.*)

When she saw me enter, a solitary magus off season, loaded down with record player and record, she gasped. The record cover was a discreet affair: a uniform navy blue with only the work's title and the names of the composer and the performer in legible letters, but she knew it was the seafarer in reverse: home came the sailor, home with the sea. She smiled a surf of a smile with those white even teeth. "So you got it," she said, but didn't ask. "So it seems," I said, following Oliver Hardy's neat advice to Stan Laurel and trying hard to be nonchalant. She immediately led me into the room and began to make a place for the record player on her night table. There was a socket beside the bed but plugging in the record player wasn't everything. How did it work? I had seen Olga Andreu make it work with smooth skill, but since I was in her house to listen, not to look, I had never noticed how the machine worked and I forgot to ask her, of course, the night before. Now I had to look like an

193

expert to Juliet, as I scrutinized the hermetic surface of the record player (now out of its case but no less inscrutable) and saw the different cybernetic buttons and the pin to place the record on, in a mechanical copulation, barely understanding a thing. But lady luck always comes to the rescue of the lost lover. I placed the record on the pin and moved one of the many handles around the platter, and the arm with the needle came to rest precisely on the edge of the record. In a moment "The sea from dawn to midday" began to make musical waves. But in my memory I don't hear the vaguest *jeux de vagues:* I'm all eyes when I turn around and find Juliet nude, not a *maja* in bed, but rather Man Ray's *Nude de dos*—Juliet in bed but heightening her curves: her soft and shapely shoulders, her hip or half a hip, her beautiful bottom and her fascinating face half turned to me to beckon, a beacon of beauty. She now says "Let's" and in less time than it takes me to say fuck, despite my occasional stutter, I've taken off my clothes and embrace Juliet standing and together we fall on the bed, kissing as we never have before, I climbing on top of her, she seeking my penis with her hand, directing it, putting it in and with a movement of her hip inserting it like an outsized suppository. Dildo will do. She begins moving like yesterday, as if floating on the bed, which is not to her a solid piece but a colloidal medium, another sea, and I feel that I'm going to come but I contract my belly, bend my plexus, withdraw the penis and the imminent orgasm never happens, until she begins her swaying movements again, back and forth, like the tide, and today she doesn't cry out like yesterday because of course she's listening to *La Mer.* But I don't hear a thing except the blood throbbing in my temples—and now comes the great coming I can no longer repress and she feels, above or below the sea, that I'm coming and begins to hurry her orgasm without a word, warning screams, or guttural groans, and I'm feeling it and though it's too early in my sex life to know the value of orgasm *a duo,* I'm still coming while she's enjoying her climax, swaying the surface of the bed and apparently the whole room and for me really the whole world, sun, stars, and universe—waves swaying, waves moving, waves expanding to infinity. When we finish, when the undulations have ceased and only a throbbing remains in my flaccid penis still inside her, Juliet says below: "Isn't Debussy wonderful?"—and I can almost swear that she hasn't gone to bed with me but with old Claude Achille, failed mariner, triumphant Neptune, god of *La Mer.*

Then she insists on hearing *La Mer* one more time, leaving me out of the tune, the sea without sex. But I'm getting worried about this second session because it's much later than eleven and Vicente must be on his way already and it would be hard for him to believe that we are naked in bed together only to listen to *La Mer.* I suggest this to Juliet and she flares her nostrils, breathing deeply, a symptom of annoyance more than of foul odors, and says: "Will you let me listen to *LA MER* in peace"—in capitals to show her exaggerated emphasis. Of course I let her listen to *La Mer* on her shore of the bed, but meanwhile I'm getting dressed and ready to leave the room, the apartment, and Old Havana as soon as possible. Fortunately the dialogue of the wind and the sea ends, like all conversations, in silence. The coda has not yet ended but, without waiting for the vehement applause, I'm already taking *The Sea* off the turntable, the record still revolving, returning it to its cover, closing the record player, pulling out the plug, and putting the cable away in its ad hoc compartment. Meanwhile, Juliet is still in an esthetic ecstasy that I wished were erotic, and she says: "It's a pity you have to take it back"—not referring to my penis of course or to the record player or record but to *La Mer.* "Yes," I say, without affirming that it's a pity, "but there's nothing we can do," as if separating from *La Mer* were a fatal disease. "Anyway, thanks a lot," she says. And while I wonder if the thanks is for my performance or the orchestra's, knowing that she must be referring to *La Mer,* I say: "No, thank you," and I should have added thanks for letting me go to bed for the first time with a woman, thanks for your beauty, thanks for having repeated that occasion which will be unique: I'll remember that incredible initiation all my life, eternally grateful for I'm still doing it now, more than a quarter of a century later. But something like profound gratitude must have been in my voice: she, still naked in bed, smiles to me with that seaborne smile of hers and says: "Favor for favor." But Vicente's presence is pressing and I already hear him approaching the door, opening it, entering, and I have to tell Juliet: "I'm off." And she says: "I know." And I ask her: "When shall we see each other again?" "Tomorrow if you wish." "Same time?" "Yes." "Okay. See you tomorrow," and this time I stoop over her naked body to give her a last kiss. I intended it to be a nice gentle farewell kiss, but Juliet turns it into a vulpine kiss for Little Lord Ridinghood. Bite and devour.

The next day I received a lesson. Speaking of which, my class attendance at Journalism School was getting lower and lower. I was leaving my studies behind for Juliet, as I had left them behind before for the arts, for reading, for literature: my true education, a vocation. The next morning I was again in Juliet's (and Vicente's, I can't forget) dark and spare apartment (how dare I speak of spare rooms?), making love, as she says —not fucking as I prefer to say. After the first fuck, she said, with one of her gentle euphemisms, with her horror of vulgarity: "Kiss me below." It was the first time I was to do divine diving, and though I had read in naughty novelettes meticulous details about this oral operation, I hadn't the slightest experience with underwater kissing. So, obeying Juliet, I stopped kissing her mouth to slide down between her breasts, down her stomach, and below the belly to where I went to kiss her, literally, and I encountered an unexpected dampness. Even for her, always wet. She was now flooded. A strong sour smell of semen came off her. I bounced back up, a diver with cramps, to her face, which was the surface of my love. "What's up?" she asked, noticing my grimace. Careful not to utter a vulgarity that could hurt her, I didn't say it was full of cum or crammed with cream, but rather explained lamely: "It's very wet." "So what?" she

195

asked, almost threateningly. "It doesn't smell good." Then she moved her face away, inhaled deeply, and looked at me with the expression with which she must have looked at Germán Puig in that pluperfect past when she told him: "Your life is a fraud. You don't read anymore," to say to me now: "Dear, love is wet and doesn't smell good." I am still indebted to her for her frankness, showing me the diverse tactile tactics and olfactory forms sex takes: she helped me overcome an aversion, an atavism from small-town life. But at that moment I was even more grateful to her for getting up and going to the bathroom.

When she returned it was obvious that she had washed herself because she said: "Try it now." I tried, but my tongue was made for talking and, aside from the excessive saliva, I immediately got a hair, or rather a pubic hair, a long one, between my lips, in my mouth, in my throat, like a soft thorn forcing me to make horrible, gross noises. I withdrew my face from her mask to see, enormous to my myopic eyes, the labia majora and the clitoris and I recited: "Madam, there are two Latin leopards beneath a juniper tree," before donning the beard again. Her sex, her not-at-all-menacing vagina, her vulva, in vulgar Havana style her comely Cuban cunt was opening itself to me: the first I ever saw opened, welcoming me like a house, inviting me to knock and enter. I began to kiss her, but from above she indicated precisely: "Use your tongue." I used it, "Tip, a little more tip." I tipped more. "Now the rosebud." I obeyed. And she began to move as if my member were inside, twisting, turning, gyrating.

At one point, while resting, I brushed her clitoris and she screamed: "Yes! There!" I again brushed her clitoris with my tongue, surrounding, turning circles around it, rubbing it, and she began to moan, to scream. She directed me, without words, with her hands on my head, in the operation of rubbing my now hard tongue against her clit, gift to the tongue, till all was wet from my saliva and then from her discharge, bursting out from all sides, fragrant fountain, smelling as much as it flowed but it was a sweet smell, intense but not at all unpleasant like the lye stench of semen, odious odor though mine. She groaned gutturally, twisted, turned, and raised my face with her revolving vulva, saying: "Yes! That's it!" many times in a row—and finally she was still, totally inert. It was then I knew she had come and, as it has never made any sense to me to kiss a corpse, I stopped rubbing my tongue against her clitoris. I heard a voice: "Come up here." It was she, back to life. "Come inside," she ordered me with a commanding yet languorous voice, a mellifluous tone from mellow Mélisande to polite Pelléas. As my first master was a mistress, I obeyed her order to climb on top. Though she seemed lethargic, stretched out with her arms along her collapsed body, she received me with a shiver, which instantly turned into a reflex movement, some sign of life. Before I had time to marvel at how quickly she had recovered, her hips escaping and seeking me, her vulva volant, her covering cunt moving around my naked penis, adopting, adapting it, the two tethered by that other umbilical cord, moving us in unison, like the mother with her son in her belly, my fanatic fetus fused with her—and in this fantasy we climaxed together. In love's lewd labor she finally gave birth to me.

I tumbled back on the bed, as if just born and at the same time lying beside her, dead, still, inert from that post-coitus lassitude, born an adult, which I now felt for the first time: I was born again and born dead, stillborn. It was the first time I enjoyed, suffered, experienced this little death—translated from French à la Juliet. Before, it had all been a continuous fuck, one after the other, but today I reached that often praised afterglow. It made me almost doze off, awakened only by my awareness of Vicente's return: thinking of Vicente I almost fell asleep to half wake up still thinking of Vicente: if the sex had been a session, this Vicente thing was an obsession and, as she had phrased it in her lost letter when speaking of Van Gogh, "Poor Vincent!," I had just discovered that I felt sorry for Vicente. So I got up, said good-bye and went away with new knowledge, the experience of my new birth, but also with sadness: the idea that I was deceiving Vicente. Although, after all, what did I care, a distant friend, if Juliet was deceiving Vicente (or not)? I didn't care, said my censor, and so I would be able to face Vicente, be in his company, look him in the eye and not blink even once.

Around that time María Valero was killed. She was a famous radio actress, adored by ladies, housewives, and even charwomen, for the soupy soap operas she starred in. I had heard her many times and, despite her velvety voice, she didn't seem like an extraordinary actress, though my mother thought she was the Eleonora Sarah Duse Bernhardt of radio. For immortality's sake, María Valero died in a tragic way. Late one night she had gone with a group of actors (among them María Escalante and Orlando Artajo, a specialist in heavenly bodies) to see a comet flying low over Havana at that hour, and they chose the Malecón to go and find what the newspapers called the "comet of death." As they crossed the deserted avenue, out of nowhere—or from fate—came a speeding car. The group of amateur astronomers split up in panic and most of the pedestrians grouped on one side of the street while María Valero remained on the other alone, and the driver drove the car, apparently out of control, toward where there were fewer people—barely anybody except for this black-haired woman in black, almost invisible in the night. The vehicle dragged her almost a hundred yards and, according to Orlando, you could hear her bones cracking like shots, her death as resonant as her radio life. There was a national commotion and station CMQ decided to render her a posthumous but macabre homage, consisting of a program in which María Valero would be speaking for the last time. This speech from beyond the grave would be composed of many pieces of dramatic recordings by the actress. Juliet, who knew the actress and was herself an actress, wanted to hear it but she didn't have a radio, and she asked to come to my house. Our radio was old and, what's worse, given to strange waves, letting you hear when it wanted and broadcasting loud

197

and clear when you least expected. But I told Juliet that she could come to my house to hear the program. My mother liked the idea of her coming. I had told her that Juliet was an actress and you already know how my mother loved actors: at the movies, on stage, on the radio—but especially in person. With Juliet came Vicente.

When it was time for the program to start, we turned on the radio and the presentation came out very clear, with an echo that resounded not from the radio station but from across the River Styx. But as soon as María Valero came on the air from the world above, the radio, mediocre medium, began to emit strange noises: trills, fritters, buzzes: the whole gamut! But the voice from beyond could barely be heard: it was a half hour of parasitic static and here and there some strange intervention by María Valero. Finally the program was over as well as the torture by radio—then another kind of ordeal began, softer but harsher. Vicente was talking to me about brushes, palettes, and painters, and I was trying hard to look him straight in the face as we talked. Adding insult to injury, Juliet, who liked to play with danger, had crossed her legs to reveal a naked piece of thigh, then uncrossed her lusty leg and, upon doing so, brushed her foot along my calf, deliberately, her shoe tartly touching my trousers. I thought everybody in the room had realized what she had done, but fortunately nobody noticed, while Vicente continued talking about painting. Finally, after an embarrassing moment in which Vicente almost confessed that he was thinking of leaving the bank to dedicate himself fully to painting—"I don't want to be a Sunday painter all my life"—Juliet and Vicente said good-bye and left. My mother said, as a résumé of the visit: "Juliet's husband is very good-looking," and I felt a welcome jealousy, which made me forget the embarrassment of his presence.

The next day I went to Juliet's house, as usual. I told her, as she undressed, how uncomfortable I'd been the night before. "Yes," she said, "that radio doesn't work well at all." I had to be explicit and tell her I wasn't talking about the radio but that I'd been embarrassed in front of Vicente and that even at this very moment I felt guilty. She stopped undressing to look at me: "Guilty about what?" "About what we're doing to Vicente," I said. "It's a dirty trick." She took a deep breath and when I thought she was going to slur me, to tell me that I didn't write anymore, that my life was a fraud, she said to me: "Love has no morals." She silenced me with that response, and not content with leaving me speechless she added: "But, if you feel that way, I think you should go," and she began to put her clothes back on, now declaring that morality has no love. I knew that my scruples were going to deprive me of my life with Juliet, which was the best thing that had happened in my life—and I didn't move. "If you don't go," she said, her body almost dressed, "you're a hypocrite." This time she was totally right. I had scruples about going to bed with Juliet and at the same time what I most desired in the world was to go to bed with her. "Why must I go?" I asked her, thinking that she was angry at me. "It's very clear: because of Vicente. You feel guilty for what you're doing to him, so you should stop it." I thought of a new slant: "And you don't feel guilty?" "I?" she said, looking truly amazed. "Why should I feel guilty? Vicente is not man enough for me in bed. The most natural thing is for me to look for my satisfaction elsewhere." Her logic was irrefutable, my censor said, why the hell did you have to talk about Vicente? Now I had to go, not forced by my censor but by pride. "Okay," I said, "I'm going," sadder I should have added but also calmer—and I left, hesitating only a moment at the door to see if she'd stop me, say something. She was now fully dressed and didn't say a thing to stop me.

How long did that calm spell last? By the next day I was no longer tranquil, remembering, seeing that naked body covered with desire. It wasn't love I felt for Juliet but desire. A goddess was the name of my desire. It didn't take me long to venerate that venereal goddess again. But the next time I went to see Juliet, not love but a surprise was waiting for me. She wasn't expecting me so early, but instead of her amazement I produced my own. I found another visitor who had come even earlier than me—and it wasn't the milkman. There, sitting on a chair in her living room, was Max Mature, who greeted me with a suspicious smile. Max Mature was an old Communist, or rather, he wasn't old (though much older than I) since he belonged to the party youth. I don't remember where I met him, perhaps at the newspaper *Hoy,* or preparing the takeover, a Hegelian putsch, of *Our Time.* The truth is, my annoyance at finding him in Juliet's house (I had considered her all mine, after Vincente) grew into an argument over the virtues of the Orthodox party and Eddy Chibás. Max Mature won by simply using his calm tone, his poised party dialectics, designed for power, and I lost by losing control of myself, almost shouting like Eddy Chibás in his historic hysteria—in a word, by not being mature enough. But it wasn't politics that was at stake, of course: it wasn't who was master of words but rather slave of Juliet. Upon entering I had noticed a stain on Max Mature's lip and could have sworn that this stigma extended below, that it was a slow drop of blood —and nobody shaves his lip no matter how much it droops. I already knew Juliet's kind of kissing too well not to know that that clot came from a bite. In short, it became a disturbing image: I, Vicente's delegate, had caught them in fraganti. Thence came my anger, which I couldn't control and which made me reveal myself as a political idiot to this man who was no contender for me in an argument—neither he nor his ideology nor his rigid dialectics. Besides, why show so much sympathy, even support, for the Orthodox party when not even Eddy Chibás, in his madness without method, really mattered to me? It was, as Juliet would have said, the trace of a kiss that unhinged me, making me an erotic double of political Chibás. I was so impassioned that I don't even remember how I left that house, but I must have gone out hating Marx Mature and hating Juliet even more, double deceiver of her husband and her lover. But I couldn't hate Juliet for long because she was love—another name for lust.

I don't remember how we got back together, I only know that we organized a rendezvous in no man's land but on love's territory. Juliet wanted to go to a *posada* as in the past she had wanted to go fuck in the cemetery or listen to *La Mer* as she made love. To me it seemed like a waste of money (which I didn't have: it was like wasting nothing) when we could be so comfortable in her house, now that I had conquered the fear of the unexpected or rather expected return of Vicente. At least the immature polemics with Mature helped me there: spending half the morning arguing as if we were in Central Park or at party headquarters convinced me that one could do everything in Juliet's house with impunity—even make love. Vicente would never debank inopportunely: what better proof than that argument? (It was hard to imagine Vicente's face, upon returning unexpectedly from the bank and finding his house turned into the stage of a political convention.) But Juliet insisted (your desires are my sires, O goddess) and I had to gratify her. I had to borrow money. Though a *posada* didn't cost much (*hôtel de nuit,* my Frenchified Juliet insisted on calling them even in daylight), anything was too much for me then, a poor journalist in bloom.

We went to the infamous inn. Juliet let me choose and I chose the fabulous—it was in all the sexual fables of the era—*posada* on Second and Thirty-first. In the late afternoon but not too late. We walked from where the bus left us on Twenty-third and Paseo. We got off discreetly so as not to cause suspicion in the conductor and strolled up Paseo until finding as if by accident (the precaution was mine, Juliet had other ideas about desire and decency) Thirty-first Street, which at that hour reverberated under the sun: the dust like reflecting sand, the sidewalks, fallen mirrors, the two of us characters in a Cocteau movie. Near the *posada* door was a group of boys, peeping tommies, evidently registering everyone who went in and out—especially every woman, all projections of Godiva under her horse. But Juliet walked like a queen those few blocks to the enchanted building, passing regally through the big entrance for cars and even accompanying me to the front desk (is that the expression?) to request the room, not remaining discreetly behind as I had been instructed that women should do according to Havana's amatory conventions. They gave us a downstairs room and we entered, she first, a novice about to leave the world outside. Juliet surveyed the room not only with her eyes but with her legs, as if measuring its exact symmetry, examining each corner, parting the curtains, which kept out the violent afternoon light, entering the small bathroom, opening the faucets, returning to the room: a complete inspection, while I waited for her to take off her clothes. But instead of getting undressed she disclosed: "You know," she said to me, "I've never been in an *hotel de passe.*" *Ça me dépasse!* I should have said, but she surprised me and, what's more, pleased me: it was like violating a virginity with her. Her frankness led me to ask myself how Vicente hadn't taken her to a *posada.* I answered my own question: I was forgetting that she reserved her virginity for marriage. Again I asked myself where she had bedded down (chastely), with Felix. Answering myself that perhaps he had scruples about taking her to a *posada*. Adding myself that Felix was too poor to afford a *posada*—I was in this question-and-answer session when I heard a sweet-voiced order, polite but peremptory: it was Juliet, not the spirit, who was saying to me aren't you coming and I saw she had taken off all her clothes (she wasn't wearing much on that hot afternoon: only a flimsy madras dress) and had lain down on the bed, completely naked, less *maja* than woman. I asked myself when she had gotten undressed but didn't waste any time in answering and I joined her, an absolute minority, putting in practice *in corpore* all the theory she had taught me.

This time Juliet (who liked to moan, not mourn, but to exclaim in ecstasy) let go as soon as my labile, now agile, tongue began touching her body. She began to sail on other seas of madness: moaning, sighing deeply, cries from the deep of her committed body. From there she passed on to groans, then cries, then howls, and as she twisted and turned, making my labor more laborious, she meowed at the top of her lungs, a coarse cat, her howls filling the room and ululating throughout the universe, filling the void and culminating the cosmos. It was because of her coloratura that I didn't hear people knocking until after they had knocked twice, ten times, an uproar outside the door that awoke us both. Juliet interrupted her broadcast from deep Debuseas and I went to see what was wrong. It wasn't the firemen at the door but rather the ticket tout, the superintendent, the innkeeper, who in a whisper (any human sound was a whisper after Juliet's cosmic cries), asked if we could make a little less noise—and that request really surprised me because they had to be used to all sorts of sentimental sounds in that place. But I wasn't too surprised, realizing that Juliet's unholy howls could very well establish a record of decibel tools in that house of attrition. When I returned to Juliet I didn't explain when she asked me, "What's the matter?" but rather said: "Nothing, it was the wrong room," when I should have said: "Everything, this is the last round!" Juliet's smile relieved me of such semantic games. But it wasn't a commentary on what was going on but rather the same expression she'd had for a while, before I closed the door, and she now said: "I had one." I didn't understand until she elaborated: "Alone, all by myself. Do you know why?" No, I said, surprised at her statement: I knew that Juliet was a man baiter but not a *pajera*, a masturbator. The orgasm hadn't come from her hand, though, but from the house: "It's this place," she explained. "It excites me. From the moment I entered I was wet. It excites me to know that this building is made exclusively for the act of love, that people come here only to make love, that the whole place is organized for making love. Architecture at the service of love!" A typical statement of Juliet's in those days. I never told her that she had attracted the attention of the architect himself. I imagined it was the first time that had happened. Then I thought Juliet had moaned so much only to establish her presence in the *posada*—or perhaps to excite the other guests? (Can *posada* patrons be called guests? I don't know. I don't have another name to give them, but somehow *guests* doesn't seem to be the proper term. Nor *patrons*. Perhaps Juliet, a master in the language of love, would know what name to give them, us. But I never asked her.)

Somehow I found myself thinking (finger on forehead, hand on temple, thumb on jaw) that I was reading too much D. H. Lawrence. Juliet had lent me the translation of *Lady Chatterley's Lover* when she was still living in sin with her parents, and it was very difficult to get that book in Havana then. Today I tend to think she got it for me as an aphrodisiac, but at that moment I thought it was her interest in English literature. Her comment, when I returned the volume, could or couldn't have been literary. "Isn't it truly powerful?" she said. After she initiated me I started looking for everything by Lawrence that had been translated into Spanish, since it was easier to get books in Spanish than in English: there was no English lending library that I remember in Havana but there was at least one that lent books in Spanish—Lawrence at the Lyceum. I read every bit of Lawrentiana, even the letters of Lawrence, a postal prophet. Perhaps I was excessively influenced by Lawrence, but whether or not I was, one day, without being truly in love with Juliet, I did tell her that we should elope. I had a plan of escape, to go together to a desert island (it should have been a quiet key, since we were already on an island, Cuba), to commune with nature, abandon Havana and its Havanity. I don't know if you know me this early in the book, but if you do you would realize that I'm incapable of surviving not only on a desert island (or key), but even in the city without the help of my family. Despite my working-class origins, born in poverty, living in misery, I'm a mama's boy who runs home for shelter at the slightest difficulty and who always goes to bed early. But I'm also daring in theory and might have gone with Juliet to another island—or deserted key.

This escapist proposition had the perplexing virtue of bringing Juliet back to bed and reality. She leaned on the pillow, rising from below the sheet, her islands of full fleshy breasts floating golden upon the white edge, foam of Venus, and said to me: "Are you crazy?" "No, not crazy," I said. "Simply in love." She paid no attention to my declaration of love but rather stuck to her former wrong impression: "Only a madman would think of such an idea! A desert island? Do you know what you're saying?" "Well, yes. We should go to an uninhibited—I mean uninhabited—island." "How? Swimming?" I suspected she knew that I didn't know how to swim. "No, walking over the waters. Don't you believe in miracles?" "You're out of your mind!" she said, and with that diagnosis our separation really began. Though, thinking it over, we were never together. Only sex joined us: my penis, my tongue, my arms: my members—and though I thought then that love could unite us, I think I would have accepted this version or verdict, had someone suggested it. "Let's see," said Juliet, the logician, "what would we do on a desert island that we can't do here in bed?" Her argument was unbeatable. What's more, she could have added that in bed I could do something I wouldn't know how to do on a desert island: swim. But, wrangler that I am, I thought of a counterargument: "We could be together all the time." By the look Juliet gave me I knew she was going to say she didn't want to be with me *all* the time. But she said: "We can be together a lot here," almost like a schoolmarm lecturing to the lower classes, which I really hate. "You can also come in the afternoons, if you want." "And at night?" I asked, totalitarian. "That leaves only the nights and at night one sleeps." What about two? I almost asked her. She wasn't going to make me believe, of course, that she only slept at night, meaning, the nights were used by her (and Vicente) only for sleeping. I told her so: "And do you use the nights only for sleeping?" "Of course," she said, convincingly. But I said: "I don't believe you." "Besides," she said, continuing her arguments without recognizing my contradiction, "how would we live? You can't even support me right here in Havana. A desert island!" She didn't say this sarcastically but rather like a sigh, after a deep breath and almost exclaiming: "Your island is a fraud!" But it sounded sarcastic and mocking to me: I had lost all notion of the meaning of words at that moment, with the desert-island idea floating in my head like a tropical Laputa. I was completely disoriented, or rather had lost the Orient of Juliet's precious words. "Besides," she said with a besides beside the point, pointless. "Even if we could, *I* don't want to live on a desert island." She didn't say: "And that's that" or "Period," or the Havanan *"Sanseacabó,"* but it sounded definite. That morning I would have left without my quota of flesh if I hadn't taken the precaution of suggesting our escape to a desert island after making love, as she said, and not before.

But this argument didn't put an end to my relationship with Juliet. What did was the real fact that she moved, and false folk wisdom. She moved to Twenty-eighth Street, almost on the corner of Twenty-third, and I visited her there for the last time one afternoon. Unlike the beginning, on those cold mornings in Old Havana with its seedy, somber, and sinuous streets, it was the hot afternoon of El Vedado, with its straight, spacious, sunny avenues, too exposed to the sun, summery. The apartment—much larger than the one in Old Havana—was on a first floor, and when I rang the bell (an electric bell, not the twisted bell of Catia's house or the three theatrical knocks—"Destiny calling on Beethoven," Queta Faría would have said—on the door of her former apartment) Juliet came to open the door, dressed, as the first time I visited her, in an apron except there was a slight difference now. She wasn't wearing anything under the apron—covering her from bellybutton down to her knees—and that was her outfit. Above, her breasts bulged bare and, when she closed the door and turned around, her buttocks were exposed. I wondered what would have happened if one of the workers from the construction site on the corner had rung the bell—and the schoolmarm had opened the door wearing nothing more than that figment of a figleaf, as she did with me.

But the physical display enhanced by the domestic touch of the apron was for me: she was expecting me. "Excuse me for a moment while I finish," she said. "I didn't expect you so early." She wasn't expecting me: being dressed or undressed that way was only a reaction to the afternoon heat, exorcising the stifling summer. "It's okay," I said. "Don't worry about me. Take your time." She bustled around the room, all the while talking about Michelangelo, though she might as well have been talking about Raphael or Leonardo because I didn't get the prominent pictorial points she was making. Instead I sat down to watch her scrubbing, running the wet rag over the floor tiles near me, turning around to present her round ass, double truncated spheres, which I contemplated, like Pascal, out of an interest in geometry. She finally finished. That is, she took off her apron as a signal that her domestic tasks had ended and she could now begin her labors of love. She came toward me and stopped in front of my face—stark naked. "Come to the room," she said, when I gave signs of being capable of coitus *sur place,* as Silvio Rigor would say.

Havanans have this superstition, probably backed by facts or myths, that fornicating after eating can lead to a sure stroke—and not exactly sunstroke. Havana had adopted me, which is why I felt obliged to tell Juliet: "I've just had lunch, but let's go"—and it was as if I had mentioned a chat with the Devil in front of the Pope. *"What?"* Juliet exclaimed. "You're not going to go to bed with me after eating!" "But it doesn't matter at all," I answered her. "It doesn't matter? No, my dear, none of that. I'm not going to let you die in my arms." I thought that, in her quick Havana accent, she was saying it with love, caring for my health, watching over my life. But she added: "I'm not running that risk." In that fatal, final phrase I saw that she didn't care a figleaf if I died, as long as I didn't do it in her bed: the truth more brutal than her words. I still didn't know if I was or wasn't in love with Juliet, but now I had found out that I was little more than a penis capable of more than one erection: for her the *Homo erectus,* a handy dick. The scene would have been amusing for an objective third party: this naked woman, with her well-made body (more than well-made: perfect) and her beautiful head discussing with her ill-starred lover, not matters of love, but rather the pros and cons of dying of a brain hemorrhage in her bed. I imagine that she must have already been calculating how to get rid of the corpus delicti, thinking up a perfect alibi, figuring out how to seem innocent in front of Vicente.

This is what I imagine but the actual argument was tiring because it wasn't dialectic, nor even didactic (Juliet-style) but rather repetitive, and it lasted too long. There was no way to move Juliet, to change her mind or heart: she wasn't going to go to bed with me for all the gold of El Dorado or for a silver-plated Potosí. That's my saying, because virtuous Juliet wasn't motivated by either gold or silver: money didn't matter to her. Only the flesh, but live flesh, not dead or dying flesh—and I was about to die if I had eaten just a little while ago, and then fucked. Finally, fatigued, I said I was going and I said good-bye in an ominous manner

—which she didn't register. She said it was okay, that I should come back another day—fasting, I suppose. But, I added, if I walk out that door I'm not coming back, almost pointing like a stage husband. "It's all right by me," she said, taking me at my word. "Don't come back," and I never returned to those kisses on her lips or on her labia. O goddess, odious goddess, golden goddess, never to see your nipples *e poi morire.*

Later, some time after our breakup (or whatever you would call that long argument and short good-bye), Juliet met Pablo Perera, a pianist with a penchant for boys. She decided, as she wasn't Virginia, that if Pablo wanted to be a concert pianist he should be named Paul, and Pablo liked the sound of his new name, Paul Perera. (It's curious that Juliet didn't try to change or Frenchify my name: it would have been comic had she persuaded me to call myself Guy.) So Pablo called himself Paul from then on, and, at the same time he changed his name, he changed his sex object, becoming Juliet's lover. (Surely Juliet initiated him in the mysteries of the Bona Dea of sex, as she did us all.) Apparently Pablo, Paul, didn't have lunch and spent all his afternoons with Juliet. But it happened that Vicente, predictable painter but unpredictable teller, came home from the bank inopportunely one day and found Juliet in tune with Pablo, Paul. He didn't catch them in bed, but, what seemed worse to Vicente, he caught (I don't know who was more caught) Paul wearing his dressing gown, decorated by him, at Juliet's request, with Japanese waves on the China Sea, yellow sun over magenta fabric. Vicente started punching Paul and in the squabble Paul bit Vicente's ear (perhaps the other way around, I don't know: it was a confusing fight or story). Vicente didn't touch a hair on Juliet's adorable, adored body but left the house, without taking a thing, not even the hand-painted robe (oil on silk), while Juliet remained to lovingly cure Paul's wounds. He didn't complain— that's a Perera for you. When I found out about the fisticuffs (from Juliet herself, who told me everything and finally added, inhaling to exhale: "Imagine, how vulgar!," accusing Vicente of fakery: his life was, without a doubt, a bank fraud), I thought that I could very well have been in Pablo, Paul, Popol Perera's place, and that I was spared the guilty embarrassment and the beating (Vicente Vega, daily toiler as teller, Sunday painter Vincent, was also Vicente the Avenging Angel and high-school athlete), saved from that double affront by a Havana superstition—or rather, by Julia Estévez's firm belief that (after eating) making love kills.

VIGIL OF THE NAKED I

By chance or by the design of ironic gods, we were now living in El Vedado on the top of a hill—yet another Havana hill. Avenida de los Presidentes ends here, at the monument overlooking the central gardens: to these august heights my country cousin Gildo Castro and I had climbed one memorable day, scaling the pretentious portico, classical in its academic arcade but rococo in its hybrid details. Cousin Gildo, on a visit from town to buy blow torches for his repair shop, saw all of Havana with me but nothing seemed as portentous to him as this bleached tomb in memory of all the dead presidents. Gildo (a mechanical magician) had brought with him a movie camera he himself had built, and set up shots I never got to see on the screen—or anywhere else, for that matter. My cousin Gildo, naïve like all inventors, or at least enthusiastic, said of this monument fixed forever in film: "Solid marble!" He then added, turning around to admire the avenue going down to the sea in the distance and all its arboreal adornments: "By God, all this was made by man!," the highest compliment he could pay the view, having inherited from his father Pepe Castro (a mechanical genius) his love for the works of man rather than of mother nature.

All this was near the Palace building, where Catia Ben Como had lived and where Olga Andreu was still living. Across from them, in the Chibás Building, lived Tomás Alea, alias Titón, whom I called Tomás Alea Jacta though he was not a boasting jackass but rather the opposite, modest to the point of being invisible. Néstor Almendros, already a photographer, introduced me to Titón, through whom I met Olga Andreu through whom I met, in this daisy chain, Catia. Titón—whom I visited often in his large, neat, upper-middle-class apartment—was now a friend who would soon take a doubly desired trip to Rome to study cinema. All these visitors from the past, and voyages into the future, made the neighborhood gratifyingly glamorous, especially after tenement life at Zulueta 408: so hard to leave and impossible to forget because it had been not a season or stopover but a lifetime among the concentric circles of hell. All thanks to a minor miracle made possible by my mentor: a countryman of his was off to Puerto Rico and left us his apartment—after taking a gratuity.

But we were still as poor as ever and soon, with my father out of work, we would be even poorer. My brother was still consumptive and would get worse, his tuberculosis spreading to both lungs: he almost died. Thus I was the subject of a movie, not of a portrait, of the artist as a poor young man. After my grandmother joined us, we had yet another resident in the incredibly elastic room at Zulueta 408. (We had practically solved the insoluble medieval conundrum of the number of angels who can stand all at once on the head of a pin, upon proving that six persons could live all at once in one room.) My green-eyed cousin had captivated a good neighbor and married, but they had gone off adventurously to live in a foreign country of the future. Our move was an escape, and thanks to the help (always depending on the kindness of friends) of Carlos Franqui, a *Mañana* newspaper van, and a truck my father somehow got hold of (perhaps through Eloy Santos, still the motorman, always mutinous) we moved secretly, late at night, like smugglers negotiating a border. Surviving the hazardous journey, we found ourselves in a furnished apartment with a telephone—and with a private bathroom! After the forced collectivism of the tenement, a toilet for us alone was a clean luxury. "And with a *bidet*!" my mother completed the inventory, adding the word *bidet* to my Havana vocabulary, though she never specified the nature or history of its usage. For a moment I thought she meant Bizet but had mispronounced it. The whole place smelled of roses, since its former tenant, an illegal chemist, made perfumes there, transforming his apartment into an attar. My mother looked younger now, not only because of the new habitat but because she stopped using the cheap black dye that made her look so somber with all that blackness around her, and her premature gray hair was a perfect frame for her hard, strong face and dark olive complexion. Her image was consecrated—an oval portrait—not by a poor man's Poe but by our Cocteau, Germán Puig. An eternal esthete and forever a flatterer, he told her: "Zoila, now you're a platinum blonde, like Harlow, better than Harlow," and though my mother's feminine ideal was Joan Crawford and not Jean Harlow, she gratefully accepted to be baptized by Germán Puig as the Natural Platinum Blonde.

In our new atmosphere we enjoyed both privacy and communication through that rare privilege, a closed door. Though this building (which one entered by a tall wood-and-glass door) was only four stories high, it was on the very top of the Upper Vedado hill and, since our apartment was on the last floor (reached by a simple marble staircase with iron banisters), we could view all the buildings in the area as well as the distant sea. Our heaven was also our hell, however: we were caressed by the morning breeze but invaded by the direct afternoon sun, declining but oppressive. In our high tower, now a lover's lookout, I learned at night the low art of the voyeur.

I must say that it wasn't really a discovery but simply that what had been a hobby before had now become an art. I began cultivating this cult when I was barely thirteen, in the second year of high school, thanks to our anatomy teacher's indifference. (I can't believe it was carelessness, and it certainly seemed more like a natural grace than a compulsive caprice.) She was the youngest teacher at school and her name was (and still is, I hope: though she may be an old lady now, she'll always have my gratitude) Isabel Miranda or, more respectfully, Professor Miranda. At the Institute the rostrum was always on raised platforms (inspiring in me, coming from informal primary school, an awe and respect that have lasted till today), which maintained the teachers over a yard above their students' intellectual level. The table and chair on the platform increased the distances, but Professor Miranda, unlike her colleagues, always sat to one side of the desk, not behind it. She usually crossed her legs, allowing her skirt to rise accidentally, showing not only her legs but parts of her massive thighs, looking as solid as the monument's marble to Cousin Gildo. She must have been around thirty then, for us an ancient age, but she made a bridge of flesh between her years and ours. I had Room 2 for that course and, double luck, the first row, feared by all the students in the algebra class (from there one went directly to the blackboard as if to the mathematical gallows), but desired by the boys during the anatomy lesson, thanks to Professor Miranda's generosity—with her anatomy? Like the women of her generation, she usually wore only a slip underneath. At times her dresses were sufficiently low-cut to allow one to see more than the beginning of her breasts: they were small but seemed surprisingly solid: more marble. When we were working with the microscope (placed on the table over which didactic Dr. Miranda bent to give us a better view of her skill), we naturally paid more attention to her magnificent milky-white breasts than to the milky vision of the magnified life of microbes. Her breasts now lost their mythic character (seen from our desks) to become neighborly, accessible, almost within reach of the impatient hand at the microscope. But they soon recovered their professorial distance and Professor Miranda (her eyes hidden behind green glasses which I have since then associated with a controlled but dangerous feminine sexuality, capable of being unleashed at any moment: like the adulterous Miriam killed by crazy Bruno in *Strangers on a Train*) again became the stuff smut myths are made of, discussed in the groups we formed in school corridors. Some of the students of comparative anatomy even swore that the teacher, whom we knew to be single, was easy—when actually she proved to be very difficult. None of us hit on her true nature, but I know now: Miss Miranda was Admiranda, exhibitionist extraordinary.

My second encounter with voyeurism was really the first. It happened that day I climbed, ailing, hanging on for dear life to the railing, the staircase to the roof of Zulueta 408 and looked out of boredom toward the Pasaje Hotel, façade of empty rooms, to discover the naked sleeper, all iodine and some peroxide—and that single vision brought me back to earth. I see her now as if through inverted binoculars, sequestered by time but also by the distance at which she slept naked. That was the true anatomy lesson and not those obscene closeups of Professor Miranda. Paradoxically, the more distant a body is, the closer it is to the revelation of the flesh. In Havana, where voyeurism was a kind of native passion, like cannibalism among the Caribs, there was no local word to describe this occupation that was a form of popular art. In Old Havana, profuse with open balconies protected only by a wrought-iron railing, a plank—known as the *tablita*—was usually erected to knee level, guarding desirable thighs from the sharp eye of voyeurs, eager eagles now grounded. This barrier could be seen on balconies as high up as the third or fourth floor, where visibility was, if not impossible, certainly difficult for even the keenest vision. Could it be that the inhabitants of those apartments —and visitors on those balconies—were provoking more than avoiding the enemy eye? There was a word for touchers, flesh feelers in Havana dialect, *rascabucheador* (meaning belly scratcher, but I prefer to preserve its tenuous local mystery, which gets thicker for foreigners) and this expression was also used, incorrectly, for voyeurs. The Spanish word for voyeur, *mirón* (from *mirar,* to look), indicated someone who looked a lot or persistently, but it isn't quite the same as voyeur or peeping tom, a kind of pervert who in sexology manuals is called a scopophiliac. But under any name that amorous activity exists and it was in the apartment on the corner of Twenty-seventh and Avenida de los Presidentes that I became a virile voyeur, a peeping thomas, an adult in pursuit of pubescence—finally an anatomist.

The apartment building facing us, the Santeiro, was lower than ours because it was downhill. (I would live there one day, and have described it elsewhere.) In our building many balconies opened toward the south side of the building facing the back of our apartment. Ours and this other building were separated by barely twenty meters of old one-story houses. From our balcony the view of the Santeiro apartments, though slanting, was complete. After dinner I used to sit out there, as if taking in the fresh air, the French windows to the living room closed, I alone in my nightwatch. Curiously, this was the most exciting part of the visual hunt: waiting for a nude to appear. It didn't matter if partial or total. In my eyes the stalking was more exciting than the actual presence of the naked body. Waiting was the art to be learned. Before, the naked bodies that had been inviting to me—Etelvina's diseased body, the black whore's invisible in the dark, the brief white visions of Xiomara, the repeated golden contemplation of Juliet, in which I did not tarry, urged on by the force of fornication, and the anonymous body innocently exhibited in the Pasaje Hotel—were not pursued by me to delight in their nudity: they were a beginning, not an end. But now I expressly sought that exhibition, which was, of course, unknown to these women—or girls. I was going to catch them in their intimacy without their even suspecting it: victims of the voyeur's visual violation. I think that if any of them had exhibited themselves ex-professo, the vision would have ipso facto lost its charms —the rules of the game, or rather, the precepts of the art of peeping.

I had fixed my attention, which is like saying my whole consciousness, even my physical being, my body, now all eyes, on the Santeiro Building. In the apartment facing ours lived a woman (I can't say her age but she obviously wasn't a girl) who often offered a concert of screams, an aria *a cappella*. I expected such shouting at Zulueta 408 but not in El Vedado, in one of its (apparently) most decent buildings. (I'm suggesting that the building wasn't inhabited by decent people when it really was, which I was able to verify when I lived there years later. Let me also ask you to forget the phrase *decent building* because it's a poor, pathetic fallacy, pure prosopopeia.) But this woman went from talking tantrums to horrible howls in the one-sided arguments she had with an always silent consort. Later I learned that this mute man was not her husband but her lover, and that he was a radio comedian famous for his gift of gab. I also learned that the woman was a hard drug addict and that many of her fits of fury occurred when she lacked not marijuana but morphine. It's curious how much one could find out about those supposedly watertight compartments, the big buildings of the neighborhood: Santeiro, Palace, Chibás—with their elegant architecture, hermetic appearance, and such seemingly solid middle-class tenants. Perhaps the climate had an influence: in these apartments people lived with their windows (if not their doors) opened to mitigate the heat—isolating air conditioning was not yet in general use. But perhaps the explanation was more historical than geographical: it wasn't the tropics but rather the Cuban character that made people reveal themselves, literally and metaphorically. Mexicans, for example, live in the same climate but are much more reserved. The Indian is inscrutable while the Negro is always expansive, and although all the neighborhood families were white, they had more of the talkative Andalusian in them than the taciturn Castilian. I must point out that the neighbor across the way was as exhibitionist physically as she was with her emotions. I had only to catch her at the right moment, though she was easy prey (I can't avoid hunting language), and soon she would appear more or less undressed, perhaps naked. But I had to wait several watches, in which as soon as night fell, after dessert and coffee, I perched at my post on the balcony. Only on Saturdays and Sundays, of course: the rest of the week I went to work nights as a private secretary, and when I came home it was already too late. But on these two brief holidays my long wait expanded time, while my spying became an obsession as I abandoned the movies, girls, friends, cultural congresses, literature itself for this vigil, a word that the dictionary defines, with unconscious irony, as intellectual labors executed at night. I didn't execute these labors of love at any other hour, but I couldn't say they were intellectual though all my activity was mental.

One night—nobody can measure the duration of time for the voyeur

—I saw this woman come out of the room. I believed then that every apartment in the Santeiro had many rooms (the grass is always greener in the eye of the beholder, an old saw or sore from Zulueta 408), but when I moved there, by then married, my apartment had only one bedroom. Then she entered the living room. She was wearing a short, transparent lounging robe, and what I couldn't see I could guess beneath the gauze (or a more modern fabric, nasty new nylon): her tits seemed erect to me, her thighs smooth, her back divided by the spinal column—the absence of flesh which is more erotic than flesh itself. It was only a walk-on but it justified my hours spent observing her house, waiting for her appearance, desiring her nudity. She hadn't come out naked but to me it was as if she had pranced the dance of the seven veils, salacious Salomé, Herodizing me, and I would have given her not only the head of the Baptist but both of mine. It was my first reward for being a dedicated voyeur: chance had not intervened as in the chemical combine (three quarters iodine, one quarter peroxide) of the sleeping girl in the Pasaje Hotel: she didn't leave much space for the voyeur—which I still wasn't. But this night's undressed or half-dressed display had made me an incurable addict of the voyeur's vice.

I waited patiently for another similar moment. I knew there wouldn't be an identical occasion: no two naked women look alike, just as one can't hunt the exact same bird again. (Though it has been hunted before, and has escaped and been hunted again in the same place, the same bird becomes two different birds of a feather.) It happened later one weekend —or several weekends later—when I least expected. The living room was lit up (on the previous occasion, all the light came from the bedroom and from the kitchen), messy and empty. I was waiting on the balcony, bent over so as not to be seen by my prey, but not so huddled as to awaken suspicions in the next-door neighbors, who would usually come out on their balcony for fresh air. Suddenly the woman came out of the bedroom —totally naked. My first reaction was total amazement: what I had been waiting for so long (or not at all) had actually happened. I also had a reflex reaction (as I had years earlier, hunting in the woods near town): I flattened myself against the edge of the balcony, my parapet and protection, trying to become invisible, that is, nonexistent. But my eyes were above the edge, eagerly looking. What I saw was a woman who was quite old (for my age), with overflowing flesh that *habaneros* like so much on the street but here, freed from the constraints of clothing, her huge hips moved side to side as she walked, forming a double hip at the top of her thighs—and these were regrettably *capitonné*. (I owe this useful French word to Juan Blanc de Blanco: it designates flesh forming waves, fatty tissue that makes invisible cracks, the divisions protruding as in a quilt: padded cakes.) Her legs, which I had seen before in stockings, were revealed to me as varicose bottles (or rather, jars), her back lacked a canal because of the foul, folding fat, and finally her buttocks drooped over the beginning of her thighs, like brown half toilet seats made of fatty

211

flesh. She went to God knows where in the house and returned, revealing a stomach that was a beer belly and tits that fell flaccidly almost to her deep belly button. It was an absolutely anaphrodisiac, anti-erotic spectacle, and I couldn't understand why her comedian lover put up with the roaring rages of that woman who was everything but my idea of a mistress. Mon Dieu, I hadn't suffered such a deception for a long time.

But this fiasco in the art of looking, confronted with a model in reverse, didn't cure me of my voyeuristic habits. You see, we are a race of peeping toms and not content with looking through dark glasses, I got Pino Zitto, who lived around the corner on F Street, to lend me his powerful field glasses. These spyglasses passed into my hands permanently— tenacious tenancy—and allowed me to see my neighbors magnified eight times. Thus the Palace Building, a good hundred meters on the other side of the park, was now at a visual distance of barely twelve meters—closer than the Santeiro with the naked eye. Hurrah for my perspective glass, as Crusoe called it.

But first a topography lesson: on the left, closing the block of buildings around the private houses below, flanked on the right by the Chibás— inexplicably distant though it was right in front of the Palace—was a four-story building (in the far corner of the visual field was the depressing Calixto García Hospital, which I never thought of examining with my telescope), whose windows revealed only shadows, women sneaking around, getting ready for bed in low light, invariably turning off the light when the time came to undress. The blinking light made it seem as if they were using candlelight. Though the building was composed of many different apartments, it looked like a secular convent, where identical nuns or pupils completed the same dressing (or undressing) ceremony for bed, invariably in the dark. A closer examination of the situation showed that not all the female inhabitants of this building put out the lights when getting undressed. Others simply closed the windows. But the dominating darkness in that cluster of building backsides—because our apartment, despite its ocean vista and avenue view, was an inner apartment and the balcony was on the backside of the building—made it difficult to see what was happening. One must also remember that, to observe these nearby dwellings, I had to adopt the sniper pose.

The only other exploratory alternative was the Palace Building. At first I concentrated on the lower floors, avoiding all the seventh-floor windows because Olga Andreu lived there and I wasn't going to snoop at the bedroom of a friend whom I would see in her living room almost every day. Catia Ben Como also lived up there, or at least was still living there, and though she was on the sixth floor, accessible, I never thought of looking toward her apartment (perhaps to avoid discovering the malignant Jacobsen), though I knew that she, like Olga, slept in the room facing the park, that is, within my visual reach. Don't ask me how I knew what room Catia slept in, when I never even visited her in her living room. Perhaps I heard her tell Olga Andreu, giving me a hint, but it was probably a deduction. Olga slept in the room facing the street and park, that is, the best bedroom, and it wasn't difficult to infer that Catia's parents—good Havana parents—would give their only daughter the best room to sleep in, refreshed by the Gulf Stream breeze. This Cuban custom or domestic politics allowed me to have the most memorable vision of that time—and of all times.

I concentrated my binoculars on the nearest end of the building as well as on the lower windows, which gave me total insight over the inside of the apartments. I discovered several household scenes but none as interesting as those revealed to James Stewart, an invalid with one long-distance eye, in *Rear Window*. Neither did I have a Queen Kelly, Grace under pressure, to come give me a slow blond buss, distracting me from the diverse window displays—and thus I spent my free nights exercising my solitary hobby. Some might have been pathetic or dramatic but at that distance, without the help of sound, all were terribly boring. Even if I had heard them with a boom ear, I know they would have been dialogues like these: "Did you bring the bread?" "No, dear. Sorry, I forgot." "Asshole! How many times do I have to tell you to make a note of what we need?" "I know, darling, but it's just that I have a lot on my mind"—which would be a lot more garbage in my mind. Neorealisms, when I was looking for the extraordinary in everyday life. Poe yes, Zola no.

On the same south edge of the building (whose windows faced the hospital courtyard rather than the park but were perfectly visible from my balcony because of the Palace's location) I discovered, by chance or willpower, a woman who again reminded me of Madame de Marelle. Now (forgetting rosy Rosita, my painted paper posy) I had a true vision of Clotilde before my eyes, almost within hand's reach—every night. I consumed many evenings observing the comings and goings of this Clotilde. Sometimes I was looking at her windows till two in the morning: my Clotilde went to bed late. I didn't care. Around that time there were no classes to get up early for, since the School of Journalism went from two to six in the afternoon: quite civilized: the only civilized trait of that school of cretins, for cretins, by cretins: a real Moronia. But now's the time to write my version of Clotilde. Just forget the *fin-de-siècle* style (which I never reconstructed because it would have been necessary to invoke Renoir rather than remember Maupassant) and the pearl Georges Duroy saw hanging from her ear with a thread of gold gliding down her neck like a drop of water on her skin—and already that first vision of the flesh is promising. *La chair était fraîche, hélas, quand j'ai lu ce livre!* There are the late-forties clothes (we were already in 1950, but this Clotilde's clothes are behind the times: one can see she doesn't care too much about fashion, that is, about dresses: she must care then about undressing: a promise that I'll see her undressed, without a dress, naked!) and her nervous gait, so typical of the other Clotilde. I don't know if she's married or not, since I often see a small man in the apartment who disappears late at night. Perhaps he's a tired husband, who retires before the untiring Clotilde. She wears her hair in the style of the forties, not combed upward revealing the Clotilde-like neck but like the Mexican film stars, which makes her like a vestal vamp. I observed her during entire nights, sparsely lit, as if by gaslight, sitting in her favorite *fauteuil* or pacing up and down the living room (that must have been her favorite form of exercise) or detained by her conversation with that man, who seems to visit more than inhabit the apartment. I tried to see her up close, violating the strict laws of voyeurism, vacillating in my own convictions that those women—the ones discovered from my balcony—should remain virgins, always distant, true horizontals, like the sleeping girl in the Pasaje Hotel. This attempt at an approach made useless my precious, almost scientific instrument: my macroscope. I often went as far as the entrance to the Palace Building when I saw her gaslight go out, trying to find her by forcing fate. I hung around the building, risking a row with the ruffians of the club (more likely a club hand) of noisy neighborhood boys who were sitting, gathering around the first bench of the next to the last section of the promenade, I ate redundant cupcakes at the Bakery, really a reduced cafeteria below Clotilde, infected (the cafeteria, not Clotilde) by the epidemic of English names that began to spread to all Havana establishments. This became a true pandemic in the fifties. But I never saw her, I mean up close, since every night she was in full view thanks to my binoculars. I suffered frustration then for not seeing her in closeup, but now I tend to think it was better that way and Clotilde, reflected in the mirrors of my spyglasses, is as real as her literary double.

If my eyeglasses were already an extension of my eyes, the spyglasses became a projection of my body, making the eye tactile. It could touch the prisoners of my eye, and when they undressed, it was I who removed with my outstretched fingers the garment whose absence turned them into precious gems. But I got my deserts in an inverse version of my attempt with Quasi Clotilde. In the Palace Building there lived a middle-aged blond man with nondescript features who was not at all intelligent-looking and, to boot, was called Snotface. Few knew his real name and no one used it. Snotface had a wife who must have been beautiful once but now middle age, or perhaps menopause, had paled her light, if any. The family was known for its only daughter, who was a radiant beauty: tall, thin (but not so thin that the inevitable *habaneros* surrounding her would nickname her Skinny, a national insult), she had blond hair (one should say a yellow mane), which fell below her shoulders, almost to the middle of her back. She wore it luminously loose, flying in the wind that always blew at the top of the avenue, making her its live monument. She had inherited some of her father's idiocy, or perhaps it was aloofness, to which her beauty gave her all the right. The truth is that none of the young ruffians, so audacious with their words to the women crossing their blue zone, dared to come near this proud iceberg in the tropics. What's more, she had the appropriate name of Helen, her face capable

214

of launching a thousand ships, beginning a mythic war and making any of us immortal (here I have to join the admiring ruffians) with a kiss. With me she achieved that eternal effect without coming any closer than a hundred meters: the distance separating us one Faustian night. Obviously my spyglasses (which had become opera glasses, allowing me to observe dramatized human behavior) brought me close to the Palace, a kind of intimacy few could enjoy. Thus I wasn't surprised (though my heart skipped a turn) to discover that Helen's apartment was on the eighth floor, facing the avenue: that is, almost parallel to my observatory. I saw her chatting with her parents (she was really talking only to her father and I presume she didn't talk much to her mother), getting up from her seat (which I couldn't see) at the exact moment I was scrutinizing those open windows, her father already standing, the two almost the same height. (For a moment I didn't recognize him as the ludicrous Snotface.) Then she stood up with her back to the window, the night, and me. Her tresses. Nobody has used this word seriously since classical times, when women used to be fabulous creatures, precious ivory unicorns: this is precisely why I use it when speaking of her. Her tresses shone in the living-room light and recognition was instantaneous. I had come upon the house of Helen: *voilà Troie!* Figuring that her parents would follow the Havanan custom I'd already seen in Olga Andreu's and presumably Catia's home, most probably the pearl of this household oyster had the best jewel-box bed: that room whose window faced the open air, the avenue, the view of the neighborhood, the coast, and the ocean—this last transformed for her into a mere Mediterranean Sea.

That same night I saw the bedroom light go on and then she appeared, moving about the room, disappearing, reappearing. Then she must have gone to the bathroom because she returned dressed in a nightgown, which I imagine long and Helenic. She must have sat in front of the mirror since she began to brush her memorable blond tresses. She brushed again and again, all the way down, with her hand behind on her shoulder, running the brush through her hair, her long locks along the sides which weren't exactly yellow though a color lighter than sand but darker than wheat, like hyaline honey: that rara avis in Havana, a natural blonde. Helen's head, a *casque d'or,* shone under the light at each stroke of her evident yet invisible brush, a focal point in the night. Repeating the incantatory strokes again and again, she then brushed in the other direction, lowering her head, letting her hair cover her face, her head all tresses, to straighten up and brush again. When the performance was over—it must have lasted many minutes but seemed only seconds to me—she looked at herself in the mirror and, even at a distance, one could see she was content with her tresses. She admired her face, liked the combination, looked at herself taking delight in looking, with a narcissism that was charming because she really was beautiful and innocent as well. What I hadn't forgiven Beba I celebrated in Helen because she wasn't the object of my love but rather the apple of my eye, eyeglasses, fieldglasses. Then she proceeded to lower the Venetian blinds and her enchanting vision disappeared from view.

Many nights I awaited the apparition of Helen, my future phantom, though sometimes she lowered the blinds before going to bed. On other occasions she lowered the blinds before her toilette but didn't close them, and through the slats—yellow bars to imprison this mythological creature—I could see her before the mirror, brushing incessantly, inspiring me to compose a verse plagiarizing Góngora: "And Helen brushed her golden tresses in the sun"—though the poetic sun was that bulb hanging from the plaster-of-Paris ceiling. I continued watching Helen all the nights she permitted me to see her midnight toilette, her ritual to beautify even more her tresses, focal point of my eyes—and nights became weeks and weeks months, waiting patiently for a miraculous revelation, which made me adore her. There was one night, a midnight when she lowered the blinds but didn't shut them (after all, she might have wondered, who would see her so high up?). After combing, brushing, treating her hair until transforming it into her flowing blond tresses, as she looked at her face surrounded by the hair running down the sides like a golden frame, she lowered one of the straps of her black nightgown, leaving one shoulder bare. Then she repeated the operation with her other shoulder and the robe fell to her invisible feet. Nocturnal Narcissa contemplated herself nude in the mirror. I had to imagine her nudity since her back was always turned toward me as she faced the mirror, I seeing her long dorsal canal, her modern shoulders (I mean they weren't rounded like those of the false Clotilde but square, straight, and thin), and the tip of her left breast: its perfection kept me from imagining that the other, hidden by her body, was identical, so unique was tit. When she finished examining herself (without a doubt approving: I would have applauded had my spectacular spyglasses not gotten in the way) in the mirror, she disappeared from my view and the light went out almost immediately. Many legends about her circulated in the neighborhood, some absurd, like the one that her father was madly in love with her and suffered uncontrollable jealousy, thus her remoteness from the boys was imposed, not natural, and so on and so forth. I can imagine that the legendary Helen slept naked that night.

Nevertheless I waited, not content with a single appearance, watching, in my hands the telescope that could reach heavenly bodies. I closed my tired eyes a moment and opened them again immediately. I want to believe it all had been imagined or invented by memory, but the light went on again and I raised my spyglasses to my glasses. Helen appeared in the visual field. She was in the far end of the room and now I could see her completely (though legless) facing front, occupied in a feverish chore. I couldn't notice her second breast because I was fascinated by the lower part of her body: she didn't use panties to sleep (which was logical) but I couldn't see her sex. She was wearing below the navel an orthopedic contraption, apparently leather by its brown color, tied with belts around

216

her waist, covering her mount of Venus like a saddle cover, disappearing between her legs, protecting—from what? from whom?—her vagina like scales. She was adjusting it, pulling on the upper edges, like a girdle, trying to raise it, and when she turned around for a moment I could see the framework covering her ass to end a little above her long buttocks. Now she was tightening the (obviously) leather belts over her back, as if adjusting a dark bodice that was too low—altogether it was an evil machine. After these adjustments she put out the light again and went back to bed, surely to sleep, I suppose. But I could barely sleep that night thinking of the archaic contraption I had just seen covering and at the same time blemishing this version of the virgin. Sometime before dawn I dreamt that I saw Helen covered with an atrocious armor that went from her white chin to her hairy vulva, with belts, straps, and cords that prevented any movement of her flesh in public—and, what was worse, eclipsed the contemplation of her splendid nudity. It was then that I understood what this obsolete object opposed to desire was: the chastity belt designed by Goya!

Yet it was less the horror than the grace which turned the gazer's spirit into stone. Never again did I return to the balcony with my instrument made for war, which I had used to fulfill the dream of the voyeur's love and had served only to create nightmares. Shortly after, I handed it down to my father.

217

FAUX PAS WITH A BALLERINA

Have any of you, ladies and gentlemen, ever tried to make fresh French love to a ballerina offstage? Whoever has attempted such an overture will have discovered this act is virtually impossible to consummate. Ballerinas (I'm not referring to dancers, who are, on the contrary, very easy) are really vestal virgins of Terpsichore, dance devotees, married to ballet as nuns are to Christ. "The practice bar is their penis," pronounced Juan Blanco, a composer of ballet music for *ballets blancs*. They seemed to drown their love sorrows on the bar. I should know: I've known more than one ballerina. Some are internationally famous now, which is why I can't name them—being a gentleman and besides I'm afraid of the libel laws. They were young, nice, apparently accessible—please note that I emphasize *apparently*—but there's nothing more elusive than a ballerina. Some won't even accept an invitation to dance. I've dealt with those with normal names and those with strange names. The gal with the common name insisted on doing a *pas de deux* with the mirror while the girl with the exotic name affected a languid romanticism that made her eyes veritable swan lakes. They all took virginity to be sacred, not sacroiliac. Therefore the slightest attempt (in a movie theater for example) against their virginal (not vaginal) integrity was branded obscene. The author of such a false move was condemned by default to end his performance then and there. Ipso faulto. A fatal fall into disgrace was my lot several times later in my life as a ballet lover when I got too close to the tutus. But at the time when initiation was still possible I had an affair with a false ballerina—or faux fare. Her name was Honey (I would someday call her Rose) Hawthorne and I met her at the art gallery of *Our Time,* when this cultured pearl of a society was living out its heroic era on Calle Reina —not so queenly a street—and had not yet become the smoke screen for a Communist organization of the same name but at a different address (or headquarters) in El Vedado. It wasn't far, barely two blocks from the promenade so descriptively called Paseo, an important avenue in my love life and night life and which I loved for its tree-lined extension over

218

successive natural terraces down to the seashore. I strolled down this promenade many a time with my false ballerina, approaching the *posada* a block away from the end, trying to guide my little love or *amorcito*—an affectionate diminutive I owe to my friend Calvert Casey, who died of love in Roma, the city that spells love backward. My purpose was to make this love of mine into my lover. The things one must do to get that extra *r!*

I met her at Our Time but I should really say I saw her at Our Time, at an exhibit of Cuban painting. There I fixed my romantic retina upon a thin girl (I would later learn she was skinny) with outstanding breasts (I would soon see she was all tits) and blonde (a fake one, I would discover)—and a procuress took care of the rest. A friend, Cuca Cumplido (a storyteller who drifted predictably toward radio soap operas), introduced us and I retained the blonde, busty, almost Aryan vision—keeping the cunnotations of her name in mind. We didn't see each other for a while, during a peak season of sexual tension (abandoned on my island by Juliet: a castaway without a Girl Friday), when I would spend my nights on Avenida de los Presidentes—a young version of the old man with the dirty raincoat—wearing a trenchcoat of transparent green nylon which the dark avenue made impenetrable. I was anxious to find a solitary woman sitting somewhere along the promenade, a propitious pedestrian, a passerby (fantasized by me in my amorous delirium) who never appeared and thus the endless walk in my plastic cage ended in moving masturbations beneath the raincoat. This apparel served not to shelter me from imaginary or real rain (it was dry season then) but rather to protect the pavement from pollution, sperm sliding swiftly down my cape—which I always carefully cleaned when I got back home, in secret, in the privacy of our bathroom, its door bolted shut. An enigma of this esoteric era was why my mother, who always saw me go out in good weather wearing a raincoat, never wondered about my, to say the least, strange behavior—a midnight Mornard in search of a transvestite Trotsky to penetrate with my feverish alpenistock.

Around then I completed my second survey, this time limited to Havana and its neighboring boroughs like Marianao, Regla and Guanabacoa—the former on the other side of the river, the latter two across the bay. Asking questions from door to door (either about political preferences for the national survey or about people's favorite television programs for the local survey), I met up with the most perverse persons and was pursued by dangerous dogs. And I almost ended up in bed, late one afternoon in Guanabacoa, with a black woman who looked like a Maillol *femme* in scanty dress, but who might or might not have been married to a black stevedore capable of appearing at any moment. It was the formidable figure of this black giant of the Mandrake comics that prevented me from turning into what I always wanted to be, a libertine Lothario. When I went to pick up the paycheck for my weary work at the offices on Galiano Street, I met up with, of all people, Honey (whom I still

219

couldn't call Rosie) Hawthorne: she also worked for a survey society. She was coming out as I was entering and I told her to wait for me, that I would be right out: maybe it was these harsh words on my part—since I barely knew her—that did the trick. She agreed to my request, which was almost a threat. After completing complicated transactions (the company was really remiss in paying, so much so that it was the last time I interrogated prospective television audiences, despite the glamour of the job, which almost turned me into a young Philip Marlowe, a private TV eye), I was finally able to rejoin Honey.

She was reading a book. I forgot to mention that she had literary pretensions: thus her friendship with my friend the Cuban story writer. Honey, of course, wanted to write poetry. She was reading a volume of poems, perhaps Neruda's *Twenty Love Songs,* because when we left the headquarters of COCROO (Company of Crooks) and walked to the bus stop on Galiano Street (though it was only I who needed to catch the bus: she lived on San Lázaro almost on the corner of Galiano, a few steps from where we were, as I later learned), I made a dreadful and daring reference to Neruda's poems. I was then what you call opinionated. I had conclusive opinions on art, literature, and poetry. "A love poem is a declaration of impotence," I said to her, and she rapidly replied: "I think you're wrong." She paused a moment, perhaps to consider my reference to poetic impotence, and continued, overlooking or perhaps forgetting it (she probably hadn't understood what was clearly pure provocation), "A love poem is a feat of love." I don't know if this was a challenge, provoking me in turn to write her a singing sonnet or if it was a sign of her literary innocence. I know that, almost following in the lost steps of Juliet, I lent her my copy (I then had the necessary notion that there weren't many copies in Havana) of *Lady Chatterley's Lover.* I have to confess that I was still a reader of Lawrence and I even read his fallacious *Fantasia of the Unconscious!* Honey read *Lady Chatterley* (for her: for me the emphasis was on *Lover*) and returned the novel to me all underlined and annotated, as if taking possession of my book. Her underlinings were certainly unexpected, but not as much as her notes. For example she had marked the phrase "The sun was setting" and beside it noted "Plagiarizing Horacio Quiroga!" How she had been able to connect Quiroga with Lawrence was as mysterious to me as the banality of the line she indicated as copied was self-evident. But this incident (in all senses of the word) shows the kind of relationship we had at the beginning.

I never brought her home but I did take her to what would become a ritual retreat: a nightclub, one among the many that had proliferated in Havana during the last decade and which were different from the cabarets. The cabarets (like the Zombie Club, near Zulueta 408, and the Montmartre, not far from Avenida de los Presidentes, on what would later be known as La Rampa: both were destined to disappear dramatically, one in the forties because of a fire and the other in the fifties, after an alarming assassination) were for dining and dancing and were clean, well-lighted, spacious places with orchestras that were actually bands. The nightclubs (very different from other nightclubs that emerged later, almost in the sixties, where one went to listen to music, singers and songs) were known as love nests (or tests), places where couples went to kiss, neck, make out, and more: some, like the Turf, had Pullman seats on which one could practically lie down: ottomans for ottomaniacs—all was fair except being in the buff. (There were, of course, bluffs.) Thanks to Juan Blanco, the club's legal consultant, I became acquainted with the Mocambo, on L Street, a few blocks from home. It was Juan Blanco who suggested to me that at the Mocambo one could "score even" (before, I had heard the word only in connection with sports commentators, talking about baseball), adding that one could use, in his vocabulary, "all the boneless organs, except one," meaning, as he had to explain (I was as thick as a hick) that they let you use your tongue—and not only for talking.

I should tell more about Juan Blanco, a singular lawyer (who freed me and imprisoned me: he got me out of jail, but he also married me off), a unique composer: the only piece of his that I admitted knowing was his "Valse Blue," which he was always trying to forget. I went as an artistic militant with Juan Blanco to the Auditorium concerts, to demand that they play more modern music. I also went to the ballet though it would be better to say the dance, since I had begun to detest the eternal Alicia Alonso (whom Juan Blanco called "The Menopauseless Giselle"), and at one performance I appeared with a long Czech smoking pipe, my war pipe, which I had to sustain with my hand in order to smoke, and from the balcony with bravado we boomed one-way boomerangs from the ranks of modern dance like Brooklyn's Artful Dodgers.

On our way home on the bus from one of these Auditorium outings (I still lived at Zulueta 408) a tall woman got on at Línea Street. She had light but not blond hair, a fine figure, and a face that wasn't beautiful but was attractive. She recognized Juan Blanco and bent her head, a little like Lauren Bacall in *To Have and Have Not,* which, as greetings go, is not very emphatic, not at all Havanan, and she then sat down in the front. We were sitting (in a group, my brother among us) on the last seat, allowing us to gossip. "Do you know her?" I asked Juan Blanco, and he told me: "Yes, vagrantly." It was obvious by his tone that there was a story behind that portmanteau adverb. "Pray tell," said someone, perhaps Roberto Branly. Juan Blanco was at first reticent, but that was pure histrionics. Finally he said: "I had something with her once." (Juan Blanco, we all knew, was inexplicably attractive to women.) But he remained serious and then said: "After that we didn't see each other for a long time. One day, years later, she came to see me at the office and, without even saying hello, she spit out a surprise: 'I'm having sentimental troubles,' she said, and without a bar rest she added," Juan Blanco paused, more serious than ever: "she said: 'Give me thirty bucks for an abortion,' and that was all she said." Juan Blanco was now silent but had told it so well, relentlessly, but making all the necessary pauses, without a transition between sentimental trouble and abortion as if that phrase and this word had an identical value, that we all broke out laughing, making every passenger turn toward us—except her. But I think that even the strange traveler felt shaken by our racket rumbling the springs of the bus.

Many witticisms passed from Juan Blanco's mouth onto my blank page. But there's one *bon mot* I never quoted, mainly because it has to do with Juliet Estévez and he hadn't spoken about her before. I already said that Juliet became not our mass muse but Initiatrix: the list of friends and acquaintances initiated sexually by Juliet would be a long one. List, oh list! Not only of those who went to bed for the first time but for the only time, perhaps: some chose the foreign penis for pains of love they do not cease to suffer, but I'm not saying or even implying this was Juliet's fault or was a result of the encounter with her: Juliet key to all nightmares. Some went to bed with her in places as remote and exotic as the pond at the Country Club or the Cojimar quarries—this place, the port not the actual quarries, became fashionable in the fifties with *The Old Man and the Sea* but she never even acknowledged it. The other place, the calm beautiful pond, was the site of a notorious double political assassination. But I don't want to talk now of the young who died, justly or unjustly, in the quiet quietus of the Country Club, but of Juliet, lover of cemeteries and of nature, real and false, of Debussy's *La Mer* and Van Gogh, who now belonged to Havana's sexual mythology—I mean that she no longer belongs to me exclusively: myths belong to everybody: to the dead and the living, to folklore, to you. Thus I can relate this story which is not even a story but a phrase, a flourish or (as Juan Blanco is a musician) a pavane flourish. We were discussing Juliet's beauty, her doe's eyes and the perfection of her body: her bounteous breasts, her hips of a hind in flight, her golden thighs that ended in luscious limbs. "Yes," Juan Blanco agreed emphatically, "but when she opens her legs, green smoke emerges from her cunt." This visualization of Juliet's promiscuity as an infernal green smoke conferred on her sex a swamp quality, of musty marshes and mires, of brutal backwoods inimical to all human life: *Lasciate ogni spelato voi ch'entrate.* It was a witty, wicked, and unforgettable remark of Juan Blanco's, and the green smoke went on to be a part of our chosen vocabulary: *cherchez la phrase.*

This same Juan Blanco recommended the Mocambo to me as a slaughterhouse (I'm not sure he used this brutal Havanan expression, more in use toward the end of the fifties, since Juan Blanco's glossary had solidified by the late forties, so much so that his nickname in his student days as diving champion was Iron Cream, after a soda pop then popular in Havana which I never got to know, getting there in time for *caficola* (the Havana name for soda counter), Ironbeer, and Rootbeer but not the era of Iron Cream. He must have said hideout or den or perhaps Fingal's Cave, with all its Inner Hebrides connotations. Anyway he gave me precise instructions about the Mocambo—which I really didn't need. I could have entered as cocksure as any other customer: it wasn't a private club but the most public of nightclubs. (But Juan Blanco considered me a Green Young Man with a case of blue balls.) I invited Honey, who came dressed to kill—and looked pretty good under the artificial light. Now I must make two revelations. One took place that night, and the other, the day I saw her in the offices of those survey scoundrels. She was white-skinned, almost livid, but one could see she had black blood. Her racial composition was undefined and, as Cuba is a country of many mixtures, perhaps her African forefather was further back into the Dark Continent than that black-faced grandfather who peers out of the family tree. But he was certainly present in her hair, which the yellow tint did not keep from tending toward a kinky currant color, even though it seemed to be straight. Just as I had done in my adolescent years at Zulueta 408, Honey avoided giving me her precise address. But the night I went to get her I insisted upon meeting her at her house. Before, I had met her on a corner or had traveled to the distant house of our writer friend, Cuca now more Cupid than Cumplido. Or simply, she had called me at home, and I went to get her at the entrance of a moviehouse. Actually, we had gone out very few times. Now, upon ascending the naked steps of her building (which was not a fatal fantastic phalanstery), I was struck by how similar its ambience was to Zulueta 408's. Honey Hawthorne, exquisite reader of pure poetry, erudite annotator of my D. H. Lawrence novel, my personal discovery at an art exhibit, lived in a tenement—just like the plebeian women of my past.

It wasn't a large tenement, however, but rather what today, when it's become fashionable to use the prefix *mini* to make even a ministry seem like a brief mystery, would be called a mini-tenement. That night I met her little sister, who, in a jump back in racial regression, revealed herself to be a true *mulata,* much younger than Honey but of a Polynesian beauty that would have excited Gauguin. (Years later, when I saw her again, now a grown girl, I regretted not having cultivated a relationship with the family: she was a *mulata* who promised a high Havanan passion.) But I never got to see the mongrel mother. Besides, I hadn't gone to her house to establish family ties but to fetch Honey, the only real promise. Her sister was waiting for me on the staircase like a reception committee, to tell me Honey would be coming right away. As she in fact did—a half hour later.

We arrived early at the Mocambo, which didn't sponsor the dark at night as during the day (such reflections would occur later, much later) but it did display a low light that, if not procuring, was at least compla-cent. We sat (novice that I was) up front, ostensibly (or at least visibly) facing the bar. I chose a table for two, facing each other and not, as I later noticed, where a couple could sit side by side, as on a love seat. Instead of a live band, which I stupidly expected, there was a big juke box, as showy as the one that became my still-life object of passion in the Martí

223

Theater lobby. But this one was, regrettably, much more modern, leaving behind the coral-colored whirling whorls, the curved conches, the fluorescent flourishes of the early forties, to slouch toward the detestable design of a square cabinet, the music box of the fifties. There still wasn't, as at the Turf Club a few years later, a system for selecting records from the table by remote control. Therefore, I had to get up to select what we wanted to hear—which was almost always what I wanted to hear. Unlike Juliet, Honey had no ear for music, thank goodness, that is, I was glad she was Honey and not Juliet, who would have insisted upon listening to Debussy in the Mocambo! Though one day I would get to hear a fragment of the overture to *Lohengrin* in a Colón bar, Wagner the sonorous cook to spoil the brothels. This gem was discovered by Carlos Franqui, a lover of romantic music amid the decadence of perfumed flesh. But I was sure that at the Mocambo Club, patronized by satyrs more than Saties, I would never hear the lapping sounds of *La Mer* at night.

Convinced that the whole universe was observing me through an inverted telescope, I had to get up the courage to walk from our table to the juke box and mark the numbers I'd like to hear—which were sung mainly, at that time, by Olga Guillot. Or Beny Moré, swinging out of the orbit of the mambo to achieve the apogee of the bolero. (Of all the male singers, he could be called the king of the bolero. Its feminine realm, however, seemed to belong entirely to Queen Guillot, whose greatest successes contained the lyrics of our satiric sayings: "Tell me more of your lies, they make me mad and happy," "Being bad was your way of being good to me," "You can always tell a loser by his loss," etc.) And though those were the years of the chachachá nobody would go to hear chachachás, with their compulsive rhythm, in a club where every couple's objective was everything but dancing. The other unavoidable selection then was Nat King Cole, a favorite since the days of my brief impersonation as copyeditor, in English! at the Havana *Herald,* when his "Mona Lisa" was in fashion. This tuneful illustration was incarnated in my brief encounter (that's how long my job lasted) with an enigmatic American copyeditor, a silent galley slavey beside me, who never even smiled, she a sphinx who knew how to spell. Those must have been my selections on the automatic memory of the juke box—inscrutable in its musical designs. Finally I returned to the table and to Honey (still not Rosie) Hawthorne—sitting pretty.

I noticed for the first time in the cloistered night her makeup, which was on the heavy side. She smeared her lips in the style of the late forties, which were the mid-forties in the movies, and so she wore another painted mouth over hers—loud lipstick falsies planted on her thin, real lips. If her mouth recalled Joan Crawford, her nose (also made-up: she was one of the first very made-up girls I knew, except for Carmina, whose makeup was a mask) was almost exactly Marlene Dietrich's nose—which isn't strange when you remember that Dietrich's nose is quite negroid. Come to think of it, many German noses are, which must have bothered Hitler not a little: Afro Aryans all. Honey, on the other hand, was an Aryan Afro. But her eyes were very black. (This is not surprising because black-eyed blondes abound in Cuba, as they would everywhere, a few years later, an archetype of the fake blonde: the strawberry blonde with dark eyes like pits. I'm referring to Brigitte Bardot, who had an unforgettable double in Havana—but it was still seven years before I would meet the one who, though named Lola, I never knew carnally, alas.) Black-eyed Honey had a sweet frank expression in her eyes: they knew how to look straight ahead and sometimes produced winkings and blinkings, either from false modesty or true timidity, which made her look incredibly like Marlene Dietrich, coining that coy chastity she sometimes assumes in movies. I'm sure now that Honey was imitating then the mock-maudlin Marlene, who got the most out of her flaring nostrils, and that the very lips Honey painted so exaggeratedly were not following fashionable Crawford but were a fake facsimile of Dietrich's lipline. But maybe I'm wrong and Honey, a slave of fashion, was only following the style of the day.

I don't remember much of what we said. (As you see, I remember her appearance more than her conversation, though I'm sure Honey would have liked to be remembered more for her discourse than for her mouth and lips uttering it, certain that her personality was the reality of her person, and not her mask.) But I do know we talked a lot, talking hours over the music, which from background became foreground, the dance of the hours. I didn't wear a watch then (I couldn't afford one, and now that I can, I can afford not to) and we talked and talked and between the cracks (rather than the intervals) in the music I could hear (or pretended to hear) what she was saying. But what I wanted was to get close to her, have her in my arms, kiss her—despite her dated daubed lips. I've always hated lipstick and nylon stockings and Honey used both cosmetics as obstacles between her body and mine. But finally I managed to give her a brief kiss, mere contact with her lipstick, a perfect word since it combines lips and stickiness. At the end of the kiss, which lasted seconds perhaps, she looked around, blinking cosmetically coy, as if thinking someone had seen her. But the public surrounding us, now diminished, was only interested in its private affairs, each man with his mate, no-nonsense Narcissuses, and they weren't thinking about us as possible partners in a *ménage à quatre*. It was then that I got up the courage to ask her to dance. I hadn't danced in my whole life, though since childhood I have always liked to watch others dancing. I don't know where I, who ain't got rhythm, acquired this voyeuristic passion for dancing. During carnival, I would go with some schoolmate, like Silvino Rizo, to a fancy-dress ball at the Galician or Asturian Center, only to see the masked couples dance, their fancy dress not succeeding in veiling their art. When the public carnival *comparsas* were allowed back on the streets after the war, my father sometimes got me a pass to the press box beside the Capitol and I delighted in watching the costume dances of the

Saturday-night parades along the Prado. On Sundays I was amused—the word is *excited*—by the parade of fiesta floats, decorated extravagantly in papier mâché but adorned with girls, girls, girls, all in bathing suits, beauties in bikinis, showing off their long legs in the early spring afternoon, which were, as it were, a summer sight for sore eyes.

Now I stepped out to dance with Honey. A slow bolero was playing and all I had to do was to stick to her and simulate that I was moving, an imitation of dance steps that in time would become a technique, looking extraordinarily like dancing without ever being it. (This first occasion reminded me of Abbott and Costello's indelible skit in which Costello emphatically declares that he doesn't like dancing. "Why?" asks Abbott, puzzled. "What's dancing?" answers Costello with a question. "A man and a woman hugging to music in the dark." "And what's wrong with that?" Abbott wants to know, and Costello clarifies definitively: "The music.") The only bad thing between Honey and me at that moment was the music. But I'm not being fair with the music. In this my first faux pass in a long career of slower than slow boleros, I achieved the proficiency of a professional dancer without even knowing how to take two steps— nay, not even one: all I did was to move my doremifasolar plexus against my partner's hips, if she allowed it. On some occasions this rubbing was too daring for my dancer, and upon moving away from me, a social slap, she left me alone to move my hips by myself. But I didn't hear the music now: I was all ears to the contact with Honey's body, drawing her toward me with a slowness similar to my pelvic rotation, wanting her to stick against me, and at the same time making sure this coupling that wanted to become copulation happened precisely while the music was still playing, in exact hip-synch. I was able to draw her so close to me that any other movement that wasn't the rotating rubbing of her body against mine would be practically impossible. Also, from the moment I'd taken her into my arms (there was something comfortable about her height, about Honey's slenderness, about having and holding her in my hands— which is more than a metaphor), I was subjected to an erection. At the time I suffered the embarrassing condition of *erectio praecox* and I can use the verb *suffer* because these erections barely let me talk to a woman or girl without being their victim—of precocious erections, not of the women or girls as predators. Often, on a bus sitting next to a woman who wasn't beautiful and not even young, the mere vibrations of the chassis produced an erection in me. This made it extremely difficult to stand up, ask my fellow traveler's permission to leave, pass her with my back to her and get off with a bulk in my crotch that not even my hand in my pocket (and getting off the vehicle with one hand, as a one-armed bandit of flesh, was complicated) could lower, no matter how hard I pulled down the rebellious member, my swine erect. Thus, I often ended up traveling to unknown regions of Havana, not at all included in my itinerary—Arroyo Arenas, El Diezmero, Nicanor del Campo—waiting vainly for the swelling to go down. The opposite, of course, occurred: the length of the trip increased in direct proportion the size of my penis, reaching shameful dimensions. I sometimes managed to leave the bus because my travel companion had gotten off first. Other times I risked the charges of gross indecency (more improbable because the legal term wasn't in the popular lexicon, though *pig* was), descending from the vehicle in motion at an unforeseen point of the route. But I usually reached the bus stop without having diminished the dimensions of that organ for which I had scored so many fugues.

Now, dancing with Honey (I must say that she was no dancer either, despite a later statement she made to that effect), I was rubbing my bump almost raw because my pants were as thin as a veil. (This initiation to dance must have occurred in the summer or at least during a heat wave: such hot spells appear in Havana when least expected, converting the traditional white-heat Christmas into an oven for the suckling pig and its eaters, all roasted Cuban style. Or sometimes it's a hot wind from the south, a sirocco that blow-torches Lent. It could have been either of these occasions, since we have only two seasons: the dry hot season and the damp hot season.) And so I was bumping my rub against her dancing dress—not a tutu but made of tulle—grinding her flat stomach since she was shorter than me. Honey not only let herself rub my rod but stuck to me, and for a third party in tune we must have formed a united steps. I'm being ironic, you must have noticed, but we really were glued to each other, dancing without moving, I frankly (or rather, shamefacedly) scrubbing up and down her dress, her midriff, her stomach, she letting herself be led by my perpetual motion, almost collaborating with me in that labor of full frontal, vertical, ventral love. That's the rub. We didn't even hear the record end because one slow number followed the next (despite the fact that it was three in the morning or somewhere around there) and we didn't have to separate to wait to continue the dance of Honey and the Bear Who Tasted Honey. Thus we were dancing (in a manner of speaking) the rest of the night or what was left of it—which wasn't much.

When we walked out it was getting light (I insist it was summer, when the days are longer, though this be the land of the eternal equinox) and I decided to accompany her home, gentleman that I was that first night. Our course was to go a few blocks up L Street and then down San Lázaro to Galiano: a long night's journey into day. Or what was left of night. Suddenly we were on Infanta and San Lázaro. L Street subtly becomes San Lázaro at the University, and one barely notices the change: this is, I'm sure, a gentleness on the part of L Street, which is modern American and pleasant and brand-new from its very beginnings, while San Lázaro is a border street but not Tijuana brassy, characterless, boring, neither in Old or New Havana. Following it up toward the University hill is like seeing how the ugly duckling *calzada* becomes a street swan. At this junction I learned once again that man proposes and woman, a goddess, disposes. There and then, almost at sunup, Honey decided she had to go home early! Hold back the dawn, Charles Boyer, so that Olivia D. will never have to cross the border late. Furthermore, she wanted to return in earnest immediately, right now. As of yesterday. There was no way I could make her see that it was impossible to find a taxi at that hour, but as he who greets dawn with an imperious Greek goddess is aided and abetted by some sister goddess, so there appeared, as if created out of an old dry pumpkin, an ancient hireling, which was what they called taxis then. It was the first time I had taken a taxi in Havana. Though Gibara was a small town, my mother was (once) obliged to call a hired car because I couldn't take a step—and I wasn't dancing then. Leaving for the movies early that night I jumped off the high sidewalk to the stone street and twisted an ankle, but I continued toward the movies, limping a bit but acting as if nothing had happened: immune, brave, determined to get to the movies at all costs. Cagney goes to his movie. It was there that my foot swelled until it couldn't stay in the shoe and we had to leave the show because of the pain, the greatest I've suffered my whole life full of tooth pain, migraines. (Perhaps I should have said I would suffer my greatest pain as an adult, with an abscessed tooth, but this wouldn't keep me from walking.) The family doctor, which was like saying the town doctor, diagnosed not a fracture but a novel synovial effusion. Without suffering an early seminal effusion, this second taxi trip was successful, I taking advantage of the vehicle's slow pace. (Later, after becoming a taxi addict, I discovered that there were only two kinds of taxis: those that go very slow and those that go excessively fast, their respective drivers trying the passenger's patience or nerves.) That night I didn't care if the cab driver on duty was cautious or daring: to hold Honey tight was what I was doing now, not only cornering her on one end of the seat but fondling her tits, touching her hips, running my hand over her thighs, and at the same time kissing her—as she was kissing me. Fortunately—this time, *un*-fortunately—San Lázaro is not a very long street. Or it wasn't sufficiently extensive for me that morning, and we reached her house too soon. Now I saw the manor being born, not eclipsed by night but rather aided by dawn in the tropics. It was about two stories high, the shoddy façade painted that almost mustard yellow with which so many Old and Middle Age Havana houses are plastered (the city has its ages, like history: there's a prehistoric Havana beyond the Malecón wall), modest, without the fearful face of the phalanstery at Zulueta 408, but just a neighborhood house, plain and simple: Honey's present was my past. We were joined by a common bond of poverty—despite the taxi, despite the dancing night at the Mocambo, despite the clothes she wore, dressed as if for a great occasion, her dress now withered by my many moist hands. But she had to go, enter the building, reach her room as soon as possible, imperiously. I opened the taxi door, kissing her on the way, and escorted her to the sidewalk and perhaps a little further, near her front door. We kissed for the last time and she disappeared from view without leaving behind a broken old slipper, like a fairy tail. In her wake she left a nod, promising, assenting, consenting, and still nodding that we would see each other again—next week, a date delayed because of my night work. Could anyone have had a more improbable job than night secretary? Not night clerk or night watchman but night amanuensis. That's what I was. But, after all, many of my jobs have taken place at night: copyeditor, movie critic (which meant going to the movies at night and writing after the show), and I was almost a night guard at a factory. Only the rule about wearing a revolver as work tool prevented me from accepting that dangerous post at a time when it would have been a lifesaver in a sea of misery, when I even envied a friend (a forgotten amateur actor, unforgettable because he had the symmetrical name of Jorge Luis Jorge) his night work at a hotel—which is not the same as work in a night hotel. Night porters for nightcaps. Alone, in front of the door, on the sidewalk, letting her gain the gate, I wasn't going to walk all the way back up San Lázaro, climbing the hideous hill to descend L Street and continue straight to Avenida de los Presidentes. So I decided to return home in the taxi—an extravagance permitted by my fleeting affluence after the chain reaction of interviews that make up a poll, but not thanks to my good pay, which was bad pay, even for a mere Marxist like me, then.

We took our time, taxi, taxi driver, and I, and when we reached Twenty-seventh Street and I entered the building it was already day. I was greeted at the door by my grandmother (which didn't surprise me: my family, except for my great-grandmother, who would get up at noon and was now eternally asleep, were all early risers: of my grandmother, my father, and my mother—an inveterate insomniac who slept in fits and starts—I was the only late riser in the house) and I immediately noticed her unwelcoming expression. My Oriental grandmother was almost as scandalized as Catia's cosmopolitan grandmother at the alarm bell. Her stage fright increased as she said: "Where have you been, boy?" I said oh, just around—made null and void by the vague gesture of my tired hand. "Well, just around is where your mother and father have been looking for you all night!" my grandmother said, adding: "They haven't slept the whole night," implying that that double insomnia was my fault. This was news: my mother was looking for me, an adult, as if I were a lost little boy. It's true she would usually stay up until I returned home from a concert or a play (if she wasn't with me) but this was too much, enough to make me furious. Though I was more worried than angry. "Where did they go?" I asked my Grandmother Grace. "How do I know?" said she. "Everywhere, probably. They went out quite a while ago." But where the hell was my mother going to go find me, dragging along my father, so easy to set in motion, so difficult to move? I remembered their search party the day they discovered the ripper at Zulueta 408, but I was sixteen then and besides it was during the day. I wasn't going to stay seated, waiting for them to return, so I left the house again, to search for my searchers. Knowing my mother, I knew she wouldn't come back till she found me, the corpus delicti.

On the street I decided to turn left down the avenue, since I didn't think they'd go looking for me among the hospitals and the Príncipe prison—though one day I'd be a patient in one and a prisoner in the other. I don't know why I thought of taking Twenty-fifth Street, toward the Mocambo—perhaps a compulsion to return to the scene of the crime. It was an excellent choice: on Twenty-fifth Street, passing the spearlike lancets guarding the gate to the medical school, came my mother, Communist Rachel, a fury followed by my father, who looked even smaller —perhaps it was the distance, or the height of the gate, or my mother's height. She seemed taller from the quest, walking tall in her anger, a giantess upon seeing me appear beyond the spears, safe and sound, my mother the Fury. The meeting among the lances must have seemed like an El Vedado version of Velázquez's "Surrender at Breda." But Victory's condescension toward the vanquished turned into an invective: my mother directed a string of insults against me but also against herself for making it her duty to not only stay up all night waiting for me but to search for me late at night (*contradictio in argumentum ad noctes:* it was already morning) and I didn't know how to pacify her: my mother, you see, was capable of having a real bad temper.

When she finished, subdued not by me nor by her words but by some early wayfarers, she hissed: "Where were you?" I told her the truth: life is not literature: "In the Mocambo." She knew what the Mocambo was: my mother seemed to know everything human—and sometimes the divine. "Alone?" "Of course not," I said, "with a girl." "With a girl?" This question echoing my answer seemed to increase her rage. "With a girl?" she repeated. "I've spent the whole night without sleeping, looking for you like a madwoman, while you were out with a girl?" My mother's raging reaction upon knowing that I'd been with a girl the whole night is curious. Let me explain, please. Only a while ago, on our last visit to our town, she was talking to a girl in Colón Park (same Columbus, different park) when I passed by with my brother on our way to the movies. My mother called me over and introduced me to this girl. She wasn't particularly pretty but neither was she ugly. For some reason (maybe timidity) all I did was to shake her hand tepidly, say how do you do and walk off. Evidently my mother expected much more of me (and maybe from the girl) because later that night, back home, she scolded me. My mother could be quite caustic and chided everyone in the family, including my father of course, over whom she had an advantage not only in height but in character, her dynamic vitality—which she maintained all her life—contrasting with his passivity, his almost Oriental patience that had allowed him to survive the cruelest catastrophes since he was a little boy. My mother took me to task for not having paid enough attention to the girl, who had told her how good-looking I was and all I did was to give her a stiff handshake and turn away. "You should take more notice of women," she finished, forgetting she had once scolded me with equal vehemence for paying too much attention to Beba and neglecting my

230

English lessons. Perhaps it was because by then (the time of that encounter in the town park) I was eighteen, no longer a minor, and therefore it was my obligation to be attentive to the opposite sex. But now, this night, no, this morning (by now the discussion was continuing amid bread-laden pedestrians passing by and staring at us, at my mother, a platinum fury with disheveled hair in the full light of day), she was infuriated that I had told her the naked truth. I even thought it would have been better to travesty truth and say that I'd been with Juan Blanco or Franqui or Rine Leal, or with some vague group from Our Time. I don't know if it was the bright light or the many indiscreet wayfarers or if my mother had consumed her store of invectives, but she was suddenly silent, stopping as if she'd been wound up till then, and she started walking, another invention of Maelzel: the mortified mother.

My father, calm, conciliatory, and Cuban, said: "Come on, let's go home for breakfast." Or could it be that he, a secret womanizer, revealed by my spyglasses, understood my predicament? If this were a family saga and not a rosary of memories, memoranda, I would tell how my father, despite (or because of) his morality, was crazy about women, how tactile he became when greeting them—squeezing a hand, touching an arm, even patting a shoulder: approximations—and how he had trysts with women who worked at *Hoy* or green correspondents who came to Havana and stayed with a *camarada* (in Spanish comrade, *camarada*, visibly comes from *cama*, bed, and it means bedfellow, not necessarily strange to each other) or, later, even neighborhood maids. Fina, my uncle the Kid's wife, who was very good-natured, would often say to my mother when visiting our house: "Zoila, your husband is cowpunching me already," which my mother ignored, not interested if it was true or false. My father would smile his shy smile—but continue his sexual politics by other means. My mother used to seek asylum then in reading romantic novels. Before, it had been radio soap operas, or going with me to the ballet, the theater, or the Philharmonic. Now, in El Vedado, the Zolaesque *solar* left behind, the soap operas had been relegated to the past, Tolstoys in the attic. We went out less frequently together because I went to the Philharmonic or ballet with my artist friends: I was more involved in active culture and writing and, on my way to becoming an adult, I had broken the affective adolescent umbilical chord, my theater tether. Now she returned to the refuge of her youth. But, either because of my influence or because her taste had progressed, she read, instead of Daring Dan (whose real name was José María Carretero) or the curious Colombian Vargas Vila, the Brontë sisters (who knows how many times she read *Wuthering Heights*), *Rebecca* in her regression, or in a game of romantic Russian roulette *Anna Karenina*, a book she read time and again until my Argentine edition in two volumes was worn and torn in pieces, their old blue covers becoming glaucous green, metaphors of my mother's absinthe. My father, on the other hand, armed with my former spyglasses, locked away on the balcony late at night, secretly scrutinized the buildings across the avenue, perhaps without my prejudice against spying on the windows of Olga Andreu—an old acquaintance be forgot.

My next date with Honey (no, not Rosie) Hawthorne was cheaper than our night at the Mocambo: I was saving my money for a nearby *posada*. I convinced her that we should watch the moon together from the Malecón, and somehow I managed to persuade her that the moon could be seen better in El Vedado, for her the South Seas, rather than nearby (she lived a block away from the waterfront). We walked up the Malecón beyond Maceo Park and the old San Lázaro Tower, passing the ramp of Twenty-third Street (which was beginning to be known as La Rampa) and the rocky promontory on which Hotel Nacional sits, my mute escarp, and the lavish lamp, an unknown masterpiece of Art Deco, a beauty beacon. We continued past the end of Avenida de los Presidentes but I kept my eyes on the sea, the horizon made visible by the fluorescent moon, as she made some analogy I can't remember (perhaps about the influence of the gaucho epic *Martín Fierro* on Thomas Mann: "The full moon shone") and we went on walking, thanks to the foresight of the Minister of Public Works, who extended the Malecón—if not, we would have had to stop right at that point, called The Bend, because of the bend there before the avenue. In the spirit of the place (or compulsion of the moment) we had a milkshake at the stand called, without much mental effort, The Bend—which Silvio Rigor, mortal, always called The Bends. My brother and I spent one afternoon there with Harold Gramadié, composer of serious not serial music, our first outing that far west. That afternoon at The Bend, Harold finished his Coca-Cola (or perhaps a Havana soda like Materva), but still thirsty he took my bottle and drank from the same glass lip I had drunk from. He must have seen my horrified expression (sharing things, when I have to put my mouth where others put theirs, has always disgusted me) because he said to me: "I know you wouldn't be capable of doing the same thing with me. But you have to learn that dirtier things are done in the name of love." A foreshadowing of the lesson (leading to the worst) which Juliet Estévez gave me on love and lips and labia—or words to that affection. Perhaps I could give lessons to Honey that night and lead her to the best.

We sat on the Malecón wall. I couldn't say how often I'd sat on the Malecón wall since that luminous summer afternoon in 1941 when I discovered it, Columbus of the city, and it charmed me forever, fortune and my eyes making Havana into a fairyland. I sat on the wall then with my mother and brother, she showing me Maceo in his park, while my father and Eloy Santos were talking probably about politics. I sat on the wall with my uncle the Kid on lucid, translucid cloudless autumn afternoons in 1941. Later I went with high-school mates, this time sitting in the parks facing the Malecón, to watch all the girls go by on their way to the amphitheater or coming from the Prado. I returned to the wall with literary colleagues from the review *New Generation,* the view seen at night, sometimes accompanied by old Burgos (who wasn't old, really: exile had aged him), to listen to his seemingly erotic but actually pathetic stories, told in first person, an impossible Casanova not only because he was ugly (his enormous Spanish nose, a probing proboscis, made him more like Cyrano than Don Juan) but because of his passive, sedentary life among books, first editions, and Cuban paintings in the modest apartment on Galiano Street he shared with his mother and sister (even uglier than Burgos because she was his female version), telling tales of virtuous women offering themselves to him. There was a story about eroticism made with mirrors: through a looking glass rosy Burgos saw how a shameless woman undressed for him, the specular surface an accomplice to the vision of her naked flesh—perhaps a quickie via quicksilver? But he hadn't accepted any of them because they were the wives of friends, therefore sacred. One day, however, his virility wouldn't stand passively for these visions—and would stand up and be cunted.

We adopted the Havanans' custom of sitting with our backs to the sea, watching the cars go by, a habit which amazed me the first time I noticed it. For me, despite my fascination with fast cars, that is, with speed, the spectacle was on the other side of the barrier: it was the sea, the bare coast of reefs, the flowing tide, and a little further, barely a nautical mile or two out to sea, the Gulf Stream, a purple mass, almost solid but fluid, flowing, moving uncontrollably from south to north, seeming to be on the move from west to east, away from the sun, a river within the sea. At night it was a mysterious blackness, where the lanterns of deep-sea fishermen shone like catfishes' eyes, during the day a fascinating habitat because of the fleeting arrows of flying fish, the slow-motion flight between surf and deep waters of the sting rays and the fearful fins of the sharks. Beside us on those nights of literary conversations or erotic boasts were the coast anglers, fishing from the wall, casting long lines into the sea, carried there by boats specialized in this urban type of fishing: from the shore to the deep. This varied sideshow, changing yet eternal, was lost to the *habaneros* watching the speeding cars go by, making the Malecón into a racetrack where all speeds were possible: crossing the road was indeed a fearless act: imported civilization turning its back on nature: the island that scorned the sea. Here in Havana, on the Malecón, her most characteristic avenue, the focal point was Maceo Park, with its monument to the Bronze Titan: the eponymous warrior, equestrian and martial, his mortal machete held high, turned his back to the promenade, his stamping bronze horse offering its rear end to the sea, shitting on the surf, turning the Atlantic Ocean into a septic hole eternally flushed by the Gulf Stream.

We were seated, Honey and I (I had to turn her around so that she'd face the sea), on the wall watching night and the sea, seeing the full moon reflected in the smooth, calm ocean, with scarcely any waves, no surf, no foam, the moon shining in a cloudless sky. I remembered Earl

233

Biggers's luminous moon over Honolulu, from one of the first detective novels I ever read: a moon more memorable in that story of deceit, mystery, and death than in real life now. I was going to talk to Honey about this literary moon over Hawaii but I was assailed by the fear that she would immediately argue that Biggers's description was stolen from a precursor, the Argentine Ricardo Güiraldes in *Don Segundo Sombra*—the moon over a pampa pond turned into a bigger moon in the Pacific sky. Honey (Rose and the Compass) Hawthorne had a nerve-racking knowledge of Latin American literature, which not only led her to make analogies, which is permissible, but also to instantaneous discoveries of unexpected steals, she the feminine and Havanan version of Charlie Chan, detective. Actually she was ahead of her time, and what she and I least suspected then is that this vision of South American precursors in other later literatures was going to become fashionable one day—even among critics, especially among critics. Thus I was sitting on the hard cement of the wall beside a scholar and critic—and I didn't know it then. Of course I didn't say a word about Charlie Chan's revealing moon and simply asked her if the night wasn't beautiful and almost released, with my overture, a Cuban rhapsody: "It's beautiful! *Bellísima!*" she said. "One of the most beautiful nights of my life!" looking at me with her black eyes beneath her blond hair (she wore it in a kind of page boy, with lank bangs that came down almost to her eyes, which would become the fashion—the haircut, not her eyes—three years later: ahead of her times again. At least in her hair style.

But I was going to find out that very night if she was also ahead in sex: not all Havana girls, of those within my reach those days, were as daring as Juliet Estévez. Would Honey Hawthorne be one of the audacious roses in the old poem? I was going to tell her, on the brink, that that night would never be repeated again, relating my theory or notion that nobody looks at the same moon twice to my devotion to *carpe diem*—in this case, seize the night. *Carpe noctem.* But I didn't say it for fear of frightening her: after all, it was only our second date. Or perhaps I feared another avalanche of the Rose of yesteryear.

My caution didn't prevent Honey from expanding long tirades into dissertations on the beauty of the night (my fault), life in Havana, her difficulties (not my fault), and literature—partially my fault because Honey knew I was writing, had earned crucial critical comments, and once almost won the prize in a literary contest that our mutual friend won, the same young woman writer who had introduced us, who encouraged me to go out with Honey, and who, I'm sure, persuaded Honey to accept my invitation. Behind her writer's reserve and thick near-sighted glasses hid a sexuality revealed in the man she chose for mate, a hirsute hombre, a brute, a kind of beast in this clear case of Mrs. Jekyll and Mr. Hyde.

Honey, apprentice writer, and her long lecture that night on *The Vortex,* another of her South American masterpieces, led me astray: I was completely lost amid the underbrush as I asked myself what the sea had to do with the jungle and couldn't answer myself. But my literary censor came to the rescue, half replying for me, connecting the sea with the desert, both a man-made measure of eternity—though perhaps the jungle was, my censor cited, the third measure of eternity on earth. "The sea and the desert and the jungle are natural labyrinths," my saving censor expressed. But I myself didn't accept the jungle except as a fantasy: Tarzan's jungle, *The Jungle Book* jungle, the jungle according to Rider Haggard, yes, but I could never accept the South American jungle, not even Horacio Quiroga's (Honey's favorite author: "He's like Poe, better than Poe," she used to say. "It's Poessible," I admitted.). If only she had spoken about the sea, even about sea literature, not Conrad's, which Honey never discovered, but even Lino Novas Calvo's sea, I could have conversed with her. But the jungle stream pleased her consciousness more than the Gulf Stream, while for me the country was not a conscious stream but a dream I had when I was a boy—besides, the jungle had disappeared from the island quite a while ago, geography devoured by history. Furthermore, I didn't talk about literature with women then: the only thing to do with women was to speak of love, to try to make love to them, in four letters, fuck—a word Juliet hated, and which would horrify Honey. But somehow I always managed to get together with women who were, in one way or another, priestesses of literature. It was literature's fault that my relationship with Juliet hadn't been more profound, more satisfying, she crazed by poetry as she was mad about boys, living a literary life reading Isadora Duncan's autobiography too religiously, making me scandalously scan Eliot, ponder Pound, and even reacting literarily, poetically, between quotation marks and amid quotes, to everyday life. Now here was Honey expounding on the verdant vortex of the jungle in the Havana night, where the domestic palm trees on that stretch of the Malecón called Avenue of the Port were burnt by brine from the sea, where the Malecón itself had been stolen from the sea. And I had to listen to her or, what's worse, pretend to be listening to her, trying to look as if I were concentrating on her honeyed harangue—to rhyme with meringue. (A future Venus would choose as her farewell an absolutely literary formula. Let me hasten to add that she was the least poetic of the women I had known till then. Ah, art and ardor!)

"Why don't we walk a bit?" I asked, taking advantage of a pause in her stroll through the jungle of books which I feared would reach the horizon but never a horizontal bed beyond. Besides I already had an idea about the direction our stroll would take: toward Paseo, in a live reckoning. South by southpaw. Faux paw. Fortunately she didn't ask where we were going.

"If you like," she said. That was good: a yielding young lady. Very good.

"Yes," I said, "I'm a little numbskulled," but literature kept her from catching word plays, even that facile, folkloric pun. So I added a scholium on the ilium: "I'm a little numb from so much sitting." But I refrained from telling her where, precisely, I was numb.

She got up. That is, she swung around on her buttocks, turning in the direction of the sidewalk, street, and promenade. I helped her off the wall though she really didn't need my help since this sea wall, which has so many different levels all along it, was quite low here but not as low as where the Malecón borders the canal at the port entrance. I took her by the arm to cross the avenue, which was quite a feat: without stoplights, waiting for the dense Amazon flow of traffic to wane. We were finally able to cross and to begin our walk up Paseo, the hill relieved by the crisscrossing of successive terraces. This promenade, like its twin, Avenida de los Presidentes, is quite dark at night, but the moon, no longer the Pacific nor even the Caribbean but the Atlantic moon, still shone, shedding light on the road—though I would have liked it to be a less livid light. All the same, once we passed Línea Street, near a stretch of the promenade which one day, one night, some nights in 1958 would make unforgettable, I dared to pass my right arm around Honey's waist—and she didn't put up the slightest resistance, not even verbal. Did this mean I had taken possession of my carnal territory? We advanced from terrace to terrace, joined by my arm on its way to becoming a true tether. A little beyond Seventeenth Street I bent over (despite her nighttime heels she was still shorter than I) and kissed her. She let me kiss her. It was the first time I had kissed her since our night at the Mocambo, but there and in the tolerant taxi the rums and Cokes she had consumed (cuba libres as she called them correctly) could have been liberating her. But now there wasn't much time left—or was it space? Before reaching Twenty-third I turned her around and kissed her hard. She returned the kiss, with some lipstick thrown in as an extra. Pungent Tangee flavor. Smearme.

Now I must explain that a little beyond Twenty-third Street Paseo gets darker, and the avenue, instead of ending in a monument—well deserved, no doubt, since it's another prominent Havana hill—simply peters out. Its end, further up, could very well have been the amazing jungle of Honey and her South American boys. Actually, what was there at that time was a vacant, barren lot, a wasteland filled with sleeping goats, which one day in the future would become a wide street of reinforced concrete. Still ill-illuminated, as dark as today, it would be crossed by speeding cars on their way to the Civic Plaza, the faster the better. But now, that is then, we approached the street's end and Honey, wary when she saw us pass the Paseo Building, the Palace's twin, began to slow down her slow pace to slow motion. I wanted to hurry her but not frighten her, and so, a warning without warning, I made a sign near the house of assignations and quoted a passage: "We must get there before the monsoon!"

"What?"

"We'll see the moon soon."

"What are you talking about? We've been watching the moon all night."

"Have we? How strange! I never noticed. I must have been blinded by your beauty. Ill-met by moonlight."

"What's the matter with you? I can't understand a word you're saying."

"It's Esperanto."

"Come again?"

"Any time you say, dear. It's the language of the tongue that always waits, expectant."

"You know what? You're beginning to sound crazy."

"The gift of the tongue is a form of madness. A divine lunacy. Did you know, by the way, that lunacy comes from the moon? Too much moon. Moonstroke."

Suddenly she stopped in her tracks. It was a full stop. "Now tell me, where the hell are we going?"

"Pray, my lady, those are harsh words for a gentle woman."

"I don't give a damn! All I want to know is *where* you are leading me."

"Taking you."

"All right, where you are taking me?"

"To La Luna."

"La luna? What's that?"

"A resting place near here."

"Never heard of it."

"There are many more things between here and the moon than you've heard of in your philosophy."

"Are you being ironic?"

"No, merely caustic. Lunar caustic."

"Well, what about it?"

"What about what?"

"Where are you taking me?"

"Then it's whereabouts but not whoreabouts. In my case now, hardabouts."

She grew silent. Stayed silent. Sulking.

"You should have said: General, you are trampling on me with your grammar."

She still was still and silent. Bad tidings.

"That's from a Mexican novel, you know."

She looked at me quickly. Good tidings. "Which one is that?"

Gotcha!

"Underdogs."

"By Mariano Azuela?"

Gotcha bitcha!

"Mari Juano Allswell, high on a reefer. That's him."

But Honey, a partisan of the well-made novel, was inoculated against paronomasia, and I could figure my exact latitude and longitude by her painted astrolabia. Dead reckoning.

"Can you please tell me where we're going now?"

How could I explain to her, really? I opted for a subterfuge, subterranean refuge. Fox Pa gone to earth.

"It's here close by."

She confronted me squarely: "Where?"

I don't think Honey knew where Paseo Street ended for me. I think (it's typical of memoirs that people write them when they're beginning to lose their memory) that I've already spoken of the unforgettable visit with Juliet Estévez to the Second and Thirty-first *posada,* which seems an arbitrary sum and is called thus because it's on the corner of Second and Thirty-first streets. (There is or was a *posada* in Miramar on Eighty-seventh Street, and it always seemed a lapsus of perverted Havanans to have baptized the meeting of Neptuno and Galiano streets as Cunt Corner—simply because old habitués and roués chose the rues to watch the women go by: all big buttocks and huge hips and thundering thighs, exposing themselves through their tight clothes more than if they'd been naked. And there was the old moviehouse on Neptuno and Belascoain, whose name I forget but whose nickname I remember: the Palace of Hot Cream. These Havana perverts were gallant in deeds—in the sense given to the adjective *gallant* by the pornographic novelettes—and generous with their sexual allusions applied to buildings. Why, then, didn't one of their enterprising architects build a *posada* on Sixty-ninth Street?) I'm thinking all this now, of course. What I thought then was how to lead Honey on course—amid euphemisms, cheap cheats, and skirmishes—to the port of call girls in the *posada.* Cool Cream Palace.

"Well, you'll see. First let's go to the end of this street." I stopped. Verbally, that is, for I was going to add: "Where the moon of May shines bright," but it seemed a bit too Donjuanesque after Molière. Hot air. "Then we turn down Second Street."

I stopped—physically.

"And then?"

She wanted to know the exact topography of the surroundings, but I couldn't give her more information. Not now. This was wartime and it was dangerous for my destination to be known. One of our crafty members might be missing.

"Let's walk a little more and you'll see," I said.

Honey seemed to accept this proposition, which was obviously short of a subject. We continued our leisurely promenade along Paseo, though I really wanted to speed up our pace, but Honey, this Honey who was like a casual caricature of Juliet, thin, almost hipless, hapless with her hair absurdly bleached blond, was suddenly imitating Juliet in her reluctance to reach the top of the walk, the last terrace of the promenade, though Juliet had gone avidly. I held her by the arm and was trying to get her to walk fast, but the last thing I wanted to do was frighten her: Honey was

238

already quite skittish. Kittled kitten. We got to the top of the hill and she turned toward me as if about to say "Quo Vadis," but before she could speak in pig Latin I herded her into the rugged, risqué terrain that led to Thirty-first Street. I could have taken her by Zapata Street—which we had just crossed—into Second Street and from there down to Thirty-first, but I saw an open bar on the corner (where there was also a small but clean and well-lighted gas station) and perhaps people peeping, so I decided to take the more difficult path, *per ardua* from the physical point of view, but at the same time easy from the social point of view, *ad astra.* Fortunately the moon (which had ceased to be Earl Derr Biggers's, Charlie Channish and mysteriousa, to go back to being a mere moon) lighted up that wide-open space. Honey let herself be led by me, not without tripping and slipping several times in her high heels over what must have been a vacant lot or, at best, an unfinished street built by some dishonest Schubert of a contractor. But in these *rejendones* (a country word meaning the pits, and so a propos now: there's no other way to describe this backland) that the night made as virgin and dark as the thickest thicket of the Cuban countryside, Honey was, without realizing it, in the midst of the jungle Havana-style. We fatally approached the erotic enclave of the *posada,* sheltered by its high wall opened on two sides, gaps that weren't doors but rather entrances for cars and taxis and the occasional couple on foot—that is, for us. Finally we arrived, and what I most feared happened.

"What's this?" asked Honey without raising her voice but with the tone of one who's been trapped in an ambush. I tried to explain, an explanation that should have been given before. After all, she had given me an image of her (from the day I met her at the offices of the survey bandits) as an emancipated girl, almost a liberated woman, open to life —at least to opening her legs, to sex.

"Well, you see," I began, with difficulties even before beginning, "this is a place where we can spend some time—"

She didn't let me finish. "What? You've brought me to a *posada?"*

Her voice suggested that I had committed the crime that has no alibi.

"It's only to spend some time together," I insisted. It was the only thing I could think of, honestly.

"But it's a *posada,* right?"

"Well, actually it's a hotel."

Nothing could look less like a traditional hotel than that walled, almost fortified place, hidden by the wall and the trees: a *maison de rendez-vous* in Hong Kong is what it looked like, and it could have been a hideout in Mexico as well. But I had to say something to her.

"A *hotelito?"* she said and, as always, a diminutive sounded more sinister than the word itself. A small hotel.

"Well, yes, if you say so."

This city-wise phrase, "if you say so," which I had acquired during my years in Old Havana, completed the sentence emotionlessly and provoked the passing of my sentence immediately. Guilty.

"But I can't enter a *hotelito!*" and this sentence ends in an exclamation mark because Honey had begun in almost neutral tones to complete the verdict in a state of outrage.

"But it's only to spend some time together, to talk," as if we hadn't talked enough, especially she, "in private and then we'll go."

"But I can't," she insisted. All this time, while the argument (that's what our intercourse had become) was going on I was leading her by the arm, closer and closer to the entrance of the *posada, hotelito,* infamous inn, house of assignation, or whatever it was, crossing the unpaved, stony street that made it seem like a colonial cobblestone court, Trinidad revisited. We got to the very wall of the fortress of love. (How old Ovid, who talked about love as a battlefield, would have liked this erotic enclosure.)

"Why?" I asked her in an almost imperious manner, summoning her to define the reason why she couldn't enter the *posada* with me: a lack of love that dares to speak its name.

"I'm a virgin," said she.

"What?" I asked, pretending to hear the wrong article, "The Virgin herself?"

But she wasn't up to irony, much less grammatical grace, or a lesson in divinity.

"No, just a virgin," said she, a little confused.

"That's beside the point," said I, actually meaning it was a moot point. "We're not going to do anything. It's just to be alone, just the two of us," who else, anyway? "For a while, and then we'll go. No harm will be done."

She seemed to be thinking it over, now a mere step from one of the doors—or doorlike openings: the real doors were hidden like slits in this pillbox of love.

"No," she said. "I don't want to."

"The most we'll do is kiss a little. I promise you."

"We've kissed enough for one night already."

"And how about Mallea's *Story of an Argentine Passion?*"

"What? What?" she asked, totally lost. She probably hadn't even heard of that Argentine author: he wasn't one of her select South Americans. He didn't even write about the pampas, much less about the jungle and wild rivers.

"Nothing, nothing. I mean I agree with you. Too many kisses for one night. Though you must remember that we kissed only on the last leg of our walk."

"I still don't want to go in."

Nevertheless, she didn't budge from the door. I was remembering one afternoon—not long ago, so it wasn't a feat of memory—when I substituted a friend of mine as proofreader at the newspaper *Mañana.* I had done it before but that day was memorable because this anonymous *amigo* had had an embarrassing accident: he had swallowed his dental bridge and, given the jeering atmosphere in any Havana printing shop,

240

he had asked me not to mention it. I told him that he had had an illustrious precursor in Sherwood Anderson, though I didn't say Anderson had died as a consequence. My friend insisted I keep it to myself and I promised that mum was the word. But somehow they all found out about the dental disaster, and not only the printers and linotypists but even the old doorman asked me bitchy questions. The most brazen remark was about this being an amazing trick, like a person who could bite his own ass. The wayzgoose was over no sooner than it had begun. They forgot all about me as a source of amusing but unpublishable news and started their afternoon game: watching those entering the *posada* on the corner of Amistad and Barcelona, especially attentive to the open entrance door on amiable Amistad Street and the sidewalk across the road. I began my work, reading galley after galley at the worktable on one side of the shop, but not far from the grated back door through which the newspapers were passed in bulk to the distributing vans. Suddenly there was a commotion among the printers—though that wasn't what they called themselves: they belonged to the union of graphic artists—who were getting a kick out of something going on in the street, and they kept calling me to join them. I was already a queer fellow at the offices, considered the eternal student, a stunted adolescent, my status as journalist (proofreaders were considered journalists then in Cuba) allowing me not to participate in their ways of a goose, but I felt obliged to join them. I went over to where they were all clustered, the making of the newspaper having come to a standstill. They were near the grated windows but far enough not to be detected from the street (besides, the midday glare outside sank the inside of the shop into deep darkness) and I saw what they were watching with intense interest and lecherous laughter. The performers of this farce were a couple on the verge of entering this inn of ill-repute, but something was making it impossible for them to penetrate that lovers' hideaway: she was a reluctant lover, fair and fat, and refused to enter just as stubbornly as her companion was trying to make her cross the threshold. Soon the argument, which at first must have been verbal, became a venereal version of tug-of-war. He was pulling her by one arm, one of his feet anchored on the jamb of the door, hauling her in vigorously—but she was grabbing with all her might onto any support: the smooth wall, the outer frame of the entrance, the door itself. Her feet slipped on the sunny sidewalk, while the man's leg seemed firmly implanted inside the dark doorway. Both (and this was curious and comical for the peeping toms of *Mañana*) seemed to completely forget, with all their pushing and shoving, the passersby passing by. Eager onlookers all. I thought some man (there were still some Cuban gentlemen left) might champion the cause of the dumpy damsel in distress, but her unrelenting lover knew better and kept pulling on his mismatched mate. Checkmate. Check-in-mate. Perseverance (or perhaps brute force) finally triumphed and the woman was dragged through the entrance by her caveman, the two disappearing in the black hole of that eternally open door, which hid (as I would know years later) another access, accessory before and after the fuck, to ingeniously block the outsider's view of the inner inn: from there on in there was a staircase to the first floor and ticket office (what else can one call the clerk's cubicle?) and to the unrest rooms: the double door was really to insure discreet entrances and exits—in this case, in theory only.

Remembering that predicament (in which the remiss mistress surely soon allowed herself to be enjoyed and to enjoy herself at the same time in the same game), remembering my reaction to that brutality, to that hauling Havanan's lack of elegance, I didn't try to imitate him and make Honey enter by brute force—anyway, there was no door frame but only the smooth opening in the wall, which would have made easier for me what Wanton and Tagle, printers at *Mañana*, would have qualified, not without admiration, as shove come to putsch.

"Okay," I said. "Let's go," and I started walking toward Zapata Street. She must have felt that she'd saved herself from a destiny worse than death, emerging from the academic shades of the grove around the *posada* to slip away along the tall wall (looking like a cemetery wall, even though on the other side was life or, at least, the opposite of death) and walk past the humble houses neighboring the *posada* on Second Street. She caught up with me on the corner of Zapata, giving the habitués (or perhaps casual customers) of the bar the rare opportunity, fat fuck, to see a couple coming from the *posada*—without having entered. Because I didn't doubt that the tardy tipplers, now looking at us as they drank cold beer and aguardiente, *knew.* I was sure they guessed it by the vertical position of our bodies—I in front frustrated, she following fearfully—that the score was nil. They were doubtless as knowledgeable about the *posada*'s instant inhabitants as the graphic guys on the *Mañana* newspaper were about the guests at Amistad and Barcelona: they could always guess when a couple were heading for the *posada* no matter how innocently both walked on the street, no matter how respectable she seemed, no matter how nonchalant he looked. Tagle and the others were capable of guessing when a sexual squabble, or a fuckers' fuckup as wanton Wanton would say, had occurred—and they would occur more frequently than one would think, believe me. As I learned in the two years I proofread there, religious education, social conventions, and sexual fear were stronger than that powerful sensuous temperament —the climate, nature, sex, and customs—which gave Havana women the "impulse to sin," as another woman, girl, would put it in the near future. And me, myself, and I had just performed in one of those fiascos!

Disappointment gave way to anger, making me cross Zapata without attending to Honey at all, marching down the Second Street hill to Twenty-third Street—until I heard a voice behind me saying: "Wait for me, please." It was she. This made me stop and wait, moved to stand still —a good place for an oxymoron, Twenty-third Street—detained by her tone. When she was next to me I could see her—despite the fact that the

242

moon had disappeared and the street was darker than the end of Paseo. For the first time, I noticed her silly sheeplike face. She didn't look at me but it couldn't be modesty: more likely it was fear of my reaction, though she must have imagined I could be a friendly lover. My friendliness could also, however, dissolve into anger: nobody is more capable of fury than an easygoing guy. Perhaps she sensed this. Or was it her experience that dictated her behavior with me? I realized I knew very little about Honey. Except her last name, the house she lived in, and one of her friends (or whom she called a friend—aside from the South American authors, all dead, of whom she seemed to have a carnal knowledge), I knew nothing of her past: how many boyfriends she'd had or not, and if she'd been in this same situation before. Maybe she had previously confronted a disappointed and therefore furious friend about to become a lousy lover. I had never asked her about her past—perhaps, now I see it, because we didn't have much of a future. Or maybe because I was afraid of unleashing another of her literary lectures, a glib gloss of asinine annotations, like the ones she adorned my book with. If I let her tell me about her years "copied from Horacio Quiroga," and her past "taken from José Eustacio Rivera," I'd find myself forever lost in the successive South American jungles of her secret recesses. She must have had a life of her own already: she was no little girl. Though younger than I she could easily have been eighteen or older—which at that time made her an adult woman, especially in Havana, a city matured by the tropics in a nation born with the century, where youth was a cult and the occult.

While I reflected in the dark, I continued walking and it was the milky lights of Twenty-third Street (though it still didn't have its present-day lighting: I always hated that ashen tungsten) that snapped me out of my meditation. I halted, nearly faltering, at the bus stop sign. The trolleys had already vanished (a pity), replaced by white, English, banal buses, which did the same run with less noise, but none passed Honey's house. We had to take Route 28—the same that took me to my work on Trocadero. We waited a while, in total silence. I was still enraged (or simply angry) and Honey must have feared my possible reaction to her words, to the mere sound of her voice, which is why she didn't open her mouth. After several Route 32s went by, all luxurious GM buses, Route 28 finally arrived, modestly delayed, domestic made. We got on, I letting her go first but without offering a helping hand. A few blocks later, coming to Avenida de los Presidentes, I informed her that I would get off at the corner of my house because I had to get up early.

As I got off, almost smiling, with the sheepish half smile she now wore, the whore, she said: "See you soon," wanly.

I thought of Branly, and said: "So long," which in Havana was a substitute for good-bye. This was a strange Havanan superstition: saying good-bye could imply a final farewell, a separation and perhaps death, and *so long* was therefore substituted in situations where one didn't expect to see again the person to whom this foreboding *adiós* was ad-

243

dressed. What I meant to say to Honey was I'll be seeing you with my adopted adieu. I think she understood perfectly because the next day, a little before I left for the School of Journalism, she phoned me at home:

"Forgive me," she said. "I was acting naïve last night." Her readings allowed her to say *naïve* instead of *silly,* as a present-day *habanera* would have said. I would have preferred *silly,* or even *foolish,* but I didn't correct her. You see, she was a faux-naïve. So she continued: "I shouldn't have done what I did. It was very immature on my part." She was the one calling her actions immature: for me they were completely middle class. That is, more mature than immature, or rather, rotten: at that time I thought being bourgeois was as bad as being an academic: the latter debunked art while the former vilified life. I didn't say a thing; she did all the talking: "But it won't happen again, I promise you. Shall we go out tonight?"

I hesitated a moment before answering: "I can't tonight. I have to work."

I wasn't playing hard to get. I really had to work. I could skip a night every once in a while, or leave work early, which I had done to help the Cine Club. But I couldn't do it two times in a row in the name of love, that lost cause. You see, I had already sneaked away the night before.

"When then?" she almost bleated. The roles were reversed: now Honey was after me. I should have told her that she was the virgin of virgins, since I had never done it with a virgin. But I replied: "Saturday, maybe."

"Saturday?" quoth the black sheep, as desolately as if Saturday was in the time of nevermore. I was suddenly happy: I knew that Saturday would be an unholiday, the bitch's Sabbath. It was the taming of the screw.

"Saturday is the loveliest night in the week," I said in my broken English. But broken or not it was Greek to her.

"What did you say?"

"*Sí,* Saturday."

"You'll come get me?"

No. That would be a concession and I didn't want to give her any, yet. Besides, picking her up meant going to San Lázaro, sleazy street, and confronting the enemy façade of her building. I decided on no man's land.

"Why don't we meet at Radiocentro, on the corner, at eight?"

I had already begun to like the Ur-urbanity of La Rampa, marginal now but it would soon be central. I would end up living and dreaming that stretch of Twenty-third Street from L to the Malecón, just five blocks five but a world in itself, an avenue of adventure. I remember one summer night returning from work early and streetwise. My work hours, you see, were variable if not capricious, my job a moveable feat. I could begin at eight and finish at ten, or begin at eight-thirty and stay till ten-thirty or even eleven, doing my major task, which was talking to Ortega, or reading and writing for *Bohemia:* I was already beginning to read the short stories submitted by Cuban writers, to suggest foreign literature that should be translated, and to write some brief and biased bios for The Profile of the Week. That night, made memorable by my mood, instead of getting off the bus at Avenida de los Presidentes, I hopped off (literally) at L and Twenty-third, at the fun fair on the site where the Havana Hilton would be built years later. I crossed the street to the cafeteria, to give myself the triple treat of a ham and cheese sandwich (I should have ordered that Havanan sandwich, the *medianoche*), a papaya milkshake, my favorite, and a demitasse. The occasion was highlighted by the décor. The cafeteria was then new, with shiny Pullman seats, gleaming chrome on the stools, *varía* wood on the bar, and the diffuse lighting gave every-thing a sparkling radiance that was like a mild hallucinatory drug: I was enchanted by the food, the milky Musak and the ambiance of glowing glamour. It was a new luxury for me, which I could afford because I had just been paid my measly salary, making me a Croesus for a night. An-other memorable meal around then took place before our move to El Vedado. I had also just been paid and at that time the money I earned was all for me. It was a golden afternoon. Or so it seemed: perhaps it was cloudy, but it was October when it's not as hot and the sky is usually clear in Havana, and if there are no hurricanes, rain is an April memory. It was noon. Anyway, it was before class. I entered El Carmelo on Twenty-third and ordered toast and coffee. The toast came surprisingly wrapped in paper napkins, hot and slightly glazed with Danish butter. I had never before eaten such a snack, and though I would repeat it in the future in the same place at the same time, it would never again be so memorable: those are the treasures of poverty, in which a mere cup of *café au lait* and buttered toast become a luxury, a Lucullent feast. I can easily com-pare those moments, that delicacy in that restaurant and that cafeteria, with another source of solitary pleasure: masturbation, those first unfor-gettable manipulations. Memorable masturbations bring me back to my want of women and to Honey and our date: evidently her words sighed on the phone signified what she would call her surrender. At least that's what she called that action, that act, chatting on the Malecón, sitting on the wall, her words eclipsed by a brilliant reflection on the literary moon, I listening while I looked at the Hawaiian moon, bigger than Biggers's. She had spoken then of another woman, from way back, probably one of those innumerable Uruguayan poetesses on whose lives, all musical words and madness, she had modeled her own.

I took her straight from Radiocentro to the *hotelito.* This time I used a taxi, without running the risk of a long walk to bed that might dissuade her. Getting out of the taxi, she suffered a moment of indecision, or rather almost reversed her decision, as if wanting to stay in the car, as if she were totally refusing to get out, Celia Margarita Mena as a moralist hacked to pieces and now torn by terror: first an ankle, then the calf, later a knee, and finally the whole leg—but it was only a moment. We entered

245

the *posada,* I the Virgil of virgins, the connoisseur of that den. (I use the term not only in the social but in the poetic sense: it was a true cave. But I was a spelean.) Actually, I had been there only once, with Juliet Estévez, and the visit occurred in daytime. Now, at night, the multiple corridors seemed even narrower but better lit. The inside was designed (and constructed) to protect visitors from furtive eyes, with a hallway that led to the cubicle where you paid (this seemed more than ever the ticket window of a cheap movie theater), and then there was another passageway leading to the rooms. A maze. We got Room 7 in this lewd lottery (seven in Havana was the sign of sex: I could never figure out the connection: Pythagoras was usually clearer), which was the first room upstairs, and thus Honey could follow me without further trouble, the procuring clerk quickly disappearing—a pimp's discretion, or perhaps just to put the money away. Before that, however, I had ordered and paid for two Cuba Libres, knowing that the combination would please Honey and would help conquer her shyness—and mine. (Yes, I was still shy with women.) I opened the door and turned on the light. The *posada* had still not fallen into the decay (vegetation, not the flesh, finally claiming the building) that would take hold of the *hotelito* in the sixties. The bed looked clean, well-made, as if no one had ever slept there—though they might have made love in it (I'm still a disciple of Juliet) just a few minutes ago, and only Eros knows how many couples fornicated there that day. Or more countless: how many had balled on it that week. Innumerable were the couples who had copulated upon that mattress that month. Infinite in number were those who rocked the bed in a year: the vertigo of cosmic coitus that inebriated Juliet to the point of an ontological orgasm. Out of the cradle endlessly fucking.

The room was completely furnished, with a side door that led to the bathroom and a large shuttered window: Honey entered behind me, looking around as if she were seeing a *posada* room for the first time in her life. If her reaction wasn't authentic, I had just discovered a great actress. I closed the door and the two of us stood there without knowing what to do with each other. I moved to the center of the room and looked back at Honey—who had remained beside the door, having turned into a salt statuette. I foresaw another night like the one before, a crisis of innocence or playing the virginal, but she opened her mouth to tell me, ask me:

"Could you please turn off the light?"

I didn't expect her to say that exactly, but in some way it didn't surprise me, though I felt a little cheated: I wanted to see her undress more than undressed.

"Of course," I said, and turned the light off. The world was in the dark for a few moments. Just as I was getting used to the darkness and was about to take off my clothes—there was a knock at the door.

"What's that?" asked Honey with fear in her disembodied voice.

"The police, probably."

"The *police?*" she repeated, but in her repetition there was now alarm. I don't know why she should have been afraid of the police: the sex police had not been created yet: it would be years before that infernal machine was invented. (I'll confess, though, that I was always afraid of the police, which is why my allusion was doubly dumb.)

"It's a joke. Must be the drinks."

I got to the door as best I could, opened it, and from our dark night of the body I retrieved from the fully lit corridor a tray with two glasses filled to the brim with a Coca-Cola-colored liquid, looking and smelling like Coca-Cola: they must have been Coca-Colas with odorless, colorless, but intoxicating Castillo rum.

"Free Cubas," I announced. "Rescued from the claws of the dry law."

I was happy. Since the violently distant days of Juliet—what's-inaname?—and our swarthy (me) seaworthy (her) love, all overshadowed by the fear that vindictive Vincent would appear (always at an inopportune moment), I had not been with a woman in a room, in the dark and wet, all set to fuck—or at least ready to. Go! I gave Honey her glass, in the darkness somewhat less thick now. I left the tray on one of the night tables and took a sip, or rather a drink of my cuba libre.

"Shouldn't we toast to something?" asked Honey with what was at times a pathetic naïveté—at least it seems so, looking back in *Angst.*

"Of course," I said, and got closer to her. "What shall we toast to?"

"To us," she said. "What else could it be?"

"To us," I said as she knocked her glass against mine.

"To us," she began but I didn't let her finish, kissing her. "Let me finish," she insisted. "To the two of us," she finally exclaimed and drank from her glass. I let her drink more. Then I took the glass out of her hand and returned it, with mine, to the tray. I turned back to her and hugged her. She embraced me. Nine o'clock sharp and all is well. I kissed her hard, forgetting her little painted lips à la late Joan Crawford or early Marlene Dietrich: I felt something coming, overcoming me. It was a song. Becoming more a dresser than getting dressed after seeing her lying beside me paler than the moon over the sheets, beyond the pale of my dark and proper pale, I addressed her with a silent chorus fit for a dumb chorine. To you I sing O how the moon is fair tonight above Havana: from between your legs there comes the breath of new-moon lays, while my practice bar just like a tallow candle is gleaming—and the old satellite's a full syrupy Honey moon. O, O as in my moon, as in my moon! (All together now.)

"Hold it," she said—that was my line or rather my prick I wanted her to hold, to be held, spellbound by—forgetting her refinement acquired in late Latin American readings and which she normally enforced, a policeman of her own delivery. That "hold it" was like a passport to the other side of the tracks: Honey was not only Havanan but of humble stock. "You're mussing up my dress," she added and to my surprise started taking off her clothes, not beside me but placing her many articles on a

247

low table that in another more expensive *posada* would surely be a dresser, but equally intriguing. Still submerged in darkness I watched her as she took off, after her dress, a half slip. (Honey was more modern than the women in Zulueta 408 but still hadn't reached the era of the stiff hoops that souffléed skirts.) Then off came her bra and finally her panties. Instead of coming over to me she ran stark-naked to the bed and hopped in, covering herself with the sheet. She didn't say a thing, wrapped in sheets to her chin: enveloped in her sweet shroud, motionless, paralyzed by fear, looking at the wall or ceiling because I certainly couldn't see her eyes: black dots in a dark room. I took off my clothes. I now had the habit, which I wouldn't relinquish in the hottest summer weather, of wearing a jacket. I rarely went out in shirt sleeves or sport shirt, and only did it out of necessity in those terrible times when I had no money to buy a suit. Perhaps it was to hide how skinny I was then or to make my shoulders wider, to seem more mature. I undressed as quickly as I could, despite my feet, so as not to frighten Honey, my fairy queen, with my flair. Even though she was under a sheet and on top of another, in the bed, in the room, inside the inquiet inn, I didn't want her previous reluctance to be repeated. Or, what was worse, to suffer a version of that lacklove now. When I finished disentangling myself, my legs finally free, my body naked, my penis waving like a flag all pole, I sat carefully on the edge of the bed. Honey had occupied the side closest to the door, which made me uneasy. I could see this virgin fleeing naked in the face of imminent penetration, opening the door without my being able to prevent her and rushing downstairs, down the labyrinth of corridors, through successive doors, the opening in the wall, and finally out on the street, quoting at the top of her lungs a passage from Rómulo Gallegos, Doña Barbara barbarously screaming prose in the night. But this vertiginous, virginal vision of Honey vanished the next moment, after getting under the solicitous, salacious, single sheet. She stayed still without even saying my lips are sealed. I reached out and placed my hand (which must have been wet with sweat) on her stomach, flat but soft. She still didn't say a word: the static sphinx. I moved my hand up (didn't want to move it down too, too soon) and more than finding I bumped into one of her tits: it was big. Honey's tits protruded under her dress but didn't look that big. Now under my hand, undressed, naked, they seemed to have grown. At least one of them, the right one—the one furthest from my body and therefore most accessible to my outstretched arm. I looked for the other tit with the same hand (I still didn't want to turn toward her: it was the seduction of Honey) and found it equally large: a fearful symmetry: her two tits were big. Compared with the tits I had seen up till now they were exceeded only (perhaps because I hadn't really seen Honey's tits yet) by Etelvina's precocious but prohibited tits. The other breasts I had touched naked were Juliet's and those were perfect, the suitable size for her height (or rather, dimensions) and weren't large because Juliet herself was small. But Honey's tits, the two of them, went beyond the measure of known tits: they were unknown tits: my first physical, palpable, three-dimensional encounter with mammoth mammas, orbis udders, the Grands Tetons. I enjoyed that first encounter with mammary abundance, though one day (perhaps returning to the maternal breast: my mother had small tits, which were well-preserved until she was well into middle age) I would be surprised to learn that my true ideal was the basic bust or rather little tits—but that knowledge belongs to the future. At this moment in which my hands were occupied in creating nipples on Honey's tits (it was the first time I learned that big boobs often lack nipples, or perhaps it was that the last tits I had in hand, Juliet's, had notable nipples) her breasts were too large and, like Etelvina's tits, had a certain tendency to spill over, each falling incredibly down the side, flowing over the edges of her body. I left off caressing her nipples (seizing her udders was like trying to utter the ineffable) and ran my hand down her stomach, past her nigger's navel, to her dark pubic zone—kinky with wild and woolly hairs. Later I would learn that the pubes (that singular word is a plural) tends to have curly hairs, at least in Havana. Honey's pubes disclosed the black man hidden in the bush of her ancestors. Even the Havana blonde (true or false) grew curls on her mount of Venus. I imagined Gulliver trying to masturbate (he couldn't do anything else: his penis would be a pin) a colossal Brobdingnaghag and having to make his way through the acacia grove of dyed pubic hairs, each as tall as a false acacia but entangled in a thick African thicket.

I returned from the second voyage to insert a finger between Honey's mute labia, which opened easily. I could feel her clitoris (which many theories and the solo practice with Juliet taught me to distinguish) and I was trying to go deeper when she closed her legs, one almost on top of the other, prohibiting my entrance to her main lobby. But by then I was excited enough not to stop at preambles, vestibules, or porticos, and skillfully, as if it were my twentieth-century job, I got on top of her. I began to kiss her and she returned the kisses, my flat chest cushioned by her tits but my hips rubbing against hers, almost as thin as mine, pelvis versus pelvis, bones against bones, my penis hanging around her vagina. While I kissed her I tried to separate her legs with one of mine—soft by softie. It took countless kisses, savoring her sticky lipstick—sweet cherry—feeling her teeth, penetrating her mouth with my tongue, seeking and finding her tongue, repeating or prolonging our wet kiss, a continuous performance until I managed to get my legs between her thighs, my lever of love, I Archimedes. Soon I had my two legs between hers, my penis seeking her entrance. She offered some resistance to the complete opening of her vulva, much more to the actual penetration. But how could it be otherwise with the Virgin, I mean a virgin? I insisted without ceasing to kiss her, with one hand caressing her breasts (or perhaps a single breast) and the other still holding her down, fearing that her resistance would become a rebellion and then a plan for escape, a flight for freedom. After all, hadn't she, my little turtle dove, done that once already? That was the first step toward a repetition. But now her evasions were little by little becoming inverted invasions. The head of my dick (the language of pornographic novels serves better than the prose of sex manuals to describe my situation) rubbed against her clit and amid hairs and kisses it finally found the opening. At the same time I strained forward, letting myself drop, pushing horizontally—and I entered my Honeycomb with astounding ease. Was that how one pierced a virgin's hymen? Was that a defloration? Had I torn to shreds Honey's *virgo intacta* with my push? I knew nothing about nothing: I had never gone to bed with a virgin, only with two hookers—if those fiascos could be called going to bed—and with Juliet, hardly a virgin. I knew—from my classics and my classmates' banter and chatter, from other sources, mostly sexual manuals—that if the membrane was abruptly extended, it would break, resulting in bleeding and sometimes hemorrhages. But I didn't feel blood on my penis, surrounded only by Honey's dew, which made it more slippery, penetrating deep and easily, entering and coming halfway out thanks to an oil-slick access. I also knew (from books) that there should have been a greater resistance to penetration, that when her vagina was stretched Honey should—had to—have felt pain and even cried out ("Women are very sensitive in their click," said Manuel Malaprops, confusing click with clit) but she didn't cry or click but rather moaned slightly, in time with my to-and-fro motion, without my letting my penis completely out of her vagina (still the fear of her flight), she moving together with me but not with Juliet's wisdom, moving her hips vertically while I moved horizontally, penetrating her, though she, Honey, moved a lot and soon I forgot my diligent vulvar investigations of her virginity. In any case, that was the past: so enjoy the present, her presence, which was her lips and her tongue entering my mouth mimicked by her other lips. I knew from the *Encyclopedia of Sexual Knowledge,* by Costler and Willys, how the feminine sexual organs were placed, and not only did I know the existence of vulva, vagina, and clitoris—these technical names were pale words compared to popular language and the erotic penny dreadfuls that imitated it—but also the existence of the major labia. (Years later I would find out how correct was Marcel Duchamp's metaphor of the vertical smile.) As she caressed my other tongue, like hers horizontal, boneless, like hers capable of producing a saliva, another more viscous, whiter, more fragrant one, a quick stream instead of a slow secretion, shooting out at this very moment, my ejaculation met by Honey's orgasm; she discreetly moaned in a low soprano voice, as if from some slight pain—not the screams, howls, clamorous Apache cry of Juliet. Honey and I came at the same time, which spoke highly in favor of her performance, being the first time and all. But was it the first time?

"Can you get off of me?" It was Honey and this seemed to be a direct allusion to my weight, though I was anything but heavy and at the most considered myself a precious cargo. I humored her immediately and lay down on my side, satisfied, smiling at the ceiling, not feeling the sadness the classic phrase attributes to all post-coitus. My flesh was in her thorn. Haw, haw! Honey shot out of bed like solid semen and went over to the window. She opened the curtains to let the moon rush in, still full: *like the moon that cursed Larry Talbot.* I saw Honey illuminated, milky white. Her breasts at this moment seemed enormous udders compared to her slight body, with her brief hips and thin legs. I got up and went over to her not merely to accompany her. I caressed both breasts. Udder joy.

"Can you leave me alone now?" she said, not angrily but almost with embarrassment and perhaps sorrow. In any case, she was so persuasive that I left her by the window and returned to my side of the bed. She stayed there, in the moonlight, amid the smell of the honeysuckle in the patio, my Honey suckled, awhile—minutes which then seemed to me a long lustrum. Finally she left the window and returned to the bed. As soon as she got in I began to caress her—but she stopped me, first with her hand, then with her voice: "Can you wait? I have something to tell you."

"Of course," I said, smiling. She didn't see the smile. Moreover, she didn't speak immediately. She didn't have me in emotional suspense but I was suspended sexually.

"I want you to know," she said seriously, "why nothing happened tonight."

I thought at first that she hadn't really come, that her official orgasm wasn't real but pretended—a pretender more than a usurper.

"Nothing happened?"

"I mean," she said, "to me. If you look at the sheets you won't find blood."

Who did she take me for, an ardorous Arab? I didn't even think of looking for traces of blood on the sheets, signs of the crime. Or perhaps I did think of it for a moment and forgot, upon seeing her breasts, satellites in the moonlight.

"But I was a virgin. I've lost my virginity with you tonight. The thing is, I studied belly. Ballet."

Ballet? What was she talking about? What did ballet have to do with us now, horizontal, in my joyous afterglow? Why this worry, after the orgasm and the moon, both full?

"You studied ballet?" I had to ask her something since, upon falling silent, she had left the implication out in the open, like her breasts.

"Yes," she said quickly, "I took ballet lessons. A few but enough. I don't know if you know that certain ballet exercises, the positions, the leg stretches stretch the hymen."

"Stretch the hymen!" Shit, I had forgotten, what with the fucking, that Honey was a literate lady. There's nothing worse than the apparent richness of a literary woman's vocabulary. I had known some, Juliet herself, though only a reader, who were capable of literary turns. But Honey was a practitioner of both the ballet and literature and she stretched her vocabulary as much as her legs. She continued with her queer explana-

251

tion—or choreography: "That stretching makes the hymen open totally, like a diaphragm, and so there's no blood, pain, or difficulty for the man during the first penetration," she turned toward me—until now she had been talking to the ceiling more than to me—"in this case you."

Fuck! (I usually detest obscenities but when I use them it's because other words are futile: where words die, foul words are born.) That was some alibi for the crime worse than death! She owed me nothing. I was prepared to accept that Honey wasn't a virgin but I didn't feel willing to accept her excuse. What's more, I didn't even believe her explanation. Why did she have to come up with such a theory on bloodless defloration? And now she was looking at me up close, crossing her eyes in the moonlight reflected on the polished floor, her sheep face converted into kosher mutton—bloodless—waiting to be spoken to. I had to say something to her and I almost said that she was a sphincter without a secret. But I said: "It doesn't matter."

"Yes, it does. I want you to know that you're the first man I've gone to bed with."

That could be one of the false pledges of Isolde the fake blonde. I was the first man she had gone to bed with. With the others she had balled standing up—or on all fours, a position favored by Havana's sexual folklore. But she continued: "I swear to you by my mother."

From such corn mighty oaths grow. But what was my next line in this faux play? I would also have sworn by my mother that I was a virgin to Juliet, just to get into bed with her—and in some way it was true. Juliet was the first woman I had really fucked, but not the first person I had gone to bed with. As for Honey and her virginity I could have told her on that night of cries and creams that I didn't place the slightest importance on virginity—not even on the Virgin's virginity. It wouldn't have been a lie. I knew that Juliet was anything but a virgin, and this didn't diminish my enthusiasm to go to bed with her or my pleasure, just as the notion that I was giving her my virginity, reversing the roles, didn't really matter. Most Havanans placed a lot of importance on the fact that their woman—their wife, that is—enters marriage a virgin. The Spanish heritage, or rather, the Arab aura. I myself, a Cuban after all, was gratefully convinced that my future wife was a virgin. But now, the night I had gone to bed with Honey, the last thing that entered my mind was her virtual virginity. My only worry was not her hymen but her hemming and hawing the previous time, when I had hopelessly tried to get her into the *posada:* this was what I presumed would be the physical obstacle to penetrating and stretching what she called her diaphragm. On the vagina considered as a Kodak camera: the hymen the focus, the vulva the lens, the clitoris the shutter, the secretion the silver salts, the pubic bush —*basta!* Not in vain did they have a popular saying in Cuba that to see a naked cunt was to take a photograph of yourself.

"You don't have to swear to me," I said, a hypocritical raunchy reader, or like her a Latin American reader. "I believe you."

"Really?"

She didn't believe that I believed her. I don't blame her: I'm the worst actor in the world.

"Really."

"Thanks." She smiled to me. "I was so worried. When they explained to me what ballet did . . ."

"Smoking is more harmful."

"What did you say?"

"Nothing. Consider it an aside."

But a digression would never be an aggression to her.

"As I was telling you, I stopped ballet immediately. But now I see it was too late."

"Evidently."

"The damage was already done."

Impelled more than compelled by her explanation of how a virgin was deflowered by a pirouette, I put my hand on her head. It was the first time I had done this and I felt my fingers pass over a coarse, wanton wig: her hair was her thorn.

"My Rosie Thorn." This escaped me, believe me, I didn't say it willfully: I'm not usually cruel to *mulatas*.

"Honey," Honey said, ratifying her name as her identity.

"No, Rosie. You're my posy and my Rosie Hawthorne."

I had to justify with flowers my defloration of her sex and her being. I thought of improvising a poem to her. But better than a passable poem were quaint quotations, quoting to her various verses to the rose—she would like that better. The first I remembered, regrettably, was "Where the virgins are soft as the roses they twine," which referred if not directly to virginity at least indirectly to virgins. Easier than Byron would be a bolero: "A French rose from France, whose sweet gentle fragrance . . ." But *le parfum* sharpened my sense of smell and I sniffed a whiff rising from down below. Does the rose smell of roses in the dark? This Rose exhaled secret secretions, smegma, an essence that sexologists insist is fetid. Asafetida. Fetid flower to treat flatulence. Rotund Rose, perilous perfume, parlor poem, and from poetry I extracted an essential quotation, an attar:

"There is no sting greater than that of the thorny rose," I recited, cited as if it were my own invention.

Honey looked at me: "Do I sting?"

I wasn't going to tell her that she stinks.

"Well, you are at least a Whore Thorn."

"Yes, I am a Hawthorne," she admitted.

"A thorn is a thorn is a thorn."

"What's that litany?"

"A quotation from Old Gertrude."

"Lawrence?"

"No, not D. H. yet," I said.

She let out a giggle, which turned into a wide smile, stretching her mouth like an open membrane. She drew near me and I could feel that before her horizontal lips brushed mine her breasts touched my breast: those were the undoubtably biggest tits I had ever come into contact with. She passed an arm over my shoulder and I embraced her, placing my right arm under her left tit, which rested, burdened by its own weight, on the bed, and encircling her tiny body—with its narrow shoulders and thin neck and frog's legs—which made her breasts seem even larger. Remembering that they looked erect beside the window in the moonlight of the Caribs—I care a bit—I felt an erection coming, and I pressed my pelvis against her hips as I turned over gently to get on top of her. There's nothing more similar to one coitus than another coitus, which is why I'll spare the reader the repetition. I'll only add that we were in the *posada* room for a long time and that we didn't spend the time talking in spite of the fact that my ballerina was so garrulous. I don't think I outdid my performance (sex is another theater: *le ballet du coeur,* the duet of the deaf, the movies of the blind) with Juliet, but the rest of the night was free of the tensions Mrs. Vega Estévez had created with her mania for teaching her sessions on sex, giving instructions in intercourse that one should execute like a trained dog in the circus. This was a union, a mating of mimes, a true collaboration in which Honey and I learned together. Obviously ballet or a *faux pas de deux* had relieved her of her virginity but she didn't know much more than I did about the art of loving. The rest of our relationship wasn't always peaceful but I still remember those nights with Honey Sucked Rose, the reluctant ballerina, easy lay, foul fucker, lusty busty, with special affection even though I was never in love with her: from the beginning it was solely a sexual relationship for me. As for her, she might have been in love with me but I'm not very sure about that. Maybe she was comparing me to some character taken from her sacred jungle, and had arrived at the conclusion that the profane city had swallowed me up forever, engulfed by the Gulf Extremes, devoured by a vortex, vain urb. Burp. That's the cuba libre. *Vivat.*

That night was the last time I took Honey home in a taxi. Or rather, the taxi driver took charge of depositing his blonde cargo at Galiano and San Lázaro since I got off at the corner of Twenty-seventh Street and Avenida de los Presidentes, kissing her good-bye on her mouth that was again excessively lipsticky: rouge subversif, by Marx Factory. We returned to the *posada* on Second and Thirty-first, of course, like a recurrent recollection. There wasn't the inviting moon of former times (the Havana moon lasts less than the lupine moon of Larry Talbot) when she'd open the window and stand beside the blinds, Braille beauty. But there was always the smell of honeysuckle, which formed part of the vegetation surrounding the hotel, and perhaps of the aralias, a less literary plant than the *madreselva,* her Honeysuckle, but for me more memorable. One night I had such an impressive revelation that it could have come out of the Apocalypse. Honey complained of not having had time

254

to shave her legs and apologized—I didn't see anything wrong with this oversight and told her that it was of no importance.

"But they're prickly," said she. "Touch," and she directed my hand not to her calves but to her thighs. I knew that women shaved their legs—though my mother didn't need to—but I had never heard of anybody shaving their thighs. Honey made me verify that such a depilation was possible, I an expert in hirsutism, Inspector Hare. She also showed me that women shaved the region between the navel and the pubic hair: "Touch, touch it," she insisted, guiding my hand to her tight tummy, like a guide showing a visitor an unknown masterpiece: the hairy Venus. All the skin there was prickly: she really was Rose of Thorns, but I didn't laugh. I felt repelled: I saw her livid thighs in the moonlight covered with hairs and her flat, milky, soft stomach, which was a pleasant contrast with her enormous white breasts—but that too was hairy, like a man's. Or worse, a wolf woman, Laura Talbot. Lupine horror, ever vulvine, didn't keep me, however, from going to bed with her that revelatory night. But there was something worse than hair everywhere: it was a fault in her personality. Honey had a defect in her upbringing that showed itself as a mental tantrum. She was very spoiled, and when she got annoyed, almost always over nothing: she knew she had the key to sex, or rather, I had the key but she was the keeper of the gate to the garden of delights and just by joining her legs together she could control our relationship, going to bed with me but literally closing, contracting her vagina, despite my efforts to win her over to love by begging for a kiss, she'd squeeze her lips (now without lipstick) and turn them inward, practically swallowing them and leaving her mouth without edges. The effect was comical, almost ridiculous but at the same time grotesque, like a grimace from a dirty old clown—and as onerous as a closed buttonhole, a sealed mailbox, a sex without access. I must confess that I pursued her pursed lips doggedly, madly, obscenely, and her disappearing-lips act was for me inconstant pain.

Despite her readings (or maybe because of them) Honey wasn't very intelligent, as Juliet was, for example. Juliet did share, however, in that exaggerated native kind of corn called in Havana *picuísmo,* untranslatable into Spanish as well as English. Carmina, Juliet, and Honey were all *picúas,* each in her own fashion. But Honey added something extra to her corny style: a certain childishness that would have been lovely in another woman but which in her seemed almost moronic. There were occasions when I might have felt offended, but she took offense easily, and yet was often humiliated without becoming offended. In that labyrinth in which the two of us played the two-backed monster, Minotaur and Sister, sexual Siamese twins united by my porous cartilage, it happened: one night (remembering my mouth-watering visit to Juliet that afternoon under the sign of Libra) I asked Honey to practice fellatio with me. I used other words, of course. She wouldn't have understood these: *fellatio, cunnilingus,* and *soixante-neuf* don't form part of the jungle's sexual vocabulary.

255

She had such control over her lips that she could be a superb sucker. Give that sucker an even break. There she blows! But she told me that she had never done it, to which I replied that there was no time like the present. She added that she was afraid and I assured her that she had nothing to fear—I became thus an amorous acrobat, the fearless Jules Léotard, inventor of the leotard and the flying trapeze.

"You yourself can control the *immissio penis.*"

"The what?" She sounded scared, as if Latin hurt.

"The ins and outs of the penis," I explained. "You know what the penis is, don't you?"

"Of course," she said, "that thing," and she pointed to the above-mentioned part.

"Shall we do it?"

After giving it a little thought, she said: "Okay, but just the tip."

I inserted the whole glans into her mouth, which inevitably grimaced, but now she couldn't eat her lips without swallowing my member, a purge of the pudenda. I began to move back and forth and she withdrew her mouth.

"You said I was going to do it alone."

"There's nothing in sex that you can do alone. Even for masturbation you need your hand."

This argument ad hominem—stolen from Juliet or copied from Harold—silenced her. I again inserted my message into her mailbox and she immediately learned the rhythmic, ritual movements. But suddenly, as I did a horizontal turn, she moved her head away.

"What's the matter now?" may I ask.

"Too pig."

"A toothpick?"

"It's too big," she said.

"You're imagining things," I explained. "The sex organ is all in the back of the mind of the holder."

"It makes me nauseated."

"You mean that it disgusts you."

"No, I'm not disgusted. It doesn't disgust me but it makes me nauseated."

"I want you to know that love makes you dizzy but never nauseated."

This argument ad nauseam convinced her and again we formed that malevolent monster with a head among the pubes: love in the place of fauces, as Juliet would have quoted upon giving me her lesson in poetic kissing, transforming me into a Yeats man. To make sure that Honey wouldn't interrupt this unique act again with her soliloquy, I took her by the head with my two hands, and while she licked my other tongue, I moved my hips vertically, leaning on her straw-blond hair as my support and fulcrum. I wiggled now as she sucked my incubus like a succubus, moving more, much more swiftly and successively, a head coitus. But she tried to pull away, which I prevented, holding her in place, firmly grabbing her hairs, electric conduits of her resistance fighting my grasp while I moved on the edge of orgasm—but she managed to break loose, uttering a "faugh pas!" and vomiting, covering my stomach, pubes and prick with a vitriolic viscosity, almost colloidal, without food remains. Perhaps her poverty hadn't permitted her to eat that night and all she had in her stomach was the conjugal cuba libre. An awful mess anyway.

"Oh, I'm so sorry," she said, a sorry sight, wiping her mouth with her hand. "I couldn't avoid it."

She tried to apologize once more, but the next time she opened her mouth I inserted my penis into it, firmly holding her neck and head like a soft pillory, pillows, ordering her: "Suck, Honey, Suckle!" I again began moving inside and against her oral orifice, my *bálano* battling between her fluffy tongue and velar larynx, evading her lupine fangs—and the ceiling of her mouth was the witness of my ejaculation, which inundated her buccal cavity, my faucet flooding her mouth with not precisely mother's milk.

Taking advantage of my northern lassitude and abandon of my prey, she pulled away from me and ran not out of the room, as I no longer feared, but to the bathroom, perhaps to wash her soiled mouth, perhaps to vomit. But upon coming out she returned lovingly beside me in bed: such was the loyalty of friendly Honey, man's best friend after Ready. Nevertheless, when I tried to initiate another coitus—or rather coitus itself, the coitus circuit—she crossed her legs and pressed her knees together, squeezing her thighs. She wasn't a ballerina preparing for a fouetté (there was nothing about her legs to remind one of ballet) but she bound her members to make the penetration of a third member impossible for me and for anyone who wasn't a crowbar that night. At the same time she closed her mouth. Upon swallowing her lips and making of them a hermetic lock, not only was it absolutely impossible to kiss her, chastely or caustically, but I couldn't even gaze upon the melting wax of her mannikin grimace. She had sealed her face inscrutably upon deliberately closing her eyes. As I've always detested sodomy, she left only her virginal ears open for penetration, offering her eardrums as the sole stretched membrane that could be deflowered, bleeding upon breaking as they never took part in the rituals of ballet—aside from the fact that none of the ballerinas I knew had a musical ear. They were mere gymnasts accompanied in their eurhythmic movements by some more or less synchronized Tchaikovsky or Stravinsky.

But it wasn't that night or any other night that brought to an end the corny course of our relationship. Bear in mind that despite the defects in her character there was her body, the carnal devil of this story (a Cuban Faust, a parody for pederasts: it wasn't her soul I wanted but her body). I was going to say her titanic tits but tit would imply that I didn't enjoy her whole body, including her virgin mouth and reluctant slit, as well as the sexual apprenticeship we initiated together and almost completed. Our sex was interrupted not by love but by matrimony—not her matrimony, curiously, but mine. I left Honey (sometimes called, mockingly, Posie Rosie) Hawthorne because, without realizing it, I was getting ready to marry. Our relationship's decline might have been detected by a third party simply by observing the kind of vehicle we traveled in—or the absence of sexual means of transport. We began in taxi, continued in buses, and ended on foot. Finally I didn't even take her to the remote, romantic *posada* on Second and Thirty-first streets, but we went, the ironies of fate, desire, or wanton will, to the *hotelito* on Amistad Street! She would come from her house and I would leave my nocturnal secretariat and, parallel paths, we'd meet along the way, rushing down wide Galiano to narrow Barcelona, from high street to back street. I left Honey definitively after one of those nights, or half nights, on Amistad, and our separation shared in the street's symbolism: we parted amiably, mutual friends. This place was to serve me as a graphic omen: it was here that I noticed the correct sense of a howler emitted, committed by Tagle, the veteran linotypist of the newspaper *Mañana,* who instead of keeping his eye on the written material, was paying too much attention to the afternoon visitors at the *posada.* Thus in the society column *matrimony* was spelled *martirmony*—a neologism I once used in parody. But I should have known that words are not only the matter the past is made of, but also form the compound future: two distinct destinies and one real destination. I therefore didn't understand that my matrimony would be a real martirmony.

On my last night with Honey, I remember we were practically flying down Águila Street—spurred by my *tempus fugit*—when we bumped into Germán Puig, exhibiting a new young companion: a stranger, with the look of a Delphic (oral) disciple. Germán introduced us but I didn't catch his name. Puig was just about to go off to Paris, to consolidate the Cinemateca de Cuba through the Cinématèque Française—and for his *education sentimentale.* But what I remember of that night is not Germán's French farewell, calling us *les visiteurs du soir,* but my hurry to get to the *posada.* It was getting late, and the luxury of lust became a dire necessity with each passing minute. Germán, as innocent as always, took us for strollers killing time. I could have killed him! In his passion for the movies he insisted on talking to me about the silent era while what I most wanted to hear was the erotic soundtrack of Honey's many moans— perhaps accompanied by a chorus of neighboring voices. While Germán talked about French films, Honey, silent beside me, squeezed my arm, indicating that, as usual, my tumescence was her urgency. Finally we went away, socially obliged to walk in the opposite direction from our delicious destination. But finally, at last, taking the roundabout romantic route past Juan Clemente Zenea (a street all of us called Neptuno—even the marble muse of the poet deserting him to become a Naïad of the old man with the trident), we reached the *auberge rouge* or purple *posada* —also called hot *hotelito* or hellhouse of assignations, none of which (names or place) now frightened my old virgin. We went up the narrow staircase: Honey ahead, I behind. I could observe that she ascended each step with her feet tilted, toes pointing outward, ankles at parallel parallel —and for a moment I thought she was wearing satin ballet slippers. Upon seeing her outstretched right hand slide up the wooden banister, I could have sworn that she was grabbing onto it like a practice bar.

THE AMAZON

There's something very vulgar about love, even without calling it sex. *Vulvar* is vulgar enough but *love* too is a four-letter word. Verbalized, love invariably becomes a narrative of vulgar vagaries. But, let's face it, love is tremendously popular nowadays. "Love is in control," claimed some singer in *Top of the Pops* not long ago, as if making the find of the century. I'm afraid, lady, it has always been so. Listen to what the DJ of VD, *Venerius Doctor,* Ovid the Precursor, had to say in his *Art of Love* on the love craft as practiced in Ancient Rome—in 1 B.C., precisely.

> Young man, here's what you should do.
> Each evening, as the sun stops all ado,
> Go stroll along dark Lover's Colonnade,
> Where well made-up girls go on parade
> To stomp at the old haunts with their loose limbs.
> Surrounded by so much young willing beauty
> Oft you don't know where to perform your duty.

Why, that's what I've been doing all my life! Doing it and telling it throughout this book you're now holding in one hand. Some kiss and tell! Though he, old Ovid, can be much more daring than I when he asserts: "The very courts of law are hunting enclosures for passion." Courts of love, indeed! You can argue of course that Ovid is only a poetaster while you consider me merely a Poe Taster. All right, what about a venerated though not venereal poet then? What about Homer himself? Well, what about him? This great, great Greek poet, whoever he was, blind in legend and deaf to lust, composed or recited two long, long poems (a couple of homers, in fact) everybody knows by name but nobody actually reads. One poem seems to celebrate war, while the other sings a paean to a pigheaded man's intention to return home early come what may—and what comes is love and sometimes haste. The first poem really expresses (the poet's) feelings about blind rage, about the will to revenge and perhaps about compassion and respect for your elders even if it kills you.

The tone is grandiloquent, eloquent, and quaint, but its hero's famed wrath erupts not so much on account of a loved friend's death but because of the loss of a concubine, which led to his crisis or to his brisance, whichever came first. Furthermore, the whole poem is about a family feud. In fact it's a rather intimate war, the aftermath of adultery in high places, later a menace to Trojans. The other poem (I don't think I have to tell you which one I've read twice) exalts a wandering hero who can't go home again—and this proves to be a gain: a blessing in many guises. Back home there is only his wife, an eager weaver, but along the way of the wanderer with the cunning tongue other women offer him diverse forms of love and even one sings erotic hymns to him, hymeneal hums. As to be expected, this second poem was labeled inferior to the first for centuries, both in its epic breadth and poetic achievement. To diminish it even further in men's eyes, it has been attributed to a woman, a deft, derivative lady writer following in the faltering footsteps of the blind Homer. But more than epic poetry, this narrative seems to belong to a genre that will be invented a thousand years later. Love has downgraded the epic tone of the second poem to novel level: the tapestry Penelope had been weaving all those years was a well-made yarn. No love's lost in the novel.

If instead of love we speak of sex, which is, naturally, older than love, we will find that vulgarity wins the day (and some nights too) romping rampant in all popular glossaries. The word now most at hand, *penis,* which at first might seem to belong in medical jargon, means tail in Latin. As any music-hall skit or burlesque show will tell, if I remember them well—and I do, I do. (Ah, Ann Corio!) The use of the word *vagina,* in the other hand, comes from a vulgar Roman comedy about a candle and the possible uses of both its ends. *Vagina* means, unsurprisingly, *sheath.* In Spanish, *vaina:* can't you see the vagina in it? Now about *vaina.* According to the Spanish Dictionary of the Royal Academy—less of an authority than the Oxford Concise but sterner than Funk and Wagnalls—*vaina* also describes, in a figurative and familiar sense, a despicable person, a jerk in modern usage but not yet as in soda jerk. It's curious, or perhaps not, that in French a *con* also serves to designate, if you pardon the expression, a sucker. The term comes from the origins of the cancan, from French *fin de siècle* cabarets where the show dancers, all female, were not only young and gay but used to perform their high kicks *au poil.* As to *cunt* in English, you can't deny you know who that is. *Con* and cunt come from the Latin *cunnus, coño* in Spain but not in Cuba. In the whole Caribbean basin a *vaina* is an idiot—though as a child I was allowed to say *coño* but not *vaina,* since it was considered vulgar, while *coño* was a swear word devoid of meaning! So much for *vagina* as a sinonym of *vulva.*

Erotic literature, however, has always been condemned to the randy ranks of vulgarity—with some brilliant exceptions in the Roman world after Ovid, a few Renaissance examples, and the well-known *rara avis* (*avia* means granny in Latin) of the eighteenth century, that happy age when you could rape everything in verse, even a lock—and get away with it, stock and barrel too! Prudery's condemnation seems implicit in the very expression of love itself. There's yet another great Greek poet (to scholars all Greek poets are great, though they are reluctant to bestow greatness on, say, Bulgarian poets) who twenty-five or thirty centuries after Homer sang to Greek lore and love. Today he is praised for his historical poems dealing with the passing of politics and men while his love poems, on men on men, though more deeply felt, are inevitably termed vulgar for they reek of sweat and semen. The poet, Greek to the core, used masculine rhymes but was a sodomite. Oral literature, however, does not fare better than oral sex. Sex, though, is now more popular than ever.

But believe you me I have nothing against vulgarity. On the contrary (my typewriter, so close to Sappho, almost wrote cuntrary) I, we thrive on it: it is caviare from the general, ambrosia to the gods, the full-fat mother's milk of humankind. Yeah! Let me give it to you straight from the arse's mouth. I want you to hear me loud and crystal clear but above all, loud. Vulgar comes from *vulgus* and *vulgus* is whence (wench!) I come and where I'm headed. Schopenhauer said that one must choose between vulgarity and loneliness. He hated women, I hate being alone.

Nothing pleases me more than vulgar sentiments, vulgar expressions, vulgarity itself. Nothing vulgar can be divine, that's true, but all vulgarity is human. Concerning the expression of vulgarity in art and literature, I think that if I'm a movie addict it is because of the movies' moving, living, lively vulgarity. I've become less and less tolerant of those movies that demand to be called films—serious, significant, and selective in their expressive form and, what's worse, in their intentions. In theater, the movies' predecessor as entertainment, I prefer minor Shakespearean comedy to the steepest (is that usage suggested to me by the use of the cothurnus?) Greek tragedy. If there's something that makes *Don Quixote* immortal (besides its author's intelligence and the creation of two archetypes) it is its vulgarity. Sterne is for me *the* eighteenth-century English writer, not the moralizing Swift or, saddling the turn of the century, Jane Austen, so proper. I am charmed by Dickens's vulgarity and can't stand George Eliot's pretensions. Given a choice, I prefer *Bel Ami* to *Madame Bovary*—an example of that vulgar artifact that is the nineteenth-century novel, all art and facts. Fortunately Joyce is as vulgar as he is creative, better than *Bel Ami* married to *Madame Bovary*. In the second half of the twentieth century the raising of pop products to the category of art (and, what's more, of culture) is not only a vindication of vulgarity but in agreement with my tastes. After all, I'm not writing a history of culture but rather putting vulgarity in its place—which is close to my art.

Somewhere else I've exalted the precious character of the Havana idiom: so vulgar, so alive, and I miss it so. It has been struck dumb to make us deaf and blind to life—closer to Helen Keller than to Homer. It's from this dead language (or language of the dead), gone with the hurricane of history hurrying over cane fields, that I've exhumed a phrase straight out of the hunters' jargon though applied to the conquest of a woman, influenced by Maupassant, en passant, no doubt. (It was Maupassant who, talking of game hunting in Africa, said, all of a sudden, that woman was the only quarry worth pursuing. Hope of finding her, here and there, is what gives life its meaning and makes it worthwhile. I approve.) The standard huntsman's phrase "I'm on the hunt" is the most appropriate when describing the winning of a woman's heart or whatever other female organs, say Fallopian tubes—after all they're a less vulgar symbol than the heart. Hunt the slipper, hunt the *sleeper!* The Greeks already used this metaphor of love as a hunt and the Romans provided Eros with bow and arrow to make him into a Cupid, as Ovid vied. But didn't the Bard bombard me too with his "she is woman, therefore to be won"? And now! For that Havana phrase! From venery to venery! "He who seeks her, sicks her."

I don't remember when I heard it for the first time, but I remember it as advice given to me in my pursuit of woman. It was said aloud by the older brother of a high-school mate of mine, graceless Raúl García. I'd often go to his house in Old Havana to study my lessons—thus I learned more from life than from all my books. That graduate student brother of his told me the phrase as a white hunter's tip upon hearing me speak of an elusive girl who was known to me only as the Dark Girl of the Horse. "Good," he said. "You're on the stalk." Did he mean *talk?* To her? I've already spoken of her and her distant nearness to me, an oxymoron for a moron. Talk, *stalk?* That black mane was a mirage in the desert of my love life and she remained as unattainable after as before this venatic piece of advice—perhaps given to me with a pinch of salt rather than at a salt lick. But the phrase proved to be wise after the fact, though then I thought it merely meant to encourage me in my pursuit of love, of girls. Or of one love: a dark girl with a brooch in the shape of a horse: a colt, a bolt. It was many years later that I put it into practice, unwittingly—and I remembered it only when it proved to be a sex axiom.

I used to write down in my mind, like a scholar of sex, the vital (at least to me) statistics of lots of girls. Thus my gray matter became my little black book but for better use than punishment: I'd break their necks with a rose. I always kept them in mind, waiting for the moment any information would be useful—but mostly it remained as the storage of persistent visions in my memory. I always hoped though that someday somehow my inside info would dig up a nympho. I say dig up now but I never expected a mummy from my forays but rather the opposite: a chick, called in Havana then as in Rome now, a *pollo,* or a *bird* in that country of bird watchers that is England. Ah, woman! If not game, they're reared as poultry.

I knew or suspected that in some artistic circles there were girls who would be easy, sometimes sassy with a sissy but willing, and besides there was my will to love, which the Phantom of the Opera called "the Will that lives on!" When there's a will there's a lay: those girls were the promised lass. Or, as the Irish publican Paddy O'Vydd, so nosy, said to Yeats in warning: "Our own Abbey Theater has always held danger for our least purty lasses." (Did he say purty or *pursy*?) Be that as it may, I feared many of them had never read Isadora, of the Duncan clan, Isadora whom I could now call Easydora. A greater fear was that they hadn't even heard about the *Ananga Ranga* or Indian Love Code. But there was the radiant precedent in my poetic-erotic relationship with Juliet Estévez, the woman who mangled men and was a menace to poets. Juliet loved the theater so much that, when her marriage foundered on the soft rocks of the bed, she decided to take the stage by storm. She, so accessible, still not past her period of mutilating Eliot, was already hitting the boards with some, as they say in the theater, *éclat.* Besides there was, remember? my own contact with the Prometheus Group, which I was so close to that only my stage fright (or an innate incapacity to express emotions) kept me from becoming an actor, even an amateur. But I didn't find any accessible girl there, then, though many seemed to be. *Videlicet:* the spectacularly beautiful María la O, so plebeian, vulgar, and notorious for her public lack of inhibitions, like that famous statement when she received from her fiancé (she convalescing in the hospital from her second appendectomy) a bunch of flowers with a card saying *Señorita:* María la Oh exclaimed: "Miss my ass! Those flowers don't come from my fiancé. He knows better than to be Missing me this late in the play!"

The closest I got to falling in love with an actress was with the little, lithe, long-haired Elizabeth Monsanto (in my onomastic passion her name seemed to me the most amorous part of her) but she was always escorted by her mother, an old pest who kept urging me to become an actor, insisting I had the voice and stage presence (how did she know? I had never stepped on stage) of a leading man. She repeated this prophecy so often, now accompanied by the beautiful Betty Monsanto, that I reached the sad conclusion that there was a vein of madness in the family, a mimic mania.

I could have had access to the hunting grounds of another group, the ADAD (poor dad) Theater, almost a family concern. Menstrual mimes, they performed their plays once a month, staged by neighbors of the classmate whose brother gave me the phrase that became my motto. But among the ADAD family players there were too many older women, almost contemporaries of my mother: he who scores in-laws scores out-laws. The third possibility, before discovering the bottomless pit of the Drama and Art Academy, was the University Theater Group, whose offices (actually a room or two) faced the Varona Roman Theater. I knew this place well because of its so-called art film series and also its Summer School of Film Art, where I won that scholarship, beating Carmina by a year into the world of movie madness. With that mixture of shyness, shrewdness, and cunning characteristic of the fabled fox, I closed in on the chicken coop of the University Theater Group—where they welcomed me as an intruder. It wasn't that I intuited or felt I was intruding: I knew it from every look on the faces of those budding buddy actors and actresses in full bloom, of those students with dramatic gifts, of all the professors of theater history who detested my disdain for Greek tragedy —merely Homer on stage—and of those dictatorial directors. (I've never known a director, from band to bank, who isn't a dictator: Sick semper tyrannis! said both Booths.) I was allowed to roam that promising province only because of my friendship with Juan Mallet, who could have been called Johann Malletus (or better, Malletus Maleficarum), what with his thin intensity, blond hair in a Prussian crewcut, and military bearing. Fortunately Mallet was completely mad, in spite of (or because of) which he studied psychiatry, and was essential to the University Theater Group because he was their only light technician. The night of the performance, all wired up, he seemed more active than the lead player, going from spotlight to headlight and taking care of the light in each scene, a protagonist in the dark. He handled electric cables, switches and switchboard with a hand as expert as it was gloveless, and with such recklessness that I feared his imminent electrocution at any moment without having committed any crime other than abiding and abetting the scenic illusion. I don't know if it was my long-standing admiration for electricians (my homage to ohmage: a light technician was closer to an electrician than an artist) or the negative magnetic pole of his madness that brought us together. Perhaps it was chess, the positive pole of my erratic game, Capablanca of the pawnbrokers. Mallet, a checkmate maniac, invariably admired how good a loser I was, something I'd always concede but conceal.

But with Mallet as my lighting Virgil I was able to descend into the Dantesque domicile of the University Theater Group and, if I wasn't accepted by those who occupied those dark roomlets burning hot beneath the Medical School (practically a cellar), at least I wasn't looked upon as an intruder anymore. This means I could leaf through the catalog of beauties that the casting desk offered. There were, of course, uglies, but I suppose it's the exposure of one's beauty, exhibitionism, that makes someone want to be an actor or actress, especially an actress, and thus there were more sirens than gargoyles in that mythological enclave. (The word is *enclosure*: there one was familiar with the complex Oedipus, inhabiting the house of the Atrides, hanging around Electra—Mallet's favorite Greek—and conversing with the Sphinx.) One of those belles, a vestal virgin of Thalia, attracted my eye, first, and then the other, and later all of my attention. (I still didn't know Juan Blanco and couldn't ask him what he thought of the relationship, if any, between classical actresses, always standing, and whether or not that verticality invited horizontality—or at least an inclining or Pisan cant.) She was of average height (perhaps shorter than I though she didn't seem so then) and not too well-proportioned. Her most outstanding features were her big green eyes. (I've already spoken of the mythology of green eyes in Cuba, where a song, "Those Green Eyes," has done for them what another song, "Black Eyes," did, I suppose, for black eyes in Russia. There is, besides, my kissing cousin, *opera prima,* now as distant in space as before in time: a love I suffered as a childhood disease.) Aside from her eyes there was her mouth, which looked full under the lipstick, with shapely lips—that double arch in her upper lip plus the long uninterrupted wave of her lower lip—so common in comic-strip gals and often in movie stars too. The most outstanding parts of her body were her fabulous breasts: they were, despite what I said, in exact proportion to her figure. The sight of her filled my eyes so that I can't remember any other girl seen that day and thus, when she passed me, wearing a dress that was closed snugly to the neck (outstanding not only because of the heat of the summer season but also because it made her breasts stand out as if it were a sweater), I looked at her so intensely that she, feeling my eyes all over her, looked back but didn't see me. What I mean is that she looked in my direction but right through my body, piercing me as if I were all air, invisible, a man invented by H. G. Wells. She didn't even notice my intruding presence: the source of my stare (my eyes behind dark glasses) never existed for her. That reduction to the absurd of nothingness with an annihilating, unseeing glare made her unforgettable: I didn't see her for a long time but I didn't forget her. You see, it's impossible to forget the eyes of the unwitting Gorgon.

I don't know if she had been in some of the university productions (invariably dramas in verse: Lope, Calderón or the trio of gift-bearing Greeks: one more menacing than the next) but she did attain a minor position on television. One day (I was still living at Zulueta 408) I saw her walking down Obispo Street, slowly, almost strolling, and I went over to say hello. She looked at me and didn't return the greeting: but this time she saw me distinctly. I asked her if she didn't remember me (who could remember *l'être* as ether?), that we had been introduced in the University Theater Group headquarters (I cited the luminous name of Mallet, who shed light upon my credentials) and she then exclaimed:

"Oh yes, of course! Please forgive me," and I liked the fact that she lied: "I didn't recognize you."

How in hell was she going to recognize me if she hadn't ever seen me? Her voice (which I hadn't heard before) went well with her body: it was low, soft, and refined in that artificial way actors' voices are cultivated: not learned in childhood, from high birth or breeding, but as an adult, from practicing good delivery. She was carrying a libretto in her hand and it was obviously a cheap script, but I asked her if she was still working in the theater—perverse, as I can be.

"No, not in the theater. In television," she said, and named the mediocre author who had written the obvious scrap of crap she held in her hand as if it were the first folio.

"I know him."

I knew him only by name, then for me despicable for merely literary reasons, not from a political or personal point of view, as later on, when he was a Shakespeare of the trade unions.

"Oh yes?" said she. "I don't know him, I'm afraid."

The walk—walking with her really became a pleasant stroll—down Obispo, the two of us alone among so many unknown pedestrians, became somewhat unpleasant because of the conversation and its subject, that third man in Havana. But suddenly she had to go, she told me, and I didn't ask for either her address or telephone—a fatal fault in my character, which later provoked an emotional earthquake. Damn it! As a desperate recourse I cursed myself audibly and visibly when she vanished. Not because she was gone but because she hadn't left behind any trace except the memory of her eyes. That is, she literally disappeared because a long time passed and I didn't see her again either in person or on television, that interposed intruder. Her vision, though, lingered on.

Then one night, just before we moved to El Vedado, I caught her walking through the porticos of the Apple Arcade. I say I caught her, but I didn't catch her, because that would have been a shock and would have also drawn her attention to my action. I caught her because I'm not a camera but rather a movie camera. If I had been a still-photo camera I would have captured her, fixed forever, like a butterfly impaled by the lepidopterist. Now I had her moving but in full focus between one column and the next under the arcade: seen at night, with the light from the streetlamps facing the Asturian Center: partially illuminated, seen at night for the first time, she looked more beautiful than ever, now visible, again visible, a fluttering gypsy moth. But unfortunately she wasn't alone: she was on the arm of a tall, dark, good-looking man with a vaguely foreign air, not European or American, but definitely not Cuban. An entomologist perhaps, but she obviously was very much in love with that hideous hunter because she was walking almost pinned to him and at the same time looking at his face: smiling contentedly, apparently more dependent on than attentive to any word of his conversation, a meticulous male monologue that seemed to extend the row of columns to infinity—and I accompanied them, both happy and sad to see her. I followed them closely, to get a good look at her, and she of course didn't even suspect that I was almost next to her, looking at her with discreet intensity, since this discretion assured me of not being detected by her and also protected me from the size and strength of her companion: it's good to be able to be the invisible man at times.

Many years and many women passed in my life, and then I got married. Of some of those women, girls rather, I have already spoken, but in all this time I didn't forget that Venus unveiled in the depths of the University Theater cellar, seen other times, but apparently vanished, returned to the Caribbean Sea. After the body had disappeared only her name remained, which I had found out with my expertise for this kind of research (I was once a pollster, remember?), I a minuscule Marlowe of love. Her name was (and it had to be a pseudonym) Violeta del Valle —Violet of the Valley, as it were. I didn't forget her face—her kissable mouth but above all her eyes—or even less, her body—her sinuous breasts: my mammory—and neither, how could I? forget her mnemonic name. Thus four, five, perhaps more years later I found her again, in of all places in the world—that is, in Havana—in that gathering site that for me seemed to be the vertigo of memory, the vortex of knowledge. Of recognition this time—on a bus, a vulgar *guagua*. I was on my way, as every or almost every night, to my nocturnal notary office, by now a custom like household sex—a bad habit. I had caught as usual the Route 28 bus: tame, domestic, incapable of surprises. But a few stops later she got on (I recognized her immediately of course: one always remembers his dreams, especially daydreams) and I watched her walk the narrow aisle, and amid the lurchings of this gondola on land I saw her take a seat as if ascending a throne—without seeing me, of course. As always. She sat down alone and, as soon as she had paid, thus eliminating the conductor's interference, I got up and sat next to her, greeting her with my usual hullo, which for some reason seemed exotic in Havana. She looked at me and didn't say a thing, not even responding to my greeting or looking at me very long: the invisible man barely visible amid the rain of time.

"Don't you remember me?"

"Please," she began as if ready to complain to the first available authority (the conductor, probably) about my impertinence. How was a vassal to sit on the throne beside the queen? The distance she had put between herself and me on that same seat was such that I wondered if I hadn't made a mistake. But I had no doubt: it was she. Those big green eyes, that beautiful mouth, and in the middle that nose with flaring nostrils, not for air to pass through but to give a more dramatic expression to her face, could only belong to the alliterating beauty discovered by desire, so often seen, so often craved.

"Violeta—Violeta del Valle?"

She looked at me again, this time not hostile but attentive.

"Do I know you?"

Though the question was formal, her tone was friendly.

"Of course. From the University Theater Group. We've spoken many times. When we met on Obispo one afternoon we had a long talk about television and theater and scripts and scriptwriters."

I tried to be as polite as possible, but she made the first step toward familiarity, breathing content: "Oh yes, I remember. Forgive me for not recognizing you, but that was so long ago!"

Yes, it was long ago, but not too long because I had seen her in her enraptured passage through the ancient colonnade at night and thought of her many times, wanting to find her again one day, wanting her, period. Of course I didn't say so.

"Yes, quite," I said. "Probably three years since I gave that lecture on television, theater, and acting as we strolled down Obispo."

She laughed. Or rather she smiled. But her lips were generous and her smile seemed like a silent laugh. Still smiling she said that she had left the theater but not television. Now she was an actress in Caracas. She also told me she had married a Venezuelan—doubtless the tall, dark, good-looking hideous man who didn't look completely like a foreigner but who wasn't exactly from Havana. Without my asking she added that she had gotten divorced and was here for the summer. I told her that since Caracas was a mountain city it was cooler than Havana in the summer, and the logical thing would be to spend the winter in Cuba and the summer in Venezuela. She agreed with me, but in an evasive way, and without saying so she led me to believe it was her divorce and not summer that had made her return. Regrettably her stop was too soon, right there, and I couldn't get off that night with her because I had to put in at least an appearance at the odd job which my duties as a movie critic and my daily task as proofreader were making more and more obsolete —not to say tautological, since I saw my mentor more than once every day at his *Carteles* office. In any case, before getting off she gave me her phone number and I repeated my name to her! So that she wouldn't forget it I gave her what was really my pseudonym. I've always felt that my real name, long and disorderly, is also forgettable. I gave her my number, but, advancing with caution, Cartesian that I am, I gave her the one at *Carteles,* land of all men in the war of love, where my ideal trenches were my dugout.

I called her, of course, the next morning at daybreak: my dawn patrol roundabout noon. We spoke a while and her voice sounded even more captivating on the phone (that evil talking machine that turns traits into caricatures: the telephone is to voices what the photograph is to features) that day—perhaps because she wanted to sound captivating. I asked her where she lived and she told me. Though there were nice buildings on her street, she explained to me in detail, she lived on the side near the Espada Cemetery. I was surprised that, being an actress on Venezuelan television, she lived in an area that was rather humble, on the poor part of San Lázaro Street, which is not a street one can call Saint Lazare easily. (I'm being ironic, of course, with San Lázaro a holy street today.) But she added immediately that she was living with her sister now since she soon expected to return to Caracas. I called her again another day (the telephone now a mellophone, tinkle bell) and we made a date. I wasn't too enthusiastic about picking her up at her house, imagining rather than verifying the character of her sister (what was she like, an older ogress?) and we decided to meet that Saturday in the lobby of the Rex Cinema, at four o'clock. She told me before hanging up that she would be delighted to see me again—which seemed to me an adequate addendum.

That Saturday I left *Carteles* without wasting time with any of my friends, old or new drunks, and I went straight home to shower, shave,

269

and spruce me up for a date I had made years ago. I told my wife that there was a preview of a Japanese film without subtitles, truly inscrutable, and as usual when exercising my twentieth-century job, I didn't take her to the movies, my church, the critic as priest—celibate celebrating a mass in black and white. I was now in the lobby of the Rex Cinema. My old haunt, once the acme of elegance and glamour, where I found a fleeting one-sided love, but today, curiously, I knew I wasn't going to be disillusioned or tricked: two tits in sight. It was exactly three in the afternoon—when Folk Lola was killed for fucking the wrong man—so that there wouldn't be the ghost of a confusion. I sat in an armchair overlooking the double glass door and settled down to wait for her. Before I did this I looked at my watch and saw that it was three-thirty—Lola become a stiff—and not three as I had thought before, evidently confusing the second hand with the minute hand. Obviously I still had problems reading time. I settled down to settling down to wait for her. Between three-thirty and four there was a space that lasted more than a half hour. At four she didn't arrive and I didn't really expect her to be punctual, despite her television career. I said to myself: more than an actress she's a *habanera* and she has the face of a woman who makes people wait. But between four and a quarter after four time became a long distance. At four-thirty I began to think that she wouldn't come, but I told myself that these were unfounded fears, pure paranoia. Why wouldn't she come? After all, she couldn't have been more friendly, more accessible in person, more inviting in the tone of her voice and even in her wide charming smile, all white teeth, when we met again, after I presented my *lettre de créance*. (This diplomatic usage would become ironic verbiage in a short while, you'll see.) But it was five o'clock and she hadn't come. I wasn't under the clock like GI Joe. I was *inside* the clock. The time got longer and longer and at the same time short, shorter: ambiguities of time, child of eternity and of the moment.

Those hours sitting in the lobby of the Rex (though I stood up once or twice and went to the glass door, not even trusting its fancy glass transparency with opaque leaves, but without going out on the street) made me feel cheated, like someone who had received counterfeit money: I had been mocked and was furious. (Though these feelings were attenuated by the hope that she still might come. Hope is sometimes mere stubbornness.) But despite the slow passage of time during my wait, the clock struck six—and then it was obvious that she wasn't coming. I didn't suffer disappointment, as had occurred in similar situations some years earlier (as I suffered in this same theater when Esther Manzano was reduced to a name, meaning just apple) but rather disillusionment—or, to be precise, deceit. Hers. Why talk to me in that intimate tone on the phone and promise to go to the movies with me and then leave me in church—in the lurch? Wouldn't it have been more direct and more simple to say that she couldn't come, to give me an excuse, to erect a flimsy barrier? Was this easy laughter a difficult lay? Or was she used to such sweet swindles?

It was very frequent in Havana, I must say, and curiously actresses often practiced this cheap cheat. I remember a famous actress, Esperanza Isis, particularly infamous for her version of *The Respectable Hooker,* acting in an arena theater. There she was, in 1955, practically nude on stage, surrounded by eager eyes: a disrespectful hooker, notorious all over the country. She had been a famous *vedette* and turned actress at the dirty hands of Sartre. Now, there was this respected, respectable drama critic, married to a former society belle, but especially addicted to actresses, who fell in love with this stage incarnation of *la putain* after Pétain, and she made respectable, sedate dates with him in crowded places, like Prado and Neptuno Street at twelve midnight, not on the corner by the Miami restaurant but across the street by the Partagás Bar, just beneath the bathing beauty in her neon swimsuit. As the actress was a friend of Rine Leal (because of his flattering review of her debut, saying that she was a hooker for all seasoning) she invited him out for a ride in her chauffeur-driven limousine (she had struck it rich as a vaudeville *vedette*) and, pointing out to him a solitary figure standing on the formerly luminous corner (now even the bather's bikini was off) she cried out: "Look, look, *there* he is!," mentioning the critic's naughty nickname. "The jerk! He's been waiting on *that* corner since twelve. The poor jerk. Isn't he cute?" Rine told me that sometimes they took those rides at two and three in the morning and there was the drama critic waiting for his present infatuation. What's more relevant is that this *vedette,* turned star through a *coup de théâtre* but *toute nue,* often used to change the tryst and the corner critic would go there trying to meet her—always in vain. Frivolity, thy name is Speranza, Espoir, Hope. Nevertheless the drama critic, now an actor in a farce, waited so much for his date, his Faith, to arrive that the actress-cum-*vedette,* now Charity, finally went to bed with him, a patient pretender, as a prize for his tenacity—which for Miss Isis was like a form of devotion. To the Three Graces.

But I didn't know then the night fable of the fickle *femme fatale* and the constant critic (this would occur only in the near future) and I was really furious. In a blind rage I found myself writing her a letter! I don't know where I got the writing paper (perhaps I went back to *Carteles,* I don't remember: frenzy has a bad memory) but the note I wrote her began by saying simply Violeta del Valle—which was the least I could call her. I went on to say that I regretted having made her waste her time in her zeal to jilt me and make me wait for her, time which must have been precious to her in her profession. Thus I considered myself obliged to pay for it! Period. And I signed it with my damn name. The letter was senseless enough but what I did next was utter folly. I included all the money I had on me (I had been paid on Saturday as usual) and I included it (I explained) as a form of fees for my wait. Obviously Stan Laurel couldn't have written a better letter. I also got an envelope and put the demented deposition in it, enclosing the money. Tongue and glue. There.

Next I went to her house, which took some effort to find (to boot,

271

metropolitan metaphors, she lived on Soledad, Solitude Street) because it was at the end of that solitary street, as she had told me, and I had forgotten, confused or mislaid it, between my paper and tedious (from now on only she could be odious) San Lázaro Street—where I got off. I hit on the number, don't ask me how, without asking. It belonged to a relatively new building: quite clean, well-lighted (by then, between my letter and my search, it had gotten dark), and well-kept. It had a not very wide open door and a narrow staircase, which went off to one side of the entrance while the other side opened onto a long corridor. How would I find her apartment? I hadn't thought of a private house when she gave me her address but neither had I thought of an apartment building. What could I have been thinking of? A palace in ruins? A rundown mansion? To a manor born? I don't really know. And at that moment my thoughts didn't worry me—for you see, I was thinking only of her door. I tried to find her name on the mailboxes, visible on one side of the corridor, but there were only numbers without a single name. Obviously nobody ever expected letters in this building: the postman never even rang once there. In any case not my kind of letter ever came. Finally I decided to seek the aid of that Havanan institution, the janitor-*cum*-doorman, *la encargada,* an infernal invention which not even the humblest buildings could do without. Their motto seemed to be: "There Cannot Be Hades for Rent without Cerberus." I found her den without need of any sign: it was the only ground-floor apartment that had an open door. It could become an axiom: the more one rose on the social scale in Havana, the more closed the doors were. But in some buildings the janitor also lived within closed quarters, despite the heat of Havana and the fact that air conditioning never reached the hot habitat of that tropical equivalent of the three-headed dog or bitch. (Can Cerberus be a woman?) The concierge was a stocky middle-aged *mulata,* obviously used to work and attentive to what was happening around her. Her mythical job was not only to watch over the hygiene and social order of her barge but, a true Charoness, to keep an eye on the souls on board and Styx them up.

I didn't have in mind these underworld allusions then but only wanted to extract from her the information necessary for my mission impassive. I asked her for Violeta del Valle's apartment. She almost answered: "Never heard of her," a foul form of folklore meaning she really hadn't heard of and much less knew a person or persons unknown. I told her she was a television actress. She still didn't know. What's more: she didn't have a television set, she said. I described Violeta then, with green eyes and pouting mouth in a last effort to come across her apartment, convinced somehow that she hadn't lied to me, that she did in fact live in this house. The janitor took a year and a half to answer this time. "Ouch," she said finally, as if memory pained her, "the one that lives in Venezuela." That's the one! But she added: "She doesn't live here," and there was a patience-trying pause before adding: "The one who lives here is her sister." Now how could I ask her where she lived? In that precise moment she added: "Of course she's staying with her sister now." I had hit the jackpot! *Per aspera.* It was she, Violeta del Valle, who lived in Caracas and now was spending the summer with her sister. *Ad astra.* Obviously the janitor's mental process was contagious: I was catching it. Or was it that I too lived in a *Solar?* I interrupted her as she was entering into another of her clarifications ("Of course that's not her name. At least not her sister's name, that is.") to ask her the apartment number. "You mean her sister's apartment," said the *emendatoria janitora.* That's the one, and I was almost going to add a please when I remembered how dangerous that strange extra can be in Havana.

She gave me the apartment number and told me where it was: the first to land her. (She meant the staircase, not Violeta. Hearing things, obviously.) Before I left her she added, knowledgeable as she was about everybody's comings and goings: "But maybe nobody's there now." I thanked her for the information, also did an about-face, went down the corridor leading to the street, and reached the open door. But, instead of leaving I went up the steps: beyond hope and despair I climbed the third stairs. On the landing I stopped before a closed door, bent down, and without any difficulty delivered, by hand, the envelope (which I now realized I had had in my hand all the time) that contained my Marxist missive, all non-sequiturs plus all my money.

Fortunately I wouldn't have to explain to my wife, who took care of the bills, what had happened to my salary that week. Come Monday, with the help of the usual usurer, my money-lender: man with three balls, intimate alien, lovable loan shark: my pawnbroker Bishop, I would have more money and credit and perhaps a credible explanation of why I hadn't been paid on Saturday, value of the variable, but would be by Monday. Where's your lost weekend? According to Marx according to Ricardo, that's gone with the weekend. But you can call it surplus value, dear. But I don't understand! That, my dear, is precisely the point. Contradictions of Cuban capitalism, you see. Labor, elaborate, equivocate.

Coming Monday, before my interview with the thieving magpie, I sat on my bench, proofreading. To read proofs is indeed a reproof: the types are mostly agate and minion, with some bourgeois thrown in for good measure. Cairo can come too. It sounds exotic or Hammettish but it's hell to the naked eye. Stereotypes all. Sternotypes. Stymie bold, though tough, is my favorite type, a prototype and then, when it's printed, it is Stymie Bold. The conundrum in proofreading is a paradox: all proofs require a previous proof. This proof is not meant to be read but merely to be the proof *avant la lettre,* so to speak. The proof that there will be proofs. Not the proof when it's still set in type, inlaid in lead, ready to become proofs, but the proof of the proofs. O cruel Zeno, Zeno the Eleatic, Zeno the erratic. An infinity of proofs is to me the most hideous nightmare: a universe of galleys sailing toward Byzantium in space, becoming that light that travels at the speed of light, running in a shift toward the red end of the visible region of the spectrum. The read, that's what's already been read but it's yet to be written: the Flying Dutchman of proofs that at best are yet to come. Fool's proof. What the hell am I talking about? Must be the spirit of proof spirit.

I stood corrected. So I sat correcting a hundred-proof novel by Corín Tellado, our olive-skin version of Barbara Cartland pink. I read a rosy *roman* that was the degenerate descendant of *Le Roman de la rose:* a novel of impossible loves made possible by tell-all Tellado. *Carteles* had changed editors and *Vanidades,* our *Vogue,* had changed owners but Corín Tellado, pink penny-dreadful, damn dime novelist, abideth, like the Spanish earth as the sun rises and sets and rises again. She was always there, eternal, the Sea of Galleys in which not only my galleon but even literary *Titanic*s foundered: the unsinkable sunk on its maiden voyage. Corín Tellado was the Asturian iceberg, the Rock, more popular than Cervantes has ever been, now gone with the windmills. I was involved in that labor of hate which was my weekly love when I got a phone call. There were no longer the arbitrary restrictions (journalists make the calls, workers won't get them) of the former firm of facetious Fascists and I could receive the call, any call. *Hullo?* I heard a clear, perhaps slightly mocking birdlike voice saying, evidently contaminated by my sickly read (proofreading is also a form of translation) of Corín Tellado:

"Hello. It's the green-eyed Venus speaking."

It was she! She was obviously being ironic in calling herself the green-eyed Venus, since on the bus, upon asking me how I remembered her years after that walk down Obispo, I told her (without ever admitting I had seen her on another occasion) how could I forget those green eyes, a little defensively, quoting the popular *habanera* "Green Eyes" but really calling her Venus. If I didn't mention this before it's because the phrase was really so literary (actually a love quotation from a *poème maudit*) whose preciosity I overlooked since it allowed me to get near this creature, a verdant vision, without being seen. My main aim was to go after this prize, following her intermittent tracks, after a long hunt in El Vedado, off-limits, and in Havana proper. Besides, the sound of the bus engine somewhat muffled my venatic voice.

"Oh, how are you," said I, in a neutral tone, a deliberate delivery because beneath there was an anxiety that I tried to disguise, poorly. It must have been obvious to her. I measured the sugar then with love spoonfuls. Love? Spoonfool!

"Comme ci, comme ça," she said. Her French was execrable, by the way. "I was calling you only to tell you that I received a letter addressed to me, so I opened it. It was from you but it wasn't for me, though I read it because it was intriguing, I must say. You know, Bluebeard's wife, the locked room and all that. Feminine curiosity, if you wish. It seemed to be a very interesting letter, though it wasn't for me, like I said. But I want to tell you something that would be better to say in person. Besides, I have to return something to you, since it's all yours."

"You don't have to return anything to me."

"Yes, I do insist," she said in dramatic overtones. I felt embarrassed.

"I'd like you to forgive me for that letter," I said to her.

"I have nothing to forgive. I already told you it wasn't for me." (Pause.) "But I do want to see you. When do you think we can get together?"

It was my moment to make myself hard to get, and besides to postpone facing her and my lethal letter. *Corpores delicti* all.

"I won't be able to till Saturday. I'm working all week long."

"I know that you're a very busy gentleman." She was again using that slightly ironic tone of hers. It hurt. "But I imagine that we can see each other. Right?"

"Yes, naturally, of course. By all means."

"Can we get together Saturday?"

"Yes, in the afternoon we can. Or at night. Or on Sunday."

"No, Saturday's fine. Same place, same time?"

I was silent for a moment. Superstition about places. *Religio loci.* But it was only a moment because then she added: "I promise I'll be there on time. As if for television. Saturday, at four then, in the vestibule of the Duplex."

"Yes, that's fine. Saturday at four," I agreed with a certain tremor in my voice, which increased as I spoke. But she didn't sound triumphant upon signing off with that odious adieu: *"Ciao."*

I hung up and remained looking at the phone, which is not only a futile but a stupid act. I couldn't believe it. I simply couldn't believe it! I didn't want to believe her call or her tone or her voice or her words. Or anything. I didn't want to believe what she said to me, much less the date she made with such precision. Certainty's the word, Heisenberg. I didn't want to believe it all through the working week or on the Sabbath. Saturday came and I believed it even less when I entered the lobby. She called it vestibule: not because she was cultured (for some reason she seemed less so than Juliet Estévez, vapidly vicarious reader of Eliot) and even less than Honey Hawthorne with her comparative readings of all literature within sight and the few works of three or four Latin American authors—and I thought it was due to her life in Venezuela, South America further from the United States than Havana.

I came in at exactly three-thirty, so that no chronometric failure of the mean standard time (I've always lived in mean times) or any stopwatch failure would allow her to escape my tenuous trap. Besides I was thus eluding the fatal hour for Lola. (Lola's lore.) I sat not in the same seat as the previous occasion, not out of superstition but out of place: the seat was virtually flooded by a fat woman. So fat she needed a sofa. (The pun was spun not then but now: language is a lazy lady.) I settled down to wait somewhere else. I'm an early settler, the son Esperante. I fixed my eyeglasses on the entrance, observing the two glass panes unfortunately decorated with some allusive, elusive, vegetation engraved in opaque glass, impeding my keen vision: *pâte de verre.* The Rex Cinema was like the America and, more modestly, like the Fausto, all typically forties: a movie theater made in late Art Deco style—only that nobody knew it. Not even I who believe that architecture always aspires to the condition of history.

Time passed with its strange petty pace, an indifferent slowness that could only be intentional. Many people and at least a couple of couples walked in and out of the engraved double doors, through fancy glass decorated with bleached palm trees. Doors à la mode. It was almost four and I was already getting ready to drum up a new coup, not literary but *de théâtre* this time, to abolish chance meetings and get me somehow nearer to that slippery broad, when precisely at the designated hour (I can't avoid smiling upon writing *designated,* when I'm thinking more of assignation) she pushed open one of the palmy swinging doors—and for a moment she was lost. It was almost as if she didn't know whom to look for amid the public in the lobby (the show had just ended) until, without moving from the entrance, pale palm leaves behind her, letting future spectators and past patrons surround her in their hustle and bustle, she saw me as I stood up after getting a good look at her: my mirage. More than pretty she looked (or perhaps was) beautiful, her wavy hair falling like a gentle crown along the sides of her head and face. I still couldn't see (because of the mob and my myopia) her violently green eyes. But I did contemplate her fine figure for a moment, noticing for the first time, I think, her legs—as perfect as Juliet's, perhaps firmer, fuller, but well-formed, with long ankles. (Not as long as those of a girl who had still not crossed my path, who had not entered my field of vision yet, whom I would find later in life when I knew how to appreciate the beauty of an ankle per se not because it formed part of the leg.) Her stylish skirt covered her knees, and I was glad because I always find knees ugly or at least grotesque, except when women are sitting—then they are taut domes of grace. She was not wearing a blouse and skirt but a tight sleeveless dressy gown with a high neck that revealed her breasts beneath (not as large as Honey's big balloons, nor as perfect as Juliet's: those tender tits which one would have to see nude to appreciate), exposing her arms, which were as well-formed as her legs, surprisingly shapely in their fullness. Perhaps she was too short-waisted—but this was becoming a beauty-contest count and I wasn't a judge, or a jury, but rather a witty witness. Her light color (and what I could most appraise from my short-sighted point of view was colors), her brunette pallor, her complexion, though not as moon pale as Honey's, nor as golden delicious as Juliet's, was beautiful *à la habanera* and the glaucous green tone of her dress, with some gray hues, a lovely lovat, was obviously chosen to bring out the green of her eyes—which I reconfirmed moments later when I came over to greet her—as well as her scarlet mouth. She smiled at me and her lips were as charming and common as the words they uttered:

"Hi. How are you?"

"Good before," I said. "Very good now."

She caught the allusion without my having to tell her the story of

276

Esperanza and the expectant critic—which I didn't know yet, besides.

"I'm terribly sorry about last Saturday. Believe me, it wasn't my fault."

"It doesn't matter now. What matters is that you're here, that you are, that you exist."

I was going to say to her that last Saturday never happened: she had just canceled it. The past was now abolished. No more time. But I feared that it was more like something to be said to Juliet (who would force me to read again "Aldous I do note Hope to turn a game"), perhaps to Honey (who would doubtless find that it had been said before by Jorge Isaacs in *María*), but she seemed too practical, too intensely feminine, and perhaps too down-to-earth for literary statements. How wrong I was.

"Well, here I am," she said. "What shall we do?"

"Where would you like to go?"

"Wherever you say. I decided to dedicate all of Saturday to you. I spent the morning making myself beautiful, the afternoon waiting to arrive on time, and now I'm available. So say the word."

If I had been younger of course (not too much younger: I had just recently made that kind of date into a habit, maybe just a few months ago) I would have invited her to the movies, but I couldn't picture her watching newsreels and shorts in the Rex Cinema or ecstatic before the art film at the Rex Duplex. (Were they still showing fragments of *Fantasia*?) Fortunately I knew the area like the palm of my hand, had its topography at my fingertips and whatever other handy metaphor: not for nothing had I grown up a few blocks from there. Child of the city.

"How about Ciro's?"

"El Ciro?" she, not having any English, swallowed the possessive, that confusing equivalent of the French *chez,* and left the nightclub as naked as a bar. "I've never been there."

"I haven't either. It must be new."

"I'm new in town myself, remember?"

"It's either that or we are both new." She smiled but I decided to part with the repartee. "It's near here. We can go and if you don't like it we can take our muse elsewhere."

"Perfect," she didn't catch my muse instead of music. Perhaps she didn't hear but I heard her perfect diction. She pronounced her *c*'s and *t*'s, rarely heard in Cuba, as *k*'s between a vowel and another consonant, revealing her theater training for television. Juliet pronounced them softly, except when she was displeased—which wasn't rare in Juliet, a too frequent fury. But it was Juliet's thirst for culture that carried her to the extremes of pronouncing her every *s,* usually silent in the idiom of Havana. Honey was marked by her living quarters: she had inhabited a tenement too long. My wife, despite her convent education, pronounced them reluctantly—perhaps because the God of the Catholics is not abstract. (See Gnostics.) Now, hearing Violeta del Valle, I could reflect on these hues of feminine phonetics. Women chat, men just talk.

I had taken her by the naked arm and moved to one side of the lobby to look attentively, almost intensely, into that beautiful but not banal face: at her nose that flared as she spoke (somewhere between the dilations of Honey and Juliet), her full mouth and her green eyes: even in her green eyes I could see for the first time that she had some black in her: a very slight accent, a bit of tar, a remote ancestor. Paraphrasing a popular poet, there was if not a grandfather at least a great-grandfather who had left his black African scar on those deliciously impaired, imperfect features. She was a genuine brunette who nevertheless reminded me of that false blonde of my childhood, Jane Powell, all total tits and green eyes. Perhaps someone, somewhere else, hadn't noticed her blemish. But I know of another writer who would have detected it in his Deep South inhabited by mutilated mulattos who dared pass for Hungarians. At the same time it was such a blend that it seemed a mirage of masks: there beneath her face was another face and at the same time that face wasn't hidden if you scrutinized her carefully. She was like the sixth essence of the *mulata* and yet she was completely white. I interrupted myself in these reflections in the race river—which lasted less time than it took her to complete the word *perfect* with perfection—to again grab that grabbable arm. Not without first brushing my hand on my trousers to wipe any possible sweat off my palm. I pushed with my other hand the palmed door for exits and we left the lobby that had made me miserable a week ago and happy now, to abandon the chambers of the twin theater, turn right, walk a few steps on the sidewalk tattooed with exotic designs (in fact, copied from the streets of Rio), turn once more to the right on the corner of the Poetic jewelry shop, Raven and Sons, turning our backs on the Royal Palm Hotel and its frayed elegance of potted palms, to march almost at the same pace past the open *bodega* bar (which she eyed almost in distrust), walking a little further down Industria on the opposite sidewalk from Glamour, the decidedly French boutique (the first to declare itself so in Havana, a city full of Cuban shops, Spanish stores, and Americanized department stores), and before entering the tough territory of the Campoamor and Lira theaters I led her down the abrupt staircase.

Which took us into the cellar called Ciro's Cabaret, which had been a nightclub and was now a mere daytime club. It regaled us with its perfume that was unknown to me (the only other nightclub I had been in was the Mocambo and I went at night) but would be as memorable as the smell (strangers would call it the stink) of the Esmeralda: cheap moviehouse scent, with its intoxicating essence of bottled but unbottled liquors, stale air-conditioning fumes, and stagnant cigarette smoke. I remember that mixture of smells almost more than the perfume Violeta del Valle was wearing, Colibrí, so fashionable in the forties and now a little unfashionable on her, dressed according to the dictates of Dior.

Ciro's was, of course, deserted at this hour except for the ghostly bartender and a waiter here and there—or perhaps the bartender was doubling up as a spiritist waiter. But this emptiness filled me with joy. All I wanted in the world was to be alone with Violeta del Valle, to hear her speak, to look at her face, whose beauty was more and more captivating, to smell her perfume—even though it was Colibrí. What's more, I thanked her for regaling me again with that aroma, which reminded me of the first time I went to the ballet, when I sat in the orchestra and in the seat just in front of me (it was a matinée, the showtime I like most in the theater, at the movies and now in a club) was a woman exuding those same subtle vapors which my mother, I don't remember when, told me were Colibrí.

"What do you want to drink?" I asked Violeta del Valle, when the waiter arrived a bit too quickly, his solicitude a response to his solitude.

"A margarita, please," she said, and I liked her mouth so much when she pronounced that please, so exotic in Havana. I don't know what reason, what urban pride or decay of manners, what lack of class, what perverted education made it a taboo to say *please* in Havana, when in my town it was always mandatory—just as it was obligatory to say, "Yes, sir," "No, ma'am," right, left, and center. I still remember the day I went to a corner coffee shop in the capital and said, "Coffee, please," and the *vendorette* stared at me and said: "Come on, kid, what's with that *please* nonsense?" Perhaps she wanted to indicate that she was there to serve me and I didn't have to please her—and that was that. But I haven't been able to forget this indelible Havana custom—a trademark of bad breeding.

"What?" asked the waiter, puzzled. Perhaps by the *please.*

"A *margarita,*" she repeated.

"What's that?" asked the waiter.

"A cocktail."

"A cocktail? Really? What's it made of?"

"It's made with tequila and—"

"Ah, but we don't have any tequila, you see."

I stepped in to mediate. I didn't want the occasion to begin with a fiasco. If they begin that way, they tend to end the same: fruits of failure.

"Why don't we order, say, two daiquiris?"

Of all the drinks created in Cuba, the daiquiri is the best they make in nightclubs and American bars in Havana. Besides, if my eyes could climb stairs, pierce the block of the Campoamor Theater and bore through the Galician Center, pass through Central Park, and cross between the Asturian Center and Apple Arcade, I would be able to see next to Alvear Park (the small square and still statue both built in memory of the builder of our aqueduct) the Floridita! This bar is supposed to be the inner sanctum of all drinks called daiquiri—where it flows like colloidal water. If they didn't invent it in this Florida fountain of youth they act as if they had perfected the formula: the potion of a Havanan Dr. Jekyll who after swallowing several samples becomes multiple ubiquitous versions of Mr. Hyde gone ape and then called Mr. High. (There are many allusions to Jekyll and Hyde in this book, I know. It's probably because the fable of the intellectual and the beast is a sexual metaphor disguised as a moral dilemma.) I had addressed the waiter and Violet at the same

279

time and she, still with her green eyes, laughing with them before smiling with her lipsticked mouth, eager for margaritas, said to me:

"That's fine!"

"Two daiquiris," I ordered and the waiter went away. I imagine him glad not to have to experiment with cocktails he didn't know with spirits he didn't have. When he took refuge behind his color bar, she opened her purse, took out an envelope I immediately recognized for its creases and my handwriting in crisis, and gave it to me: "Here's your message."

If she had added "to García" she would have been perfect. I was glad she didn't say it: I hate perfections.

"I want you to know," she said, "that my sister was furious. Was she mad! She didn't even want me to come see you today. What's more, she doesn't know I'm with you. She told me you were treating me like a prostitute, though she used another word. Whore."

It was then that I really realized what I had done: it had been a ruse that worked, another trap for my prey, trick or tits. This diminished its enormity in my eyes—though it's true I hadn't behaved well. Objectively, the letter could be considered an insult. Actually with its contents I was treating her like the opposite of a whore: for services not rendered. Nevertheless, it was a rule of the game to offer my apologies:

"Forgive me," I said, "but I was furious. I waited for you for such a long time. Besides you had assured me that you would come."

I didn't say that I thought she had made fun of me as the future actress would mock the critic. I couldn't say it even if I had wanted to: neither of them, Esperanza or Esperanto, existed then.

"I know," she said. "But believe me, I couldn't come. I did everything possible but it was *im*possible."

"Well, that doesn't matter now," I said, taking the envelope and putting it in an intimate pocket.

"It's all there," she said, and I imagined she was referring only to the money. "I didn't want to keep the letter either."

"I understand and I don't blame you. It was hideous of me."

"It shows that you're very passionate. Just like Alexander."

For a moment I tried to place the unknown Alexander and his passion. Was he the one called Alexander as well as Paris? The one Helen made mortal with a kiss: a tawdry passion for pretentious art? The Greek conqueror of Greek boys? Alexandre Dumas, father and son, mulattoes both? Finally I remembered her Venezuelan visitor. Her husband she called him. Her lover probably: that man with the shadow of a beard but without the shadow of a doubt a future shadow over my love. *That* Alexander! I exclaimed silently and I felt instant jealousy. That's me. I suffer from a jealousy more total than my recall of it: retrospective, introspective, prospective jealousy. I'm more jealous than God. Like a Moor I should live not in a harem but behind jalousies. To save me now from an oncoming attack of grand jealousy (I was already sensing its green aura), the waiter arrived with two deep daiquiris in which to wash away my *petit*

280

mal. Are love pains wash and wear? They can be drowned, can't they? But no one here was going to jump into the icy lake of those glaciers, *glasses:* they were unnecessarily frozen: the blended ice turned tundras contained in arctic circles of sugar icing. Adding cold spells to the gusts of air conditioning that made the bar into a Yukon just for you, Venusiceberg—and for me, amusing Amundsen adnauseam. The *albedo* from the twin tundras was so intense that I had to wear my dark glasses again. I didn't have my snow goggles with me, you see. You do but I didn't.

She picked up her ice sea shaped as a glass with such grace under snow pressure that Captain Oates would have admired her as intensely as the antarctic cold. Then she put it as near as possible to mine, icicycles tinkling against icefloes, and said, "Chin chin!" My teeth ground now as much as the ice in the daiquiri I was already holding in my gloveless hand. But it wasn't the antarctic drink that grated my teeth—it was her toast. "Chin chin" is to my teeth what "Ciao" is to my ear: that alien knife that makes us all versions of Van Gogh without being painters. You can cut off one of your ears with a sharp *ciao*—especially if you are not in Italy nor were you born there. But the number of Italians who immigrated to Venezuela must be staggering! So much so that Bolívar could have said, "I have plowed the Tyrrhenian Sea" and still be a South American patriot. But I smiled and touched her icepack gently. At least I thought I did it gently. But upon seeing the daiquiri in her hand and watching with horror how her glass shook between her frostbit fingers (so much so that her iceberg tipped to overflow a bit), I realized my mistake—due no doubt to snowblindness. A later reckoning showed that I had miscalculated the distance between the icebergs. (Icebergs befuddle the soul.) So I saw the glacial fragments falling on the table only too late. I apologized for the ice waterfall but she said: "It doesn't matter. You know it means good luck?"

I didn't know. Besides did she say good luck or good fuck? Cold weather can permanently affect your hearing. Anyway, good fuck to you too, dear. A rabbit's foot, hairy and hard, for every good fuck. For a better fuck, a rat's tail, smooth and erectile but, alas, not sterile. On the contrary, quite fertile—all of them, rabbit or rat. I smiled a rabbit's grin and she smiled too. Naughty and natty. Had she been reading the dirty tale of my mind? Then she laughed and I had to laugh too. We laughed together. Cocktails and laughter—what could come after? Only one thing. Who would come first? Coward, that's who. Cowards always come first, even before women and children. Do they really? Did he actually? I can't remember—or else I forget. Else who? Elsa Popping. Your eyes are popping even before she shows you her tits. You've seen her teeth and eyes, Popeye. What about her lips? That's quite intimate, you know. Fair's fair. Fair enough but not far enough. Enough!

I don't remember how many daiquiris we managed to negotiate in that frozen darkness of the arctic night where her originally young warm flesh became thirtyish marble ice. She growing old, my limbs growing cold. What with my dizziness and seasickness and my sea legs becoming numb, I should have worn snowboots. I felt like Admiral Byrd but not really very admirable: a navigator with no North Star on the Hudson Bay of the bar. There was snow everywhere, even behind the counter, where there were snowshelves with frozen bottles. Icicles formed everywhere and our glasses, including my own glasses, were all snowbound. We should have ordered whiskey, damn it! But then they would have served it on the rocks, ice rocks. Scotch of the Antarctic.

To forget about the Arctic show in the tropics, I talked. She talked. We talked. You could see our breath make foggy sounds a mile away. Talk and chat like a chat show, a talkathon. What did we talk about? About her of course, about her career, trials and tribulations. About her as a stage actress in Havana, condemned here to the inertia that comes not from movement but from stagnation—and when she said this word, she froze.

The Greeks were right, there must be an Antarctica somewhere. They meant it to be opposite the Bear but it's closer than they thought. Forget Ursa Major! Ciro's is your place, *hoi polloi*. We were inside the Polar Bear, colder than the whale and the seal—even than seven seals put together. Huddled. The star, Stella Polaris, and the smaller bear so near. This polar star with her stiff upper lip and her frozen stage smile was talking about Greek tragedy. What about Greek comedy? The Greeks were right about the Poles even if they spoke Spanish at the University. That theater group stagnated my beautiful statue of frozen salt. What was she talking about now in such cold undertones? Television, that's what. Apparently she was complaining of the fact that she actually got very few roles on Channelle 5 (isn't that a French perfume?) here in Havana, where the snow is falling heavier than her sorrows. Migraine. So she decided to emigrate. To warmer climes, no doubt. Venezuela, the capital of Caracas, where things were going well for her. Congratulations. A bow. Next or next to next she talked about her marriage. My deepest antipathies. I got my sled ready and alerted the huskies. I wielded my whip, about to shout, "Mush!" But unfortunately—hold it!—it had gone sour on her. Her marriage foundered in ice sea near Caracas.

Stagnant waters being warmer than polar undercurrents in Don Juan pond, I profited from this stalemate (or from my mate being stale, whichever came first) to initiate a faint feint that in time would become a thrust and finally a plunge. From there onward it was a quick step to the clinch or *corps à corps*—before my quarry could parry. This foil fencing is my contribution to an updated technique in the wars amatoria or duel of love. If I sound like a cross between Ovid and my mother's favorite *author et amator*, M. Delly, it's because in love one can only repeat words, like Romeo and Juliet, or bandy them, like Ovid's Roman lovers, or echo clichés—and who's better to create them than a dime novelist? (Such pigeonholing does not imply literary value: it's a mere stating of price at the bookstalls.) *Au fond* then: I told her that I too was married.

(In the future I would get used to uttering that phrase "I'm married," like a declaration of principles of independence—which means that I must be taken as I am. That's the civil state I am in now and I don't intend to change it in the immediate future. Unless of course—)

"I feared as much," said she.

"Do I look the part?"

"Something told me. From the moment I met you."

We were obviously talking about different versions of my life: when she had met me, I had already known her previously, and when I first saw her I wasn't even engaged yet, not to say married.

"Do you care?" I asked her.

"Not really. There's nothing to prevent two married people from establishing a friendship."

Was she still married? Last time she told me she was divorced. Strange. And intriguing. But I didn't want to begin an inquiry. I was afraid that the name of Alexander might crop up again, so detestable for me. Not because it belonged to this tall phantom from one night in memory—the columns were taller—but because of the materialized present: because he had been or was the husband of this benumbed beauty beside me. I tried to talk about other things—the theater for example. But it was obvious that her connection with the theater was as remote now as mine. Since the days of my sexual safaris to the University Theater Group many things had happened. Among them important things like the true loss of my virginity, my intimate relationship with one or two women, imprisonment because of words—the prison of words and even my marriage as a consequence of the (prison) sentence. The theater was as ancient as the age of the works the University Theater Group performed. Should we talk about movies? But that was almost like showing off my profession: I could just as well talk about proofreading. Without a doubt the delete symbol was as much a tool of my work as the images on the screen. I was the only movie critic who corrected his own galleys. I hit on the right note—we would talk about television. Delete vision? I wasn't like the writers of my generation who bragged about despising television without realizing that it was the same scorn the movies had met with early in the century. I liked television as a spectator, I was even interested as a writer and I had almost written scripts for television, doing some adaptation for a mystery program called "After the Scent on Channel 5" and which despite its comic monicker would allow me to depict Havana as hell. I never wrote it of course but I spoke of television.

"Ah, television," she said, in a tone that wasn't declamatory because beneath her expression there was always a popular lilt, doubtless a product of San Lázaro and its tarts with high tar. *Mulatas, mulaticas.* "It's a pain, believe you me! The only good part is that you earn good money. At least in Venezuela. But those marks on the floor!" (The intensity in her voice almost made me look under the table.) "That little guy stooping in front of you! He looks as if he were going to look under your skirt, if it

283

wasn't that he was wearing those earphones." She said, clearly, "airphones," which has an impeccable logic but is not exact: I've written "earphones" because I don't want to be implacable with her memory: besides it sounded so well in her irreproducible voice: "And a libretto in his hand, always leading you around."

She meant the script, of course, as she was doubtless referring to the coordinator, a floor official not a dwarf, who despite his technical name was only someone who performs the hateful job of an itinerant prompter. I was afraid she was going to go on that warpath of all actresses who complain about the intrusion of technology on stage. I tried to erect a barrier that would keep her from entering that gentle jungle of laments.

"But they must do a lot of closeups of you. One doesn't see eyes like yours every day of the week and much less in Caracas."

Never scorn corn because it can be as effective as soap. She smiled and if she had known any English and known the old saw, she would have said: "Flattery will get you knowhere." But it was obvious that she felt it and like many of the women (I've never heard a man say it) who express this saying, even correctly, she enjoyed the bouquet of paper flowers. Adulation can lead to adultery. Though one mustn't coin new phrases but rather mint counterfeit clichés.

"Oh, closops! The most terrifying part because you feel naked." Closops, Cyclops, TV. *Video meliora, deteriora sequor.*

"And what do you have against feeling naked?"

"Nothing, when there's a spectator," she said with a certain smile. "Perhaps very little when there are many spectators. But it's terrible when you're naked in front of nothing, only looked at by that mechanical creature with an empty eye in the middle and a red gizmo winking on the side."

It was a good description of a television camera.

"Polimorphous Polyphemus."

"What?"

"Nothing. Go on."

But there was no need to encourage her: she was an actress after action was called.

"When they do a closop of me is when I feel most vulnerable. I'm afraid they'll see everything."

"But all that they'll see is what's visible."

It was doubly true: besides her mouth, her lips bordered symmetrically spotless rows of teeth, with even, white teeth set in perfect rosy gums. I've already described the rest of her face, and though she might develop a double chin one day, now her chin completed not an oval but an outline without blemish. She smiled again before continuing: pearls in a pearl.

"What I mean is that the emotions may show too much or not at all or might seem false. It's an agony! That's why I'm enjoying so much this time I'm spending in Havana."

"Among the natives."

"Among my people."

I was glad she didn't say she had enjoyed the time of her marriage, as she must have, judging by the joy she displayed under the total possessiveness of her hideous husband that Havana night full of columns so long ago—and really so recent. All the time we talked we had been drinking, shivering amid passing penguins—the waiters. Besides being frozen I felt quite cheery. Call me Dayquiri. Wisecracking the ice. Mental exercise is an antidote against arctic cold and now I was threatening to be brilliant but also drunk, therefore capable of being a big bungler. Besides time was passing but nothing else was. I decided it was time to make a daring move in the dark winter night, calculating according to the compass rose that we were heading north, picking this Violet of the Valley, greenhouse not hothouse flower, testing her in a *tête-à-tête* but keeping in mind all the time that she was divorced. Besides she was an actress who seemed lewdly liberated. But how to begin? I should try an original move, a Ruy López opening made to take the queen. No nights, no king. All power to the pawn.

"How would you like to be alone with me for a while?" He who has seduced more than one woman is condemned to repeat himself: the first time in a drama, the second in a farce. She looked at me, looked around the bar, as solitary as Lapland in winter, which the two waiters (now looking like awks in awe of extinction) made seem even more desolate.

"Don't you think we're sufficiently alone?"

I had to concede a point to her but I wasn't there to keep score. She was right, though, even in amorous chess. Check.

"I mean the two of us alone."

She smiled. "You mean you want to be alone with me all by myself?"

It was time to put the cards on the table: chess was becoming mere poker. Decadence of the games of love.

"That's it."

"In a room?"

I paused a moment before answering. Would she have a hidden face, an ace? "Yep." I feared that she would react if not violently at least negatively.

"All right."

I couldn't believe it. Was she bluffing? Cardsharp. "Yes?"

"Yes."

"Really?"

"Really."

It would almost seem as if I wanted to convince her of just the opposite. Or as if I were dealing with a risky virgin. It was obvious that matters of love had changed a lot in Havana (of Cuba I don't know: I lived on an island that was my city) in only five years. In 1949 Juliet was an early settler, a pubic pilgrim who risked the title of whore (without the

285

vox populi admitting that whore was only one who was paid for it) for going to bed with the man she loved—or only liked. (So as not to boast that she might have loved me at one point.) The rest, all the girls I knew, were professional virgins or puritans like Catia Ben Como, who considered sex dangerous if not mere love ("mere love," if only Ovid could hear me!) as a dangerous province: a kind of contamination down there against which one had to be vaccinated. If their adolescence lent girls some charms that were their main attraction, it wasn't their fault: those charms had to be eliminated. Thus Catia's final solution was her resolve to use eyeglasses when she wasn't even near-sighted! That's why Juliet remained as a vestal of love, a virgin in reverse to whom one should render tribute for her surrender to sex—Saint Giuletta, neither virgin nor martyr. Many of my friends, even today, remember her fondly (is that the adverb?), considering her a true initiatrix: not only did she initiate almost all of us in sex but she herself initiated a lewd liberation, which culminated now in Violet's being at ease more than easy in accepting a proposal that was more awkward than irresistible—my poor poker against her canasta.

I asked for the bill and paid—with my money: not Violet's, the money she had returned to me, those *billets doux.* We emerged on the street and summer received us: the hot kitchen, furnace, drycleaner's atmosphere that I was now grateful for after my stay among the Eskimos. I was glad to be alive in Havana, following behind her, walking slowly. Not only to admire her frank, Harrisian hips, but also because I had had too much to drink and you already know what that other Frank, Rabelaisian, says about the divine bottle—though he doesn't say its forms are like a woman's. This woman had the form of my content.

The violent summer light had turned into a gentle twilight, more pink than mauve, as we walked toward the urban *posada,* I holding her by the arm as though it were mine, making her turn right and down Industria Street barely two blocks to Barcelona—the street not the city. But, when I had taken her by the arm upon leaving the bar, she had said: "If they say something to me, don't do anything, please."

I didn't understand. "Come again."

"If someone gets familiar with me, don't react. I don't want any scenes, you understand?"

"Nobody's going to get familiar with you," I said, to assure her though I wasn't too sure. Violeta had provocative tits, which were indeed very noticeable, and her body was very womanly and she wore besides her beautiful face very visibly. She was what was called in the venereal vernacular a great lay, and this last word isn't a misprint for lady. On the other hand I still had my damned juvenile physique, despite jackets with padded shoulders and dark glasses, and it was obvious that she looked like too much woman for me—thus spake Silvano Suárez on Beba Far, much to my fury. But Violeta had nothing to fear. I wasn't violent, at least physically: I could be a citric critic, with acidic (not Hassidic) humor, but I was a pacific citizen, obeying not only traffic laws but the laws of physiques too. What's more, since my high-school days, after passing my first inexperienced year in a Havana primary school, miraculously surviving the abuses of the local bullies, I entered the Institute with my right foot forward. Since then I had avoided being among the victims of violence by dint of wit, with a joke here, a wisecrack there, a grotesque gag yonder: playing the clown though at first I was one of those who were considered the weaklings, the four-eyed eggheads, the bookworms hated by the bullyboys, the tough guys. Thus, when my sea change happened, instead of studying textbooks I read books, instead of playing ball I helped organize stage performances, instead of going to the movies in a noisy gang I helped create a film club. I left violence behind without even feeling touched by it, like a duck who doesn't know he's waterproof. Thus I avoided street violence and was fortunate not to have to confront it when out on a stroll with a woman. It's also true that these outings almost always occurred after dark in the dark on dark avenues—and few of my female companions could be considered popular beauties. It was quite a different kettle of fish, however, to be walking now with this excessively, spectacularly beautiful woman, along a crowded street in downtown Havana by day. Fortunately I had only one block left to go in this dim dusk, escorting this husky beauty.

When we entered the room, which she inspected almost with a face of: I've never been here before. But I've been and who cares? Dingy shades in a thousand rooms furnished like this. Leaving her purse on the dressing table, she said, "Would you mind closing the curtains? I detest the light."

Women of the world unite. You have nothing to lose but your quirks. Fortunately when she used such a cultured verb as *detest* she didn't employ the inflection that Juliet Estévez would have lent it, which would seem if not false at least a wasted slang, an eliotism. Or the bookish barbarism—inevitably South American junglese—that Honey Hawthorne would have boomed. But rather she said it with such sweet simplicity. On that note, she went into the bathroom. I was always wondering what women did in the bathroom before coming to bed with a man. (If I had gone to the Nice Theater and seen *How Ladies Bathe* I would have known. I would have even known what they do before going to bed with another woman!) Dutifully I closed the curtains. *Posadas,* like European houses, made generous use of curtains, with the intention of promoting a darkness that would perhaps invite commerce between the sexes, but they also lent an exotic touch—immediately contradicted by the furniture. (As Cuban as could be, it was called what I considered an incomprehensible neologism when I first came to Havana: a room set.) I went to the door of the bathroom to see her not undress but reflected pale and upside down in the mirror, the cold-cream fluorescent light lending a distant quality to her warm flesh as she proceeded to wipe off her lipstick —before scarlet, now purple—with toilet paper. As the only customers in the frigid eyrie, closely observed by the waiters, we hadn't even kissed because of their attention or perhaps because of the cold climate, numbly aware of the possibility of a chill, or of freezing to death, frozen lovers. I think once or twice I held her benumbed hand with my frost-bitten fingers. And here we were, without even having bussed, in the bathroom of a *posada,* ready to leave it to get into the propitious bed and make love! That gallicism I learned from Juliet as the only decent way of saying fuck. Oh that the words, not the actions, were sentenced by morality! The language of love is always obscene, even if love itself cannot be.

I moved to one side when she came out of the bathroom and I followed her—and lost her. When she turned off the light we were explosed (pardon the misprint, exposed: returned to the quality of negatives which we have before birth) to the total dark of the room—as much an enemy as the cold of the club. I remained standing beside the door waiting for her to get undressed. Or rather listening to her take off her clothes with the rustling of satin or silk (or was it that other enemy, nylon?) without enjoying the pure pleasure of watching a woman disrobe. Now she was a shadow unveiling itself, a sinuous silhouette I could barely distinguish from the squares—squat and big but all black—of the furniture. I heard her (it's amazing how much you can hear in the dark) get between the creaking sheets and then her voice coming from south-southwest (after the nordic night of the nightclub everything was goin' south for me) say:

"Are you coming?"

Of course I was coming! (In the literal sense.) But first I had to get undressed. For some hidden reason—or would it be better to say dark reason in the gloom of the room?—I hadn't even taken off my perennial jacket, now brown, waiting for her to offer me the eternally new spectacle because I had waited so long. It was easy to rid myself of the jacket and shirt, which had not had time to become sweaty after having frozen during the winterkill at Ciro's. The difficult part was the pants: always my difficulty is taking off my pants, erratically: it comes and goes. Today it was coming. My balance is pretty precarious, to tell the truth. In fact I walk with one leg in the correct position, but the other, at foot level, makes a weird kind of centrifugal turn, which thrusts itself outward while the centripetal force of the other leg returns it to its center. I would never have noticed this leg anomaly if my mentor, fearing for all his cats' lives, hadn't told me about it once when I was advancing along the narrow corridor of his apartment toward the kitchen. But there had been more than one friend who had asked me why I walked so strangely, with that quick step that never quite becomes a foxtrot. Now, one of my pant legs always gets caught on my shoe, even on my bare foot, and almost makes me fall—which is why I carry out the operation of taking off my pants either seated or leaning on some propitious piece of furniture. This time there was no chair nearby but I didn't want to sit on the bed, which seemed markedly marital to me and would take away the clandestine character of that encounter—and so I keeled over so noisily now that she asked from her darkness amid the pillows:

288

"What happened? Did you fall?"

"No, no," I hurried to assure her, "I only tripped in the dark."

"Forgive me," she pleaded, "for insisting on it being so dark but I've never been able to be naked in the light."

Just my luck! Did she mean that I would never see that covered coveted body uncovered, contemplate that flesh awaiting in splendor, that seemed succulent just from the bits and pieces she revealed: arms, legs, neck? *Morceaux choisis.* I groped my way to the bed and lay down beside her, imagining her image.

"Are you okay?" she asked me with her voice that lost for me its phony euphony and only sounded refined. She was probably still referring to my fall.

"Yes, yes, I'm fine. It was nothing."

"No, I mean are you okay with me here."

How could she ask that? I had no choice but to make exterior this interior voice: "How can you ask me that?"

"Oh, I don't know. It's the first time. I imagine you must feel strange the first time. I feel very odd."

"Odd?" Did she mean cold? "What do you mean?"

"I don't know. The two of us here, so quickly, without even knowing each other's real names. You've only given me your pseudonym." True. For reasons of sexual security I had given her the name I signed my writings with. But there was also the problem of my longest name, which had never been in close harmony with my short body, but she? "And I have given you my stage name. Do you know why I ordered a margarita at the club?"

"I suppose because you like it."

"No, it's just that my real name is Margarita del Campo."

Well, calling oneself Daisy of the Fields is almost as florid as calling oneself Violet of the Valley. Even worse would be naming oneself Lily Lagoon, Poppy Park, or Rose Gardens. Stop it! I told her so. In Spanish and without the "stop it" bit.

"But my last name isn't even del Campo. It's simply Pérez. Margarita Pérez."

Margarita Pérez. For some dark reason (and I don't mean here now, but before) I had gotten into repeating mentally what I heard and saying out loud what I was thinking. Echolalia and confessionism. I decided that we had talked enough already, perhaps too much, and tired of Violets and Daisies and Lilies of the field I turned around to kiss her—which I didn't do exactly on her mouth. You see, she was still lying face up or recumbent, sublimely supine, as a cordial coroner would say if she were a corpse—and for all erotic effects she was, and I'm no necrophile. Just the opposite is true. But her supine position didn't last long and she turned around to me to return the kiss. This time the two mouths kissed: the four lips and finally the three tongues: for a moment it seemed as if she were a two-tongued tigress. But it was an illusion of her amatory art. She knew how to kiss, as much as Juliet and much more of course than Honey, infinitely more than my wife: a trio of comparisons that despite its difficulty (it's much easier to compare two things than three: triolism is always tough on one of the components) I made immediately. On the sex spot. We kissed: I smelled her real fragrance above the aroma of all the alcohol, which is not a stink to me. I don't really like the taste of alcohol, but there's something supremely attractive about its smell. I suppose that if I could get drunk by inhaling instead of drinking I would be a dipsomaniac by now. Though alcohol blocks the tasting of a woman's intimate breath. Consider me a breathtaker.

I pressed my body against hers and felt all her soft splendor tactilely (the way of the dark), the smoothness of her skin all along my body, and I reached then and there the conclusion that, even if I hadn't read all the books, alas, I knew that *la chair n'est pas triste*. On the contrary, the flesh is joyous, pleasing, exhilarating, and once more I told myself that the theologian who punished it for opposing virtuous continence knew what he was doing. The flesh condemns us to contemplate, to love it, to adore it. It's our version of Paradise Last. I gave thanks for having in my hands, in my arms, between my legs all that coveted flesh I had dreamt of for five years—a lustrum of lusting—for which I had wished upon a star or two, whom I pursued awake and in my dreams, seeing her from afar or having her close by but remote, who ignored me as I explored her pore by visible pore—like the Stanley of this unknown dark continent. Such a long lust-time and now she was in my space, truly but incredibly because I was possessing her and soon we would be in the moment with no time, lust in space, in that human-sized eternity that is coitus, fucking. (*Singar* in Cuba's a verb that somehow seems to say that one comes singing.) I still hadn't entered her, only penetrated her mouth with my tongue, converting a hole into an instrument of penetration. And as my soft segment pierced her, she executed her own entrance into my mouth. I stopped kissing her for a moment with those well-aimed, relentless, implacable kisses of mine to seek her breasts, to find with my mouth those tits that were always her bust beneath her concealing clothing, forever green, and I lowered my head till I came upon one of her nipples: which I kissed, sucked, almost perforated with my tongue, making for her the orifice maternity would someday provide, creating artificially what mother nature did with a purpose, with another intention, but both of us, *natura* and I, blindly: I because of the darkness she imposed: *fiat tenebrae*. I tried to find with my other hand her other breast.

"Don't!"

She said it so suddenly, so firmly, so out of character, that she disoriented me, and before asking her what was wrong, what I had done dastardly with my mortal tongue or hand, she said: "No, please don't touch me there. You can continue as you were but leave my other side alone."

She was referring to the right tit, the one I tried to find, the one I would never find. It was enough to make anyone worry. But I was so happy to have her in bed, naked, between my members, she now opening her legs, that I forgot her prohibition, a mere caprice, and got on top. All penetration is knowledge and the time would come when in order for me to deal intimately with a woman it would be indispensable to go to bed with her. Until now my practice with carnal knowledge was limited because for a hunter the only pieces that count are the stuffed ones. Juliet was already a married woman and there was in her a didactic mania that made her indicate where and how I should enter and when I should come out. Honey was worried only the first time about disguising her deflowering —real or fictitious?—with dance steps: it was all the fault of ballet. Thus my first penetration of Honey was masked by her hypocrisy, by choreographies, by the dance that never began with my Missadora. The encounter with my wife was not with a virgin but with the virgin. Her religious education, her real religiousness, plus a peculiar tendency toward hysteria, turned our first time into the only time for several days, a perforation more than a penetration, provoking hemorrhages that reminded me of my brother's hemoptysis and even the childhood vision, back home, of a boy who had nose bleeds without a known cause. This first disastrous experience with a *virgo intacta* didn't keep me from pursuing virginity like a domestic version of Don Juan (Silvio Rigor, always attuned to musical metaphors, would have said that it was my interpretation of Don Juan Strauss's *Sinfonia Domestica*)—I was convinced then that the only way to achieve a certain immortality in a woman's memory was going to bed with her before anybody else. Deflowering created a tie, in some cases of love, in others of hate, but it never bred indifference. The breaking of a mere membrane therefore brought unforgettable consequences to its proprietress, hereinafter known as the property, and the first penetrator becomes the property owner—not in the sense of possession of the body but of the soul (the Satan in me), which seemed to reside behind the hymen and thus liberated would come to lodge in the lover like an incubus. Or rather succubus. Curiously, with the act of defloration, man becomes woman a little. A fib for infibulators.

But now Violet was opening her softest flesh like a shell and I was entering the threshold of her womb. She was receiving me as if I were coming home, entering her castle, pawn taking queen. She began to move with a naturalness that didn't intend to teach me anything, hiding nothing from me, offering her orifice without artifice. At the same time it was all done with an artful simplicity displayed, for example, by certain Japanese painters who seemed to have been born painting and nevertheless their age, the size of their experience, the atemporal quality of their work indicate an apprenticeship because, in effect, an art is always learned. I didn't feel jealous at that moment over the many lovers or the single, singular lover who taught her to move—and not only move because it was more than movement, more than the skillful suction of the vagina, more than the apparent thrust of an embolus created to receive a piston—her body as if in flight, stretching toward a horizon while leaving behind the vigorous vulva, surrendering her pelvis to me as she stole away her torso. She broke into two as if coitus sawed her in half in a vicious vaudeville act: it was as if she fled to surrender, half and half, half escape and half embrace.

It was all a disposition (indicating not only the activity but the position, what ballerinas and pilots call *attitude*) showing that sex is a mental exercise performed with the body—and it didn't even matter to me if it was that distant Alexander or an alexander all *crème de cacao,* brandy, and cream. Now she was effectively all mine just as much as I was hers. When she reached orgasm, when both of us reached the climax, she didn't even scream with the vocal din of Juliet, who seemed to consider the beautiful art of coitus as murder, revealing as her true self that expression she so much hated: vulgarity. Or would it be better to call it vulvarity? Violeta (though for me she had already begun to be Margarita) moaned or rather bemoaned quietly but with an intensity not destined for the gallery (in a manner of speaking) but for the galley slave, for me alone, a particularly long moan giving not only the measure of her orgasm but of a genuine, sincere feeling of joy, rejoicing: she achieved pleasure with me but, mainly, for me.

No sooner did we end than we began again, Fin again. But we did it only twice, and I had the impression I hadn't performed well. That sensation assaulted me the first time I was with Juliet, but she was immediately giving me instructions *(How to Achieve Coitus in Four Quartets),* which didn't allow me to become conscious of my inefficiency. The same thing happened with Honey: her haste to explain to me ridiculously, comedically, why she wasn't a virgin even though she was also kept me from noticing, as I should have, any fault in my performance. Now it was a fact that for some inhibition I couldn't extricate (or would have needed a lot of time to investigate, in order to discover its deep cause) I was a poor *palo* the first time. That first time with Margarita (or Violeta del Valle as she still should be called in television, now, alas, playing the roles of mother or perhaps grandmother: I never asked her her age but she always seemed older than I—or was it an image projected by her experience, her wisdom, her quantity of life lived?) I was not satisfied with my performance test nor had I satiated my sexual appetite. The latter dissatisfaction I kept to myself but I did state the former, a performer's self-criticism, with an explanation that was the truth but was also a cliché to save face.

"I'm not usually very good the first time."

"Don't worry," she told me. "You did fine."

Was there something in her tone of the mother who doesn't reward the son but who doesn't want to hurt him either? Or rather than a friendly maternalism, was it the encouragement a stage director gives to the actor who's not happy with his performance? In any case she revealed one of her bedroom qualities: she took part in the sexual act but knew how to dissociate herself from her participation enough to be able to judge it. An actress addicted to the *Verfremdungseffekt* or V-Effekt, in which the V stands for vagina. In the future I would see some women capable of this doubling-up as actress and audience, but none of them carried it off as completely as she did. At the same time she showed me more than once that she could be a passionate woman—perhaps too passionate.

"Do you mind if I get dressed?" said she, the spectator now.

"No, not at all."

She got out of bed on her side of the dark. She walked in night, the beauty moving barefoot, invisible and silent, to pick up her clothes (rustling of silk—or was it nylon?) and enter the bathroom to get dressed: *per speculum in enigmata.* She closed the door (sound of Yale lock) before turning (click) the light on. I struck a match to light a cigarette and smoke in darkest bed. I smoked cigarettes then, exotic L & Ms, after having abandoned the war pipe of adolescence, without having adopted the cigar yet, a Havana brand of hand-rolled coronas. But I was, like Thomas Mitchell, already partial to the weed myself. All habits are a repetition and a synthesis: a man who smokes is all men who smoke—even if it's in bed. Smoking after coitus is a habit not created by Rodrigo de Xeres, the discoverer of tobacco—that is, of the smoking of the leaf—for all Europeans. Nor by Sir Walter Raleigh, who brought it to England. But possibly by Raleigh's contemporary, the irreverent poet Christopher Marlowe, who claimed that all who didn't love tobacco and boys were fools, after pleading "come live with me and be my love." I can imagine him inventing the habit of smoking after fucking.

I waited for her in bed, in darkness, still under the sheets, still naked, an Indian in his tepee, leaning on the pillows against the headrest. Smoking the invisible, silent cigarette I saw her come out of the bathroom: dressed as elegantly as when she emerged from behind the smoke-stained glass doors—mirrors with leaf images multiplying her passage from reality to the unreality of our encounter—in the Rex Duplex, double cinema. She was fully made-up again: her swollen mouth now overflowing with lips done in pasty red, her hair combed in long waves, her body contained in her gown. She seemed ready to leave forever. But no, wait! She came to sit on the bed. She leaned forward and became such a closeup to my purblind eyes that I thought for a moment, despite her big red lips (wet paint), that she wanted a kiss—or a smoke.

"You didn't notice anything?"

When? When she came? When she came out of the bathroom? When she sat next to me now?

"Notice?"

I hoped she didn't mean the wet-paint sign.

"When we were doing it."

She didn't belong to the school of Juliet, who would have said making love. Or of Honey, who would have avoided referring to the sexual act

293

unless it was to relate it to some obscure Peruvian writer who perhaps never even dreamed of it. Ciro's Alegría was never to cry over spilt cream. Violeta used a verb, pronouns, and a participle. Grammatically it was a sentence.

"No. What happened?"

I imagined she was going to refer to her evident lack of hymen, or some difficulty in the sphincter. For a moment I thought it had something to do with me. Was it something special—a gift, a quality, a specific and hidden anatomical characteristic? Not the voracious *vagina dentata* but that vulva-versa sucking with contractions, practically an inverted birth, the penis becoming a fetus on its return trip—which my concentration, caught in the act, had prevented me from noticing.

"Nothing happened. It was something that should have been there but wasn't. Simply because it doesn't exist."

I didn't understand a thing. She looked me in the eyes. "You know, you're very innocent. Or very sweet."

"Choose both," I said to her in jest.

"No, seriously."

She looked even grave. "I have to tell you something. Remember when I told you not to touch my right breast?"

Yes, I remember. I have a good memory."

"Well, when I was little we were very poor in Santiago. My parents are dead and the only one left in the family is my sister. I was very little then and at home there was no electricity, but next to my bed my mother always kept a kerosene lamp. One night because of a movement I made or because it was very close to the edge, the lamp fell on my bed and set my bedclothes on fire. I had a very bad burn on the whole right side of my body, but not on my face or my neck or my legs. Only on my chest. They took me to the hospital and bandaged me and I took a long time to get well. When they finally took the bandages off the wounds had healed but my arm was stuck to my chest. The only importance this had then was that I couldn't move my arm. My arm remained immobile like that for some time, I don't remember how long, and finally they operated on me. As you can imagine, it was a pauper's hospital and a shoddy job by some butcher with a title, and I lost part of my right breast. It was still not a breast because I was little, but it should have grown like the other breast, which, in addition, is big and round. On the other side there's just the old scars and the breast I'm missing. I became an actress to earn money and have plastic surgery done on me. But I went to earn money in a place where there are not very good surgeons! That's one of the reasons why I've returned to Havana now, to be operated on. But the plastic surgeon here, Dr. Molnar, a Hungarian, says that I've lost a lot of muscle and the glands didn't form. In one word, the operation is more difficult than was believed. If not useless."

She had spoken nonstop, as if reciting from memory or as if it were about some other person. She obviously didn't feel any self-pity. She was still staring straight at me, the bathroom light from the open door falling directly upon the bed, like another lover.

"Well, now you know everything about me. Don't you have anything to say?"

I was going to say that it didn't matter (my standard usage when something matters a lot), but before I spoke I remembered that it was her breasts more than her eyes that had attracted me that eventful evening in the University dim cellar and how I had seen so often their evenly clothed splendor. Well, one of those breasts was a prop, a falsie, mere fill-in. It was as if she were revealing that one of her big beautiful verdant eyes was of glass. Verdant my eye! Verdantique.

"It doesn't matter," I said finally. "I like you all the same. All the way."

"But it means you'll never, ever, see me nude, that there's a part of my body you'll never be able to touch, that part of me, so to speak, is off limits for you."

Woman as El Vedado.

"All the rest is left," I said. "Quite a lot."

Perhaps too much for me—her body I mean, with that quality the English define with a word both comical and imposing: statuesque. She was a version of Venus lacking a piece of marble: the one found in Cyrene, ancient Africa. Her flesh of stone had always produced erections in me. A masterpiece to masturbate before—and now after.

"Well," she said, "can we go now?"

It seemed as if it bothered her to spend a minute more in that room for stripping naked, for the splendor of the flesh, for total love-making. She was the anti-Juliet, a vestal of the *autel de passe*.

"Let's go then," I said, and when she got up I got out of bed. I dressed quickly. I always dress with more skill than I undress—but still my pants got stuck on my bare heels. We caught a taxi which refused—not the vehicle but its driver—to enter her dead-end street, and we got out at San Lázaro, which you perhaps know is not my favorite Havana street. But, after all, I'd have to get used to it: we weren't always going to meet in the lobby of the Rex Cinema.

Walking the two blocks to her house I suddenly remembered why this piece of street was familiar to me. It wasn't because of the Espada Cemetery, in which nobody had been buried for at least a hundred years, the cemetery now closed, even forgotten. I had been there before—if memory didn't betray me. I remembered having visited two sisters with Roberto Branly. One of the sisters had a pinhead and was grossly fat. A hopeless cretin who grew all over while her head got thinner and thinner, as if she had been kidnaped by the Jivaro Indians and they had shrunk her skull alive. A walking *tsantsa*—or at least a sitting one, because she was always sitting in her rocking chair and moving back and forth all the time. The other sister, a clear mirror, was a true beauty: red-haired, her body too adult for her sixteen years—but also kind of silly. In any case I was the only complete fool because I accompanied Branly on these amorous excursions (which were, on the other hand, four-handed exercises: Branly's occupied and mine useless), and I had no role to play. Branly came with his shiny yellow guitar, burnished by time or by beat, by music, and sang his own boleros. Or rather his solitaire songs in double time but introducing caustic chords, since Branly was ahead of his times and already in the late forties was composing songs with intricate harmonies, indifferent to the obligatory tonic-dominant harmonic pattern that dominated the Cuban bolero. Then this girl, who was all the public Branly could have (apart from the pinhead who rocked smiling like a happy metronome, moving her microhead like Maelzel's pendulum—now allow me a digression: isn't there a certain sinister symmetry in that Maelzel, immortalized by Poe, after stealing the metronomic invention, took over and perfected a robot still known today as Maelzel's Chess-Player?—the German was obviously a genius in appropriating what wasn't his), this red-headed beauty, called Barbara no less, smiled exactly like her sister. In fact the two smiles, one on the pinhead and the other on the beautiful face surrounded by lots of red hair, seemed the same, bestowing beauty on the pinhead while her perfect sister, the redhead, took on the grotesque quality of the deformed smile, indicating that they came from the same family, that they were doubtless sisters and at certain moments, on certain nights, seemed identical twins. Barbara listened to Branly's music, he singing in a low voice after long introductions and capricious chords with his small tenor, his avant-garde songs like wandering scouts of a lost patrol. From time to time she said: "Oh Robertico, what a pretty melody!" when the sounds Branly produced modestly on his poor guitar—unresolved, inverted, dissonant chords—were everything but pretty melodies. At times I thought that Barbara was really the house cretin and that the silent girl (she was as young as Barbara: even her minuscule head made her seem like a little girl grafted onto a fat woman), who moved metronomically on her rocking chair, as if trying to keep time with Branly's offbeat songs, was an extremely discerning music critic, who reserved her comments—doubtless ego-puncturing—on Branly's compositions, those solitary solos, those Branlyburg Concertos, those serenades for six strings to seduce Barbara, which her sister censured silently, as a present form of posterity. If Barbara, in turn, was not a moron, she was an oxymoron: the ugly beauty.

These memories took me barely a few yards. Only the space between abandoning the reluctant taxi and the moment when Margarita—no longer Violeta del Valle for me—took me by the arm, making me her Armand, she my condemned mistress, the *fin-de-siècle* tuberculosis exchanged for mutilation: the invisible imperfection converted into a disease capable of being more visible than her scars. I was convinced I would never see her naked, she who when dressed was a beauty, what they called in Havana a womanly woman—and in that instant, when I returned from remembering the ugly sisters, I felt her soft arm on my arm. (The softness wasn't in her skin, which I couldn't feel through my shirt and jacket, but in the lightness with which she placed it on mine.) It was then that I knew I had fallen in love, perhaps for the first time in my life. I know I had to review my past (and perhaps rewrite it) to reach the conclusion that in my previous loves, or so-called loves, I only believed I was in love. I was never in love with Juliet and, much less, with Honey, and the brief love, a fault in my character, that I felt for my wife had been immediately annulled upon knowing her intimately. With Margarita, however, it was love and I would feel, enjoy, and suffer it despite her personality—or perhaps because of it.

We walked slowly. Margarita walked slowly. As if in delayed action. Her flesh stayed in its place in more than one moment, statuesque, as if unveiling her in all her green splendor. Come to think of it, none of the women who had meant something in my life, from the distant Beba Mauri parading down the corridors of Zulueta 408 as in a slow bolero, to Margarita now, not one of them walked fast. The only exception was my wife, who moved with ill-balanced speed. But Juliet, for example, was a slow-motion show, descending Inquisidor Street, moving her hips from side to side, invariably inviting improper *piropos* (in Spanish street language, obscenity in the form of flattery, or vice version), showing her small great body and slowing down on purpose as she passed through the narrow streets as if on a gangplank flanked by amorous, staring, shouting, and gesturing passersby, who sometimes went so far as to touch her, evoking from Juliet the eternal expletive: "How vulgar!" Perhaps these *habaneras'* leisurely passage through life (even an adopted *habanera* like Margarita, now a night visitor as Germán Puig would call her) had to do with the tropical atmosphere, the balmy night seducing one to stroll, as the song says, caressed by the sea breeze. *O lente, lente, currite noctis equi.*

We finally reached the door of her building and stopped there to say goodnight, I desirous to make our next date amorous, she morose: since we had left the *posada* I had felt her eluding my allusions to a future encounter. Could Margarita be a daisy for a day? I decided to ask her directly, like bold lightning: "When shall we meet again?"

She still paused before answering. "I don't know," she said finally.

"Tomorrow night?"

"No, not tomorrow. I have to go out."

"Who with?"

She looked at me as if reproaching me for seeming so inquisitive, perhaps possessive. "With a person," she said, eluding me.

"With a person, of course. You weren't going to go out with a ghost," I said, alluding to the cemetery with a grave gesture.

She smiled. "Why do you want to know?"

The theory of knowledge, I was going to say. The problem of our times. This age of Kant. But I said: "Just to know."

"It's a person who doesn't mean anything to me, much less to you. An insignificant stranger."

"Well, I want to know who that strange dwarf is. As you know, my real name is Velázquez. I know one midget or two."

She didn't laugh. She didn't even smile, but paused again, to take her time, which was my time warp.

"He owns a radio station. The one on the top floor of the Palace Building. That's all there is to know. Satisfied?"

That putrid Palace! Always coming up in my life like a stone intruder. Haunt of all Jacobsens.

"What do you have to do with him?"

"It's a date I can't break."

"Did you have something to do with him?"

"Why do you want to know?"

"Just to know."

They fucked for sure. This age of cunt!

"If I did, it was in the past. We're in the present now."

"Tomorrow is the future. It will be the present for you two."

"I had nothing to do with him. He's an older person. It's as if he were my father."

"But he's not your father. Besides, there are incestuous relationships."

She smiled, showing off or merely showing her perfect teeth but by smiling she was already showing them off: a double row of Oriente pearls. But aren't pearls a nuisance? Margarita's teeth (Zorrilla's simile now barely a smile) were like solid pearls that invited you to eat them the way Don Juan drank his lover's tears, liquid pearls. Teeth and tears being of the loved woman precious but opposite jewels. Pearls are a pest. Her teeth, if made liquid, would flow like a vicious source of lies to poison your soul. She was a liar from teeth to tits, all genuine but capable of flagrant lies. Imperfect tits, perfect teeth were foul fountains not of Lethe but of lotus water that made you forget what she was, even what she had done only a minute ago. Worst of all, this strange stream could also make you forget who you were. Her teeth, like a pearly potion from a certain Celtic chalice, could render you uncertain.

From a new Ireland come, this green-eyed Isolde with a bit of black knew that you simply must love her after drinking from her well of teeth, as I just did today. But she never knew, naturally, that you could hate her for this also: to drink from her teeth a poisonous philter in a poison phial to soil your soul. Smiling she would tell me one day that she never had a filling in her life, meaning that her teeth were free of cavities. Was it a slip of both tongue and teeth that she said *feeling* instead of *filling*? "I never had a feeling in my life" was what she actually said and then she smiled a Cheshire cat grin to prove it. "See?" But you know moral caries can begin with tooth decay. It takes a whole set of teeth (or even dentures) to laugh for joy, but one tooth is enough to feel pain. Margarita's painless, stainless pearly-perfect teeth laughed at me and then smiled so charmingly that she charmed and disarmed me. Pearls are for carnal swine. I remembered Carmen—as a matter of fact I never forgot Carmina, the deceiver with a smile over her lies. You see, I have a sweet tooth for teeth. Now she, my Margarita not alien Carmina, smiled again. Pearls can be paste. Tooth paste.

"You must be joking, darling."

But I had no intention of making a joke. Incest is a serious matter. At least you should consider it so if you are about to become a father. Incest is for fathers—and for mothers too. Sometimes it is for sons and daughters, especially daughters.

"You're funny."

"I'm being perfectly serious."

"Then you are silly, which is worse."

I was going to say something more acrid, acid, when I saw in her face —her head leaning against the frame of the dumb doorless door, my back to the street—that something was happening behind me.

"Here comes my sister."

I turned around in time to see a woman who was coming up to us. Margarita was suddenly downgraded to pretty because this apparition was truly beautiful. The perfect bone structure: her mouth wasn't as large as Margarita's and she had even lips, the upper a mirror image of the lower: her cheekbones were higher than Margarita's but better formed, sunken cheeks, and she had big brown eyes which seemed to dominate all the other features of her face. But they weren't brown: her eyes turned yellow right in front of me, a light yet radiant yellow, which made her gaze more intense. Opal eyes, oval face. She didn't have on any makeup and was dressed simply, almost casually. She didn't have Margarita's body (that is, the one Margarita revealed with her clothes on), since her slight waist made her hips seem wide and her figure was quite coarse. She needed a corset, I decided. She was taller than Margarita, yes, but something was amiss.

"My sister," said Margarita, abandoning her position at the door.

Her sister smiled wanly as her only response. There was something profoundly sad about her: in her clothes, her body, her face, and even in her even smile and her eyes, which fixed on me for a moment.

"Look," Margarita said to her, "this is the boy I spoke to you about. The one who wrote me that letter the other day. This is my sister Tania," she said to me.

"A pleasure to meet you," I said and was about to shake her hand, a gesture which she seemed to consider as archaic as kissing it.

She didn't even respond to my greeting but said: "You do very strange things, you know." I thought she was referring to my extended hand. "That letter of yours. My!"

An intolerably embarrassing silence ensued, but Margarita came to my rescue: "It doesn't matter, sis. He already apologized."

But I had to insist. I always do. "Please forgive me. It was a sudden impulse."

"Well, you're quite impulsive," she said without even complaining: it was just a statement.

"You're right. It was very stupid of me."

But she continued on to the doorstep without paying any more attention to me.

"I'm coming right up," said Margarita, turning into a popular version of Catia Ben Como: Catty. The good sister instead of the well-bred granddaughter. Righteous Rita.

"It's okay, don't hurry," said her sister. "Pepe's coming right away."

She turned her back on me at the very moment I was extending my hand to shake hands with her, to say good-bye with a friendly gesture or perhaps both. Or was it my old social reflex, still active? I was left holding my hand out when she had already disappeared upstairs.

"I'm sorry," I said to her.

"About what?"

"About what happened, the effect on your sister."

"Don't worry. It's always been that way. It'll take years for her to forget."

A bit exaggerated, don't you think? It was obviously hyperbolic to be talking about years: it had only been a few days, barely a week.

"*Years?*"

"Yes," said Margarita. "It's been five years now. More."

Five years? More? What was she talking about?

"What do you mean?" I asked her and was already about to add: "Seems more like seven days to me," when she elaborated: "My sister Atanasia," she paused. "Her real name is Atanasia but it's such a hick name! I changed it when I was little. But she's still Atanasia for the records, and she even insists on giving it as her true name when required."

"I would bet that your name isn't Margarita either."

She looked at me, surprised but more amused than bemused. Her amusement took over: "How did you know?"

I was going to say that it was onomastic science but I said to her: "I'm a good guesser."

"All right, you're right. My name isn't Margarita but I'm not going to tell you my real name. It's so horrible that I hide it under wraps. My parents had no idea how a name can brand you for life."

Until now I had been the one to change people's names, and thus Julia had become Juliet and Honey came to be called at times Rosie or Rose. But this was my first encounter with names used as masks: covering a stigma with the letters of an alias. Though I myself used a pseudonym often (I had used five in all), it would be some years before I met up with people who changed names like outfits—especially women. But I have spoken of these metamorphoses elsewhere. Now I simply want to mark my first encounter with a person who discarded names like a snake changing skin. Perhaps the next encounter with her would signify a new name. "Call me Ishmaela." (Though Juliet Estévez gave her husband and lover French names, these were mere translations, not baptisms.) But more than her name under her name I was intrigued to know the secret behind the sister's sad smile.

"What's the matter with her?" nodding at the woman upstairs.

"Well, she was married to a man she loved, madly. We're very passionate women. Let that be a warning to you. He was a very handsome man and he loved her a lot. This all happened in Santiago. One day they went out for a walk and someone new in the neighborhood, or a troublemaker, I don't know which, said something to my sister as they passed by. Something rude and nasty, showing no respect for her husband's manliness. Anyway, he challenged the gross guy to a fist fight. But the other guy stuck a dagger in his heart."

Margarita didn't pause here but I do now to reflect on her use of the word *dagger*. A little more and she would have said stiletto, making her narrative a Renaissance tale. Why hadn't she used a more usual word like knife? That was, probably, the weapon the gross aggressor used.

"My brother-in-law fell dead right before my sister's eyes. They never caught the other man, the assassin. But that doesn't matter. What's terrible is that my sister's life, so happy before, turned into a nightmare. She almost went crazy, unwilling or unable to admit that her husband was dead and buried. She not only had recurrent nightmares at night but hallucinations during the day. Talking to the deceased and all that. I was the one who finally persuaded her to come to Havana. You know what: to top it off her husband's family accused her of being the cause of his death for being so alluring. Can you beat that? Tell me, was it my sister's fault for being beautiful?"

At that point it all seemed a truculent tragedy, or maybe a didactic drama—a destiny that could be repeated. What would happen if someone said something ugly, something brutal to Margarita while she was with me? How should I react? Would the beast with the knife still be lying in ambush? Perhaps a premonition or the mere memory had made her act so cautiously on the street with me earlier that evening. Perhaps she feared there was a dagger destined for her companion's heart, surging out of the distant memory to become a mortal wound. I was able to reflect upon that destiny later, at some other time. Now I felt sorry for her sister's fate, condemned by her beauty. But sometimes, then and especially now, I tend to think that Margarita was heeding James's dictum: "Dramatize, dramatize," and that that symmetrical drama about beauty never took place: the possession of beauty, the lust for beauty, death because of beauty, condemnation because of beauty. It was in fact a tragedy in four acts. In any case I maintained a silence that was neutral but must have appeared respectful—which lasted until Pepe arrived. Evidently Tania's present husband (I decided to accept her Russian name together with her Spanish tragedy), he greeted Margarita and I watched him pass by to go upstairs like the prototypical Cuban (or rather

Havanan: in my town, perhaps because of the poverty, most people tended to be thin, quasi-Quixotes, with very few passing Panzas), his hips as wide as his shoulders, his hair thinning from the forehead without giving his face an intelligent air, walking upstairs with his regular pace. Obviously from his voice, his appearance, his clothes he seemed to be a decent person, perhaps the owner of a grocery store or of a corner café. In any case someone who didn't deserve that sad beauty with her smile that was never quite a complete smile—a beautiful grimace implanted on her perfect face. A grim grin.

After a while Margarita said to me: "I'm going up now. I want to go to bed. I don't know why I'm so tired."

I wasn't going to explain it to her, but sex is tiring—especially her kind of sex. Carnal knowledge causes flesh fatigue.

"When will we see each other again?" It was me, relentless as I am.

"I don't know. I'll call you."

"Okay."

As consolation prize for playing patience she gave me a gentle kiss, taking care not to smear me with her scarlet lips. We were under the entrance light of the building, and at that time one didn't see many people kissing on the street in Havana—where it was a crime against Cuban mores, a violation of public decency and an offense to good manners. (We are not in Paris, you know.) It would be a whole other matter barely three years later. Many things would change by then but Margarita wasn't going to change them now with a single night kiss: the light was still on, current morality was still on the prowl. But for Margarita a kiss was just a kiss.

"Go," she said. But I didn't budge. "Aren't you going?"

"No," I said. "Here I stand. As I cannot do udderwise, I'll play the luther. I want to see you walk up the stairs."

She smiled in her naughty way. "Are you thinking by any chance that I'm going to go out again?"

"It never entered my mind."

She would never guess my private motives, which I had to make public. "I only want to see you going up the steps, one by one."

She was surprised a moment. But upon seeing my face, the absolutely serious expression of Charles Voyeur, my seeing-eye-dog's mug, my hands all peeping thumbs, she said: "All right," and entered, proceeding immediately to go up the steps, an action in which her body became elastic: she pushed herself upward, losing her balance for a moment, and regaining it again as she reached the next stage, her haute-coutured hips forming balanced and beautiful flesh patterns underneath, her long thighs disappearing under her skirt. It was a carnal ascension—*femme habillée montant un escalier.*

Sunday was domestic more than tame because I had her beast caged inside me. Monday followed Sunday and I spent the day dreaming of her: of the afternoon at Ciro's that was an education, my Cypropedia, sex in

302

the dark (what color is the pubic hair in darkest night?), the tactile tremor of her flesh in the palpable obscure, she Braille to the touch, and her body with the softness of a sponge from the deep—all drew me down twenty thousand leagues under her skin. But there were also my present tortures: waiting futilely for her call, cursing her for not calling me, knowing that she wouldn't call me. (Women have reasons that the human heart won't understand.) Desiring, desiring all the time, between dreams and hallucinations produced by her Fallopium poppy, to see, to see her, to see her again. When I finished my forced labor, Ben Hur of the galleys, liberated by the movies, I went to the cinema since it was first-run night but barely saw the film. (It was a story of impossible love, Visconti's *Senso* or *Uragano d'Estate: Summer Hurricane*.) After which I was cured of my whirlpool obsession with Alida Valli to begin a descent into the maelstrom of Margarita, always falling down but never touching bottom of her Mare Tenebrarum.

The desire to see her in four dimensions, the three dimensions of life and the fourth dimension of memory, turned into a need like a hard drug, into an imperious thirst that it was absolutely irrational to quench now because I could easily wait a day or two for her to call me. Impelled by this insane anxiety (Poe was my power drive) I found myself walking from the movies to her house. After all, the real distance wasn't so great: all the first-run theaters, with the exception of the Payret, the Acapulco, and the Rodi—the same goes for the Trianon across the way—were a short distance from her house. Going down unredeemable San Lázaro, a most lazar-like street with vile and loathsome crust, as if poisoned with juice of hebona: leprous distillation poured in the portals and façades. That's why I turned on Soledad so solitary to reach the end of the street with the warm Havana night heating my body as I walked, after the exotic cold of excessive air conditioning of the Infanta Theater, which made my jacket necessary, now unnecessary, carried in my hand, held by the tips of my fingers and hanging over a shoulder like a Spanish cape of hope, allowing the warm land breeze to dry the shirt on my back, sweating from the trek, which was now reaching its end, like the street pugnaciously named Espada. But now we won't call a spade a spade but a sword an *espada* or *epée,* which is what it means—so, *en garde!* Fencing stolen brides.

I looked at my watch. It wasn't late for Havana, now a night city that had left behind its Spanish village ways to acquire more and more the mores of a cosmopolitan city. Nightlife was life! My ideal was to live at night, attend to my affairs of labor and love, sleep during the day, and to end my life when faced with a reversal of luck or adverse edict before the verdict: to open my veins under a warm shower. Petronius, servant of Rome and my Caesar. Back from Nero's nights I didn't think Margarita would have gone to bed yet. With that certain feeling I climbed the steps that would be so familiar to me in a few hours and knocked on the door. Nobody answered. I thought that perhaps, after all, she might already be sleeping. I was deciding whether to go or knock again, throwing into the air an imaginary coin, Raft's Medusa's engaging trick, when the door opened, just a crack. A segment of face appeared in it, which I didn't recognize until the door opened more and the face was Margarita's without makeup and altered by sleep but no: it was her sister. Sleeping alter ego.

"Oh, it's you" was what she said.

"Yes, excuse me for coming to bother you at this hour. Is Margarita in yet?"

It was a good thing her sister had told me her name was more or less Margarita because it would have been ridiculous to ask for Violeta del Valle in the wee hours. But immediately a doubt came over me: what if her sister knew her only by her *real* name, hidden like a stigma?

"No, she hasn't come back yet."

She must have noticed the consternation on my face (or grimace to that effect) because she opened the door more and I could see she was in underdress to slip into my mind. Faithful to the image of the women of her era, she slept in a slip. She didn't have a bad body. At least the body visible down to the half-breasts that emerged from the pseudo-satin: there was a certain perfection in her even olive skin. Gauguin would have approved. So did I. Margarita and her sister looked a lot alike, even in their slight, tenuous, almost imperceptible mixed blood. The sisters— what the hell were their true names?—like normal natives of Santiago had that essential Ethiopian element among their racial components. Of course my Ethiopia was as literary as Pushkin's. Here it was necessary to speak of Dahomey, of Calabar, of the faraway fields of Nigeria where the Yoruba roam. After all, wasn't the heroine of the island's favorite fiction from the nineteenth century, our Cecilia Valdés, a mythical *mulata*? Neither Margarita nor her sister was a *mulata* in the street sense of the word, but they were close enough, believe me. She was, of course, unaware of my reflections, reflecting solely solitude in my face, as if contaminated by the name of the street out there.

"But she must be on her way back," she said, referring to her ever-elusive Eve with no tomorrow. "Would you like to wait for her inside?"

Poor old girl. Violently awakened round about midnight by someone who was almost a stranger, an intruder, an ugly bean, she did not react with anger but was hospitable and invited me into her home. That's Santiago for you.

"No, thanks. I'll see her another day."

"Do you want to leave her a message?"

Was she provoking me to write another letter, some more incoherent insults? Or trying to release the Laurel and Hardy in me? Or perhaps just the Lawrence and Hardy?

"No, just that I was here." Kilroy's the name—that was a secret, silent joke.

"Okay," she said, and closed the door gently. Poor unmerry widow. I descended the stairs in defeat because I was thinking not about Cecilia Valdés nor about myth and *mulatas* but rather about where the hell could Margarita be and what was she doing now and with whom. I came out on Soledad Street and started walking in search of San Lázaro, but upon reaching the corner I did an about-face—and returned to the building where she lived. I decided to wait for her return, to see who she returned with and to confront her with the fact of being out so late—because suddenly it was midnight. Only a few minutes had passed since I verified that it wasn't too late to visit Margarita. But time is obviously relative and my mood proved it with more precision than those silly theories proposed by that moonraker Einstein. Time playing marbles with mood. Engrossed in the physics of feelings I leaned against the door jamb, all set to wait: after all, she would probably be back soon. I looked at the cement staircase that she had filled with her clothed flesh and I thought of her naked flesh, of male hands passing over that trembling warmth I had felt in the pitch-black tunnel of love. Who the devil was Margarita with? Fucking with, spending the night with? Moodraker. Raker, rake. Twelve o'clock along the roaches of the street. There they go! Held in lunar ecstasies. Moonrake.

To avoid growing desperate while waiting and rejecting what were actually erotic fantasies by Sacher-Masoch, I decided to review the history of the street as another way of passing the time while measuring it. Bergson's time. There at the end were the remains of the Espada Cemetery—the corpse of a cemetery so to speak. The churchyard (that's what it was) was called Espada because it was built upon the advice of the Bishop Espada in the nineteenth century, after the many protests of merchants and bankers (who were dead serious on this matter of the seriously dead) of this boom town which was becoming a city. They disliked the custom of burying corpses in the churches. Obviously by then there were more corpses than churches—even in such a pious place as eighteenth-century Havana. Thus the brand-new Espada Cemetery was founded and built in an outlying area that was already called San Lázaro—which must have been as ugly a street then as now. Here the dead were buried in niches, a practice that soon made it obsolete—or at least overcrowded. Too many dead Cubans, apparently. Today there was nothing left of the cemetery. Or at least I couldn't see any remainders, sitting as I was on the upper step of the two that led to the entrance of Margarita's building.

But beyond that dark zone was the spot where some boys played with a skull and two shinbones without realizing that these were the symbol of death. They were medical students, thus their familiarity with skeletons. But they also had the misfortune to be carefree, under a tyranny. While waiting for an anatomy lesson, they were wheeling each other about in a wheelbarrow, which previously had been less fun and more funereal. They stopped playing when the bearded professor appeared, but their game had a deadly ending. Someone noticed shortly afterward that the glass of the niche of a Spanish grandee had been maliciously scratched—that is, desecrated. Immediately the rumor spread that the tomb of a Spanish hero had been profaned and the accusation against the Cuban students followed suit. They were indicted for sacrilege. There was soon a summary trial and finally several medical undergraduates were sentenced to death—among them some who hadn't attended classes in the cemetery that day and others who weren't even in Havana when the so-called crime or mortal offense had been committed. All the condemned were chosen by a lottery, justice having become an aleatory art. Eight were shot (by firing squad) and their murder—the execution can have no other name—revealed, politically, that the colonial government was becoming a totalitarian power. Soon after, the dead students became immortals. Their monument is a great square on the place where they were shot—Martyrs' Mall now. No one remembers the cemetery and the supposedly desecrated tomb. The profaned deceased fell into oblivion, a fate worse than death. But all Cuban students remember the murdered medical martyrs, and their innocence has conquered not only their sentence but death. Is memory imperishable when life isn't? Can memory save us from death? Is there a life after memory?

I was caught up in these questions and foundering when I returned from historical memory to the deserted street, to the present city, and to the night. Two alma maters that matter have I: Havana and the night. But somehow it seemed late. I wanted a second opinion and consulted my watch: it was twelve-thirty. I must have spent a long time amid martyrs and tombs for time to pass so abruptly. There were no signs of Margarita, now a midnight daisy. I stood up and walked to the corner. There was nobody, not even a night owl or a soul. A block further, on night-walking San Lázaro some buses and cars passed by. I began a long habitual process that started in anxiety, continued in despair, and ended in fury. But it was still at the beginning. Fazed one. I could still return to the door of her building, but my purpose was obscure because she was obviously not going to come back from that dead end, a heroine amid the tombs. I was not waiting for a shade from the cemetery but her living flesh. Perhaps I felt it was more natural to wait at the entrance of her house than on the corner. But what's natural in waiting? Waiting can be an art or a philosophy. What's natural is impatience. Besides I was afraid she wouldn't return alone. I sat on the hard step of the entranceway again, cold as a tombstone, without a tale to tell myself, without the mirror of martyrdom in which to see myself, without a slow reflection to make, forlornly looking at the staircase she had ascended fully clothed. Goaded by that lucid frenzy which jealousy creates, projecting obscure images, I again saw Margarita, this Queen Margot, in a bed and naked (a prodigy of the imagination: my magic lantern), with another person (more than possible), and the mere idea that she could not only give but feel pleasure with someone who wasn't me was intolerable. I was now my own zealous Iago playing up to my jealous Othello.

Lente nox, festina lente. Time passed slowly but since the minutes were equal to themselves, without anything to mark them but my periodic glances at the circle of the watch (though if someone had asked me the time at that moment I would have had to fix my attention on the hands to be able to give it), just as the quarter and half hours were indistinguishable, time passed quickly—except for my mood marking changes that went from discouragement to anger and back to a futile calm because I immediately thought of her, withered daisy, faded Marguerite. I imagined her in sexual positions (I couldn't say love-making) that were unbearably lewd, lecherous, and obscene. If she had been with me, however, they would have been immortally beautiful, an inexhaustible fountain of eroticism, fun forever. Ziucker-Masoch. But as I hadn't seen her naked, Venus in a fur, and didn't know her anatomy beyond what I could imagine under her clothes (the more exposed the further she was from sex, as when she climbed the stairs dressed: Marguerite Duchamp), they were totally imaginary positions of her body during coitus. I didn't know it then, but those fuck fantasies helped me smite my turbaned jealousy thus: that woman in a grotesque sixty-nine wasn't she. It was a vision, a double, fantasmata. Perhaps even taken from the Gallant Novelettes read so long ago or invented by me now not for pleasure but for torment: the sexual daisy wheel, the rack for Margarita, pliers for her nipples. I'll confess! I had never felt such jealousy. Yes, there was a remote occasion when my first cousin, almost my sister since we were brought up together—again the green eyes as love and hate: the principle of pain—amused herself in innocent games with Langue, the blond boy from the neighboring house in town, after she had kissed me all over the day before—and she was only eight! But that vision belonged to remote childhood, to the time I discovered that love and jealousy could be transmitted by the same person: a double-agent vaccination: the vaccine working before the virus sets in and the two mixed in the test tube of that boyhood memory. Bodies, antibodies.

I looked at the watch and saw that it was the Spanish hour: three o'clock. Three in the morning! I had happily cracked many jokes about that hour considered as a title, the name of the waltz my mother liked so much, the crowning hour before dawn and now here I was in the open, suddenly caught in its exact measure, or beat. Waltz Street. Three o'clock in the morning: I had looked at the watch and it was exactly three A.M. Not a quarter to three or three-fifteen but three o'clock *sharp.* Before a desirable duration, now a desperate hour. I must have looked at the watch other times but I didn't register the occasion and suddenly it was the decisive o'clock, what's called the moment of truth: I was, like pathetic Vicente Vega, like my wife, being deceived. The painful difference was that I knew it. I was a cuckold from the start, crowned before having ascended the throne, sentenced before the true edict. Besides, it was *three* in the morning! Shit! There was not only Margarita's scandalous flight with God knows whom, the devil knows where, but the fact that I had never been out so late since I'd been married. What excuse would I give? What would I say? How could I explain my passage from an evening screening, from a daily duty, into an inexcusable night absence? I stood up to return home. While riding a hobby horse, I tried to figure out, undying Tristan, a stern invention worthy of a master of digressions capable of concocting a domestic philter: a spectacular accident of an absent friend. One of Fausto's test tubes exploded on him—but no: Fausto was inescapably connected to Margarita. Everything would be found out. Another improbable, or better, implausible incident would have to be invented: the bigger the lie, the best. Courtesy of the admirable Dr. Goebbels.

But at that very moment a car came down the street and continued to the corner of Jovellar Street, where it stopped, gaily illuminating my somber mien briefly. I thought someone had made a mistake and taken the blind alley for an open street, when the headlights shone right in my face again. I knew then, without zither music, that it was my concern. I hid behind the door frame but watched the car carefully. Single-minded, I saw a black cat cross the alley—an alley cat no doubt. A woman got out, closed the car door, and stopped to talk to someone, obviously the driver. Since in Havana then it was impossible to distinguish a private vehicle from a taxi, I thought she might be paying for the trip, the woman scrupulously fixing her fare or checking the change. But Madame X was taking too much time beside the automobile and, a naïve onlooker, I even thought that the driver was having trouble with the change—conversion instead of conversation. But soon I realized—or rather, guessed—that it wasn't just any anonymous woman, that her name was Margarita—or whatever her name really was. What's worse, it wasn't a taxi but a private car taking her back home, the vehicle prevented from going as far as I was, her house, because it was a difficult maneuver to get out of that dead-end street, and besides it was obvious that the driver—not the chauffeur but her lover—was going to go down Jovellar. A coup of headlights will never abolish road hazards. The woman—that is, Margarita: by now I had no doubt about her identity—left the car and walked slowly (not even the night turning into dawn nor the desolate street nor the lack of moonlight made her speed up her adopted Havana pace) on this side of the cul-de-sac. When she was almost in the doorway, the car did a half turn in the background and disappeared beyond the lighted corner. It was then that I came out of my hiding place, enveloped in darkness, and advanced like a larva toward her. She was scared stiff! Obviously she mistook me for an assailant: Jack the Rapist when I was really Jack the Wretch. For a second she didn't recognize me, but when she did, when she saw it was only me alone, Frère Jack the Risible, her fear turned to anger.

"What the hell are you doing here at this hour!"

The words, now dead and horizontal in memory, cannot transmit the hiss of her voice that had completely lost its caressing tone: Eve turned

serpent. It was her venomous voice full of juice of Habana in my ears that kept me from saying it was I who should be asking that question.

"I," was all I said, as if asserting myself.

"Who do you think you are?"

"I was—"

"Who do you think you are—my husband or something? How dare you keep an eye on me like that!"

"But I wasn't watching over you."

"Really!"

"I was *waiting* for you."

"It amounts to the same thing, don't you think?"

"I wanted to wait for you."

"Why should you?"

"It's three o'clock in the morning already."

"I know what time it is. Thank you."

It was obvious that I should have been stronger, shown more conviction in my arguments, been more assertive. My lack of conviction condemned me. My innocence was my guilt. She was right. Who was I to be watching over her comings and goings? I was convicted though I hadn't confessed. First the sentence:

"I don't like to be controlled. I'm an adult woman, a free woman, do you hear me?"

"Yes, I heard you. You're right. You're an adult and a free woman. And this is a free country. But I wanted to see you tonight and I came after the movies but you weren't back. So I waited for you, thinking you would be back in a half hour and between the Bishop and the medical pawns and Death's gambit—"

"Who's what?"

"Nobody."

"What are you talking about?"

"Nothing, nothing. I simply lost track of things waiting for you."

"You could have very well been waiting till the cows came home! I almost didn't come back."

That meant she had spent the night in Buick—I mean, in bed. With the invisible driver. Jealousy drove me on faster. "Who was that guy?"

She looked at me with derision. That had to be his name. Don Derision.

"What do you care? Let me pass, come on."

I was still in the doorway, she on the sidewalk, and I was effectively blocking her way. Besides I was taller than she. To this day I wonder how her movements could have been so forceful as to win over my winning position: a queen in check who achieved checkmate. But I had lost the game since my opening in the dark. Black's move next. I stepped down from my square, resigned my position, and let her pass. She climbed the stairs without looking back. I didn't say anything either, not even goodbye. I didn't watch her in her ascent. Queens always win, even when a

pawn is queened. That's bigamy! Queen won.

At that hour I began my return trip home, defeated, on foot, a retreat climbing up Jovellar as if going down it until reaching the University, further down L Street to Twenty-fifth Street, and from there along the medical-school side of the street, all gates and railings, I finally gained —in a manner of speaking—Avenida de los Presidentes and Twenty-seventh Street, in utter defeat. When I opened the door to the apartment I found a welcoming committee—I would have been disappointed if there hadn't been one—composed not only of my wife and my mother, but of my father and even my grandmother. My wife and her belly were there to reveal her pregnancy, accusingly. *J'accouche.* I never ceased to be amazed that, with all the women I had gone to bed with, none had gotten pregnant, and my wife, after three months of marriage, was already with child. But I congratulated myself on her condition since it allowed me a freedom, sexual and otherwise, which I had never had before my marriage: it was reason enough to play a fanfare on her Fallopian tubas. She didn't say a single word but retired to our room with a face of distress. Retreat.

It was my mother, always the DA, who asked me: "Where have you been up till now?"

It was evident that it was my wife who should have asked me that question. But my mother took her side, as she had done since our courtship: poor little convent girl. Little Orphan Annie meets the Mother of the Gracchi. Cornelia and Hornelia.

"Around."

There was a reluctance in my tone that made it definitive, and it was really that I had nothing to say: I was absolutely empty, vacuous, cleaned. Null and void. My mother didn't ask anything more that night. I went to the bathroom, urinated vile, entered my room, took off my clothes, and lay down beside my wife—who was obviously awake and crying. *J'accuse.* I felt guilty several times but never condemned. No verdict. I wasn't going to spend my life through the looking glass.

The next day I received a call at *Carteles* and I thought it was my wife, who hadn't spoken to me all morning—but immediately I recognized the voice.

"Guess who."

"Who?"

"You don't know?"

"Haven't the slightest."

"You have so many female admirers?"

"Phew."

"It's Margarita."

"Hello." *Non serviam.*

"I was calling to apologize for last night."

"You don't have to. You were right. I had no right."

"Your two rights won't make up for my wrong. But you scared the

310

living hell out of me! The last thing I expected was to find you hiding there."

"I wasn't hiding."

"Well, in the dark." She laughed. "At least admit that you weren't very visible."

"Nobody is in the dark."

"But you were in the dark, don't you see?"

I didn't say anything. *No lo contendere.*

"Well," she finally countermanded my guilty silence, "I was calling you not to talk about last night but about tonight. I would like to invite you over to my house."

What was I going to get out of going to her house? Another humiliation? Find the traces of her lover—whose memory she wanted to erase from my mind? I had no doubt that the invisible man in the jealous jalopy was her lover. One didn't have to be worldly or wordy to know what they'd been doing together so late. The missionary monster.

"I don't know if I can," I said.

"The two of us will be alone," she said insinuatingly. "My sister's going out. Come."

I didn't say anything for a moment, but even my silence signaled that the idea of seeing her alone in her house was tempting. It tempted me already.

"Please," she insisted. "Don't play hard to get."

"I'm not playing anything," I said, and said no more. Silence is more cunning than words.

"Come on! I have a surprise for you. Come."

She never said please but I still loved surprises then—especially announced by a woman's voice, caressing as Margarita's was now, so different from the sibilant snake of the night before. (I remembered that night again and the illusion almost collapsed.) She was now inviting me to uncover her surprise in her company. A surprise party for two, a teasing party. She repeated so much the fact that there was a surprise and I was weak, I am weak, the flesh is weak and mine trembled like Jell-O, jealousy or not, at the memory of contact with Margarita's invisible but so memorable flesh that—of course I went. I can resist everything but the irresistible.

I arrived after dinner. My dinner. I didn't know about hers. I never found out. It was as thick a mystery as what she had done with the invisible but too present man. I hadn't yet gotten to inviting the women I was after to dinner, as I would do later. After dinner, I limited myself to walks with them or to a fashionable nightclub or to the movies, which I had done with other less important women in my life. With Margarita it had been a nightclub (turned icy dayclub) and openly, without further hypocritical to-do, with a frankness I was grateful to her for—we went straight to bed. After, dinner. Now I was in her house, presuming she must have had dinner, sitting in her sister's small, modest living room:

decorated with the inevitable chartreuse-green, stone-hard, and nylon-covered furniture (fashionable in the mid-fifties for a Havana lower middle class aspiring to the heights of an haut bourgeois elegance), with a brass standing lamp wearing a citron shade, and the *de rigueur* reproduction of a painting with a wild menagerie scene (either an incredibly stylized black panther over pink branches or a flamingo in a blue lagoon blooming with lilies), done in colors and lines that were artificial, but not so stylized as to be considered suavely surrealist, a school of painting (more Dali gaga than Dada) that insulted even domestic Cuban sensibility like Kultur Kommandos, taken as an esthetic assault on ethics. It was a kind of corny nonrealism that seemed to fulfill the middle-class Havana housewife's desire for exotic fantasy, doubtless copied from a design originating in Miami—if anything could have its origin in Repro City, Fla. The atmosphere of Margarita's sister's living room (a succession of full possessives) prefigured that Miami identical building where there would surely be chairs like those, paintings like these, a settee like the one Margarita came to sit on softly beside me gracefully (how did she manage?) with two filled glasses in her hand. I felt like a Billy the Kitsch. I wondered what rigorous Rigor's response would be to this ambiance. Rigor mores. Our art belongs to dodos. Sofa so good.

"Here," she said, giving me one of the glasses. "Here's my surprise!"

My surprise was great but not as great as when Juliet slipped me the slim volume of verse with Eliot's elitist poetry, and I turned *Ash Wednesday* into *Hatched Wednesday,* laying an ashen egg after she pronounced her Here, read to me on Inquisidor Street. Margarita was now ordering me to Here, drink this on Soledad. "Solitude," Ellington would write. Better music than Eliot's, anyway.

"I'll bet you can't guess what it is?"

I hadn't the slightest idea. I told her so in so many words.

"Try it," she summoned me.

I tried it. It tasted like strong stuff: harsh, sour, a bit bitter.

"You still don't know?"

"A drink, isn't it?"

"Yes, but what drink? That's the question."

"I haven't the foggiest."

"I knew it! I knew you wouldn't guess. Silly boy! It's a—margarita! I took the trouble to get the tequila and the other ingredients. This very afternoon. All for you. Drink a little more. Come on!"

I obeyed her. It tasted like a Bulgarian bacilli brew. I used to take them as a boy. Good for your tummy, sonny.

"Do you like it?"

What could I say? It was water witches' water. Ugh! I said yes, of course.

"I knew you would like it. It's my favorite drink and it has my name. Isn't that perfect?"

Evidently she liked symmetries. I would hate to drink anything that wore my name. To begin with, I didn't even choose my name: it was imposed on me and I detest it. Aliases probably taste better.

"Drink. There's more where this comes from."

I obeyed. But it seemed ominous to me that there was more because it was quite a potent potion. It also had the power of increasing the reigning heavy heat, making the loud little living room into a furnished furnace. Kirsch versus kitsch. But she was ecstatic, a veritable Venezuelan ovenbird. Come to think of it, I noticed that she wasn't drinking as much as she should—that is, not as much as she was compelling me to drink. Did she really want to make me drunk? That wouldn't be difficult because I really wasn't a drinker, though I fulfilled the social obligations of my sex like an amoral duty and went out for a drink with my *Carteles* companions, all lazy buddies, *bebe* bums. On Saturdays after we got our pay checks we'd sneak into the bar on the corner, called La Cuevita, a grotesque grotto, a mere hole in the wall with a Wurlitzer that was always on. Other times we ventured further: to the waterfront bars on the Alameda de Paula, where there was a dark, secluding place called Alley Oop's (in honor of the cave-man hero, as we were a rather antediluvian bunch), to have Dinny with King Guzzle and Chairman Moo, and usually we ended up on Virtudes Street in a place called Cave Cane, barking our heads off on the border of the Colón colony, lupanar zone, from bar to *bayú*. What a howler that was—drinking wolfbane juice with a *lupa vulgaris* or rather, *vulvaris*. There were other occasions to toast to, almost all of them before meeting Margarita—which takes me back to the strange strong brew I had in my hand. I raised it from time to time to my mouth while she looked at me, glancing from the glass to my face, trying to scrutinize the inscrutable: my Chinese face, a Pacific half moon, Charlie Changai. I never liked the taste of straight liquor, rum or whiskey, and always chose cocktails like Cuba Libres or daiquiris, in which the Coca-Cola or the taste of a sweet lemonade disguised the alcohol. I didn't like the taste of this—or should I say the?—margarita, with its bitter aftertaste. However, Margarita made me drink more margarita.

"Drink, don't think," she said to me, and leaned back to watch me imbibe. At one point she got up from the sofa and sat in one of the green armchairs facing me, looking directly at me, not with the half profile, which was all the sofa permitted, but face to face, observing me. She was a now voyeuress, Avidog, Godiva in reverse, and got pleasure out of watching me drink till I got drunk. Scopophiliac of dipsomaniacs—the Greeks have a word for everything. This magicaRita in her eyrie, surrounded by painted panthers, watched how her potion turned me into a swine. It tasted bitter and bitterer. Angostura, now called Ciudad Bolívar. Rita smiled a strange smile (I'm sure her smile was sane, my glazed glaze insane) and finally said:

"I have something to tell you. A true confession."

What a child I was! I didn't know how dangerous it was to stay and hear a she-wolf talk. But I thought it was a confession about her traitor's tryst the other night, and I tried wholeheartedly to prevent it (I am the scourge of my conviction) but I only managed to wave my arm lamely. Sign tongue. An Indian from another tribe approaching, or a deaf-mute mate. Excluding excuses. But she seemed to be preparing a declaration of dependence. I have the right to remain garrulous. But, despite my gestures of a man drowning in a margarita, she said:

"What would you say if I told you I had put poison in the drink?"

"That you're a poisonous Ivy, because Marguerites are as pure as Daisies. Roses on the other hand have thorns—"

"It's not a joke, I tell you. I'm dead serious. I put poison in your drink."

I'd say she was deadly serious. Or that, if she was serious, I was a dead man. Dead men don't joke. I stopped smiling (that is, it was when I realized that she was smiling in all seriousness that I also got serious, or rather I became earnest) and I stared her in the eyes. They were as honest as her face. We were all serious all of a sudden: I, she, Ernest, and her eyes, which looked loudly luminously green. I thought of the color green and the sea, of the green-eyed monster. Did I look green in her eyes? Am I not too green to die?

"I've just poisoned you," she announced. "You only have a few, four or five, more minutes to live."

I had never really thought of the duration of the act of poisoning, between its beginning, its execution, and its end. Does it last hours or seconds? When does the poisoning begin? When the poison is administered? When it acts upon the organism? This wasn't the time for such investigations because I really felt poisoned now. What effects does a poison produce? A stomach ache? Convulsions? Asphyxiation, death rattles, and finally the Big Sleep itself? Or a violent collapse. A sudden death or a slow one? Poison, where is thy sting?

"When you drop dead," that was she, continuing, "I'll drag you out of the house, down the stairs, through the street, and I'll leave you beside the wall."

That is, my mortal remains among the remains of Bishop Espada Cemetery: a modern corpse among the ancient but equally dead corpses. I would be less alive than The Students, who had a monument in the Colón Cemetery named after them and a day in the patriotic calendar: *November 27th—Execution of the Medical Students.* Mournful ephemeris. All of Cuba remembered them. In fact, nobody could forget them: it was not permitted: martyrs are never forgotten. Martyrs are forever, like Martí. While with me, a mere ephemeron, the death squad, as the newspapers call it, would have a hard time identifying my body. I would have to wait lying there, dead in that dead end, until the coroner certified me dead—a phrase from journalese that has always intrigued me. Did the coroner himself give a death certificate to every corpse left on the street? The guy could have a hard time signing autographs to dead fans these days, you know. The strain could give the man a heart attack. Coronary coroner. *Coroner Drops Dead from a Coronary on a Corner.* A coroner's inquest will follow before a coroner's jury. *Coroner's corner.*

I was in this dreadful drama playing possum in my delirium (doubtless produced by the poison: some Venezuelan venom with curare components: green I hate you green, deathly green, all green will make you perishable: gangreen) when I heard a tremendous laugh, more than a cataract a waterfall, an Angel's Fall of laughter close to my closed eyes, in my strangely peaceful agony, my come sweet death as I lay dying, still death doing me apart. With a great effort I managed to open my eyes—and I saw Margarita, laughing! All lips and teeth, to eat me better no doubt, her green eyes shining in the dark like the twin moons of Mars. She was sitting next to me, almost on top of me. Now she was taking the glass out of my hand, lifting it, and drinking the rest of the sloe poison quickly, a suicide pact no doubt. But it takes two to make a compact and I hadn't given my consent to be killed. I want to live! Then she spoke, with a very happy voice, not the voice of someone who's about to die, *morituri,* as she naturally would have died unnaturally after drinking the poisonous potion point blank. Strict strychnine. Rictus, ridens, ridicule. *Te salutant.* She was laughing. At me. Comic relief. It was *la scena delle bèffe,* the joke scene, the yoke's thing.

"You believed it!" she shouted. "Don't say you didn't because I saw you. I saw you. I saw it in your face. You believed it!"

What what? What did I believe? Green in one's eye.

"Swear by your holy mother that you didn't believe you'd been poisoned? Why, you were already dying, sweetie pie!"

She laughed again, this time less vociferously or perhaps not so close to my ear. I have a pierced eardrum from listening to Wagner's *Ring* full blast. But she was a heldensoprano. Odin's din. Now she pierced my soul with her green-vitriol eyes.

"Am I or am I not a good actress?"

I suddenly realized that Margarita had put me, in her parlor, in a parlous situation. A new and more deadly pallor seized me. Craven that I am, to palliate it I looked for the bust of Pallas. There was none. Appalling Poe. Kitsch off! I turned red evidence now. Blushing I came out of my sopor, my stupor, my stupration really, for she had raped me emotionally in one bold stroke. It was all playacting! It wasn't the Rape of the Hemlock after all. I was Socrates without a sympoison but with a xamed Xantippe. No hebona in Havana, Romeo. That's from another play. This is the play within the foreplay, remember? Now, antidote, do your work! I'm not ashamed to tell it to you today but was I ashamed to face her yesterday! Greendel.

You see, I was so naïve then that I thought she had really poisoned me, merely by the suggestion of her voice, of her fulgurant green eyes and the vile taste of the cantankerous concoction she had cooked up as a cocktail. Besides, there was some kind of greenhouse effect in that chartreuse living room. Suddenly, she drew near me, nearer, and gave me a kiss on the mouth: wet from the drink but also from saliva: saliva sap: soupy: a salacious kiss full of savvy, all lecherous lips and tender tongue.

"My poor poisoned puppy!"

She smoothed her hair with a problematic hand, then put a record on the Victrola and sang silently to the music: my mistress's mouth miming Olga Guillot's sobbing, crooning, and cooing till her cow of a sister came home. Do I dare? And then, do I dare? Should I part her hair in front— or behind?

I didn't dare. Her laughter tinkled among the prowling panthers and the still flamingos. Flaming. Goes. All green shall perish. Perish the thinker. Perishcope. I looked at her with my only eye. She sat back again: to look at me: see me better. Gradiva, what green eyes you've got! Proud she was. María Marga meeting a most lazar-like Lazarus near San Lázaro: have faith and ye shall rise again! Lazy Daisy kissing leopards. Lepers. Mist metaphors. Must be the mixture of before.

"If you believed me, dear, then you're capable of believing anything!"

Rise to the occasion. Rise!

"Anything."

Finally I reacted to her last words, delivered Juliet-fashion, all flaring nostrils and high sighs: "I didn't believe anything! I was putting on an act just like you, playacting too. Why would you poison me? What for? Who for? Only motives can create a crime."

"Oh yeah?" she sneered triumphantly. "I have an answer to all that. I'm taking revenge on man unkind. On all mankind, in fact. I'm doing it to strike!" and she paused so that I could catch her agent double-entendre (more later) "man down. He done me wrong and so, tit for tit, as you would say, dahlin! You see, I've got a chip on my shoulder, so I enjoy poisoning my lovers—"

"Dans la Tour de Nesle?"

"—just to see them suffer and die asking for forgiveness. Aren't these motives enough?"

"You don't have any chip on your shoulder—"

"How do you know?"

"—or thereabouts."

"Well, maybe not on my shoulder, but you've never seen me as I really am. And I don't mean naked." Then, without any transition, she added: "Let's go. My sister will be back any minute now with her husband. Enough gallant games for today, loverboy."

I still had the ultimate naïveté to wonder where we were going. It was obvious she wanted to go to one particular private place: that closed room where one is alone in company, where two make one and then they are none. *La petite mort* is the perfect crime. Though there could be several sites for the same beginning and different ends. I calculated the possibilities within reach (I was about to say at hand) and decided that the best place was the *posada* on Eleventh and Twenty-fourth. Ordinal numbers for cardinal sins.

In the taxi her beauty was highlighted, like the star in any movie, by the streetlamps and the shadows of San Lázaro Street, before ascending the dark University Hill, called thus because of Romemania: those Latins wanted to be true Romans. But one of the hills—there were not even seven—insisted on being called, vulgarly, Burro's Butte, a beaut, instead of *Mons Asinorum.* Her eyes growing more intensely green in the darkest corner of the car, Margarita was at the same time beauty and the beast. From her hiding place she insisted on her innocence, insinuatingly guilty. But at first I didn't understand what her purring was all about.

"What?"

"It wasn't belladonna."

"What pretty lady?"

"Poison."

"Pretty poison?"

I swear I didn't know what she was talking about.

"Yes, deadly nightshade. I mean, no. What I mean is, what I gave you in the drink wasn't poison."

"It wasn't? That's news. Good news. Great news. Thank you."

"But it was something more sinister."

After those wireless words she paused dramatically, radio soap-operatically, since at that moment the street became dark and I could hear only her voice: a candid coloratura: "Do you know what it was?"

I decided to hear one more time, one more tale from the Havana Nights, told by her, aside.

"No idea, dear."

"I know you know but I'll tell you anyway. It was a love philter."

There was no denying that her job was to dramatize, falsifying what was never true. She must have also been a radio actress in Caracas: Soundwaves unsound.

"A *love* philter! Come on!" I scolded her, not for the sentiment but for the word. "Where did you find such a tautology?"

"I didn't find any tautology! As a matter of fact I don't even know that ingredient."

"It's a word. Greek. It means repetition."

"Ah. Sorry. I didn't know."

"Why don't you say plain potion? Or Spanish fly or cantharis? Or just say *bilongo,* as they say in Santiago."

She looked at me, her face visible again as the taxi went down L Street, approaching Radiocentro and the limelights and the new neon noises. She smiled, her teeth reflecting the myriad bulbs from the marquee lights. "Well, if you wish, I'll be vulgar then. Honey, I put a hex on you."

She had used the appropriate witchcraft word, lost in translation even into Spanish, as she had said the Havana black magic word *amarre,* which might mean a tie but it means a lot more than a knot. So, what the heck, *hex* will have to do. The window on my side was down and, despite the speed of the taxi and the night air coming in gusts from the sea, I couldn't avoid a certain disgust, a revulsion, emanating like the smell of stagnant waters from this Nausicaa, now a nausea. You see, I knew exactly what she meant and what that Cuban version of the Celtic philter was invariably made of: no hellist Homeric hellebore or medieval concoctions or romantic "magistral medication." None of that. A woman's *amarre* always contained drops of menstrual blood, period. It can be a powerful knot to tie you with. No Alexander could cut it with his Greek sword.

But she didn't know that I had the Great Sinistrari on my side and that he could give me his recipe against the incubus: "Sweet flag for patriots, cubeb seed, roots of aristolachia, the philosopher's weed, great and small cardamos, unforgettable Ginger, long pepper to make the short penis grow, clove-pink against the pink, cinnamon and clove, an anti-Gabrielles, mace as in a mood maze, nutmeg, resin, benzoin, aloe wood and family roots with fragrant sandals." What a prescription! I could burn all this in the bowl of my pipe right now and have me an infernal *potafeu* to smoke her out. I could also obliterate her spell by making a covenant with grace. Witches cannot injure a good man. But the conundrum was, was I a good man?

I looked at her and was about to ask her if it was true about her brew, but her beauty, her half-opened mouth (not out of sexual heat but because she was about to tell me something), and her luminous eyes staring at me from their green jungle of love didn't let me speak to find out the truth: beast and beauty left me speechless. But not her.

"Do you know why I did it?"

"I suppose to put me under your spell. Isn't that the usual reason?"

"I want you to love me forever."

She was capable, like Juliet, of saying these things without blushing. Now she was helped by the night. But how could one respond to such a statement?

"Forever looks like a long time seen from here."

"Forever and ever and eternally! Even when I'm no longer here. I know I'm not going to be here one day but I want you to continue loving me even when I'm gone."

"It sounds so definitive. Why are you going to go?"

"I don't know," she said, and suddenly her voice took on a truthful tone. "I suppose I'll have to return to Venezuela one of these days and you're not going to come with me. I know that."

I couldn't understand her change. She switched from witch or bitch to distant like last night to become today, tonight, to now a devoted mistress, a loving slave.

"What made you change?"

"What do you mean?"

"Since last night."

"I haven't changed at all. I've always been the same, but last night, after you left . . ."

318

"After you forced me to leave."

"Well, whatever. After that, when I was alone again, I started thinking about you, about why you had waited for me all that time. I realized that I meant more to you than I ever dreamed. It was your strange letter, our meeting the other day, and your waiting last night which made me realize this. I thought that you meant something to me. Not as much as Alexander once. But you have a purity, an innocence—"

"Don't be so sure. I can be quite a devil too, you know." I interrupted her. I *had* to.

"Whatever you say. But Alexander was not nor will ever be as virginal—"

"Virginal? But that's an instrument played mostly by young ladies!"

"Real virginity then."

"Why not Virginia reel?"

Fortunately it started to rain, a sudden spray. Prayers, somewhere in the desert of the night, were suddenly answered. Havana in the sudden summer rain over well-lit Línea Street. Electric light drops poured all over the city and lights made white the lace of the shroud enveloping dark nature to entomb it in the open skies. This tropical aurora borealis sometimes began almost at sunset. Then night was light, heaven was on fire, and hell became a beacon. The rain stopped as suddenly but not the fireflies. Glowworms. Firelights. Electric bugs. Bulbs. Luminescence aloft. Now Havana, a night goddess, had her halo. Hail! I remember when Havana was not just a ride in a taxi. Night was then a recurrent dream of trolleys flashing greenish signals amid the constant yellow hue of streetlamps above each corner. Bad verse probably but good electric rites. Writes. It all happened when lights learned to spell names in the dark, a foreign name or a domestic one looking foreign above: the neon-lit era. Signs blue and red, on and off, saying things with a blink. Blinkity-blank, blinkity-black. Black. Night is black. Black is back. She was back too. Or rather, she was still there. Her voice that is.

"Call it inexperienced, unspoiled. In one word, angelical—"

I thought of the fallen angel, in hell a bore, of Mephisto and the true felicity of evil—but I didn't say a word. Of things you cannot talk it's best not to talk at all, as Wittgenstein just said. Then the pianist turned to the composer to say: Ah, M. Ravel, I'd give my right arm to play your concerto! *Taisez-vous!*

"Alexander lacked something," she was still playing her Alexander's Rat-Time Bondage. "Though he meant a great deal to me, I have to admit. But something was amiss."

She signed off with a sigh and then fell finally silent into a dark pit in the taxi. I was glad she did because I couldn't stand hearing her talk, a mere monologue, about that ancient Alexander, who was almost mythical: a vanishing point, a source, a nameplate. But I knew he existed not only because she talked about him but because I had seen him. What's more, he was with her and I remembered the joy she exuded then, like champagne bubbles in the Havana night: a bottle-green happiness very visible in the summer warm air under the bright yellow lights of the Apple Arcade, that forbidden fruit of the good and evil of the town: where harlots and faggots used to prowl round about midnight, where suicides stalked the opportunity to join death in their tryst under the arcades at noon. She, Margarita, in a glass bell and in slow motion not in sudden death in the Apple Arcade, Eve of the evening in the central square of a haunted city of columns: always full of mischief like the night, always present in the moon night: her face all green eyes, her gait gay and her joyous way of holding on to the arm of that mean man, between two columns and then a twist, 'twixt the next two columns, the columns coming rather than the man to interrupt the everlasting joy of the moment—or the memory. Memory, coy deceiver. Memories the only key to the past.

But when I opened the keyless door she warned me rapidly like a conditioned reflex—an air-conditioned reflex, in fact: "Remember not to turn on the lights."

"And how am I going to enter the room then? By groping my way in the dark, like an Oedipus octopus? You might be a trueblood nighthawk, birdie, but I suffer from nyctalopia too. Didn't the doctor tell you?"

"Come on! You know very well I don't mean now, this very minute, but *later*. Besides, no long words, please."

"Right. Into the inn then."

Am I a rotten reactor! Of course I knew what she meant. But I wanted to pull her leg as much as I desired to grab her ass or snatch her body. Anatomic possessions. I turned on the lights, we went in, and I closed the door. Cerberus with two heads, that's me.

"I'll change in the bathroom," she said. "But *please* don't forget about the lights."

"You better watch it, cat's-eyes! There will be a searchlight closing in on you when you come out."

I was going to say something about *seins et lumières* but that was crude and cruel. Besides, I wasn't too sure of her French. A *lumière spento*. She showed off her teeth and entered the bathroom smiling. I got undressed with the lights on. I wasn't going to add to my natural bent to be maladroit when taking off my pants by doing it by touch again—an artificial act this. Against nature. First touch and go, then touch and come. I turned off the lights and immediately got into bed to lie down in darkness, my nightwatch ticking time off: waiting. I saw the bathroom light go off (actually it was the crack under the door that went off) and heard the door open, but didn't hear anything else. (Her bare footsteps were feline: a black panther in the dark, her green eyes burning brightly in the forest of the fuck.) Then I heard her or her double getting into bed, sneaking under the sheet, and coming toward me: side by side by sex. Now she suddenly climbed on top of me! I felt her single breast on my chest, soft and hard, her body made tactile flesh on my body: her softness to be sung in silky sonnets. Like the Dark Lady, this Lady in the Dark was unique—a woman, all woman, my first woman in my life. Whoa, woman! It's a man you womanize now, you know, not mankind. She was the first woman I had had on top of me (Juliet, disdainful, called it mountain climbing) and it was a strange experience: the roles reversed, inverted I patiently passive, her cunt aloft. Though she wasn't there to let herself be penetrated from down under, but rather for another activity, which was more memorable. (See below.)

"Do you know what I'm going to do to you tonight?" she said to me, invisible, a pitch from the dark, all radio voice now. I hadn't the foggiest.

"I haven't the foggiest."

"I'm going to mark you for all the world to know who you belong to. That's what I'm going to do."

I still hadn't any idea what she meant by marking me when she began to bite my neck, my chest, my arms—and into my armpits too. They were not exactly bites but sucks at my flesh as if wanting to drain out the nerve juice. *Sucus nervosus.* Succubus she. Actually all this sucking was more pleasant than painful, like a gentle green-eyed leech working on me silky softly. I understood then the pleasurable but morbid reaction suffered with delight, though not in daylight, laylight, by the numerous but all passive victims of vampires in the annotated avatars of the Count Divine, the Un-Dead, the Immortal. Could she be a Cuban version of Lady Dracula? Or: Marguerite de Transylvalley? Vulgarian Violet? Princess of Darkness? I managed to play passively my active role among her marked possessions, she on top, below, to the side—always feeling her breast like a tame and soft unicorn. Ah the beast with two backs and one horn! She had been me tonight and I was hers now. *Maleficia!*

I returned home late at night but not so late as to find everybody up. That's one more parental paradox for you: you come home late and everybody is sleeping, you come home later—and everybody is staying up waiting for you. Amor vincit omnia—except of course insomnia! I felt satisfied not because the holy night was a still night but because I'd performed well tonight. The bed considered as a stage, I know. As if waiting for the reviews in the morning. Though ours was a tactile theater: the Bard in Braille. My participation had been more effective than the first time on the bed or boards. She was becoming my Alma Mattress. But I was worried about the marks of Margarita. On tiptoes (tiptoeing amid daisies: I almost spoiled everything by laughing out loud!) I went to the bathroom, locked the door, and turned on the light to open my shirt like a curtain. There on my chest, on one of my shoulders and almost on my neck were the unwanted imprints: cow-punched, the traces of ecstasy like *X*'s on my skin: Daisy-tattooed for life. Stigmata. I tried to rub them off with my forefinger, with other fingers, with my whole hand—to no avail. Like the stains of Lady Macbeth, they were indelible. They would be there till Judgment Day: signs advertising a mortal sin, *stigmata diaboli.*

I turned the light off and gropingly again came out of the bathroom —not without first opening the door. I entered the room silently, going toward the chest of drawers on one side of the bed, a risky operation I pulled off in the dark with commando expertise—or rather like a photographer in a darkroom. I opened a lower drawer and took out a garment. I returned to the bathroom, closed the door, and turned the light on again: precautions of Margarita that because of Margarita were mine too now. This time I took off my shirt and seeing my whole body (or what was actually a piece of me) covered with this smallpox of love, variolate, I peeped at myself with some pleasure: a masturbation not of the foreskin but of all the skin. I had been erotically branded to become a Queequeg of the West Indies, a polygamous Polynesian, an antic poet. In joy I put on the T-shirt, obstreperous underwear in Havana, that I didn't even use in that cool summer we call Winter—and which I now had to wear all summer—*real* summer. It felt like a hairshirt. Margarita would brand me regularly in the future, a singular Circe watching over the ownership of her single head of cattle: the ox of the pox, Swineborn, the painted pig. I had to justify the use of the undershirt when my wife asked me the next day, as a cure for a sudden touch of bronchitis—I who didn't even cough from a cold, the best lungs in the family, a man who once thought that *The Magic Mountain* was a novel set in a ski resort! Only her innocence —or conventual coyness—got me out of the mire of marks with such a lame excuse. Playing possum by feigning a club foot.

At one point Margarita's love marks overextended high up my neck and I had to search all over Havana for a scarf, in August! and wear it as the latest craze in summer wear in Hollywood. This garment provoked more than a few jokes at *Carteles*—and in the neighborhood, where street arabs shouted nicknames at me: *Scarfo!* Rine, *in seiner Art,* called me Scarfmouche because of my dash that was actually panache. Silvino Ruiz just coughed his disapproval: scarf, scarf. And Silvio Rigor claimed that I was *le fou du foulard.* Only Branly limited himself to some humming out of tune. The most uncomfortable passage was that, with my undershirt turned *sudario* or sweating shroud, prickly heat now marked my neck as a new stigma not made by a love leech. Fortunately I didn't have to be naked with my wife because she was modest and I became suddenly chaste. As far as making love to her was concerned, around that time the big belly she sported maternally, covered or uncovered (with which grotesque biped can one compare a pregnant woman? The dodo? Ubu?), prohibited us from sex, as if we were out of the heat season. Our contacts now were mere tactile recognitions, ways of assuring her that we still belonged to the same tribe.

O lente, lente, currite noctis aquí, for not all was violent love with Margarita. Nor even sex was all. There were many times (now we saw each other almost every evening: my dull nights as an amanuensis became forlorn with the pretext of the movies, my métier, to the greater glory of glamour) when we'd take walks around her night neighborhood, which she obviously liked. She was charmed by this lower-middle-class urban domesticity aspiring to be a higher heaven in Havana: a petty-bourgeois brotherhood of Cubans. The most free-enterprising homesteaders chose San Lázaro up University Hill, where on any day (air was the only clear thing in Havana then) you could see the West Indians a mile away. The true pioneers ventured into the unknown territory of El Vedado, the wild West, where the sun always sets fiercely. There the street became colonial, curiously *Calle* L. The zone was actually postcolonial since San Lázaro had prospered and become livable with the Republic, being born as a street at the pantheon to pacifist poet Zenea (the one with the statuesque marble muse sitting next to him) to die at the feet of the robust bust of Mella, always green bronze when he was a Communist student leader, as rival factions would point out regularly by smearing the heavy head with red paint: the monument to the martyr from Moscow.

If there existed an exclusive enclave on San Lázaro's first block it was the Unión Club (gentlemen only) while on the last block there was Havana's mecca of middle-class bad taste: The House of Quesada Lamps: Aladdin's embarrassing choice of hundreds of candelabra, bed lamps, table lamps, and floor lamps. The whole store was a glass case crisscrossed with enormous chandeliers hanging from a mirrored ceiling over polished marble floors: woods of weeping willows of cut glass with lusters like perennial tears: mourning become electric or the kitsch of death. Within reach of such splendor in glass was L Street, suddenly Americanized by default. It was not christened with a proper name, an anniversary, a governor general from colonial times, a *mambí* patriot, a Republican president, or a more or less friendly or faraway nation or a forgotten martyr. It was simply L Street, clad only with a letter where other streets are drawn by numbers: Havana emulating New York in its least New York-style areas, exactly in the green zone where the streets are truly tropical marked in their green exuberance by the abundance of gardens protected by iron fences, all upright spears and tall gates. This didn't exist in Old Havana—where green was hidden behind stone walls. Nor in the Havana of the turn of the century, colonial *malgré elle*, all arcades and colonnades, columns in a mirror. Nor of course in that temporal and spatial limbo where Margarita lived, with neither mansions nor gardens nor grand gates. In fact, quite a dump.

Occasionally we went in the opposite direction down Jovellar Street to Maceo Park and across the Malecón. Sometimes the night became her and suddenly there were invisible flowers: night daisies, *marguerites de la nuit,* Greta's grotto, meregrot, *grutas de mar.* Since Maceo Park didn't have trees and on the other side little Colón Park (probably erected by Bobadilla to Columbus's eternal ignominy: Havana's hideous homage to the Discoverer after he was sent back to Spain in chains of shame) was a tiny amusement park which was my first zoo and much later the refuge of my ménage as menagerie: the double dates with my wife, then my fiancée, and her sister escorted by Rine, who would one day become her husband, all for friendship. Being spouses together we didn't lose a friend but gained a brother-in-law. Talk of the devil's disciple, one night I brought Rine along to meet Margarita in his double guise, disguise rather, as connoisseur and as oral chronicler of my conquests as Don Juanito, as Rine called me. He also named me Casanovalis. Or Kirk Egaard. Shaw of Sheville he, I invariably told him all about my amorous adventures, which he enjoyed vicariously, prevented from joining by his successive failures. Sexual fiascos that he finally overcame thanks to modern science and ancient alchemy: he medicated himself with liberal dosages of yohimbine, an old aphrodisiac, and its antidote, new Nupercainal, its antagonist rather, a topical anesthesia. A double-dater this: a philter and its chaser. Had Dr. Faust known this formula he wouldn't have sold his soul to the devil, perhaps. Rine was, in his spare time, not a chemist but a drama critic. "She's an actress," I assured him, meaning my Margarita. "She was with the University Group Theater under Mallet and now she works on television in Caracas." I was selling her to Rine as if I were her public-relations agent or as if she were a play and my comments, program notes.

Margarita, on our way to Maceo Park, the meeting place of our critic's choice, was worried without knowing why (alliteration). I told her there was no reason at all to be anxious about anything. I assured her that Rine Leal was a real, loyal friend (play on words), not an old pro getting ready for the kill, a hit man, a matador. Pshaw! I dismissed her qualms quietly. But no nervine agent was necessary. When we met Rine by the crumbling tower of San Lázaro (my modest Martello) and I introduced my green-lustered pearl, she showed night was her oyster: she smiled a smile I hadn't seen on her before. It was shy, bashful, timid, as if she were facing not an audience but an audition. Rine was very witty that night, a diamond cutting a dash to face a pearl. Not only did he make jokes on Dumas *fils*'s creation and Violet's violated vows ("A marguerite capable of withering all camilles," he said to her, and then addressing me: "You've managed, Count, to deflower the Daisy," and later mock-generalizing: "Love more than a daisy chain is a daisy wheel"), which were all too predictable because Rine moved between Silvio's rigor and my facility awhile. But he also told a story that at first seemed inappropriate to me but which finally was of mutual enjoyment because Margarita liked it. It's all about a flowering fruit: a *maricón*. Being on the Malecón is what probably brought on Rine's version, as it happened years later to Allen Ginsberg: fag's end. But it was really about romantic fist fucking, Rine an avant-garde erotic storyteller. Anyway, this Queen goes to the doctor because he has a pain in the ass. "His *anus mirabilis*," Rine scholiasted, "not just any old jackass." The doctor decides to explore the rectum— "What's up, Doc?"—to reach the sources of the pain. He's wearing a pith helmet. "The Vaseline wasn't necessary," explicated Rine. "The old boys in the band never used Glostora." Past the right rectum and still climbing. Doctor: "Does it hurt?" Faggot (playing himself): "Not at all, doctor. I'm quite comfortable. You may proceed, please." The doctor continues probing. "Auscultating," according to Rine, who pronounced it "asscultating." The Galenist doesn't find anything in the creases. He increases. The probe. Moving on to the north face. Doctor again: "Now, does it hurt?" Fag: "Not a bit." Doctor Miraculion is about to give up and pull out, when he bumps into a vile body around a bend in the cavity. He touches it, feels it, grabs it—and retrieves it. Doctor Amazed: "But—it's a—*flower!*" Fag, unfazed: "What a turn-up for the book!" Rine finished it off by saying that of course that flower wasn't a blue violet but a rose, no less red for being lost in the dark.

Rine continued with a bitter suite, a bawdy tale told to us by Virgilio Piñera once. Virgil waxed wordy about the boy who got lost in a body sitting in the paradise of a picture palace. Virgilio was our guide through that dirty *Story of Oh*—O as in the orifice of storytelling on the opposite end of the blooming ass: flowers of evil smell.

This dirty joke, all pains and puns, delighted Margarita, who some time later, some other time, or even that evening, told me how much she had liked Rine. But she also implied that she had thought it impossible for her to like any of my friends. How *dared* she? This was her bouquet of barbs to me, distilled from her inner self. Do you know what I should have done? I should have brought Branly along, with his disconcerting concertina of conundrums without drums, so discordant in concert, and his totally unexpected jokes with background music—paronomasias *pour le piano.* But of course without a piano. This Latin satin Satie, born the day Left Erik died, was some sort of Red Erikson: Satie was the punative father of Bon Branlemain Branly. *Sans branler dans le manche.*

He was a better, or worse, composer than singer. However he sometimes wrote himself into spoiled childish corners, as he did with his *"Pieza para Cuatro,"* composed not for four hands but for his own *tres,* which he called a *cuatro.* The *tres* is the traditional Cuban guitar and the *cuatro* comes from Venezuela, though they all have six strings, just like the original Spanish guitar. Branly was only mocking such nonsense nomenclature as arbitrary and misleading. He later wrote a piece after Debussy called *"Très tres."* Always the romantic, Branly specified that this composition was *pour la guitare d'amour.* After Satie he composed his "Gymnastics for the Guitar," which, as he explained, was *"Très inusité."* Unusual especially for the guitarist: he had to do all the gymnastics, not on the guitar but *for* the guitar, which remained idle as long as the music lasted! But, more than an impersonator, Branly was a *Mimus polyglottos,* a *sinsonte,* a mockingbird forever singing the national anthem of Utopia.

Branly claimed to belong to the fraternity of the Pre-Ravelites, who always live in *cités auriculaires.* This is none other than Satie's site, inhabited by parasaties. They composed before Ravel's time: *avant Ravel.* They knew there was no such thing as a Ravelaisian world, and each time he, Branly, wanted to send up a composer to oblivion he shouted, on a barbed cue: "Up against the waltz! But don't shoot until you see the white of his hard-boiled eggs." When I told him egg didn't mean *that* in English and explained why, he retorted: "Save me the balls!" Then to wash his hands, musically speaking, with a melodious metaphor, he composed his famed opera titled "Piece in the Form of a Pear's Soap Bar." It was, it had to be, a soap opera.

I think I must reveal now that Branly never wrote a single one of his songs—not a note! (I can still hear him saying this.) He refused notation because, he claimed, the modern musical score was created by a Renaissance musician called Cyprien de Rore. Branly, a man of his generation, always called the scorer Chypre d'Erore—a perfume of mistakes. Why then, you might ask, this homage of mine so late in the book? Because Branly is dead. He died of lung cancer two years ago. Cancer can explain his small voice but not his personality. Consider this then an explanation for any late-blooming Margarita who might ask about Branly with a *Who he?* As to my Margarita, she never knew Branly. She didn't even meet him.

I wasn't bothered by Margarita's opinion later that night, but I was vexed with Rine's verdict the next morning—more like a trial than a hangover. Rine had found Margarita gorgeous (the adjective was aptly chosen for once), but he added that he was convinced she wasn't an actress. "If she is," he ruled, "she must be very bad." He didn't explicate his sentence and, annoyed, I didn't inquire into the nature of her crime. The jury voiced consonantly but with finality: "If she's an actress my name is Lear." A tame, lame allusion to his last name, Leal, meaning Loyal, and which time proved was the appropriate one for him: Rine Loyal. But at that moment, piqued, I thought he was just a fool. Love, you see, made me disloyal.

Another of Margarita's passions was the movies. But, alas, she had a facile *faible:* a sort of weakness for Mexican motion pictures. Mexican movies were like an extension of her fondness for San Lázaro Street. More than once, instead of going to an opening to do my duty, I found myself on the way to the conveniently nearby Florencia, a theater around the corner—on San Lázaro of all places. There the recurrent repertory was Mexican movies or one Mexican movie in an eternal rerun—as if Nietzsche had been born in Xochimilco. An Anatole France *malgré moi,* even there I was pursued by masterpieces! But those too always made a comeback, sooner or later. I visited the theater after Margarita had vanished and even then I saw *Beyond Oblivion,* in which Hugo del Carril, an old tango singer, loves a woman, but she dies and he sorrowfully goes off to Europe by boat. In Paris (where all Argentines go when their wives die) he finds a faultless facsimile of the dead woman—with whom he falls passionately in love again. But his love, returning eternally like Mexican movies, finally kills her. Here love, the theme of the double, and necrophilia were linked in a dream, more than a crime, of passion.

At the Florencia I saw with Margarita at least one surreal master-piece, which, in spite (or because) of its emotional intensity, was uninten-tionally funny. I had already seen it but watching it with Margarita was a weird experience—at least for me. The movie is called *An Abyss of Passion* but is based on *Wuthering Heights.* Isn't it weird? Starting with the title one can see Luis Buñuel, who directed it, ready to debauch the prim and proper Emily Brontë. He later proceeds not only to rape and torture and confuse her but he totally betrays her—and one finally loves Buñuel the more for it. Abyss here must be pronounced abbess, as in De Sade.

There's nothing more distant from *Wuthering Heights* than this Mex-ican version, perversion, inversion. Either because he is stone deaf in real life or because of the producer's delusions of grand dewan, the cast couldn't have sounded more ludicrous merely by opening their respec-tive mouths. Heathcliff becomes Alejandro (accursed name!—no matter how it's spelt it casts a spell) and is played by Jorge Mistral with a strong Spanish accent: when he tries to sound Mexican he only manages to be an Andalusian hound dog. Catherine is Catalina all right, but she is spoken for by Irasema Dilian with the thickest possible Polish accent in Spanish. Mistral was swarthy, while Irasema is blonde. So, racially, they are not such an odd couple—if you plug your ears. Otherwise the moor becomes the Moor. Edgar is embodied, disembodied rather, by Ernesto Alonso, an epicene Mexican actor who lisps, then stammers. His enact-ing of an Englishman is as weak as tea. As strong as tequila is Isabella, Heathcliff's wife. The moment she becomes Alejandro's spouse she's transformed into an impossibly refined version of a waterfront torch singer. I give you Lilia Prado! She, more than a Mexican mestiza, looks like a Cuban *mulata.* (Or perhaps she's a Mexican *mulata:* nobody's impossible with Buñuel as casting director.) To top it all off, the evil Hindley is impersonated (the only good acting in the movie: the baddie's the best) by López Tarso, always a deadly Mexican verbose villain, who could be more comfortable among Pancho Villa's troops than in Buñuel's troupe—such was his ferocious mien. This is best seen when, completely drunk, he tells the incredibly modest, timid Lilia Prado, who sees him coming toward her bed (terrified she grabs the sheets to cover properly, even prudishly, her naked shoulders): "Don't be silly, you fool! You don't have to be afraid of *me.* I'm not going to rape you." And with his plosive, implausible verb as an assurance he accentuates the negative—and in this spectator turned writer the certainty of an imminent rape-*cum*-murder that should be a double treat and trick to Lilia Prado. The vil-lain's violation is never seen, alas. Nevertheless, there I was laughing perversely in the dark like a lesser devil, while Margarita sobbed at my side, crying over the impossible love of Jorge Mistral and Irasema Dilian, the tongue-twisted lovers.

At one moment however the two of us almost got together as in a sentimental orgasm: she laughing, I crying. It happened at the end of the

movie, with Catalina dead and buried, and Buñuel and Alejandro stray-
ing further than ever from the book and from life. Alejandro goes down
the steep steps into Catalina's tomb, deep set in a cold catacomb or crypt,
to pry open her grave and rape her dead body or desecrate her living
memory—whichever comes first to his deranged mind. Perturbed by the
pain, Alejandro, disturbed, delirious, or just plain mad, sees his dream
come true when he glimpses Catalina's phantasm, in her wedding dress,
poised at the top of the stairs. It's she all right. No doubt about that. He
calls to her: "Catalina!" As an answer, he gets shot almost point blank
with López Tarso's elephant gun, the vision of Catalina disappearing a
moment before the blast to reveal the hideous killer, obviously a crank
and a crack shot. The body of Alejandro remains in the creepy crypt
beside Catalina's corpse. López Tarso, triumphant, blows away the
smoke from his double-barreled gun, closes the tomb forever—and with
the falling gravestone the movie ends on a romantic note. During this
surprising finale the "Liebestod" from *Tristan und Isolde* has been playing endlessly—just as it played while Joan Crawford died of too much
music in *Humoresque.* When the sound went off, the lights went on—
Wagner's own invention. Amid tears, I handing her my handkerchief
(with some misgivings: I could only hope it wouldn't become stained with
her telltale scarlet), she drying her evergreen eyes, Margarita whispered
to me: "Isn't it a beautiful movie?"—and I had to agree by nodding. I
couldn't tell her it was bad Brontë but good Breton. She would have
thought I was choking.

That night, in front of her house (perhaps under the influence of the
images of love and hate), she kissed me incessantly, in a damp atmosphere of kisses without hugs, kissing in the air, between my mouth and
her lips, both of us highlighted by the bulb above. We were a private
spectacle in a public place: a show nobody saw, though it was free, because it was too late for other eyes that weren't mine to see—but my
eyeglasses detached me from the moment. Before I left for the night,
breaking away from her kisses, Margarita grabbed my hand and suddenly (did I hear a whisper: "Infirm of purpose! Give me the daggers"?),
without revealing the slightest intention, never betraying her crime
(caused no doubt by the passion of the abyss), she stuck the nails of her
right hand into the back of my left hand, not violently but with deep
intent. Margarita had long, beautiful, curved nails, painted red. That
night I discovered their hardness and their cutting edge. They were nails
for all senses. She hurt me! *Damn you, you bitch! You bitch witch!* I
withdrew my wounded limb abruptly and reacting to pain and pride I
raised my hand (perhaps to slap her, perhaps to save it from her claws),
when she said to me, the hussy hissing: "That's so you won't forget me!
As long as the scar lasts, I'll last in you."

I stepped back and my withdrawal really began then. I examined my
hand. My wounds were deep, especially one made by one of her armed
fingers, perhaps the forefinger, which ran along the back, from the flesh

on the other side of the mount of Venus to the base of the thumb. How could she do this to me? I mean, did she have a concealed weapon? I tried to stop the blood with my handkerchief, now stained scarlet: streetlights can be tricky. But my wound kept bleeding and I left her without a word, without retaliating, without desire for revenge or even just desire, now only wishing to be safely out of reach, recoiling toward home, retreating from the eyrie that she kept watch over, still standing there, watching, as I began to walk toward Jovellar Street, watchful bird of prey in paradise, all talons and eagle-eyed. But before turning the corner I heard her call me, not calling out but just calling, beak and call, a harpy turned harp: "Will I see you tomorrow?" I didn't say a word and she repeated the question again, repeating it three times, each time more musical, a mockingbird, beckoning me—and upon turning around, Orpheus condescending, I saw that she had followed me to the corner. She stood there looking a lot like Lot's mistress.

But I had no intention of even acknowledging her distress signal, occupied, preoccupied as I was about my bleeding furrow, now wrinkle of worry. What other marks would this woman brand me with, labeling me as cattle, she a ranchowner among rustlers? This was a dangerous scratch test. I would have to scrape through by more than one mark—blame or blemish. Margarita was becoming a flower full of thorns but no bed of roses. I had done my best to keep our love sub rosa but now—damn it! Damn the flower of her sex! Damn the flower then, now damn the flow of my pen.

When I reached home, without further incidents and no trace of blood left behind by my telltale heart throbs, I was about to go directly to the bathroom when I found the damn door closed—the *front* door. Closed and locked. I tried to open it silently, single-handed, by inserting the key in our Yale of tears—to no avail. Wrong key perhaps? No, right key, wrong insertion. Tried again—and the stupid door opened this time, just like that. You must give credit to Yale: they might make lousy scholars but they're excellent locksmiths. I'm a Yaleman myself, I must say. I rushed to the bathroom: door open, no Yale lock, but I entered to bolt myself in the lavatory and wash off the clot: it proved to be thicker than spilt blood and running water. I had to increase the jet to waterfall pressure to be able to see that the scratches were not, as she hoped and I feared, terribly important, except for one: the one at the base of my thumb was a gash. I was aghast. Those nails could become such offensive weapons—or were they really a defense? I put a bandage on the cut, which had started bleeding again, and went to bed trying to imagine what explanation to give my eternally sleeping wife when she awoke. What if I said I had hurt myself with my typewriter at *Carteles*? But as obsolete as a typewriter could be (and the magazine machines could belong to the Remington Museum) it would never get so aggressive: typewriters are more masochistic than anything. They receive direct blows and beatings docilely and none ever attacks man. Maybe this one was on

329

the make. "It's an old Underwood, you know. Very complicated affair this machine of mine." A fine excuse for a finer mess. What's more, it couldn't be an explanation or an excuse. Actually it was an alibi for someone else's crime. But passion made me an accessory after the fact. Roman love, English law. Besides, my wife was a practicing typist and knew all about Underwoods and Remingtons—in her pregnant state she surely even knew about my Hermes Baby! What alibi then would alleviate my love injury? I could get tetanus and it would become a *Liebestod!* Should I wake her up and tell her about the wound and the arrow? Let sleeping wives lie. I must lie down now and lie some more tomorrow yet.

Next morning, before getting up, still drowsy, and my wife, like the rest of the family, all up and about, I decided I would tell her there had been a confused fight at *Carteles.* To make it more difficult to confute I'd be confusing, leaving it ambiguous: I could either be fierce contender or peaceful mediator. My marked hand could very well be an honorable injury. It could work, you know. It would work! Let sleepy husbands lie. I also decided (Decisions Day) never to see Margarita again. Perhaps I had been considering this for some time. Perhaps I had formulated this decision just now, as much a part of the morning after as a glass of cold milk. The truth is that her violent nature added to the burden of back-street love. Though I'd never hesitate to deceive my wife with the first female voyager, fellow reveler, to appear on a bus, such encounters were fleeting fugacities of the fly. But this was more serious, more involved, a deadlier affair: a love that wanted to become eternal. I often got my designs for living out of books, most of the time from movies, and now a book and a movie joined together to warn me that violent loves end violently—and I no longer doubted Violet's violence, in and out of bed. I never told anything to my wife or my mother about the case of the wounded hand that became a wounded heart. I just stopped seeing Margarita. For good.

Or rather, until the next time she called me at *Carteles*—not long after I took my vows. Now I had to swallow them whole but it wasn't crackers or the Host: I hadn't sought asylum in holy orders yet. I must confess, though, that I simply couldn't resist the lure of her voice. She wasn't crying in the wilderness at all: she didn't sound like she was pleading for mercy or begging. But she asked me twice that we get together at least once. One more time. That was all. As you can see, it wasn't a *plaidoyer* for pardon or parole. Instead, the quality of her voice promised tragedy and love—a passion beyond oblivion. It was a heady philter, believe me. Hard Cora twice wouldn't have been more effective as a stimulant. Perhaps Rine was wrong after all and she was an excellent actress, even a great one, better than all the divas that had ever lived before. Who knows? Show me a critic and I'll show a reviewer who has Ziegfeld's follies of grandeur. To me Margarita was then a histrionic trinity: Sarah Bernhardt on the phone, Eleonora Dusa with Marconi for an agent and Ellen Terry meeting *Alexander* Graham Bell for a chat. And there was her deeply felt body on top of that—or on top of me, if you please. With her I had discovered that I wasn't cut out to be a missionary all my life. Margarita had been my cannibal, eating me alive bit by bit. But that was merely carnal. On the spiritual side, she had a sincere lilt in her voice that, well, moved me. Besides, as Virgilio wrote of the man who wouldn't leave hell even forcibly and then explained why: Who can give up a dear habit?

I returned to her house, of course. To her sister's house, to that well of loveliness to which I climbed now instead of descending—the hell above. It was Saturday afternoon, the time and the day we could be together longer for longing. For us, Saturday night was the longest night in the week. Night began at noon, lasted through evening and still at midnight we craved for more. Saturday might be Saturn's day but was Saturn's night for us, a saturnalia, and its other name, *sábado,* was in our mother tongue the witches' Sabbath. God rested on the seventh day but we didn't. He blessed the seventh day—and so did we. But it wasn't God who breathed into my nostrils the breath of Life, it was Margarita. God surely must have created woman first and then forgot, because I was born from my mother and then reborn by Margarita. We shall become one flesh, yes! To belie Genesis we were both naked, as man and wife, but she, Margarita, was ashamed even before the fall. At least that's how she sounded over the phone.

Her remote sister, a minor mystery enveloped in an exotic enigma veiled in burlap (the cloth the devotees of San Lázaro wear as a promise of penance), the eternal widow hidden behind black jalousies: never merry, never married—Slippery Beauty wasn't home. Heil Lelujah! I knew it the moment Margarita came to the door: when she opened it she fell into my arms with such abandon that I could easily have made the moment eternal. I stood on the highest pavement of the stairs and leaned on an ardor's turn. Or, more precisely, it happened when she began to kiss me and became an all-stem margarita that just couldn't hold me: she was all petals now: See love, all lips, no hands! Then she spoke a scroll of words of love, almost a whole chapter of old Blasco on TV as he had been *Torrente* Ibáñez in silent movies: torrents of this dark Greta flooded my Valentino blood and the sad sand—her torrents of verbal passion, my own spendthrift blood and the sands of time in hour ourglass: time, a double-dome of pleasure.

She spoke of how much she needed me, darling. How much she wanted me, sweetheart. How much she loved me dear, *dear!* But not even once did she ask, the bitch, in passing in her passion, how much I had bled from her stabs. Did she keep tabs? She never alluded to or eluded the subject of the scratches marked on my hand with her branding iron —indelibly so. Though I was no longer wearing a showy bandage or a discreet Band-aid like a badge of honor, the largest wound had become a pale scar on my tanned skin. It's still visible now when I type these complaints I'll never file. There it is on the back of my left thumb: a little further up than the gash I inflicted on myself, clumsy with knives as I've always been, when I was, how old? Oh, nine years old, I suppose. Both are injuries that occurred far away and long ago so suddenly, but I still bear the traces under my skin. Flesh is the saddest, said a poet. Perhaps. But what about the soul—and the body yet? Without waiting for an answer, Margarita, in one of her swing moods, doing an about-face without letting go of my neck, said in a neat contortion, keeping the contour of our courting:

"Let's go out. Now!"

I thought that the end of a summer afternoon in Havana was hardly the best time of day to face (almost to confront) the effrontery, the challenge, the double insult of the ever-vertical sun and the horizon of cement: demential, treeless Maceo Park or the burning asphalt dedal of the Malecón, maze and molten Moebius strip looping the loop around the city —this desert now with mirrors in the dunes. Explorers without a pity helmet, take your pique: sunstroke or dementia praecox? Pithy! I told her so. Though not in so many words, of course. She did a mock double-take.

"I meant *else*where, silly!"

She smiled, red lips moist and dry green eyes: sources of feeling and desire. She was clearly inviting me to the place of poses, the *posada,* where the passion play is in constant display. Though there was no vestige of the little girl in this fully grown woman, she reminded me of a little girl, my cousin from childhood years in town, the one who was only *days* older than I. With her depraved innocence, a gift of love, this amorous Mozart called the tune with me already at six or seven: a perverted prodigy, she invited me, an ignoramus, to the precarious privacy of the privy, closing the tall wooden door with a bang, then taking her doll dress off, getting rid of her tiny panties that looked more like diapers: clothings for a small sinner. But it was an exposure devoutly to begin anew forever. The creaking door of the outhouse will close again and again, as Nietzsche's spider and the moment and myself and the moonlight on the gateway will be repeated forever—even if the price to pay is hell. Once more, all will happen over and over again in the *escusado* where she lay eternally across the top of the wooden toilet seat to show me her little body with no breasts and no hair—and right there between her little legs, belonging to her but not really hers, I saw the minute center of the world. Not an aleph but my *prima's facie.* That strongest, strangest point where all points converge: the flesh that was no flesh. She had no bird, only a *void!* A revelation for me that still holds, as if once known and now forgotten: I still look for that knowledge and every time it's shown to me it's the same as that original time. If you want me to be ethical I can say that it was an education: until that miraculous moment I was an innocent, but after it I became a sinner. If you want me to be physical, it was an anatomy lesson to last forever. If you want me to be metaphysical about it you only have to look again and you'll be once more on the brink of the abyss. That's why, vertigo of the void, I understood perfectly what

Margarita meant with those enormous green eyes still grinning at me twenty years after she showed me in the primeval privy the place where all fortunate men go to die. Fortunato murdered by *son trésor* in treason. Every man is in the end killed by the thing he loves. *L'appétite morte.*

"*Capiche?*" said Margarita with a wink, Italianate Caracan that she was.

"*Capisco,*" said I but I didn't wink. I can't. I never could. I always do it with both eyes, you see. I must look blind to all. Milton with his private paradise, Homer with his Troy to play with, lost in the dark. That's me.

On the corner of San Lázaro and Hospital, painful bends, we found a taxi soon to be wrapped in the double vertigo of speed and blinding light. Queta feared as much on the slow night train from Cumbres to the city of the plain. I told the driver to take us straight to Second and Thirty-first. He assented with a sideways head movement that was neither nod nor shake. Neither here nor there. I hoped he didn't do it in complicity or complacency. You never knew with Havana taxi drivers: they all made Mercury and Hermes look like vaudeville comedians. Today I wanted to change sexual stages, to visit with Margarita another venereal venue, a foreign flesh spot. Then, later, to all the neighboring *posadas* I'd take her, supposing she didn't object to this *via volupta.* Perhaps, if our intimate interlude lasted (this is the mot juste, the word with most juice: the whole relationship was under the sign of Precarious, preserved by the lasting of a moment that we wished to extend into some fleeting eternity), we'd go off to Eightieth and Miramar, where there's a small hotel right on the exotic border, on Hades Edge, that riverbank I'd never reached before. In spite of what the song says. So songs must not be believed—or at least some sad songs. But on top of these reflections, almost over my request, she said:

"Oh no! Not *there.* There's too much daylight now."

Before telling the driver to change directions (an assent that would be a consent: a priceless procurer), I suffered an acute attack of jealousy, *grand mal:* almost a fit of foul fury. Her correcting my reckoning clearly meant one thing and one thing only: she knew the place. Though I had no claim on her past life, such precise knowledge of that *posada* in daytime could only mean, no more, no less, that she had been there before —and not exactly with Dante Rossetti. I was tempted to say this to her (to kill her unkindly with my erudition) but I adjusted a silencer to my mouth, dangerous gun that I am. The answer demanded by me would exact from her an inexact explanation, of course. This falsity in turn could only lead to another question by me and a new false statement from her, probably under oath over her mother's grave. All this would cascade as an ensuing argument, finally flooding the afternoon in a Niagara of screams, vicious voices, a wordfall. In a word, a row. On the other hand (how I hate this handy metaphor!) she didn't matter to me as a totality but as the moment—or several moments in a chain, a chain game. Whatever had happened before me was as far from me now as the future.

333

Besides, there was in the present the almost uniformed presence of the cab driver, as attentive as if we were sitting in the front seat with him —Margarita on the window side, naturally. The battered cabbie's scabby face caught my worried eye in his rear-view mirror and looked up in the direction of the heavens or the sky—or the roof of his car. No, it was at his hat. Was he trying to tell me something in his deaf but not dumb language? Eyes up. Up, up! Taxi cab, taxi cap. Was that it? *Cap?* Cap Dodge? No, it wasn't a Dodge or even De Soto. I know those cars: they often tail me. But Marlowe always can tail, tell. A Daimler then? Cap Daimler? No! Another make, another car? Perdiem car? That's it! *Carpe diem!* Latin's immemorial carp seen in the rear-view mirror. Seize the day. Don't wait for the night but shoot it day for night. Now! Scene one, take one. Harpo's carpo.

Once inside the inner sanctum of her preferred *posada* (where we arrived safe after she gave the driver an address that sounded like the combination to a safe) she repeated the ceremony of innocence (we'd be drowned in light if the curtains—the sun still shining blindingly over Havana—were not drawn quickly) again now like a nameless ritual. As well as turning off nature's lights, the interdiction included the bulb above and other electrical appliances everywhere, lest another sun indoors might wither this night daisy. She always had something to say on her way to the bathroom: it was her version of the *esprit de l'escalier:* a *bulletin des salles de bain.* Now she said something in a confidential tone, *paroles d'amour* or rather a heart murmur.

"I have something for you today. It's my specialty, dreamboat. I'll be back with you in a minute."

She said no more but I was by then already used to the young lady's whims: garrulous one moment, laconic the next, mysterious some time later. She was the sibyl of Cuba, a pithy Pythia, a pythoness around my neck: the oracle with the hourglass figure. Whim is feminine in my mother tongue. Resigned to being in the dark, I got undressed as usual and as usual I climbed into bed in blackout Havana. Only the narrow beacon from the bathroom, visible under the invisible door, told me that there's always light when it's darkest. How could a room be pitch black at midday in the tropics? It was a midnight mystery to me. After a while (it's amazing what light can do to time: I had discovered that time's progress is slower in the dark—should I tell Einstein?) I heard her call. It was not a cry for help. She was simply saying something—from behind the carbon curtain of the bathroom door. She shouted now. Somehow voices sound louder in the dark. That's how whispers were born.

"You have your glasses on?"

At the time I used to wear dark shades during the day in such a fashion that they looked like fashionable sunglasses. I had begun to wear dark glasses again, but they were a shade darker now. The first spectacles I was medically forced to use at eighteen were dark green, or rather black, by choice, to disguise the fact that I was nearsighted, therefore a weakling, almost an invalid. I was bowing to the prejudices of the super-male, then rampant at the Institute and directed against students (especially boys) who wore glasses—a sign of the worst kind of schoolmate. That is, hard-working. At the same time eyeglasses despicably betrayed the user's weakness—not all of it located in the eyes. That is, the eyes were where you showed your *cojones* when you were not naked. Dark glasses were then like figleaves against superserpents worn by us timid Adams. They were supposed to make the bearers almost spiritually immune to the shameful sickness of weak knees.

Now I was again using green-black eyeglasses during the day to look fierce: a Tom Macoute. But one night I went with Margarita to the movies and wore my usual glasses, for her unusual: with lucid lenses, those I usually called normal—if you can call wearing any eyeglasses normal. No wonder the most prominent writer in the language to wear glasses, Quevedo, was a small man with a clubfoot who had such a vile temper that he had to become a swordsman to fend off attackers upon his precarious life. That night at the movies she asked me if I really needed (pointing) those? It was almost like asking a clubfoot less pugnacious than querulous, quarreling Quevedo, why he needed only one high-heeled shoe. But I was already used to that kind of remark coming from people who had twenty-twenty vision, from cradle to crypt. My God, Cuban heels were not named that way for nothing! Nor Cuban shades for that matter. So I said yes to this beauty made of eyes. "Yes, dear, I need eyeglasses, especially at night and in dim light." She, Margarita all eyes, laughed like a mad maenad and in mid-laughter sputtered something silly about her never ever thinking of falling in love with a man who wore glasses: "Imagine, me married to Four Eyes!" Then she corrected herself, quickly: "Well, not exactly married." But she didn't withdraw the remark or remove the label of four-eyes. Or, as she said, Four Eyes. I came to be a double Cyclops for her. Less than that, I was her updated version of Harold Lloyd: slightly funny for being slightly blind. Lucky of me that I didn't have, like Branly, eyes so close together that they precluded three-dimensional vision—not only in daily life but in the movies too.

"*Sí,*" I answered her from across the room, almost yelling yes in the dark. There's no better sound barrier than a closed door.

"Well," shouted she, "take them off then. When I say 'when,' put them on again."

What was this? The ocultist playing oculist? Or a game of musical shades? But I did exactly what she asked—what she ordered me, in fact. I always obey a woman's wish, so as not to let her think that her whim is my command. The definite darkness became blurred but not less dark for it. From my myopic point of view I saw the beam under the bathroom door getting bigger and bigger, like dawn in the dark room. The square of light was no longer limited but overflowing as an ill-defined source from the now obviously open door. Then the shining stream of faked daylight, that luminous lamp, disappeared again and her voice said to

335

me, now from inside the room, now closer (but not close enough), something silly, something sour:

"Glasses on. Now!"

I did what she commanded, covered my eyes with my glasses to see
—*presto chango!*—a spectacle! For it was a spectacle, unique and unforgettable. Truly unforgettable. It happened over a quarter of a century ago
and I haven't forgotten a single moment of it: not a fragment or a frame
of what I saw—not even one scintilla. Or is scintillation the word? She
was standing next to the half-closed bathroom door and a ray of light
slipping neatly through the crack, which before could have been intrusive or indiscreet for her, was now her accomplice, a tool of her witchcraft. The light hit, or rather touched, her body. But only half of it—the
left half. The right half remained in darkness and I could see nothing of
that zone of eclipsed body, her umbra. The illuminated flesh (illuminated is the key word here) was what I saw. The left half of her body
revealed a thigh (I couldn't see her left leg because of the dumb bed, but
it didn't really mattress, matter: I knew both her legs by heart), rounded
and long, with a curving shape that reached the beginning of her hips
—her hip. A thigh is not a thigh: a thigh without a hip is only a sigh for
me. Now about her hip. Her hip, her only hip to me, was high and round:
it was the hip of nothing less than a full woman, and though she wasn't
fat it had enough flesh to look more Rubensian than like Velázquez's
Valencian Venus stolen by Rokeby—or only abducted? At the same time
she was much more modern than Boucher's O'Morpheus lewd little lady.
There was nothing eighteenth century about this twentieth-century
Ovidian ophidian, who tempted me like a surrogate sexual sage. The
double curve of both thigh and hip reached very high, to her waist, which
was short. (I had already guessed as much despite her clothes, but now
she confirmed my guess.) At the same time it was a perfect match for the
lower part of her body, in a harmony of Watteau waves. The upper part
was dominated by a large, round, and sound *teta,* whose nipple stood out,
central, in the beam of light: the same bud of flesh I had felt in my mouth
so many times—soft Lifesaver or light lemon drop, which in my fingers
became a doorbell button. I was in ecstasy watching her only tit without
regretting it didn't have a constant companion, this nonpareil dome that
made visible the music of the semispheres. Exploring that hemisphere
I had traveled blindly, a Magellan at sea, Braille with no fingertips but
fingerprints. Now I could see Margarita bare but barely. Her neck wasn't
long but not short either and it looked paler than her face now. On her
neck her beautiful head was as well placed as on an Ingres odalisque—
those beauties with a *cou de déese qui jamais n'abolira l'art.*

When I told this to Silvio, as I always did, he rigored and smuttered:
"That's no muse, *mon ami.* That woman's a damn museum!" But I knew
better, best. She could look like many paintings and be compared to the
women in them. She could be a gallery of women, all the women in the
Love Museum put together, but she was not made of oil and canvas and

turpentine. She was alive, *vivante, viva,* to say it in all the languages I know. Her naked neck and fully lighted face, topping off her divined body divine, from lips to labia, completed the carnal portrait she had sat for and, as Alton always advised, had painted (being both artist and model) with light. Though deep inside me I knew the painter wasn't Alton, John, of whom she had never heard tell. Actually, a better painter was the author. Below, barely visible in the shadows near her left leg, there was an inscription, also made with lights: *Malletus pixit.*

There was now a smug smile on her daubed double lips and a certain defiant look in her eyes (as you must know by now, my myopic movie pupils were trained to see a lot in the dark), as if daring me to compare that half body she was showing off in pome perfection to any other complete body I had seen before: in my life or in my dreams or of course in the dream life of the screen. I thought she really was an ancient amazon. I almost said so out loud—as aloud as a shout or a report. But I didn't—I didn't have the time, you see. She came to me rather abruptly. She came to bed without turning off the bathroom bulb, with perfect control over her light source: a sorceress who was a graduate student of Master Mallet in stage lighting. I could see her whole silhouette when she climbed up toward me and I didn't try to find out where which breast was *not* now because the fullness of her body filled any absence. She wasn't fat, you couldn't even say that she was overweight. Only that her flesh, a happy tissue, generously covered the infrastructure of her body like a superstructure. Besides, she created her own canon constantly.

"Did you like it?" she asked while bending over to kiss me.

From between her spreading lips I managed to say: "A lot!"

"Do you want me then?"

"Too much!"

"Never say too much to love, dear," she almost sang in my ear. "Always ask for more. Greed in love means being generous."

She was bordering the abyss of corn in passion without ever falling in it, like the lyrics of a bolero. Like the time when she told me that something was wrong with her breast for the first time she almost advertised it like an airport announcer: "One of my tits is missing." My fear with *habaneras* (other women were all alien corn) was that their corniness a-plenty would make it impossible for me to have our têtes-à-têtes pronounced tits-à-tits, as Silvio Rigor loved to jest at night, like a light surrounded by *bonne* moths.

But Margarita was a *mariposa,* a butterfly, an *Aphrodite fritillary,* with her scented breath now perfumed by the sweet Bacardi rum in the Cuba Libre she drank down in one gulp (forgetting that it wasn't a margarita), still kissing me with her sugary tongue flooded from the drink, her lips soaked in my saliva, salty from our tongues engaged in deep-kissing—salt and sugar, plus the vision of her. I'm talking of that motion picture in slow motion she ran only for me. For it could only be a movie. Television was too flat with its crude lighting in gray. And the theater always has a spotlight for each player, as Mallet used to teach: words must be seen to be believed. Only the cinema offers that *chiaroscuro,* that dramatic lighting, that fusion of lights with shadows as a narrative form: to create moving highlights from the interplay of total darkness and a harsh source of light. What she had created with that naked light bulb in the bathroom, the crack of dawn in the door, and her own body sawn in half by the crude beam as if it were a magician's circular saw, was an image almost shot in black and white: a scene taken unwittingly from the visual repertoire of both Von Sternberg and Orson Welles, the latter dabbling in stage magic, the former more like a camera conjurer—a dramatic duo now playing with the body of a carnal Cuban copy of Marlene. Why did most available beauties in Havana then look like Marlene Dietrich, with or without the peroxide mane—from treacly Honey to pungent, poignant Margarita: bitter Rita, sweet Circe?

That she had produced such an elaborate number (really a big production) just for me, especially mounted for an audience of one, excited me terribly. I never stopped to think then that her dumb show implied multiple undress rehearsals, trial runs, and previous performances. Nothing could be further from my mind. All I cared about then, *now,* was a three-letter word and two bodies in unison: two to make one: sex. There's nothing as erotic as a glimpse of instant eternity. Even if it's done with mirrors. She was Eve's apple but already half-eaten by the serpent of fate: a forbidden fruit with a hideous bite on its side. According to her, early in her life she had had an encounter with sharks. This could only be a legend: the past as literature. But now she had shown me her half body and left me guessing what the other face of her moon looked like, my imagination running wild.

Like a lunatic, a mad Adam, I immediately spread-eagled her on the sheets and penetrated her swiftly (like Swift, demented), almost violently, wanting to make her womb into a tomb for the little dead as I kissed her on the mouth, then the neck, then her bouncing breast, and now her bombed breast—or rather crater. I felt the stretched tissue flatten and wrinkle in diverse directions, forming new tissue, scars, the flesh almost macerated but taut. All in contrast with her soft, single, singular breast: beauty in my eye, in my hand, in my mouth. I was already longing for that show in the shadows and her sawn-off body she displayed in part with art. It wasn't sad flesh, it was wise carnage. Feeling my love for Margarita turn to pure passion I realized that she was coming: fast, faster, vastly—and I hurried my movements inside her, making myself into the piston of her cylinder. We were piston rod, greasy cylinder, block, head, cylinder press, rod, head, piston twice, piss piston, cylindroid! She and I became a soft engine and we came together. Almost immediately after, we began again in perpetual motion of the first kind but not mechanical toys. Never like a fucking machine: we were the flesh.

We interrupted our performance, our fusion, for an infusion, cold

338

Coca-Cola cocktails, to imbibe a *déjà-bu*. Since Margarita liked to drink (luscious lush from Caracas, sipping señorita from Havana), my ordering of Cuba Libres, getting up, getting them, paying for them, and finally settling down to drink the drinks, avidly, avidly! were our only intermissions. When we really finished, all she did was to mutter "Love" and then to say or sing, "Oh love, oh love!," those lyrics of a song being sung sometime earlier that earful year by every mouth in Havana. It went comically corny, like this, still talking of love: "Was born in me, was born in you, was born in hope"—hope being Bob Hope, no doubt. But Bing didn't sing it: he was too busy at the time trying to learn "Be careful, it's my heart" by heart. Be careful, it's my cock you're holding in your mouth. Thanks for the mammory anyway. The missing mammory.

It should be obvious by now that Margarita gave little or no importance to getting from me more than one repeated orgasm, as Juliet did. It was as if it were my mission—or rather my emission in life. Come, thick night, and come thick, knight. Ah Lady M! Unsex her here. There was no bottom, none, in her. All the cream in her kind of man could not fill up the cistern of her lust. Now, lying face up, my mate only by proxy —that is, known by touch only—she was looking almost blindly at the invisible ceiling. Eyes in the dark, going green and burning with a light of their own, she became Daisy Day's Eyes. For a moment I thought she might tell me to come to her woman's breast. But she didn't. She was undoubtedly thinking of something other than her breasts, full or foul. I was about to know how wrong I was! Since what interests me most about a woman, besides her body, is her mind, I wanted to possess her completely, bad breast and all. As I had already tamed her bountiful body, now I had to control her mind. Do you mind, love? But she canceled out my standard sentence, a standing order: "What are you thinking, dear?" Before I asked her, she made her move:

"I have a confession to make."

I looked in the direction of her voice. I have a confection to make.

"I'm going to be a father soon, but not a father confessor, I'm afraid."

She sat up in bed. *"Seriously.* I must. Will you get angry?"

"That depends on the sin."

I said so somewhat facetiously but also somewhat fazed. I couldn't guess why. She grew silent but not sullen. Suddenly she spoke up: "I have been unfaithful to you in my fashion. I said it. *Vaya!"*

I felt violently invaded by a Moorish jealousy more sudden than her words. But this revelation was reduced in size by the notion that the women in my life history tended to repeat themselves twice—as in a Feydeau farce. *Mais, Margay, pourquoi donc tu te promets toute nue?* Your skin is akin to the panther's hide. Margarita had just now employed the same cultured, therefore false, phrase that Juliet had used on a similar occasion years ago. Why didn't she just say, I cheated on you? A true natural phrase cannot exist in captivity. Women used to be more natural in Paris once apparently—and therefore the opposite of the dandy. Contrary candy. In Havana now they lived in a green and wild ambiance—except two or three that were like a French perfume. Now *je croyais respirer le parfum de son sang sauvage.* That was an odor of henbane. *Colibrí probablement.*

"Well, not *totally* unfaithful," she explained. "That's why I'm saying I've been *half* unfaithful."

I visualized immediately, as in a *camera obscura,* the enormous green Buick that brought her home that fateful night. I know—I've seen too many pictures. But I hadn't seen this one. Not yet. I was only making it as I made it up. I shot the aging owner of that monstrous motor car, in close up: getting on in years—the driver, not the car. Getting out of it. Getting into her. Then performing a coitus interruptus. Not by being interrupted (he had her whole that fatal night) but because he had too many children already: pregnancy is the mother of the condom but also of many a roué's ruses. Was that form of abrupt concourse an uncoming together: what she called "half unfaithful"? How can you be half fucked? Did she mean halfway insertions, sperms served in halves, like canned pears? Ha' penis? Ha!

"Is it that radio guy?"

"No, it's not that guy. It's not any *guy.*"

Did she say *that?* Did you hear? Did she actually say that? I didn't understand, I swear. It was *not* a guy. Was it a boy then? Corrupting a minor with a minuscule mick and in the nick of time to take the mickey out of her—I mean, of him? Technically you can go to jail for that. But not she. Not here anyway. No Cuban judge worth his salt wit will convict a woman for fornicating with a fourteen-year-old yet. No offense. The defense rests. The defendant then lies down. Not guilty! Honorable members of the jury. There are no juries in Cuba. Your Honor then. Could it be an old man perhaps? Pedophilia or gerontophilia? Necrophilia with the half dead? Count Dracul? Confusion she made into a masterpiece.

"It's a girlfriend of mine."

Was I startled! Mentally I mean. But I also must have jumped in the bed. Physically I mean. Springs used to be very sensitive in *posadas* down Havana way. So were the summers. This was the summer of my malcontent then.

"A *girl*friend?"

Did I gulp or swallow or choke?

"Yes, an old girlfriend."

Sapphic sex! Having truck and tricks with an old woman! There's the rubbing! *De la male Sappho qui fut amante Secrète.* Baudelaire *et maux de tête.* She must have been reading my literary mind in the dark: mental Braille to blind me. The amount of things she could do in the dark was truly amazing. Well, not really. After all, she had spent most of her life in the dark. But not me. She was determined to enlighten me tonight. *Secrets et lumières.*

"She's my age and we've been friends for a long time. We used to play doctor when we were kids and I was the patient. She's always been very insinuating. Dropping hints and making advances concealed as compliments. You know, that kind of thing. Until the other night, when she came out and proposed—"

Pro*what*? I never thought women could propose to other women as men do. What about etiquette? A formal or an informal proposal? What attire then—evening dress? What would they say to each other? "Will you take me, Daisy, to be your beloved wife?" What about banns? Would the announcements be published in the newspapers? In the social column or in the sports section? What of a full front page? *Diario de la Marina,* so Catholic, so parochial, should be appropriate. *"Engagements.* It was announced today at Saint John Lateran's Church that two of our most beautiful and desirable *jeunes filles* formally proposed to each other in the dead of night. In the absence of a groom the brides will use a broom." But no, oh no! It was all too ridiculous really. Though even more ridiculous was my question.

"Did you say yes?"

Her perfume reached me undulating. Colubrid. A snake in the bed. Poisonous smell that bit me in the ear.

"No, I didn't say yes. But things happened."

Great Greek goddess! It was the first time I had been involved with a woman who had a "Sapphic soulmate" as Silvio Rigor called them. He used to say (and I didn't believe him), "Tribadism is more common than tribalism in this Indian village." He called it Anabana but sometimes he would call it Afrodissant: "Our long-lost Lesbos lies by the ocean now." I helped him by saying in my mock civil-engineering manner that all *Male*cons are dikes by another name. Then we would laugh like twin stooges for having handed Havana over to the Latvians. I even concocted a slogan: "Lesbians of the world, unite! You have nothing to lose. Not even your hymens." As you can see, I could make light of lesbians before as I can now detach my penis and my pains from my bedfellow. I would agree, though, that there is drama in lesbian love. There could be even tragedy, as in the case of Sappho herself. But, believe me, there was much comedy. Like Marie Bonaparte, of all people, calling lesbian sex the revenge of the clitoris! Obviously some sort of virago version of the pit and the pudendum. What women do they'll do and pronounce it dildo: a leather condom, or Boswell's amor for amours. O Lesbos, olisbos!

It's easy to be blasé now, even nonchalant. But then, when Margarita confessed to me her act against man or woman plus some women versus man, I was at first surprised, almost astonished. I had known few women as feminine or as decidedly a female of the species as she. Though I should have remembered the revelation made to me once, when I was a greenhorn from that *Zolar* 408, by an aristocratic *habanera.* (Can such beings be?) She stated flatly that when a woman is very womanly and very ardent (she said amorous) it matters little to her if her lovers are of the opposite sex or of her own. That is, women lovers. I had heard this years ago at a literary party at the Pino-Zittos' in their *salon* in El Vedado, surrounded by paintings by Portocarrero, Victor Manuel, Lam and Lydia Rubio—and by some of the painters live. Upon seeing all the distinguished guests laugh either politely or heartily at what was considered a witty, naughty, and even intimate remark, a revelation even, I also laughed. First grinning, then smiling, and finally my laughter giving way to guffawing, timid as I was, when I listened to this descendant of the fabled Countess de Merlin. (The noble beauty by betrothal had come back from France to the tropics she was born into, not on a visit in verse like Heredia the French but in the lovely flesh to write her *bouquin,* upon returning to Europe, on how she discovered Havana while revealing what Paris was all about to those *sales métèques* that looked like macaques in drag—meaning of course us.) But this respectable lady, herself an aristocrat by birth, was insisting now that she was speaking in earnest. So much so that she, a baroness, sometimes felt like a baron born. A daring thing to say then, I must say now. Considering that in Spanish there's no difference in pronunciation between *barón* or *varón* —except that the latter definitely means not a nobleman but a human male. Now, as I realized that Margarita too could get interested in women, I felt scandalized, shocked, and finally furious. Mad at the girl —or rather, boy.

"Are you being serious?"

"Do you want to know what happened?"

"No. I'm not at all interested."

Margarita, obviously (like the baroness who could become a baron for a night in the tropical moonlight, where orchids are fetid flowers: their name means testicles in Greek), was speaking perfectly seriously. It wasn't a joke like the poisoned margarita she made me drink one night. She was a poisonous Margarita now—a green-eyed snake within my grasp.

"But *I* want to tell you. I want you to know *all* about me."

"I don't want to know."

She went on talking anyway. What could I do? Was I going to stuff my ears with wax and let this siren sing of sin? I couldn't cover my head with the pillow or, better or worse, suffocate her with it, Desdemona become a Yago and I the Othello who knew that Emilia picked up the handkerchief out of love, as a *memento mulieri.*

"This girl," Margarita began, like all women, by taking off years before taking off her clothes: she was about to make a confession about her contemporary but she had to call her a girl. She herself was thirty if she was a day. "She's an old friend. A friend of the family too. From Bayamo. She came to spend some days with my sister, who's her godmother. There are only two rooms in the apartment and my sister's husband never sleeps at home." It was obvious, from the time I saw him, that the relationship between this indistinguishable gentleman and Margarita's sister was just like ours: he was her lover, period. "She had to sleep with me in my bed, which isn't very big, to say the least. One night. The other night, two, three nights ago, we were chatting in bed in the dark, with my sister already asleep, and she began to remind me of our childhood days spent in Bayamo. She talked about our house, the chickens in the yard and how I loved the little chicks, so tiny and so yellow that they looked like canaries. A fancy of mine, of course. Never mind. She also reminded me how we played house under the house because it was built like that, perched on a, a, how do you call it? When the ground goes under a house, down a slope like this? You know of course."

"An incline." Words always lead me astray. I shouldn't have answered her query but I had already begun to grow an interest in her story: you never know when a story might turn into a short story.

"That's it. An incline. Because of the incline the house was perched on poles and there was a kind of dark, damp cellar where we'd go under. To play, you know, like in a cave. She told me about the time we played at being married in there and how she, who's older than me, always played the husband. I remembered, of course. It's true that we played house and that she was always my husband."

She stopped almost in mid-sentence. She did it for effect. I know. I couldn't see her face but I could imagine it as she was telling me: "As she was telling me all this, almost toward the end, she put her hand on my breast and did it so suddenly, so silently in the dark that I jumped. She then asked me if she had frightened me and I said no, not really. You see, she hadn't frightened me. At all. There was actually nothing to be afraid of. I was startled only because she brought me back from the memory so abruptly. All this time she left her hand on my breast. Without touching it but touching it. As if."

She stopped this time because I'd made her stop. Because I'd deduced that it was her good breast and that therefore her girlfriend was lying on her right. I was on her left now. This deduction, as you can see, didn't take me long. Besides she didn't let me dwell on it because she carried on with her continuing story:

"Then she removed her hand and I heard her move in the bed. Kind of jerky but careful. The next thing I knew, she was naked beside me! She had taken her slip off. I knew because she took my hand and brought it to her breasts and they were out in the open. She forced me gently with her hand at first. But when she took away her hand I didn't remove mine. I left it there on her breasts, on both breasts, touching one with my fingers, the other with my arm. Her breasts are not at all like mine. That much I can tell—and—that's all! Nothing else happened. I swear. She insisted on going further. She wanted me to take off my clothes. All of them. My nightie, my underpants, everything. She was frantic! But always whispering because she realized my sister could hear us if she went on insisting. Finally she put her slip back on in the dark and then came to cuddle next to me, playing sister. Right then and there I fell asleep. It was all too tiring!"

She stopped her narrative for good. Or for bad, because I didn't say anything. No scholia, no commentary, no footnotes. Nothing.

"Does it bother you?"

I didn't say a word. I should have told her that it was only an anecdote, that there wasn't meat enough for a story. Besides, it lacked an ending. Too much like Katherine Mansfield and not much better told, if you ask me.

"Tell me, *please,* if it bothers you."

That please moved me to repay her courtesy with a response: "Of course it bothers me."

"Does it bother you that it happened or that I told you?"

"Both."

"But if I hadn't told you, you'd never have found out."

I obviously wasn't going to give in to her reasoning—which was correct, of course. She had what you could call a point. A pointless point, however.

"I would have found out somehow. One always finds out."

"But this happened between two people, *alone,* in a room, behind closed doors—and you don't know the other person at all. You haven't even seen her, for Christ's sake!"

"I would have found out. There are always third parties. Truth will out."

"You don't even know her name, damn it! Besides, I swear on my mother's grave that *nothing* happened. Only memories of childhood. Games and that we fondled each other. That was all."

"It's more than enough."

She stayed silent for a while, I remaining as priggish as a priest. Father Logan hearing confession from Otto's Alma in the dark in a booze, booth. A confessional, just like this book. Then—

"I'll admit that she's still insisting. I'll admit as much. She's around. And whenever she gets a chance, she makes a play for me. Looks at me, touches me as if by accident. But she lingers, insinuating herself, you know. Even though I don't want any truck with her. She doesn't have a chance with me. Not a chance. Not a ghost of a chance, I tell you! But I've talked to her about you, I must admit. About my love for you, about how much I like you. As a man. But she still insists. She insists. Oh how she insists!"

She was silent again. I was silent too. We were both silent. But we didn't remain silent for long.

"Tell me something," she said. Then a pause. Then again: "Would you like her to go to bed with us?"

Silvio Rigor always said that inside me there slept a double of mine who was a part-time puritan—and he was right. Doubly so. Even if I was an insomniac in a king-size bed. Here with Margarita now, the Cuban Quaker awoke from his somber slumber. "Rain" in the Antipodes. I spoke to her in harsh tones, almost violently. Was I angry! Or was I merely

344

afraid? Refusal is only another name for fear.

"I'm not interested! *File* it."

"I suggested it to her and she seemed to like the idea. But if you don't like it, then, well—"

"I don't like it at all!"

"All right, okay. Don't get mad. It was just a thought. That's all. But this is the only way I'd agree to go to bed with her. The three of us. You and me and her. She yes but if you first."

Good God! Even her grammar was being perverted. Syntax must be a sin too.

"I'm not interested in triolism."

"In *what?*"

"Triolism. Combinations. One man and two women, naked, in bed."

"Oh, I see! I thought you meant something political. You know me, I hate politics."

"It's *not* politics. It's sex. S-E-X. Haven't you heard the word before?"

"Of course I have. Sex. It's sex."

"Then how many times do I have to tell you that I don't want to share you sexually with anybody, man, woman, or beast? *In* or *out* of bed. Understand?"

"Yes, yes! I understand. You won't have to tell me twice, believe me. You are my love, my only love."

"I wonder how many men you must have told that to."

"If you only knew! Few, very few indeed."

"The sappy few."

"What?"

"Forget it."

"But I can't forget you. I'm telling you it's only you. There's nobody else in the whole world!"

At that moment, as if on cue, there was a knock on the door. It wasn't someone, man or woman, to share our bed but a catamite to evict us from it. No sex allowed in excess of two hours. The knock didn't mean destiny at my door as in the Fifth but rather that our time was up. How dared they? Impudent Proustian prowlers! Huxleys in Havana. All is Wells. Time must have all the stops pulled out, like rotten teeth in a mouth organ. The moment of tooth had arrived. The allotted time at the *posada* was over. Allotropy had expired. Bodies must separate. Kindly leave the room. Instantly. Spunk punks. *Allons Infantes de la petrie. Contrepeterie.* Good-bye, I must begun. Rite a Magritte. Was I relieved of being relived! A base relief. Everything was up, except my vain weathercock. I had absolutely nothing else to do there. As a parting shot I told her I wouldn't see her the next day, Sunday, because I was going to Guanabacoa for a *toque de santos.* African drums beating to a Catholic saint's name. She wasn't interested in ceremonies and much less in Afro-Cuban drum rites. Certainly not in Cuban music, either songs or boleros or ballroom rumbas. So how could she ever be interested in such raucous ritual? Singing

345

in archaic Yoruba with the backing of an all-drum percussion, chanting and beating the tam-tam for hours on end, until one dancer, usually a woman, "gets the saint"—but the *santo* resembles the *grand mal* more than religious ecstasy. The dancer develops all of a sudden rhythm fits as if suffering from aural auras, to fall on the dance floor with arched back and twitching limbs and spasms as if in a violent tetany. Then she will babble in tongues till she faints and is taken unconscious out of the room. The epileptic experience becomes an epidemic until all or most of the celebrants—the all-dancing, all-chanting chorus—are visited one by one by the saint. In this case called Babalú-ayé. Also known as San Lázaro.

But, before parting, some sweet arrow, she made me promise to see her afterward, meaning the late afternoon of the same saintly Sunday. At first I was reluctant, but later I thought—perverted prejudice—that otherwise she would perhaps then pass the time with her girlfriend, in lighthearted lesbian links that could lead to her partner's rubbing her dirty: both rubbing pubes: the other woman's crude sex manners rubbing off on her: butch and bitch. If I wasn't there she would be her placebo. She her lover. A love match. Yes. I would come back to see her. Delighted to. I didn't tell her why.

Back from Guanabacoa I left Branly and my able brother in Fausto's car, Fautomobile and fautotum, and got swiftly to Infanta and San Lázaro, Aladdin's din, to confuse Fausto, always curious, always wanting to know more, to know all, Sir Knowall, and I went down San Lázaro Street. It's my curse that my course is to travel often down that dreadful street in my Havana dreams on an everlasting phantom chariot called Route 28, the green-and-red bus a Cuban version on wheels of the Flying Dutchman sailing down the detested street, *via smarrita,* always the area around Infanta, the more than abhorred, aberrant way, deformed, disfigured like a mirror version. It's that I'm returning to Margarita's haunts once more in the dream, as I will until the Day of Judgment: traveling in on the *red* ship because I didn't find a woman faithful enough.

Ah San Lázaro! Saint Lazare, Lazar, Lazarus. But in spite of the different names still the same street: the leper simply cannot change his spots. Neither can I as I walk now slowly toward Soledad, the memory another kind of dream, and on that street, surprise! I see her coming toward me. In memory the street doesn't look like San Lázaro either and I always think the encounter occurred on another parallel street. (Do parallel streets only meet in infinity?) But topographic logic makes me backtrack in my footsteps to believe we did meet on San Lázaro, because I was walking westerly heading east, while she was coming from the east: like the earth meeting the sun. I should have said the moon, though: Margarita didn't have a light of her own. All her light was reflected, while other girls I knew then were radiant, sun girls. Like Juliet. Jeweliet looked the most glorious glowing blonde one night. (I must admit it happened years after we'd been lovers.) That night she entered the University Film Club—on the surprising arm of Fausto. He her new lover now: a dashing young version of Fausto. They came to sit right in front of my unsuspecting wife and me—to my chagrin, the evening spoiled forever. She, Juliet, with her hair cut short, marceled by the waves of the ocean and splendidly blond from the same sun that made her golden all over: a vision of happiness because she was in love. She showed a demeanor so sublime: a blonde and not at all beat Beata Beatrice. She never had it with Vicente, a crude Van Gogh. Or, I must confess, with me either. Unlike certain magic jewel boxes I, *l'étuis que je suis,* can treasure true baroque pearls but I don't know how to make perfect pearls sparkle. I can keep them though as an—amulet. *Ah, mulata!* See Margarita now: look at her harlot skin, kin to Queen Margot, fickle wife of lousy Louis the Stubborn, who had her head cut off for being a she-debauchee. *Mucha Margarita!* A lot of woman. Lot of women. Lot's lot: a wife and daughters-in-love. Once she had a talisman, a tallish man. She walked in night then dressed in columns like the city. *Puella pulchra* this girl was, later *margaritam ante porcos.*

The city eternal yesterday, for a while a Roma, aroma now, a fragrance preserved in memory like a flower in a book. In remembrance green goes she in alien eyes. Gringo's he. Greener I. Not a traffic light on *go* but a jealous monster. I look back in agony and she turns into a pillar of sun. The clouds of time dust forming other couples with light years ever since. But she was the only oneiric form complete—the flesh dreams are made of. But Funny-man Freud had to make his German joke about Violet and violate and Dante, to infer that to give a girl flowers is to deflower her symbolically. Symbols, my roots! Immundus Sickmonde should have met María Sans! What about giving a girl white flowers? Obviously Freud knew nothing about venereal diseases. He learnt all about the mind but ignored the body—and how can you ignore this body? Be a busybody, buddy!

She was a single shadow in my sideshow: a flower freak, a delicate monster, a crippled doll: a beautiful baclanova in my own Ten-to-One carnival. Baby Browning, that's me—*im Verklaerung und Todd.* Baroque Margot was a *barrueco* pearl. Havana, mother of pearls, contains her as she lies in the viscous flesh of edible bivalves: Havana is her world oyster. But for me she (the city of course) is a fixation, while Margarita was never my perpetual motion, my emotion. Two pearly gates have I, night and the city. Remembering is opening that Pundora's Box to let all puns loose, all pains too and that fuck music of moans—and the small smells as well. Two brides have I, her and my hand. Or is it two in one? Punctiliously must I cross with my forked tongue that *puns asinorum* that goes from the twin of hearts to the cunt of diamond to the ass in the hole. Punnilingus. The pun of no returns. She's getting warm. Every writer with more than one tongue should speak with green smoke signals. Warmer. She's closing in on me now. Hot. She's coming alone. She's coming by herself. Come of comes. Is woman an island that can lie alone? Sweet Sargasso sea sí seaweed. Partial to the weed myself, ma'am. Two former fatherlands have I, the City of Words and *das kleine Nachtmusik.* Chamberpot music. *Petite morte et la musique.* Moosick. Read softly, reader, for you're reading my dreams. Here she is, there she was. In dreams begin awakening. Too much woman. Too-muck woman. To mock woman. O Silvano so vain! She's my bane and I her weathervane. I proved that not even an amazon is too big for the spear I shake. Milkshake. Ice and lemon juice and ice and rum and ice. Day query. Margarita has grown in my memory, mamory vane, my mory. Memento memory. Megalomamma. Grandma Moss still growing, Mother Moth: *le moth juste.* She opens her mammoth mouth. To suck me better? Back to her cunt, Conte.

Now she's looking at me with pleasure, approaching me with a smile (a vale of teeth), holding out her hands to take mine, touching it with her fingertrips. Tips. On the sidewalk, side by side, women come and go talking of Velázquez. But she doesn't care if we are on a public path or a crossroads or even on a *carrefour,* making Havana a *Paris à deux,* never paying any attention to the pedestrian passersby, those invisible minders of their own business, because they had disappeared from the until then all-buses busy street. Which always made me think that our enclosed encounter never took place on San Lázaro but on a side street that, curiously and curiously, wasn't Jovellar either. This simply won't do, topographically. It won't wash. Despite the mnemotechnical efforts I've made to prove the opposite, it's evident that, as in dreams, there's another logic ruling memory. Wittgenstein should play dreams with his right hand—to unravel 'em. Margarita, this side of my dreams, pressed too close to me to say:

"I like you a lot like this!"

"Like Lot's wife or like his daughters?"

"The way you're dressed today, *tonto.*"

To go to the *bembé* (a magical word I hadn't pronounced before so as not to reveal its secret to Fausto, but listen carefully: it's the black mass with everybody being black in white: I walked with a *zambo*) I had rid myself of the sports jacket I always wore, come rain, come shine, even in that dry September. The rains of the storm season had in fact been a fire in dry grass: a weather right for rumors and stories. I had cast it aside as a garment, not for climatic reasons but because in a *toque de santos* (see *bembé*) any formal wear would have been as out of place as shorts in church. I had on a buttoned-down-collar shirt, light blue with white stripes, now unbuttoned and opened at the top, showing the usual male awkwardness of my species, making me look like a hairy drone about to take off or a male mantis praying to a lord of the flies. I always try to hide this hunch of mine with suits or jackets: my legs are too long for my torso and my narrow shoulders arch a wider chest than they can disguise while my thin arms hang apart from my body—an ape so sedulously simian, trying to walk erect just like normal men. The shirt now masked that awful anatomical trait, and though the sleeves were rolled halfway up my arms, showing my weak wrists, these didn't stand out as much as if I were wearing a short-sleeved shirt. I don't know why Margarita liked my appearance so much now. Quasimodo is always somewhat stunned by what Esmeralda likes and dislikes about him. Years later I wouldn't even have been surprised. By then I was used to women finding me attractive for my most hidden assets: my voice, the shape of my mouth, my thin hands or, good God, my ears! My Tartar lips were either a liability or an ability when I spoke. But Margarita that day, that afternoon, that sultry September Sunday liked my attire. Women have always been an enigma to me. They are like another country. Paraphrasing Pascal I can say, what a strange monster is woman! But I was ready to play the sedulous ape to my playmate, a fay ray.

"What's there about it you like so much?"

"Oh, I don't know. You look so—manly."

No doubt to rhyme with Branly. It's true though that I've always looked young for my years. Too young in fact, even boyish then. But it was precisely the suits, the starch-stiff collar and the tie, and especially the jackets that I thought were hiding not only my physical defects but my youthful excess, always going to extremes, like living in the Antipodes. Climate, anticlimax. I was trying to add on years to those I already had (when people asked me my age) by wearing somber colors and even planning a beard—a political ploy no doubt, the model being more Gavrilo Princip than the Prince of Wales. Now Margarita liked the absence of a jacket with which to cloak (and dagger) my adolescent appearance. Ah ardorous apparel! I made my pun a coat.

"And you like that?"

"So much so that I could chew you up right here on the street! Tear you limb from limb, have you drawn and quartered and then munch and crunch you all over!"

"I believe you."

I believed her. I remembered her registered marks. *Marcas registradas.*

"I'd eat you up right now!"

"You are an anthropophagus, you know that?"

"What Gus is that?"

"A cannibal."

"Ah! That I am, if you are my main dish."

I realized that we shouldn't be there, standing, on the street, dressed. Our mutual drives had only one direction on the compass—not compassion but passion. A tropical climax. But we couldn't vary the vertical plane to have a lay. Not that Sunday evening anyway, since I had already exhausted my excuser. My sources were all used up, what with my brother whisked away by Fausto together with old Branly—salvation through speed for all. He was surely back home by now and my wife would be waiting for me as if for a lost husband. Call me Ulysses. After all, I met Polyphemus quite young. Thus we limited ourselves to talking for a while and exchanging looks from eyes to glasses in a dry toast of desire. Finally I left my Circe, cousin to Cyclops, without even a kiss. Ananthropophagy.

I don't remember what happened that week and for all I know the week itself never happened either—but I'll never be able to forget what happened the following Saturday as long as I live. I went to pick up Margarita earlier than ever, after a quick lunch at home *en famille* and a parting pretext for my wife: "I have to give Fausto a few alchemy lessons." On how to translate printing lead into printed gold: something vague and obscure. Poor Penelope, spinning her web day and night and weekends too. I must have arrived at Margarita's house a little after one. It must have been before one, in fact. Which makes me more of an Achilles than a Ulysses. Could I, in a crisis, have Briseis? Gagammemnon.

Be that as it may we were already in the *posada,* naked, the two in bed by two. She didn't talk about her girlfriend (in fact she didn't mention her again for a long time) and just drank her first Cuba Libre avidly. Ovid I was avid for something else. It was a desire to be inside her, which turned into a drunken fury to penetrate her immediately, dipso facto, with her glass still in her hand: which I heard from the clinking of the ice, which I felt because it spilled on my chest. Such impetuousness made my penis immediately reach further inside her than it ever had before, my scrotum turned into another instrument of penetration, banging frenetically against her vulva, its shrunken skin making it a blunt object, banging her where her loud lips form a mute bell, balls becoming bell tongue, then a clapper—what good old Ovid called the *plausor.* Ding dong! (Or was it bang bang?) She received me with her usual soulful softness: her skin smooth, her long limbs couched in friendly flesh, warm inside and all wet: a place to dock a soft ship. The commencement coitus —which she in her Havana ways called the first fuck—was very quick but no quickie. I continued fucking her with the same dense desire that meant not to hurry but to completely possess this my first woman—all that Margarita had revealed herself to be to me. For me.

But beneath the soft-hearted woman there was a firmness that confirmed the Havana seesaw: "She's tough dough, kid. Real tough!"— which I heard for the first time one night while passing by the Florencia and its Mexican mural movie stills. Perhaps those blighted bullyboys only meant to say a tough cookie or something or other and weren't even alluding to her. In any case Margarita grabbed me firmly by the arm and hurried to cross the street perilously, perhaps believing that what we overheard was just a poor *piropo,* wary of my reaction to that impudent insolence and fearful of my offended and therefore dangerous reaction to the bullyrag. Even imagining an ensuing argument followed by a fight and finally, after somebody in the crowd of spectators called me by my name, a naked dagger would shine in the sultry night, seeking, as I was now, an immortal wound or a suave sheath. Margarita received me without reluctance, with a warm wet welcome, and at the same time she corresponded with her movements, her queen's moves, in an agile twisting of her pelvis that not even Juliet's naturally expert hips could compare with favorably. There's the mauve memory of those risky but randy mornings on Calle Lamparilla, the street of old oil lamps, I a Havanan Aladdin, rubbing her soft lamp to be magically transported into her cave not out. Then there were the more obscure but secure interludes in the *posada,* but there was nothing like this, nothing! Moreover, I don't think there has ever been anything similar to Margarita in my love life my whole life—and I don't mean just sex but finding the being in the place of dying. *La morte, ma petite!*

I took a rest after the third coming in a row. Crowd roars, crows caw. Through all of the bouts I simply had to think "Open Sesame" and she did! Thus my orgasm was transformed into an organon: means of communicating not just knowledge but carnal knowledge. I had decided to stop for a moment to rest and taste my tepid drink, when I looked at her for the first time: I saw she was staring, observing, scrutinizing me avidly, Ovidly, while on her face, all but inscrutable, there was a satisfied, almost smug smile. The evening sun going down had managed to sneak in through some crack to make doors and windows into the seventh veil of this Salomé as she lay veiled in darkness, for whom the moon was a silver coin, a quarter of a dollar, a dime shining bright to dance to: she was naked. Like the night.

But this was the sun not the moon peeping at her now! There was light enough to see her with no veils other than skin. I didn't dare think of trying to peer into her absent breast or even to look at the marks such absence must have left, like an ogling ugly Ovid glossing the name Amor amorally. She was already caressing me, urging me to get on top of her again, I a missionary doing his daily duty religiously. I was returning to my labor of a lover's loss, making of love a gain through knowledge, turning love not into something that will last beyond death (as the eternal melody in *Tristan* promises), but rather knowing that as long as memory lives love will last. Peeking into the orifice of eternity I realized that we had fornicated, fucked! five times. Really! A recess from her recess was in order, and so I ordered on the intercom (one of those New Latin obscene words) a couple of inCuba Libres, following the pressing though whispered suggestion of this hard-drinking, hard-fucking Margarita: *fiat voluptas tua,* Lady Lay. A Circe of pleasure. No Hermes could drag me to Arcadia tonight. But I am nevertheless aware of the damp souls rising from the semen on the sheets. Shades of shame. Bedroom surfer!

The drinks arrived promptly *(pourboire, pour boire, pour voir?)* and I went to open the door, dragging myself and my pants to get out the money and pay, to then return dragging pants and cocktails, cod resting peace. Out of carelessness or fatigue (or both: slob's sloth) I didn't close

351

the door completely but only knew it when it opened wide, suddenly, silently, as I was on my way back to the bed. A violent stream of light, much like Munch, entered the room, the sunshot ricocheting off the sheets like a golden bullet—and I saw Margarita plain: in bed, stark naked now, her body as Olympia with so many curves or one single curve originating at her feet: thin, long ankles, one of them anklet-ornated, dipped deep in the Styx of light, the other ankle neither limp nor vulnerable but bare with its curve twisted into the strip of her calves (one beauty spotted, the other with a mole) that sank in turn into her knees and then surfaced again to sketch her long thighs before entering the beginning of her haughty hips and then, crowning curves, the double helix of her loins—hellish spiral, descending vertigo or climbing ecstasy, a voluptuous volute: the hirsute center of her cosmos. There were other curves indenting her waist but the last curve reached her shoulder and then turned down into a gentle curve, in curves toward her arms—as shapely as her legs. The whole was an interplay of curves by Courbet. My God, this woman had no straight limbs! To fuck her was really to cupolate. It was then, reflecting upon a reflection, that I noticed she did nothing to hide her breast. (The breast that was her Hyde, a shame hidden in one's own hide. The other one, the good tit, what I had already seen so dramatically highlighted, fell a little to one side, leaning toward a pillow and slightly under the armpit but still was not emotionless, a moving still-life: a breast heaving with every breath that preserved its unimpeachable peach form: like the Olympia she was a *chef d'oeuvre* revealed by masterstrokes of light. That girl was a living museum in daylight!) Now I could see it all distinctly. What remained of her left breast was the nipple. The rest was flattened on her chest, obliterated. Not a deflated balloon but as if the blast zone were made of muscle, like the torso of an old body-built man who had stopped his weight lifting long ago. The skin toward the sides stretched into streaks, scars and stripes forever toward her armpit, where more scarred tissue extended down her arm, reminding me of lean, jerked meat, but as she moved it showed that it had been kept alive somehow: fresh corned beef. Before turning around but never averting my face (this vision of her netherflesh must have lasted only seconds), while hurrying to close the door, pants still on and panting, to kill the streaming light, I could see her smiling with her long, lovely lips, as if pleased that I had seen her. Or rather, that she had let herself be seen by me, overexposed, in a complete striptease. Now I knew all of her. All of Eve. She was a moon goddess and her mutilated breast was her crater Alphonsus, visible to the naked eye when she is naked.

I returned to the bed in the dark now, without giving her her glass and with an erection I hadn't noticed before. I mounted Margarita. To mount her was to ride Pegasus, pony of poetry. Was this the famed Greek love, when Greek meets Greek? At least all my reference vessels were now bound for Greece. Homo Plato was the man who invented love, though he had in mind a love whose name he could say freely then but which for twenty-five hundred years nobody ever dared to say again. At least not in print. Infamous Sappho, also a platonic, originated lesbianism almost all by herself: before the poetess lesbians were rare, if at all. Now Margarita, with a little help from her friend, was being Greek to me sometimes. I'd correct all that (like a galley proof) and mend her ways. I swore. Pearl, with my little rod I'd touch your source of light and change the iridescent orient of your being—away from the dark! Penetration is a good word to begin with. Once more I sank between her legs, deep into her darkness—to realize that it really wasn't necessary to enter her so deeply. I withdrew to surface level sensing that we could be urchins together: she a sea urchin, I the heart urchin, both street urchins streetwise in the shallows of the bed.

Ardor versus ardor in Arden Forest of mock night. Ardent spirits we both. A penistree on the Mount of Venus. Panting panther, tiger lily, the sexpot and the poet: I'd find shelter in her loins, her crotch crutches, cock reached. I'd find shell in her. *Concha, coño.* Southern synonyms. Margarita, so that I would go deep into her now, needing my crutch in her crotch, my long stiff staff, inverted the notion: she supported my body, then raising her legs over my shoulders (this position must have a name in Hindi: the *Ananga Ranga* has a title for every coitus) while staying in her place and, later, later, her heels rested on my back—then she pulled me forward, toward her, more inside, insider. *Con concha.* I kept on moving, realizing it was taking longer for my longing now, that I was taking more time to ejaculate this time. I felt the sweat running down my brow, down my nose, my face, my belly, and into my belly button: a deep purple pond. Upon caressing her other breast, oddly enough, I felt it slippery. Perhaps the sweat was from my hand, perhaps from her skin, damp dermis. Damned dreams! But dreams can be another name for desires. Then, that very moment, she took my rhetorical hand and put it on her breast other and let it lie to rest on that crippled shape of lust. I felt flatness first. Like a man's chest, my chest, very much like a man's tit, like my own nipples. Tissue tit. The scars were rough, very, and the skin folded over itself—and odder than the other udder, I came there and then, *sur le con,* sperm spasms squirming among cunt contractions. *Coño cálido.* It was only on feeling her vulvar spells that I knew she too was coming in silence, like the night. Over and doubt. But I was too tired to care. Out. I threw myself down beside her and immediately, a reflex arc, I grabbed for my glass, *de la glace qui sonne,* in cubes, a cold incubus in my mouth, exactly where her hot succubus tongue had been: ice in the place of love. She also drank from her glass. Gulps in the gulch. I could hear her big, strong, masculine drinks. I tried to imitate her drinking habits, gulping and gurgling—and I soon felt dizzy, giddy, and nauseated. I thought it was from the stifling heat of the heats. Air-conditioned dream, where were you when I most needed your electric breeze? I was unable to answer this frigid question.

No sooner had she finished swallowing her beverage than she murmured a regal command: "Come." She defined the ambiguous word with a decisive action: she pulled me toward her. More than moved me she dragged me, an inert body, to climb her north face, which I ascended as we the dead do. Finally she placed me on top of her like a beloved corpse. Here we go again. Or rather I began afresh: each coitus is really an initiation. I moved as much as my exhaustion allowed and all it permitted me was to drag. A drag. Or a drag race run on a dead battery: I was sure I wouldn't come again. It was then that I felt her hand reaching for my shrunken scrotum and one of her fingers began to rub my epididymis (Greek again) from the exterior. An outsider trying to become insider. It was a gentle frottage at first, then becoming increasingly intense. Tense. It wasn't agreeable. "Let me do," she advised expertly. "You let yourself go." She continued with her fully fornicatory friction. Now her rubbing was too close to the anus for comfort. "You've never had a hood?" What the hell was she talking about! Seeing green she must have thought I'm Robin. What's a hood? A condom? Boswell's amorous armor or armorous amour? "What's that?" That was me talking, naturally, trying not to sound unnatural. "Never mind. I'll do you a riding hood. Okay?" "What's wrong with young little Red?" *"What?"* "Never you mind." "All right. Ready for the hood? Here comes the hood." Then she began ball-rubbing me, down under, rubbing the isthmus down below, close to the anus, *very* close to *my* anus. Was she going to fuck me? Do it onto me as I did to her? A woman's revenge! But then again, who's afraid of the virgin wolf? Once more love had pitched its tent in the place of excreta. Excrete a secret. It's in *Cratylus*. What's in a name, any name, given or borrowed or even stolen? Are names significant by nature? Or is nature just another name for the known that's never understood? My sordid sword, Excretabur, was it hidden in a hole like a poker ace? A labiarynth in ex Crete for my Minotaurus. Born in the cruelest month. Be that as it May, Excretures. "It's very good," she assured me. If only she could read my thoughts or even this page now. "It helps men come." "What about women?" "They don't need it, dear, they just come. But this is great for men who can't come. It works wonders." She sounded like the Midwife of Bath: to help big men give birth: the womb in the colon, anal labor, anurous parturition. Life in the place of excreta. To excrete, to be born. Birth of a turd. Absurd!

Wise or unwise cracks apart, I felt my penis grow, the erection harden, the thickness thicken. Night comes thick, Lady M. The threshold of pleasure was extended—on both bodily edifices, I imagine. I crossed her portal to look for her beneath the arches, in the arcade between the colonnades where I found her pale face in the moonlight to put my tongue like an Apache arrow in her pioneering mouth. She was already waiting for me, open wound, with longing lips. All her lips, large and small, horizontal and vertical, major and minor chords, were taking in my moist organ now. Somehow her tongue found a way around mine to enter my mouth, in a play of penetrations. Two tongues in cheek. Mean-

354

while, hordes of Semen from South Yemen went in search of the green oasis all over her Arabia Felix. Four horsemen of the puckered lips galloped to the walls of jelly—aposiopesis now!

A cloaked night in ardor, upon losing his head, cried out: *"Chapeau!"* Kisses resounded in the last, late afternoon: "Hail thee, Thane of Glans!" Jelly Roll used to play ragtimes with three hands on the pianola with his prick as an extra hand: that Jelly Rolly, Morton *meme, me salutat.* The adamant dagger becomes an intimate jelly knife. Couteau of the deep. Meet Meatloaf. The battle of the Unsex Continent had just begun (with my reinforcement, Taras Vulva, arriving on horseback in the last real) when a hysterical event occurred: spasm, jisms, seisms. It was a flesh-quake! The fault is mine. Vast deferences in my *vas deferens* are summed up and the Last Coming occurs: a Yeats man. It is the richest climax in sounds, her howling becoming echoes of cries of dependence I had never emitted, committed before: inside her mouth my cry. You have the right to remain silent. Your remains must be righteous but silent. Margarita is responding with an orgasm with all stops pulled out but her pipes are mute. She was a Greek organ, born before sound was invented at the end of the Middle Ages. She had a splendid windchest but a bellow for her was something beautiful in the language of Caracas, Italian, *bello.* Her will to blow was gone. Out the window. In flew Enza, pumped by Jay/Jay. Besides, she was reserved, even restrained in the way she signaled her every climax, all tropical. This was a one-man show, a unique private act for an audience of one: in this play she was no actress. She was rather an escape artist. Motion was her tone mode of expression in bed, but motion to stay put: she was a contortionist, all twists and torsions. But now she became really frantic in her contractions, Houdini gone berserk. Houdinia. They were actually tetanic spasms: her head jerked back, her trunk extended, her back arched and her body become a true bridge of flesh, resting on her head and heels only, as one span. Then she was shaken by a new wave of spasms and doubled over forward like a suave sword or a soft cutthroat razor: each contracture striking me as strych-nine posing, poisoning. *Moi le venim?*

Love is a kind of warfare and she was my battlefield. Now her Cuban heels nailed my kidneys to produce a vague lumbago. Ah sweet virago! Stop kidding! My kidding, I mean my kidneys are killing me! Relax, kiddo. She stayed doubled up in this tender tetany, her legs then sliding slowly down my back. Titania. An anaconda in the groins. That snake sneaked in from the Orinoco. *Poco a poco.* All of a sudden all convulsions ceased: her motor movements, reflexes, and action replays stopped for good. In a word, she became still. She was inert. Motionless she, a calm cadaver, an exquisite corpse: a dead body under me, inverting the crimi-nal metaphor. She remained regally rigid. While I—an anacoluthon goes here. But I collapsed on her in sheer exhaustion, my pipe now an exhaust. Our nature does pursue a randy evil, and when we fuck—we die. She in turn all of a sudden received me with open arms—to close them around me, beatific boa, kissing me with busy fire lips. Where was this firebird hidden, hey? She didn't have such body heat barely a minute ago! Had she been playing possum before as she's playing passion now? Whence did she elicit this energy? What elixir? Out of semen? Or was it the Caracan *arepas* she had for breakfast? Only God understands women! Not even He. Eva's the sample.

She suddenly declared, declaimed, claimed: "Do you realize what we've done?" I thought of some guilty act more sinful than adultery. Did she have sodomy in mind? No, sodomy's for the birds. Dodomy. On its way to extinction. She didn't give me time to ask her about that new guilt on the edges of my soul, a recently opened sin tin for men like me, more fucked-up than fucking, for she intoned, Wagnerian soprano that she was, all lyrics: "God, the number of times we fucked this afternoon!" I was going to tell her I didn't have much to brag about if she compared me to the legendary Chinese warlord nicknamed General Fifty-six! The nickname didn't allude to his actual age, if you see what I mean. This evergreen, or rather, everhot general was discovered by Silvio Rigor, *homo ludens,* in some lewd or ludicrous book of erotic epics. General Fifty-six was famous, in peace, on both sides of the Great Wall for his feat of having fought and won fifty-six consecutive bouts—with as many concubines—in a brothel in Nanking. Apparently every orgasm was greeted with a cry from the general: *"Kam beh!"* According to Rigor this means in Chinese bottoms up! I didn't want to speak to mah Maggie of this Chinaman, a stud. Studious of sex as Rigor mentis was, I found him velee leliable. Besides, I don't want to extend myself in eulogy of this riotous race that has been first in almost everything and now threatened to furnish every orgasm with a people's commissar. To think that I could have been one of them once! The man who would be Chink. Pray, why quibble and diminish before her, my prey, my prowess? Pry I didn't mean to.

I climbed down from her as if from a conquered Everest that nevertheless is still there. I lay down beside my mountain. She covered herself with the sheet up to her chin. It wasn't snow all over the ever-esteemed mount but, probably, pudency. (By the way, *pudency* means to be ashamed but is a word akin to *pudenda.*) A woman can be discreet and indiscreet at will. Double pudenda. Now I was witnessing this extraordinary behavior at the same time in the same place. Seeing her in her unholy shroud I began to fall asleep dreaming of women: all naked, on a beach, cavorting in the dunes that shone like mirrors in the sun. The glare didn't let me see her distinctly: a mirage in a movie. I woke up. She was looking at me and smiling: lips unpleated, eyes pleated. Was she planning to go Chinese on me? She's turning yellow, glaucous, greenish —like absinthe. Wormwood boring holes in the green dragon. I'm still green according to Silvano. My eyeglasses are tinted green. Now she sees me in her green room. But all green will have to perish. Green, don't want you green. Gang green. I grinned, she greened her white shroud just by opening and closing her eyes at twenty-four blinks per second. The two of us were falling asleep into a green dream at the same time. A double orgasm of sleep. We would have all our dreams together. Monotonous monochrome. Oneiromance of the rose. Rosy. Pink. In the pink. Copulation as a sleeping potion. Fly. Tsetse bug. Sleeping sickness. Going to sleep: back in our town meant fucking or rather fornication. Don Lotus slept with his own daughter. Margarita and I had already slept in unison. Unisonge. But in Havana sleeping is only an image of death, like the funeral phrase that's a social must at every wake: "He seems to be asleep." *He* must be a male corpse of course. Margarita in her winding sheet seemed to be deadly dead. Fallen in battle. To a body unknown a known grave build. Medieval man that I am, I decided to join her: love lasting beyond the little death to become a gothic marble couple lying side by side: Francis of Brittany and his consort Marguerite de Foix in the famous tomb by Colombe. It takes two to *tombe. Tombeau.* Now, at five o'clock sharp, when the late Lorca lamented the death of his bullfighter lover, we were both sleeping *a duo.* A duetto. The Sleeping Duplex. *Dos dormidos.* In that silly sleep, in that wake with only one candle, waxing and waning, waking up spermous next to Margarita, spermargaret, she wearing my spermine as ermine, I heard her wakeful, full voice saying after the quake:

"Glove."

"What!"

"Love."

"What next?"

"Love is."

I completely awoke from my dream lying in state betwixt the Middle Ages and the Renaissance, between life and death, to the amazement of her voice, sweet and sensuous, and not the sex sexton's (Seyton's the name), the same that came to announce to me that Juliet embarked upon alarum and excursions: "It's the cry of women," he said succinctly. Sucksaintly. To suck a sin. He was due any minute now to knock knock on the door in *Macbeth,* making me call the gracious dunce in anger: "You creep! In this petty place from day to day! Today and tomorrow and tomorrow and tomorrow!" He smiled sheepishly. All he wanted of course was to warn me that my time was up as they had forewarned when I came into this maze, a mess. The impudence! As if that body bare beside me were not an hourglass of flesh, now made of sand. A lying living statute she is, even when her mouth is unsealed: a body emptied of desire. Finally and utterly unsexed. His impudence, my impotence, her importance. I looked at my stylus, sundial, or minute hand—then I shook her veiled shoulder, shrouded flesh, enraptured mummy.

"Time to go to hell," I said sweetly.

"What?"

"The burning forest has come to Dunce's Nine," I said, becoming the poor player that struts and frets his hour spent fucking.

357

"What did you say?"

Unbelievable! She just wouldn't register. She wouldn't wake up even if I set this house of assignations on fire. Nevertit wanted her remains to remain in her tomb a little longer. A couple of centuries or so. Mummies can be more possessive than wives.

"Go we must!" I shouted.

"Come again?"

"Oh no! It's time to go now, not to come."

She didn't understand. Like all women she didn't get the allusions, be they literary, historical, or mythological. She didn't even understand wordplay! Only swordplay—and only if it had to do with fate and her sister. What she understood needn't understanding. It's called illusions. She could be a magician and a conjurer and be her own audience too.

"Gotta go," I repeated myself. *Repetitio est mater illusionis.* Or just *mater,* for that matter.

"Already?" she asked remotely, probably speaking from her happy Egypt.

"All ready. Time. To depart. To tear myself from the native soil. Away. Awake, native soul!"

"I'm awake, I'm awake!" she protested.

If she didn't get allusions she certainly wasn't going to know of quotations and puns and parodies. Not so late in the day anyway. She just sleepwalked now to the bathroom, turning on the light with the door open: letting the relentless bulb bathe her body like a shower of light and revealing her anatomy, which I knew now by heart—or rather by eye, like a gray Galen, knowledgeable in those forbidden though no longer private parts. At least no more forbidden though still forbidding. If I mean what I see. Adam was always wary of Eve, especially after biting the apple—above all *after* the bite. She closed the door now and I heard that din of rude dew, the actual not the metaphoric shower. My jet of words can sound more like a shower than the real shower. I decided not to shower, so I began to dress. I didn't want to bathe that day but to conserve the smells of her body on my skin like another branding mark. I was careful though to put my undershirt on first to hide the many visible bruises on my torso. When I stood up to stick myself awkwardly into my pants, I fell over on the bed, not because of my old awkwardness but because of a newfangled fatigue. I was really sinking: my legs trembled, even my arms were convulsed with muscular tremors. Tetania. A reflex is the memory of muscles, I reflected.

Finally I managed to get dressed when she was already coming out of the bathroom, naked, leaving the door open, her flesh exposed (until Margarita appeared in my life I didn't exactly understand what those innumerable naughty novels meant with a single repeated word, *morbid:* she was a morbid moll) and visible against the light: now not afraid that I would see her naked, that I could know her as intimately as any man could know a woman. Even more intimately, since I knew about her breasts and her breast. She dressed but didn't put on her makeup. She was the ghost of a girl I knew. She looked very pale indeed: her bloodless lips were the same color as her face, almost ivory, her neck now a version of the *turris eburnea*. Before leaving, putting out the light, taking one last look at the land of love to see if we had forgotten something (the ectoplasm of sex: sperm and secretions: séance on a wet room), I looked at my watch again and saw that it was nine o'clock: we had been in the *posada* almost seven hours. It wasn't a record but for me it would be a floodtide: that height of love produced only by her sexuality was a splendor that would not occur again. To complete the night, adding risk to rejoicing, we went to an American bar, a restaurant rather, on K Street, only three blocks from home, halfway between the Medical School and the Palace: the joint around the corner. There I devoured a filet mignon, wrapped in bacon, which was one of my favorite dishes then. Margarita didn't touch hers, resigned to watching me meticulously, my voracity her satiety. Then I wolfed her portion too. I walked her home. One long-lasting kiss. Returning home, a third provocation, I decided it was time to sleep without the coy cover of the T-shirt. I never found out if my wife got to see the marks that made me into a leopard, an animal with natural spots, a copula cat. From then on I no longer cared if I was seen naked.

The next day, Sunday *do ut des,* in a fit of bucolia Margarita insisted upon escaping from Havana. I hated the country as much as I loved the city. The furthest I would go into the countryside was a compromise: the Country Club pond, beyond Marianao Beach and its luminous cabarets obscured by the sun, but without entering what was for me no man's land: the sumptuous Biltmore suburbs or the residential area of the Country Club with its many millionaire mansions. This little lake, like the distant lagoon outside my town in the country, was a false landscape, a still life, Monet's lily pond, which is why I was drawn to visit it often. But there was also a morbid interest. One morning two men appeared there, lying together on the lawn, dead. "Riddled with bullets," said the press, which is the last refuge of clichés. I can solve that riddle now, thirty-five years later. Gustavo Massó and Juancito Regueiro were two punks I once knew: two kids who pushed their luck too far, too soon. Massó was slightly older than I, but Juancito was younger, almost a boy. The two were different Havana versions of Billy the Kid—and as deadly. But never as infamous. Billy was scruffy, dirty, and prone to treason. Contrarily my contemporaries were the victims of treason, both betrayed. Massó was blond, clean-cut, blue-eyed, thin, and fragile, and had been led to violence because (for the cause) of politics and political infighting at the time. Juancito was husky, taciturn, and a born killer. They weren't friends of mine but both had been high-school classmates —though we never were in the same class together—and I always felt they didn't deserve their fate. Probably the last man they killed (who wore the name of a Nicaraguan poet, Rubén Darío, but was no poet: he was a crooked cop) didn't deserve his fate either. Nevertheless, Juancito and Massó pushed open the swinging doors of the waterfront bar where Rubén Darío was having a drink by himself. They say it's not salutary to drink alone. True or false, it wasn't healthy for Rubén Darío that day. Both newcomers were carrying Colt .45 pistols, a weapon Billy the Kid would have loved. The two walked calmly to the bar and said so low it came out as a hoarse or coarse whisper:

"Move aside, gentlemen," said Massó or his friend. "Our business is an exclusive deal with this patron here." The craven customers moved speedily away from the counter. The lieutenant, still named Rubén Darío, didn't have a ghost of a chance even before being called a corpse. Both, Juancito and Gustavo, opened fire at once and Darío fell dead over the counter. Juancito gave him the *coup de grâce* in the back of his head. Then they both walked out of the bar and into the harsh light quietly, with restraint, but never turning their backs on the counter—as if they too had seen too too many Westerns. They had not. They didn't have the time, you see. What with being busy being killers together there was not much time left for movies. Now they were gunsels in distress: apparently hoodlums at large but actually lambs on the lam. Though they had killed in cold blood, they were killed with even colder calculation out of political expediency. Their sudden death impressed me then: how they were brought to the pond and right there on the lawn got what was coming to them: a coup de grass. But now—that is then—I thought that barely a decade later nothing was left of the pair, except in the memory of a few friends and foes. I myself came to the place of the killing, today verdant and placid, not to remember them or to think of death but to live my life fuller: to complete my erotic education and to learn how to love over the same violent land, under the same relentless sky.

By cultivating Margarita I sponsored her sylvan fantasies: the lakeside had vegetation enough for her craving, with its giant trees, leafy ficus, and even deceptively wild bamboo, bamboozling you with its chinoiseries. We sat on the grass (another concession: I detest sitting on the lawn: lovebirds on the grass alas) and suddenly I noticed she was silent. Not sullen, just silent. It wasn't usual: all Havana girls were born after the talkies.

"What's the matter?"
"Life is such a chore time!"
Did I hear well? "What did you say?"
"That life is so *short.*"
"*Ars* longer."
"What did you say?"
"I said *that* before."
"No, truly. What was that?"
"Latin. A proverb. Of course *vita brevis* comes first."
"Sometimes I don't understand a word you say."
"Neither do I."
"*Really?*"

"Who's writing your lines?"

"Me and myself. At least two of us."

"I guessed as much."

"Life is still short."

"So are your lines."

"Yours are longer."

"Art always is."

But nature was longer or at least bigger, even when it's tame. The air was sweet that day, with the fragrance of flowers in the garden. All of it had to be embalmed but it was a balmy day nevertheless. Orchids in the afternoon. Barmy! Orchids smell only in the wild. Roses then, honeysuckle roses. Jasmine? I breathed deeply.

"Nice smell," I said. She smiled. I smiled too.

"It's me," said Margarita. "Laliche."

"Labiche? That's a French—"

"Yes, it's French but it's pronounced *Laliche.* It's my favorite perfume."

"But I thought you only wear Colibrí!"

"Colibrí! You gotta be kiddin'! That's for old maids. There are no old maids or spinsters in my family. My mother died early, consumed."

"Phthisis?"

"What's that?"

"Tuberculosis."

Margarita looked at me askance, askew (ask me if you want but I won't be able to describe her stare), and lifted her chin to talk to me, *l'auteur,* from all her *hauteur,* though she remained seated.

"My mother was consumed with passion," pause. "I come from a race of Balkan women."

"First or second Balkan?"

"What the hell do you mean by that?"

"Never mind. I believe you. I've met Balkans before."

"Balkan? But I mean *volcan.*"

"You mean volcanic then."

"Yes, that, volcanic. We all are volcanic women. My sister, my mother, myself. My mother was very volcanic."

She must be ashes by now. Or at least cinders. That's what I thought —I didn't tell her, of course.

Now she turned to stare at some invisible point between the green pond, somewhat dirty with mud, and the blue horizon that the trees hid tenaciously: nothing can kill a view more thoroughly than trees. All trees. The tree of life won't let you see life because of eternity. The tree of knowledge of good and evil, because it is forbidden, won't let you attain any knowledge and they'll kick you out of the garden if you insist on tasting its fruit. Indeed you cannot see the wood for the trees: all you see is bark. A rose could rise but a tree is a tree forever.

"What are you looking at?" I asked her, though she could very well be looking at the spreading fig trees ahead. She didn't jump back to me but returned from her point of view, a long shot, to a closeup of my face too quickly to focus the lens on me.

"I was trying to recover things past."

"Pure Proust."

"What's that? A drink?"

Oh God! "Forget it." She could do that. But how could I? I wasn't surprised that she used such a Proustian phrase (after all, according to Proust, *l'homme*, literary property is theft) but rather by the intensity of her tone. My automatic reaction was the quick quip from the hip, as in any Western. I handle my pun guns as Wild Bill Hickok does his twin pistols. I've killed more than one memorable occasion with my bullets of wit: on target, sharp, implacable. Though my guilty conscience when confronted with the corpse always cries for punishment.

"What were you thinking about?" I begged of her, trying to reform and through words to gain my pardon. A parolee.

"I was actually comparing the past and the present in my love life. In one word, I was thinking of Alexander."

She hadn't mentioned this name for some time now and today it only reminded me at first of Buñuel's cruel parody of *Wuthering Heights*. But as she elaborated the other Alexander reappeared, a ghost of Old Havana, a stooge on the stage among square columns: a checkered shade in the evening's colonnade. Alexandria by the Stream was that memorable metropolis of memory—founded by an alien Alexander.

"I was also thinking of you. I cannot do otherwise. I was really comparing you with him."

I felt annoyed at being measured against that tall, handsome, strong stranger. He was everything I wasn't. It wasn't fair. Or at least I wasn't. Was she?

"On my honeymoon I thought it impossible that anyone else could fit in his shoes."

"Have you seen my feet?"

"I mean to be a better lover. Now you have shown me that you're better in bed than he."

With a single sentence—and my interruption—she had changed not only my mood but the landscape: all those deep green trees were oil paintings, the sky was a backdrop painted blue and the two of us on the lovely lawn were *Le Déjeuner sur l'herbe,* for two, by a modern Manet. (Everybody must get dressed though.) To complete my sexual fantasy she only had to identify me with the Cuban Superman with his powerful penis. (His pudenda was a must in all provocative pictures of the past, despite his public protestations of passive pederasty.) But she surprised me when she spoke again. Not what she said but the way she said:

"Do you realize how many times in a row we made love the last time?"

It could have been Juliet Estévez speaking! She avoided all obscene mines on the field of love, where violently vulgar battles must occur despite all conventions since Adam and Eve. I didn't accentuate the negative the two women had in common (vulvar, vulgar, remember?) by asking her why she didn't call a cock a cock in daylight. Or, by the same token, a fuck a fuck after dark. I decided I should insist on my modesty: I'm vainly modest.

"We can always better that record, you know," I said smiling. "The Olympics aren't over yet."

She looked at me as if in pain. "Don't laugh please. I'm being serious."

I too was being serious: that day I felt capable of calling old General Fifty-six's bluff, in the laundry of his choosing, to defeat him on a clean set of sheets. But she didn't continue sailing down the romantic river of remembrance. In fact, she didn't speak for a long long time, looking at the calm surface of the pond, that enormous pool, an artificial lake form-fitted to the terrain. It was natural only to the extent that some water was deposited there during the rainy season, which the National Observatory called, to spare us the shame of being taken for Hindi, the hurricane season, eluding the word *monsoon* like the Punjabi plague, therefore deluding us: we Cubans are whiter than the Indias. No monsoons allowed here. The rain must fall, but with any other name even if it rains from April to November. Maughams must leave. Now Margarita was looking at the orderly but apparently wild shrubbery (mere pruned bush) all around us, with those green eyes of hers: green on green. All green will grieve perennially. I didn't speak but rather observed her profile. It wasn't her best side, I must say. Jane Powell never was Hedy Lamarr but in profile she looked somewhat puckery. For the first time I could compare her with my wife, to the latter's advantage. My wife had a pretty good profile. Not pretty but good, a good profile as profiles go. On the word *profile* I began to reflect on how a face in profile is always different from a face facing forward, how the face contradicts the profile facing us, frank Dr. Jekyll hiding hideous, devious Mr. Hyde in his profile. Thus I was theorizing on how one could base conclusive evidence according to physiognomy on these differences alone (Lombroso, a criminal anthropologist, did no less when he signaled the stigmata of the criminal classes, meaning not mystic marks but the brigand's brand, and he invented, all by himself, the mugshot) when she made her profile disappear—just by turning to talk to me:

"I have something to tell you."

She was serious, too serious, much more serious than in profile, when a woman is at her most serious: profiles never smile. She had faced me with frontal frankness. Earnestly now she had something to tell me. She always had a revelation devoutly to be visited by me.

"Yes? What is it?"

"I have to start thinking about returning to Venezuela."

"So soon?"

"I have a contract there waiting for me."

"But do you have to honor it right away?"

"No, not immediately. But I have to begin to return."

I never remembered if she said start to return or think about returning. I didn't want to speak to her of her purpose in returning to Havana in the first place—which wasn't myself, of course, but plastic surgery: the reconstruction of her mutilated breast. She seemed to have completely forgotten about it.

"Why don't you stay in Havana?"

"The truth is I've tried to get work in television here. Even on Channel 2. But I haven't gotten anything. I only have sure work in Caracas and I have an idea."

She paused. I had no idea what idea she had. Then the report—"Why don't you come with me to Venezuela?"

She caught me completely by surprise—which was hidden behind my dark glasses. But I couldn't disguise my voice. The voice always betrays you. It's not the heart that tells tales but the mouth. *"What?"*

"Come, with me, to Caracas."

She was pleading. It was in her voice, in her face, but above all in her eyes. I think that she even pleaded with her hands. All this paraphernalia of gestures, some truthful, some true According to the Method, gave me time to recover.

"To do what in Caracas—play the maracas?"

Wit can be my witness for the prosecution but she was in earnest, so she didn't hear the rhyme. Besides, there's no tradition of limericks in Spanish. Even though there must be an old man in Peru. But she had a trump card, a trumped-up card, a strumpet's card.

"You don't have to work if you don't want to. I'll support you. We can always live on my salary. I get enough. More than enough. Come live with me, my love."

The words were almost Kit Marlowe but the sentiment was all William Faulkner. It was the ideal situation for a writer according to the author of *Light in August* and "Dry September." The Southern gentleman said once that the perfect habitat for a writer was the brothel: supported by harlots, with a secure roof over his head and all the sex he would or could want. That plus spending the day writing and the nights conversing with beautiful women. The fatal Faulknerian fascination— almost. She wasn't inviting me to a Caracan brothel but to her house in Caracas. But she was certainly proposing that I be a kept man, locked in her seraglio for one. Any woman can become a witch, you've seen it before. But all witches, starting with Circe, source of sorcery, aspire to the condition of housewife. All they want is a broom with a view. But, she went on, I'd have a roof *on* my head. She made it sound like a hat—a Panama no doubt. But what about a roof over my tongue? It was she again: I would write during the day and have intercourse, social or otherwise, with a beautiful woman, namely her, every night. She was virtually offering me all the sex I could covet—and more, much more. Love in my afternoons. *L'après-midi d'Infante.* The offer was as tempting as she was

364

then, now, *here,* can you see her? right in front of my eyes: her day eyes looking intently into the green of my eyes as a reflection of hers. That's what I think she assumed: the eyes of a daisy become modest toward evening. Daisy wheels, Daisy chains, and Daisy whines. Days of whines and rosary. A daisy in my rosarium to end in gloria, morning glory. But night must fall. Something wicked my way gropes. Moon daisy me now. Then, one day or one nightfall, I'll be pulling sex while pushing sixty. Suddenly or in pain, I'll be pushing up the daisies. Gone to earth, the way of all foxes. Moonshine from a moon Daisy to a moon rake. Daisy, Daisy, you are my posy. Dressy in Havana, nude in Caracas. *Maracas registradas.* The offer, I must say, was tempting: as alluring as she was. Lure of laurels to rest. Temptation from a temptress: an allure I cannot resist. She should insist. I did desist.

"I'd never leave this place and I don't mean the lawn, the park, or the pond."

Eve, evicted, became speechless. But only for a moment. "But why not?"

"My life is here in Havana." Adam turned adamant.

"But you would live very well in Venezuela. Besides the fact that we'd have an apartment in Caracas, we could go away for the season"—I'll never forget that she used that endearing expression from Oriente and not *vacations*—"inland. Or better yet, to Margarita, which is a marvelous island. I like it a lot."

Did she like the island because it bore her name? How boring. Margarita was the pearl around which an oyster of words grew. Wasn't the island of Margarita near Trinidad? In that case what she was proposing to me was the Apocalypso. But her gift was pearls to the swineherd. The swine in me never heard anything.

"No, I can't. Besides, I don't want to."

"If you like, we could live on the island, stay there all the time we want. I have money saved in Caracas. I can make a lot more now, when I return, in next to no time at all."

Could she have read D. H. Lawrence years ago, like me? I felt a prisoner of that island, Île du Diable. I understood Juliet now in her firm refusal to follow me to my mythical and literary island: impossible islands, flying Laputas.

"I hate islands," I said, to dissuade her definitively.

"But Cuba is an island!" she protested.

"I don't live in Cuba, I live in Havana."

"Then you could also live in Caracas. It's a modern city with long avenues and high buildings and besides—"

I interrupted her catalogue of Caracas's characteristics. "Now, see here, Margarita. Let me explain once and for all. I'm not going to leave Havana. I'm not going with you to Venezuela, be it an island or *terra firma.* I never intend to leave Havana."

She seemed profoundly disillusioned. I compromised: "It would be something else if you stayed to live here."

"And always play second fiddle? No, thanks."

"You would never play second fiddle to anybody. You're first fiddle in any orchestra," a little laugh. Seriously now: "What's more, you're the most special thing that has happened to me in my life," which was true, at that point. "I was looking for you for years. When you didn't even know I existed I was already looking for you. Now that I've found you, I don't want to lose you."

I was going to tell her that Havana was not only my beginning and my end but my middle queendom. I was afraid though that she didn't know about Mary Stuart or understood mottos or mortal games of love and restoration. *De Civitate Dea.* Better bitter: "But I don't want to lose myself either. I want to keep you, keep us together."

"Oh, really? Like this? And continue as we are, meeting on the weekends, you on loan?"

"We can see each other more often, as long as I do my job."

"Your family's your job too?"

Job's family, I almost told her. But she was right. Treason has its reasons which the heart doesn't know yet. There was nothing else to be said, so I didn't say it. There ended our afternoon in the country—an urban countryside, amid private gardens, cut grass, and an artificial public pond open to all executions. It was not only the last afternoon we had in the country but the first and only one. Now it was the mauve hour, a violent hue: violet, purple, and deep blue.

I thought all was over when she called me on Friday to see her Saturday early in the afternoon. I got to her house around two and both she and her sister—whom I was surprised to find in the house: she was the vanishing woman: now you see her, now you don't—were getting ready to leave.

"You're coming with us," said Margarita and it was more an order than an invitation.

"Where?"

"We're going to the doctor," and upon saying so she looked toward the rooms. Then in a medical murmur that was a theatrical aside, a leftover from the classical university theater, she added: "My sister's going to have an abortion."

I don't know if I escorted them wherever out of curiosity or inertia, that old bad habit of spending Saturdays with Margarita. Thus I found myself walking with the two sisters, not between them but rather on the sunny side of the sidewalk, Margarita's side. Tania or whatever was on the inside and looking somberly at the ground: without saying a word, in an obviously dark mood. Margarita looked at me from time to time but without saying anything either, without even smiling. The three of us marched up Jovellar to L Street, then down Twenty-fifth Street, two blocks from the medical school—to the office of the abortionist, an Aesculapius without scruples, the serpent with albino skin. I had never seen a member of his secretive profession in action: for me he was a kind of killer in white, denying hypocritically the Hippocratic oath, taking life instead of giving it, the worst sort of scavenger. According to my acquired morality I was entering a den of iniquity. In effect, the death doctor's office was in a cellar (as rare as they were in Havana): we descended dangerously steep steps painted black, funereal, fetal: back into the womb, the tomb. But once inside I was surprised by the whiteness of the place, the hygienically-painted walls, the decorous receptionist, and the animal adornment of numerous fish bowls filled with green water and live goldfish, visibly swimming. Were they adults? Branly's banter to better adjust myself to the presence of expectant patients, all women. Evidently the criminal surgeon (these scandalized epithets really did cross my muddy mind then, recurrently, like the fish passing in their pond) worked wholesale: he performed abortions in a row. Among these women, between Margarita and her sister, sat I: a conspicuous accessory before and after the fact. In fact the only *visible* man since the doctor, at his twisted task, was invisible. He was also inaudible and nobody spoke: the waiting women mute like Margarita's sister, like Margarita too. Silence was so pregnant that you could hear my dandruff drop. Suddenly I heard a hiss and for a moment I thought it was the Aesculapian serpent, sibylline, but it was Margarita murmuring in my ear. Not a theatrical aside this time but rather her voice off, copied from the movies by television: "Why don't you take a walk and come back in an hour?"

Then why did she ask me to come, I was going to say: I wanted to see the whole process. As I had never gone to war, my *nom de guerre* in name only, I was substituting this fetal slaughter for the historical kind. After all, the massacre of the innocents could end like this, with a hysterical Herod baring his hatred beyond the womb. Fetuses as cannon fodder, father. I was also about to ask what I was going to do at that hour for an hour: stroll along the Malecón until melting, a foetus of Phoebus? Watch the girls go by in El Vedado, off limits, now forbidden to me, no longer a passive peeper but an active member? Go home to visit? This wasn't such a bad idea though it seems parallel, morally, to what the abortionist did. So I went home to have a snack with my wife and mother, both expectant now. I don't know what excuse I gave for arriving unexpectedly. An unusual version of Ulysses, I found my Penelope weaving baby booties and my mother, Euryclea in Amnesia, didn't recognize me: you, here, at this hour, boy? I don't know what words escaped from my sacred set of teeth but I had to invent another excuse to leave again in an hour: "Fausto wants to hear Wagner listening to the record of his life." It wasn't a good excuse but at least it was great music.

When I returned to the office (or morgue) the operation was over: a happy event: a successful abortion. Have a cigarette, my boy. Since Margarita's sister insisted on walking home, I had to urge her to take a taxi with us. It hadn't been a birth and her behavior couldn't be compared with that of those peasant mothers, child-bearing heroines, whom I had heard praised in my childhood because they gave birth standing in the fields, then picking up the infant from the ground amid the produce (potato, sweet potato, papoose) to take it home and to return immediately to work the crop—doubtless against science but not contrary to Mother Nature. But that day, in the heart of the city, in Havana, Tania's stubbornness revealed an elemental nature. There had always been in her face and her body a certain primal aura which, after all, could be called a quality. Pearls and pigheads. When I left them at their house Margarita, ascending the stairs, said to me, almost in a murmur:

"I'll see you tomorrow."

She obviously took for granted that I'd be there the next day, available as on a weekday, at her majestic service—which was also my pleasure. After all, we both shared the same weekend double bed and its joys. Though we rarely met on Sundays for anything besides conversation as we walked around the neighborhood she seemed to appreciate so much and which I hated—only the topographical coincidence that it extended to the Tower of San Lázaro and the miraculous Malecón, sea and wall, made it bearable under the ubiquitous sun god. But that Sunday contradicted the gentle breeze of September on its way to being October, the halcyon days when there are neither hurry nor hurricanes, when the lazy sky curves high, intensely blue, cloudless, and there's barely any heat: the burning of Havana in September cooled by the Gulf Stream. Our aura was different now: no longer the torrid zone of summer but the October city I learned to discover that first autumn in Havana when I explored both sides of the Malecón: getting to know its urban side, examining its sea side. That sweet Sunday what emerged from Margarita's lips were bitter recriminations, incriminations rather, after she insisted once more (always punished in the pillory of language was I: is it possible to insist once less?) that I should go with her to Caracas. I became thus a heterosexual Humboldt Humboldt, with the same bait and the same bite of the apple. But now came the threat: an ultimate ultimatum: either I agreed to abandon my family, my country, my city—what was more threatening: Havana or life?—for her or it was all over. There wasn't much logic in her reasoning: if she was really going to Venezuela it was obvious that our relationship was over. I didn't point this out to her, of course, so as not to contribute to her despair, which was extreme indeed. At one moment she gave me the measure of her anguish by saying: "I really should have put poison in your drink that night!" For a moment I had to make a mnemotechnical effort to remember her Venezuelan Valpurgis night: green passion poison. Yesterday's heady love potion is today's hate antidote. It was also painful for me: after all, I loved Margarita. She was not only sex: she was love. But she didn't see it that way, and upon completing our walk, which was like a cycle, an orbit, another ring, at the door of her house, she announced to me that it was all over. "I mean it," she said, and crossed her thumb and forefinger to kiss them:

"Cross my heart and hope you die!" She climbed the stairs rapidly but I was able to notice that she was wearing sandals that afternoon: her feet were perfect.

One night some time later I was writing a rage review after having shot the movie down with my Marey's gun to give it, as a parting shot, a coup de gratis, when the telephone rang. Un coup de phone. I was surprised that someone would be calling at such an unseemly hour: nobody knew that I had begun to write at night at *Carteles*, a nighthawk of criticism in his eyrie. I picked up the black and rotund receiver (they could kill you with it: un coup de grâce de telephone), raised it to my ear, and a low voice mumbled musical and memorable: "Hi. How are you?" It was Margarita of course: Margie's gun. There's no other, there was no other like her. But I was so amazed that she had found me at the magazine at that unusual hour that I had to make sure: Meg the sniper, Peg the crackshot.

"Who's this?"

"It's Margarita, a magic wonder."

"Then you're magic Wanda, escaped from Ouida."

"Just Margarita."

"My magic Rita! A creature for a critic. My most magic write!"

I could have punned all night! To celebrate this auditive but tactile contact with Margarita, *Marguerite des marguerites*, I was willing to become a Seigneur de la Môle—little did I know that then. But now her voice sounded happy, her tone festive: it all seemed very inviting, ready for fucking. Accessible to scrutiny and screwing, as Silvio Rigor would say. Being a disciple of both Ortega and Gasset is an asset but Silvio was a gass. But how did she know I would be there—*here*?

"I just guessed." She was a guesser. "I was alone, I wanted to talk to you, and I knew immediately where to find you. As simple as that."

Sentiments more than presentiments. Predilections rather than predictions. Intuition not tuition. She was a guest.

"When are we getting together?" I wanted to know. Perhaps tonight? It's a good night for night games. Shapes and things to come. Things that go bang in the night. But all there was was a silence followed by her speaking in a comically serious voice. Women *really* kill me.

"Well, darling, in reality we're not going to see much of each other in the future. In fact, not at all. I won't be seeing you anymore. That's what I wanted to tell you. I'm going, my dear, to far Oriente tomorrow." Wander: escape as in *huída*. "But I wanted you to know it, I'm going with my girlfriend. You know which. The one—"

"Yes, I know which witch."

"Never mind that. What counts is that the two of us are going together. I plan to spend some days at her house in Bayamo. Then I'm returning to Caracas via Havana. You can call it a farewell voyage. A last good-bye to the provinces."

369

"Or a second honeymoon," I said more mortified than wishing to mortify.

"Or *the* honeymoon. Why not? After all, if I asked her to go with me to Venezuela she wouldn't hesitate for a split second. You know what? It wouldn't be a bad idea to ask her. Not a bad idea at all. Coming to Caracas."

A carcass in Caracas, I thought. But I said nothing. Her tone was purely provincial: a pure provincial-town player. An awful actress. Worse than the actress in the movie I'll have to shoot at dawn.

"Aren't you going to say something? After all, dear, it's probably the last time we're going to talk."

I remained silent. Lack of breath more than of words.

"Dearest, say something to me. Come on. Wish me well. Tell me to break a leg. Anything."

This stagy vulgarity of the unwell-wisher was like a verbal ball rubbing. An oral hood in all likelihood. Who's afraid of big but dead Thomas Wolfe?

"I wish you well. Wherever you may go, with whomever, blessed be thy name—whatever it is." Adieu, Artemidosa.

I knew the importance she gave her names.

"Thanks," she said and hung up. Our love was an umbilical cord and she had just cut it with a click. I couldn't continue working that night and the critical chronicle turned into a photo collection of starlets, more or less dressed, courtesy of Twentieth-Century Fox ("Fox in the Chick Coop" was the title), with more or less naked descriptions in crude, cruel captions. What had begun as literature had ended as publicity. Once more love, vulgar veneris, had come to ruin the possibility of a perfect paragraph—but I would have given all literature to achieve such valid vulgarity!

I heard from Margarita again in an unexpected manner. About a week later a telegram arrived at *Carteles.* Its delivery surprised me because, though I received letters from readers (most of them angry), I didn't think they'd be in such a hurry to communicate with me as to do it by telegram. Besides, it was addressed to my proper name, not to my *nom Daguerre* for pictures. I opened it and the message almost bowled me over. It said:

TIME AND DISTANCE HAVE LED ME TO REALIZE I'VE LOST YOU
VIOLETA DEL VALLE

The words must have been heartfelt but their effect was irresistible derision. Laughter in daylight. Writing that open poem and signing it with such a name and giving it all to the telegraph operator at the Bayamo post office was a daring and hard act to follow. For years I kept that tender telegram with its sick sense. Elsewhere I've made jokes about its text but in the context it was moving. Evidently it meant the end of Margarita, now lost in her pompous pseudonym. I knew that our relationship was going to end sooner or later, but I didn't want it to end in such a literary, "poetic," *relativist* way. Had she been reading Eliot in the loo? British can can. Toilet poems. Nevertheless I was resigned to that loss, knowing besides that I'd probably never find another woman like her: I had reached my sexual peak beside her, on top of her. She was a kind of climax after which everything would be twilight loves, changing partners, positions. If you do this, I'll do that. Nothing unites people more than a separation. Thus I devoted myself not to cultivating my garden but to caring for my wife, a potted plant. All that attention almost made me into a widower. One night I took her to visit the Almendroses' house, since Néstor was going to New York to study the wild life. We walked all along El Vedado because I had read that it was good for pregnant women to walk and my wife had been condemned to stay indoors all that time I spent with Margarita, sitting or lying down with her barrel belly growing each day and seemingly also each night. The thin girl I had married became an obese woman, her slender neck lost amid the fat, her gracefully curved back now a hump—only her hands conserved their original grace.

We chatted with Néstor's parents, model monogamists, the only couple I knew to be united by fidelity (my father, sneakily, continued his hidden hot adventures), they talking about maternity, implying paternity in passing. Even Néstor, a bachelor but not celibate, took part in the conversation and their solid solidarity made me feel like a scoundrel, a lewd Don Juan. My docile wife smiled before the Almendroses' admirable model of love—which I now appeared to emulate, seeing myself reflected in that domestic mirror, radiant in my image of a libertine without making any progress, calling a rake a rake. Taking Línea Street, we walked all the way back home. But she was barely able to climb the Avenida de los Presidentes hill, gasping by the time we reached the top of the avenue—and suffocating as we made it up to the fourth floor without a break and a breath, her face all purple, almost mauve. But, after a while, thanks to my mother's solicitude—with her four childbirths she knew about pregnancies and labor pains—she got her air back, thank God. I would have hated to become a widower! Better a father.

Asleep, deep in dreams, I was violently awakened at midnight (or perhaps it was already morning: it's always midnight for the sleeping sloth: I too lived in Hibernia) by my wife sitting on the bed and moaning, moving her body as if about to vomit, convulsed: she looked like a gasping fish ashore, but it was labor contractions. I had already seen them in the movies, *Birth of a Baby* or something or other. (Was it at the Niza or at the Monte Carlo?) Besides, my mother confirmed it with a prompt, precise prognosis: parturient pains. We were a medical family indeed. At that hour, at that ungodly hour, I had to leave the bed, get dressed, and go looking for a taxi, while my mother packed my wife's maternity gear in the small suitcase bought ad hoc or wherever.

Fortunately the god who watches over early-morning taxi searchers,

Hermes, favored me. I found a taxi waiting, throbbing. I, tired, myopic, throbbing too, and hesitating between two wives, hailed it as a savior. We reached the clinic (the one with the impressive name) in time—or perhaps too early. At the hospital there was a doctor on duty who explained to me that these were merely the first labor contractions, that there were to be others yet and until they had the regularity of I don't remember how many stabs of pain a minute (a very scientific way of measuring) there was no chance of expulsion. (That's what he said: science speaking.) Therefore, I could go back home if I wished since, once my wife had been admitted, I had nothing to do there but be in the way (scientific bad manners), so I returned home. Then I went to Caracas—to *Carteles.* Not to work because, when I explained to Ortega (not the Gasset one) my situation, he advised me to take the day off or whatever time was necessary. I was liberated from my daily galleys! The duet sung by Rine Leal and me, "Oh, how I hate to study journalism!" was followed by the aria, "Oh, how I hate to read these crime proofs!" a plainsong I wouldn't leave behind until I quit proofreading forever, almost three years later, to become like Errol Flynn a full-fledged film pirate, or Robin the Hood garbed in green.

I returned home in time for lunch, the moveable feast now an anniversary: the birth of emotions. Then I calmly marched down the avenue like a couple of swells to Twenty-third Street, walking leisurely to the expensively lettered Maternidad Privada de El Vedado (deeper breath), scientific clinic for suckers, private maternity ward. Along the way I found the sky cloudy (I always have my head in the clouds), overcast, and filled with those bulging dark clouds Silvio Rigor would always call clouts. They were grouping mostly over the sea, which had lost its everlasting flat blue, later streaked with the purple seam of the eternal Gulf Stream, never mauve. But I didn't pay any more attention to these smoke signals than I would a full moon: seascapes for Debussy, sounds on Juliet's balcony or bed, visions on the word by Honey, due the moment you mention the noun *sea* or even the article *the, thé dansant.* I'm fed up with that thalassic fauna!

The moment I reached the clinic and heard a long, loud cry I recognized my wife—though I'd never heard her scream before. She was more primeval than primipara. It was like a desperate version of Juliet's lovemaking. I looked for the reception desk (which wasn't in the entrance but to one side) and they informed me that Dr. Fumagalli, the director himself, was taking personal charge of the delivery. How deferent. In a little while Dr. Fumagalli appeared. There was something odd about him, but I wasn't sure what it was until I realized it was his head. He had not a deformed but an ill-formed head, elongated, with a skull like a blimp, which he tried to counterbalance with round dark tortoise-shell eyeglasses and a thick mustache, also dark. This made him look scientific on the one hand (the glasses) and slightly sinister (the mustache) on the other, while the rest of his dirigible head was prevented from taking

372

flight by the double anchor of the mustache and the round tortoise-shell specs. Different. The heady head of the clinic told me there was absolutely nothing to worry about, that it was an easy delivery, that I should take a seat. *Donaferentis.* The best place, furthest from the cries, was the wide porch with disorderly ordered columns. The clinic was installed not in a modern building ad hoc but, contradicting the pretension of its name, in an old mansion of El Vedado—though its adjective, private, must have come from the neighborhood. Here I sat in an enormous wicker and nylon chair—to watch it rain, because it was raining torrentially—and in Havana this adverb means something! It was the end of summer. Upon saying this phrase to myself I was repeating the disguise elaborated by the press and approved by science (from the National Observatory, secular dome across the bay) and sanctified by the Church (from the Belén College Observatory, Jesuitic enclave: astronomy under the Cross) that on this tropical island, in the torrid zone, there were seasons and not seasoning. In reality there were only two climatic periods, the rainy and the dry. The dry spell was over. Now the rains came.

Every time it rains something happens after the rain, right after the rain stops. It's not always a rainbow. But something always happens after the rain. Not necessarily something evil or good either. What I'm saying is that something happens after it lets up. Perhaps it's only the memory of the rain. Perhaps it's what the rain really left behind, like the silt of a happening. It was then that a nurse—female, thin, ugly—came too: to bring me a cup filled with an evil-looking rusty water. It was steaming hot. "Tea," said the nurse and disappeared. She was no ghost, she simply moved swiftly. So much so that she went away before I had time to tell her that I didn't like tea. In fact, I hated tea. But suddenly, with the rainstorm raging outside, I felt a certain perverse pleasure in sipping tea while it rained. Not many people in Cuba could boast of having a teacup in a tempest. Inversion is what they call that figure of speech. But in Spanish an inversion is synonymous with an investment. I invest in these small private inversions expecting to be word wealthy one day. In the meantime I drank tea while the storm raged on.

Watching the rain fall I almost fell asleep myself: what with the rounding, rocking rhythm of the rain all around me adding to my leftlover lack of sleep from last night. Sleep, shlep, splash. At last the dissonant chords of my wife woke me up to a wake alas! But the mournful cries were more frequent, as predicted. Nobody told me they were to become higher and closer: louder. I never went to the opera before but this much I could tell: she was no coloratura. A new nurse (or perhaps the old one after being caught in the rain: she was uglier—if that could be possible: my God, what an expensive clinic this was and yet so crummy it couldn't afford one decent-looking nurse!) came to me abruptly. She told me that she had just broken water. For a dumb moment I thought she was talking about the rain and herself as its creator: a weather word. Or worse, akin to break wind. Earthwake up!

373

It was a medical metaphor: my wife was giving birth and they were asking me if I wanted to watch! This is the dawn of the age of the eye and they offered me a stall seat for a new spectacle, childbirth. *Son et lumière! Dar a luz.* Light not in August but early in September. Here comes my baby—and without a net! Look, daddy! Head first! I followed the nurse to a room that in another era must have been the living room and was now an operating theater. There, on a surgical table, center stage, was my wife struggling amid cries, her only means of communication: birth is always primeval. She screamed and they put a rubber mask over her face. She stopped screaming. They withdrew the mask and she screamed and screamed again. Back to the mask and heavy breathing. Stop. It must have been some form of anesthesia, but it seemed to me that in her silent lapses she wasn't screaming only because the mask was suffocating her howling. More cries, more gag. The perfect cure for bold sopranos. Spotless in surgical linen and white mask, Dr. Fumagalli didn't even look in my direction, busy with the delivery as if it were a difficult work of art: the birth of Venus but more out of blood, pierced placenta, and broken water than out of foam. But Botticelli or not, the good doctor owed me an explanation about his poor part, his odd art: this bad birth. After all, I had paid for my wife to give birth without pain and here she was, not only in pain but in a lot of pain and expressing it screaming her head off. Paindora's Box. Unable to bear that atmosphere of improvised performance in impeccable costume, I tried to leave the dying room, where there was a confusion that was anything but scientific, orderly, and sane. As a matter of fact it all seemed to enact that metaphor to which I would resort in a not distant future: the chaos that must have reigned on board the *Titanic* when they counted lifeboats and heads. I returned to the porch, where with the same inevitability of things natural it had stopped raining. Order. *Calme. Voluptas.*

The sun was setting in absentia, a twilight by default: it had rained on the parade of red tropical fires that always tend to become silkscreen copies of the image of hell according to De Mille—those that Juliet used to collect on her honeymoon. There was instead a predominant, dominant greenish hue filtering through glaucous clouds: a peaceful aura reigned now after the rain, all bathed in green light—as if we all were inside a fishbowl whose glass bowl we didn't see anymore.

Visions of Venus! Night had not yet fallen when another nurse came to tell me that I was the happy father of a little girl. Just justice: surrounded always by women I would be continued in woman. *Che será, seraglio.* I entered the room: a small room: it was now a becalmed room and not the disorderly operating theater that had once been a quiet drawing room or a noisy *salon* but never the theater of pain and panic. I saw first my wife, still fat but obviously deflated—and the first thing that occurred to me was that the swelling had gone with her screams after breaking water, whatever that was. From somewhere in the wings they produced a baby, made of foam rubber, a prop of course—no, wait! It's moving! It's alive! My daughter if she moves. The faceless nurse said something about teeth and the general surprise about it. But I was more frightened by the grimace she made when she smiled. The most amazing part, though, was that her eyes were open and were green. Crystal-clear green! Neither my wife nor I had green eyes and I definitely had to discard the possibility that her mother had been unfaithful to me with a green-eyed milkman. Those green eyes were, in fact, another form of adultery: they were the eyes of Margarita, Violeta del Valle, whatever was the name of that woman who had been so close—she had been inside me, not I inside her—and was now so far away. Then they returned the little girl to the place whence she originated—backstage. (A modern clinic this though contained in an ancient house: the babies never shared their mother's room after being born.) Giving my wife a lame excuse, Byronian that I was, I abandoned her room, left the motherly manor, and limped down Twenty-third Street, seeking, curiously, a place to get drunk —not precisely to celebrate my daughter or drink to my wife's health but to the memory. Memory lame. Now at the end of that street there's a slope aslant the seawall. Going down that ramp, called with an excess of imagination La Rampa, I saw that there were several nightclubs. One might be the one. It was sheer beginner's luck that on turning down O Street as if falling into a black hole I found the bar that only a lustrum later was going to have all the luster of sin in its name but now was a loud, lackluster Cuban-American bar: hybrid, inebriate. I went in and walked nonchalantly to the *barra*, a better word for bar than just bar. The bartender welcomed me, smiling like old chums. Be debonair. I waved.

"Hi, James."

He nodded, still smiling.

"I'm a different man, James."

"Sorry, sir."

"Don't be, James, please."

"I mean my name's not James, sir."

"It isn't?"

"No, sir. It's Santiago."

"Pity. Well, never mind. I'm still a different man."

"Are you, sir?"

"Yes. I'm a different man and so are you now."

"If you say so, sir."

"Polite for a Cuban barman, aren't you?"

"I'm Asturian, sir."

"Sorry about that."

The Asturian cycle is over.

"That's all right, sir. No one's to blame. What's it going to be?"

No longer vicariously into American stichomythia, a myth, but seated precariously on a high stool that was too tall for me, my bony hands on the mottled mahogany *mostrador,* a counter to steady myself even before having had one drink, a seasick sailor on shore, I ordered the only concoction I could order on that occasion. At least it seemed like the right stuff at the time. I wasn't going to ask for an Alexander. So—

"A Margarita, please."

Suddenly alien, the bartender looked at me with confusion—or was it misunderstanding? He squinted but that didn't make him any wiser—just like James Finlayson. Double take, double talk, double think.

"A what?"

"A margarita."

But it wasn't the capital M that bothered him, it was the whole damn name. The nondrinker pursuing the undrinkable. Double drink.

"Sorry, brother, what's that made of?"

He was no more a brother to me than I to Abel, obviously, but a twin to the waiter at Ciro's, the one in furs. His brother's barkeeper.

"Forget the margarita."

Though I lacked Margarita I didn't want to appear lackadaisical. "Bring me a Cuba Libre then. In a dirty glass."

The last line was a wisecrack said with more hope than zing. But it really wasn't a celebration or the time for daiquiris, such a festive drink, beginning with its aspect contrary to the tropics, an iceberg from tip to bottom. The brim of the glass always lined with frozen sugar, a true icing plus the icy surface of the drink, rather like a glacier—damn it! Damn! Damn! How I miss that torrid day when I melted Margarita's ice cream! Steady, boy. Even the shape of the glass itself, fit for champagne, was a reminder as remembered from the mock toast in *La Traviata* when the dipsomaniac in *The Lost Weekend* went to the opera. In Havana gaseous cider was always drunk on champagne occasions from wine glasses. The holiday it gives you just to look at it! As it was joyous to watch Margarita naked, a marguerite smiling margaric grins with all her lips, mouth, and vulva like damp oysters in the dark. She glowed all over, this Iceland poppy transplanted to South America, to an island named like her where they fish for pearls. Symmetry thy name is woman. A glory to behold! I don't mean her now, an asymmetrical pearl, I mean the daiquiri the bartender is mixing this very moment. It's a damn milkshake made of rum and crushed ice, not poured but shaken. It's a beaut! Even to me who's not a drinker. Which is why it was so queer for me to be doing what only drunkards do—drinking alone.

There was nobody in the bar except a daiquiri-drinking couple who occupied a distant table to make my solitude greater than a song. Why is this man drinking alone if he's no lush? *Rara avis bibere.* If we were at least two we could sing, the *cabrón* consul and I. What would you like to sing, sir? "Il Brindisi from *Traviata,* act one. Sorry I'm so late." It's all right, sir. What key? "Try C Minor. I can't afford more." Very well, sir. At a one, at a two, at a three! *Libiamo, libiamo ne' lieti calici*—what the hell is that! Italian for let's drink, let us drink, the champagne glass is now overflowing—or lyrics to that effect. Now Violeta sings the second stanza and the chorus joins festively, champagne glasses in hand. All together now! They all sing to love and life—and death, eventually. Death always comes in the end. They should be singing to jealousy, but that's in another opera, though the wench also ends up dead. The strumpet theme played by the trumpet. Virtue dies before vice.

Ah, il vizio! From vice into eternal darkness, into fire, into ice. From ice into eternal drunkenness and back into vice. *Dar a Dante.* But vice is so strange a state. In any case it's a strange thing to be one. To be what? A vice. Vice presidents, viceroys, men who never achieve fullness. That sort of thing. Vice is a monster of so frightful a mien. Amen. Wait! I think I've got it. Life is a monster of such fearful means! She has ways of making you talk and in the end she justifies the means. The means, the bads, and the uglies. But you can't complain, bud. After all, you've been alive most of your life, haven't you? One can do worse than that, you know. Knights must fall too. Now toward the barman comfortably leaned the stool, like a tower of vice about to fall *e caddi come corpso morto cade.* Caddy! Men are never so serious, thoughtful, and intent as when they are at stool. That's so Swift, the other was too much of a Pope to swoon. Vices of versa. Opposite English both, contrary natures, odd fellows. What about you? Who, me? Yes *you. Cameriere!* I'm the odd man in. My God! I've been talking nonstop since the dawn of woman. *Please,* somebody stop me before I talk more! Waiter! Wait! I also do Don Juan in different vices, voices. Let me see. Ovid in exile on his isle, Petronius Arbiter bloodless but not lifeless, Johann Faustus (isn't it ironic that this avatar's major feat was to predict a "very bad year" for the *Venezuelan* expedition?) and Mañara and Mañara and Mañara. Too many voices. My Master's Vice. My mouth is very dry now and so is my throat. So's my soul. SOS. Thirst is worse than thrift. Drift. Adrift. On the extreme of consciousness. Now. Daddy!

I should have been celebrating my fatherhood (hava havana), since at that time I considered paternity a privilege, not a life's sentence: children, like crime, never pay. I had proclaimed my wife's pregnancy to my friends' joy and to my mother's greatest content. Only one candid voice wasn't in tune with that candy chorus—Ortega, editor, my mentor, had repeated sarcastically my stout statement that I was going to be a father: "So you're going to have a child?" Ortega, who always remained formal with me, said this as if I had just contracted an incurable disease that was not only long but painful—and contagious too. But I wasn't celebrating my daughter's arrival: I was bemoaning or rather lamenting Margarita's departure, even more painful since it was a double flight: she had gone with her gifted girlfriend and they were perhaps already in bed (peasants go to bed early everywhere) at their labor of love, or rather, sexual chore, Margarita under (I always imagined her in her so active yet passive position) while her fiendish friend slipped and slid slickly on top of her, obscenely rubbing against her, trying to produce the penis that nature had denied her (but which I was born with), mimicking with that frottage the penetration I achieved so often effortlessly. But Margarita was not letting herself be had passively. She was responding with urgency, turgently corresponding—she was a correspondent! It's a common notion everywhere (but especially in Havana then) that there's no cuckold worse than the man who's been deceived not by one but by two women: perhaps it's this double woman, fully à deux, that makes public punishment so severe. So Severa. Severed Head with Horns. Cuckolds can live in bliss of ignorance. Not if Bliss is the name of the other woman. Besides I had been forewarned. Served with notice. My woman and her woman were now making the bug with eight legs: they do the spider in different poses. It was my own fault that she'd become Ariadne. The unsexed monster Ariachne in her webby labyrinth. Unpenised yet unpunished. Not castrati but unique eunuchs singing, singando like marimbas, with contralto voices made of timber, their timbre of wood. Clarinet players in the night but with no instrument. Like Othello I should kiss the instruments of their pleasure. I should have made it a trio. Triolissimo. Now they are a female duo singing a cappella. That's the way the world will go. Virago mundi. Virgo, virago, go! Now, this very minute, somebody other than I was going over the transom in the dark, daringly. Gentle Genitalia inter pares. Swanking, an instance of swans wanking.

Like the base Indian, I threw a pearl away. My Margarita, my! was a pearl and I didn't know it! Etymology, the deviation of words. Worlds. Deviants. Catty people. Cats in hell's chance. Potions pottle deep. I understand a fury in your words, sir, but not the words. Speak the spite. To make myself clear to myself I reverted to a literary character betrayed by his own crosslines, all hidden meaning and pregnant patter. I'll deliver. Once again I was enacting the role of the suntanned playboy, in color, made a fool more than a cuckold by a woman and a woman. Blonde on blonde or two dark ladies in a single sonnet—what's the difference? They're all women wearing masks. Now the name of the bar, Johnny's Dream, became Dirty Dick's. Dikes served after sex o'clock only. Drinks that money can't buy. Dreams. Dreams are on me, ladies. No, dreams are in the house. On the house. Some dreams later my man St. James came back bartenderly.

"Anything else?"

Bebe said the voice but I heard vive.

"Everything else?"

"I mean, is there anything else you want, sir?"

I pretended to think it over—but only a little bit over. Let's not overdo anything, shall we? Agreed? A greed. "What about some cither?"

"Cider? Sure. Let's see, we have hard cider, sweet cider, and champagne cider. You name it."

"Not that cider. Cither, zither." I spelt the name but not its spell. "Zeether music."

"Music? On the radio or from the juke box or piped?"

"To drink, my good man. Here. Now, over the counter."

378

"To *drink? Music* to drink?"

"That's the idea. Haven't you heard the phrase the evening air is like wine tonight?"

"Never in my life, sir. Besides this is not a wine bar."

"Never mind the wine! Music is like zither tonight. Haven't you seen *The Third Man* yet?

"Not tonight."

There must be a third man. That's what the loud, lewd logician proclaimed. If there's a second, then there must be a third. A third man. Is that clear? Am I making myself ferpectly clear? Crystal clear. Like glass. Pour. Down.

"But he might show up later. Who knows?"

"Who will?"

"Your third man."

Now he looked at me queer in the eye—and winked! I winked back of course but I didn't like it. I didn't like it at all. But if I didn't wink, what was I supposed to do with my eye? Gouge it out with my screwdriver? Besides, I was drinking daiquiris. Was I?

"What are you going to drink in the meantime?"

I looked at him straight in the eye. The one he blinked at me.

"In these mean times let's drink to Violeta Valli, the actress!"

"Is she Cuban?"

"Half and half. Half Cuban, half Italian. A cross. To bear."

"Is she any good?"

"Good? That category won't do, mate. She *creates* her own canon, you see. Naked she's unique but when she's fully dressed she can be terrible. A panther in reverse."

There must be a third man, sure. But what if it's a second woman? Top banana. Caught in the act.

"That's too bad."

"You can say that again but please don't. I don't want to hear it again."

I grew silent so suddenly. But he didn't, diminishing my laconic stature. Stoic men shouldn't talk.

"What are you going to have now?"

"I don't know. What are you going to have?"

"Me? Nothing of course. I'm the bartender here, remember?"

"I don't want to remember."

"Well, mister, what are *you* going to have?"

I didn't like his tone. But then again I'm perhaps a bit too musical. I carried the tune, though.

"Something I'm keen on. Too keen. Something green."

Yes, that's it! Something verdant like my valley. How green was *my* Valli! At least her eyes were. So was her forbidding, hidden husband's face. Green and mean. Like a dream, that night. Green Valley, green nightmare. Light Mare. Dreams last longer but nightmares can be indeli-

379

ble. Like birthmarks. Or lovemarks. Green-eyed is the worst monster.
"Though green, I want her green—"

"You want a peppermint frappé then?"

I looked at him. A bartender. Behind bars for life. A prisoner of my desire. Better to reprieve him, governor.

"What about some absinthe?" I asked him as a parole.

"Absent you said or accent?"

"Forget it, Saint-Iago. I'm absintheminded tonight."

I forgot the French interdiction of 1915. A flavored spirit. No wormwood though. Too late to save Verlaine, though it didn't do Lautrec any good. At least he wasn't any taller for it. Pity!

"Give me *un pernod* then."

"Per no?"

"Pernod is a greenish imitation absinthe. When you add water it turns milky. It tastes like liquorice and has a good uplift."

"Sorry, brother. We don't have any left."

"You know what? This is becoming a rather long repartee."

In fact it had become too long already.

"What do you want then?"

"Something good to spook memory."

"Spook memory?"

"Yeah. Give me anything to forgive and forget."

"Then, sir, it's Lethean water what you need."

Did he say *that*? Did he *actually* say that? *Lethean* water? My God, waiters are worse than writers!

"All right, that'll do."

"What will?"

"Lethe water."

"Lethe, sir?"

"Lethe, Lethean, lethal—any water."

"Seltz sir?"

"No, not Alka-Seltzer! Firewater. Vodka, whiskey, aguardiente. Anything. But make it double and make it quick."

"On the double."

"That's the spirit."

Sat I never on so high a stool that I sat but upon my tale. The rest of the night was pascalian silence.

Next day everything returned to normal. It was clear in the morning, cloudy at midday, and rained in the afternoon. The nights were damp and filled with press previews. Nothing really happened, really, except in the house of dreams for hire. No more wandering along meandering streets late at night alone. No more drinks at Johnny's Dream solo. No more lines borrowed in order to live in disorder in this order. No more life copied from books. No copycat's nine lives like tales anymore—and of course no sea change for me. Never again.

My wife came home from the clinic, armed with the advice and prescriptions of Dr. Fumagalli, all mustache and glasses and zeppelin-like head, who answered my questions by saying that my wife had had a difficult but natural parturition, not at all abnormal for a beginner and a healthy offspring (*his* word). Nothing to worry about. Really. One hundred and fifty pesos, please. A swindle, for sure, but a legal one and, what's more, a scientific swindle. My mother was delighted to have at least a little girl to take care of. My father made a few comments about the fact that nobody ever told him anything about anything. (I hadn't a clue what he meant by that.) But as usual his comments were on God knows what subject and nobody paid any attention to them. After all, with my mother busier than ever, he'd have more time now to dedicate to his treasured spyglasses and pet peeping. I continued my routine as proofreader (those galling galleys!) during the day, and some nights I wrote my reviews for the magazine, both jobs oddly done not far from the maddening crew at the printshop but certainly too close to the linotypists for comfort—they were all getting more and more avid.

Ovid more than *divo* was I engaged in those labors of my excess in daytime, read and write by rote, when the telephone rang—and the call was for me, which wasn't strange. "It's a woman's voice," said Rine, gagging the receiver and thus shutting up the disembodied lady. Not for a moment did I suspect it could be my wife because according to Rine the caller used my pseudonym. Which admirer could she be? Known or unknown? Both. It was Margarita, of course, who had vanished from my life but not from my memory. Memory spoke now. Her voice was as caressing as before and my reaction followed sweet. The soul is weak, you see. So was her tone. She wanted to sea (sic) me. (And the misprint as pun was very appropriate: she was water all around me, making me into an island where all desires wreck ashore: man as a woman-made isle.) To *see* me, she needed to see me, when could she see me. Where could we get together? Thus she moved from requesting to direct action: we *had* to see each other. Not at her house (she would explain) but on the corner of Soledad, that very day, that afternoon, now—and I saw her. The flesh is weak but the vision of flesh can be very powerful. It was.

She was prettier than ever but she was no vision: she looked very physical indeed. I suppose that contrary to the Latin not latent lesbians I knew (figures of Havana's cultural life, a zoo of Sapphos, each more of a boss than the melodious mistress at Lesbos, real inverted matrons), for Margarita the trip with her friend, the bed they shared, the caresses they gave each other, playing not the spider but being both moths in the dark, had really beautified her. Or was it the passive posture? Or pose rather: cobwebs spun by spiders for the weary fly. I told her so. I mean, I didn't appraise in disdain her love life but praised her beauty highly. I didn't have to lie: she was ravishing. At least she could have ravished me. My God, was she beautiful! She smiled sadly and said:

"I suppose that wisdom and pain, if you survive them, are a form of beauty."

It must have been live lines from one of her Venezuelan television scripts, soapsuds. She had been fed her own corn, as the radio had formed more than deformed the sound of the voice who invented radio love, TV was the TB of the soul for her, video her VD, Pandora's Box but without the hope. Should I tell her? But now she took a finger to her lovely lips and put it straight into her mouth. For a moment I thought she was going to suck it. After all *Baby Doll* was all the rage in Havana then—out of her cradle endlessly a suckling. Suck your finger, little doll. Sucklethumb. Sugarbaby. HoneySuckleSuck. Cunt! No, not cunt: cunning lingus. She stopped sucking her finger.

"Sweets are killing me!"

Had she read my mind? Or read the book already?

"What?"

"Sweets are bad for me."

"What's the matter?"

"I ate a candy bar. Now something's wrong with my teeth. Damn!"

Was that the pain she was talking about? I asked her.

"Silly!" was all she said, tongue in cheek. Now I understood her talk of wisdom: she had a pain in her wisdom tooth. Tooth, truth: too true. Her naked body exposed to scrutiny on the bed of cheap one-night hotels, she looking like a patient etherised on a truth table. But what if she were Vronsky playing the role of Anna Karenina. I should call her Anna Cariesnin then. Cunt Vronsky. Dom Karenina. DK. Decay.

"Did you get my telegram?"

What was she talking about? Sweets to a sweet. Truth's sweet serum. Probably her toothache was affecting her thinking.

"What telegram?"

"The one I sent you from Bayamo, remember?"

"Ah, *that* telegram. Yes, I got it."

"What did you think of it?"

What did she want? Literary appraisal? Or a sentimental evaluation? Untruth serum. What had begun with a letter ended in a telegram. Sign of the times. Wordcount.

"It was very you," I said, avoiding any opinion with such a precise yet vague phrase. Critical serum.

"I wanted to see you," she said. Here she paused for a while, as if she had forgotten what she wanted to see me for. But she hadn't forgotten. "For the last time. I'm going tomorrow."

"Oh," I said, a word I often repeat: a lack of sound and fury signifying everything.

"Yes, I'm on my way to Caracas. But I wanted to tell you something first," she stopped for a pause. Then: "Remember that day you accompanied us to the doctor?"

"To the abortionist?"

"Well, yes, if that's what you want to call him. He's really a very good doctor, very dedicated to his profession, very understanding."

I didn't say anything. Faced with that praise of an expert in curettages as if he were Dr. Schweitzer playing doctor for his natives I had nothing to say. But I couldn't help imagining the abortionist palpating the organ at night. Performing an abortion con brio, allegro abortando.

"What I wanted to tell you is difficult for me to say and I didn't want to tell you. But I think that you definitely should know."

Another pause.

"It wasn't my sister who had an abortion that day. It was me."

There was yet another pause that I should have called an after-pregnancy pause. I looked at her upon such a revelation, plus pause, out of *A Kiss Before Dying,* seen not long ago at the Atlantic for professional reasons which had now become personal motives. But she didn't look like Joanne Woodward with her blonde, close-cropped California hair, blue eyes, and moronic, or innocent, smile. She didn't look like her at all. She looked more like her sister, dark Virginia Leith, who belonged beautifully in the fifties—that era when life itself was seen in CinemaScope. She was as slenderly plump as Margarita, this Virginia Lee. But she wasn't the pregnant one, remember? It was *Joanne.* It was her *sister* Joanne, do you hear? Her sister! Joanne Woodworm. So I wouldn't have to get myself into all that trouble to kill her. Her *baby,* I mean. I wouldn't have to kiss her before dying. Murder is messy. I was saved by a movie in the last reel. Holy cow! That was close! Real close! We had so much in common. A lot. I said sex, she said sex. But then she had to bring love into the affair. So, if I said lust, she said love again, and feelings and affection and the cream of human kindness. She said. "And jokes," said Robert Wagner. "Don't forget about jokes." I smiled, Wagner-like. Try-stand. "Jokes can glue a plot," I revealed. I was going to tell Margarita my Marxist joke on unions and reunions, a familiar plot. It goes like this: "Oxen of the world, unite! You have nothing to lose but your yokes." But she never had what you could call a sense of humor. A sense of sex, yes, but not a sense of pun. Besides, she was waiting for my reaction not my erection or my derision. My reaction was of course utter amazement. Utterly faked, of course.

"You?"

"Yes, it was your child. It was also the first time in my life I had got an abortion. It's the first time anyone ever made me pregnant. That blood clot could have been your, our child."

I couldn't avoid remembering a sad song that says: "To think that that son of yours/Could have been also mine," despite her seriousness: she was so serious that she looked almost deadpan—or just dead. A deadpan tragedian, like Medea. But to become deadpan serious she had paused again, this time not dramatically as before but tragically, as befits Medea after killing at least one son. Her feelings were visible beneath the mask of her makeup. What could I say to her, not being skilled in tragedy, no Sophocles? I really thought it was terrible but I also refused to believe her. *Il gran rifiuto* is silence. I didn't say a word. You see, I couldn't.

Stammer the speech. I should have laughed like an irresponsible foetus.

"I thought it my duty to tell you," she told me. She was now about to cry. Oh my God! I hate to see women cry. It's not funny. Men crying is funny but not women crying. Tears isolate like any other stream. Besides, something always happens after the rain. Luckily she didn't sob but added: "That's all," a pause, "take care," another pause. "Good-bye."

A pose? No she simply turned around. She turned her back on me. Lotsa woman. In turn she turned into a column at the Apple Arcade. Nothing divides two people more than a common past. She just turned around and headed for her house next to the old cemetery: its wall was its tombstone now. I just stood there on the corner of Soledad, watching her, watching all the girl walk away. Just watching. This time I couldn't pick out any of the parts of her body to compose a memory: she was a human being. But I couldn't help noticing that her slip was showing.

That was the last time I saw her but not the last time I *heard* her. As in a radio serial version of herself, she said good-bye again but in voice only. I returned home sadder but freer, thinking along the way that Margarita's revelation made of my life a full circle: a lack of love that produces a green-eyed daughter, a green-eyed love that had its climax in abortion. It was all too pat. Too well-balanced, too symmetrical. There had to be an asymmetrical note somewhere, a dissonance, a cacophonous chord to resolve such complete harmony. I hate unison singing. I reached the conclusion that Margarita was lying. It wouldn't be the first time she had lied to me. Even her Sapphic story ended up seeming some sort of invention. Who saw her kiss? But I wasn't a hundred percent sure. I wanted a second opinion.

I consulted my friends as if they were oracles—but they turned out to be toilet-trained sphinxes with guesses. But what are friends for but to rewrite parallel lives to our own by rereading them? *Traduttore traditore*. All. Pearls before sin, Margarita to some sound advice. All Branly said was: "You're looking for the lost chord, buddy," but he pronounced *buddy, body*. I told Rine Leal the story of her alleged abortion and he found it to be a fake pregnancy. "She's an actress" was his last judgment. "Have no qualms. She's always on stage." I was going to correct his proofs as inadmissible evidence, claiming that she was on television not the theater, but I preferred his verdict of two. However, I told Silvio Rigor her recounting of her encounter with her girlfriend: the shared bed, the caresses in the dark, their trip to Bayamo together. "It's not an invention. It's the version of a perversion," said Silvio, and then stiff with Rigor mortis all over his upper lip, he added in clipped tones: "Our dancing *habaneras*, mac. Those who aren't tramps are vamps or have cramps. The rest are dikes." Margarita before sundries. Before all. Before nothing, before nothingness, before being.

One night—I don't remember if a week or two days later: time is memory—I was home, sitting in the living room four floors above the street with my mother and my wife, alone. We had already had supper and my brother had gone with Branly to some concert and my father had disappeared onto the dark balcony to hide in a corner, binoculars ready, on the prowl. As we still hadn't contracted TV but had lost the habit of overhearing the radio, and the record player, like all electrical appliances in the household, was out of order, we took refuge in conversation, which more than an art was among us an early stage of a craft. My mother loved to talk and my wife, as a conventual habit, sometimes recited litanies. I who talked a lot with my friends, practicing verbal crisscross or rather playing oral tennis matches (love naught, loveknot), and who also used to talk to talkative girls and loquacious women and note-taking old women: a garrulous garland, now kept mum before these two mothers. Having lost the custom of family reunions since I began to have literary gatherings, I listened and stared at my mother and wife getting into a long exchange about the novelty of certain kinds of wash and wear diapers and about the harmful friction against a baby's tender skin as opposed to the virtue of Mennen talcum powder for heat rashes. Fascinated, I was about to ask whatever happened to the Johnson baby —when the telephone rang abruptly, loudly, like a shot in a cathedral. Stand all! I got up quickly to answer it, and before hearing the voice on the other side of the void, I knew it was she. She had to be Margarita. There was a brief silence after my hello, and in that pause, dead phone in black in hand, I asked myself how she knew my number, which was private, which wasn't in the book, which I had never given her: of that I was sure. A backstreet lover is always ex-directory. Perhaps she knew my address but certainly not my phone number, and the company that had been such a stickler for rules that it refused even to give my address to the police already in possession of name and number, two years earlier, wasn't going to give my number now to her, just like that. It wasn't telephoning but telepathy. For it was she, no doubt about that: the very silence following my habitual hello had betrayed her. Finally, without having to say hello again, she spoke:

"I want to see you," she paused and for a moment I thought she was drunk: actually she had been crying, she was still crying: women don't heavy-breathe. "I have to see you. Let me see you. I need to talk to you."

She was once more on the verge of quoting the lyrics of one bolero or two but didn't quite quote any. There was a certain dignity not only in her tone but in her repetition: Greek tragedians knew a lot about decorum. "We have to see each other, to talk, today, tonight."

After my response as greeting I hadn't said anything else. I think I didn't even breathe. Now I observed, under the intense, tense light of the living room, floodlight bulbs hanging from the ceiling, my mother wearing a brown dress that didn't become her, sitting on the dark green sofa and my wife in a mauve gown in a wicker chair painted white, both still on the side of the room I had left to answer the phone. In fact they were very still, as if waiting for I don't know what: perhaps some distress signal coming from the phone. For my mother the telephone had substituted for the telegram as a source of sorcery—more often than not it was bad medicine. Weeping wires. But my wife should know better. As a matter of fact, I think she did know better. Mother and daughter-in-law looked absurdly, absolutely unreal: a waxwork family group in any Museum of Ideal Home. Awesome wax portrait! Both were actually looking at me, with keen curiosity at my rigid stance at the phone. I was waxworks to them too. I had said only hello and then responded to the voice of the void with utter silence: a still of the author as a young man. However, she, Margarita, continued: "I want to, need to see you. Tonight."

It was obvious that two verbs together were not going to advance her discourse or cause. Or change my course. Finally I said: "I can't."

"Please. I beg of you."

"It's absolutely impossible."

She was the sound. Mother and wife, the sight.

"I want to tell you that my friend is with me and if it weren't for her I would have committed a terrible act."

A folly à deux? An act against nature? Or against man? She didn't elaborate but I thought vaguely of suicide and then with precise horror —I remember it now as clear as the floodlit room—that she would come to my house *presently*.

"I'm sorry but I can't tonight."

"I'm leaving tomorrow. We won't see each other again, you know it. But I want to see you one more time. I've never begged a man."

"What about a woman?" Sing Sapphic strophes. Sappho's stuff. Sapphires. That's what I intended to say but didn't. What I said was: "I can't. Sorry. So long."

She, now without a trace of tears, had a last word: "Good-bye."

I think we hung up at the same time. Or at least that's what I like to think: coming to an end together. *Adieu à deux.* As Waldo Lydecker said, that was the last time I ever heard her voice. She was no Laura though. No shotgun of mine was going to kill her ever and this is no portrait of her either: more than a shooting art gallery was needed to erase her image. But what I best remember of that white night is that my wife, in the spotlight, never asked me who called. Neither did my mother. Ulysses at home, I'd stopped their ears with wax.

Days later, perhaps weeks later, months later maybe—memory is time—I was sitting for hours on end on a stool at a forgotten bar. No name on the souvenir. No memorable name at least, though there was a constant flame burning behind the counter and a wreath. So it must have been the monument to the unknown bar beneath the arcades: the arches of defeat or any other arches in this city of drunken columns, daisy arcades, apple colonnades. It was in there, thanks to the lousy rum and Coke, acid to melt pennies but not to erase the memories, I got stinking drunk thinking of Margarita, a pearl for this swigging swine, formerly a swain. Impossible not to think and remember and sense with memory all her sexual splendor in the green, her ardor, her ardent verdant eyes.

Also, of course, to celebrate, why not, the fault in her beauty, the stigmata, the breast she lacked, which made of the other breast a rare unique ferpection, *perfection,* damn it! The precious horn of the unicorn for a literary lion. *Mon Dieu,* her *droit!* Or was it left? I can't remember.

But I remembered the first dazzling vision in the theater's fruit cellar and the long chase through the years along the streets of Havana (mire, maze) and the encounter, the broken date, and my awkward stratagem that was nonetheless spidery effective: spinning my web for the wayward green fly. I thought of how I had won her and owned her and lost her and how possessing her had been an education, an apprenticeship, a master grade—though I didn't exactly know what for. *Gradus ad digressus.* Mock-Latin phrase, of course. All this and haven too was offered me by that Roman *à clef* who first said, *Courez, lentement, chevaux de la Nuit!,* which I cited, recited not in the bar but barging into the street and the night and the musing, walking in now, *night,* by myself, finding myself by myself in verse and worse: on hateful *Calle* San Lázaro, a *rue* to rue, a street I never learnt to love, not even like, though it was the street nearest to where she lived. She was gone but the street was there and will be there for me to pass. But I was compelled to hold my horses in the night for all of a sudden I was on beloved but somber Soledad, going down the deadend that ended at the wall of the cemetery of dead metaphors. Run, run fast, hearses of the night! I had reached her door, that dour, doorless doorway, climbed the steppes, the *steps* I had climbed before, after her, chasing her, that she climbed with me, the ones I saw her climb like a champ, alone, step by step: tap, tip, top. I was then a spectator of her body behind her back: the legs, the calves, the feet I never complimented her on (I should have, you know), only praising her other perfections: green eyes, scarlet lips, teeth like pearls before me. That girl was born for Technicolor, Mrs. Kalmus! But I stopped short right there, afraid of insulting her by praising the breasts that could only be singular. The breast. Knocker. Knock on the door. Hold your heart, knight! But before I had time to realize what I was doing drunk, repenting rapidly, suddenly sober, the door opened—and there was Margarita! It wasn't a ghost or a fullfigment of my imagination or a mirage. It was she, in 3D. In all the dimensions. Splendid spectacle! Weave, weave Nietzschean night, the moonlight in her hair! It was Margarita's return. Or she hadn't gone away as I had suspected, as she had made me believe. I had only thought so. Here she was! Just like Catalina. Margarita, only teller, *taller* now (probably high heels) but broader, with higher cheekbones and more slanty eyes. She recognized me and said with fuller lips:

"Oh, hi! How are you? Come in, come in."

But that wasn't her educated, low, caressing velvet voice: it was her sister's voice. It *was* her sister! Tatiana, Sebastiana, whatever her name was: Rosy, Russian, Rosicrussian. Anunshe. Not the other with the seared breast of a warrior woman. This was Isis' sis, now being hospitable. Come with me into the convent. She let me in. I've been, I thought, in a thousand furnished rooms before. Then she sweetly had me sit in one of the chairs covered once more with hideously chartreuse-green nylon. Obviously green ran in the family. There I was in full green-chartreuse regalia among panthers cavorting with unwary flies, flamingos, and before knowing what the hell I was doing in that fantastic zoo, I found myself crying—a unicorn in love. Unique corn. What's-her-name took my hand, and sat in the other equally hideous chartreuse-green nylon-covered chair. I let myself be dragged more by remorse than by gravity to the floor, where I fell crying as a dead body falls but with my head at the level of her knees, feeling all the pity in the world for myself by myself. She caressed my hair and said something. I told her in silence speak lightly I can hear young Daisy grow. But she wouldn't listen and had to say this to me:

"You're crying for her. I know."

Shit! She spoiled my fun, the nun. I stopped crying of course as soon as she mentioned my tears for Margarita. But I didn't remove my head, all face and tears, from between those shaved legs with clean clogged feet. She was wearing wooden sandals, sandalwood, slippers, called in Havana *chancletas:* another new word. When words collide. Slipping you are. Not me, my hand! What I did afterward was absurdly audacious: I caressed her leg, soft to the touch—but she didn't pull away her leg or my hand! She, like Night, stood still. Her complexion was pale, paler than Margarita's. Not too tar but two tarts, the sisters. Nuns. Black Irish from Saint Jack. Daisy O'Heaven, Daisy O'Hell.

"You know," she said not too softly or too subtly, "you have very fine hair. Like a baby's."

I didn't answer. What was I supposed to say to that—want to see where my hair is finer? I have a pubes just like a baby's but without the diaper. So I simply continued calmly caressing her leg, from the ankle to the knee. Sof, softly. Softy. Drunker than I thought but able was I: here I saw double. Two legs, equally soft. Soft you now, fair ophidian. My hand soft-pedaled between her knees to caress her thighs. Soft hand for very soft caresses: *deux Dumas avec doux doigts dans ses fines fesses.* Love in the place of feces. She took my hand but not the one caressing her, the other hand, the left I think. I'm not too good for hand signs. She stroked it—as my other hand hid between her legs, out of shame and into her body.

"And this scar?" she asked me. For a moment I didn't know what she was talking about. What scar? I've never been to war. I'm a pacifist and a coward: a certified objector. I didn't have no scars. I had never been wounded, nor been in an accident or in bar brawls. What's with the scar? But I saw her pointing to my hand and I looked and saw it too. Visibly white on my swarthy skin, on the back of my hand (playing poker?), between the thumb and forefinger, there it was. Uncanny! Margarita's memento, a mere scratch, converted into an indelible mark. Curious! I had forgotten all about it. Curiouser! Now I remembered the moment she cut into me, why she marked me. But, mark my words, for the life of me I couldn't remember what she said then. Scars last longer than words.

"It's nothing," I said to her sister. I insisted: "A manicure accident."

Corny cuticle, careless cutie. I would be lying to you if I say I didn't remember Margarita, cutting cutie that she was. I remembered her all right, there and then, but she was absent, gone with my monsoon that summer the waters broke, and she was now the stormy past. The present was her sister with her strange, strong beauty, reminding me of Margarita and at the same time making me forget her. She was like a dark version of Gene Tierney, my favorite film face: more unreal even than the Gene Tierney of the movie shadows, a version of life. A diversion, then a perversion. Laura, I leave you to heaven as I shave your legs with my razor's edge. Legs, let's go, let's. I picked myself up and her sister too to go to bed—where else? During the whole clinch of legs (shaved, unshaved) and arms and the array of lips and disarray of the senses and the sheets I didn't think once of Margarita or give much thought to this trampy trashy treason—but I was worried about being in bed with a version of utter aversion for me: a widow. Like the spider of her name she could kill: her glossy black beauty and her shiny scarlet spot on the belly were signs as deadly as sin. I saw myself knifed like her dead husband by Pepe (a butcher no doubt) for possessing this woman no less delectable (an expression picked up at the movies: when words collapse) than her vanished sister but much more dangerous.

When we finished it was all over. This time there was no sexual marathon or amorous bookkeeping and of course no *posada* to pay for. Nor do I remember how she was when naked between kisses: I never knew her hidden fault that was her greatest asset to be shown to the whole world. There was no passion or compassion, just sex: *ars amatoria*. I walked out of her room, out of the living room zoo and out of the perfectly hideous chartreuse-green house. Staggering, still drunk, putrid potion! I reached the corner of Espada (these Havana streets with symbols for a name: sword is the password: *clef de l'aube*) and looked at my hand, one or the other, in a reflex move: it was the right one. In the unerring streetlight I could see the pale scar on my skin and I thought that, after all, I had really been knifed in the back, of hand or mind: a last twist of the knife for her sister's sake. It was the beautiful Margarita herself, perfectly perfidious, bellicose but beloved, an amazon, who pierced me with her dagger.

EPILOG

MOVIES MUST HAVE AN END

I saw her. I saw her again. I saw her again years later, when it was apparently too late because she was already inside the *cine,* one more face among the lobby cards, in black and white but tinted. Wait! She hadn't gone in yet. No sirree! Nothing is more deceptive than these Havana deep purple or mauve twilights. Without the doubt of a shadow she intended to enter the picture palace, but she was still buying her seat. Or rather, a sexless and disembodied hand was offering her a ticket to the gods while she fumbled for coins in her purse, aping its gape with her mouth. Waitwaitwait! She was in fact looking for the money in the five-and-ten maze of her handbag, disregarding for a moment—as in oblivion or in the limbo of the absent-minded—the tantalizing ticket to the show. But, come to think of it, she could have already paid her fare and was now merely returning the change to her bag, pocketbook, purse—whatever—taking the ticket like a deft or daft patroness of the art of the cinema.

But it was all immaterial, really. What matters is that, before, she had her back turned (to me, to us) but now she was glancing at me and me only—though on the sly, out of the corner of her eye, like a silent movie vamp. That's the only way a single woman could look at a stranger in that Havana, west of the bay, nicknamed Felix but sometimes rather Deserta: that Arabia where she must have been living happily ever after before she met her fate in a movie. Back home her bedsheets could be her tent pitched in the desert of the night but here I had the cheek to abduct her, via Valentino.

She peeked at me obliquely while showing off her profile (before, she only showed her beautiful bare back) and the pale crescent of her ivory face: a *prima facies eburnea* that rose ever so gently over the dark horizon of the ticket box or booth or both. Her chin's sheen shone bright, her slanted eyes arching in a circumflex reflex, and that yellow shock of hair gleaming like new-mown hay (curly I believe, straight I think, but surely bleached) to frame her perfect features bathed in the iodine of the lobby lights. (Tinting too.) Finally her livid, long, languid neck stood out against the dark box office: a cool cameo displayed on black velvet. I don't know why, but for a moment I thought of a platinum version of Anna May Wong—an impossible casting indeed! But now, in a clearing of my jungle of puns, I can see she was an early punk.

She looked at me again for a moment (barely twenty-four blinks a second) and then cowered to lower her coy eyelids cutely. The things a woman does at the movies! Now she smiled secretly, invitingly—at nobody. Of course it was an open invitation to the dance of life: perhaps to the movies and perhaps intended for me only—or perhaps not. I cannot say. Women were a foreign film then. Havana women at least, who passed from passive to active voice when they started to conjugate the verb *amar* so suddenly sometimes. Or at least in fewer tenses than before, all syntagma go. So I had no choice but to respond to the lure of fate like a marlin to the mackerel bait. I turned to my student Fausto and as a *pater seraphicus* gave him a lasting lesson in angelic art—there and then, right in the middle of the Prado Promenade, a prowess no doubt. I started to say *"Arcades ambo,"* then I stopped. My friend, though a Latin, had no Latin. I knew it was odd even then. Should I translate the Virgil I saw as a barbaric bard, "Bad boys both"? No, that would have been more Byronic than ironic. I thought of inflicting him a lesser wound by inflecting it to *"Arcadia ambae,"* meaning the girl and the movies. I expected that at least he would approve of me by saying there's a blessing in this guy. He didn't say a word, however. Would you believe it? Ungrateful bastard! But didn't the other bard, the one who talked of a rhapsody of blue words, say also that the play's the thing? The play was mine then, therefore I took a golden bow.

"I'm leaving you, Fausto, for some fun in the Fausto," I said meaning the cinema, as she was now, fairer than the evening air, moving past the swinging doors and into the darkened hall, also called the Fausto Theater —surely the Fausto Moviehouse for her, commonly. *Comme* ill Faust, my friend said simply: "Hell!" I had to retort Goethically, "Come, this is no time for artistry." Somehow this moved my friend Fausto to say again, "Hell," with such sweet sorrow that I had to check his private hell before a public heaven with a correction. "Hell is for heels. In this case for Cuban heels," I stated, a variation on a theme. But then, as if of hell he had a great disdain, Fausto muttered: "Fuck!" And I said nothing. I only had words for hell, you see. "Fuck, fuck!" he fuzzed and then suddenly shouted: "Fuck you cunt!" Fustian phrases puffing frustration, which I increased by saying: "That's exactly what I intend to do." Now you know. I was being a mean Mephistopheles for a false Faust.

Falling off and out of his dashing white Sunbeam convertible (used by me so often as to be called Abuse), I responded to his chagrin with my usual felicity in verbal games. "As you can infer, Luz y Fer, bilinguists, we are. Both at your service, mate," meaning no *maté* but *mate*, in Cuban, just to let him know that what I was pursuing was Ambrosia Belle

Candycunt—both entering now the charmed circle of the cinema, to the sweetest, happiest end. An ardor to adore!

Thus, with the curse of Faust but resolutely, I got out in the nick of time of the already moving topless. He blindly crossed with his car the scars left by the old tram tracks on Colón Street: visual vestiges of a vanished culture he never knew. Then I saw Fausto speed up Paseo del Prado, passing like a volley at dawn by the executed poetaster and his morbid muse, Erato turned Urania with her rod, both etherised in the intimate moment of their monument: an intercourse made a matter of course by being performed in public. Seemingly all his hot bronze was penetrating her cold marble, but it was actually the impaling of the dark poet by his frigid friend, a white marvel with a stony stiletto: still, stiff. Faster, Fausto, faster! Fastest, he left behind the Martyrs of Love's Lane to disappear along the Malecón of memory forever. Faustus is gone, mused I, Marlowe. Nobody will ever follow me in my footsteps again in a convertible. Cut is the branch and now he'll grow straight. Well, that's life, folks. There's no performance without vexation.

I must have bought the ticket and entered the theater at the speed of light through the swing doors and under the sign that said "NO SE ADMITEN INFANTES"—which I didn't even see. Then the den's darkness (no usher cared to ferry me to my seat) always contrasting with the glare outside —either day glow or light electric—hit me right between the eyes like a blinding shot. But I still could see (thanks to the searchlight from the screen, which at that moment opened a crack in the black wall), cut out in the dark void, in a vacuum flash, her white dress rising like a phantom gown: actually she was trying to sit down without creasing her skirt. Venus à la mode that she was, it was a stunt for her to ride so fast the ceaseless waves of crinoline on the surf of the starched slips beneath her dress: the foam of fashion no doubt. So I didn't have to run to catch up with her ghostly image after all. Calmly I sat behind her scented body first and then, without a visible pretext (there were only shadows at the movies: motionless in the seats, moving on the screen), I got up to sit in her row. Seemingly fickle, I suddenly changed seats again and came to rest at last beside her—a technique that was the creaming of the experience gained during days and nights at the flicks, movie man that I was, to seek love in the dark like a mystic. If sex could sanctify, I would have been a saint long ago, believe me.

But she never looked my way and I began to think I had sat not in the wrong seat but really next to the Wong girl. Probably the lancing glances in the lobby had been a loose look, all empty eyes and faked frenzy zignifying nothing. I didn't say a word. No introduciton, presentation of credentials or mere greetings. Not even that rude ritual, considered casual but refined in Havana, of a man asking a woman alone in the cinema, Is this seat taken, miss? before sitting down—an approach without reproach. Roaches. How rotten! Besides there were loads of vacant seats and empty rows at that time of the day and between performances to boot. I looked at her at first feigning surprise that she was sitting next to me, with so many seats null and void around us. Then I looked at her as if recognizing her features, wondering where I had seen that cameo face and those bleached waves before. I started giving her long and then longer side glances, across my glasses and under their frame. Finally I stared straight at her, learning her perfect profile by heart, her everlasting profilm, Nevertiti! I reached the conclusion that I was watching a cameo role more than a guest appearance.

But while I sat there looking at her I thought of all the connotations of cameo, from the perpetual profile to its silly syllables. (In my smother tongue, Spanish, the word *camafeo,* broken in two, means bed and ugly. She beddable, me ugh! Carving this cameo I was being sardonyx, of course.) But I stopped looking at her face to peek at her knee glowing phosphorescently in the dim light of her legs. (It's amazing how many things you can see in the twinkling twilight of the movies, *entre deux lumières* as it were, once your pupils get used to the bright blinking of the images, performed in the flicker of an eye.) One of her legs was straddling the other, taking turns, but always leaving one knee afloat, tenebrously, like one tenth of a brown warm iceberg of flesh swimming softly in the enveloping dome of the dark. I looked so hard at her knee that I began to think of *knee* as a four-letter word in my translator's English, the language of the movies and maybe of love too. A knee could also become a need. That it can come from the Latin *genu* is ingenuously ridiculous: it obviously is an arbitrary English word, like *pun*—a nonce that overstayed its welcome. But why was the knee called knee and not soft rock or dermal dome or ivory incline? It could have even been called Glibaltar! I thought, though, of the platonic knee incarnadine, incarnated infinitely in hordes of dead dames and herds of live leggy lasses: the metaphysical knee from which I returned gladly to the physical one: to that knee, to the owner of this knee. A rotunda. Thinking about her knee and my hand and her knee and my hand on her knee I jumped from theory to practice and put a hand on her knee. Just like that. My hand on her knee—and she didn't say a word! I had followed Ovid's advice—what of it? All Ovid—so familiar therefore forgotten: except she wasn't a Roman *puella* at the circus but a Havana *pollo* at the movies. Leg of chick. Leggo? Never! She didn't say a word. Believe me. Not a word.

Her only reaction, I swear, was to look at me, and though I couldn't see her features well because a sudden *nuit américaine* fell like day for night on the screen (it was one of those white nights of the movies in which the midday moon casts a midnight shadow) and because I was looking at her knee, now eclipsed by my hand, I knew she was looking at me, just as she had eyed me outside, in that long hot summer afternoon where all mortals live. *Doux doigts dans ses fesses* that were not caresses. I took my hand off her knee because both hand and knee were clammy, slippery, wet with the anxious sweat of my tropical palms. But before figuring out what to do with that hand of mine I saw it cupping (autonomously, like Orlac's, independent of its author) one of her breasts! Rather, it was poised on the filmy fabric over her tits, as hard as her knee. She was all domes, this girl. She didn't smile but laugh. Yes, she laughed! She was laughing so loud she bounced my hand all over her breast. Actually she wasn't laughing at my act but at the action up there on the screen. It was a cartoon of Pluto: in suspended animation, walking in the air, over an abyss—and not falling because he didn't realize yet he was stepping on air. She laughed for quite a while.

When she had had her laugh, almost as an extension of her last laugh, she took my hand off her breast—and returned it to its point of departure: my skinny, clothed, trembling knee. I saw my hand leave her breast in the silvery light of the screen and alight on my pants in the dark, having been carried part of the way by her hand, carefully, like a rocket with a dangerous warhead: animosity was her thrust, my friendliness her payload. But later I saw her hand flying in free flight to my alien hand, catching it between its bare fingers, and placing it where it had been before—on her fleshy and smooth knee! (As soft as her tit it was.) Trust me, that's exactly what she did. When she took my trespassing hand off her breast I thought she was going to stage a skit (say something, do something), her hand quickly quitting my knee to hit my face hard, to nail me with her fingernails, stick pins in me, stab me with daggers and call the absent charnel usher, the invisible doorman, the spectral cashier —or even the projectionist with a hundred eyes. Well, she did nothing more threatening than returning my hand to her knee. She could do better than that—and she did. She slapped my hand twice, gently: both hands, hers and mine, on her knee: pat pat: my hand like a slim slice of damp ham on the warm toast of her finally friendly flesh. I almost heard her say, I give you my knee! (left or right) knee and my hand, also indistinct through the thick of postures. Then she started pressing her knees together, as good little girls (and some big bad women) do when they don't want to show whatever they're hiding between their legs. So that not only the tender tips but the nails, knuckles, joints, and skin of my hand (made up of bones, tendons, muscles, etc. according to the anatomy lessons of Professor Miranda) touched her other knee. Or rather were nailed to her flesh and crushed against her bones, the hardness of it all felt for the first time in the evening as she pressed her knees together even more. She squeezed my hand between her knees and continued to crush and crack until my hand was a nut in a nutcracker *tout de suite*. Sweet toets, did it hurt! So much so that I almost screamed. To no avail: even a howl would have been muffled by the riotous laughter in the movie. Literally she had a crush on me. No man knows what evil lurks between a woman's legs!

Then I managed somehow to ease my hurting hand out of her rotary press: a device, a vice she had against all intimate flesh. I withdrew my fingers but not the sweaty palm or the lame hand entirely. She was laughing loudly now but it might have been Pluto again, his feat as invisible to me as her feet because I was looking neither at the luminous screen nor at the dark beneath her skirt. In fact I was looking at her breasts rising and falling above. They rose and fell too quickly for such movement to be the effect of breathing. It wasn't her laughter either. Could she be that moved? Rising and falling, rising and falling, high above the smooth domes like twin starry skies in the night. Commotion, emotion, motion—and then some. Stand still, you ever-moving hemispheres! It was then that she opened her legs. I knew she did because her billowing thighs blew many a warm gust over my hand like mild monsoons. But I didn't budge an inch, my hand stuck by capillary action to her knee. Besides, it was a nice nesting niche down there in the minty monticule of her knee. At least that's what I thought. But my hand, a Frankenstein's monster of flesh and bones, had ideas of its own. A creeper on its way after opposite flesh, a sexual climber, my hand entertained fantasies above its station in life. I should know that, for at the time I still thought I owned it.

Now I saw it crawl by itself up her garter. Funny that! I didn't notice before (until the change of skin, that is) that she was wearing nylons, so tough to the touch. But I came to feel the smooth stickiness of stockings upon crossing the bulge of her cheap old-fashioned garters. They were wrapped in her stocking tops and rolled up in a hump above her kneecap. (Ugly word that.) It was only over the top that I felt her cold thighs. Not really cold but cool, smooth, terse, soft, fleshy as my roving hand crept all over them. Then they began to grow lukewarm: warm: hot: hotter: burning—a fiery flaming furnace of a woman she was! My hand (*the* hand by now) tried to divide all that flesh into two separate limbs (two legs, two thighs) without knowing (my hand) that they were divided by nature: twins about to become separable Siamese. All she (the girl) had to do was to open her body for my hand to find its final cradle, endlessly crotched. I made then another discovery in fashionable wear, as anachronic as her garters: the moviegoer belied Amelia Bloomer. My Marilyn Monroe, like Lady Godiva, was riding bare and a tom-tom my heart beat became. Suddenly from Godiva she was transformed into Pandora, opening her hopeful music box for all the world to whirl. Smells are only terribly potent perfumes.

And we hadn't been introduced yet! Or even spoken. Could you believe it? I hadn't tried to speak to her before, it's true. Moves speak a lot louder than words, you see. But when I tried to speak to her, she didn't answer. All she did was to laugh again and make some demented Mona Lisa smirk. She didn't let me speak to her but it's not that she gagged me or pressed a finger on my lips or said hush hush. Nothing like that. She didn't do anything to keep me from talking but it was obvious that all she wanted was to look at the screen—so I merely opened my mouth, formed an O with my breath, and then shut it again. But I *had* to speak to her.

397

I couldn't help it. It was important, imperative, paramount: I couldn't go home *without* my ring.

"My wedding ring . . ."

It was my voice finally—or firstly. But she didn't pay any attention.

"My ring."

I had spoken louder but still she paid no attention. I was talking so loudly that now I was shouting, when someone told me to shut up by hissing from somewhere—an unidentified sound coming from an unexpected audience. I took my hand out from amid fat fast lips and thin hairs: away from that other face, and I sat up straight. A stickler for cleanliness, I wiped my hand dry fastidiously on the right leg of my trousers. I looked at the screen—and saw nothing.

"What is it?"

It was she, speaking for the first time. But she wasn't looking at me. I almost thought she was talking to Pluto. We were so damn close—not to each other but to the screen. So near in fact that sometimes we were projected onto the sheet and straight into the picture.

"What happened?"

She didn't glance at me sideways as she had outside, with that fascinating mauve look of hers in the Havana twilight.

"What made you stop?"

I turned to look at her for a second time and twice she continued in profile, watching the action, movements, motions of Pluto. Double takes.

"My ring."

I would have been her eternal slave if she had said "With that ring I thee wet" or asked incredulously: "Wagner's ring perhaps?" But all this Valkyrie did was to utter a coarse and common: "What?"

"I lost my ring—" call this aposiopesis if you will, but I stopped in mid-phrase. She laughed. She laughed again and then looked at me for the first time since I had entered the theater—or her.

"—my wedding ring. It fell off."

She laughed even more and more than ever she laughed at Pluto's plight and flight.

"Fell *in*," I corrected myself in a whisper.

"I know, silly."

She laughed, was laughing, will laugh forever, convulsively, convulsed—like a carnival doll.

"What should I do now?" I said in a lament that expressed my regrets about having to go home without my wedding ring and confront my wife with such affront. Besides there was my mother, a stern prosecutor—a hanging judge in fact.

"Go look for it."

I was stunned, speechless. I didn't know what to say or do. But she led me by the hand. That is, she transported my hand free past nylon stockings, old-fashioned garters, and fashionable slips onto mildly massive marble thighs burning bright before the forest of thickest night.

"Go ahead, look."

As I obeyed her, or a moment before, piqued I peeked at her and saw that she was once more into the movie, gaily concentrating on contemplating all that gaiety. Was she a fan! Meanwhile, all by myself I looked carefully along the sides, my fingers slipping on wet edges. I felt the change of atmosphere, of both ambiance and texture, inside. I inserted an exploratory hand and the edges tightened around my wrist, just as her knees had trapped my hand before. I tried and verified that I could move my fingers. I could. I probed to the very end and hit against an obstacle, a wall, a deadend possibly. But there was no ring to be found anywhere. Nothing! I looked some more. No trace of my ring and it was the one that joined me in holy matrimony till death do us—I abruptly pulled out my hand but my wrist got caught on an edge.

"Damn it!"

"What's the matter now?"

She had completely taken her eyes off the screen. Even in the chiaroscuro of the theater one could see she was annoyed, her movie eyes burning like carbon lamps, double daggers of light.

"My wristwatch slipped off."

"So what?"

"What do you mean *so what*? It's gone! Safety wristband and all. I don't want to lose it. It's a present from my father."

I lied (with what proficiency I couldn't tell yet) so that it would sound less like a new watch and more like an object with some sentimental value attached. There will be a reward for whoever finds it and returns it to its legitimate owner.

"When I say *so what* I mean so what? So what?"

"But what am I going to do now?"

"Don't be such a cry baby! Just bend down and pick it up."

"Pick it up! It fell in the same place I lost my ring."

"Go in and get it."

Was I hearing right? "Go—*in?*"

"And get it!"

She was once more glued to the screen but had left a wake of annoyance: "It's up to you, of course. I don't care one way or the other."

I cursed (in a whispered aside) my luck. Now not only did I have to look for my wedding ring but also my father's watch. What a bleeding pain, family heirlooms: always looming. Meanwhile, back at the movies, she was shaking with laughter, erupting guffaws. As for me, it might seem easy to find a watch where before you've lost a ring, but it isn't. I began to look, groping and reconnoitering the places I had searched before—and found nothing. Not one thing. Nothing at all. Nil. Besides, I had a pain in my neck from stooping so low for so long and the seat's arm was now prodding my ribs. I must have felt cattle, for I decided to go down on my knees. I squeezed myself between the back of the seat in front and my own seat, carefully avoiding her dangerous legs, a real vise.

I didn't want to disturb her for fear of having my head turned into a nutshell between her murderous kneecaps.

"Ouch!" she howled. "What's the matter with you now? Are you nuts?"

I wanted to answer her "Not yet" or "You bet" but I didn't. You see, I had really tried to kneel on the floor but had landed on her foot instead. All I did in fact was to raise my head to whisper an explanation, but from down there she looked still more furious, even imposing now, what with her eyes burning and her yellow hair almost in flames. I wasn't in the best position to be convincing, jabbering on my knees and trapped between her legs and the row in front. This was a pose fit only for praying to a wet goddess.

"It's just that—"

How easy a row becomes a row!

"Will you please let me watch this movie?"

The reviewer in me was about to correct her, a persistent viewer, and explain to her that this wasn't a movie. But it seemed better to clarify my position first, a nonbeliever trapped in a pew.

"Can't you see it's not my heart? It's my *watch* you're holding. First my ring and now my watch—"

"Good grief! How possessive can you get? *My* watch, *my* ring. Is there anything in the world that doesn't belong to you yet? It's your own fault, anyway!"

How can one answer double-talk dialectics while kneeling? I decided the next best thing was to concentrate on my quest and the best thing was to avoid her body. (Around here there's no logic in my narrative, I know. That's because there was much madness in my method for a search party.) I stuck my hand all the way in but couldn't find anything. Nothing. *Nada,* a word less than nothing and yet much more. Where could they be, both watch and ring? She *must* know. She should, you know. I tapped her arm to get her attention but she wouldn't listen. All that interested her was the damn peep show! Such blasted blasphemy. I had cursed at the movies! I'd be punished for that. Suddenly I was paralyzed by religious terror. In this state of catatonia, I couldn't stoop to stupor. If she could see me now. Put on the lights! Then catalepsy would set in on this isle of the dead. But after a while, seeing that not even a blinding bolt fell from the screen to my seat, I recovered. I even got up enough courage to move an arm, then the hand and finally a finger to rap, then tap her again. But she wouldn't pay any attention to anything that wasn't the screen and the light coming from the end of the cavern, as if Pluto were Plato. That's why I stretched the length of my arm up and up and up, as far as it could go in some sort of SS salute. But my arm wasn't long enough, mighty midget that I was, to reach her eye line. Though I moved my fingers and even crossed them, she obviously didn't see me. Exhausted (Nazis can be tired heroes too) I began to lower my arm, when my hand, accidentally I swear, bumped against one of her breasts. She jumped as if it were a booby trap.

"What the hell is it now?"

I detest women who curse as a matter of course, but I wasn't in a position to show her my aversion, a diversion from her show, obviously. Besides, she would have thought it a version.

"C-c-can I—?"

I can stammer when in a gaffe or annoyed, and I was embarrassed, suffering from that Cuban combination of pain and shame called *pena* —a peaky pun for rock also: "Thou are Peter and upon thy rock I shall roll."

"Cut that out!"

Was she religious too?

"Sorry. I only wanted to—"

"What is it now?"

"Can I—with my other—hand?"

"Of course you can, as long as you don't touch me."

"But to look, in this darkness, I have to touch."

"That's your problem, not mine."

"But how am I going to explore then?"

"I don't mean touching down there, I mean *elsewhere.*"

It seemed absurd to me but not confusing. Not then anyway. Now, to my purpose—but before: "I mean . . . with *both* hands."

"Do it once and for all, damn it!"

I obeyed. It was an order. To the oven then. I felt around with both hands anxiously, extensively, meticulously, to my own amazement or with my mind in a maze. I was shocked that this exploratory operation could be so easy. Methodical man that I am, I searched the left side first with my right hand and the right side with my left, measure for measure. Or centimeter by centimeter, going by the decimal system, which in Latin countries—I didn't find a damn thing! *Nothingnothing.* I decided to cross hands and make the left do the work on the left and vice versa, following the antipathy of opposites and the sympathy of the similar. Nothing! I searched the whole area, sifted the ground, probed the terrain further—to realize that I was getting nowhere and fast. I took out my speleological hands and sighed. I inhaled deeply but exhaled painfully because of the smell: my reaction to the secret secretion, stinking stigma, also called smegma in man.

"Will you shut up?" It was she from above, like a thundering goddess, an Artemis for whom I was only Act One.

"But I didn't say anything," I said humbly: I was in the ideal position to be humble.

"All those noises you're making, *dearie.* People will talk. They're going to think it's something nasty and complain and throw us out. Or worse! Believe me, *I* know what I'm talking about."

There was no doubt that she was right, as there was no doubt that I had neither ring nor watch, lost in a sleight of hand that will not abolish magic.

"So what should I do now?" I consulted her.

"Don't ask me. You just do it quietly—or else."

"No ring, no watch."

In dramatic desperation I put my hands on my head, using her transudate suddenly as pomade and I saw—the cuffs of my shirt hanging *loose,* lying beyond the edge of my jacket sleeves. Oh demigod!

"My cuff links!"

People, a crowd indeed, shushed me from all over the theater. A very strange behavior this! As if they were in church, zealous parishioners all of them. Obviously, I became the pagan in a temple! Acteon Part Two.

"That does it!"

It was she, not the audience. She was angry, against me, furious—a fury. Had she heard my silent quip? I had no time to answer myself in some sort of quip pro quo, because she was a hydra now, with all those hundred hideous heads howling at me. She was an unhappy Harpy, an eerie Erinye in her eyrie, Flash Gorgon, and more, much more. Right this way, ladies and gentlemen! See the Show! See the sideshow! Salome, Messalina, Catherine de Medici and her snow-white sister the Great, Eva Perón and Ilse Koch and, finally, ahead of her time and just to see heads roll, Madame Mao—an army of mean maenads bent toward destruction and on top of me: terrifyingly atrocious, formidably forbidding forever, a menace a minute!

Shiva shivered! But because of her incarnadine and apoplectic color, red of rage and purple patellas in sharp contrast with her bleached hair, she was in fact a many-mitted Kali, now waving a single flashing sword in one of her four hands. She whistled like a pressure cooker in distress:

"If you're ssssso inneressssssted in thossssse thingssssssss—get in there immediately and fetch them!"

"WHAT?"

But she didn't answer. She opened not her mouth but her purse in the dark and rummaged around. (Was she again the girl I had seen outside?)

"Here!"

She was handing me something metallic, shining and reflecting light from the screen. A suspicion in the shadows grew in me—her dagger? Or a sword? Kali's chalice? Or a soup spoon. Soupçons so soon that truth would out sooner.

"There!"

"What the hell is this?" I asked before taking the offering.

"My flashlight, what else?"

She slammed it into the palm of my hand and at the same time opened her legs as wide as she could, placing a leg on either arm of her seat. I felt my head growing lengthwise like a blimp, then my eyeglasses had tortoise-shell frames, and a sinister mustache was growing on me. Oh the things one could do at the movies in Havana then! First I could pick up a girl, any girl. I could also become a doctor and hide if I wished. And I didn't have to drink any potion to achieve my metamorphosis. Should I

402

tell her? But I saw that she had stopped paying any attention to me to concentrate once again on what was happening on the stained screen. I switched on the flashlight, opening a hole of light where before all had been touch and tell. Before peering over the brink (È pericoloso spor-gersi), I had a touch of prescience. All present say I. Untying the laces of one of my shoes I fastened the earpieces of the spectacles around my ears and the back of my head. Purely on specs I advanced boldly, unheeded, cutting a path through the bushy hedge. At my back a lion roared—or perhaps it was three leopards in unison. Back into the jungle in reverse motion.

The moment I poked my head inside all sensations ceased—noises, textures, smells, bitter tastes ended. Everything except the vision pro-jected by my, her, flashlight, which had a strong light indeed though it wasn't much larger than the Pelikan in my pocket—in my pocket?—yes, ever-ready and firmly fastened to my jacket pocket it was. This peri-phrasis was the German influence of my pen, apparently. (Or was it I, still beating about the bush?) I was right to insert the flashlight first but wrong to go in arms and head first. The very instant I raised my head, my narrow shoulders also entered (involuntarily), and when I tried to get them out for fear of getting stuck, using my elbows as fulcrum and arms as lever, I achieved the opposite of the effect desired—and the entrance became a chute. I fell inside downward in a big swallow. The word of mouth should be phenomenal. But I did not lose the flashlight, doctor.

I got up to find out that I was limping on the one foot of mine that was always independent and wild, with a life of its own but more reasonable than my hand. It felt wet, sticky, uneasy. Was I hurt? Once, when I was a child, I jumped from a tall tower and tore a ligament. Perhaps a born-again Byron, I had developed a club foot of my own. Chubby and clubby George Gordon said, Join us! Enough of this musing. Something amiss? I flashed the light on my feet and saw that one of my shoes was missing, the left one. The other one was firmly fastened. Before beginning the search for my lost sock I was bemused to see how well my gray sock looked in contrast with the damp red floor. I was amused by the pattern but forgetting my sudden post-Impressionist bent I aimed the flashlight at the walls, which were shiny pink or coral-red or reflecting perhaps scarlet dots. Toward the back the light faded around a purple bend. I lit up the entrance but the shoe was nowhere to be found. Could I have lost it *outside*? I climbed as well as I could up the slimy slope through the orifice into which I had fallen and tried to peer at the outside world. All I saw was I (appalling dome) facing a dark lobby with a mauve bell up above and some deep purple hangings along the sides. But no shoe. Nymphs I didn't see either. Lymphs neither. No nodes. I was going to cross the threshold when there was a sudden tremor (an earthquake?) and I slid downward again, almost to the end of the room. But I didn't lose my flashlight.

I stood up once more and tried to find the entrance ramp, now invisible. I never called it La Rampa, of course. I had obviously slid into another space. I started walking in what I thought was the right direction toward the exit and immediately realized that instead of stepping out I was going further in. I lit up walls, roof, and every corner within reach of my flashlight. I took meticulous mental note of what seemed to be a thoroughly purple plot. Though the color varied at times from deep purple to pale pink and the floor was first grainy and then striated, I was always in a soft cave. Neither ring nor watch nor cuff links appeared. But upon carefully examining the area, bit by bit, and tracing its exact topography I knew I was inside a pear-shaped salon. A literary lion on the lam. My success would be my exit.

I reached a fork in the road, and following the peasant advice that recommends the straight path as always greener (a metaphor) I decided to take the forking path on the right, which looked if not green at least wider. I walked ten steps (though I can't say how many steps there were from the entrance: I was obviously in some sort of space warp) to come face to face (a commonplace) with a smooth, fast-red wall. Could this be a cardinal chapel? But a careful inspection showed that long red uneven firm thin stripes went up and down the wall. There was nothing there. No traces of the objects to be found. Not a thing. I went all around, my eyes glued to the damp floor and the bright ring of light that was my guide. Upon returning to the fork, on the left I saw a white spot that *ran* to disappear beyond the bend. It looked to me, as horrible as it might seem, like a rabbit foot! I also ran to the corner but saw neither trace nor tail—trail—of it. Was it a hallucination? No one answered my question and I discovered that I was alone in a woman's world. Or almost alone: I had my flashlight for company. When one is alone even a flashlight is a soulmate. Unless, perish the thought, I was in some solitary confinement. Search, search! *Felix qui potuit.*

I turned thus the corner—to find another fork. *Rerum cognoscere.* I was in a labyrinth. For the snark was a *bollo,* you see. There was no doubt about that. *Causas.* Following a rule of thumb I established at that very moment, I rejected, also without a doubt, the wide peasant path for the straight and narrow footpath. After walking a few steps along this way I found myself in a cul-de-sac. (Also called blind alley or dead end in pictures.) Was I lost? Impossible! He who has found himself is never lost. The exit, and ensuing success, was right there on the right. On the right? Was the exit to the real of the movie on the right or on the left? I was going to pull out a coin to use it as a compass and decide my reckoning on heads or tails, a Raft toss-up, when the earth and the walls trembled again and the whole cavern, measureless to man, shook in spasms. It was I who was tossed and not the coin! I found myself pushed by movements that were more and more seismic—toward the back. Or was it toward the front? This time I managed to maintain a precarious balance and didn't let go of my companion flashlight either—though I lost the coin in my pocket: the coin of my spitting image. I skated now at an even pace (a foxtrot or slow waltz but not yet the slowest) to a little sour wine-colored room and right in the middle of a beat the tremors stopped as abruptly as they had started. Where was I now? The cul-de-sac had passed alongside me, pushed away by violet-colored walls and sickly mucous columns and soft modules, *nodules.* Nymph nodes. I decided to reflect upon my situation—mostly because I was afraid to move from where I was. Quietism on a quiet isthmus, I suppose. My course suggested the steeplechase more than a hunt, where the obstacles (hedges, ditches, water jumps) exceeded the course from starting point to the end. That's no way out, to exist in exit. Exodus too. I felt beat and in my defeat I did what all losers do when they don't believe in heaven: I looked at the floor. What appeared was as unexpected as the disappearance of my personal properties and my own dead loss. There was a book down there! Or rather, a little book, almost a booklet. I saw it as a sign. Doctor Fatso, a former friend, had said when he sold his soul to the movies, "I'll burn my books!" But I had always believed in salvation through books—even through *one* single book. I bent down, never stooping, to pick it up, and in the light of my flashlight (which suddenly seemed a magic lantern to me) I could see that it was an ancient volume bound in leather. On the cover was an inscription in Latin, the way in, in Greek to me, which said: *"Ovarium, corpus luteus, labium majus, matrix, tubae Falloppi."* I didn't understand a single word! Well, maybe one word, the last one, which doubtlessly referred to a medieval printer. It was clearly a book about books. Or printer's devil's manual! What good was it to me now? I was not a proofreader anymore. Caxton meant as much as Paxton to me now. I could even throw bricks to the latter and tell the first that the bible is only a book.

But under this inscription there were two initials, *AS.* Apparently those of the author, unknown or too well-known to print his name on the cover—or just as coy as W. H. himself. I composed a brief list of possible authors upon wondering who it could be. Adolphe Sax? It didn't seem to me a volume of musical instruments, despite the tuba. But I was under the impression that the solution was easy. Ashkenazis and Sephardim? An inverted Sofonisba Anguisciola, a Renaissance woman? All Souls? Patience tempered my impatience. But, just you wait! Weren't those the initials of—Of course! That was it! Why didn't I think of it before? Open Sesame! (In Spanish, naturally: *Abrete Sesamo.*) I opened the book eagerly. The first chapter's title was "Cave at Emptor"—but what I found were fragments from a diary or a ship's log. I tried to heave the log. It was too heavy. Sigh. Sight. *Tolle, lege:*

> *Sunday, 16 August.* Nothing new. The same weather. The wind freshened slightly. When I awoke, my first thought was to observe the intensity of the light. I lived in fear that the electric light might grow dim and then go out altogether. . . .

My legs and the log were trembling. At first I thought it was nerves but later found out that it was the floor that was shaking. Rumbling and deep-throated muted noises came from the bowels of the cavern.

My uncle took soundings several times, tying one of the heaviest pickaxes to the end of a cord which he let down two hundred fathoms. No bottom. We had some difficulty in hauling up our weight.

When the pickaxe was back on board, Hans showed me some deep imprints on its surface. It was as if that piece of iron had been squeezed between two hard bodies.

I looked at the guide.

"Tänder," he said.

I did not understand and turned to my uncle, who was deep in his calculations. I decided not to disturb him and returned to the Icelander, who by opening and shutting his mouth several times conveyed his meaning to me.

"Teeth!" I said in amazement, looking more closely at the iron bar.

Yes, those were definitely the marks of teeth imprinted on the metal. The jaws which contained them must have been incredibly powerful. Were they the teeth of some monster of a prehistoric species which lived deep down under the surface, a monster more voracious than the . . . I couldn't take my eyes off his bar which had been half gnawed away. . . .

I tried to light the log better and read it at the same time but (those who have tried it know well) it was practically impossible, what with the ground being so slippery and shaken as it was by minor tremors. Besides, the batteries must have given out for the light was dimmer, weaker. I decided to grab hold of the flashlight with my teeth and draw the diary closer to my myopic eyes, to see better. Mer sea.

Tuesday, 18 August. Evening came, or rather the moment when sleep weights down our eyelids. For there is no night on this ocean, and the implacable light tires our eyes with its persistency, as if we were sailing under the Arctic sun. . . .

Two hours later a violent shock awoke me. . . .

"What's the matter?" cried my uncle. . . .

Hans pointed to a dark mass rising and falling about a quarter of a mile away. I looked and cried:

"It's a colossal porpoise!"

"Yes," replied my uncle, "and there there's an enormous sea-lizard."

"And farther on a monstrous crocodile! Look at its huge jaws and its rows of teeth! Oh, it's disappearing!"

"A whale! A whale!" cried the Professor. "I can see its enormous fins. Look at the air and the water it's throwing out through its blowers!"

Sure enough, two liquid columns were rising to a considerable height above the sea. . . . Fortunately the wind, which is blowing hard has enabled us to get away quickly from the scene of the battle. . . .

Thursday, 20 August. Wind N.N.E., variable. Temperature high. Speed about nine knots.

Towards midday we heard a very distant noise, a continuous roar which I could not identify. . . .

Three hours went by. The roar seemed to be coming from a distant water-fall. I said as much to my uncle, who shook his head. All the same I felt sure that I was right, and wondered whether we might not be sailing towards some cataract which would hurl us into the abyss. I had no doubt that this method of descent would please the Professor, because it would be newly vertical, but for my part . . .

At any rate there was definitely a very noisy phenomenon a good few miles to leeward, for now the roaring noise was clearly audible. . . .

I looked up at the vapours hanging in the atmosphere and tried to penetrate their depths. . . .

I then examined the horizon, which was unbroken and free from mist. Its appearance had not changed in any way. But if the noise came from a water-fall, a cataract, if the whole sea was flowing into a lower basin, if that roar was produced by a mass of falling water, then there was bound to be a current, and its increasing speed would give me the measure of the danger threatening us. I consulted the current: it was nil. I threw an empty bottle into the sea: it lay still. . . .

"He has seen something," said my uncle.

"Yes, I do believe he has."

Hans came and stretched his arm out to the south, saying:

"Der nere!"

"Over there?" repeated my uncle.

Seizing his telescope, he gazed hard for a minute which seemed an age to me.

"Yes, yes!" he cried.

"What can you see?"

"A huge jet of water rising above the waves."

"Another sea monster?"

"Perhaps."

"Then let us steer more to the west, because we know how dangerous those antediluvian monsters are!"

"No, let us go straight ahead," replied my uncle.

I turned to Hans, but he held his tiller with inflexible determination.

Yet if at the distance which separated us from the animal—a distance I estimated at thirty miles at least—we could see the column of water expelled by its blowers, then it must be of supernatural dimensions. The most ordinary prudence would dictate immediate flight, but we had not come so far to be prudent.

We therefore pressed on. The nearer we got to the jet, the bigger it seemed. What monster, we wondered, could take such a quantity of water and shoot it out without a moment's interruption?

At eight o'clock in the evening we were less than five miles from it. Its huge, dark, hillocky body lay in the sea like an island. Illusion or fear gave me the impression that it was over a mile long. What could this cetacean be, which neither Cuvier nor Blumenbach knew anything about? It was motionless and apparently asleep; the sea seemed incapable of moving it, and it was the waves that lapped against its sides. The column of water, thrown up to a height of five hundred feet, was falling in the form of rain with a deafening roar. And there we were, speeding like lunatics towards that powerful monster which a hun-dred whales a day would be insufficient to satisfy.

Terror seized me. I refused to go any farther and swore that I would cut the halyards if necessary. I expressed my mutinous feelings to the Professor, but he made no reply.

All of a sudden Hans stood up, pointed at the menacing object, and said: *"Holme,"* . . .

Holmes? Sherlock Holmes as a navigator? What kind of stupid joke was this? But I was Watson enough to go on reading in the light of my dim dark lantern—and asking silly questions nobody ever bothered to answer.

Sunday, 23 August. Where are we? We have been carried along with indescribable rapidity. . . .

Where are we going? . . .

It is getting hotter.

Monday, 24 August. Will this never end? . . .

For three days we had not been able to exchange a single word. We opened our mouths and moved our lips, but no sound could be heard. . . .

My uncle came over to me and pronounced a few words. I think he said, "We are done for," but I am not sure.

I wrote down these words for him to read: "Let us lower the sail."

He nodded in agreement.

He had scarcely lifted his head again before a ball of fire appeared on board the raft. . . .

We were paralysed with fear. The fireball, half white, half blue, and the size of a ten-inch shell, moved slowly over the raft, slowly. . . .

A smell of nitrous gas filled the air, entering our throats and filling our lungs to suffocation.

So that's what it was! Nitrous gas. I knew it couldn't be nitrous oxide because this smells so sweet, like a gas used in anesthesia. Out there it is known as laughing gas—but then perhaps the indolent movie goer had her own source. That would explain her laughter in the dark. But back to the book.

Suddenly there was a blaze of light. The ball had burst and we were covered with tongues of fire.

Then everything went dark. . . . Hans still at his tiller but "spitting fire." . . . Where are we going? Where are we going?

Tuesday, 25 August. I have just emerged from a long swoon. . . .

I can hear a new noise! Surely it is the sound of the sea breaking on rocks . . .! But then . . .

Here I couldn't go on reading not because the log was terminated by the inimical elements but because the little book came to an end. *Terminat Author Opus.* Who was this submerged logkeeper? Who were his fellow travelers? Where did the journey on this raft in the lagoon, lake, or pond end? I never knew. Neither did I discover the nature of the monster. Was it animal, vegetal, or mineral? Made of flesh and blood or was it just a projection of the mind, a monster of the id in a forbidden land? Mysteries of a soul at sea or a deliberate design to provoke scholia (and thus scholars) to these fantastic fragments? Sailor or mariner? Castaway or cunning writer? In this last question mark a shock wave rocked the grotto with a force I never experienced before. Then there was another seismic jar, stronger than the one before. Could this be a Love wave? What would it have measured according to the Lacoste pendulum, by now certainly swinging wild? Had it attained the moho discontinuity —or given as high a reading as 9 degrees on the Modified Mercalli Scale of Felt Intensity? How many richters had it reached? If it wasn't a primary wave, could it have been a shear wave then? Or a Raleigh wave perhaps? I cursed myself for not having with me Benioff's vertical seismograph—but would he have lent it to me?

I also asked myself if the Lg waves were creating seismic seiches all around me. But I would not know then or ever, for a blast wave of about 13 degrees Mercalli knocked me down and I remember, just before sinking, thinking that I would never be able to decipher the initials on the cover. The A could also stand for Ariadne and perhaps the volume, more of a thread than a threat, would help me find a way out of this trap in a theater. But what did the S Signify? Sodom, solo, shalom? Oh, what a fetid enigma! It was in the midst of this soliloquy that there was another spasm in the *cueva* or cave and another and another and yet another, the tremors getting stronger by the second. It was then that I heard the sound of distant laughter!

But the tremor had now laid me out upon a cushioned carpet. Then there was another wave in the cavern and yet another, each time stronger. It was a cataclysm! How many richters had it reached? Now, believe you me, my body (and I with it) began to move along the floor! First to the right, then to the left, then we returned to the center—to immediately slip forward and finally fly out, as if we were, yes, airborne! I had always longed since childhood to fly on a carpet, but I was far from elated flying all by myself—backward. Good heavens! Where will we end up? Where? I was traveling at a greater speed on the flooded floor, sometimes sliding like a sled, other times sailing over a cushion of air like a hovercraft, and even flying as if really on a magic carpet. Now we hit a warm wall straight on, changing direction to collide with a pulpy pillar and being set on yet another erratic course. Then we, *I*, came to a halt. I had stopped amidst debris, in a pool of turbid water. We were in an alluviated area: underground pipes had broken and subsequently flooded the floor. Judging by the staggering amount of ejected mud or of a mudlike substance, I was in a cesspool, rubbing elbows, so to speak, with the jetsam and the flotsam. I could discern among them, and this included me, some torn quartz tubes. Had something wrecked poor Benioff's apparatus? Just then the muck ran amuck and everything turned red. The pool floor began to shake, rocked by body waves that rippled the muddy waters, then stirred them vertically, from bottom upward, and finally made the whole basin boil over like a pressure cooker about to explode. I was caught in the middle of an eruption! Fate had flung me in the path of burning lava, molten rock, boiling water, and all sorts of eruptive matter. Was I going to be thrown out, expelled, rejected, vomited, spat into the air? Oh my God! Then the thrust stopped.

During the halt I was nearly suffocated, but while I was moving the burning air really took my breath away. I thought for a moment of the bliss of suddenly finding myself in the polar regions at a freezing temperature, swimmingly basking in the Arctic glare while floating in a colloidal suspension of animation and with a sugar-frothed rim around me like icing on a glass dome. This collodion even tasted sweet! Obviously my brain, little by little weakened by my flights of fancy, the wild trip plus my imagination, was softening into an idiotic serum while I floated in the amniotic fluid of memories. Then I had the exact but odd feeling of true terror thrills, as if condemned to travel on a roller-coaster forever. Now I was tied to the mouth of a cannon, in a fun fear for good, just as the shot is fired and all limbs are scattered to the hot air, wind, space. Silly as it might sound, after the boom I felt proud, my pride coming from the fact that never for a dull moment had I let go of my torch, which was the light. But precisely at this moment as I was falling I realized to my chagrin that I had lost the book. Me, myself, and I, flying limbs and all, began then to spin in a wild whirlpool with no center, a mauve maelstrom, the chaos as before. Stop! Then there was light, a streak lightning or street lighting, the freak bolt followed by something like a crash in a crack, a fall into the fault, a death rattle in the spelunca and when I was about to wake up screaming—I fell freely into a horizontal abbess, *abyss!*

Here's where I came in.

PETROS ABATZOGLOU, *What Does Mrs. Freeman Want?*
PIERRE ALBERT-BIROT, *Grabinoulor.*
YUZ ALESHKOVSKY, *Kangaroo.*
SVETLANA ALEXIEVICH, *Voices from Chernobyl.*
FELIPE ALFAU, *Chromos.*
  Locos.
IVAN ÂNGELO, *The Celebration.*
  The Tower of Glass.
DAVID ANTIN, *Talking.*
DJUNA BARNES, *Ladies Almanack.*
  Ryder.
JOHN BARTH, *LETTERS.*
  Sabbatical.
SVETISLAV BASARA, *Chinese Letter.*
ANDREI BITOV, *Pushkin House.*
LOUIS PAUL BOON, *Chapel Road.*
ROGER BOYLAN, *Killoyle.*
IGNÁCIO DE LOYOLA BRANDÃO, *Zero.*
CHRISTINE BROOKE-ROSE, *Amalgamemnon.*
BRIGID BROPHY, *In Transit.*
MEREDITH BROSNAN, *Mr. Dynamite.*
GERALD L. BRUNS,
  Modern Poetry and the Idea of Language.
GABRIELLE BURTON, *Heartbreak Hotel.*
MICHEL BUTOR, *Degrees.*
  Mobile.
  Portrait of the Artist as a Young Ape.
G. CABRERA INFANTE, *Infante's Inferno.*
  Three Trapped Tigers.
JULIETA CAMPOS, *The Fear of Losing Eurydice.*
ANNE CARSON, *Eros the Bittersweet.*
CAMILO JOSÉ CELA, *The Family of Pascual Duarte.*
  The Hive.
LOUIS-FERDINAND CÉLINE, *Castle to Castle.*
  London Bridge.
  North.
  Rigadoon.
HUGO CHARTERIS, *The Tide Is Right.*
JEROME CHARYN, *The Tar Baby.*
MARC CHOLODENKO, *Mordechai Schamz.*
EMILY HOLMES COLEMAN, *The Shutter of Snow.*
ROBERT COOVER, *A Night at the Movies.*
STANLEY CRAWFORD, *Some Instructions to My Wife.*
ROBERT CREELEY, *Collected Prose.*
RENÉ CREVEL, *Putting My Foot in It.*
RALPH CUSACK, *Cadenza.*
SUSAN DAITCH, *L.C.*
  Storytown.
NIGEL DENNIS, *Cards of Identity.*
PETER DIMOCK,
  A Short Rhetoric for Leaving the Family.
ARIEL DORFMAN, *Konfidenz.*
COLEMAN DOWELL, *The Houses of Children.*
  Island People.
  Too Much Flesh and Jabez.
RIKKI DUCORNET, *The Complete Butcher's Tales.*
  The Fountains of Neptune.
  The Jade Cabinet.
  Phosphor in Dreamland.
  The Stain.
  The Word "Desire."
WILLIAM EASTLAKE, *The Bamboo Bed.*
  Castle Keep.
  Lyric of the Circle Heart.
JEAN ECHENOZ, *Chopin's Move.*
STANLEY ELKIN, *A Bad Man.*
  Boswell: A Modern Comedy.
  Criers and Kibitzers, Kibitzers and Criers.
  The Dick Gibson Show.
  The Franchiser.
  George Mills.

  The Living End.
  The MacGuffin.
  The Magic Kingdom.
  Mrs. Ted Bliss.
  The Rabbi of Lud.
  Van Gogh's Room at Arles.
ANNIE ERNAUX, *Cleaned Out.*
LAUREN FAIRBANKS, *Muzzle Thyself.*
  Sister Carrie.
LESLIE A. FIEDLER,
  Love and Death in the American Novel.
GUSTAVE FLAUBERT, *Bouvard and Pécuchet.*
FORD MADOX FORD, *The March of Literature.*
CARLOS FUENTES, *Terra Nostra.*
  Where the Air Is Clear.
JANICE GALLOWAY, *Foreign Parts.*
  The Trick Is to Keep Breathing.
WILLIAM H. GASS, *The Tunnel.*
  Willie Masters' Lonesome Wife.
ETIENNE GILSON, *The Arts of the Beautiful.*
  Forms and Substances in the Arts.
C. S. GISCOMBE, *Giscome Road.*
  Here.
DOUGLAS GLOVER, *Bad News of the Heart.*
KAREN ELIZABETH GORDON, *The Red Shoes.*
GEORGI GOSPODINOV, *Natural Novel.*
PATRICK GRAINVILLE, *The Cave of Heaven.*
HENRY GREEN, *Blindness.*
  Concluding.
  Doting.
  Nothing.
JIŘÍ GRUŠA, *The Questionnaire.*
JOHN HAWKES, *Whistlejacket.*
AIDAN HIGGINS, *A Bestiary.*
  Flotsam and Jetsam.
  Langrishe, Go Down.
  Scenes from a Receding Past.
  Windy Arbours.
ALDOUS HUXLEY, *Antic Hay.*
  Crome Yellow.
  Point Counter Point.
  Those Barren Leaves.
  Time Must Have a Stop.
MIKHAIL IOSSEL AND JEFF PARKER, EDS., *Amerika:*
  Contemporary Russians View the United States.
GERT JONKE, *Geometric Regional Novel.*
JACQUES JOUET, *Mountain R.*
HUGH KENNER, *Flaubert, Joyce and Beckett:*
  The Stoic Comedians.
DANILO KIŠ, *Garden, Ashes.*
  A Tomb for Boris Davidovich.
TADEUSZ KONWICKI, *A Minor Apocalypse.*
  The Polish Complex.
ELAINE KRAF, *The Princess of 72nd Street.*
JIM KRUSOE, *Iceland.*
EWA KURYLUK, *Century 21.*
VIOLETTE LEDUC, *La Bâtarde.*
DEBORAH LEVY, *Billy and Girl.*
  Pillow Talk in Europe and Other Places.
JOSÉ LEZAMA LIMA, *Paradiso.*
OSMAN LINS, *Avalovara.*
  The Queen of the Prisons of Greece.
ALF MAC LOCHLAINN, *The Corpus in the Library.*
  Out of Focus.
RON LOEWINSOHN, *Magnetic Field(s).*
D. KEITH MANO, *Take Five.*
BEN MARCUS, *The Age of Wire and String.*
WALLACE MARKFIELD, *Teitlebaum's Window.*
  To an Early Grave.
DAVID MARKSON, *Reader's Block.*
  Springer's Progress.
  Wittgenstein's Mistress.

FOR A FULL LIST OF PUBLICATIONS, VISIT:
www.dalkeyarchive.com